Fe: an Atom's Tale
Benjamin Bronte

Published by Elegua Editions LLC.

ISBN 979-8-9904681-8-4

For Amanda

Contents

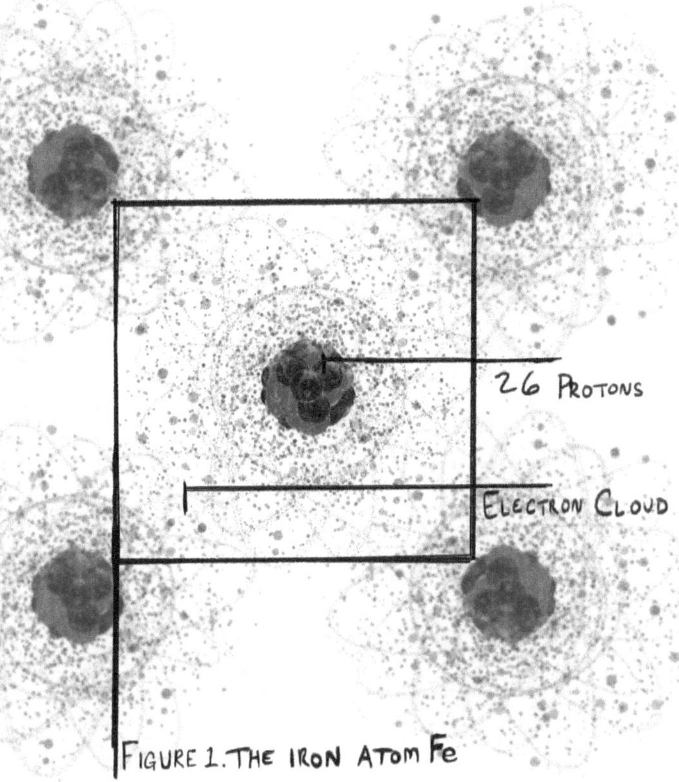

FIGURE 1. THE IRON ATOM Fe

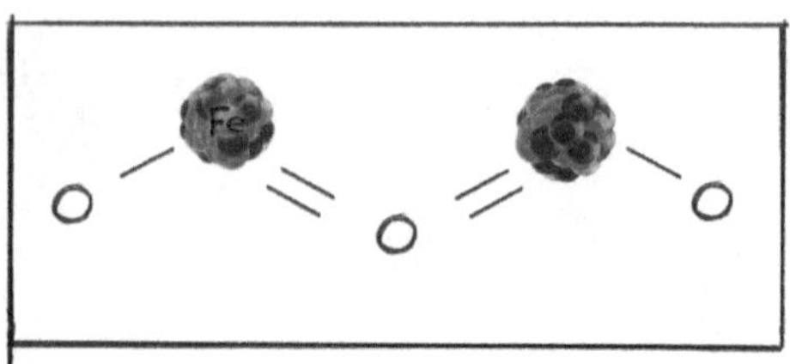

FIGURE 2.   IRON-iii-OXIDE

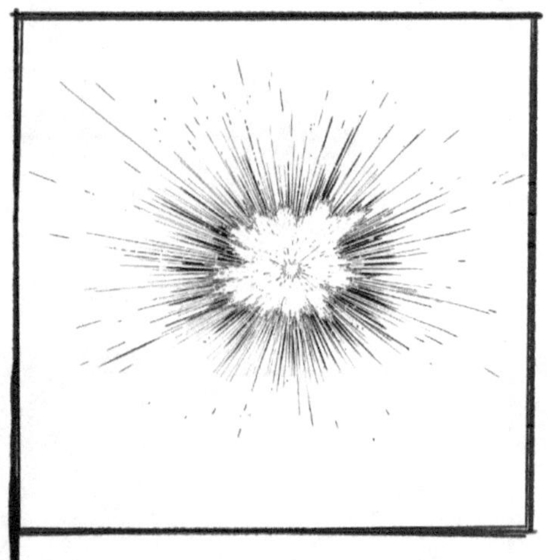

FIGURE 3. THE MOTHER STAR
(ARTIST'S RENDITION)

All matter in nature is made up of uncuttables—atoms—floating in the void. All bodies are merely temporary agglomerations of these atoms, which are too tiny to see, but they have weight, and they move randomly, drawn always, inexorably downward. It is the movement and collision of these atoms, and not the gods, that is responsible for mechanical and natural phenomena. All people are made of the same atomic material, and naturally, this makes them equal to one another...

Epicurus of Samos (341-270 BCE)

Prologue

At the instant of Fe's birth, its dying Mother shone more brightly than any object in the universe. A red giant at the end of her long reign, the Mother Star indulged in one final collapse before violently exploding, ending her existence and birthing a new era of infinite potential upon the young, sterile galaxy. Indeed, each Earthborn destined to interact with the atom Fe, including those who would learn its tale, could trace every last particle in their own skin, sinew, and nerve to that same stellar womb.

As with most stories, it all started with hydrogen. Though, a minority of helium atoms, to be fair, populated the early universe alongside their smaller cousins–the leftovers from the big bang. Hydrogen existed as a heavy, charged proton, while helium hefted a nucleus of two. However many sterile neutrons bulked up their cores, and however many charged little electrons they gained or lost, the atoms' identities remained as long as they clung to the single or double proton that defined their existence. They drifted seemingly forever before succumbing to the desire that motivates human beings and interstellar dust particles alike–the need for companionship.

Gravity, that fundamental force of the universe, patiently set to work.

In the beginning, it was agonizingly slow. The particles drifted across a vast nothingness, attracted to each other by the smallest, faintest tugs. Eon by eon, their drifting grew less aimless, more vectored–their journeys as uneventful as they were epic. Though staggering distances still separated the atoms, the most concentrated areas of space became bustling cities compared with the nothingness outside. Silent and black, each existed as a galactic necropole–light, heat, noise, and fire still a faraway dream.

An epic tug of war silently raged as each hydrogen cluster exerted its own tiny gravity upon its neighbors. Gravitationally-mediated mergers turned millions of hydrogen cities into thousands of kingdoms. Thousands of kingdoms became hundreds of empires, collapsing and conjoining into one. At long last, a single, unimaginably vast megalopolis stood proud against the emptiness of the galaxy–a newborn nebula.

Gravity was not yet finished with the insignificant hydrogen atoms. They had finally found one another after traveling stretches of time and space that defy comprehension, but the force that had once been so gentle and distant now began to grow exponentially more monstrous. Inevitably, the cloud collapsed under its own weight, gravity forcibly transforming the beautiful nebula into one of the first true objects in the universe. She possessed mass and a coherent shape. She glowed–expressing herself in floods of massless photons that illuminated the cold, dark emptiness from which she had been born.

Mentored by gravity, the proto-Mother matured, and the denser she grew, the hungrier its pull became. For the septendecillions of hydrogen atoms at the core, this crushing desire became so powerful that, when their madly-embracing protons encountered the universal barrier against two particles occupying the same space at the same time–they leaped over the law, two fusing together to become one.

Two lonely hydrogens became a single atom of helium, an entity somewhat less than the sum of its parts. Indeed, the missing quantum of its mass had transformed into pure energy during the fusion reaction, betraying a bizarre feature of a cold and calculating universe–all matter is simply energy trapped in a corporeal state.

Crushed-together particles grew frenzied by this new influx of thermal and kinetic motivation. Propelled by the font of fire, other atoms began to follow the pioneering hydrogens. More couples fused together, and the massive energies they released multiplied their neighbors' unions exponentially. Miraculously, the Mother's fiery core stabilized, and the chain reaction of ecstatic fusion became self-sustaining. She was a star, and she lit up the early galaxy.

Despite their radiant glory, her class of young stars did not represent order emerging from chaos. They did not violate the laws of death. Suns like the Mother radiated titanic amounts of energy into the galactic void, energy that had once been matter—never again to exist in a state of order. Above all else, stars were engines of chaos and profligate entropy.

Fe was still not yet even a twinkle in its self-absorbed Mother's eye in those early eons. The glowing giantess had more pressing matters to deal with. She had other children to birth.

At a certain point, her appetite for hydrogen ran out. It was no matter. The Mother was a powerful beast who could consume her helium children as easily as she'd feasted on the primal hydrogen they'd been born from. Two helium atoms were not enough to satisfy, however, but when a third joined its siblings, they turned to something new and stable—an atom of carbon. This newborn scion was defined by the six protons in its nucleus, incidentally representing the upstream destruction of six unique hydrogen atoms.

When there were no more light elements to easily cannibalize, the Mother turned her enormous temperature and pressure to the infant carbons. Two atoms entered the nuclear forge and exited as neon, sacrificing a modicum of mass to satisfy their mother's hunger for energy. Each time, her children went willingly into the fire, for they always emerged as something more—neon became oxygen became silicon. Each era of nuclear fusion represented a briefer phase than the one that had preceded it. By the time she found herself desperately fusing silicon atoms together, the Mother Star's life was nearing its end.

As her core collapsed, solid silicon became bombarded by a throng of helium nuclei, fusing silicon to sulfur. Sulfur became argon—argon became calcium. She struggled to maintain her internal pressure, each rapid new stage of fusion providing paltry stoking for her nuclear fires. Calcium was reborn as titanium, which was almost immediately transformed into chromium—the heaviest child yet at twenty four protons. It was not enough—not enough.

As the Mother Star exploded and died, the atom Fe was brought into the universe. A chromium atom, born mere moments earlier, ended its short existence at the hands of a stray helium. Under the terrible pressure of the supernova, the twenty four protons of the chromium combined with the helium nucleus to create iron.

Fe was born.

All around the baby iron atom, the womb writhed with chaos. Its siblings were madly forged into being just as others decayed–brutalized into simpler forms. Fe's existence could have easily ended then and there, should a chance encounter with a rogue helium have taken place. The infant Fe was lucky, however. Its Mother died too quickly to ensure further fusion. At last betrayed by the gravity that had created her, she collapsed in an eyeblink. Her supernova's enormous energies turned inward, turned outward, and wrenched free. A trillion trillion trillion photons screamed out into the night, messengers announcing the Mother Star's departure from the universe, then darkness.

Fe found itself hurtled outward, but not into the void. Gravity was strong near the central collection of the Mother's viscera, and a cluster soon formed–another baby nebula. Gradually, the forces of attraction asserted themselves, just as before. Hot atoms smashed into one another, sharing electrons and bonding themselves into compounds. As the increasingly fiery nebula swirled and condensed, its core grew more and more massive. Fe stayed out of the thick of things, drifting via random atomic motion, submissive to the currents of gravity.

Half-melted bits collided and stuck to others. Fe joined with sibling iron atoms, partnering with minorities of nickels and manganeses, to condense into a sizable metallic lump billions upon quintillions strong. Together, Fe and the other atoms inside the asteroid sailed through the thin, debris-strewn hydrogen soup that surrounded the protostar.

Within the central crucible, hydrogens who never had a chance to join their nuclei in the Mother found exoneration in the core of Sol–the newborn Sun. Flares and energetic particles erupted from the young star as it ignited, blasting away the gaseous remains of the nebula. Its energetic solar winds even bombarded Fe's asteroid, but the heavy iron-nickel mass weathered the storm. The system stabilized, and Sol shone brightly, settling in for eons of hydrogen burning.

Several bodies grew large enough to distinguish themselves–entire molten worlds accreting from embers of rock and metal. Sometimes two of these massive planetesimals collided. Occasionally, they merged, and sometimes, they simply tore each other to shreds. Fe orbited within the vicinity as gravity bashed two of the giants together in a spectacular display of carnage. Captured by one another's pull, each ripped into the very core of their opponent, spraying a spiral of glowing-hot debris into space. After many revolutions, the aftermath resolved–the larger planetesimal that would one day be called 'Earth' healed and regained its spherical shape, holding the smaller, defeated mass in thrall as its anomalously large satellite.

Thousands of asteroids, including Fe's, gradually migrated toward a belt accumulating around the inner planets. However, an irregular rocky chunk, unstable in its orbit and helpless to maneuver, delivered a glancing blow to the larger body ridden by Fe. Bonded in metallic lattice, the atom vibrated with a thrum of sudden kinetic energy. Chunks of alloy sheared from the asteroid's surface, cooling and floating off into oblivion. The rocky interloper careened wildly away after the impact, fated to be swallowed up by the enormous planet Jupiter. Fe's asteroid took a different path. Vectored out of the inner Solar system, it flew beyond the orbits of even the outermost gas giants and still further, until Sol became just another bright star in the distance.

Once every several hundred thousand years, measured in revolutions of the Earth about its star, Fe's asteroid would make an inevitable return to the inner system, moving along its orbital trajectory as smoothly as if it ran on rails. The metallic space-rock avoided the giant planets, hardly encountering even the smallest bit of matter during its endless cycle of lopsided orbits about Sol–one brief moment of light and heat, followed by a frigid, black eternity.

Millions of years passed this way in the young Solar system. Over and over, Fe's asteroid traced its wild loop. The inner planets were all still aflame. Mercury, scorched by its massive stellar neighbor, was dragged along helplessly by Sol's gravity. The Earth-sized Venus smoldered in its orbit, volcanoes bursting like angry pustules on the world's surface. The third planet danced with its giant moon, exchanging momentum while waltzing through the universe together. The diminutive, iron-rich Mars stood sentinel for the terrestrial planets, marking the wall of asteroids which separated them from the giants. Jupiter's surface stormed and raged, its core boiled with unknowable pressures, and lovely Saturn slowly developed magnificent moons and rings. Uranus and Neptune shivered in their distant orbits, churning global seas of frozen gasses and marking the boundaries of the planets' domain.

Fe's glacially slow U-turn eventually led the asteroid back into the Solar system to enjoy its too-brief sojourn in sunlight. Compared with its lengthy journey through the faraway empty regions, Fe's rock basked in Sol's glory for a mere instant.

Inside the nearby planet Earth, a white hot mass of Fe's sibling irons revolved like a communal dynamo, creating powerful currents and generating a strong magnetic field that protected the young planet from Sol's relentless, atmosphere-stripping wind. The young Earth flexed its gravity, holding onto water molecules, some carbon dioxide, and above all nitrogen. Large comets of frozen water—two ancient hydrogens bonded to a single oxygen—slammed into the planet's surface, dumping payload after payload until the Earth became a wet planet. Such a bombardment had given Mars a watery surface as well, and the hot planet Venus grew similarly soaked.

One billion years after Sol's ignition, fundamental changes began within its empire. During one orbit, Fe's asteroid passed a sterile Earth—on the next, it sailed above a living world. A near-infinite number of random particle interactions had formed certain compounds, precursors to proteins. These simple molecules grew in complexity via successful one-in-a-million combinations until they had become self-replicating. The proteins most successful at synthesizing chemical copies of themselves lived on, and the process of natural selection took over.

Another billion years of monotony-on-rails for Fe, but downbelow, life was busy building walls to protect itself from the outside world, drinking in Sol's light to stay alive. The metallic asteroid swung in close and hurtled back out into purgatory, silently enduring cycle after cycle of the fateful dance. Nothing ever happened to the atom Fe or its bonded, static siblings. The Earth, however, underwent changes more rapid and more revolutionary than any world for light years around.

Trillions of tiny photosynthesizing factories pumped molecule after molecule of volatile oxygen into the planet's atmosphere, leading to stranger and stranger phenomena. Eukaryotes breathed the highly-reactive gas, meeting, competing, and turning the gears of evolution ever more rapidly. As life blossomed upon the Earth, the small planet Mars began to die. Over billions of years, the diminutive world cooled and faded. Left with no magnetic field and no protection, solar wind blasted away much of its atmosphere. Mars' water evaporated, and its thin crust of organics withered. All that remained was a corpse of a world, stained red with oxides of Fe's wasted siblings.

Pass after pass, Fe's asteroid waited for the perfect synchronicity of the laws of physics that would release it from its orbital prison. Down on Earth, photosynthetic land-dwellers, colored by their chlorophyll, graffitied the world in green. Ages passed, and land animals took over the lush continents, insects spreading their wings to buzz through the low jungles. Eons of competition followed, and eventually, the very continents of Earth were shaken by colossal organisms grown to unheard of proportions–dinosaurs proliferating in their billions. An asteroid, far larger and more expeditious than Fe's own, brought down one biological empire, only to give rise to another. A new order ascended, boasting fur and warm blood, caring ever more intimately for its young. Epic dramas between predators and prey played themselves out on the surface of the breathing world. Horns clashed, teeth bit, and blood spilled. Frightened things burrowed into the ground, and seagoing leviathans lurked beneath the blue planet's waves. Fated by orbital dynamics, the wayward asteroid's path converged into the perfect plane, at the perfect distance, and at the perfect time.

It would only be a matter of orbits.

Locked in its metallic lattice, Fe completed another hundred or so, passing ever closer to the fated Earth. Meanwhile, large, tree-dwelling animals diverged from their mammalian ancestors, using cunning brains and dexterous hands to carve out a niche for themselves. Their brave descendants learned to master fire born from atmospheric lightning, and they quickly ascended to dominate the globe. They grew smarter, stronger, and taller–they trapped abstract thought in bits of mundane matter. They became human. From one orbit to the next, they wandered their world.

Some four and half billion years after its birth, the atom Fe left Earth and its crafty creatures behind once more, swinging off into the void for the final time.

Hostile climatic conditions, or the discovery of an especially fertile landscape, occasionally induced the hominid wanderers to pause their perambulations. Where they settled, the humans built cities and gods. Sitting still for so long motivated the primates to move stones into neat piles and call those who stood atop 'king'. They dug ore from the planet's skin and smashed it with rocks. They tamed the world's beasts, learning to bend the evolution of their fellow creatures toward their own ends...

Chapter 1: The Prince

Akkar stood atop a large stone, one hand shading his dark brown eyes against the glare of the afternoon sun. Nearby, the goats grazed serenely, either unaware of the heat of the day or unbothered by it. The boy was ostensibly watching the herd, keeping an eye out for predators and thieves. However, neither Akkar nor his father had seen any wild dogs in ages, and nobody in their hamlet would consider stealing the King's livestock. Goats out of mind, Akkar gazed at the tall grass, trying to catch a glimpse of his sister. Hattal was small for her age, and her tan, dusty skin blended with the sandy earth and grass.

At the moment, she employed her formidable camouflage to its fullest. Without warning, Akkar smacked his long wooden staff against the stone, creating a loud crack that echoed through the valley. He hoped to spook her out of hiding but succeeded only in rousing the goats. They started, and turned their horned heads toward the sound. An almost disrespectfully short moment later, though, the beasts quieted and returned to grazing, annoyed at the momentary interruption of their busy schedules.

Akkar habitually wore nothing but simple pants, tied around the waist with a length of flax cord, augmented by the occasional head or hand wrap. Hattal, however, had recently taken to wearing a polished stone around her neck. She found it in the bottom of their stream. It had been smoothed on all sides by eons of water and shone nearly transparent, though a pale pink hue revealed itself if the sun hit just right.

Like a glimpse of an early poppy blossom, Akkar saw the nearly imperceptible flash of color from deep within the dry grass. Wordlessly, he bent down and picked up a dried goat dropping, closed one eye, and hurled the missile toward his target.

Hattal gasped, more out of surprise than pain. She stood upright, glaring at her brother.

Akkar let out a triumphant whoop and began to laugh. Anger flashed in Hattal's eyes. While Akkar was doubled over, the girl broke into a sprint, closing quickly to tackle him from atop his stone. He landed heavily, hitting the ground near a pile of goat pellets, raising a small cloud of dust.

Hattal climbed up the stone, straightening her necklace and shaking the dust from her wild hair. Akkar stayed on the ground, staring up at the cloudless sky. A lone bird entered his peripheral vision. It flew fast and straight on black wings.

"Aaaayyy!" Hattal screeched suddenly, leaping from her perch to attack her prone brother.

Akkar watched her shadow. At the last instant, he rolled away, dodging the attack and letting his assailant land hands-first in the pile of droppings.

She turned to him and hissed. Hattal's deep brown eyes smoldered with bloodlust. Anyone other than Akkar might have been frightened by the feral girl, but long experience had taught him his young sister's preference for taking things to extremes—especially play.

"Maybe we try peace?" He said to her in the language of their people.

Rather than responding, Hattal filled her hands with the goats' shiny leavings and flung them at her brother in a wild, unaimed assault.

"Oh!" He scrambled in the dust, running away from the mad spray of feces pellets.

Akkar regained his feet and his wooden staff, and taking shelter behind the large stone, he risked a glance at his opponent. Instead of pressing the assault, the girl was busy unwrapping a small bundle she had just found.

Aghast, the goatherd watched his sister take a bite from his mid-day meal.

"Thief!" He bellowed.

It was a simple lunch of ground grain-cakes and a bit of dried meat, but it was the principle that mattered.

Akkar strode over, and ignoring the kicking of her thin legs, the much-taller older sibling reached down and grabbed Hattal by her upper arm. He pulled her part of the way up, then flung her to the dusty ground, where she landed some distance away.

"Inanna curse you!" She spat at him.

"Maybe I hit you with this," Akkar offered, slamming the tip of his staff into the ground for emphasis, "then you can go *meet* Inanna?"

"Brother–"

"You should know better than to take bread from a man's mouth." Annoyed, Akkar picked up and rewrapped what he could salvage from the meal.

"Brother!" Hattal repeated, pulling herself up. "The goats!"Sure enough, the herd had wandered down the hillside, giving the humans space to resolve their differences. Akkar called out to them, but the distant grazers chose not to notice. One of the older goats traveled further afield than the others, and the remainder were currently following her into a hidden valley.

Akkar cursed.

"Come on!" The goatherd called to his sister, their feud instantly forgotten.

The siblings scrambled after their livestock, hurtling down the hillside and letting the dry grass tear at their simple flaxen garments. They ran hard, creating more heat than they could radiate away, allowing the unforgiving sun to bake their skins and raise beads of sweat from their pores.

Soon enough, the goats noticed the hot pursuit of their masters. Rather than cowing to the shepherds, they simply picked up the pace of their excursion.

Akkar bellowed, and, running hard, he caught up to the trailing goat–an otherwise strong male that suffered from a slightly lame rear leg. The goatherd pounded his hand firmly against the animal's flanks, avoiding its horns and turning it submissively back. While he worked, however, the other members of the herd trotted even further away.

"Go around, stupid," Hattal scolded her brother, running up alongside.

"What?""Go to the front!" She ordered, holding out her hand. "Give him here."

Not wasting time to argue, Akkar left the lame goat in his sister's care. He traced a wide path around the herd as he ran, forcing himself up a steep, rocky rise and running down the other side in order to cut the animals off at the front. Before long, the sweat-soaked Akkar found himself ahead of the lead female. He stood before her, panting, staring her down, his hands on his knees. Unimpressed, the goat stared back, chewing her cud.

The two creatures locked eyes–Akkar's preferred battleground. The old nanny goat let out a bleat of stubborn protest, but soon she withered under the huffing human's fiery glare. He put his hands on her broad abdomen, turning her body in the direction he wanted her to go, but, uncharacteristically, the other goats in the herd began to moan in unified unease.

"What's wrong with you?" He snapped at the animals, hot and out of patience.

Their bleats turned to full-blown screams.

Akkar heard a subtle tone beneath the animal noises, something on the edge of imagination. For an instant, a shadow flickered over the sun, and the goatherd turned, shielding his eyes and gazing at the sky. A large bird traveled the empty firmament above. It flew straight and energetically, slicing quickly across the sky–too quickly. Akkar squinted, making out a glinting mass but discerning no wings or head. A long white tail began to extend from behind the bird, and without warning, it ignited into a blinding ball of fire.

● ● ●

The asteroid that carried Fe, its mass no greater than an especially large land mammal, plummeted toward the shimmering Earth. Green continents, interspersed with vast stretches of featureless desert, floated in deep blue waters that stretched from one horizon to the next. Long, white clouds snaked across the sky, swirling in the atmosphere and making the planet seem even more alive. Fe's asteroid shattered this peaceful scene, hurtling at blistering speed.

When the air in the upper reaches of the ionosphere kissed the face of the asteroid, it was the first time Fe or any of its sibling atoms had interacted with other particles of matter in billions of years. The air grew thicker as the reunion between cousins blasted away the face of the meteor. The metal rapidly warmed as the forces of friction converted the traveler's leftover orbital energy into furious heat. Outer layers of metallic compounds and rocky deposits ablated off the incoming projectile. Trillions of Fe's siblings were scattered to the winds as the entire mass erupted.

To the horror of the goatherds, the bird burst into flame and was now engaged in a screaming, doomed plummet. Akkar stood staring, open-mouthed. Hattal caught up to her brother and clung to him, terrified. Together, their sharp eyes followed the firebird's descent. It curved across the sky, losing altitude with each passing second until—the flaming beast dropped behind a low hill in the distance. The two humans stood still, not quite believing what their eyes had seen. A moment passed, and then a deep and terrifying rumble shook the land.

Hattal cried out, and Akkar bit his lip to keep from doing the same. The sound was like the most frightening thunder they had ever heard, but somehow alien—hitting their feet before their ears.

Meanwhile, the goats flew into an uncontrolled panic. They stomped and bleated, running terrified in random directions. It only took a moment for Akkar's shock to wear off. He shouted at his sister and ran into the herd. Together, they struggled to locate and overpower the panicking animals, returning them to the group one by one. During the demanding, sweaty work, all Akkar wished to do was to run off beyond the hills and see where the firebird had fallen, but the King's goats always came first. It took much of the latter half of the day to round up and calm the animals, but eventually, the goatherds were able to march their beasts to an enclosure.

Hattal led the herd, an impatient Akkar bringing up the rear, preventing any of his charges from running for the hills—something the boy himself ached for with each retreating step.

Night threatened by the time they completed the goat-drive, but the very instant Akkar was sure his sister had control of the animals, he sprinted off in the direction of the firebird's fall. The boy flew through the tall grass, his heart pounding a steady rhythm and his bare feet thudding against the hard, dry earth. In his mind, he knew that he should be frightened. Akkar's herd had run away from the fire in the sky and the terrible noise. The goats had sense enough to avoid danger, so why didn't he? Somehow, the fear of the unknown only added to the youthful excitement and curiosity that overwhelmed the adolescent human's mind.

His pace slowed as he started up an especially-steep rise. He was tired, and no amount of anticipation could overcome his body's limits. Akkar took a knee and caught his breath. He glanced back at his family's hamlet—a simple cluster of dried-mud enclosures surrounding a communal square. In the valley opposite, sprawling irrigated fields separated the herders from the city proper. Akkar glimpsed the star of Inanna on the horizon and pivoted, trying to trace the path of the fallen traveler. He could just make out the stones of the Kishite citadel from the flickering firelights upon its walls, burning like a bloody reflection of the stars above. Surely, the goatherd reasoned, many of his people had seen the firebird as it passed over, or had felt its terrible crash, but none were as close as he. Emboldened by this thought, and the goddess above, Akkar resumed his climb.

The rise gave way to a descent into a narrow valley, followed by yet another steep hill. Dry and winded, the goatherd wondered if he'd even know the traveler if he saw it. He reached the top of the hill and scanned the surrounding area, looking for the corpse of the firebird. Despite the demands of his lungs, Akkar's breath caught in his throat—the land in the distance had been obliterated.

An old well and the small copse of trees that surrounded it had been utterly erased. Hattal would often draw water there when their herds ventured especially far. In place of the modest oasis, now there gaped a sprawling hole in the earth, far wider than it was deep. Mist rose from the wound, making it appear as though some great god had scooped out a handful of the living planet. Stones and steaming clumps of dirt littered the ground around the edge of the steep-sided wound, the firebird's crash having raised a lip of earth around the crater's rim.

After scaling the cone, Akkar noted that a flat plane lay in the depression within the crater, and at its very center, smoke billowed from a black speck. He squinted to get a better look, but it was useless against the night's gloom. He held his staff tightly as he approached, ready to defend himself in case the beast had survived its fall. He trod upon a burning ember and gasped, but his pace didn't slow. Akkar hurtled the final lip of the wound and slid down the slope on his rear. The smoke made his eyes water, but he recklessly stumbled ahead toward the deepest part of the crater. The smoking speck was actually a shallow pit, and Akkar fell to his knees to look inside. The smoke had not abated, so he gingerly reached down to explore the cavity–

"Ay!" Pain shot through the nerves in the human's fingers, radiating up his arm.

Almost immediately he brought his hand back up, putting the scorched skin to his mouth and instinctively sucking on it. Perhaps material from heaven will always sear mortal flesh, he reasoned, or perhaps the Gods were angry with him. He examined the burn, finding it blistered, but with no markers of the supernatural. He comforted himself with the mundane theory that the fiery traveler was still too hot, and he merely needed to wait until it was ready for him.

Akkar forced himself to be patient. He licked at his burnt hand and rubbed his eyes, banishing sleep when it threatened. His night-adapted vision began to make out the vague shape of the object through the fog, and after what seemed like an eternity to the naturally impatient youth, the haze cleared. It was not until the first rays of the rising sun provided enough illumination that the goatherd finally stood and gazed down into the hole, seeing nothing but a large stone. He was struck by a rush of disappointment and confusion.

"Where is the firebird?" He wondered aloud, to himself and to the Gods.

However, as Akkar examined the stone more closely, his disappointment evaporated. It was like nothing he had ever seen–black and shiny, covered in round pits with smoothed edges. The stone almost seemed to be made of liquid, the way its surfaces shimmered and flowed. It wasn't a bird at all, the boy realized all at once. The fire from the sky came from this magic stone, crashed to Earth from the heavens. Akkar longed to touch it, but he'd learned his lesson.

* * *

News of the alleged firebird traveled with meteoric swiftness through the city of Kish and outlying areas. The temple priests were torn in their analysis–the meteor was a blessing from the Gods—it was a dark omen and symbol of destruction. Often, they spoke the two contradictory interpretations in the same breath. When King Zuqaqip, still blinking the sleep from his eyes, first heard tell of the visitor from heaven, he ordered a detachment of guards and workmen to travel to the impact site and retrieve it immediately.

Thus, the morning after the firebird crashed from the sky, four soldiers, four slaves, and a temple priest followed the directions of the townspeople to the scrubland where the meteor had landed. They brought along a two-wheeled sled, harnessed to an onager and filled with spades for digging and spears in case the priests' more ominous interpretations turned out to be correct. When the party arrived, they found a parched-looking youth standing guard above the crater, armed with a wooden staff.

Their bronze spear tips gleaming, the four soldiers in the detachment advanced on the goatherd, but the temple priest halted them with a gesture.

"Why do you stand there, boy?" He asked. "Is this where the visitor from heaven made its landing?"

"Visitor? It is a fallen star—a stone from the Gods, and I found it," Akkar answered, standing as tall as he could before the messengers of the King.

"If it fell in the lands of King Zuqaqip, it belongs to King Zuqaqip," the tallest of the soldiers thundered.

The priest raised his hand, calming the soldier. "It's here, yes?" He asked Akkar. "How do you know of its nature?"

"I touched it," the boy answered before he could think better of it.

A collective gasp issued from the King's men.

Too late, Akkar tried to conceal his burned hand, but at a gesture from the priest, the irate soldier lunged forward and seized the goatherd. The staff fell from the boy's grip as the brute grabbed his other arm, presenting the blistered fingertips to the priest.

"You have violated the will of the Gods, boy. Do you know what happens to those who try to steal from the King?"

The priest's voice rose, threateningly, but just as Akkar was about to surrender to despair, Hattal arrived at the scene, holding a ceramic jug.

"Brother," she called out, coming toward them from the other direction, "are you with someone?"

"Hattal!" He screamed.

As she beheld the small army surrounding Akkar, Hattal gave out a shriek and dropped the jug, which shattered, spilling its mixture of water and grain into the thirsty earth. The confusion that followed gave just enough time for their father to arrive, huffing and puffing, the thick patriarch having lagged behind his energetic daughter.

"What's the meaning of this?" He wheezed at the men who held his son.

"We are emissaries of Zuqaqip, your King," the priest answered, his voice hard. "A gift fell from heaven last night, and we've come to retrieve it. This boy is standing in our way."

"That boy is my son, and I assure you he means you no harm. Our family has always been loyal to King Zuqaqip—we manage his goats in these hills! It's no wonder my Akkar came upon it first if it landed here of all places. I cannot imagine he wishes to bar the King's progress." With these last words, Akkar's father gave his son a meaningful look.

"The Gods have already judged your son for trying to claim the King's prize—behold!" The priest pointed to the goatherd's blistered skin.

Akkar's father bent to examine the burn. Fear darted across his face, replaced quickly with a mask of rage.

"Stupid boy!" He bellowed, grabbing his son by the shoulders and pulling him out of the surprised soldier's grip. "What made you think you could hold something sent by the Gods? Would a son of mine have immortal fingers? Tell me true, Akkar—were you trying to claim this gift as your own?"

As he screamed, he tossed his son into the dirt and leveled a hard-looking kick at the boy, pulling back just before impacting his ribs.

"No! I did not try to take it for my own. I swear!" Akkard sobbed, curled into a ball at his father's feet.

"I see now your trouble," the father explained to the King's detachment, struggling to catch his breath. "This boy is very lucky if you ask me."

"How so?" The priest answered, surprised by the goatherding patriarch's sudden aggression.

"He must be *blessed* by the Gods to have come away so lightly after grasping such a thing, clearly never meant for his hands. Our family is very grateful for the mercy of the Gods and the King."

With that, Akkar's father produced a small gold coin from the folds of his robes and handed it to the priest, who accepted it without remark.

"Come on, boy–get you gone! Hattal!" Their father bellowed, hastily ushering the children in the direction opposite the men with spears, stumbling down the hillside and quickly out of sight and mind.

Impatient to get on with things, the soldiers prodded the laborers forward. They stood around the hole, staring down at something truly alien. Much of Fe's asteroid's mass had been lost as it entered the atmosphere, and though the melted metallic lump could now be carried by a single strong human, none of those present were willing to try.

A shallow jab from a soldier's bronze spearpoint proved enough for them to take the risk. None were burned as they loaded the shiny black meteor onto the sled bound for the city, but the enslaved humans who briefly hefted the stone made sure to rub their hands in the dirt afterward in an effort to purify themselves.

Once Fe's meteorite had been lugged safely behind the walls of the city of Kish, Zuqaqip, King of all, ordered the assembly of a small council to advise him on the heavenly visitor. The meteorite rested heavily on a stone table in the largest room of the King's palace. Generals, priests, a scribe, and one ancient artisan gathered around it. No useful information was initially put forth by the council. The military knew not what to make of it, and the priests could only offer poorly crafted superstition. It wasn't until a lull in the conversation that Quishda first spoke.

"I have seen stones of this type before," the elderly artisan offered, breaking the silence, "though never one as large as this."

"What do you know, Quishda?" One of the higher priests asked, indicating the blackened lump that lay before them.

"May I?" He tentatively reached out a hand.

The King gave a small nod, granting permission to his late father's friend and confidant.

Quishda placed his hand against the cool surface of the meteorite.

"It is a metal, Lord, like copper, gold, or silver." The artisan's voice lowered in awe. "Men can dig these lesser metals from the earth, but the material in *this* stone only exists in heaven. It is the rarest seen in my trade, so seldom worked that it does not even have a name—many magical properties, though. Such a gift from heaven would shed much glory upon your Lordship if it were to take the right form."

"Old man," Zuqaqip rumbled, "you forged copper into spearpoints and arrowheads for the armies of my father in days long past, but have you ever before worked this heaven metal?"

"None has come to these lands until now," Quishda shrugged, his voice rising defensively, though his eyes remained tactfully averted from his monarch. "I have thus never had the opportunity, but his Lordship knows well my skill."

The King's hand moved to the gold chains he wore around his neck—one that had been his father's and one made for Zuqaqip's own coronation, both from the forge of Quishda. Though each was an exquisite artifact to behold, the King often resented that the links in the newer chain were fewer and thinner.

Quishda allowed his excitement to fill the silence. "Entrust the stone to me, Lord, and I shall craft you a dagger of legend, sharp enough to pierce the very fabric of night."

This rash claim was based on little more than a feeling in the artisan's aching bones. He had grown old and had little left to lose—the chance to unlock the secrets of heaven metal was worth risking the fatal displeasure of the King should he fail.

To the dismay of the priests, Zuqaqip agreed to bequeath custody of the metal to Quishda. A blade made from the mysterious black ore would do much for his semi-divine reputation, the King well knew, and he ordered the meteorite to be secreted to Quishda's workshop. Two of his slaves wrapped the object in a wool blanket, which they held between themselves, and they carried it out of the palace, down clay steps to the waiting onager sled.

● ● ●

Fe's meteorite rested heavily on the floor of Quishda's simple hut. The old man paced around the heavenly rock, scratching his chin. He stared in silent reverence until the baby screamed. She waved her arms, out and above her head, whining, straining against the leather harness that held her.

The wailing creature belonged to Quishda's daughter, who went out during the day engaged in business of her own, leaving the infant to the dubious warmth of her grandfather and his forge. His reverie broken, the artisan stepped over to release the child from her prison—an ingenious system of slings that Quishda had designed himself to keep the babe from crawling where she should not. Almost instantly, she quieted, content with being free.

Quishda let his grandchild crawl toward the lump of heaven metal. He'd heard tales of the fallen object melting the flesh from the hand of an unworthy goatherd who'd tried to claim it, but the infant seemed unharmed as she pressed her soft hands and lips against the surface of Fe's meteorite. The metal was divine, to be sure, but it had been a gift, not a curse, Quishda reasoned—to Zuqaqip, to Kish, perhaps even to himself.

"Kee," the child babbled.

The old man remembered his task and appraised the meteorite with a critical smith's eye.

"Pellets of copper or gold can be melted and reforged easily enough," he thought aloud, "but what can the tools of man hope to accomplish when used against the metal of the Gods?"

"Kee?"

"Let us find out."

Quishda unsheathed a small copper blade from inside his boot, leaned down, and attempted to carve a slice from the heaven metal, pushing the baby aside with one foot. The copper edge of the blade bent when he applied pressure to the alloy, and the smith immediately stopped so as not to cause further damage.

"Fear not," he said to his granddaughter, exchanging the copper blade for an even smaller scraper knife.

Made from an alloy of copper and tin, the knife's bronze edge met the black exterior of the meteorite in a clash of elements. Nickel atoms and Fe's sibling irons resisted the advance of the copper-tin metallic lattice, which sent a defiant, straining force through the thin, brittle invader.

"Anu take me!" Quishda screamed as the bronze shattered in his hand.

Angered by the tool's failure, he tossed the valuable bronze scraps across the hut. His absent daughter's baby began to whimper, but he paid it no mind.

Placing the copper aside and muttering curses, Quishda rummaged beneath his sleeping furs and pulled out a tiny clay pot. Inside was the elder's most prized possession–a diminutive jade hand axe. On one side, it boasted a sharpened, curved face, like a large flat tooth. The other, duller side served as a handle.

"This is probably one of the oldest objects in the world," he said, slowly and soothingly.

"Ya?" The baby calmed, turning to listen, now curious.

"Passed down through the ancient royal lines of Kish, this." He held up the green stone. "But the King gave it to *me*. The King, I mean–not *this* King. It's jade, child, rare and precious and perhaps magical as well. Though it be formed from the bones of the Earth, it just may shave the stone from heaven."

The aged craftsman wrapped his right hand in a strip of leather and began gingerly scraping the edge of the ornate hand axe against the meteorite's surface. The iron-nickel alloy, champion against copper, yielded to jade. On a molecular level, the hard green stone terminated in a vanishingly thin edge–only a few crystalline blocks of a near-mystically tough arrangement of both metal and non-metal ions working as one. The intermolecular bonds within the meteorite could take only so much physical strain, and with great patience, Quishda scraped tiny flakes from the mass until he had a small handful of the black metal.

Still many layers deep in the alloy, the atom Fe was not among these scrapings, though the jade cleaved away trillions upon trillions of the sibling irons whom Fe had been born alongside and had shared an orbit with since time before time.

With reverence, the old man returned his jade treasure to its home and gathered the hard-won iron shavings into a pouch in his robes. He returned the baby to the harness, despite her protests, and left the cramped space. Throwing aside a heavy pair of hide curtains, Quishda found himself temporarily blinded by the late afternoon sun. He walked around the back of his hovel, where a workshop of sorts had been set up. It somewhat resembled a stable for goats or onagers, though the smith's area boasted a long flat table, a chest of tools, and a kiln the size of a fat child. With a deep groan, Quishda bent down and untied a bundle of sticks and kindling.

He set to work lighting the kiln. During more mundane times, the elderly craftsman used this rudimentary furnace to fire ceramics and for occasional metal-working. Once the kiln's fire crackled, he located a crucible and poured the handful of iron shavings inside, careful not to lose any of the precious alloy. Quishda used the same method to melt white metals, which he could then cast by pouring the molten product into a simple form of sand and tallow. He told himself that he was using the shavings to test the properties of the heaven metal, but he harbored a fantasy of keeping this small amount to fashion himself a ring.

What divine powers would be bestowed on the bearer of a ring from the heavens, Quishda could only imagine. When the kiln was ready, the craftsman held the crucible between two sticks and slid it inside the furnace. His plan was to heat the metal for three times as long as was normally required for gold smelting.

While he waited for the heaven metal to melt, Quishda prepared a ring mold. The craftsman carved a circular shape into the sand outside his workshop and carefully poured some drops of hot animal fat around the mold, forcing it to keep its shape long enough for a ring to form.

Through the evening and the night, Quishda kept the fires in the kiln burning. At a certain point, his daughter came home with food and beer. She fed the baby while the smith chewed absentmindedly at his dinner. He walked outside to check the progress of the crucible more than once, and each time he returned to his hut, he found his beer jug just a little lighter.

Quishda found himself unable to eat or sleep much during the time the kiln burned, though his daughter and the baby slept like the dead. He waited with a patience that comes only from age, keeping his mind's eye always on the glowing fires of his forge.

At dawn, the time had come at last. The old man pulled the crucible out of the half-dead fire, as quickly as he was able, using a combination of sticks and hands wrapped in clumsy woolen mitts. He set the crucible down on a flat stone and peered inside. The shavings of the heaven metal glowed a faint orange, but they were still very much intact.

"Unmeltable!" Quishda bellowed, storming back into his hovel, the crucible still clutched in one gloved hand.

The old smith found himself alone, save for his granddaughter who stared at him as though his frustration fascinated her.

"Oh!" He said in surprise. "I see that Erish has gone off to wherever she goes, and your grandfather has been a fool. Of course my fire cannot melt metal from the very heavens!"

The smith stomped around until he located a small granite anvil that he had once used for fine jewelry work.

"Was the stone not aflame as it fell from the sky?" He muttered, upending the crucible, pouring the smoldering iron scraps on the rock. "Fool! But, perhaps–"

Quishda picked up a striking stone and smashed it down on the iron. Sparks flew with the impact. He pushed the shavings together in a pile and struck again.

Tied in her harness, the baby stared, transfixed–not even managing to cry out at the spectacle.

Quishda pounded the hot iron alloy until no more sparks flew. He wiped sweat from his brow, and rummaged inside his hovel for a skin of water. He poured the tepid liquid on the iron, which steamed and hissed as it cooled.

"Keee!" The baby cooed in wonder.

With trepidation, Quishda's fingers brushed against the metallic lump. It was cool enough to touch, and he took it in his hand. The iron shavings had been smashed together into a misshapen and jagged mass. A spark of hope ignited within the old man.

"It cannot be melted or cast, but it can be *forged*," he whispered.

After all, had he not just dismantled part of the stone and then forced it back together with the powers of fire and his own strength?

The aged craftsman was right, though he had no way of knowing why. Fe shared its outer electrons with other iron atoms, locked together through metallic bonds. As the temperature of the metal fluctuated, quantum distribution of these outermost charges flowed around the metallic crystal, bonding the atoms inside ever more tightly. These intermolecular forces inhibited the meteoric iron from easily melting. More Earthly sources of iron at the time were already heavily oxidized, locked away from the people of Kish and their technology. It would take another thousand years before humans would come to master iron.

Despite the challenges, Quishda, artisan of Kish, worked feverishly through the day and into the night. He'd learned that the unmeltable metal could nevertheless be worked if it were warm enough. Doggedly, he continued to heat the nickel-iron lump in the kiln until it glowed faintly. Each time, Quishda extracted the hot metal and flattened it with stones, sending sparks and light flying from each strike. Finally, he had scraped and smashed the lump until it resembled a smooth flat coin. Again it entered the kiln. When it emerged, the craftsman painstakingly gouged a hole from the center of the coin using the tip of his jade axe.

Another heating, another shaping, another heating, and one last round of smoothing and polishing followed. By the time Quishda stumbled back into his hovel, finally finished, his bones hurt and he was as tired as he had ever been. However, the man felt exhilaration, for he had a ring of heaven metal in his possession. With the precious craft clutched in one hand, he collapsed into dreamless slumber.

"Yaya. Zee!"

When he awoke, it was morning and he and the baby were alone. Rubbing the sleep from his eyes, Quishda remembered the promise made to King Zuqaqip.

"A *dagger*," he moaned, "I promised, child. I cannot fail the king."

To give himself strength, Quishda slipped the iron ring onto the middle finger of his right hand—it felt rough and heavy against his skin. After a pause, however, he decided it would be better to keep the heaven metal out of sight. Looping the ring through a length of cord, the artisan tied it around his neck and slipped it beneath his robes.

The kiln out back would not be sufficient to do the larger job, Quishda well knew. He rubbed the baby's soft head until she fell asleep, then walked to the town square and flagged down the first man he saw wearing armor and holding a spear, passing him a message to deliver to Zuqaqip.

• • •

Quishda briefed a palace representative on the challenges of working the obstinate heaven metal, and the King duly granted his request for the assistance of several enslaved laborers for the day. Under the craftsman's direction, the palace slaves dismantled his old kiln and set to building something better suited to forging iron. They dug a deep pit for the fire, carving channels in the dirt to allow for better airflow. Instead of an enclosed oven, useful for firing pots and melting gold, the new forge was made with an exposed space above the flames. Quishda's design would allow him to hammer the metal while it was still being heated, giving him longer to work with the malleable material before it had to be once again submerged in hellfire.

Construction finished by sundown. Quishda, however, did not retire for the night. Instead, he immediately lit his new forge, enlisting a slave to shove the entire meteorite into the embers of the fire pit. For the second time in four billion years, Fe's load of thermal energy began to rise—precipitously, though far more slowly than days earlier when the atom had ridden a flaming meteor to Earth.

It took hours of stoking the flames before the meteoric alloy rose to a temperature hot enough to be worked, but when it did, Quishda eagerly pounded the glowing iron with a stone striker. Impurities flaked and broke off as the amorphous metal lump was smashed into shape. Next, the smith plunged the meteorite back into the coals until it glowed orange once again. He hammered the hot iron, endeavoring to force a flat and elongated shape. After several reheatings and furious beatings, Fe's meteorite no longer resembled itself—the metallic bonds between the iron atoms were still intact, but they had been coerced to move as a group under the forces of Quishda's hammer.

After quenching the rough iron ingot, the old smith went back inside to rest, but he could see little after staring into the fires for so long. Someone, either Erish or the baby, spoke to him, but he did not have the strength to respond. While he slept, he clutched Fe's warm metal slug in his arms like a beloved child.

The next morning, the fires were relit, the ingot went back in the forge, and the metal slowly gained thermal energy. Quishda was not an armorer or weaponsmith by inclination, so he elected for a simple design—the meteoric iron could be shaped into a long dagger, complete with blade, hilt, and guard. Crafted from a single piece of metal, the dagger would be heavy and poorly balanced, but it was the best Quishda could do under the circumstances.

Gradually, the weapon began to emerge from Fe's ingot, its blade drawn out and pounded flat. The smith hammered out a simple guard and painstakingly forged a rounded grip. Twice, Quishda burned his hand testing the dimensions of the blade. He longed for rest but knew that he must finish the dagger quickly or risk provoking the King's impatience. With a few more hours of working, the ingot had transformed into an intimidating weapon.

"Exquisite, is it not?" Quishda asked, cradling the nearly-finished dagger.

"Yaya." The baby reached out one tiny, soft finger, and her grandfather allowed her to caress the handle of the black metal weapon.

"I made this," the old man said, slightly embarrassed by his own pride. "A gift from the Gods to the King, but forged by my hand."

Quishda shared another moment of quiet pride with the child before wrapping a strip of fine leather around the dagger's grip and leaving for the palace. Once in the presence of the soldiers of Kish, the old smith requested the use of a turning stone for sharpening. The process took longer than usual, as standard copper-alloy blades yielded more easily to the rough stone than the mystical heaven metal, but Quishda ground and polished the weapon, over and over again, until he felt satisfied with its razor edge.

The dagger containing Fe was presented to the King that evening. Quishda carried it at arm's length and set it upon a soft fur pillow. The metal was almost black in color, with little sheen, and the entire weapon stretched about the length of a grown man's forearm. Its blade was sharpened on both sides, and its edges came together at a symmetrical, wickedly-sharp point—a tool for stabbing. The grip was simple goat leather, otherwise unadorned. Zuqaqip loved it.

"You've done well, old man," the King said, unable to tear his divine eyes from the heaven metal in his hands.

"It is my honor to serve your Lordship."

"This blade of yours is spectacular to look upon, but its true value is in the provenance–the abode of the Gods. Indeed, the Gods have sent me this blade so that all will know me as a living symbol of their divinity."

For Zuqaqip, the object further legitimized his reign and power. Since inheriting the throne, the young King had occasional doubts as to what qualified him to rule. He knew the crown was his by divine right, but he never felt confident about that fact until he took the heavy, unwieldy dagger into his hands.

Zuqaqip admired the blade closely. "I can feel the power radiating from within," he rumbled.

When he lowered the dagger, however, the King noticed that Quishda wore a queer expression. The old man had been acting furtively since taking custody of the magical stone, Zuqaqip realized. Sending messengers instead of speaking to him in person–and now Quishda was shrinking from his praise.

"Approach," Zuqaqip commanded.

Quishda reluctantly obeyed, his gaze cast low. Tearing his focus from the blade, the King studied the cowering smith and noticed that he was wearing something around his neck that had not been there three days previous.

The old man did not back away as the King extended his hand, reaching toward his throat. Zuqaqip gripped the cord and lifted the iron ring out from under Quishda's robe. With a downward tug, he ripped off the strap and forced the old smith to his knees. The King let the stolen piece of heaven metal fall to the floor, where it clanged and clattered against the cold, stone tile.

"Traitor!" Zuqaqip bellowed. "The gift that fell from heaven–all of it–has been given to *me*! As a symbol that *I* walk as a god among men. And you dare to sample its power?"

Quishda tried to protest, but fear had frozen the voice in his throat.

"You may have somehow earned the love of my father," the King continued, "but for this, thief, be assured that he will turn his back to you in the afterlife."

With that, King Zuqaqip plunged the iron dagger into the back of Quishda's neck. The strong metallic bonds of the meteoritic alloy easily split the relatively soft tissues of the old man's skin and flesh. He let out a low gurgle as he died.

Zuqaqip gripped the dagger in his right hand, drawing it slowly from Quishda as if the man were a sheath. Bright red blood poured down the blade and spattered against the stone below. The King wiped his treasure on the robes of the dead craftsman, staining the flaxen fabric with color—a warlike crimson created by iron atoms in human blood, siblings to Fe born during the death throes of their Mother Star.

●　●　●

The weapon remained close to Zuqaqip for the rest of his life and reign, his rule iron and uncompromising since the day the meteorite fell in the hills beyond Kish. He proclaimed himself a god among men and believed he would never die. Death took King Zuqaqip by surprise, and few tears were shed for the ruler upon his burial. The heaven metal blade, however, its existence and power known to all Kishites, remained aboveground.

King Atab, Zuqaqip's heir, could not bring himself to honor the dead ruler's final request to be interred with his iron prize. Instead, Fe's dagger found itself wrapped in lambskin and stored in a simple box in a room of the palace nearest the temple. Atab felt vaguely uneasy when he thought of his father's blade, but his own heir, King Mashda, dug the dagger out of obscurity and had it mounted above his throne. His grandson, King Arwium the Swift, took to wearing the heaven metal on his hip and even went so far as to wear the weapon into battle, though the King remained safely behind his soldiers on each occasion, his blade undrawn. Arwium begot a son, Balih, who took little interest in the dagger, leaving it to rest for decades in the royal hoard despite its legend. Strangely, upon his death, King

Balih requested to be buried with the meteoric weapon. However, like Zuqaqip before him, the King's request was ignored.

New dynasties came to rule over Sumer, Kish, and its people. With the throne of the land came dominion over the legendary heaven metal blade, though the weapon's symbolic power did not shield it from the ravages of time. Unlike the void through which Fe's asteroid traveled for so long, Earth's air thronged with grasping oxygen, eager to tarnish the metal's surface with rust. To keep the treasure from the clutches of oblivion, its keepers sharpened and resurfaced the blade many times over the years, oiling it and wrapping it in soft animal skins. The smiths and servants of Kish would use a hard stone to hone the alloy, the work often supervised by a temple priest lest the Gods take offense. Trillions of tiny irons flaked away, ejected forever with each sharpening, yet the atom Fe remained safely ensconced near the artifact's core.

When King En-me-nuna rose to power and claimed the dagger as his own, he ordered the iron treasure fitted with a handle of horn and ornately engraved with the legend of the firebird's descent. He bequeathed it to his eldest son, Melem-Kish, who died before he was able to have a son of his own. Instead, the kingdom and the blade passed to En-me-nuna's youngest son, King Barsal-nuna, whose reign ended with the ascension of King Zamug the Effervescent. Zamug's son, King Tizqar, would be the last King of Kish to wield the heaven metal dagger.

Those who best knew Tizqar often said that he'd been born an old man. Unlike most children of Kings, young Tizqar never dreamed of power. He hated playing at kingship, hardly ever sitting in his father's throne and issuing orders to the echoing halls. Prince Tizqar learned to read and write at an early age. He visited the citizens of his father's realm and would sit quietly among them, unobserved, seeing the people at their work. He watched the farmers spread irrigation and sow their crops on hands and knees. He observed the merchants weighing grain and gold and haggling with their customers. He spied on the women of Kish as they wove clothes and tanned leather. He stood on the hills with the shepherds while they guarded his father's flocks—the goatherds he left to their own devices. Tizqar would never think of joining the commoners in their labors, nor would he speak to them. Royal blood flowed through his veins, and the people of Kish knew that he was chosen by the Gods to one day rule over them all.

When King Zamug died, Prince Tizqar was still relatively young by the standards of his day. He accepted the throne with a heavy heart. In the process, he inherited his father's hoard, including Fe's dagger alongside much white-metal treasure and some lesser examples of meteoric iron. Sometimes the new King would study the ancient blade. Though he had no taste for battle, he marveled at the weapon's color and feel. Truly, the object was like no other he had ever encountered–it seemed to suck the very light from the room and the warmth from his hands. Tizqar knew the history of the blade, represented in vague carvings upon its cracked horn handle, though the engraved legend said nothing of atoms or Mother Stars.

For the majority of the reign of Tizqar, he kept the dagger in a wooden chest by his bed, wrapped in soft furs. Though he liked to keep it close, the King had no practical need for the weapon and would not wear it on his person. Months at a time would pass without Tizqar disturbing Fe's rest. One day, however, the King's six-year-old son, Prince Kaliq, came across the heaven metal blade laying like a new toy in its chest.

He had menaced away the servants, and, unsupervised, set to rummaging in his father's belongings. When the boy unsheathed the blade from its fur wrappings, his eyes greedily slid across its slick, black surface. A warlike child, Kaliq had recently learned of the pleasures that could be had from hitting other children with sticks. He liked best that they never hit back, but he hadn't yet tried hitting with anything like this before. The boy stood up, holding Fe's dagger before him in a fighting pose–it was time to find something to kill.

By the time Tizqar located his son, one eunuch slave was already dead, and a young woman in training as a palace courtesan lay curled on the stone courtyard, bleeding from a dozen shallow stab wounds. The royal child stood above her, his bloody hands wrapped around the slick, wet grip of the iron blade. He brought the dagger down deliberately, eager to make another hole in the dying girl–to watch her bright red vitality drain away.

Before he could strike, however, a hard slap across the face knocked Kaliq sideways. The Prince and the weapon clattered roughly onto the floor of the courtyard. Tiny red droplets spattered across the sand-colored tiles as Fe's blade tumbled. A bronze knife might have shattered from the impact, but the malleable iron merely blunted against the stone.

Defiant tears glinted in Kaliq's eyes as he looked up at his attacker. A thin rivulet of blood streamed from the child's nose. King Tizqar towered above his prone son, showing no emotion. He called for his guards, who appeared at once, ready to intervene only at the direction of the King. Wordlessly, he gestured for them to carry away the dead eunuch and the dying girl.

"Up, Kaliq!" The King bellowed, grabbing his son's arm and yanking him to his feet.

Next, Tizqar knelt down to retrieve the fallen heaven metal dagger while Prince Kaliq struggled for freedom in his iron grip.

"Let me go!" He whined. "I'll kill you!"

Unmoved, Tizqar dragged the young Prince into the throne room–kicking, screaming, biting, and cursing–before throwing him back to the ground.

With a weary sigh, Tizqar, King of Kish, lowered himself onto his throne.

"Men!" He called out, summoning a pair of his armed guardians. "Hold him."

With some reluctance, two of the soldiers put their hands on little Kaliq before he could wriggle away.

"Those slaves were valuable property, son," Tizqar explained, in patient tones. "They cannot be slaughtered for no reason. Would you throw a prize lamb from the clifftop just to watch it burst? Do you see how you've acted in the wrong?"In the grip of the guards, the Prince lifted his head to meet his father's gaze.

"It is improper for a prince, or even a king, to attack a woman. Whether she be queen or slave, do you understand me?"

Kaliq said nothing.

"This is why we have soldiers, or executioners," the King continued. "You know this. But I ask you–can you even name your greatest transgression? What is the reason for my fury, boy?"

"Stabbing," Kaliq answered, attempting a sneer.

"No." Tizqar ignored his son's imperious attitude, for he could read the rage in the Prince's eyes gradually giving way to fear. "Did you enter into my private chambers?"

"Yes." "Did you steal this, the most sacred weapon of Kish, to use as a toy?" The King asked, still holding the bloody dagger.

"Yes. Yes!" The boy could no longer meet his father's gaze.

"And you did all of this without my permission." Tizqar sighed heavily. "No citizen of Kish may disobey me, not even a prince."

The King rose from his throne and approached his son, dagger in hand. Kaliq withered further under his father's gaze and began to sob.

"Hold the boy's right arm." He instructed a soldier before taking his son's hand, maneuvering the dented blade's iron edge between the fourth and final diminutive finger.

The Prince struggled and screamed, but the guards held him fast. Under deliberate pressure from the King, the blade began to cleave its way through flesh. Metallically-bonded iron atoms from the strong alloy met little resistance as they sliced through a complex tangle of proteins and soft, organic tissues. Billions of Kaliq's blood cells soaked the already-tainted blade, vitality from the ordained Prince mixing with that of his property.

When his task was finished, the King wiped the meteoric dagger on the robes of the nearest guard.

"Release him," he instructed.

Expressionless, King Tizqar began to walk away, but before exiting the room, he turned back to his wailing, mangled son.

"Remember this."

Kaliq was left to writhe and cry on the cold floor of the throne room, his smallest finger laying severed beside him.

Ten years after he stole the dagger, Kaliq was given command of the armies of Kish. King Tizqar, never one for battle himself, hoped it would divert the Prince's bloodlust into proper channels, and so he allowed his young son to lead small skirmishes, hunt thieves, and put down rebellions in the outlying provinces.

Prince Kaliq grew into one of the kingdom's greatest warriors. He shied away from knives and daggers, mastering instead the art of the polearm. By his nineteenth summer, Kaliq could best any of his father's soldiers in a mock battle of spears–the men ordered under pain of death not to let their prince win too easily.

Changes were coming to the land of Sumer. Rival empires gained power in lands shrouded by distance, and city-states like Kish grew nervous. They hoarded resources and began eyeing their former allies with suspicion, choking trade. Storm clouds gathered ominously in the East. From his spies, King Tizqar learned that an army was being assembled around Susa, a formerly-peaceful city in the land of Elam.

Prompted by this existential threat to his people, the King unwrapped Fe's dagger for the first time in many years. He held it in his palms–it was truly an extraordinary piece. In the hands of a gifted warrior, the meteoric iron could do terrible damage to the enemies of Kish. Tizqar stared into the black depths of the heaven metal. He knew what had to be done.

* * *

Under orders from the King, the royal armorer took possession of the blade. He polished and sharpened the piece until its edge shone as pristine as the day it had first been finished. The stained and cracked horn handle broke away, its carvings transferred onto a long wooden pole by priests and scribes. The armorer bore a deep groove into the end of the shaft, setting the handle of the heaven metal dagger inside and securing it with pitch and sturdy leather bindings. Fe's blade now formed the tip of a handsome spear–a weapon fit for a prince.

The same day, King Tizqar called for his son. The summons reached Kaliq just as the sun was setting. The young man immediately ran from the training grounds to the palace. At the Prince's approach, two guards threw open a pair of heavy wooden doors that led to the throne room. Inside, along with several dozen members of the military, King Tizqar waited.

"Approach," he rumbled.

Fires burned in bronze braziers, providing an orange glow to the room. Shadows danced across Kaliq's face as he approached his father and took a knee. Tizqar had grown old and grey–the kneeling Kaliq was young, strong, and commanded the loyalty of the military. Overthrowing his father, however, never crossed his mind. The Prince knew his place—the King had made the lesson sink in long ago. "Rise, my son," Tizqar commanded, slowly standing himself.

Kaliq noticed that the King wielded a long and beautifully crafted spear. The aged monarch held the weapon lightly across both palms, keeping it away from his body as if it were a baby of whom he was not particularly fond. The Prince could not help but admire the spear's tip, shining very unlike bronze. When the light hit it, the color remained a liquid black.

"Heaven metal," he breathed. "That spearhead, Father. It's so long. I—I recognize that blade!"

"The sacred dagger." The King nodded. "The same that you stole from me. The same that carved away your flesh and made you into the man you are today. You are finally ready to wield your people's most powerful weapon."

Tizqar smiled thinly, and Kaliq accepted the weapon, his eyes stinging with hot, salt tears. The Prince blinked his vision clear, studying the engravings on his new weapon that told the familiar legend of the firebird's fall. The King sat back on his throne with a soft grunt, no longer young enough to do so in silence.

"Thank you, Father," Kaliq said, meaning it.

"It is now time to speak of the threat posed by Elam." King Tizqar sighed, gesturing to the assembled commanders and soldiers to step forward. "Over the past five moons, the Susans of Elam have doubled the size of their army. They've hoarded bronze. They've ignored our rights of safe passage. This, you know?"

"Yes, father," Kaliq answered.

"My spies have confirmed that this army is meant for us–meant to march on Kish."

A collection of soft gasps issued from his audience, and the King nodded, satisfied, though few present had been unaware of the news.

"The situation is indeed dire, yet, I believe that a preemptive assault is the sole hope remaining to our people," he continued. "Marching our armies into Elam and sacking Susa, before they can finish their preparations, will save Kish. It is my decree. Naturally, Prince Kaliq, it will be up to you to lead this assault and take their city."

Kaliq listened solemnly. He held the heaven metal spear vigilantly by his side, locked in military posture.

"You have never experienced war on this scale before, my son. You have grown used to leading sorties against small rebel bands and gangs of bandits. The armies of Kish can always crush foes such as these, but the forces of Susa will be something else entirely. Your own men are the finest in the world, but the army you are fated to lead will be made up of the peasant sons and farmers of Kish, untested in battle and fearful for their city. Can you lead these people?"

"I can, my King. It is an honor to accept my fate."

Despite the danger and uncertainty, a fire burned within Kaliq. It was the ghost of that same fire that possessed the Prince as a child, but now he would harness the rage and the bloodlust within for his father and for his kingdom.

The army of Kish marched two days later, Kaliq at their head. In those brief, restless hours following the King's declaration of war, hundreds of men were pressed into service to defend their homeland. Anyone who could sew or weave a cuirass helped empty the storehouses of Kish to outfit the new conscripts.

Kishite warriors marched in simple armor that covered their chests and necks, their arms and legs left nearly unprotected to allow for greater mobility. Some of the soldiers wore chestpieces fashioned from hardened leather, others only heavy woven tunics–hardy enough to withstand the slash of a blade, if not the thrust of a spear. Most carried large flat shields made of woven wicker and reinforced with leather.

Nearly every warrior of Kish, conscript and regular alike, walked with a long wooden spear. The shafts were tipped with bronze, stone, or copper points roughly the size of a human hand. Several soldiers carried heavy stone axes instead, and some canny veterans concealed knives in leather sheaths tied to their bodies in case they should lose their primary weapon. Slingers wore a pouch full of hard, smooth ammunition stones dangling from their belts. Along with their prince, the vanguard of the forces of Kish marched in helmets of copper and polished bronze, the sun glinting off their heads like a line of Earthbound stars as they advanced, leaving behind an awe-inspiring image to all who beheld them.

Traveling alongside the foot soldiers were chariots drawn by teams of hardy, barely-tame onagers. Constructed from wood, leather, and copper, the chariots represented the height of Sumerian engineering, each boasting two axles with heavy spokeless wheels at the ends. The elite of their people, chariot teams differed slightly in their outfit and specialty. Most simply held spears, longer and sturdier than those of the footsoldiers. A minority of the knightly Sumerians, however, had been armed with dozens of pots of flammable pitch with matching heavy slings.

To the rear of the convoy, teams of oxen pulled carts laden with supplies for the traveling army. Food, water, and extra weapons took up the bulk of the space. A small cadre of support personnel accompanied the oxen and the rear guard. Smiths were on hand to make repairs to any damaged equipment, and even a scribe and a temple priest followed the ranks.

The army continued through the fertile lands of greater Sumer, and it crossed the Tigris without incident. They trudged over rugged hills which formed the borderlands of Elam. In cosmic terms, the armies of Kish traveled only an infinitesimal distance. Still, the march covered a stretch of over six hundred and fifty thousand cubits, taking the warriors across much of the known world. Six days and five nights passed before Kaliq and his army glimpsed the gates of the enemy city.

Aboard his own royal chariot, Kaliq waited behind a high dashboard made from wood and leather. He wore a resplendent copper cuirass across his chest, with thick wool and leather padding at his back. On his forearms and shins he wore leather guards, studded with bronze. The Prince's helmet was exquisitely crafted, though not ostentatious. Kaliq, prudently, preferred to forgo plumage or any markings of leadership–he did not wish to make himself a target. Equipped with the same shield as his men, he held the unique spear in his four-fingered right hand. The meteoric nickel-iron alloy, harboring the atom Fe at its core, had been fashioned into a deadly blade centuries earlier. Now, the black iron represented the very vertex of the army of Kish–it tipped the spear carried by the Prince who traveled at the head of a thousand men.

●　●　●

"Susa must know well of our forces by now," Kaliq mused, standing with his men on a hilltop in the predawn gloom.

"Then they know well of their doom," Idim, the Prince's driver, replied gravely.

His onagers snorted and pawed at the ground.

Susan scouts had indeed noticed the troops of Kish the day before. The rival city-state, not yet finished building their invasion force, had to scramble to prepare for the surprise attack. Despite the haste, the city of Susa managed to put up an intimidating defense before Kaliq's army reached their gates.

"The enemy raised and outfitted eight hundreds of regular soldiers, my Lord," one of the Prince's scouts informed him.

"Anu's ass!" Urshub cursed. The foul-mouthed youth, one of Tizqar's bastards, served as the javelin-thrower aboard Kaliq's chariot.

"Eight hundreds of men." The Prince sighed, shaking his head.

"No, your lordship. Eight hundreds of *regulars*, with bronze. The common people too are taking up defense of Susa with whatever they can carry. Nearly two thousands of them."

Urshub opened his mouth, but no more profanity emerged. Idim simply closed his eyes and breathed. The Prince, however, made efforts to appear unshaken by the news.

"It was too much to hope for," he said, "to believe that our surprise attack would encounter no obstacles. Elamites may be more like dogs than men, but we can assume they fear the pillaging of their hamlets and fields as we would. They're moving their forces away from the city, yes?"

"Yes, my Lord," the scout answered, surprised by his leader's frank insight. He pointed to the lowlands. "There's a barren plain on the edge of Susa's fields."

"Then that is where we shall meet them."

"Perfect!" Urshub said happily. "Once we deal with Susa's real soldiers, laying up a siege will be easy. I wager no more than a quarter moon of fun before they give out–the terrified dogs can't hold up long."

Kaliq looked up at Fe's menacing spearpoint and smiled confidently. Meeting a professional army in open ground would be the true test of his skills as a warrior. On the horizon, the planet Mars glinted a faint red.

"Before the quarter moon turns full," Kaliq announced, "Susa will be mine."

Scrub brush and small thorny plants, poking out between rocks, grew in random patches on the plain where the two armies met. The terrain offered nowhere to hide—neither side held the advantage, and short of magic, an ambush would be impossible. On the eastern end of the plain, protecting the way to their city, the army of Susa stood at the ready, their front line fortified against all comers. In an unbroken wall, they stood shield-to-shield, each bit of leather and wicker emblazoned with complex patterns of repeating, long-stemmed cones. Bronze spears bristled out and above the shield wall, angled to skewer the vanguard of Kish.

Prince Kaliq surveyed his foes. The copper helmets and spears of the enemy soldiers blazed with reflected light. The Susans had halted and made no further moves to advance, content to let the Sumerians rush into their jaws. Just as the morning sun began to peek over the horizon to his rear, Kaliq decided to give them their wish.

He bent forward over his dashboard and nodded to Idim. Bringing his shield up below his chin, the Prince pointed his heaven metal spear toward the enemy.

"Charge!"

Idim drove the royal chariot full-tilt toward the endless wall of shields and gleaming, fiery spear tips–the forces of Kish surging behind like a human wave. Kaliq knew that the enemy stared into the sun as his own men charged.

The unsteady rhythm pounded in the dust by sprinting footsoldiers was soon drowned out by the thundering Kishite chariots and their braying asses. As they approached the fortified front line, rocks and stones started raining down from the sky.

"Slingers!" Kaliq bellowed, warning his men of the ranged attackers hiding behind the shield wall. "Sling–" as he called out again, a large stone gonged off his strong, bronze helmet, briefly stunning the Prince.

As the fastest Kishite chariots met the bristling bronze-tipped barricade of Elam, the air filled with the sounds of shouting men and dying onagers. Whipped by their human masters, the mad, fearless creatures charged straight into the Susan hedgehog. Bronze-tipped spears tore through the wild asses' flesh, their momentum carrying them unstoppably forward.

"A gift, from Kish!" Urshub cried as he hurled a javelin into the front ranks.

Kaliq deftly parried a protruding Susan spear before his own chariot slammed into a wall of screaming men. He crouched and sprung, leaping from the rapidly-decelerating vehicle and rolling to a halt in the dust. Other warriors of Kish followed suit, evacuating their own chariots and using them as cover for fighting on foot, behind enemy lines.

Kaliq swung his heavy spear in a wide circle, creating space in the middle of the fray.

"Kishites! To me!" He howled.

The shield wall had been shattered by his charge, and soldiers of Kish ran as fast as their legs would carry them through the gaps carved in the enemy line. They spilled into Kaliq's circular clearing, taking cover around the chariots.

"Death is here!" The Prince screamed at the Elamites, locking onto a doomed shield-bearer and thrusting his sacred spear forward like the horn of a charging animal.

As the weapon impacted its victim, Fe and its siblings held fast in their metallic lattice, ensuring the spearpoint's easy dominance over the hide and fiber shield it encountered. Propelled by the Prince's arm, the iron tip continued its journey into the leather breastplate of the soldier. Hard packed proteins and dead keratinocytes from the skin of a grass-eating animal gave way to the razor edge of meteoric alloy driven by the strongest warrior in Kish.

Leather split down to the skin, and the spear ripped into the soldier's chest. He died instantly with his ribs shattered and organs shredded.

"We shit on their feast table tonight!" Kaliq shouted to his allies as he braced his foot against the dead man to gain leverage.

He pulled, releasing the stuck speartip and reclaiming his divine armament.

The Prince glanced over his shoulder, just in time to see a Susan soldier charging him with a long spear of poplar and bronze. Kaliq dodged, and swatting against the shaft of the man's weapon, he redirected the path of the charge.

The warrior of Susa stumbled forward, his momentum driving his deadly bronze spearpoint into the backside of one of his unwary comrades. A look of horror crossed the spearman's face as he beheld what his weapon had done, but the emotion did not linger–Kaliq advanced, slicing the solder along the neck almost as an afterthought.

Along the flanks of the melee, several chariots remained upright, Kaliq's among them. Though Idim, his driver, hung dead–slumped over the royal dash-board–Urshub still breathed, huddled against a tangle of rocks and chariot debris with a group of Sumerian javelin-throwers, occasionally ducking out to hurl missiles at the enemy.

Nearby, flame spouted from a chariot stocked with firepots–its bronze brazier had been lit.

Carefully, a soldier held out a pot to the flame, igniting its oiled linen fuse. Shielded by a companion, the grenadier loaded the pitch projectile into his sling and cast it deep within the ranks of the enemy army.

Kaliq watched with half an eye as the clay pot sailed through the air. The sound of shattering ceramic preceded a gushing of oily black fluid, followed immediately by a billowing of sudden, colorless flame. Other Kishite grenadiers succeeded in launching firepots of their own. As each clumsy clay projectile shattered, small fires broke out among the pitch-coated enemy. Howling spearmen threw down their flaming shields, and others clawed at clumps of burning tar that clung to their skin.

As his chariot bounced over the stony ground, the daring Sumerian pulled another incendiary pot from the basket. He lit it against the brazier and loaded it into his sling's pouch, when, with a thin whistle, a javelin with a long, cruelly-sharp stone tip sailed from the inner ranks of the Elamites, catching the grenadier in the eye as he stood up. His sling dropped, and the clay pot shattered at his feet.

"Urshub!"

The Prince called out as his eyes beheld the chariot and its incendiary cargo become engulfed, but his screams were to no avail–his half-brother burned like a tallow light.

Kaliq made to call out again, but before he could, the entire chariot exploded, spewing hideous gouts of flame among the fighting men.

Near the Prince, a Susan spearman saw the flash and briefly turned his head in the direction of the explosion. It was all the time Kaliq needed to swing his spear around and bury it in the man's neck.

"I pledge your soul to Urshub," Kaliq commanded, flicking his wrist and sending droplets of blood flying from Fe's alloy speartip. "You will serve him in the next life."

As the battle raged into a disorganized fray, Sumerian against Elamite, Fe's scattered siblings fought on all sides. Under Kaliq's boots, iron atoms identical to Fe soaked into the ground, bonded to the hemoglobin in the dead Susan's blood.

Fuming, Prince Kaliq turned in a slow circle, looking for a foe to engage. All around, warriors were locked in single combat–Kish's untrained conscripts falling fast to Susa's regulars. In his peripheral vision, the Prince saw a mountain of a man approaching, wielding an enormous axe and standing at least four-and-one-half cubits tall.

"Over here!" Kaliq shouted, slamming the butt of his spear against the ground.

The brute wore no armor, save for thick leather pauldrons strapped to his massive shoulders. As he drew nearer, the Prince noticed that the man's bald head was swollen on one side. The haft of his axe resembled a still-living tree branch, with a head made of savagely sharp obsidian.

"Anu's ass–you're a true monster," Kaliq taunted. "Are you as stupid as you are ugly? Did the Gods take the clay for your penis and brains and use it to build those big dumb arms instead?"

"Die, fancyman!" The giant screamed an epithet from his dialect, closing the distance in three huge strides.

The hair-covered mountain raised his axe, bellowing as he brought it down upon the Prince. Kaliq held his spear up over his head with both hands, ready to deflect the blow and roll in for the kill. However, the Susan's stone axe cleaved straight through the engraved wooden shaft.

Barely slowed, the obsidian wedge continued its downward trajectory, impacting the Prince's copper cuirass, crumpling the metal and the torso beneath. Though the axehead did not penetrate his skin, several of Kaliq's ribs shattered under the force of the blow. Blood vessels ruptured, forcing the Prince's iron-rich vitality to drain into his own body cavities.

Kaliq fell backward on the rocky ground, gasping as the axeblow drove the air from his lungs. He allowed the useless length of engraved wood that had once been part of his spear to fall from his left hand, though Fe's blessed blade remained attached to the fragment still gripped in his four-fingered right.

As the brute made to swing once more, Kaliq rolled sideways, dodging the blow but nearly losing consciousness from the unexpected pain. Nevertheless, he forced himself up.

"Yaaah–" Kaliq wailed, surmounting his own agony. Filling his palm with sand as he rose to his feet, the Prince spun and hurled the handful of dust and grit into the giant's eyes.

The living mountain screamed and staggered.

As the giant stumbled, Kaliq lunged forward to take advantage. Fe's alloy spear tip pierced the Susan axeman's chest, its still-sharp edge slicing through progressing layers of skin, fat, and muscle. Though the cloudy quantum bonds of Fe and its iron kin held as strongly as ever, Kaliq's arm of flesh had not the strength of heaven metal.

Startled, the Prince realized that his killing blow lacked the requisite force to send his point deep enough to stick the Elamite's vital organs. Kaliq struggled, his vision spotting, unable even to pull the spear free. He made to scream at his foe, but he could only cough bubbles of foamy blood.

"I eat your heart, fancyman!" The giant swatted Kaliq with an orangutan fist.

The Prince tumbled to the ground, his holy weapon still buried in the aggressor's chest. Despite this, the mountain still held his obsidian axe, raising it for a final blow aimed at the smaller man's head. In desperation, Kaliq struck out with his foot, impacting the Susan's shin just above the ankle. The blow proved too feeble to harm the enormous soldier, but the giant's footing momentarily failed him upon the unsteady field of stones and pebbles.

Stumbling, the mountain of an Elamite flew directly onto Kaliq, the terrible axe falling harmlessly to the ground. As he flopped forward, gravity conspired with the Susan's inordinate mass to accomplish what the injured Kaliq could not–driving the speartip deeper and puncturing an overtaxed heart.

Fe and the iron blade cleaved through cell after cell of cardiac tissue, and with a final spasm, the great red organ lapsed into stillness.

His body broken, Kaliq lay pinned beneath the giant, struggling for breath. The Prince tried to claw at the massive corpse, his nine fingers grasping weakly at his foe's hairy flesh. Kaliq's strength failed him. All around, he could hear the sounds of battle–men screamed, weapons clashed–perhaps even the far off claps of thunder, Kaliq thought, suddenly thirsty for rain. Gradually, as his breathing became ragged and shallow, the sounds of the battle distorted and diminished. Screams became whispers, thunder turned to the rushing of a calming wind, and the clashing of weapons fell silent altogether. As Kaliq, Prince of Kish, closed his eyes for the last time, the only sound he registered was the steady ping-ping-ping of blood, dripping down the protruding edge of the heaven metal blade and spattering against his copper chestplate.

● ● ●

Sab waded through rows of corpses, swatting at flies as he went. The sun hung low in the sky, but the heat of the day lingered, accelerating the rot of the fetid battlefield and its garden of corpses ripe for harvest.

Nabu, his young trainee, held his nose with one grubby hand.

Sab was sweating, and he hated sweating. His skin chafed where the strap of his leather bag cut across his shoulder, now heavy with clinking gold coins. To make matters worse, the bottoms of his sandals were now hopelessly stained with thick, brown blood.

When news of victory first reached the city's rulers, they dispatched convicts, orphans, and others of Sab's ilk to the scene of the battle. It was up to these untouchables of Susa to stay one step ahead of other scavengers, animal and human alike, picking through the debris and appropriating anything that could easily be carried off.

"Put that down," Sab hissed, noticing his young protégé relieving a dead soldier of his shortsword. "Ours is to look for gold."

"Weapons are more fun," Nabu sneered. "Look at all this bronze, you ass. I could be a king!"

"You're stupid and know nothing. I've seen the blade-carriers and the bronze-scrapers get all cut up. Men die faster than dogs on that detail."

"I hate being your partner," the young orphan whined, petulantly tossing the bronze blade to the ground.

"You're moronic and you're wrong, as usual. This is a blessed assignment compared to theirs. Gold is holy. Look to the Sun–" Sab pointed. "Utu aids us in our search. There is an art to it. Observe, wretch." He knelt down by the body of a man wearing copper guards on his arms and legs.

"Who's he?" Nabu asked.

"Must have been some sort of noble." Sab sniffed and shook his head.

The body was covered with far too much drying blood to determine which side he had fought on. With both his hands, Sab rolled the corpse, slumping it over onto its back. He spied a ring on the man's left hand.

"Gold and bronze, inlaid with...a cloudy red stone. I don't know," he observed.

Sab tugged, but the ring wouldn't budge. Undeterred, the veteran tried to lubricate the dead man's finger, spitting into his hands but finding that the hot plains of Elam had sucked the moisture from his mouth.

"Hey, kid. Spit on this."

Nabu bent down to imitate his mentor, but the youth too came up dry.

"What do we do?" He asked.

"Cut it off, I guess. Where's his knife?"

"Wait," Nabu said as Sab looked around for an appropriate blade. "What if I try something?"

Tilting his head away, the orphan dug one hand into a deep gash in the soldier's leg, emerging with a fistful of thick, spoiled blood. Nabu rubbed the grisly lubrication on the ring finger and slid the treasure free.

"Utu's balls!" Sab cursed. "That's disgusting."

"No more disgusting than cutting off a dead man's finger." Nabu smiled, wiping the gold-alloy ring on his soiled smock and tucking it into a pouch.

Sab muttered and shook his head, turning his back on his protégé and continuing the search. Soon, their path became blocked by a tangle of shattered wood and stinking onager carcasses. Cursing his vocation, the older scavenger stepped over the rubble and collapsed to one knee as his front foot slipped on a slick of equine blood and viscera.

"For the sake of Nergal," Sab grunted, pulling himself up.

He wiped futilely at the foul stain on his linen while Nabu laughed. They walked on, kicking at various dead soldiers, scrutinizing clothing and belts for possible hidden treasures. They came across one unfortunate combatant sprawled against a low bush, unarmed, the shaft of a javelin protruding from his back. The man had a hefty pouch tied to his belt.

"Why don't you take this one?" Sab instructed, pointing to the corpse.

Unsheathing a small stone knife, Nabu scampered over to the slumped corpse and cut the pouch free. Greedily, he upended the contents into his hand, cursing when eight smooth stones fell out–ammunition for slings.

"Heh heh," Sab chuckled, wiggling his fingers in a rude gesture. "The man doesn't even have shoes and you look for gold."

The apprentice ghoul rolled his eyes and stomped away. When laughter turned to deep, wracking coughs, Sab decided to continue walking. Ahead lay a strange scene–a man as large as any the senior scavenger had ever beheld had died hanging in a bizarre, statuesque position. The carcass had to be at least four cubits tall, Sab estimated, perhaps as many as five. As he approached the dead giant, he realized why the man lay so strangely–pinned beneath the corpulent hulk lay another clad in regal-looking copper armor, crushed and smeared with dark blood.

Sab stepped around to get a better look at the deceased combatants. The misshapen giant was barely clothed, and Sab would be astounded if he carried any gold. The richly-armored submissive, on the other hand, looked like someone of importance.

"Bastards have been here first," he grunted, noticing that the bloody hand of the man was missing one finger–wrongly assuming it to be the work of rival scavengers.

Sab tried to search the body, but most of the noble was concealed beneath the immovable giant.

"Kid!" He called out for Nabu, who wandered somewhere nearby, distracted as usual. "Nabu! Damn you, I'll do it myself. Move, you landscape of lard–"

Sab fell to his knees and began to push the large man's corpse aside. It was pinned to the noble below, and the dead weight proved too much for Sab to handle. Yet he pushed with all his meager might, and, finally surrendering to gravity and friction, he slid backward into the dust.

"Nabu!" He screamed.

More than ready to end the day, Sab cursed, stood up, and brushed himself off. He followed up his yells with a sharp, two-fingered whistle, which eventually produced Nabu.

"Help me, wretch," Sab said when his protégé appeared.

Together, they were able to muster enough strength to roll the giant's body a half-cubit to one side, then they went to work searching the nobleman's corpse. He carried a sizable bag of gold and silver, and he wore a jade amulet around his neck, tucked beneath ruined armor. Deftly, Nabu cut them both free with his sharp stone blade.

"Look at that," Sab pointed to the strange, broken polearm protruding from the giant's chest.

The bottom of the blade glistened an oily black, and the shaft's wooden surface was covered in smeared engravings.

"Looks like black obsidian," the scavenger observed, moving closer to Fe and the repurposed heaven metal dagger.

"Obsidian?" Nabu echoed skeptically. "Is there a whole work gang for that too?"

Ignoring him, Sab walked over and studied the weapon carefully. Though he shrewdly concealed the fact from his colleague, Sab knew something about reading. The symbols he could see were mostly representative, but a winding strip of cuneiform spoke of heaven and a fallen star. Sab gripped the engraved shaft and heaved, but the spear held fast. He looked over at Nabu, who was busy pointlessly counting gold. The older scavenger paused for a moment, then he began to rock his arms back and forth, hoping the spearpoint would be able to cut its own way out. Little by little, iron sawed through flesh, and the weapon loosened. With one final pull and a wet sucking sound, the spear slid out of the giant's chest.

Sweat poured down Sab's face, even as the sun waned and the day expired. He would be glad when he could return to the relative comfort of his home. He used a scrap of the giant's sparse clothing to wipe the sweat from his brow, the blood from his hands, and finally, to clean the treasure itself. Strangely, the point of the weapon was neither bronze, obsidian, nor copper. It didn't shine like metal, yet it felt nothing like stone.

"What is it?" Nabu walked over. "That's not gold," he said, reproachfully.

"A mystery," Sab answered, genuinely baffled.

"Toss it back, let's go."

"I worked too hard for this thing to just *toss it back*."

Sab placed the broken spear in the bag with the rest of his clinking plunder, though in truth, he had simply enjoyed reading the story of the fallen star.

After the gold-scavengers left the field of the dead, they tossed their bags into the back of an ox-drawn wagon and trudged off toward their rude homes. Drivers whipped the animals lashed to their conveyances, and a circle of protective Susan officials escorted the convoy of battlefield treasure back along the road and inside the city walls.

In rooms beneath the palace, members of the royal Susan court busily divided the plunder. Gold, which made up the majority of the take, they added to the city treasury—a healthy sum embezzled along the way. Small gems and other trifles of scrip and barter, likewise, were cataloged and pocketed in equal measure.

Looted blades, armor, and bronze went to the smiths and the generals. No weaponry, save Fe's blade, made it into the scavengers' gold wagon and the subsequent sorting party. The blunted, filthy state of the broken spear belied its material nature, and during the avaricious cataloging of loot, it was eventually tossed aside into a pile of miscellany by distracted hands.

Finally, toward the end of the evening, the most exciting of the take having been claimed and hoarded, a literate noble noticed the distinctive carvings and cuneiform writing on the unusual spear fragment's shaft. He thought the fallen star tale a charming little story. It made him think of the night sky, and this made him yawn. On his way to bed, the nobleman placed it among a pile of scrolls to be transcribed.

Three days and three nights passed before the blunt alloy spear was disturbed by outside forces. During that period, news of the battle traveled back to Kish—King Tizqar had lost his son, and would soon lose his city. The evening after professional scavengers claimed Fe, unscrupulous Susan citizens took to the war-torn plains to conduct a ghoulish, starlit frenzy—claiming anything of even marginal value to help assuage the pain and poverty of serfdom. At the darkest part of the night, the civilized looters were frightened off by the terrifying visages of nomadic tribespeople, who moved in shadows and claimed body parts from the fallen. None in Susa could unravel the motive when they found the grisly remains in the morning. The next days and nights belonged to the animals, and by the time the scrolls and the spear were packed away for good, little evidence of the great battle survived.

Fe and its heaven metal siblings found themselves locked in a crate of wood, lined in soft leather. Documents detailing the battle and its particulars shared the cramped space. Some took the ancient form of tablets, but most were scrolls of rolled vellum, a sophisticated technology developed in Elam. As an added investment, the recordkeepers treated the chest with bitumen to help keep these more fragile skins intact.

The scribes' chest was placed in the palace vaults and, containing no apparent treasure, left undisturbed and unlooted for many years. Eventually the records were forgotten entirely, shoved into a corner of a corner. Dust collected dust.

Susa found itself conquered by Ur, a Sumerian sister state of the Kishites. Elam retaliated, eventually taking back their coveted city.

Earth twirled around Sol again and again, and, during one of these orbits, the forces of King Nebuchadnezzar of faroff Babylon swept across the land. Though Susa was sacked, and its treasures looted, the hasty Mesopotamian invaders overlooked Fe's decrepit chest in their pillaging. Swollen with hubris, they built a new palace over the ruins of the old.

● ● ●

As its designers intended, the bitumen-and-leather lining protected the contents of the records crate from the outside world for the length of a human lifetime or five. However, time erodes all things. It was time that had a hand in slaying the Mother Star–turning a titan of creation to a shroud of dust. Fe's treasure was not spared the travels through that terrible dimension. The chest rotted in some places and fossilized in others. The fragile, information-rich vellum of the scrolls dissolved into a protein-rich mulch, devoured by Earth's everpresent microorganisms. More ubiquitous were the caustic, destructive molecules of diatomic oxygen. Patiently and relentlessly, they subjected the heaven metal to the ravages of oxidation–the rust wars.

The surface of the blade was first to fall. The iron atoms which formed its outermost skin, those which had pierced the giant's flesh in that terrible battle, betrayed their siblings by succumbing to nonmetal attraction. They broke their fraternal metallic bonds, drawn by the electromagnetic siren-song of oxygen. Guided by floating particles of busybody waters that had snuck into the undercroft, pairs of iron atoms joined with triads of atmospheric oxygen to form molecules of iron oxide. Trillions of Fe's siblings turned to rust in the silent, ages-long battle. The same processes that had colored Mars eons prior now stained the heavenly speartip a dirty red.

Time eroded Babylon as well, collapsing the conquerors of Susa into dust. Assyrians invaded from the north and leveled the city once again. Two millennia after the armies of Kish met their doom, the conqueror Cyrus brought the unstoppable might of the Persian Achaemenids to Elam, personally taking Susa as his own throne city. Time, however, conquered Cyrus and his sons. The king called Darius built Susa into a realm of such grandeur that the untouchable Sab or Nabu would hardly have believed its unprecedented luxuries. King after king, emperor after emperor, sat atop the great city and thought it theirs. All the while, the once-mystical iron speartip holding Fe lay forgotten under Susa's deepest foundation, losing a battle of attrition.

The weapon's engraved wooden shaft and leather bindings disappeared, carried off bit by bite by sip, devoured by saprotrophs or simply sublimated into the thirsty air. Thus, the shape of Quishda's original dagger-form emerged, rusted but intact. Had the smith succeeded in smelting the iron himself, time would have won a more rapid victory over the treasure. Yet, the naturally-oxidized exterior protected the inner meteoric iron from further rusting. This protection often proved fickle, however. Each time a tremor shook the hidden chamber, outer flakes of rust would fall, exposing virgin alloy to the ravages of planetary air. The atom Fe, however, occupied a spot in the great crystal close to the center. It would be among the last to fall from the blade should time have its way.

Another hundred years passed, another hundred orbits. The Persian Empire swelled to enormous dimensions, but Alexander of Macedon emerged and launched an aggressive campaign with the aim to conquer all of Earth. His army carried iron weapons, as did their many foes. Humans no longer relied on meteorites to harvest Fe's kin. Ore from the ground could be mined and smelted in great blast furnaces that put Quishda's kiln to shame. The Macedonian King, reborn a Greek Emperor, drove his forces east and south into the lands that had been Assyria and Babylon, swarming Susa, looting its treasures, and trampling its long memory.

Alexander continued east to his doom. Centuries bled away. Susa fell to the Seleucids. It rose again with the Parothians—leveled and rebuilt, looted and replenished. Through it all, the ancient history of the land eroded like stone into sand. In far off lands, the Roman Empire built itself out to the corners of its world. The Romans grabbed Susa like a brass ring, and the Eternal City ruled for a time before falling back, like a flower slowly wilting after stretching its petals to their glorious limits. In nearby lands, some peoples rejected the multiplicity of the gods. Yahweh and Judaism spawned Christianity and, later, Islam. Muslim armies, worshiping the one God, swept into power and conquered Persian lands, leveling Susa in their wrath. Yet, the people who had always inhabited the land eventually rebuilt stubborn Susa atop its own multi-layered bones.

The ruins of so many empires lay above the ancient chamber that housed Fe's spearpoint that the tomb stagnated, rarely experiencing even the thrill of airflow. Above, generations of Susans were born and died, going about their lives all the while. Far to the east, however, another conqueror, Genghis Khan, lord of the horsemen, rode across the great eastern continent taking every land he entered. The Khan moved west, sweeping into the Islamic and Persian lands, adding his name to those who had razed Susa. After the Mongols dissolved, people continued to live in Susa, though in time, the word 'city' could no longer describe the half-abandoned hamlet.

The world changed more rapidly with each passing year since Fe's asteroid first orbited above a living Earth, and human cultures learned to study their environment as deeply and objectively as their primate brains could dare to. Eventually, they proved the existence of the atom, which had been there all along, mathematically unlocking the structure and purpose of Fe and its kin. The iron once known as heaven metal became utterly commonplace, mined and refined in its billions of tons. Steel alloys allowed enormous structures to rise across the globe. The great apes even figured out the electron, the tiny charge which motivated Fe's bonds, and they mastered magnetism and electricity. They built telescopes to look into the heavens and learned of the planets, Sol's truth, and their own address in the sprawling galaxy. They unlocked the mysteries of asteroids and meteors—the firebird finally unmasked in its mundanity. So full of knowledge and power, the self-proclaimed *Homo sapiens sapiens* began to wonder if they could harness the power of the sun to create new atoms of their own.

During all these exciting centuries, Fe remained locked in the twisted and rusted lump that had once been the grandest weapon in all of Kish. Still vaguely recognizable as a blade, the iron dagger-turned-spearpoint had lost much of itself in the oxide wars, and likely would not survive a further march of millenia. However, the aforementioned advance of human science did not limit itself to studying the natural world. The apes liked to look at themselves, after all, and human scholars became fascinated with the mysteries of their own past. Fe had been born of physics, and chemistry threatened to rip it from its siblings—yet it would be the human social science of archaeology that would prove to be the atom's salvation.

Chapter 2: The Archeologist

The ink was still drying on Patricia Haverwood's doctorate when her ship landed in the port of Beirut. She had just turned twenty nine, but displayed the vivacity, determination, and naïveté of a much younger scientist.

She disembarked from the steamer, dragging her trunk on a trailing cart. Stretching after the long journey, she checked her reflection in the window of a waiting coach—Patty believed herself a tad on the tall side, slightly wobbly, and with too-thin limbs which, in her youth, drew unwelcome comparisons to avian creatures from immature boys. She felt prideful, however, of her luminous blue eyes and enjoyed letting her hair kiss the breezes in its loose, natural curls.

It was an unseasonably warm day in May of nineteen thirty-nine, and Patty luxuriated in the sun. To think, there had been a blizzard just a few weeks earlier when she had left her native Chicago and—wet, shivering, and crying from one too many long goodbyes—boarded a bus to New York. From there, it was a nine day journey by ship to reach Greece. Once on Morea, to her dismay, the travel-weary academic had no time to soak up Greek culture, almost immediately hopping a small dirty vessel that took her across the Mediterranean to the Lebanon. Overjoyed to be off the boat, Patty found her enthusiasm nonetheless weighed down by the knowledge that she still had a long way left to go.

"One step at a time, friend of mine." She spoke aloud, giving herself a little pep-talk before taking the next leap on her grand journey.

Dr. Haverwood, as she was now entitled to call herself, was to meet the French archaeologist Roland de Mecquenem that day. Unlike some of Patty's less adventurous peers, she'd relentlessly petitioned for field work, even before completing her doctoral studies. Soon after graduation, to her delight, the powers-that-be offered her a grant to travel to Persia to work with Dr. Mecquenem of the Louvre in his excavations of ancient Susa.

The middle-aged Frenchman was waiting for her at an outdoor café near the docks. His greying hair was piled on his head, and he wore a long and unkempt moustache. Though they'd never met, Patty recognized him immediately.

"Hello there!" She shouted, waving her hand. "Bonjour!"

Mecquenem smiled, wiped his hands on a cloth napkin, and stood up. He took her right hand in both of his and shook earnestly.

"Bonjour." His moustache twitched as he smiled. "I am, eh, pleasured to meet you."

Patty smiled back, acutely aware that the archeologist's eyes had slid down to examine her body. She decided to ignore the implication and smiled wider.

"New country, new job, new life," she said softly to herself.

"Pardonné?"

"Nothing. I know we have a long way left to travel," Patty slapped a hand against her steamer trunk, "but do I have time to grab a coffee first?"

"Oui. Bien sûr." Dr. Mecquenem laughed.

Patty gratefully took a seat and flagged down a waiter, gesturing for cup-and-saucer. She spoke with Mecquenem about the excavation site and his career studying ancient Susa.

"Decades?" She whistled, impressed. "You must love it."

"Oui. N'est-ce pas?"

It was a challenge for Patty to make out everything the man said through his thick accent and her limited understanding of French, but after all, digging was her specialty. The Louvre archaeologist had uncovered some beautiful pieces of Persian sculpture, which his home country proudly displayed in Paris' fabled museum.

"It's amazing," she said, stirring her coffee. "Years of research, but we still know so little about the city back then or its people. What's Persia like nowadays? Or should I say Iran, in deference to the Shah?"

"You eh, find out." Mecquenem smiled. "S'il vous plait."

They were headed to his dig site on the western border of Iran. The pair would have to travel through the Lebanon, Lavant, and most of Iraq. The journey's length as measured in days could hardly be estimated, the Frenchman explained, since the reliability of their transportation was spotty due to the unfortunate political conditions of the day.

"It certainly is a turbulent time for anyone to be traveling through Europe and adjacent territories," Dr. Haverwood noted sympathetically, as the pair finished their refreshments and began walking to the rail yard.

"I believe, as scientists, we are quite removed from the warring factions. Expanding human knowledge is in everyone's interest. Isn't that so, Dr. Mecquenem?"

"War, eh, is hell. American words," Mecquenem replied.

"We'll be quite safe," Patty said, with conviction. "I have been assured by people in the know that 'the Middle East is one of the safest and most stable parts of the world!' At least my trip across the Atlantic was uneventful, though I've heard terrible stories of German undersea boats attacking unarmed vessels."

Around the pair, the people of Beirut acted as if there was no war on at all, and this buoyed Patty's spirits greatly. Mecquenem already had their tickets purchased, and when the archaeologists arrived at the gleaming, hissing train, he gallantly assisted Patty with her steamer trunk. They traveled aboard the crowded, clattering railcar to the city of Damascus, receiving only the most cursory attention from an inspector upon crossing the border. From there, however, the reliability of transportation withered. Unable to find a train or direct route that wouldn't cost more time than it would save, the archeologists gave up for the night and checked into a rude Levantine hotel.

"Buck up, Buttercup," Patty instructed herself, laying atop a thin mattress in the chamber she'd been given for the night.

The newly-minted antiquarian tried to remain optimistic, though she was in an unfamiliar city far from home–her only companion a Frenchman twice her age with a loose grasp of English and a lecherous eye. Her chamber, however, remained inviolate. She identified five separate species of insect crawling about the small room–four of which she was able to kill with her shoe–before giving up and retiring for the night.

In the morning, Mecquenem showed her what he claimed was a bus. The vehicle was certainly some type of automobile, Patty had to admit–a poorly-maintained relic, belching smoke from a corroded tailpipe. It appeared to have no expectation of passengers. A human driver sat aboard, but their face could not be discerned beneath a veil of linen coverings. Though the Frenchman's sleepless eyes were bloodshot and his face sallow, he seemed genuinely pleased with the transportation.

"Wonderful," Dr. Haverwood said, summoning more optimism than she felt. "I'm glad you spent the night making friends."

With Mecquenem's help, she tied her steamer trunk to the roof and climbed inside the cabin. The bus turned onto a northbound street and soon left the city behind. In the featureless desert of Northern Arabia, the driver's dust-blocking attire began to make more sense to Patty. The bus shook its way over dirt roads and sand-swept trails, covering both her and the snoozing Frenchman with a fine layer of particulate matter. Soon enough, Patty became hypnotized by the vibrations of the vehicle and the vast expanse of nothing outside.

The sun rose to its highest point, turning the ancient bus into a furnace. Occasionally the driver stopped to either refuel from large, sideslung cans or to make quick, violent repairs to the protesting petroleum-driven beast. When the sun mercifully set, Patty tried her best to sleep.

By early morning, signs of civilization once again became visible. The bus was driving into Baghdad, capital of the Kingdom of Iraq. It pulled up in front of a busy commercial avenue and shuddered to a halt.

"It's a wonder the crazy contraption made it this far," Patty muttered, her nerves frayed.

As she worked to reclaim her dust-drenched trunk from the roof, she spied Mecquenem handing the driver a small cotton bag, its contents unknown. The veiled driver nodded curtly at the Frenchman, ignored Patty entirely, and drove off into the crowded streets once the archeologists had taken their luggage.

Dr. Haverwood was hot, sweaty, starving, and exhausted. She took a deep breath of Baghdadi air, preparing to whine and beg for a rest when Mecquenem surprised her.

"Patricia, s'il vous plait—I must go." He looked slightly nervous when he said this, piquing Patty's curiosity. "Demain matin, uh tomorrow in the morning. I come for you. Hôtel Majestic."

She was in no mood to argue. "Aces! Let you go off on your adventures. Leave the soft beds and running water to me."

Despite his apparent eagerness to be off, Mecquenem escorted Patty to the nearby hotel. His hypervigilant manner gave Dr. Haverwood the impression that it was not entirely safe for a body to be alone on the streets of Baghdad, regardless of its level of education.

When his ward was settled in her rooms, Dr. Mecquenem disappeared with another hasty apology and a repeated promise to meet her first thing next morning. Too tired to even clean the dust off her body, let alone count the insects, Patty collapsed on the bed.

She woke up late in the afternoon with a dry mouth and a headache. She realized that she had barely imbibed any liquid the day before.

"I sweated out five pounds on that damned bus," Patty said to herself as she rose from the bed, running her hands along her worryingly-slim sides.

Holding her throbbing head, she staggered into the restroom and put her mouth under the running tap.

The ragged American cleaned herself as best she could, using the hotel's limited facilities. She peeled off her clothes of the previous day, likely ruined from hard travel, and changed into a clean outfit selected from her steamer trunk. She exited the hotel and turned for a stroll down a city street chosen at random. Despite Mecquenem's apparent misgivings, the locals seemed to give the unescorted woman a wide berth.

"Maybe it's my height," she said to herself after walking through a knot of Iraqi men who parted for her like water before Moses.

Confidently, Patty hopped off the walk and entered into a cramped building that she was fairly certain must be some sort of restaurant, at least judging by its smell. A bearded man with a tray came over to her after she sat. Unable to navigate the local dialect or writing system, she opted to order a cup of strong tea to begin.

"Tea?" Patty asked the waiter, sweetly.

He stared back at her with a subtle hostility.

"Thé? Tee? Chai?" She tried again, using all of her languages.

The message must have broken through, because the waiter stepped away, returning a few minutes later and dropping a steaming mug in front of her. He strode off before she could request milk or sugar.

"Oh well," she said to herself, happily. "When in Rome..."

Baghdad was truly magnificent, Patty had to admit to herself, watching from the sidelines. It was crowded, and it had a troublesome odor, she mused, but there was just something about it—history, she decided. The land positively oozed with it. The Kingdom of Iraq would always be Mesopotamia to Dr. Haverwood and her colleagues—this land, once the cradle of civilization, was where the first city-builders set down roots and began to master their environment.

Patty tapped her feet against the café floor, almost giddy with the weight of centuries beneath the stones. Ancient Sumer had once claimed this same land, she knew. In fact, though the good Doctor Haverwood had no way of perceiving it, she sipped her tea mere kilometers from the path once marched by Prince Kaliq and his doomed army of Kishites.

Though the sun still shone and the city simply begged to be explored, Patty decided that she should err on the side of caution and return to her hotel room after securing nourishment. Grabbing a few more hours of sleep seemed like a prudent move, especially considering what Dr. Mecquenem may have planned for their next day's travel.

"But first things first," she said to herself, signaling the waiter.

"Baklava?" She smiled, looking up at him.

The waiter nodded and walked away.

"I'm getting better at this."

* * *

The next morning, when Patty stepped back out onto the busy streets of Baghdad, lugging her steamer trunk, Mecquenem waited nearby. He stood next to a private, local car turned ad-hoc taxicab. Patty noticed that her traveling companion's eyes were even more red and puffy than they had been when they left Damascus.

"Does this fella ever sleep?" Patty grunted to herself before she managed to drag her heavy trunk to the cab.

On the other hand, the gangly antiquarian had to admit, the car Dr. Mecquenem had found for them looked much more modern and comfortable than that wretched bus. A driver appeared, too late to help her with her luggage. He wore a clean white suit and sported a moustache far more tidy than the Frenchman's. The elder archeologist entered the front of the cab, and the prim Baghdadi driver joined him, leaving the rear to Patty and the trunks. Forty minutes of navigating death-defying traffic brought them to the edge of the metropolis, where the car turned south.

"Where are we going?" Patty asked her companion. She had to lean forward and shout over the rattling from the uneven road.

"Amarah," Mecquenem shouted back.

"Amawhere?"

"Amarah," he repeated.

"Amarah," the driver added, in chorus.

"Oh, this is useless." Patty threw herself back in the seat and crossed her arms.

She had never been more impatient to meet the remainder of her colleagues to-be. To the best of her knowledge, in addition to herself and Mecquenem, there should be two professional archeologists at the dig—supposedly a husband and wife team from the UK.

For hours, she stared out the window at the unchanging scenery. The Iraqi motor route, if it could be given such a grand name, took a course roughly parallel to the Tigris River. Patty enjoyed watching the winding trail of green and blue cut through the desolate brown of the landscape beyond.

Occasionally they traveled through small villages and towns.

"Do they build roads to connect the existing urban areas here, or do these settlements build up along the roadsides, like in America?" Patty asked once, though neither of the men in the front seat had the knowledge, inclination, or English to answer her fully.

At one point, they found themselves blocked for five minutes as a teenaged boy led a herd of misbehaving goats across the road. Distant descendants of the goats of Kish, the animals seemed especially agitated by the sounds and smells of the rumbling gasoline engine. Through the window, Dr. Haverwood studied their gently curving horns and their intelligent, utterly alien eyes.

They drove for some time before the taxicab began to slow. The driver stopped the vehicle in the middle of a row of simple houses.

"This must be the place," Patty decided. "What mode of transportation is next, Monsieur Mecquenem? Perhaps a motorcycle, or a riverboat? Ooh? Have you chartered a biplane for us?"

"Non, non," Mecquenem said, shaking his head at Patty and signaling the driver not to stop. "Les écuries, allez."

The American felt a growing sense of dread as the driver started up again, and the taxicab wound its way through the little town, parking near some stables on the far eastern edge. Reluctantly, Dr. Haverwood climbed out and sniffed the air.

"What's that smell?" She asked.

Her question went unanswered by the driver, who hastily unloaded their bags, so Patty decided to investigate for herself. After a single peek at the stables, however, the mystery resolved itself.

"Camels!" She gasped. "And to think I was worried about motorcycles."

Mecquenem walked straight toward the camels, displaying a baffling level of confidence around the queer creatures. Patty followed with some trepidation to a canopy alongside the enclosure. A man in a white linen shirt wearing a beard large enough to conceal a small child stepped out of the shade. He and the Frenchman began conversing as easily as old friends, though Patty couldn't make out the pidgin language they employed. Soon, the stableman turned and untied two of the sand-colored dromedaries from their enclosure. As he walked them over to the archeologists, the camel smell intensified, and Patty felt the regrettable second helping of baklava churn in her stomach.

"Je suis désolé," Mecquenem told her, a pained expression on his face. "Eh, bags. Bags. Your bags."

He gestured at her steamer trunk and then again at a set of heavy canvas bags hanging from one of the camels. He repeated the motion and the message sank in—she was to leave her massive trunk behind and repack what belongings she could into saddle bags.

She noticed a worried expression replacing Mecquenem's look of impatience. In fact, quite against her will, Patty had gone nearly red with indignation, frightening the Frenchman and his hairy friend.

As quickly as she could, the flustered young antiquarian turned her back on them and busied herself popping open the clasps on her trunk.

"What?" She chastised herself under her breath, angrily snapping the trunk's brass latches. "Do you want to go back to Illinois and marry a banker? Pop out a few kids, cook pot roasts? How does one even make a pot roast—oh, I suppose it's in the name."

Behind her, one of the men cleared his throat. To allay further embarrassment, Patty steeled herself and forced a pleasant smile, turning briefly to Mecquenem.

"Un moment," she said audibly, raising one finger before turning back to complete her unplanned reorganizing.

The Frenchman was visibly relieved, and, politely, he ignored his new protégé's strange, idiosyncratic mumblings.

With the help of Roland's friend, the archeologists secured their bags to the camels after Patty had finished her repacking. Throughout the process, the huge desert beasts sat, tame and disinterested, flicking their long eyelashes and letting the humans overload them with cargo. Mecquenem pressed a few coins into the hands of the well-bearded stableman, who demonstrated how to properly mount and drive the camel for the novice Dr. Haverwood.

The American picked up the technique quickly, burying her fear and distaste under a façade of excitement—one that became real around the same time her brain gave up and stopped noticing the smell.

As Drs. Patricia Haverwood and Roland de Mecquenem rode on camelback across the parched borderlands of Persia and Mesopotamia, like the Bedouins of old, the former reflected on her adventures thus far and decided that she was having the time of her life.

"If only my friends back in Chicago could see me now!" She giggled to Mecquenem, bumping up and down unsteadily on her fragrant mount. "My sister would never hug me again if she knew I had ridden a camel."

The Frenchman smiled politely, amused by his new colleague's enthusiasm.

"Personnellement, I...like, eh, les chameaux. Les Camels. Not 'trange to mount."

After some time, both tied coverings over their heads and necks to protect against the desert sun. To the young traveler's eyes, Mecquenem appeared as if the moustachioed Adolphe Menjou had switched clothes with Valentino in *The Sheik*.

"I betcha someone on that hill who saw us two bedouins," Patty gave a muffled snort, "would have no idea he was looking at a European and an American!"

Gamely, the hired camels navigated the dry, rocky terrain without complaint or rest. Despite the utter desolation of the landscape, Mecquenem seemed to know the way by heart, leading them across a trail without landmarks or roads. Perhaps Patty had underestimated him, she thought, as her camel followed close behind his. Or, she mused dreamily, the fellow has gone mad from lack of sleep and is riding us straight into a mirage. With this last thought, she let her eyes close, lulled by the complacent motions of the tireless camel.

When Patty opened her eyes several minutes later, the landscape had changed subtly. She blinked away the sleep and noticed that to the south, in the distance, the desert rocks and sand gave way to what looked like a bog.

"Is that a mirage?"

Mecquenem noticed her looking at the wetlands, and he cracked a grin.

"Marshes, 'averwood."

"Wonderful," she said sleepily, marveling at how the world still had the capacity to surprise. "A swamp in the desert."

It took them a near-eternity of trudging to travel the fifty-odd miles from Amarah to the international dig site atop what used to be the city of Susa. By sundown, the romance and adventure of riding a camel across the desert had long worn off for Dr. Haverwood. Even her mount seemed to be tiring of the endless trudge, falling further behind the lead animal. Patty worried that if she should sleep again she may wake alone, separated from their meager caravan.

Once again, she longed for the comfort of a hotel room.

"You won't find one out here," she admonished herself at the thought. "So toughen up, Buttercup."

Mecquenem half-turned as Patty spoke, but quickly turned away and fixed his gaze ahead. The older man seemed to be growing used to his American colleague's frequent soliloquizing.

Despite her weariness, Patty did her best to spur her tired camel onward, tableau after tableau of moonlit mesopotamia spinning through her head. Finally, lights appeared on the horizon, tiny at first, but eventually, dark shapes resolved themselves, coming into slow focus. Patty could make out tents and scaffolding, illuminated by flickering oil lamps.

It was the archaeologists' camp—a smattering of temporary structures with a village of a few simple houses standing some distance behind. Hidden deep beneath the ground, a five thousand year-old chamber lay buried, filled with ancient debris that included a rusted alloy spearpoint among the dross, one whose heaven metal core long ago fell from the stars in a screaming ball of flame.

● ● ●

Voices carried on the air and a few scattered words reached Patty's ears.

"–about time!"

Someone was speaking English–to the homesick American, the words sounded so good she could cry. Mecquenem took the reins of the camel from Patty after she'd dismounted. He led the dromedaries to a small area with posts and a trough, where two horses and an elderly-looking donkey were already waiting. Patty noticed a cooking fire nearby and smelled a rich spicy aroma that she could not identify.

Beside the quartet of foreign archeologists, a few paid locals staffed the camp. Mostly young Persian men from nearby villages hired for their labor, the help included some domestic specialists–and apparently at least one cook.

Patty's stomach rumbled, and she realized that, in the excitement of her travels, she had been neglecting her belly. Before she could inquire about the food, Mecquenem returned and took her arm. He led her to an open tent where a couple were sitting cross-legged, eating from tin cups. The woman was slim and pale, the man uniformly ruddy and sunburnt. They quickly noticed company arriving and stood up, wearing huge smiles.

"Patricia 'averwood," the Frenchman said, gesturing to the man and woman, "les Nicks."

"Pleased to meet you, Mr. Nick," Patty said, shaking the man's hand and his wife's in turn, "Mrs. Nick."

The couple laughed.

"Actually, we're Mr. and Mrs. Thornburg," the man explained. "Nick is our first name."

Patty's face crinkled into a quizzical expression.

"My name is Nicole. His is Nicolas, love." The woman's accent was aristocratic, but her words came out friendly and conspiratorial, without a hint of the stereotypical anglo superciliousness Patty had expected.

"Monsieur Mecquenem finds it endlessly amusing to refer to us as *'Les Nicks.'*"

Bone-sore, Dr. Haverwood sat down on the hard ground next to Mecquenem and the Drs. Thornburg, gratefully accepting a cup of the spicy-smelling stew. It was excellent. She chewed while they talked about their experiences at the excavation site thus far and exchanged personal histories.

Like Patty, the Nicks were relatively young and inexperienced–not yet widely published and thus academically mysterious. She'd been impressed to learn that the couple had whetted their teeth working on excavations throughout Southern Egypt and the British-controlled Sudan territory before relocating to Susa.

"Well, you've got me beat," Patty said, licking her spoon.

"We were nothing but glorified pages on the Egyptian digs, I'm afraid," Nicolas bashfully confessed. "If we're telling truths, we had nothing at all to do with the most famous discoveries."

"So serving in ol' Roland's operation is everyone's first chance at a degree of real autonomy, then?" Patty concluded, resting her elbows on her knobby knees.

"Bien sûr!" Nicole bubbled in reply, her accent practiced. "Monsieur Roland's *laissez faire* operation is perfect if one desires le autonomie."

"Nicole!" Her husband admonished.

Somewhat tickled by Mrs. Thornburg's boldness, Patty studied the interplay of her new companions from behind a tired, contented grin.

"This is bad thing?" Mecquenem asked the trio, smiling slyly and playing with his long moustache. "You do well...if, you eh, travail not au liberté?"

His smile disappeared as his eyes met Nicole's.

"Not at all!" Her pale face flushed, provoking giggles from Nicolas and Patty.

The conversation, mostly centered around bringing the newly-arrived Dr. Haverwood up to speed, wound unabated into the night–social adrenaline and strong Turkish coffee keeping the four archeologists awake.

"Until last century," the Englishwoman explained, gesturing with her cup, "they hadn't the foggiest notion of how much history lay below their feet. Generations of Persians lived and died here, never knowing Ancient Susa hid below."

"Fifty years, this site, travail–eh, worked, by archéologues français." Mecquenem added, lighting a cigar.

"So far, the efforts have uncovered a good deal of pottery and some sculpture," the male Nick filled in, "artifacts dating to the time of the first Achaemenid Empire."

"There are records with mentions of Susa going back *much* further," Patty noted with excitement. "Names of undiscovered Kings, just waiting for us to find them!"

"They love their legends," Nicole nodded her head in the direction of the near-by village of locals. "Sumerians, Akkadians, Elamites–they also loved exaggerating time-scales."

"I've read legends that go back ten thousand years, or ten billion, depending on how you translate," her husband added.

"Le Big Bang!" The Frenchman enunciated, blowing smoke-rings. He turned to Patty. "Preuve? *Evidence*?"

Her smile faded at the goading, gentle and academically-sound though it had been. Inside, however, she felt a spark of motivation being kindled.

"Since long before we shipped over," Nicolas explained, "the excavations have been concentrated on two main sites: the palace of Darius and the palace of Artaxerxes. Now that you've arrived, Patricia, Nicole and I will be joining Monsieur Mecquenem at the Artaxerxes site."

"It seems to me, then, you've concluded there's not much left at the Darius site?" Patty asked.

"You want true autonomy, yes?" The Englishwoman winked.

"Oui, laissez faire." Mecquenem looked at Patty and shrugged. "You are...ah, welcome to join us–essayer–or, you might eh, take your chances."

Dr. Haverwood opened her mouth, but found herself uncharacteristically at a loss for hasty words.

"Come, love. Let's leave the boys alone for a bit," Nicole said to Patty, setting down her mug. "Otherwise they're liable to make us do dishes. Follow me. I'll show you to your quarters."

Nicolas stuck out his tongue playfully at his wife as the two women ducked out of the tent. They walked together through the meager camp, where Nicole helped Patty retrieve her belongings from the camel bags.

"Stinky buggers," She complained. "Patricia—I can't help but ask, how *is* Roland as a traveling companion?"

Patty thought for a moment, slinging a bag across her shoulder and following Nicole to the tent assigned her.

"Tireless," she replied, at last, a small smirk raising one corner of her mouth.

"Did you two…" Mrs. Thornburg let the words hang in the air, but as she noticed a frown spreading across Patty's face, she changed tack. "I mean, did he *try* anything? You know?"

"Dr. Thornburg—travel was a nightmare, thank you very much!" She replied, with pique. "And, sorry to disappoint you, but there was hardly a moment when Dr. Mecquenem and I were both conscious and present at the same time, not that it would have made a difference!"

"A thousand pardons," Nicole offered, one pale hand stretched out placatingly. "Forgive me. I was too bold. But, it's no secret that he likes pretty things. He spends his life filling a museum with them, for God's sake. And, he's *French*. It would be unnatural if he didn't notice you, love."

Now that she'd eaten and been seen safely to the tents, Patty felt the exhaustion of the last two weeks descend on her all at once, and she allowed the discussion to drop.

"This is where Nick and I sleep," Nicole said, pointing to the largest of the tents. "This one belongs to Roland, and whoever else joins him for the night. Do watch out."

"I'll be on my guard, you can bet on it," Patty said, listlessly.

She briefly wondered at the Englishwoman's fixation on her supervisor's supposed lasciviousness. "This is you over here, Patricia." Nicole pointed to a simple, sturdy-looking tent. "It's not the Langham, but it should do."

"Thank you, Dr. Thornburg," Patty yawned, "for everything."

The tent was small, sandy drab, and sewn from canvas. The interior had been lined in a thin mesh of insect netting, which hung like a ghost above the bedroll. The floor was rough, without even the thinnest rug to cover the packed dirt, and a simple wash basin lay next to the sleeping roll. To Patty, any accommodations would be acceptable after her last sleep on camelback.

Despite the implicit goodbye, the English archeologist still lingered near Patty's tent.

"We're all quite lucky, you know," she said.

"However do you mean?" Patty knew exactly what Nicole meant, but there was no harm indulging someone she wouldn't mind having as a new friend.

"Nick and I get to scamper about, barely supervised, and Roland practically gave you carte blanche to conduct your own dig at the palace of Darius. Granted, the site has likely been more than fished out, but then again...you never know. Fortune smiles on the bold."

"The laissez faire archeology thing? He was serious about that?"

"Why–*bien sûr*! Of course," Nicole replied, playfully. "Here's the dirty little secret, love: Roland doesn't really care what we do, so long as any significant finds end up back in Paris with his name on the plaque."

Once disengaged from social interaction for the night and tucked away in her sleeping roll, her body aching in gratitude, Patty's mind stayed awake, churning with excitement. It quickly turned to Susa, the fabled city of ancients–a world of potential secrets, resting just outside her tent flaps. She thanked her lucky stars that Dr. Mecquenem was such an easygoing project head. She kept her voice low as she talked herself to sleep.

"I'll find 'em all," she slurred, dreamily. "Anybody who was anybody came here. Cyrus, Darius, Alexander, Trajan–Genghis Khan. A hot spot, yessir."

Images of great empires and historic battles danced inside Patty's head. As she drifted off to sleep, she fantasized about discovering some lost tomb or ancient artifact, golden and magnificent to behold. She dreamed about having *her* name on the plaque.

● ● ●

In the morning, Patty was almost too sore to get up. Over the past few days, she had slept on boats, buses, in hotels with pillows that contained more roaches than feathers, and briefly on camelback. After a night on the hard ground, her body screamed in protest, but her excitement for the new day was the best painkiller under the sun. She sprung to her feet, changed into fresh clothes, and washed her face in the basin, soon joining Mecquenem and the Thornburgs at an al fresco breakfast.

A teenage boy was cooking beans for the archeologists. He had deeply browned skin and a thin, scraggly moustache that tried in vain to cover his upper lip. When he moved to hand Patty a plate of food, Nicolas took the opportunity to introduce him.

"Patricia, this is Mohammed. I believe he'll be assisting you while you get settled." His eyes flashed over to Mecquenem, who nodded.

"It's a pleasure to meet you, Mohammed." Patty stuck out her hand and shined a dazzling smile at the boy, who bowed slightly and turned back to the cooking fire.

"A tad shy." Nicole winked.

Patty smiled and tried her breakfast. She decided that she'd give the boy some space for now. They would spend the next dozen or so hours in each other's company—plenty of time for him to warm to her.

"How did you sleep?" The male Nick asked through a mouthful of beans.

"I'm still not used to roughing it, I'm afraid," Patty said. "Sleeping out here though... All this history, it does something to your dreams."

"Oui," Mecquenem nodded solemnly. "Je sais ce que tu veux dire. Mes rêves...fascinant, terrifier."

"He feels the same way," Nicolas translated. He chewed thoughtfully for a moment, "I think we all do."

The archeologists grew silent for a few minutes, but their reverie was broken when two burly men exited a nearby tent, arguing loudly in Farsi. They continued the debate as they received cups of beans from a disinterested Mohammed, only ceasing their discourse upon joining the Westerners.

"Dr. Haverwood, meet Karim and Jojo," Nicole said.

"It's a pleasure to meet you both." Patty reached out her hand.

Both men hesitated briefly, but they shook her hand warmly.

"Salâm," Karim said.

Jojo's mouth was already full, so he just smiled.

She returned the man's smile, deciding not to ask Jojo about what she assumed was his nickname. He was tall and well-muscled. Karim, on the other hand, was short and barrel-chested. Despite this, both men sported nearly identical beards, making them difficult for Patty to tell apart once they were seated side by side.

After breakfast, Mecquenem went through the formality of asking Dr. Haverwood about her choice.

"Avez-vous fait votre décision?"

"You know what? I think I'll take a swing at Darius's palace," Patty answered cheerfully, in spite of the site's alleged emptiness.

Nicolas translated the baseball idiom, and with well-wishes all around, the party broke up, the American heading in one direction, the Europeans in another. Before Patty began her hike to the dig site, she filled a small bag with a length of measuring tape, a notebook, and some dried fruit among other essentials.

"Today is all about observation, planning, and acclimation," she declared to herself as she packed.

Her chosen palace was located at the top of a steep plateau overlooking the rest of the excavation. After a rocky solo hike to the site, the young antiquarian walked around the perimeter of the plateau scouting for an easy way up. On the southern side of the rise, she spotted a relatively gentle slope inset with hand and footholds by past explorers. Awkwardly, she clambered up the sandstone, the soft mineral scraping tiny white lines into the flesh of her hands and forearms as she scrambled.

Once atop the plateau, Patty navigated to the highest point she could, heaving herself up a natural stone ledge. There, she breathed out in a happy woosh and surveyed the excavation, shielding her eyes from the sun. Low, broken walls outlined the various ancient buildings that had been uncovered or reconstructed.

"Missus, that big one is the palace," a small voice said beside her.

Patty gasped and almost tumbled from her roost. Standing silently below her was young Mohammed.

"Over there," he continued, pointing his left hand at an area of low stone walls in front of the palace, "the acropolis. All the rest over here in front is the royal village."

"Thanks a million." Patty beamed. "I didn't know you could speak English!"

Mohammed shrugged and lifted an arm to shade his eyes. "I thought missus might not understand me if I spoke in Persian."

"You thought right." She slid down from her perch, dusting her trousers off upon landing. "Is the palace safe to enter?"

"Yes. I have been inside many times," the youth answered proudly.

"Lead the way, then."

The two walked across the windswept plateau toward the ruined palace. Nearly four hundred meters long, the excavated structure was surprisingly intact for its age, and Patty found herself impressed by its size and complexity.

"The old man says that there are no more treasures here," Mohammed said thoughtfully. "I don't believe it missus. It is so big."

"People have been digging here for a very long time," Patty said, playing devil's advocate. "Ol' Dr. Mecquenem is very good at what he does. Also, little man, you should know—my friends call me Dr. Haverwood."

He seemed saddened, considering this information.

"So you believe there really is nothing here too, Doctor Haverwood?"

"Horsefeathers!" Patty broke into a wide smile. "Do you have any idea how old this place is?" She looked down at her new assistant. "Darius the First built this one. Do I have that right?" Mohammed nodded, a grin lighting up his face.

"From what we can tell," she continued, "Susa goes back much, much further than crazy Darius here. It was around way before Persia, no offense. Before Babylon, before most of the Egyptian pyramids. Heck—when Darius first walked into this city, it must have been as ancient to him as *he* is to us!"

They spent the remainder of their sunlit hours studying the excavation site, and Mohammed explained the informal names he had given to each room in the palace—'the King's Seat', 'the Prison', 'Battle Court', 'the Bricks', and 'the Sticks' among his idiosyncratic labels. He knew, in detail, the location and description of every great treasure found in Susa, even the finds dating back to the nineteenth century. It was likely, Patty reflected later, that Mohammed had spent his entire life at the excavation site, helping foreigners dig up the dead city.

That night, back at camp, Patty sat alone, enjoying the cool breeze on her sore ankles and drinking coffee by the light of the still-swollen moon. In the village nearby, Mohammed slept like the dead.

"Maybe I'll put the little guy's name on the plaque too." Dr. Haverwood smiled, thinking of her competent new assistant.

On the surface of the wooden camp table before her, she had arranged a handful of stones in a rough outline of her palace.

"Bones built on bones," she mused, leaning over to fill her palm with loose sand. "Where would you be concealed, ye kings of old?"

Patty buried her sculpture in a tiny sandstorm, letting the grains fall slowly from a hand sporting two fresh blisters. She scratched for more stones beneath the bench, adding another layer of simulated history to her tabletop diorama. As she worked in the pool of moonlight, Patty noticed irregular blobs of darkness begin to interrupt her work. A sound on the edge of hearing clawed at her, and she looked up, the mystery immediately resolving.

Bats—a cloudy, shrieking storm of tiny bodies flew across the moon as a nearby colony emptied from within the hollow hills.

Dr. Haverwood watched them for some minutes.

"I should go to bed," she told herself, still sipping coffee.

As the days went by, Patty became an expert on the Darius excavation's geography. She wanted to have a full picture of where her predecessors had gone before she attempted to dig any deeper. She also wanted to make sure that Mecquenem and the Nicks were comfortable with her going off on a one-woman wild goose chase. The Drs. Thornburg assured her that things at the palace of Artaxerxes were already plenty crowded. Mecquenem, for his part, seemed happy to indulge her. Patty remembered the advice she had been given her first night in camp, paraphrasing it in her rare moments of doubt.

"As long as I bring something shiny back to Paris..."

● ● ●

Nearly a week after arriving at the Susan excavation, Patty grew comfortable enough to begin her own search in earnest, starting at the lowest chamber in the palace.

"The way I see it," she explained to Mohammed, "two thousand years of history happened before they ever built this fancy palace. What if we decided to go into business together Mo, open up a high-rise Ritz right here at Susa? Sure, we'd have to build it on these ruins, and once the place goes bust, any future archeologists would have to go to our basement and start digging down. Do you see where I'm going with this?"

Mohammed nodded, understanding most of her words and deciding to give the others the benefit of the doubt.

Dr. Haverwood mapped out the site where she wanted to begin excavating, her assistant helping her mark the individual stones that would have to be moved. That evening, Mecquenem hiked up to give his approval for the next stage of the project, and the following morning, Patty and Mohammed climbed the plateau with pickaxes and shovels in hand.

Careful not to damage the structural integrity of the ancient building, Dr. Haverwood and her teen helper began to pull rocks, dirt, and sandstone from the chamber floor. They were anxious to do no damage to the palace, but progress was slow-going. For the two slim laborers, excavating away the centuries with barely-sufficient hand tools was tedious, exhausting work.

"I'd kill for a steam shovel," Patty lamented, more than once.

"No," Mohammed disagreed, "better Jojo or Karim. They could do in one hour what we move in a day."

Nonetheless, through sheer determination and patience, the gangly archeologist and scrawny teenager managed to move mountains. They dug ten feet below the lowest chamber, dividing each section of ground into quadrants, performing systematic searches of the rock and rubble they unearthed. However, after many days of labor, all they had to show were piles of historically-insignificant stone.

"All of the men say it is empty here. Maybe it is not good to dream," Mohammed, bone-sore and disheartened by their failure, bewailed once.

Patty, however, remained optimistic. To her keen mind, it defied common sense to believe that there was nothing buried deeper–the plateau was the ideal place to construct any sort of defensive fortification or ceremonial structure. On the other hand, she knew the landscape must have changed during the last several millennia.

"Something has to be here," Patty repeated as she dug. "It just has to be."

Life quickly grew into a routine at camp. Haverwood was acclimating to her cramped sleeping arrangements, and after a long day at the palace dig, she was often tired enough to sleep on needles–her stiff, spartan bedroll seeming nothing short of luxury in the moment. Elsewhere on the planet, slaughter and chaos ruled, yet the archeologists' camp remained a pool of tranquility.

Late one night, however, one of the site's animals, the elderly donkey, passed away. It went suddenly, without any apparent diagnosis save for old age. The laborers buried the beast without ceremony, moving the carcass several hundred yards away from the tents before they dug. Less than a week later, Karim led a replacement back from his supply run into the larger villages.

Months stacked up, and Dr. Haverwood had come no closer to uncovering Fe or any other significant treasure. Meanwhile, Mecquenem and the Nicks made better progress at their own dig–clearing an eroded stone facade and uncovering new rooms in the palace of Artaxerxes. Some of these new chambers contained preserved examples of ancient graffiti scrawled on their walls. Patty and even Mohammed were called in to help the team prepare the best pieces for cutting and packing.

"Dumb luck and muscular helpers are an archeologist's best friends," Patty quipped to herself, only the tiniest bit jealous of her colleagues' success.

It was a chilly night, and Patty was to join the Thornburgs for a little translation soiree in the largest tent. She found the couple surrounded by lanterns, bent over stone slabs studded with irregular patches of Old Persian cuneiform. A gold pocket watch and a half-full bottle of gin joined the ancient artifacts on the camp table.

"Patricia!" Nicole called out, her face flushed, one arm around her husband's waist for stability.

"Ooh, have I seen that one yet?" Patty asked by way of greeting, sidling around the table to get a better look at the cuneiform. "Hmm. That symbol could be 'sword' or a phallus, depending."

The Englishwoman let loose a burble of laughter.

"Either way, he's definitely bragging," Dr. Haverwood concluded.

"A disappointment," Nicole informed her. "Poor Nick was hoping for the location of the lost tribes of Israel."

"Forgive me if I'm beginning to find violence tedious," the male Thornburg replied in his defense. "There's so much of it these days." He took a pull at the gin, making an ugly grimace as he swallowed.

"History is full of thugs and killers, and yet our own nations were fool enough to appease Hitler," he continued, bitterly. "Now we're at war, on the brink of annihilation–staring the German war machine in the face. He's doing to Poland what these lads did to Susa... I wonder who will be there to dig up their bones?"

"Not me," Nicole said lightly, wary of her husband's darkening mood. "Too cold in Central Europe."

"Patrica, you and your idle Roosevelt have heard about Poland, of course? Can a lame man move no faster?" The dour Englishman asked, taking another drink.

Patty found herself in no mood to be ambushed by politics. Mercifully, before she could answer, they heard the growing rumble of a truck engine, followed by a skidding of gravel under tires. A door slammed, and a trio of voices could be heard, raised in farewell–the Frenchman's distinct syllables among them.

"Bonsoir!" Dr. Mecquenem said a moment later, his pupils shrinking in the bright lantern-light as he ducked inside the tent.

He squinted at his Western colleagues. His face was windswept, and he carried a bottle-shaped parcel wrapped in paper and twine.

"Bonne année mes amis!" He raised the bottle, shedding its wrappings to reveal a litre of fine brandy.

"Any news? The war?" Nicolas asked.

If he had intended to shatter the holiday spirit, the Englishman had succeeded. The corners of Mecquenem's moustache fell, and the giddy smile drained from his features.

"Oui. La guerre," he answered, followed by a glum, nearly-monotone account of the latest. "Ce n'est pas bon…"

"The Soviets are burning the Finns alive. More English vessels fallen to the sea mines," Nicole translated. "And it seems we're losing air supremacy, honey. Well hasn't this turned out to be a fabulous party after all?"

"Welcome back, Dr. Mecquenem," Patty said, filling a growing silence. "And a happy *bonne année* to you as well."

The Frenchman's wary expression crinkled into a smile.

"We've been translating the graffiti from the palace," she added.

"Precisely!" Nicole said happily. "We're an ocean and a continent away from the chaos and death in Europe. So let's celebrate something else tonight."

Nicolas huffed and contented himself by studying the brandy label.

"Patricia? You find eh, raison célébrer?" Mecquenem asked Patty.

"I haven't found anything as spectacular as this writing," she answered diplomatically, "but I've been making progress."

"Oh?" The older archeologist challenged, raising an eyebrow.

"In fact, I'm pleased to say that Phase One of my plan is now complete," Patty blurted, hearing her own unsubstantiated words as they flew from her mouth.

Stalling for time, she accepted the bottle from Nicolas and took a nip. Patty swirled the complex product of rot, time, and fruit around her palate, and she allowed her mind to fill itself with a plausible course of action.

"By now," she began, "the little man and I have dug out a sub-basement of the palace. Earthquakes, floods, erosion, and landslides may have shifted or shaken anything Darius built his foundations on, you know. I never expected to *find* anything in Phase One."

Ignoring the looks of amusement from her colleagues, Dr. Haverwood continued.

"This presents some unique challenges for Phase Two. From the central depression, we will need to excavate exploratory tunnels. Branching out in all directions. Of course," she added, "we'll make certain to properly buttress and reinforce them as we go, leaving as little impact to the original site as possible. If there's anything at all under the palace, my friends—I'll find it."

It was a strong finish, and Patty breathed a sigh of relief. Her plan was as good as any, and the brandy was being passed around liberally, helping her cause.

After exchanging a few sentences of French with the Nicks, too rapid for Patty to catch, Dr. Mecquenem nodded his consent.

"Oui. It is good." He nodded.

Patty smiled and accepted a small hug from Nicole.

Adding to their growing spirits, the Frenchman briefly exited the tent, reappearing with a large object, carefully wrapped in a canvas sheet. Quickly, the team packed away the artifacts, and the wrappings on the heavy package fell away, revealing a crank-powered phonograph.

Patty clapped her hands together in delight.

"Musique!" Their supervisor announced, cranking the handle and producing the promised tune in four-four time.

Safely wrapped in their bubble of science and history, the archeologists drank, danced, and observed the ticking watch, waiting to celebrate the dawning of a new year.

"Nineteen-hundred and forty, *Anno Domini Nostri Jesu Christi!*"

"Eh, em–*Aera vulgaris.*"

"To 1940!"

"Happy New Year!"

Even Nicolas did his best to put his worries aside for the evening. In fact, the only sour note came when Patty asked Mecquenem about requisitioning a supply of lumber for her Phase Two tunnels. His humorous eyes clouded over with irritation–instant, dark, and fleeting–but he grumpily consented to the expenditure.

● ● ●

The first tunnel pointed south, inching toward the bulk of the palace site and the acropolis beyond. Patty's plan called for it to extend fifty meters before they could break ground on the next exploratory tunnel.

"And after?" Mohammed asked, with some skepticism.

"If all the primary tunnels come up dry," she explained, "we'll just have to extend each of them a little further...

"...if I haven't been fired by then," she added, once the boy was out of earshot.

They had rigged up a simple pulley system to move the dirt from inside the tunnels back up to the surface for disposal. Patty hammered together a sturdy frame, attaching a bucket and a rope. Mohammed figured out how to operate the contraption almost immediately, and together, they began digging into the south wall of the depression.

They took turns excavating from inside the tunnel, one swinging a pickaxe and the other hauling out full buckets. Occasionally, they would have to cut and set pieces of their precious imported lumber, shoring up the excavation against the possibility of collapse. Both the archaeologist and her assistant were on the scrawny side, and as such, they made the tunnel just wide enough to accommodate one of their own slim forms.

"I feel like Abbé Faria in *The Count of Monte Christo*," Patty said, wedged in the tiny space between solid walls of cold earth. "I hope we're going in the right direction, at the very least," she whispered, thinking of the supposedly-mad priest.

After weeks on the dig site, excavating the area below the low palace chamber and building a tunnel system by hand, Patty could feel her body changing. Her arms and legs were as slender as ever, but they had hardened–growing powerful and wiry. Her skin tanned from exposure to the desert sun, and her long-fingered hands were as calloused as a dockworker's.

"If my mother could see me like this, she would have kittens!" She declared once, rolling up her long sleeves to reveal the muscle beneath.

Mohammed laughed, flexing his own growing physique. The once-skinny boy also underwent changes during this phase. Like an ambitious plant, he gained height and vigor by the day. Even his moustache thickened. Though still a pip-squeak compared with Karim and Jojo, Mohammed's growing strength became indispensable to Dr. Haverwood's Phase Two.

On an unseasonably warm day in February, Patty found herself crouched inside the furthest extension of her second tunnel, which by then had grown to a length of thirty meters. She knelt on hands and knees, diligently chipping away at dusty stone. It was nearly pitch black inside the freshly-carved crevice, the only source of potential light a bulky electric lantern that was almost more trouble than it was worth to haul around.

The archeologist grew used to the darkness, feeling a primal sense of comfort at times, like a memory from one of her ancient mammalian ancestors who had made a living burrowing through the sunless soil.

Without warning, Patty felt the ground give way beneath her knees. She screamed as the dirt floor collapsed under her weight–first her feet, then her legs and hips disappearing into the blackness below.

Desperately, she scratched at the dusty, uncertain ground under her hands, trying to save herself from falling. Heaving and wriggling, she came to a stop, darkness all around–the stone beneath her clawing hands holding, for now.

Patty hung, half in and half out of her broken tunnel. Her heart pounded arrhythmically in its bony cage, the thudding bass blocking out all other noise. Somewhere, light-years behind her at the tunnel entrance, Mohammed was calling out at the top of his lungs.

"Missus!" He screamed, again and again, forgetting to use her honorific in his distress.

She heard nothing over the surging of blood in her ears, but eventually, Dr. Haverwood's breathing steadied, and her heartbeat slowed. She gradually took stock of her peril. The newly dug-out area in front of her was only a few inches wide–not enough space for her to pull herself up. She kicked out with her legs, but they contacted nothing but air. The only plan that came immediately to her mind was to let go and hope the fall wasn't too far, but a deeply-ingrained animal instinct stopped her.

Her blood wasn't pounding quite as loudly then, and she heard a voice.

"Missus! Missus!" Mohammed seemed to be crawling down the tunnel after her.

From the bouncing shadows, Patty could tell he was bringing along a light.

"I'm here!" She called back, urgently. "I'm alright, but *don't* come any further, Mo! The floor of the tunnel collapsed."

"What should I do, missus?"

"Go get a piece of wood. A board. Anything!" Patty struggled to keep her voice steady. "Something long that I can use as a bridge. I don't want to fall."

"No missus," he shouted back. "I won't leave you."

"Mohammed." She made her tone stern despite her barely-contained fear. "Go! Find Mecquenem or the Nicks. Find Karim, or Jojo, I don't care who. Tell them what I told you. Go now!" Patty realized she was crying.

"No!" The boy sounded even more terrified than she was. "*I* will help."

"Mohammed, please!" Patty begged, succumbing to contagious panic, tears streaming down her face. "Please get help. I'm hanging over a pit! I can't hold on for long."

"How far? How far is the drop?" Mohammed called back.

Patty wanted to scream. If only she had a free hand to slap his face.

"I don't know!" She wailed. "I can't feel the bottom."

"Did you try to drop a stone?"

"Drop a—Oh!" The idea filtered down to her panicked brain. "I'm such a dumb palooka," she lamented below her breath.

"Drop a stone missus," the boy instructed. "We can count how long–"

"I understand, Mo. Thank you."

Terrified to let go with either hand, Patty instead used her right elbow to nudge a pebble, gradually sliding it toward herself. Without releasing her death grip on the part of the stonework that held her, she gently sidled one hand until its thumb rested near the pebble. With a flick, she sent the stone tumbling behind her, down into the blackness.

"One Mississi–" Before Patty could begin counting, a sharp click sounded from below, indicating that the stone had impacted a hard surface.

The American nearly went numb with relief. Her muscles were still frozen, attached vicelike to the earthen ledge, but Patty dropped one stone followed by another into the sucking void. Each hit bottom in less than a second. Soon, her body began to believe–hard evidence chasing away primal fear.

"Mohammed! I'm ok. It's not deep! I'm letting go."

Her muscles relaxed, and she dropped.

For a brief, sickening instant, she touched nothing, but before the thought could register–her boots hit terra firma. Patty slipped on the uneven ground, dropping roughly to her knees. There would be bruises, but she was alive. Her hands could feel the debris-strewn floor of the newly discovered chamber she'd landed in, and when she looked up at the hole of flickering light above, a mad laugh rose and caught in her long, dusty throat.

"Missus! Missus!' Back up the tunnel, Mohammed was still calling to her, more frantic than ever.

"I'm fine! It wasn't as deep as I thought," she shouted. "Mohammed? Come meet me down here–bring some rope and an extra lamp!"

The chamber she'd fallen into was small and mostly collapsed. The air hung thick with dust, and little oxygen reached her lungs. Despite the rush of stimuli, Patty had to labor to keep her breathing steady. Soon, Mohammed's lamp, tied to a thin rope, descended in a series of jerky stages, its light spilling across the cramped, underground ruin.

Patty realized that the room's interior was only about three times the size of her spartan tent. The chamber contained no obvious furniture or other artifacts, and the floor was covered with a thick layer of dust–augmented greatly by the torrent of dirt and debris that had come with the collapse of the floor above. Its walls, however, were worked stone, clearly carved by the tools of human artisans, but unlike her colleague's site, Dr. Haverwood's chamber contained no visible inscriptions, not even graffiti.

Patty crawled through her discovery while Mohammed remained above, his face poking out through the gap. The antiquarian's initial fear had given way to excitement once she realized what they'd found. Now, with the lamp to illuminate her surroundings and the true dimensions of the meager chamber revealed, she could not help but feel a twinge of unearned disappointment.

"What did you expect?" She scolded herself. "Did you think you'd fallen into a room full of gold coins and sculptures? Bruise your butt on the lost treasure of Darius?"

"What?" Mohammed called. "Doctor, I cannot hear you."

"Nevermind, Mo!"

The truth was that, empty or not, this chamber was a huge discovery for the young archeologist. She had fallen into a part of the ancient city that no living person knew existed. As she examined her surroundings more thoroughly, her disappointment started to fade. Indeed, the room seemed to have a pair of doorways cut into its walls, though both had partially collapsed, sealing the room off from whatever lay beyond. If her team could somehow travel down there and shift the rubble, there was no telling how many more rooms and chambers could be revealed.

"Hey kiddo," she called up to Mohammed. "Lower that other rope and help me climb out of here. It's time we told the others."

When Patty finally emerged from the palace of Darius, she was coated with dirt, dust, and some dried blood where she'd scraped her arms and legs. Despite her undead appearance, the young woman's luminous blue eyes shone through as she slid down the plateau and gaily jogged to the Artaxerxes dig.

"I found something!" Patty blurted out, interrupting Roland, Nicolas, and Karim on their tea break. "A whole new building, buried beneath the old palace!"

The dusty American's news hit the dig like a bombshell. Everyone working on the Artaxerxes site abandoned their current tasks to follow Patty back to her palace. However, once inside the ruins, the team of archeologists and laborers ran into a problem. As they took turns squeezing down the narrow, carved passage that led to the lost chamber, it turned out that Patty, Mohammed, and Nicole had no issues navigating the tight confines, but as Nicolas attempted the squeeze, he nearly managed to get himself stuck by the shoulders. Dr. Mecquenem, Karim, and the towering Jojo wisely declined to even attempt the journey.

That night, despite the setback, the team managed to find enough liquor and music to properly celebrate the find, each of them speculating wildly about what lay in the rooms beyond the chamber.

"My money's on storage," the male Thornburg argued. "These rulers taxed their people to ruin, hoarding oil, grain—whatever they could."

"Some gold would be nice," Patty added.

"Gold indeed."

"Why dream so small?" Nicole, who by virtue of her slim frame had actually managed to gain a peek into the lower palace, scolded them. "Would it not be grand if we found an entirely new dynasty? Kings whose names have never been written? Cultures older than words existed, you know. If they'd be anywhere, it would be Susa."

Dr. Mecquenem declined to join in the speculation, though he did watch the proceedings, sipping spirits with a benign smile spread across his features—no doubt mentally recording and cataloging the various theories, Patty suspected. The highlight of the evening, however, was Mohammed's spirited retelling of their discovery.

"Help! Help!" He imitated. "I am hanging over a pit without a bottom!"

The others laughed and Patty flushed, but throughout the telling, she noticed that Mohammed emphasized his own terror and panic far more than her bone-headedness, and she loved him a little more for that.

* * *

Dr. Mecquenem, the Nicks, and their local help all converged on Patty's promising site. Taking charge, the French archeologist ordered the initial passage widened and refortified. Karim and Jojo got to work digging out the walls of the tunnel, while the others formed a brigade to help clear the shifted rubble. They worked eagerly throughout the morning. After the mid-day meal, however, Dr. Mecquenem retired to his tent without a word. Widening a thirty meter passageway with hand tools was not a simple task, yet the team kept at it until well after sunset.

The following morning, Patty found that a crisis of enthusiasm already threatened her efforts. The tunnel remained mostly blocked, and days of hard labor stretched out ahead before they could even fully survey the lower palace. Later, after only a few hours of shifting stones, the Thornburgs expressed their desire to break ranks. When they sat down for luncheon, the tired Anglos admitted to Patty that they would be resuming their excavations at the Artaxerxes site.

"Roland as well," Nicole informed her. "However, he's given his permission for you to keep Karim and Jojo—at least until the exploratory tunnel is sufficiently widened."

Secretly, Patty appreciated that the others lacked her fire for the accidental find. She knew the eventual credit for any artifacts would go to Roland de Mecquenem as project head, but she wanted to experience the pure thrill of making a discovery for herself—the fewer people looking over her shoulder, the more likely that would be to happen.

It took three backbreaking days for Dr. Haverwood, Mohammed, Karim, and Jojo to widen the tunnel. By the time they finished, the passage leading to the lost chamber was wide enough to allow easy egress, even for the massive Jojo. However, the lower chamber still contained a building's worth of rubble, not to mention the two mysterious, blocked side-rooms. The situation in Europe was growing worse by the day, Patty knew, and her little hermetic bubble-world wouldn't stay inviolate forever. Time might soon become a factor.

For a full, uneventful day, Patty lugged stones from one end of her claustrophobic chamber to the other, trying to clear the area around one of the tantalizing doorways. Though the scrawny Dr. Haverwood had by now acclimated to the hard work of excavation, day after day of intense effort began to wear at her body. The others felt the same way, and accidents, small and large, became more commonplace.

During one shift in the darkened lower palace, for instance, Patty heard a bellowing scream echoing from the tunnel above. Karim had dropped a thirty-pound stone on his foot. The barrel-chested Persian was out of commission for weeks.

"I wonder what the life expectancy is for an archeologist?" Patty asked herself, after leaving some tea for her injured friend, feeling the cracks and creaks of her own weary skeleton as she shuffled off to bed.

Unfortunately, when the first doorway in the lower palace had finally been cleared, it became apparent that the chamber beyond was in a state of complete collapse—massive slabs of stone blocked the entrance, and most of the space beyond was filled with tightly-packed grit. Again, Patty gathered the Susa team to survey and inspect her progress.

Everyone present concluded that it would take a major effort to clear the room, but their simple, Louvre-backed dig was not even remotely equipped for such an effort. Not even the hulking Jojo could shift the confounding stone slabs. Excavating from above was out of the question, as any serious machine-driven digging would destroy the ruins atop the plateau. The sad fact hung in the air–there existed an entire lower palace buried at Susa, but accessing it might seriously damage the acropolis and upper floors. Nobody was willing to make that sacrifice, not even Dr. Haverwood.

Still, there remained the hope of a second doorway leading from the lost chamber. From the outside, it appeared even more hopelessly blocked, but it was Patty's only chance. After Roland, Nicolas, and Jojo helped shift the greatest pieces blocking her way to the second portal, the men informed Patty that they would be returning to the Palace of Artaxerxes.

"Really?" She teased. "You want to leave all the glory to me?""To us," Mohammed corrected, standing beside her, his hand on his hips.

Despite their colleagues' absence, Patty and Mohammed made swift progress excavating their latest hope. The pair found themselves driven by a renewed fervor, hungry to unlock the secrets of the lower palace before it was too late. Painstakingly, they hauled away chunks of rock and stone from the first doorway to make way for new rubble to be cleared from the second. After three tireless days, they were forced to rest, taking a long morning to nurse their sore muscles and eat extra rations brought in from the latest supply run.

Finally, their hands calloused into leather mitts, Patty and Mohammed succeeded in hauling away enough debris from the doorway that they could conceivably enter the new room. The collapse within was not nearly as extensive as the blockage in the first chamber, and a slender person could easily wriggle their way inside.

"I'm rigging up a simple harness," Patty declared, wary of further injury. "Tie this around your waist," she instructed Mohammed.

She looped the rope around a heavy boulder, affixing the other loose end to herself. Cautiously, the archeologist proceeded to duck under a low ceiling and step over a small hill of dust and stones. She shifted rubble where she had to, and when she stepped, she stepped so as not to carelessly trod on some priceless treasure. It took an effort both of physical and mental will for Patty to manage it, but after another calculated squeeze, she found herself in the hollow of the new chamber.

The space was small and cramped, with little open breathing room. However, to Patty's delight, there was junk everywhere.

"Mohammed!" She cried out, "this place has been lived in!"

"You mean squatters?" He answered.

"Not for thousands of years," she laughed, looking around at bits of earthenware vessels and other refuse she could not immediately place.

To the young archeologist, this cluttered chamber was beyond a miracle—it had survived the looting of a half-dozen marauding armies over the centuries, the trembling of the Earth, and the relentless erosions of time.

"Imagine what this place has been through, Mo. Heck—this room even survived a hundred years of French archeologists!" Patty declared, gleefully.

Upon hearing the news, the rest of the team shared Haverwood's excitement. Toasts were guzzled in her honor, and any traces of Mecquenem's former impatience evaporated—the Frenchman favoring Patty with an enormous bear-hug when she described the untouched chamber. Still, there was much work to be done at both dig sites, and, as Nicolas did not fail to inform them, time was growing ever shorter as the Germans and Italians continued their march through Europe and Northern Africa. That night, Mecquenem decided that at least one of the Nicks would assist Patty for the next few days, until either a proper inventory of the new chamber could be made or until they were forced to go home—whichever came first.

*   *   *

"If you discover anything else," Nicole lectured, "be sure to carefully mark the location where you first spotted it. Then call it out to me, and I'll make a note in the log before we actually move anything."

"Not my first time at the dance," Patty quipped back from inside the chamber. She wore the improvised safety harness around her waist and shoulders, trusting her colleague for ballast.

"Isn't it?"

"Ok, it sort of is, Nicky, but still–please shut up."Nicole snorted, a sound unexpected from one so well-polished. It made Patty start to laugh, despite herself. Within seconds, they were both choking on the dust particles floating in the stale cavern air.

"Here," Dr. Haverwood coughed at last, "I'm sending back the pieces for grid A-four."

Carefully, she packed fragments of ancient wood into a padded crate, wrapped in a safety line of its own.

"Later, we can place these back together like a jigsaw puzzle."

"Fragments from the throne of ancient Persian kings, you think?" Nicole theorized, dryly. "More likely roof supports or wall paneling."

After the petrified bits were sent back up the tunnel, Patty continued to pick through the rubble, with Nicole and Mohammed taking turns standing outside, holding the safety line and keeping the necessary logs. The newly-discovered chamber was hopelessly shattered and rotted, the antiquarians discovered. There existed not a single fragment in the debris that stood out clearly as an identifiable object. Shards of ceramic implied that the room once held pottery, and petrified goo mashed against the dirt hinted at organic matter.

"The possibility that these were books–scrolls or velum. It breaks my heart to see them rotted to illegibility," Patty remarked, referring to the smeared traces of organics.

"Corpses," Mohammed hypothesized upon seeing the stains.

"Maybe," Dr. Haverwood replied, unfazed, "but bodies usually leave bones behind, don't they?"

As the hours passed, she gradually made her way through their carefully-laid search grid. While inspecting the easternmost wall of the chamber, Patty knelt down to shift a large clod of dirt and rock and found that beneath, the floor of the chamber bulged upward.

"I think there's something buried here. E-fourteen." She called back to Nicole, who made a note in her logbook.

"Could it be a rock?" Nicole asked, stifling a yawn. "Or perhaps one of Mohammed's corpses?"

Patty ignored her and started carefully digging at the mound with a small trowel. The dirt gave way easily against the iron of her spade. Beneath, the object seemed too soft to be made from stone but too solid to be a mere clod of dirt. Selecting a heavy brush, the archeologist whisked away the top layer of loose soil, revealing the dimensions of the blocky find—a boxy rectangular prism, roughly eighteen inches in height, much of it still buried in hard-packed dirt.

"I think we have some sort of container. A chest, maybe," Patty called out.

"A treasure chest, I hope," Nicole's clear voice replied. "Too large to carry?"

"No. I've got it."

When Patty tried to free the artifact from the surrounding dirt, she found it held fast. Whatever the treasure chest happened to hold, the container was too far gone to remove intact. She did her best to excavate the area around the box, leaving its material undamaged, but much of the ancient rotted and petrified wood collapsed as she dug.

"Come on, you bum," she cursed at the fragile thing. "Just a little more..."

By the time it came free, the ancient chest resembled little more than a dirty, shapeless mass. Patty brought a light close to inspect its surface. She found a lip around the edge, marking the location where a lid may have been.

"Judgment call." Patty whispered to herself.

Proper archeological procedure would be to remove the entire object, as intact as possible, only attempting to lift the lid after every restoration and preservation method under the sun had been employed. There in the field, however, Dr. Haverwood estimated that the rotten container would not survive the journey out of the room, let alone up the rope, out of the lower palace, through the tunnel, and aboveground. The ancient chest may itself be a loss, but damaging its contents would be a worse scenario, Patty decided.

"Best to take my chances now," she declared. "I'm going to try to open it."

"I beg your pardon?"

The American raised her voice. "I am going to open the chest, Nicole."

"Shouldn't I go and fetch Roland first?" "No, it's ok," Patty answered. "I know what I'm doing. I hope."

This last she said under her breath, and with as much care as she could muster, Patty put her hands near where the lid should open and gave a sharp tug.

The container held, and Haverwood had no choice but to pull harder, employing her new wiry strength to leverage the two pieces apart. Flakes of dust and decayed matter tumbled off its sides, but the chest refused to open. Next, she wiped her hands on her trousers, took a moment to better consider her technique, and selected a penknife from her vest.

For the next twenty minutes, Patty worked at the chest, using the steel blade to gradually carve a clean space around the edge, Nicole demanding updates every other moment. The steel penknife proved itself more than a match for the crust of ancient filth, in minutes scraping away what had taken millennia to accumulate.

Humming to herself, Patty had another go. Her fingers wrapped around the ancient lid, applying leverage–a small budge. She sighed, and set to another interminable stretch of scratching with the knife before trying again. This time, Patty's strength proved sufficient, and the chest opened. With a sudden sliding motion, the shapeless and filthy lid collapsed in her hands, revealing the interior of the chest–small and full of grime. The air that escaped from within held the unpleasant funk of eons, causing Patty to curl her nose.

"I've got it open," she announced. "It stinks."

"You're speaking to me now, are you?" Nicole tried to make her aristocratic voice sound indignant, but a hint of excitement seeped through. "What do you see?"

"Hold your horses."

Patty angled her lamp to better illuminate the grimy interior. Whatever had once been inside, little remained unravaged by time. She could make out only three distinct objects among the detritus. Two took the form of pale rectangles, slablike and stacked one atop the other.

"Stone, or ceramic," Patty noted.

She tried to pick one up, but they were stuck together. Gingerly, the archeologist experimented with her penknife, investigating if the flat stones could easily be pried apart. With a small exertion of force and a flick of the wrist, she managed to separate two artifacts with a small pop.

"Oh!" She exclaimed, too softly to be overheard.

The pale objects certainly resembled ceramic, but they had been shaped into thin, rectangular tablets rather than cups or bowls. Patty gently picked up one of the fragile forms, finding it solid and undamaged. She blew off some dust and dirt and held the tablet up to the lamp. She gasped.

"Cuneiform. Nicole! These tablets are engraved with cuneiform!"

Indeed, the ceramic slabs were covered in rows of clunky, wedge-shaped characters that predated any linguistic system based on an alphabet.

"Tablets? Are you positive?"

"Yes, Nicky! It's a crude version, but I'd recognize it anywhere. Sumero-Akkadian cuneiform! This place...the lower palace, I mean, it must date back to the most ancient Elamite ancestors!" Patty's hands were shaking with the weight of the discovery, and she gently set the treasure down, "my word...it's so much older than we thought."

"Truly?" Nicole crooned. "Never doubted you, love. Not for one second!"

The other clay tablet was also engraved, but Patty decided she could examine it later, under better conditions. Blood still coursing with the adrenaline-thrill of discovery, the archeologist turned her attention to the other object in the chest. The thing was the size of a large, very flat shoe, but it was difficult to determine its exact dimensions. Running her hands over it as gently as possible, Patty realized that a mass of stuck-together detritus coated the thing. She hit it with her brush, causing the object to settle into shape. Flecks of red gleamed in her lamp-light.

"Metal," Patty whispered.

She reached down and wrapped her fingers around what remained of the handle of Quishda's dagger–the mounting tang of Kaliq's spearhead. Her eyes widened at the familiar weight of iron alloy.

"I've got something else. Something made of metal!"

"Gold?" Nicole inquired.

"No, I don't think so."

Patty held the brush in her other hand, rotating the metal artifact and clearing away its dust and dirt. It was badly corroded, but the shape was unmistakable.

"It's a knife!" She yelled happily to Nicole. "Or a dagger–some sort of weapon. It's incredible!"

As Patty's eyes greedily devoured the discovery, they caught a glimpse of her hands in the yellow lamplight. Her palms were stained a dark red. Instinctively, the archeologist's heart beat faster–she feared she had cut herself. However, upon examining her hands more closely, the distinction became clear.

"Rust," she breathed a sigh of relief. "It's only rust. Which would mean...It's made of iron!" Patty reported, audibly. "I'm sure of it."

"I don't think that's possible," Nicole replied thoughtfully, her academic's voice flowing into the collapsed room like a cool, blue stream. "If those tablets are as old as you think they are, love, your weapon couldn't be iron."

"I don't know how it's possible, but it is. Maybe they're from different eras, Nicky–I don't know. Maybe the chest belonged to a Persian archeologist or something." Patty looked down at her rust-stained hands as she held the fragile and corroded weapon. "It's definitely iron. I'd bet my life on it."

* * *

Until that moment, Fe's sullied spearhead had rested undisturbed, buried in its rotted tomb for enormous stretches of time, as humans viewed the dimension. On a cosmic scale, however, this subterranean sabbatical was nothing when compared to even a single orbit of the original asteroid. Yet, conditions on Earth proved far more hostile to the iron alloy's surface than the cold and uncaring void of space. Though a scant handful of millennia had passed since the dagger was buried, trillions upon trillions of its constituent atoms had rusted away into oblivion, oxidation devouring the artifact from the outside in. Indeed, every last atom of the unearthly black blade, once an object of awe and worship by the Kings of Kish, would have succumbed to the same chemical fate had Dr. Patricia Haverwood not plucked it from the seas of time.

After packing away her finds, Patty brushed her hands clear, rubbing away trillions of molecules of iron oxide–children from the Mother Star fallen to earthly ruin. She wrapped the artifacts carefully, first the two clay tablets, then Fe's rusted bayonet. With utmost caution, she passed the bundles backwards to Nicole.

Aboveground, the team scrambled to set up their largest tent and establish basic safeguards to examine the artifacts. Patty eagerly allowed the Thornburgs and Dr. Mecquenem to set the tablets and the iron implement in their own bins, each on a different folding table, surrounded by brushes and other tools of the trade. Someone produced a fresh pack of field notebooks, and Mecquenem even whipped out his phonograph to set the mood.

To complete the examination room's state-of-the-art setup, the Frenchman unloaded a thirty-five millimeter still camera from its leather case and proceeded to click images of the artifacts, and archeologists, in their various stages of restoration.

"Object One is a tablet, constructed from clay, likely kiln-fired." Patty spoke while Nicole took dictation. "I located it in section E-fourteen of the second room in the lower palace dig. Object is approximately twenty centimeters by twenty centimeters and is engraved with cuneiform writing."

Mecquenem squinted into the camera's viewfinder and snapped a picture.

"Object Two is also a clay tablet, found in the same container as object one, also from E-fourteen," Patty continued. "Approximately twenty two centimeters by twenty, the tablet displays similar Sumero-Akkadian cuneiform."

"Although the content is different," Nicole chimed in, looking up from the notes she was taking.

"What?" Dr. Haverwood was taken aback by the interruption. "First things first Nicole–and, how could you already know?""Look, right there," the English-woman replied testily. "It says 'Kish'. Do you need me?"

"Well, um, yes–"

Before Patty could reply, however, Nicole had dashed out of the tent.

"Don't mind my wife," Nicolas remarked, flipping open a notebook and taking a pencil from behind one red, flaky ear. "Please, Dr. Haverwood, continue."

"Very well," Patty said, taking a breath. "This brings us to Object Three, a metallic implement, roughly thirty one centimeters longways, less than ten at its widest. From the shape, the object appears to possess both a blade and a handle. Tentatively, I am classifying it as a weapon. Not much of a stretch, there. It was inside the remains of a chest found in area E-fourteen of the second room of the lower palace, alongside Objects One and Two. From extensive rusting, I can conclude that the weapon is composed of some type of iron alloy."

"Iron? That's a surprise," the male Thornburg replied, putting down the dictation to better study Fe's blade resting in its bin.

Dr. Mecquenem snapped photographs of the heaven metal.

"Fer," he said. "It is iron, certainment."

At that moment, Nicole Thornburg ducked back under the tent's white hangings, a volume on ancient cuneiform tucked beneath her arm.

"Some Elamite cultures may have used iron here and there," the Englishman replied to Roland's certainty, noting his wife's entrance with raised eyebrows, "but you must admit, a four thousand year old iron artifact may be beyond the pale. Ferrous metallurgy didn't even exist in those times."

"Précisément!" Mecquenem agreed happily, confusing both Nicolas and the American.

"See?" Nicole interrupted, her book spread before her. "This symbol is definitely Kish. The tablet is talking about a battle." She pointed at the second slab of cuneiform.

"Oh?" Patty squinted at the dozens of little wedges, impressed by the speed of Nicole's work. "And this one?" She asked, pointing at the first tablet.

The female Dr. Thornburg glanced at the tablet, going between it and her book for a moment.

"This one is boring," she concluded. "A dry accounting of gold, silver, and copper, I think."

"Native metals," Nicolas added. "But I guarantee they weren't mining iron."

"Does it mention an iron weapon?" Patty asked.

"No," Nicole determined, after a moment of study.

"Ha!"

"That proves nothing," Patty said, hotly. "Watch this."

She lifted a pitcher of water and, gently, poured its contents over Fe's terribly rusted speartip. The water turned a thin red as microscopic flakes of iron oxide hydrated and ran away to the sides of the bin. Though a full restoration would have to wait for Paris, the weapon somewhat resembled itself after its rinse. In fact, centuries of corrosion had given Fe's blade a jagged, menacing appearance that King Zuqaqip would have loved.

Nicolas let out a low whistle.

"Iron." Dr. Mecquenem voiced the word in two thick, English syllables. "Iron météorique."

"That would explain it," Nicole concurred.

"Iron from a meteor?" Her husband and colleague looked at Fe's speartip with a new, keen expression. "If that were the case, this nasty thing must have been beyond valuable."

"Do you think it killed anybody?" Mohammed asked excitedly.

He had stood in the tent for some minutes without being noticed.

"Mo, you sneak!" Patty scolded, smiling despite herself.

"Va t'en!" Mecquenem shouted, shooing the boy away.

"Conquerors always have a use for iron," Thornburg said to the adults, his tone darkening. "Even now, Hitler and the Soviets are going after strategic centers of iron ore production. The Elamites might have made this one spear–"

"Or knife," Patty added.

"Or knife," he continued, "but look out world: it's nineteen hundred and forty. Humanity has a new iron arsenal to play with. Planes! Tanks! Submarines, bombs, guns—field artillery!"

"Love, enough. Enough." Nicole gently took her husband's hand in both her own.

Through the afternoon, the team lovingly cleansed the tablets and dagger of centuries of dirt and dust, packed them away for long term storage, and scribbled up drafts of their final assessments, which were to be sent, along with segments of thirty-five millimeter film, to colleagues in Paris, London, and Patty's own native Chicago.

That night, the archeologists and laborers celebrated Dr. Haverwood's find with gusto. Mecquenem produced a bottle of champagne, and even Mohammed was offered a mug, which he politely declined. Patricia drank her portion of the champagne happily, relieved to have finally made a contribution. Indeed, it was quite the grand contribution—Fe's spearhead and the clay tablets were the jewels of the entire Susan excavation thus far. The fragments of pottery and graffiti found at the palace of Artaxerxes simply couldn't compete.

The others shared Patty's pride, though Nicolas Thornburg continued to speak darkly of the brewing war at every opportunity. Together, the team toasted them-selves and the many denizens of Susa over its centuries. Now that the ambitious American had proven the site's true antiquity, all agreed that there was far more to be found beneath both palaces.

Spurred on by the success, Patty and the team continued their mission with renewed vigor. The recently re-ambulant Karim took charge of the dig's safety, and with his help, the buried structure was excavated and mapped without further injury.

The archeologists theorized that the Elamite ancestor structure once stood as large and grand as the palace of Darius, though much of it had been eaten by the earth over the millennia. Almost as exciting as the heaven metal dagger, several fine examples of representative sculpture were discovered by the antiquarians, but even half-broken, the great severed pieces of stone gods and kings proved far too large to move by hand.

"One for future expeditions, I suppose," Patty concluded. "Know anybody out here with heavy equipment?"

"Oh, I'm sure someone will roll in, soon enough," Nicolas remarked.

Back under the Artaxerxes site, Macquenem had enlisted Mohammed as his own aide de camp, ceding his British colleagues to Dr. Haverwood. With the boy's help, the later site produced scraps of petrified leather and some unusual damaged pottery, alongside some new instances of lewd Achaemenidian graffiti, which Roland had no qualms about translating for the Muslim teenager.

Return post trickled into the isolated archeologists' camp. Not every letter they sent had been returned, but Patty at least received replies from experts back in her own neutral nation, congratulating the team on the find and confirming Dr. Thornburg's tentative translation of the cuneiform tablets. When writing back to her university, Patty declared her intent to stay on with Dr. Mecquenem for another year. She wrote it all out plainly and stamped the envelope shut, thinking the application a mere formality.

"If they want me to leave Susa," she happily hummed to herself after she'd addressed the last letter, "they'll have to come out here themselves and drag me back."

Unfortunately for Dr. Haverwood, the Second Great War chose those happy moments to breach the team's hermetic bubble of science and discovery. Upon returning from a supply trip to a nearby town, Roland de Mecquenem gathered his team. Patty had never seen the Frenchman's face so lined and haggard. He had received a communique from Paris.

"The dig is, eh, cut," he explained gruffly, in English.

"I don't understand," Patty said.

"Cut?"

Dr. Mecquenem gave a heavy sigh and began speaking in French, his tone dull.

"All funding and support for the archeological mission at Susa had been suspended," Nicole translated, the little color in her face draining away. "Apparently, Hitler annexed the duchy of Luxembourg."

"Then the Germans have declared their intentions to invade France and take all of Europe," Nicolas said, bitterly.

"Paris informed Roland that he's free to remain here until the situation develops one way or the other," Nicole continued, "but he's been strongly advised to return his team home while he still can."

Patty watched the news unfold. She could hear the blood rushing in her ears, and her face flushed with surprise and something itchy-shame. She had been so busy unearthing lost treasures that she'd forgotten that her colleagues' homes hung in a state of war.

"I understand their thinking," the male Thornburg commented. "Persia and Arabia have rich oil fields. A tempting target for the Germans, Soviets perhaps. I've spoken with the local lads. Invasion is on their lips."

Dr. Mecquenem only glowered.

"So do we stay here, or we go back?" Nicole asked the question, her voice stressed higher than its usual pitch. "Mind you all, both choices are far easier said than done."

"We should stay!" Nicolas declared, surprising everyone. "Our camp is not situated atop an oilfield. This is the barren borderlands of Iran and Iraq–the back end of nowhere. Even if the Bosch take every strategic target, we're still in the safest bloody place we could be."

"Non–à Paris!"

"Are you mad?" Thornburg retorted, "Hitler is marching *toward* Paris. We're not in the circus–I will not walk into the lion's mouth."

"Au contraire–Le Louvre, she is eh, empty."

"It's true," Nicole defended the Frenchman. "The exhibits went out on railcars–we may be able to continue our work *there*. The museum itself is of no strategic importance. Truly, who worries about a handful of archeologists?"

"Patricia may be able to get away with such a stunt," Nicolas scoffed. "But our lot would be taken as prisoners-of-war faster than you can say Artaxerxes."

"It isn't like we're the safest here, love," Nicole argued, looking her husband in the eye. "If the Turks change their minds about neutrality..."

"Syria, Iraq, I know. Iran wouldn't be far behind–"

"And then there's no going back."

Throughout much of the debate, Patty remained silent. She acutely felt the distance between herself and her colleagues. Mohammed and the other laborers were not present, and for that, Patty was thankful. She would have no idea what to say if the keen-minded boy asked her what made America different.

The team continued to discuss and process the matters of war, but when the hour grew late, Dr. Mecquenem made an executive decision.

"The dig is cut," the supervisor repeated. "Paquet les large artefacts. Retour à Paris, eh, avec le fer arme, les tablets," he pointed vaguely to the artifacts, "le plus important."

"I can take care of that," Patty insisted.

"Bien."

"Very well." Nicolas conceded his leader's decision. "It's a terrible risk you're taking, you know. The city isn't safe."

"Eh, Paris is...eternal," Mecquenem replied, his tone strong and serious. "Ville des Lumières. Lutèce. *La Dame de Fer...* "

* * *

The team packed as carefully and as quickly as they could, though the effort took several days. During that time, the swiftly-moving German blitzkrieg managed to engulf the Netherlands. Patty dreaded saying her final goodbyes to Mohammed, but at last, the moment came.

He stood among Karim, Jojo, and the other paid helpers, looking more a man than ever.

"Be good, kiddo," Patty said, ruffling his hair.

She regretted how weak it sounded, but there was nothing else she could think to do or say without breaking down completely.

"Yes, missus," Mohammed replied, remaining nearly as stoic as his mentor.

Dr. Mecquenem and the Nicks shook hands and exchanged hugs and certain parcels with Jojo and Karim, promising that somehow, they would all see one another again some day.

They would be taking the first leg of their journey by truck. Patty at least was appreciative to not have to spend any more time on camelback. However, wary of the rough and uncertain nature of desert roads, she decided to take personal charge of the E-fourteen artifacts. After removing the dagger and tablets from their wooden crates, Patty had them wrapped in crinkly cellophane and layers of tough, breathable linen. She placed the parcels in a canvas shoulder bag, stuffed with rags and padding. Dr. Haverwood kept at least one hand and one eye on this bjorn of fragile treasures during the team's long journey to the Louvre.

Their odyssey from Susa to Beirut stretched over five hundred miles as the crow flies. Unfortunately for the archeologists, their industrial Ford Model-AA was hardly a crow, and the local roads were poor at best and nonexistent at worst. Patty prided herself on her skillful handling of the boxy, bouncing machine–its manual steering and bronco-stubborn clutch no match for her wiry, excavation-toned physique.

Yet with each rut in the ill-maintained road and each new mile of mesopotamia, billions upon quadrillions of iron atoms from the Mother Star, long lost to rust, flaked away from the main mass and settled on the bottom of Dr. Haverwood's jealously-guarded bag. Patty had been careful when she rinsed and wrapped the treasures, yet the journey overland hit the artifacts like a rock polisher. Still, most of the ancient iron and nickel atoms remained locked in crystalline matrix, safe within the same bonded formation they had occupied for the better part of five billion years.

Though the region they traveled was ostensibly neutral territory, crossing borders between nations was not nearly as easy as it had been for Patty and Mecquenem the previous year. Fortunately for the multicultural team, even with war enveloping the globe, there were few places where British, French, or American citizenship did not hold significant sway. The archaeologists only occasionally found themselves briefly delayed and questioned by the tense border guards they encountered on their journey.

Once, Patty was ordered out from behind the wheel at a rural checkpoint by men with rifles. Nervously, she complied, clutching her shoulder bag and fearing the worst. However, it turned out that the local authorities were disturbed solely by her gender–they sent the team happily on their way as soon as they were assured that either Nicolas or Dr. Mecquenem would take over the driving duties.

Several days of rough travel and even rougher sleep brought Fe and the four archeologists at last to the eastern coast of the Mediterranean, washing up in Beirut, where Patty had first met Dr. Mecquenem one long year before. Once secure in the first lodgings they came to, the team took time to recover and gather information.

By coin and wire, Mecquenem managed to get in touch with his contacts in Paris, who were pleased to hear that the team had followed the advice to evacuate. The Nicks had worse luck, and neither Nicole nor her husband could get through to England by wire, though each wrote and dropped off hopeful letters to loved ones and colleagues. Patty also composed a letter to her family in Illinois, assuring them of her safety in every other line.

There was, of course, the temptation to remain among the comforts of civilization. Beirut, after all, boasted electric lights at night, diverse foods, and hotels with hot water. Compared to the rude desert camp, it was the last word in luxury accommodations. However, the group knew their next challenge lay in finding passage to somewhere west, with the hope of ending up at any port in the South of France.

Upon his first visit to the Levantine harbor, Mecquenem found a paucity of passenger vessels willing to cross the Mediterranean since the commencement of major hostilities in Europe.

"Politics are the true obstacles we must navigate," Nicolas warned.

"All these countries are neutral, though," Patty said. "It doesn't make sense."

"Neutral. Huh." The Frenchman pronounced the word as if it were a vile curse.

"Officially yes," Nicolas replied, "but there are underlying politics at play. Italy is controlled by fascists, very friendly with Hitler. Like little boys, they call themselves the Pact of Steel."

"Modern man is a complex beast," Nicole observed.

"Italie attendez eh, waits for opportune moment to...enter le guerre," Mecquenem explained, with disgust.

"Like a vulture," Patty blurted, the image coming suddenly and unbidden into her mind.

Forcefully, Mecquenem ruled out any voyage which involved a call in Italian ports.

"Rome, Naples, and Tripoli are no longer options for anyone. It's his final say," Nicole translated. "I for one agree."

Days passed before they finally found a promising way to leave Beirut, Dr. Mecquenem silently raging at every delay. He took to chain smoking and roaming the streets at night. Everyone in the group waited uneasily, but the Frenchman's desperation became hard to ignore. It was palpable to the team that Roland felt trapped, tortured by the need to return to his home before the Germans destroyed it. Eventually, though, fortune smiled on the four travelers, and from a less-than-reliable-looking vagabond, they booked passage on a boat going to Athens.

The vessel's youngish, one-eyed master would accept only gold or silver coins, but the Europeans seemed to have no shortage of payment for the budding war-profiteer. Not for the first time, Patty found herself wondering how her colleagues, especially Dr. Mecquenem, were able to so easily produce gold when called for. In any event, she didn't ask, deciding instead to be grateful for the private charter.

"Thank you again," she said to Roland, standing beside him by the deck's upper railing. "I've never been to Athens. All that history–it's bananas."

Mecquenem smoked his pipe and looked out at the water.

"Greece, eh, like Poland," he said at last, "is eh temping target for the warmongers."

"If Hitler sacks that beautiful city, I'll kick him in the teeth myself."

Mecquenem nodded. "Angland, France. We eh, pledge to protect Grecs from invasion."

"You know," Patty said, grinning and watching smoke billow from beneath the man's moustache, "your English is better when the Nicks aren't around to translate."

"Anglish is eh, not my preferred." Mecquenem shrugged. "Je ne parle pas Américaine."

"Athens goes back six thousand years, or more—right?" She mused, leaning on the boat's railing and looking out to sea. "It's funny, but compared to the oldest artifacts from Athens, our iron relic is as modern as a typewriter.

"Is safe and dry?" Dr. Mecquenem asked, tapping his bowl empty.

"Of course." Patty nodded, putting her hand to the shoulder bag.

"Excusez-moi, Patricia. Désolé."

Vanishing almost as quickly as his smoke, the Frenchman disappeared belowdecks. Patty hoped he was finally catching some sleep. There wasn't much else to do on the boat—a chugging, unimpressive vessel so small that its master had christened it '*Mīkrós*'.

Though the late spring weather was sunny and clear, Patty couldn't enjoy it. Pacing aimlessly, she could hear voices whispering and felt a low sense of dread until she realized it was the Nicks, out of sight but around a corner somewhere, speaking quietly. Patty turned and walked in the other direction, deciding not to eavesdrop. The strangely rhythmic nature of their voices, however, made her wonder if they were praying.

She was beyond relieved to land in Athens, grateful for even a bit of breathing space from her glum, travel-weary companions, whom she had never been more than a few meters away from on the tiny boat.

Dr. Haverwood was first to jump out onto the Greek docks, leaving the *Mīkrós* and the salty waters of the Mediterranean behind. She let the history-laden air of the land enter her nostrils and escape her mouth—after her lungs had stolen some of its oxygen. It was good. Patty felt there was something reassuring about spending the night in a seven thousand year-old city.

Unfortunately, the antiquarians' much-anticipated night in Athens turned into two, then three—eventually stretching over an entire week. Under other circumstances, it would have been a dream to explore its famous ruins, taste the local cuisine, and maybe even visit some shops. However, much of the team's time was spent scrambling about searching for acceptable transport. Thousands of miles still separated them from Paris, and traveling by land would be all but impossible. Thus, the archeologists resigned themselves to another voyage by sea.

Even in their hotel, Patty remained protective of the Susan artifacts that she carried with her nearly everywhere.

"I'll be damned," Patty said patting the bag, which she wore over her belly, "if I pulled you from the lower palace with my bare hands and brought you halfway to the Louvre just to lose you to a Greek cutpurse."

Around her, the hotel bar thronged with characters, many just as strange and travel-worn as the archeologists or their mysterious Mediterranean captain.

"Talking to yourself again, love?" Nicole asked sweetly, walking up to Patty and taking a seat, Nicolas in tow.

"No, to the artifacts this time."

"Uh, how dreary." Nicole mock-swooned. "Those tablets are terrible company. They speak of nothing but gold and silver, blood and war."

"Definitely boy-stuff," Patty agreed.

Nicolas huffed and searched in vain for a bartender. The days of fruitless questing for transport were beginning to pile up on them all. While the team sat restlessly in Greece, Hitler's army was making inroads to empire.

"Belgique is, eh, fallen," Mecquenem said darkly, joining them later in the evening, relating what he'd learned between throatfuls of spirits.

"He says Germany is using the Belgians as a runway to the heart of France," Nicole translated as Roland muttered. "They're leaving Paris to die."

Together, they processed the news of Calais and Dunkirk, the trapped Allies surrounded by Hitler's ten-million-man army. That night, Patty dreamed of conquerors. Centuries pulsed beneath her head, vibrating the stones of the sleeping city like hoofbeats–Athenians falling to Macedonians falling to the Romans. She dreamed of the Byzantines, the French, Spanish, Italians, and the Ottomans. All were marching for war–marching toward *her*.

After almost a week in Athens, much of its classical charm having worn off, Patty began to feel more trapped than secure in the ancient city, and she was thankful indeed when their passage was finally booked. Dr. Mecquenem, looking as grey as the sky, had neglected to retire with his colleagues the previous night. It had taken an impressive combination of charm, bribes, and alcohol-tolerance to arrange it, but after far too long in Greece, the archeologists gratefully boarded a trade ship pointed west to North Africa.

The homesick Frenchman had somehow persuaded the ship's captain to veer off its scheduled itinerary and dock briefly in Tunis, another ancient metropolis with more than its share of history. He informed his colleagues that Grand Tunis was a good luck charm—it had avoided hostilities during the last Great War and was, at the moment, still loyal to France. Unfortunately, unofficial travel arrangements meant unofficial accommodations, and the archeological team spent nearly three days in the loud, damp hold of the ship, feeling like their own artifacts—packed and stuffed. When they finally disembarked, setting foot upon the Maghreb and the northern tip of the African continent, they felt positively reborn with relief.

To their eyes, the storied city of Tunis appeared untouched by war. By that point, the atom Fe, still secure in its spearpoint, had journeyed further in Patty's bag than it had since arriving on Earth. Even the most well-traveled soldiers in Kaliq's army never glimpsed even a hint of the Mediterranean's great breadth. Once property of kings, Fe's heaven metal had made its way across the great sea at the breast of a commoner and was now tucked beneath a Tunisian café table, swathed in rags.

Emotions ran high as the humans stretched in the sunshine and ordered coffees and plate after plate of richly-spiced food. The archeologists were optimistic that the final leg of their Mediterranean travel would be the simplest, but the team had reached a crossroads. Mecquenem argued that transport from Tunis to Southern France would be a far easier proposition than any of their previous passages.

"No one wants to get *into* France, love," Nicole sighed.

"We can really just walk in and out like that?" Patty wondered.

"If anyone wishes to get *out* of France," Nicolas said derisively, "he missed his last chance at Dunkirk."

Mecquenem, however, remained intent on continuing on to Paris. He wished to bring the artifacts to the Louvre.

"Tout le monde, eh, would be safe," he argued. "L'automne dernier…"

"Last autumn," Nicole translated. "They packed away the museum's entire contents, relocating them–he doesn't know where."

The Frenchman gestured with his hands as he spoke, and his translator's jaw tightened.

"I don't believe it will make 'the perfect hiding place,' Roland."

"He has a point," Nicolas said, playing devil's advocate. "So far at least, Hitler's left the majority of his conquests intact."

"Exactement!" Mecquenem slapped the table in triumph. "Les Boches, eh, like Alexander, les Romains. Dominion eh, non plunder. More interest to occupy Paris. Le Louvre, no plunder. *Safe*, tout le monde."

"You're forgetting, love," Nicole said, her tone growing stern, "*we* are still far from home. It's easy and noble to go down with the ship when it's your bloody ship."

"Soon it will be too late for us to even attempt to find a way home to England," the male Thornburg argued. "The risk is already near foolish!"

"Ça alors!"

"I'm sorry, Dr. Mecquenem," Nicole said at last, her blue eyes shining with moisture. "We will not travel with you into France. We are to remain here. We'll find our own way home, by sea, somehow."

Nicolas clasped his wife's shoulders in solidarity.

"Patricia," Mecquenem said, turning to Patty instead of answering the Nicks. "You have been, eh, calme?"

"I'm torn really," Dr. Haverwood said, breaking her uneasy silence. "But you shouldn't ask *me*. I can conceivably travel home easier than anyone here."

"Do you wish to go home?" Nicolas asked her.

"Of course not."

"That makes you the only one, love," the other Dr. Thornburg replied. "You're more than welcome to come to England with us. Plenty to study, Patricia, and an *ocean* away from Hitler."

"Patricia, venez à Paris avec moi."

"You can go to Paris when it's not bloody occupied!" Nicole flushed.

Patty looked at her friends. They all stared across the table at her. The young archeologist looked down, thinking, retreating within her own mind.

"Well, I can rule out going home. I signed onto another year of this fellowship, and dammit–a Haverwood sees her contracts through. I did not sit through dry lectures for a lifetime and travel halfway around the world just to turn tail and run back to Illinois when things get hairy!"

"Is she talking to us?"

"Je ne sais pas."

"You're more than just my colleagues," Patty told them. "I can't leave you alone. I've decided–I'm bringing the pieces from the lower palace back to the Louvre."

She nodded once, firmly. The Thornburgs gave her looks of pity. Mecquenem, on the other hand, gazed at Patty with barely-contained relief.

Their future paths decided, the group relocated to a crowded bar, intent on one last signature celebration.

"A good ol' fashioned Susa-style soiree," Patty quipped.

After some time, however, she noticed Roland drinking too much, and she began to question him in her typically blunt, American fashion.

"Listen, Dr. M. I know it's unfair that my family are safe, a million miles away from this horrible conflict. Is that it? Do you feel guilty too–is that why we're heading to the front lines?"

Mecquenem didn't answer, but he set down his glass.

"I've heard what you say about Hitler's Nazi Party," Patty continued. "If they nab me, it's no big deal, but you? I don't know about sneaking back to France..."

She joked, trying to get a rise out of him. "Wouldn't these artifacts look just aces back in Chicago? We could use some Sumerian stuff in Illinois. Too many feathered headdresses, if you ask me."

Roland drained his glass, ran a hand across his damp moustache, and stood up from the bar.

"Je suis navré," he said at last. "I never thought eh, I live to see another Great War."

Moving stealthily, the Nicks had come up behind him.

"Allons enfant de la patrie…" Nicolas sang in a ringing baritone, a tumbler held loosely in one ruddy hand. "Le jour de gloire est arrivé!"

Nicole joined in harmony with her clear, liquid mezzo-soprano.

A smile crept across Mecquenem's lined face. He didn't sing at first, but more than one voice from around the establishment rose up to join the Thornburgs in the "Marseillaise Hymn". Before long, much of the bar thundered together, Patty trying her best to hum along with the melody.

They talked and drank until deep in the night, and with local lodging clogged by travelers fleeing Europe, the antiquarians contented themselves to sleep together in the tavern until the morning light woke them.

As she slumbered, cuddling with Fe and the tablets, Patty dreamed of Tunis. Hannibal Barca atop a great, tusked beast. White-clad Islamic conquerors on horseback and French Enlightenment colonizers in their blue coats with their long rifles. And finally, a new German reich, oozing red on the northern horizon.

The omen of conquest turned out to be just the rising sun illuminating the blood behind Patty's eyelids. Her friends were awaking as well, moving stiffly from their rough night of unconsciousness. Thus, with little ceremony, the archeologists parted. Hugs and silent handshakes were exchanged–everything that needed to be said had already passed their lips and gone down with the liquor. Upon exiting the building, Mr. and Mrs. Thornburg turned right along the clean-swept streets, while Mecquenem and Patty turned left, toward the rising sun. Within her shoulder bag, two ancient manuscripts and Fe's alloy spearhead rode along, bound for the world's greatest museum.

● ● ●

After a hastily-purchased breakfast, Patty caught the silent Frenchman's eye, and he blearily brought her up to speed. There were a number of port cities which could serve as their entrypoint into France, but he would need to spend some time in a wire office, trying to contact the mainland.

Patty used her idle hours to walk amongst the locals. The impression she gleaned from snatches swirling amongst the polyglot was that most of the ports in the South of France were safe, though flooded by refugees coming to Tunis, on their way to other places.

That very afternoon, in fact, Mecquenem returned to her, having located a passenger ship employed in the ferrying of refugees from Nice to Tunis. Since the invasion, few opted to take the return voyage, for once making passage easy and cheap to secure.

"I probably could have managed to arrange a ride to France myself, they're all going back empty," Patty remarked, "but thank you for the ride, *monsieur*."

"Thank you for eh, the company."

Though the seas were thick with warships flexing their muscles, the passage of the French ship proved an uneventful, if psychologically tense affair. No one knew when Italy would decide to join their German allies in slicing apart Western Europe, and when the ship arrived in Lympia Port, Patty saw firsthand evidence of what people were calling the Second World War. Badly damaged vessels hung in the oily harbor, some under repair, some doomed derelicts hastily towed out of the shipping lane by stout tugboats.

The instant the ship from Tunis docked, a flood of harried passengers filled its hold, cramming their way inside and leaving the archeologists little room to climb down onto the wharf. There, at the port of Nice, they observed a scene of barely restrained chaos, and after disembarking, the pair valiantly shoved their way into the city proper. Lines of hollow-eyed people queued everywhere, and Mecquenem found no open wires with which to contact Paris. The archeologists learned that the war department had taken over most available lines of communication–most train routes as well.

As they walked among the sea of people, Patty tightly clutched her artifact bag, terribly wary of the thousands of refugee hands with their tens of thousands of grasping fingers, and, at the same time, she was ashamed of herself for those feelings. Displaced Jews had been in the city the longest, fleeing pogroms and ghetto raids. Later, Poles and Belgians fled west when their lands were trampled by Hitler's war machine. In a reversal of the archaeologist's itinerary, many of the refugees traveled to Nice in hopes of securing passage to North Africa. Mecquenem told Patty that hiding in the French colonies seemed a popular plan for surviving the war. Some, apparently, were trying to relocate as far as the Western Hemisphere—noticing her accent, or possibly her teeth, more than one desperate European begged Patty in broken English if she could take them to America.

Though the rail station appeared fully mobilized, Patty was surprised to find that there were still trains to Paris running, though few passengers opted to take the trip north. On a departing platform, the archeologists overheard news of the occupation of Boulogne-sur-Mer and Calais, though Paris, for the moment, still stood out of reach of German hands.

Once safely aboard the northbound passenger coach, Patty and Mecquenem tried to relax. The young American placed her bag over her belly, covering it with both hands. The elder antiquarian rested with his eyes closed. Patty looked around the cabin, noticing that the few other passengers looked either half-dead or utterly terrified.

"Into the belly of the beast," she whispered to herself.

She heard the Frenchman snoring beside her and experienced a moment where the whole adventure seemed absurd.

"Now is not the time to question the sanity of one's decisions," she said resolutely, squashing the feeling.

Eventually, Patty slept. The ancient tablets and Fe's spearpoint remained safely tucked away in the bag, children of the Mother Star cradled in the human's arms. Hours slipped away with the hypnotic clacking of the rails. Night fell and the train continued north. As the locomotive chugged onward, so too did history. Italy, receding rapidly behind the night train, finally decided to shed the paper-thin veil of neutrality and declare war on France and England. The archaeologists had crossed the sea just in time. Patty woke to the distant rumbling of thunder, or artillery—she could not tell which.

She didn't remember falling asleep.

"We are safe," Dr. Mecquenem assured Haverwood at an uncomfortably long stop at Orléans. "Eh, 'istory is bigger than nations."

When the train pulled into Paris, it arrived during the deepest part of the night.

"Oh, my," Patty yawned. "I thought this was supposed to be the City of Lights?"

Few lamps were lit, she noticed, and the windows of the buildings had been firmly shuttered or covered with heavy hangings–those who hadn't left Paris hardly wished to advertise their continued presence.

Patty and Mecquenem stepped off the platform, and they watched the handful of other passengers wander away. A larger throng, fleeing the doomed capital, took their places in the empty car, filling it with their babies, bodies, and belongings.

With a hearty yawn, Mecquenem took Patricia's hand and led her away.

"I've never been to Paris before, you know?" She said, keeping her voice low. "Like most American girls, I guess I dreamed of visiting this city–fantasies of its romance and history can be overwhelming when you only get to see her in *Camille* or *L'Atalante*, you can imagine."

In fact, when Patty won the grant to assist the French archeologist, she constructed dreams of striding into Paris, triumphantly holding a lost treasure from ancient Susa. Remarkably, she had the Frenchman at her side and the treasure in her bag, but there was no triumph in her step as it echoed hollowly against the paving stones. This was not the Paris she had dreamed of–nobody dreamed of that frightened and dark place, save in their nightmares. As they made their way toward le Louvre, winding through darkened streets cluttered with piles of garbage and castoff belongings, Patty and her companion caught a whiff of something horrible–a dead horse, decomposing near a wrought-iron fence that enclosed a public garden.

"I'd bet this place was beautiful before the war."

Roland nodded, turning his head from the scene of death and neglect.

The world's greatest museum loomed sadly in the dark, its magnificent architecture and regal feel lost in the shadows. Not a light burned in the cavernous structure. Optimistically, Mecquenem strolled up and tried the doors. Patty followed him up the palace's outer steps, and though he rattled their iron, the locks and bars held. Like inept burglars, the antiquarians walked around the grand building, Roland systematically pounding on each window and door they came across.

"Jean! Hélène!" He shouted the names of his colleagues. "Bastien! Putain!"

Each time, no one answered, and Patty noticed his shouting gradually turn from names to French profanity.

"Le musée," he concluded at last, "she is dead."

"Then what are we still doing here?"

Mecquenem shrugged. "I am, eh, chief conservateur, now."

"Those fellas usually have keys."

"Néanmoins."

Shrugging again, Roland de Mecquenem, acting curator of Le Louvre, continued searching for a way inside the palace. With nowhere else to go, Patty followed him. Soon, the journeyman archeologist stopped, turned, and smiled at Patty, pointing to the window of a small water-closet three meters off of the ground.

Dr. Haverwood looked up at the thin window, unimpressed. As she contemplated the angles, Mecquenem picked up a stone from the ground and hurled it at the building.

The window shattered, and Patty gasped.

The night's oppressive silence, however, quickly recovered. If any latchkey Parisians had witnessed the act of vandalism, they weren't telling. Roland pointed again to the window and then to his shoulders.

"S'il vous plaît."

"The world has gone insane," Patty declared.

Suppressing her disbelief, she awkwardly clambered onto his back, clutching at the stone wall to gain purchase. The Frenchman grunted as Patty drew herself to her full height. She extended her fingers and felt the ledge under the window.

"A little higher." With a grunt, Dr. Mecquenem unfolded from his squat, raising Patty like an elevator until she stood at a comfortable height before the broken window.

Taking one hand off the wall, she reached into the frame, looking for a latch. Instead, she found a window shard–the sharp silicon oxide crystals of glass carving a line of bloody skin from her hand.

"Ah, hell," Patty moaned. "I need a minute!"

Below, Mecquenem could only grunt in forlorn, Atlas-like resignation.

Deliberately, Patty switched hands, placing her bleeding appendage against the wall for support. With her other, she swept the ledge, looking for a stone or anything hard enough to knock away the broken glass, but she found nothing that fit the bill. Guiltily, the airborne archeologist looked to the bag of priceless artifacts slung over her shoulder.

Patty slipped her free hand into the bag. Using a millennia-old stone tablet as a cudgel was out of the question–she'd rather chew her way into the Louvre. After a moment of contemplation, however, she grasped the tight cloth wrappings of Fe's iron spearpoint.

Pommel-side first, she gently tapped the pieces of broken window out of the frame. Inside the heaven metal, every atom locked in their metallic crystals vibrated with the tiny transfer of kinetic energy from each strike, and Patty's careful application of force prevented any damage to the artifact more significant than dislodging a few flakes of rust.

With the path clear, she stowed the iron tool. The intruder's injured hand left a bloody smear against the museum wall as she shifted against the ledge and, with a small shriek, pushed down with her feet and jumped from Mecquenem's shoulders into the building.

"Oof-" he cried, collapsing to the ground.

Patty stood up inside the pitch-dark room, patiently waiting for her eyes to adjust. She stepped over to a stand of ghostly white porcelain and fumbled with the knobs until she produced a stream of cold running water.

"I broke into the Louvre," she said to herself, enjoying the cinematic absurdity. "I'm a cat burglar!"

Trillions and trillions of water molecules gushed from the faucet, sweeping the fresh blood from the human's hands, the cold constricting her blood vessels enough to stem the thin flow of vitality.

Her task finished and her night-vision somewhat serviceable, Patty located the water-closet's door and stepped into the empty, creaking upper-floor hallway of the great museum.

"Burglars are scary," she reminded herself. "We don't *get* scared."

Walking through the empty Louvre, however, proved a ghostly experience for the antiquarian. The walls were bare, discolored where paintings had covered them for decades. Patty felt like she was at another excavation site. The building seemed like it had been abandoned for far longer than a few months. Some rooms contained haphazard stacks of wooden frames, empty—like mummies, she thought.

"It is not at all uncommon," Dr. Haverwood addressed the echoing hallways, affecting the gruff, self-important tone of her thesis advisor, quoting nearly verbatim, "for the working archeologist to come across the odd mass grave here or there. Hold your nose—and remember human nature. As surely as people stack stones to the sky to hold up their dreams, they fill pits in the earth to bury their hates."

The echos proved hollow company, however. Just a year previous, Patty imagined, the Louvre would have been brightly lit and positively swarming with tourists and excited schoolchildren alike, perhaps even pairs of wandering Parisian lovers. Now, ghosts and dust-motes served to patronize the empty galleries.

Eventually, following gravity's guiding path downward, the self-proclaimed burglar's wanderings brought her to a final flight of stairs and the foremost of the palatial museum's entrances. Happily, she noticed that she needed no key to release the locks from the inside. Patty unlocked one of the heavy doors and swung it open to find Mecquenem waiting outside.

"Bienvenue au Louvre." She spoke officially, trying not to smile. "L'admission...est cinq francs."

Mecquenem stepped inside, betraying no expression. As he strode past, into the echoing lobby, he tossed a small silver coin to Patty, who caught it and threw it back with more force. The little circle of silver impacted the back of the Frenchman's coat and clattered to the floor. He looked back, only showing the slightest surprise.

Neither archeologist made a move to pick up the coin.

After a relatively thorough walk of the museum's darkened halls, the two felt safe enough to slump uncomfortably onto benches and close their eyes, surrendering to a cold and broken sleep, shifting and shivering until they were prematurely awoken by rays of morning sunlight.

Dawn revealed a city even quieter than it had been the night before. Even some of the birds had evacuated the grand capital. From windows in the Louvre Palace's upper stories, they watched the desolate streets. Patty preferred the more dynamic view of the river to the south, though even it seemed empty and haunted. If the archeologists had located the small radio in one of the janitorial closets, they would have heard news of the French government decamping to Tours.

"I confess, it's a little shocking," Patty said as she looked out at the tense, half-empty capital.

"Paris eh, non defend," Dr. Mecquenem replied sadly.

"Nobody wants it to get broken." She sighed. "It's like the city is waiting...an empty apartment ready for its new tenants, no offense."

The Frenchman waved his hand dismissively.

"Les Boches," he said, with some bitterness, "we eh, safe. Nous pas Juifs."

"Safe feels an awful lot like trapped," Patty remarked to herself, not caring if Mecquenem overheard.

In the daylight, the Grande Galerie possessed a forlorn sort of luminance—its arched glass ceiling letting in sun to light nothing but dusty wooden floors scattered with pieces of empty, ruined frames. The American and the curator carefully kept the E-fourteen artifacts in their possession as they further explored the cavernous halls. To wind away the time, Mecquenem, like an especially laconic tour guide, occasionally supplied his colleague with a tidbit about the famous structure and its history. At one point, close to the day's end, the pair found some canned goods in a storage area, alongside several bottles of marginal French wine.

"Wanna get drunk?" Patty offered, noting the left-behind stash.

Mecquenem curled his nose and shook his head.

"Wine not worth to take is eh, wine not worth the drinking."

Dr. Haverwood had no interest in drinking alone. Thus, the pair contented themselves eating a cold meal by candlelight. With little else to do but wait for sleep, Patty wrote letters to her friends, describing her experiences and travels.

"Burn them," Mecquenem ordered, seeing her growing pile of potential correspondence.

Her face flushed hot at the indignity of such a request, but Patty complied, conceding that she had no experience living through war.

The next day, the trapped archeologists spent most of their time watching the doomed city from the museum's stately windows. Once the birds stopped singing, the din of distant battle seemed to creep closer by the hour.

On the night of her first uncomfortable sleep, a distant rumbling was all she made out. By her third sleep, however, Patty had to cover her ears to block out what sounded like the advance of a thousand German tanks. A statue of Charlemagne melted into one of Napoleon, dissolving at last into a screaming, laughing bust of Hitler.

● ● ●

Dr. Haverwood could not tell for sure whether she was still dreaming when the sun rose on the fourteenth of June. An amplified voice boomed throughout the streets of Paris. Groggily, Mecquenem translated as best he could—the German army had seized Paris, they meant the French people no harm, curfew would be imposed at sundown, and resistance would be punishable by death. As these contradictory messages continued to play in German-accented French, the archeologists were once again driven by curiosity to their haunt at the windows. The silent streets had finally come alive, intermittently swarming with German soldiers and vehicles.

An hour passed, and a sense of unreality swept over Patty. Soldiers in black clothing crawled over Paris like ants. Columns marched in the city streets somewhere—she could see their dust. Red Nazi swastika banners were popping up everywhere.

"Some postgraduate adventure this turned out to be," she mused to herself.

Dr. Mecquenem stood at the other end of the museum's long, northern hallway—out of earshot, lost in thought and gazing through his own window.

Looking at his expression, Patty immediately cursed herself as selfish.

"Roland has it far worse," she chastised. "they're trampling *his* home."

Below, the occupiers were engaged in ripping doors from Parisian apartments. Most buildings were spared this treatment, though Patty noticed that trucks would come to haul away any valuables reaped by the soldiers.

Late in the afternoon, she noticed a cluster of young Germans in grey uniforms just outside, examining the museum door. The tallest among them, clad in a deep black coat, curved hat, and a bright red armband, appeared to be in charge.

Above, Mecquenem stepped over to speak quietly in Patty's ear.

"Schutzstaffel," he said, indicating the officer below.

"If he's SS," Patty said, aware of Hitler's elite military police, "he may be better educated than some Nazis. That could be good for us."

"Educated man with a pistol." Roland scoffed.

As Patty and Mecquenem watched, the man in black turned his head and looked directly up at them.

"Wer ist da?" The Officer shouted, his hand darting to the gun at his hip.

Patty's blood turned to ice, and she instinctively ducked down out of sight. Mecquenem was more pragmatic, however, and remained in place to placate the soldiers. He held up his arms, palms spread wide, signaling to the Germans that he was unarmed.

"Frieden!" He shouted down at them in broken German. "Ich archäologe!"

"Öffne die Tür!" The German pointed at the door. "Jetzt!"

Mecquenem grabbed Patty's hand.

"Come," he said, pulling her to her feet.

The pair left the windowed room and headed along a second-floor hallway adjacent to an atrium. They could hear pounding coming from the main entrance below. Patty choked back her fear and allowed Mecquenem to lead her down a staircase, around a bend, and toward the waiting Germans. When they arrived at the entrance, the Frenchman unlatched the door and backed hastily away.

The SS Officer strode imperiously through the portal, his soldiers trailing behind. He sniffed the air and looked around.

"Wer seid ihr?" He barked.

Patty and Mecquenem did not understand. The officer repeated the question, and his men began to fan out and search the building.

"Parlez-vous français?" Mecquenem asked the officer.

"Oui," he sneered, "si je suis oblige."

Patty watched them speak for a period of time, trying hard to understand. She picked up only occasional words among the banter of the French archeologist and German officer, who, after a time, still seemed not to understand their reasons for squatting in the Louvre. He was irate when his greysuits returned from their quick search of the sprawling palace.

"Leer," one reported.

"Niemand," the next confirmed.

The Officer seemed satisfied and barked a new command at his men, pointing to the archeologists.

"Merde–ah!–je n'ai rien." Mecquenem bristled. "Quelle honte!"

Patty tried not to let her fear show as the German soldiers grabbed her. They stripped away the shoulder bag and began rifling through her pockets and taking her papers.

"Hey–be careful. Goons!"

She tried to throw an elbow at the solider on her left whose hand had ventured too close to her chest, but he caught her arm and returned Patty a painful slap across the face.

She glared back, the image in her eyes growing wavery.

"Merde," Mecquenem cursed, though he did a better job acquiescing to the Nazis, who found nothing. "Je n'ai rien," he said gently, "trés embarrassant."

The youngest greysuit picked up Patty's shoulder bag and upended it. Some rags floated to the ground–the artifacts tightly stuffed inside.

"No!"

He gave the bag a violent shake, dislodging everything. Gravity seized Fe along with the clay tablets. The latter, tumbling from their wrappings, made a terrible cracking sound as they struck the hard floor.

"God, no!" Patty gasped, feeling sick to her stomach.

The ancient spearpoint, however, still partially cushioned in its cellophane and linen, bounced against the wooden floor with only a slight clatter. Inside, chaotic kinetic forces vibrated Fe and its sibling atoms, the impact creating minute fractures and shaking loose still more sheets of rust.

The German officer knelt down and inspected the former contents of the shoulder bag. Uninterested in the broken tablets, he reached for the heavy iron artifact and ripped away its wrappings. Scaly flakes of iron oxide tumbled away as the Nazi revealed Fe's black, pitted alloy blade. Triumph shone in the man's small eyes.

"Artefacts," Mecquenem offered, with a shrug and a weak smile.

"Waffe," the officer said accusingly, holding the alleged weapon in his hand.

He disdainfully tossed the alloy blade to a soldier behind him, who carried it outside and out of Patty's view. Another soldier handed him the papers found on Drs. Mecquenem and Haverwood–their personal identification documents.

The Officer flipped through them. "Amerikanisch?" he asked, looking at Patty.

She could only nod, not knowing what the implications of her American citizenship would be to a member of the SS.

Mecquenem came to her rescue, interjecting and speaking in rapid-fire French to the officer. He had to repeat himself several times, but eventually he seemed to make the German understand. Patty caught only the words 'Archéologues' and 'Amerikan'. The self-important officer then proceeded to deliver a monologue, to which Roland occasionally nodded and oui'd. She anxiously watched, her eyes darting from Mecquenem to the officer, hoping to glean any knowledge of her fate.

The German did most of the talking, and he and Mecquenem paced the first floor hallways. Patty found herself left alone with the greysuited Nazis, feeling the young men's eyes on her and wondering, not for the first time, what the hell was happening. Though she badly wanted to speak, Patty bit her tongue and kept her mouth closed. Every few seconds, however, she glanced painfully at the broken tablets, her eyes moving of their own accord to the brutalized remains of her ancient charges. More than anything, except perhaps avoiding gunshot wounds, she wished to rush over and inspect the damage. She seethed, knowing the slabs had survived for thousands of years just to be carelessly shattered by a thuggish boy in a swastika armband.

Finally, the men's prolonged discussion apparently having reached its conclusion, Patty was shocked to see the officer actually shaking Mecquenem's hand and more shocked that the Nazis left of their own accord. Somehow, Roland had done it.

"Heil Hitler!" The black-clad German yelled, throwing his arm up in salute.

Not waiting for a reply, he turned and marched out the front door, leaving the museum as abruptly as he'd arrived. The greysuits followed, though two remained posted at the outermost door, which the Frenchman pulled shut with a bang.

"What the hell is going on?" Patty demanded of Mecquenem, raising her voice above the echoing slam.

The journeyman archeologist's face was a study in weariness–topographical lines of compromise. Even his normally buoyant moustache drooped somewhat. Slowly, he summarized the situation to Patty. He had explained to the Germans that they were archeologists working for the Louvre. The greysuits wanted to take Dr. Haverwood with them, since she was a citizen of a neutral nation, but Mecquenem had convinced the Germans that it would be better if she stayed at the museum.

"Better here than on a U-boat," Patty shuddered. "There's nothing in my fellowship agreement that covers war, so I suppose I still work here, right?"

"Bien," Mecquenem nodded. "I eh, told them."

He went on to say that the Germans wished to reopen the Louvre as soon as possible, and they would be bringing in new art once they deemed the city secure. The museum was to be repurposed as an example of the cultural benefits of German dominion, Mecquenem explained, not bothering to chase the disgust from his tone. As for the two antiquarians, they were to stay on and help organize the reopening.

"We are safe as long as eh, we have value. 'oo else will take care of her?" He concluded, looking around at the museum's silent halls.

"But what about the iron artifact from Susa?" Patty demanded, suddenly annoyed that her fate had been decided for her. "The bayonet? Did you tell your pal Lord Nazi how old and important it is?"

"Non." Mecquenem shook his head and sighed. "It is eh, already gone."

"What? Why?" Dr. Haverwood asked, incensed. "I pulled that damn thing from the lower palace with my bare hands."

"They say weapon. *Waffe.* These men—they are non eh, élastique. Try to hide it, they will killed you." Mecquenem put his hand on Patty's shoulder and looked sternly into her eyes. "No artefact is worth le sacrifier—Patricia, *you* are priceless."

Patty shook off the Frenchman's arm, and biting back tears, she rushed to where her eyes longed to take her, and she knelt to the ground.

Dr. Haverwood shook for a moment, but didn't weep. Instead, she gingerly untangled the broken bundles, careful not to disturb the dust—eventually revealing all of the fragments from the shattered clay tablets.

"Please Roland, see if you can get me some more light," she said, starting to put the pieces back together as best she could. "And find gloves!"

Chapter 3: The Pilot

A German private carried the ancient heaven metal blade, which contained Fe and trillions of other iron atoms, out of the Louvre museum and down its stone steps. He was pointed to a row of soldiers waiting by a truck, where, without ceremony, he tossed the priceless artifact into a crate full of confiscated weapons. Wary of armed resistance, the fast-moving German army had been quick to relieve their conquered populations of any knives, guns, or other objects arbitrarily deemed dangerous.

Packed inside its wooden crate, the blade was kept company by a few knives and old swords. All were made from steel, an alloy of iron allied with a minority of much-lighter carbon atoms—even the most tarnished example gleamed more brightly than Fe's corrosion-covered spike. Simple rifles and revolvers, seized from the people of Paris, populated the contraband crates. These sophisticated instruments of death relied on steel for strength and ease of manufacture rather than for the metal's cutting edge. By this era, some of these ballistic killing machines had grown old enough to be considered relics themselves. Indeed, more than one three-hundred-year-old musket, ripped from above the fireplaces of Parisian homes, joined the ancient Sumerian spearhead in the ranks of nominally threatening weaponry.

Eventually, the truck rumbled to life and carried the crates of contraband through the winding streets of the conquered French capital, out toward the countryside—further and further away from Dr. Patricia Haverwood and the Louvre. Its engine burned petroleum in a cycle of controlled explosions, propelling it east toward Berlin. The truck bounced across the rough French roads, clattering Fe's Sumerian relic against stacks of hardened gun barrels. Large and tiny flakes of oxide shook loose from the corroded surface, hours of abuse in the truckbed doing as much damage to the structure of the brittle alloy as centuries of neglect beneath Susa.

Mercifully, the ride smoothed somewhat as the convoy made its way further east. After refuelings, some checkpoints, and two days of intermittent travel, the truck eventually crossed the border back into Germany–its destination a military outpost near the strategically-located city of Bonn.

For the second time in its millennia of existence, the heaven metal prize found itself sorted by the functionaries of a victorious military action. Most of the assorted firearms that Fe rode with were thrown into large piles by uniformed German teenagers, their cloth-wrapped hands indiscriminately lobbing even the most ancient of French family hunting weapons into the heap. Most of the knives, along with some guns that turned out to be nonfunctional, or merely toys, found themselves tossed into an enormous pile dominated by scrap steel and all manner of broken things.

A calloused hand reached into the crate and pulled out the Sumerian dagger. With no archeological context, the once-legendary weapon was a sorry sight to behold–badly corroded, dull, and seemingly useless. The eyes attached to the hand barely scanned the remains of Fe's blade before tossing it carelessly into the scrap pile where it impacted a chunk of hardened steel from a tractor. Powerful waves of kinetic energy pulsed through Fe's metallic lattice. Internal resonance broke down along one crucial avenue, and the stress from the impact caused the brittle spike to crack down its middle–splitting the artifact into two jagged pieces.

One of the corroded chunks, encompassing the handle, guard, and a small segment of broken blade, slid forlornly down the pile, far away from the fragment containing Fe. For the first time since the accretion of the iron-nickel asteroid in the early Solar system, the atom found itself separated from the bulk of its siblings, its own smaller bit of blade wedged between a broken firewood axe and a length of heavy steel pipe.

The sorting process persisted until sundown. Thousands of items had been confiscated from France and Belgium and forcibly appropriated for the German domination effort. Useful firearms would be refurbished and placed in the hands of soldiers or military police. Useless artifacts made primarily of iron or steel were to be recycled. Many humans had died recently over Earthly mines of heaven metal to feed Hitler's steel-hungry war machine. Before the outbreak of hostilities, Fe's scrap would likely have been cast aside, left to rust into obscurity. However, at that time and place, every possible atom of iron was collected by the mobilized state like sips of precious nectar.

New trucks rumbled up to the pile of scrap, where a shift of sweat-stained, unshaven men shoveled the pieces of iron and steel into their waiting beds. The fragment containing Fe separated from its companion forever as it was shoveled from one pile to another–the weighty lower half of Quishda's creation fated to go on a different trunk, never to reunite with its sharpest point.

Octane explosions thundered inside an engine, and soon enough, Fe bumped along another road, this time into the German heartland, where the truck off-floaded its contents at a busy depot. Teams of men, some with shovels, others driving heavy loading equipment, moved massive quantities of scrap iron and steel, transferring the piles from trucks into rail cars. Parts of automobiles, appliances, weapons, and pipes crowded the cars, keeping Fe's Sumerian scrap company, all of the packed iron atoms distant, long-lost twins, each and every one born in their stellar matriarch's last dying moments.

The train pulled away from the depot and headed north, rattling through serene countryside, seemingly untouched by war. No enemy soldier had yet set foot in Germany. However, when the train passed its urban centers, evidence of destruction became difficult to ignore. Bombing campaigns from Britain and France attempted to flatten German industry, and many towns displayed scorched buildings and debris-lined craters.

Following the iron rails, the locomotive and its cargo chugged their way at last to a stop in Essen, the heart of Nazi steel. Simultaneously prosperous and devastated, the city was a scene of wartime chaos. Factories belched smoke into the air, busy workmen ran from one place to another, and the railyard screamed with activity. Almost immediately, a worker lowered a large, industrial electromagnet into the train car.

The device boasted a flat disk of featureless iron for a face, and once the operator activated its current, it transformed into a stronger magnet than any found outside the Earth's core. A pull of a switch induced electricity to pour through a coiled wire, the energy flowing from each copper atom to the next via buzzing clouds of busy electrons. In an instant, the current flowing through the copper coil created a strong, artificial magnetic field–irresistible to the scraps of iron and steel below.

An invisible force washed down from the electromagnet–its magnetic b-field affecting every iron atom in the train car. Fe had never before found itself subject to such a strange force. Inherently, every twenty-six-protoned iron atom possessed a unique magnetic moment, and each could act as a tiny magnet on its own. Under normal circumstances, Fe and its siblings never manifested this potential, their electrons' random spins canceling one another out.

However, as energy coursed through the wiring of the electromagnet and its b-field saturated the quadrillions of irons, each tiny cloud began to reorient itself. Fe's bonds with its neighbors remained intact, but an invisible string of force realigned its electrons, spinning the atom's magnetic moment in lockstep with its fellows.

Trillions of trillions of atomic-scale magnets all pointed in the same direction, appearing, in essence, to the world outside as one large magnet. The attraction to the overhead source was immediate. An irresistible force seized the broken blade.

An instant, and Fe's fragment of speartip shot upward–out of the train car and against the flat, iron disk. Together with a tangled mass of small scraps and twisted steel plates, the fragment of heaven metal clung tightly to the electromagnet's underside, stymying its old foe gravity.

The revolutionary magnet swung away from the train, bringing the alloy along for the ride–Fe and its fellows forever pressed to the magnet's face by the invisible hand of electromagnetic force–then, the intense attraction cut away as if it had never existed. Without current flowing through its coils, the industrial magnet lost its b-field, and the many atoms inside the ferromagnetic scrap immediately reoriented themselves back to their random arrangements, choreographed no more.

Gravity once again took control, and the broken Sumerian speartip tumbled away from the magnet, landing hard amongst ferrous debris filling the bed of yet another truck. The electromagnet made three more passes, flooding the scrap pile with its powerful field only to pull it away, again and again, piling heavy steel atop Fe's fragment until it became utterly buried, with no light shining through.

● ● ●

For the meteoric iron, the short trip from the rail yard to one of Essen's steel mills was the final leg on a four billion year journey. Even as the atmosphere's fires burned it, and the forges of Kish heated it, the heaven metal remained chemically unchanged. In Susa, the blade rested and rusted for thousands of years, but Fe itself escaped eventual oxidation, plucked from time by Dr. Haverwood and whisked halfway around the world, going from ship to boat to crate to truck to train and to truck once again—remaining always in the same crystalline chemical structure, contentedly bonded to the most familiar of its siblings.

Outside the iron-laden truck, humans shoveled scrap metal into large buckets. The grime-covered steelworkers wore forlorn expressions, their glances often straying to the armed men who walked among them. To feed its mission of conquest, the German army needed able-bodied men to serve in its armed forces, and, deeming that work in a steel mill could be done by others, the Nazi government drew upon its vast supply of prisoners. Conscripted French, Belgians, and Poles made up the labor force, as Germany's own Jewish population had been put to hard labor for years, and only a scant handful remained healthy enough to work at the foundry. Antlike, the conscript steelers passed iron scrap from one man to the next.

At the end of the chain, one sinewy, emaciated worker piled Fe's broken blade, along with shovelfuls of steel bits, into an enormous bucket—open at the top with a trapdoor hinged below. Shovelful after shovelful joined the mass. Once the bucket was filled nearly to its brim, an operator moved levers to command a machine to hoist it in the air. Sparks, slag, and steam billowed beside it. For a time, the hopper remained suspended above exhaust vents, where hot gasses enveloped and warmed the scrap.

Below, molten steel sweltered and swelled, roiling like the early surface of the Earth. In the bucket, the metal's temperature began to rise precipitously—its constituent atoms pumped with titanic quantities of kinetic energy. Fe had not been heated to such a degree since the ancient days of Quishda's kiln, though the fires of Essen would prove to burn far hotter.

A worker, far below the suspended scrap, pulled a lever, and the trapdoor floor of the hopper fell away. Piles of steel and bits of iron tumbled into thick molten goo, gravity forcing Fe's fragment on a vector down toward the planet's center. A modest ball of fire erupted from the furnace as the new arrivals splashed into the molten metal, igniting slicks of grease on the surface of machinery and automobile parts.

Though Fe's fragment had fallen into the crucible, it would not fully melt. The mass of the added metal was much greater than the molten puddle remaining in the furnace. Thus, as heat energy transferred between solid scrap and liquid steel, cold seemingly won, and the molten metal began to thicken.

As the roof of the furnace closed, a group of electrodes descended and hovered above the sea of smoking scrap. Undreamed of by the smiths of Sumer, the German foundry workers were employing electric currents to more efficiently heat their steel.

Somewhere outside, a human hand summoned an electric current with the flick of a switch, and an arc of energy lashed out from both electrodes, boring like lightning into the highly conductive metal below. Locked in its lattice, Fe and its sibling atoms were subjected to the violent and sudden influx of energy. Above the pile of scrap, the very air of the furnace had been split apart into its constituent atoms, ionized as massive torrents of power flowed between electrode and electron. Soon, the inefficiencies of energy transfer between atoms began to manifest—friction turning to heat. Much the same process had happened on a cosmic scale, billions of years earlier, as the collapsing universal dust cloud kindled stars from nothing but the rubbing vibrations from colliding crowds of primordial atoms.

The German furnace acted far more quickly than did galactic gravity, forcing high-voltage electrons to blindly navigate the metallic matrix of Fe's meteoric alloy. The temperature created in these furnaces by modern humans was something truly impressive—even during accretion, Fe had never had so much thermal energy forced into it. However, no matter how furiously the furnace pumped pure power into the molten steel, it could never touch the conditions inside the Mother Star. Fusion, at least for now, lay outside of human control.

More metal melted under the electrodes, and before long, the furnace no longer contained a collection of heterogeneous scrap. It was now home to an ocean of liquid metal. Inside the steel sea, Fe's companions from the original asteroid slowly floated away, heaven metal intermingling with trillions of trillions of more Earthly atoms. The molten mass held elements other than iron, and these impurities collected and separated, lighter compounds rising to the top of the soup and heavier interlopers sinking below in much the same process as when the cooling Earth first differentiated. The remaining rusted casualties from Fe's spearpoint's millennia of neglect floated to the surface, joining the layer of slag atop the purifying steel.

When the process finished, heavy machinery below turned massive gears, producing enough torque to tilt the entire furnace sideways. A sheet of glowing-hot liquid metal cascaded down from the upended crucible. Fe rode the molten waterfall down into an enormous ladle. Suited workers stepped back, and sparks flew as the liquid steel flowed and splashed. Before the dregs of impure slag could follow, the machine's gears turned the other direction, righting the furnace and cutting off its molten flow.

Fe's tub of incipient steel moved on rails to another part of the foundry. The entire melting process had taken less than an hour, but Fe was no longer constrained by the metallic bonds it had held since the dawn of the Solar system. As it cooled, a new alloy formed from a sprawling lattice of floating irons, bonded to one another and forming a cage around random, unbonded, carbon atoms.

The atom Fe was now part of a human invention—steel. If the Kings of Kish had seen Essen steel, they would have had to reasssign the name 'heaven metal'. Steel was easier to shape, easier to clean, could hold a better edge, and shone like the finest silver. The Essen mill could produce long steel girders, pipes, plates, and pellets, all forged by different species of heavy machinery, themselves beasts composed redundantly of iron and steel, doing in seconds what it took Quishda days of labor to only scratch at.

Factory workers rerouted the cooling metal to where it could be shaped. Fe's batch was destined to be rolled into sheet steel. Far from molten, the hot metal slumped onto a surface where industrial hammers pounded it flat before it was sent through a set of massive rollers. The atoms' crystal cages flexed and flowed with the mechanical manipulation, but inside, the carbon-iron alloy kept its structure, even as the machinery pounded and pressed it into a smooth, flat plane.

An unstoppable, massive wedge of hardened metal crashed down onto the newly-formed sheet steel, cleaving through an entire meridian of metallic bonds and portioning it into uniform lengths. Fe ended up in a rectangular section, a shape far removed from the pointed, deadly spike of the dagger-turned-spearhead. After forging and cutting, the sheet metal moved to a storage facility, stacked by workers and rolled into a shed, interred alongside hundreds of other identical pieces.

Fe's sheet sat in the warehouse for many days. Objects in every shape and size waited patiently for shipment inside the building, the clamor and thunder of the foundry and railyard rarely subsiding. More resistant to rusting than raw iron, the steel and its atoms rested peacefully, nearly untroubled by the ravages of atmospheric oxygen. It was the first time since its long sleep beneath Susa that Fe had remained stationary for more than a handful of hours.

Outside, in the fast-moving world, the war continued to rage. Hitler began implementing plans to invade the British islands, ordering an effort to increase his air force, the Luftwaffe, in preparation. It was this impetus that spurred the piece of sheet metal containing Fe to finally leave the Essen warehouse. Workers carefully packed each flat steel segment into a wooden frame to protect it from bending and surface damage during transit. The frames were loaded onto a train car at the same railyard where Fe's confiscated speartip had first entered the foundry.

The steel train roared to life and clattered out of the station, its line of cars appearing little different than that which had fled the Louvre—a caravan of carefully-packed works of fine art. Bound for the distant city of Leipzig, the train rumbled across four hundred and fifty kilometers of Central Germany, bypassing the main station when it arrived, instead pulling directly alongside a private, industrial bay at the Junkers Flugzeug und Motorenwerke factory. From the train, the sheet metal pieces were unloaded, one by one. Two men, healthier than those in Essen, gripped each framed package and stacked them gingerly against nearby walls.

When the train had finally been emptied, its engine roared again to life and the long metal snake chugged away in the direction from whence it had come, bound to find another load to pull.

● ● ●

Inside the Junkers factory, hundreds of workers busily went about their tasks–drillers, riveters, toolmakers, die casters, machinists, technicians, and supervisors. Those in charge were German men, often too old or too rich for military service. Forced laborers from conquered nations had not yet reached Leipzig in large numbers. Instead, highly-trained workers, too important to the war effort to be drafted into cannon-fodder, served the Junkers plant. Some German women and children even populated the ranks, working unskilled jobs to contribute to the glory of their Führer.

Rows of aircraft in various states of construction lined the vast factory floor. The process of manufacture had changed a great deal since Fe first landed on Earth. Instead of a skilled artisan such as Quishda slowly creating an object by hand, every task in the Junkers factory was efficiently orchestrated–large groups of humans each performed relatively simple tasks, the work going down the line, until, gradually, a finished airplane emerged. Not a scrap of steel went to waste, and the workers' skilled hands rarely slipped.

"Nächste!" A tall worker ordered, pointing to the row of newly-arrived steel.

Near the delivery entrance, a line of men cracked Fe's sheet out of its frame, tossing aside the protective wood. They brought the thin steel into part of the factory where a giant iron beast divided the room in two. Black and dirty, it stood taller than an adult human, sporting oiled tubes along its unsightly length. The tall German slid Fe's sheet toward two young workers who stood in front of the device, crouched over a waist-high table.

"Bitteschön," he said. As he leaned over, a swastika pin on his chest glinted in the artificial light.

The younger workers grabbed the sheet and carefully maneuvered it into the beastly machine. They were not yet party members like the tall man, but the fairer of the two had put in his application and harbored high hopes for acceptance. His coworker, however, had delayed applying for Nazihood—he feared complications of his trace Indian ancestry, once a tastefully-exotic family feature now turned dangerous secret.

Together, the steelmen slid Fe's sheet into place below a set of titanic jaws, which, with an incredible amount of cutting force, sliced it into two clean pieces. On the other side of the giant machine, an older worker with an oil-stained moustache took the segments in his gloved hands and stacked them atop layers of identical components.

From there, another worker eventually took custody of the stacks of cut steel and brought them to a second part of the factory. There, a man wearing a protective mask composed of a visor and a flat transparent shield took the sheets and carefully lined them up on a workbench.

A veteran of the Great War, the masked worker was a survivor of the trenches with the scars to prove it. Another machine, far smaller than the beastly shears, hovered over his bench, suspended by a system of tubes and mounts. Before touching the instrument, the masked worker placed a large sheet of paper over the layers of metal. It had been printed with distinct shapes—two tiny and thin, the other large and semi-ovoid.

Long ago, the steelman had operated similar machines in the manufacture of boilers. The economy had worsened, however, and after seven terrible years of post-war unemployment, the masked worker felt deep gratitude for his new position at Junkers.

Gripping its handles, he activated his machine, and with a deafening whir, the device came to life. A hardened metal bit spun up to thousands of revolutions per second—a stream of machine oil dripping down onto the moving parts. The burr dipped into the surface of the sheet metal as easily as if the steel had still been molten. Its veteran operator skillfully traced the rotor head over the paper guide, cutting out a stack of shaped pieces.

Fe ended up in one of the larger, ovoid segments, the castoff bits of its steel swept up for later recycling. The finished shapes were given to another worker, a child this time, and slid onto a long elevated pathway made from hundreds of rollers. A number of different human hands—some calloused, some burned, some old or far too young—touched the steel, diverting it one way or the other.

At one junction, the small skinny pieces went off to the right, while the larger pieces, including the atom Fe, were sent straight ahead, directed toward yet another intimidating industrial hulk. A massive black metal box hung suspended at each corner by a long column, which moved the assembly up and down, applying enormous hydraulic pressure to whatever lay beneath.

Four Junkers employees clustered around the building-sized machine. One stood near an operating panel covered with gauges and switches, while the other three lined the rolling pathway and flat metal counter that extended into the machine itself. Each man wore black pants and a sweat-stained khaki shirt. The youngest, who experienced an intermingling of shame and cunning-pride over being the only one out of five brothers not serving in the army, handled the steel with a heavily-bandaged left hand.

Fe's form and the other pre-cut shapes slid on rollers toward the four men, who plucked them off the line and stacked them on a three-tiered shelf. From the other direction, a large tray-shaped die slowly moved before them. Over two meters long, the industrial die sported a variety of abstract-looking three dimensional protrusions—some long and pointed, others shallow and cored. Each Junkers man turned to the shelf and pulled out a single pre-cut metal blank, placing it on the die's correspondingly-shaped protrusion. Once covered, the workers moved the mold inside the giant machine, positioning it directly under the colossal black box. The man nearest the panel hit a switch, and a mountain of hydraulic force pressed down on the trapped steel plates.

When the machine had completed its squeeze, two of the employees came to collect the pieces. Each thin sheet had been pressed irresistibly into the form of a three-dimensional shape. The workers loaded the now-empty die with fresh steel and repeated the process. It took two more cycles of stacking and pressing before the bandaged youth took Fe's sheet in his good hand and placed it onto the die. It sat atop a protrusion with a rounded, semi-symmetrical shape, resembling part of an egg–ovoid and narrow at the top but cleanly horizontal at the wide base.

A terrible pressure squished Fe's steel plate, heating its atoms and forcing the body of the metal to bend and take on a new, three-dimensional shape. Like blows from Quishda's hammer stone, the press shifted but did not break the molecular structure of Fe's alloy.

The die slid out, and two workers lifted Fe's partial-eggshell, dropping it into a wheeled cart filled with piles of identical pieces. Once full, the heavy load moved down the factory floor toward a short-term storage area. There, numerous shelves, baskets, and crates full of parts waited for the next step in warplane manufacturing.

Some of Fe's neighboring components were also made from steel, though the bulk of the prefab parts in the warehouse were composed from a material that would have been utterly alien to the ancients and their seven native metals. Back inside the Mother Star's core, long before the final panicked moments of fusion that lead to Fe's traumatic birth, other light metals sprung into being. When her hydrogen fused with the light metal magnesium, it released a flood of energy and brought a new element into the universe–one composed of thirteen protons.

Aluminum.

For humans, Fe's rival metal boasted impressive physical properties, weighing far less than iron while mimicking much of its strength.

Aluminum and steel pieces alike found themselves busily claimed by antlike lines of German laborers. The quarter-shell forms hardly had time to gather dust before they were plucked from storage and hustled toward assembly lines that stretched across the main body of the crowded, cavernous Junkers factory. At the far end, nearly-finished airplanes rolled out of the warehouse doors, already capable of moving under their own power.

Hundreds of meters back down the line, the planes-to-be existed as nothing more than scattered parts. Workers busily manufactured components in bays around the facility. Near one wall, a pack of Junkers men swarmed around a half-dozen metallic skeletons in the shape of giant wings. Dwarfed by the structures, human specialists moved in repetitive, nearly-mechanical motions. One did nothing but drill holes. Another placed small metal rivets inside each drilled bore, and still a third wielded the corded riveter.

Fuselages in various states of completion took up much of the factory floor. Some, like the wing sections, were simple framed skeletons. Further along, others had begun to receive their metal skins and interior fixtures. Long cables stretched down from the ceiling and attached to great hollow tubes at different points along each aluminum fuselage. At every station, at least five humans lined the sides of the plane bodies, some riveting, some drilling. Children carefully walked behind and around the workers, sweeping the floors clear of twisted metal castoffs.

When a section finished, a man with a small flashlight would sidle up to the plane's body and run his beam along each line of rivets. One such inspector made fussy notes on a clipboard as he worked, marking the metal with a grease pencil at specific points. He had been a party member for years, and his wife was the daughter of an important man at the Reichstag. The inspector did his job well, though his mind was full of thoughts of moving on to bigger and better things as the fortunes of his Fatherland multiplied.

Near another loading bay, men wielding crowbars cracked open enormous crates, revealing complicated, resplendent aircraft engines, shipped over from a different facility. After an inspection, metalworkers attached aluminum skins to the engine mounts with screaming drills and steaming rivets.

Adding to the growing behemoths, ten meter wings floated in on cables to be mounted to the nearly complete fuselages. The factory's machines boasted the brute strength of teams of oxen, but they operated with the grace and precision of a hummingbird.

Workers fitted tail sections, rudders, and cockpits onto the growing warplanes. Heavy equipment roared forward to hoist the newly unboxed Jumo-211 engines for mounting on the wings. Three dramatically-twisted wooden blades, forming a bare propeller, protruded from each of the two engine assemblies. Soon, workers brought in the shaped steel blanks, one of which counted the atom Fe among its trillions.

Fe's half-shell was tossed up to a diminutive worker perched atop the wing of an unfinished bomber. Though fourteen years old, the boy resembled a kindergartener in stature. He lay flat on his stomach and, biting his tongue with concentration, mounted the steel form around the propeller, fitting it over the forwardmost section of the engine like a spinning conical shield. Below, a much-more robust worker on a step-stool fitted another piece, securing it symmetrically to Fe's form. When the humans had finished, the stamped steel came together to form a bespoke armored spinner-cone for the gestating bomber's port-side engine.

Over the next few hours, the aircraft came together rapidly. At its forward nose, a skeletal dome filled in with glass panes, and a single tail fin sprouted from the metal bird's rear end. From the factory ceiling high above, machinery kicked into gear and pushed the nearly-finished aircraft forward to another bay.

There, various components underwent a final installation—kilometers of electric wiring twisting from the cockpit and spreading throughout the body of the plane like synthetic vasculature. Workers wired and screwed a complex panel of switches, buttons, and knobs into place before bolting down equipment lockers and chairs for the pilots.

They added gunnery sections—swiveling, inertially dampened mounts which anticipated machine guns. The metal bird received its final layers of aluminum skin before inspectors swarmed the aircraft, armed with flashlights and clipboards, closely scrutinizing every instrument, every weld, and every rivet.

Beams from their narrow flashlights swept over the engine cone containing Fe three times before the Nazi inspectors were satisfied.

Only a matter of days after the train laden with sheet metal had arrived at the Junkers factory, a newborn aircraft rolled off of the assembly line—the Ju-88, a fearsome schnellbomber and a key component of Hitler's Luftwaffe. Fast and light, the bomber had been designed by devious primate brains to drop explosive ordinance upon targets, ground or sea, while simultaneously outrunning any pursuers. It was a machine optimized by its human masters to sow death and conquest as efficiently and reliably as possible. Thus, for the second time in its existence, the atom Fe found itself part of an instrument of war.

* * *

A drop of crimson blood fell from the straight razor, diffusing slowly into the basin of foamy water beneath. Karl continued shaving, unaware or unconcerned that he'd been cut. Strengthened by a sprawling molecular matrix of iron-carbon cellblocks, the steel razor's edge scraped over leathery human skin, cleaving cleanly through the scaly protein towers that were the pilot's facial hairs.

He dipped his razor clean in the pink-tinted water, staring straight ahead at the dirty mirror of the barracks washroom. Another pass, another triumph of steel over flesh, and another line of skin rendered somewhat smooth. Tilting his wrist, the Major deftly avoided a patch of scar tissue near his chin, finishing off his shave by scraping the blade against his upper lip.

Karl splashed a handful of water on his face to clear away the last of the suds and a few drops of lingering blood. Even cleanly shaven, Major Fleisher wasn't much to look at. The scar on his chin had been earned the previous summer during Adlerangriff—the eagle attack—two weeks of blistering raids upon Britain's coastal airfields. Other blemishes and grooves wound around the pilot's face, neck, and hands—scars from his losing battle against time. That day marked a milestone in the relentless conflict, for it happened to be the Major's birthday.

Karl Fleisher had been a pilot for most of his adult life. When the last Great War broke out nearly thirty years earlier, he served with distinction. Flight was young in those days, and Karl took to his training like an infant learning to walk. Fleisher mastered everything he flew, starting with the primitive biplanes of the time and advancing to more custom-engineered aircraft as the war drew to a close. During those mad days of wartime technological innovation, he sat behind the controls of inventions his superiors weren't sure would even fly. He knit together a knot of friends, bonded with them as brothers, and subsequently mourned them as they fell, one by one. It was also the singular time in Karl's life when he allowed himself to fall in love, only to watch the man die in a bow-gunner's seat months later. Over his career, three planes had been shot down from underneath him, but Karl always survived.

Political and economic upheaval had made the stretch between World Wars hard on every German, and as lean years stretched into decades, even his status as a high-ranking hero pilot barely saved Fleisher from destitution. But now, the Fatherland had once again risen, and the Luftwaffe was revitalized. Skilled pilots were at a premium. Karl, pushing sixty, had turned down offers for leadership and instructor positions–he belonged in the sky. He argued, and he threatened colleagues in Luftwaffe command until a bomber yoke was again in his hands.

A yoke, a lever, a switch–these were his killing tools. Karl's surname meant 'butcher' in his language, and he lived up to the name while keeping his hands clean and unbloodied. He wore a token of party membership upon his lapel, but the politics of the Führer mattered less to the old pilot than did his access to aircraft. Karl had no strong feelings about the Jews, no deep resentment toward communism or the decadent Western empires. He had, and always would, put country first. He took no pleasure in bringing death to those he was ordered to slay, aside, of course, for professional pride in a mission well-flown. At night, the pilot slept untroubled by demons.

Outside the stillness of the washroom, the barracks clattered, noisy and chaotic. Karl believed the young airmen overly brash and enthusiastic to a man. He could never remember having such boundless energy at their age–at any age. They talked and laughed loudly as Karl walked by, not troubling themselves to salute his rank. Half-uniformed boys played cards for rations, others simply lay on their bunks and looked at their bibles, only some of which concealed lewd periodicals.

Major Fleisher moved into the common room, finding it too overcrowded with other consciousnesses. Voices raised in argument or simple conversation filled the space, and the clacking of game balls and some crewman's radio added to the din. Karl noted more than one fellow sleeping in a random, slumped posture, but he grimly conceded that airmen, by their nature, were an informal lot and to be forgiven.

He stepped around the sleepers to find an insulated spot–a well-worn armchair, located away from most of the adolescents. Karl spied a folded publication trapped under the leg of a rusting metal table. He leaned over to grab it, and when he flipped it over, the pilot found it to be a cheaply printed copy of Goethe's *Faust: Der Tragödie zweiter Teil.*

"-momentum and triumph. In Poland, Belgium. Even France!" A confident voice declared in educated German. "We're almost done with England, mark my words."

Nearby, a trio of young leutnants sat around a table, engaged in banal discussion. Karl tried his best to ignore them, opening the Goethe folio.

"Tommies are never going to surrender or capitulate," a second voice argued, emanating from a man with 'Lt. Lemming' on his nameplate. "Mers-el-Kébir, boys. Britain is a tough egg to crack."

"We're the eierköpfer then," the first voice replied dismissively. "Just another stepping stone to Hitler's dominance of Europe."

Karl had not read the first part of the play and was finding he could not follow the plot of the volume he'd opened.

"But Oberleutnant Floss," a third, bespectacled airman interjected, "it's not as simple as rolling a few panzers over the border and gaining quick victory over the natives. England is an *island*. The Tommys' navy ruled the world for a hundred years."

"Is it a hundred years ago?" Floss sniffed, arrogance saturating his voice. "No. Herr Gabelkhoven? No. Air support is the chief factor of warfare. Without their guardian angels, even the grandest navy on Earth would stand no chance before us."

"I'll drink to that," Lemming replied, pulling a flask from his jacket. "Burn the island to ash from above, I say. Make it easier for the army's landing party, those lazy socks."

"Oh, how I wish I were in the army," Karl moaned. "I'd settle for the SS, Christ forbid, if its boys had some damn discipline."

"What was that?" Floss said, noticing Karl for the first time.

Major Fleisher locked eyes with the younger pilot, but said nothing.

"Have something to say, Red Baron?" Oberleutnant Floss mocked.

Karl folded the copy of *Faust* with a sharp snap. "Don't you understand, schwesterlein? Your generation receives its education by being tossed into the fire like logs."

"What does that mean?" Gabelkhoven whispered to his comrade.

"We're losing pilots faster than we can replenish them," the Major clarified, staring daggers at Floss. "Have you been sent on an unescorted mission yet, airman?"

"Of course," the Oberleutnant sneered.

Karl had no idea if the baby pilot was telling the truth. Unescorted bombing runs were sheer terror, even for an experienced, businesslike hand.

"Meanwhile," Karl continued, "Poles and Czechs fly for the British. Franzmann too. They are better trained and better experienced than most of you. They fly with hatred for the Reich in their hearts. Do you know what it's like, schwesterlein, to have someone who *hates* you try to *kill* you?"

Blotchy, crimson patches bloomed across Floss's face and neck as he struggled to hold his tongue against Major Fleisher's scathing impudence.

"This is why we've been flying at night," Gabelkhoven nervously broke the silence. "A good strategy, ja? Avoid the Tommies entirely. Escort or no. Large scattered runs. Take the smaller hits where we can find them."

"More crows fly in the Luftwaffe than eagles now," Karl muttered, disgusted.

"'s a smart strategy," Lemming slurred.

"It's a strategy of necessity, born of a lack of experienced German bomber crews." Fliesher's blood ran hot in his veins—he was beginning to enjoy the dogfight with his junior colleagues. "Dropping a bomb without aiming is easy enough a baby could do it, and it is precisely *babies* who now fly for the Fatherland. I pity you for never knowing the discipline and the grandeur that the Luftwaffe once possessed! Like rogues, we fly sneak attacks to terrorize the townspeople because we are not bold enough to face their warriors in the skies."

"Your words are treason!" Oberleutnant Floss spat. "Major or no Major, I'll take you—"

"Ja?" Karl rose to his full height, looming over Floss.

With clattering chairs, Leutnants Gabelkhoven and Lemming pushed them-selves from the table and stood at attention.

"Herren!" A new voice, sharp and crisp, cut through the conflict.

Its owner, clad in a smart black uniform, marched into the common room, heralded by echoing footfalls from polished boots–his sudden entrance aborting the airmen's brewing fight. The officer wore a black, wide-brimmed cap, lending him an air of authority. Though decades younger than Fleischer, he outranked everyone in the room.

"Guten tag, Major Fleisher."

"Guten Tag, Major Rohr," Karl answered.

Rohr turned to the leutnants and nodded. "Heil Hitler."

"Heil Hitler!" They shouted back in unison.

"Brighten up, Herren," Rohr said before turning back to Karl, his voice cheer-ful, "this will be a good month for the Luftwaffe. We've got iron and aluminium flowing in from the Reich's newest territories, and now the factories spit out better aircraft every day." The Major flashed a brilliant set of teeth. "One of the freshly minted bombers they're sending has your name on it, Karl."

"Danke, Major Rohr."

"I mean that quite literally. I've had it christened *Fleischerbeile*."

The young airmen chuckled, even Floss let out a small snigger.

"It will be my honor to fly a warplane yet undamaged and undented by any previous, less competent pilots," Karl answered, pointedly.

"They'll be landing any minute. Walk with me." Rorh signaled to Karl, who followed him from the building and into the bright sunlight.

The two Majors marched down the airfield toward a row of nearly-empty hangars at one far end. The thrumming of engines filled the air, the din waxing and waning with the movements of dozens of aircraft.

"What were you about to do to those boys?" Rohr hollered, playfully. "Don't they know that few other men in history have a body count as high as yours?"

"Does Luftwaffe command know?" Karl retorted. "You don't act like it. You put me in rotten planes, each less reliable than the last, and my crews grow younger by the week."

"You won't complain once you see your new Junkers."

"I know what you've been doing, you rat," Karl accused, unplacated. "Orders to fly a single mission with a batch of raw airmen, only to rebase somewhere new the next week. I'm being moved from crew to crew to train the Luftwaffe's greenest. Admit it–leadership thinks I can be tricked."

Rohr shrugged. "You wanted to remain an airman, ja? Part of that is taking orders. You took great effort to remain in military service after the Great War, and now Karl, you complain. Do you desire a promotion to leadership?"

"Christ, no."

"How about a teacher? You'll survive the war–unless one of your pupils should give into temptation and stab you.""I'd sooner be test-pilot for the Führer's manned-missile."

"Things will improve for you, Karl. The equipment now is better than the Gothas, I trust?"

"Honestly, I'm in awe of our engineers, sir." Major Fleisher smiled in spite of himself, recalling the yoke-in-hand feeling–the thrum, the acceleration.

The capabilities of this war's breathtaking, mechanical beasts captivated Karl and kept him among the airmen's ranks.

"You flew in the first retaliatory strike after they bombed Berlin, yes?"

"Ja," Karl said, remembering the cold-sweat tension of the flight, the pilots ripped from the skies around him.

"That's right. You've flown in every mission, haven't you? You must be the oldest active pilot in the Luftwaffe.

"I've never bothered to check, sir. But I've also never been as old as I am today."

At that moment, a group of newborn planes from the Leipzig Junkers factory vectored in toward the airfield. The gleaming metal craft were resplendent in the sunlight. Karl watched from below, his hand shading his eyes from the glare, testing his still-sharp vision by trying to read the planes' tail numbers as they landed.

Locked in the metal lattice of its steel half-shell, the atom Fe again soared through the lower atmosphere of Earth–like the firebird descending over the outskirts of Kish. This time, however, landfall proved far gentler.

Each aircraft downed its landing gear onto the manicured grass runway and bumped along to near-stillness before taxiing toward the hangars. A larger cargo plane trailed the incoming aircraft, landing and idling nearby. As soon as the pilots in the new arrivals had finished their deliveries, they popped out from their '88s and jogged back outside, climbing aboard the waiting transport for a ride home.

Karl followed the aluminum marvels to the hangar, Rohr trailing behind. Upon entering the cavernous, shadowy room, it took the pilot's keen eyes a minute to adjust.

He stepped over and read the identification markings on the nearest aircraft, pleasantly surprised to find that it matched that of his orders. Walking around the hulking bomber, Karl passed Fe's spinner-cone and read the moniker '*Fleischerbeile*' painted in stylized script along the fuselage.

"Alles Gute zum Geburtstag!" Major Rohr clapped the birthday boy on the back and admired the plane alongside him.

Specially outfitted for night bombing operations, Fe's twin-engined schnellbomber was painted a matte grey with dark accents on the wings. The rear fuselage, tail, and wingtips bore the distinctive balkenkreuz–the same iron cross emblem had adorned each plane Karl piloted in the Great War, many of the contraptions now only foggy memories.

A swelling of pride for the Fatherland burst inside the old pilot's chest each time he saw the ancient Teutonic symbol. Still, some things had changed since Karl's youth–on the tail of his new Ju-88, a black swastika had been painted, four-armed and outlined in white.

"I'm glad you like your present," Rohr continued, "but I must be off. I'm late. Heil Hitler. Oh, your crew arrives tonight, Karl."

After the young Major made his exit from the hangar, Karl climbed inside his new commission and maneuvered toward its cockpit, where he fitted himself into the pilot's chair. With a scatter of gentle taps, he ran his hands across the instrument panel before letting them hover above the yoke. He had flown other Ju-88s, but Karl believed that in many small ways, every plane was unique. He looked forward to taking the aircraft up and putting it through its paces.

For a few more minutes, he lingered in the pilot's seat before rising to give the plane a thorough inspection. To Fleisher's eye, far less discerning than those trained in the Junkers factory, everything appeared to be in place and in working order. Indeed, the machine was in mint condition. Karl inhaled the new-vehicle aroma. Its seats were freshly upholstered, no bullet holes riddled the fuselage, and the smells of gunpowder, motor oil, blood, and fear-vomit were refreshingly absent from its bays.

Eventually, the Major tore himself away from the resplendent metal bird. He was to meet and debrief his new bomber crew later that day, and he wanted to come at the task well-rested. Fortunately, when Karl returned to the barracks, he found the common room nearly empty. Of the cluster of young leutnants, only the bespectacled Gabelkhoven remained.

"Do you have the time?" Karl asked after slumping into an overstuffed arm-chair.

The Leutnant pulled a watch from his coat.

"Seventeen forty-six," he read.

Karl still had hours before his support crew were due to arrive.

"A lesson, baby airman, since you alone seem to possess half a brain. Perhaps the greatest skill of a war pilot, I contend, is the ability to endure long periods of boredom."

"And?"

"Liken it to being a feuerwehrmann in a large city. Hours or even days of waiting, then—alarms! You slide down the pole and you're off to a life-and-death struggle. The real trick is keeping your mind sharp and your body energized. To that end..."

Karl leaned back, opened the discarded copy of Faust, placed it over his eyes, and promptly fell asleep.

● ● ●

Hours later, the roughly-rested Major looked at the crew assigned to his new Ju-88 in disbelief. Only one man stood at attention before him.

"One man? Fucking Luftwaffe," he muttered.

Immediately, Karl regretted the outward display of disloyalty in front of a subordinate.

"True words, sir!" The crewman answered, betraying no expression. "One man to fly the plane and one to drop the bombs. They must think there's no need to aim, no need for complex navigation. I've heard the men call them 'skeleton crews' for a reason...sir!"

Unsure what to do in the face of such substantiated support, the Major decided to move along with the interview.

"Name?" Karl asked the young man.

"Quale," he answered. "Oberleutnant Maximilian Quale."

"Wie alt bist du?"

"Dreiundzwanzig."

Karl shook his head. The man was only twenty-three years old and already somehow up-jumped to the rank of Oberleutnant. The Major wondered how long ago Max completed his flight training but decided not to ask for the sake of his own sanity. He studied his strange new crew of one. The boy must have connections, Karl decided.

For his part, young Quale stood at attention with his hands clasped behind his back. His grey uniform was neatly pressed and excruciatingly well-maintained. Max had wavy blond hair, conservative in length but meticulously styled. His blue eyes and small smile hinted at something Karl interpreted as a combination of arrogance and fastidiousness. Good, he thought. A subordinate with bravery and confidence born from stupidity would be far more useful to him than one filled with fear derived of wisdom.

"At ease, Quale. My name is Major Karl Fleisher. I've been flying since you were a sperm of a sperm."

"Yes sir, Major Fleisher."

The boy was properly respectful at least, Karl determined. He signaled for Max to follow and led the young crewman to the hanger where their sparkling new Ju-88 waited.

The bomber was even more fearsome in the shadows, Karl thought. Max seemed unimpressed, keeping his attention focused on his new captain rather than the *Fleischerbeile*.

"This Junkers here is ours, Quale. The '88 can be anything from a night fighter to a spy plane, but for us she'll be a schnellbomber. Have you served aboard one of this type before?"

"Nein, Major Fleisher. She'll be my first posting, of any kind, sir."

Karl looked at his new bombardier and blinked several times. Only one man and pure green, at that. The Major began to feel his face warm as angry epinephrine mixed into his blood. He took a shallow breath and found his calm, circling around the aluminum bird and mechanically explaining features of the bomber to Max, who, for his part, seemed to absorb the information quickly and unquestioningly.

"Little point to these, ja?" Karl observed, noticing the array of machine guns bristling from the plane's turrets. "With no men to operate, they're just dead weight, Quale. Find some groundcrew–I'd appreciate flying a few hundred kilos lighter."

"I'll take care of it, sir."

The next morning, Karl and Max took Fe's Ju-88 on an official acclimation and rebasing flight. The old pilot moved through the pre-flight routine more slowly than normal, allowing his subordinate to observe. A touch of the ignition, and the craft's powerful engines roared to life–consuming injections of hydrocarbons in fiery combustion reactions. Mechanical power was routed to the propeller blades, which spun forcefully enough to drive the entire lurching vessel and its inner humans forward.

Within the twelve-cylinder Jumo-211 engines, massive megawatts sprung from the controlled combustion of petroleum, the hydrocarbon remains of eons-old plant and animal life, recovered by mankind to power their energy-hungry machines. It was thus that an atom originally from an asteroid flew again through the Earth's lower atmosphere, this time pushed against gravity by burning the carboniferous remains of the same green creatures that Fe had once passed on its long, eccentric orbit.

Held tight in metallic crystal lattice, the atom vibrated with the surging kinetic forces all around it. Soon enough, gravity's cold grip was shaken off and the *Fleischerbeile* took to the sky—the spring sunlight's blinding rays streaming down onto the metal wings of the soaring warplane.

Seated within the fresh-smelling cockpit, Karl Fleischer took to the machine instantly, feeling beyond satisfied by its technical perfection. No unexpected problems had popped up, and patiently, he walked Max through the operations procedures, giving a version of the same lecture he'd delivered to more young men than he could remember. Once or twice, Max seemingly could not restrain himself from showing impatience at times and jumping ahead, having already studied for his assignment in depth.

Karl dealt with know-it-alls the way he always had—meeting eager blabber with dead silence. When the Major had finished covering the basics, at his own pace, the airmen still had some time left on their flight.

The new bombardier seemed in a sociable mood, and Karl let Max chatter endlessly about himself, speaking over headset to defeat the din of the engine. "...an uncle in the SS..." was the most salient detail Karl absorbed from the monologue, only partly listening as he brought the bomber North toward their new airfield.

"You know where we'll be based, Quale? That makes us almost certain to fly over Britain in the near future."

"I assumed so, Major," Max agreed.

Too eagerly, he began to question Karl about his experiences in the months-long chaos of the Battle of Britain the year before.

"You're lucky to have missed it," Karl answered grimly, offering no personal details. "Those missions are *why* we're running on a skeleton crew. Probably part of the reason you were promoted, Quale, no offense."

"Maybe, Sir. But if you ask me, Luftwaffe command has pulled too many of our resources south, to aid Italy's idiotic invasion of Greece." He paused for breath before continuing. "And there's rumors of war with the Soviets."

"I would do anything for the Fatherland, Quale, but flying over *Russia…*" Karl trailed off. It was common knowledge that Germany had decided against a Soviet alliance, and the whispers of an eastern invasion were growing louder. Karl hoped the rumors were untrue. "Bailing out over Soviet territory would be a fate worse than death," he continued. "Best case—we freeze to death in the Russian tundra. Better than getting captured by Stalin's army. Better to be captured by the English—"

"—or drown in the channel," Max finished, darkly.

The remainder of the flight proved uneventful, the German countryside appearing absolutely serene when seen from the sky. Just before sunset, they reached their new airfield, where ground crew took custody of the *Fleischerbeile,* and Max immediately fell in with a knot of young Airmen.

Karl stayed with Fe's plane until he was sure his official duties were over, then he struck off, looking for a comfortable place to sleep. He'd been based at this particular airfield twice in the past, and, as was his custom, he quickly found the quietest spot in the barracks.

Before the tired old pilot could settle in for the night, to his surprise, Max broke off from the laughing and back-slapping of Luftwaffe youth to pay Karl a visit.

"Abend! I've learned some things from the airboys," he announced. "*All* the schnellbombers are running skeleton crews until they can train more men. Your hunch was right, too, Major Fleisher—word around base is night sorties above Britain. And they say the cook here does schnitzel on weekends."

Karl nodded, not moving from his bunk. "The job of the Luftwaffe is changing," he said. "If we can't invade England, we can keep them from trying to get into Europe. Command wants us to cripple their shipping, if we can."

"Isn't that the job of the U-boats, sir? Harassing convoys and the like?"

"Stopping the Amerikanisch gravy train, you mean?"

"They haven't declared war, but their factories have." "Equally dangerous, Quale," Karl answered. "Now turn off that brain, find a bunk, and get some sleep—that's an order."

● ● ●

Fe's Ju-88 would fly its first bombing run several days after Karl's birthday. Orders came down for an attack on the port city of Plymouth, rousing the airmen to scramble from the warmth of the barracks into the dark, chilly night. After Karl and Max jumped into their thermal flight suits, they jogged across the starlit grass field to the hangars. The base had come alive, and already the thrumming of enormous petroleum engines shattered the night's silence.

Max reached the *Fleischerbeile* first, sprinting on his young legs far faster than he needed to. By contrast, Karl worked to keep his jog steady. He needed a level heart rate to fly effectively. Sprinting to the plane did nobody any favors–youthful exuberance and adrenaline be damned. He reminded himself to have a word with Quale later.

None of the other crews boasted a pilot as experienced as Major Fleisher, but many of the young pilots were already veterans themselves–as familiar with their planes, and their enemy, as could be expected.

The only truly green airman to fly that night was Max, and his fear visibly leaked through the facade he endeavored to maintain. Redundantly, Karl guided his young oberleutnant through the takeoff procedures, trying to keep the man's mind too busy for it to become consumed by fear.

Max nodded along with his commander's words, his lips pale.

Within minutes, the blistering trio of laminate propeller blades screamed their dervish dance around Fe's steel cone, their identical counterparts matching them upon the other wing. Masterfully, Karl guided the '88 onto the runway and took off into the black sky, where the waning moon hung, still bright enough to see by.

"The Luftwaffe likes to run night bombings by moonlight," he explained to Quale over the headset. "The easiest way to avoid using our navigational beams, which, to the Tommies, are like spotlights."

Karl guided the bomber carefully and evenly through the lower atmosphere. Other Junkers craft thundered through the dark firmament alongside, and the Major settled into formation, fitting the *Fleischerbeile* into a pod of light bombers–flanked by a thin escort of agile and deadly fighter planes. Max seemed to have recovered some of his nerve, and he read navigational data from the instruments in a calm, clear voice.

Navigating by the half-light of the moon, the positions of the stars—it reminded Karl of his youth, though he had been older than Max, even in those early days.

Although they maintained radio silence, the cabin of the bomber was far from quiet. The twin aircraft engines boomed through the night and shook the body of the plane, vibrating the humans, the iron atoms, and each of the trillions upon trillions of nearly-frozen aluminums that formed the outer skin of the great flying machine.

Karl shivered, taking his gloved hands briefly from the yoke and rubbing them together, hoping for warmth from friction. Quale was worse off, as his vitality had not yet acclimated to the cold conditions of night-flying like the older pilot.

For nearly thirty minutes, the moon passed behind a thick cloudbank, causing Max to lose their position.

"I can't see a thing," he said, more than once, the panic rising in his voice.

"Keep the other planes in sight as best you can, Oberleutnant. Losing our position is nothing so bad as losing our escort."

Max bit his pale lips, nodding, and the pair worked to stick as closely to their allies as possible in the thin, black air. Soon enough, the moon returned, and Quale could better find their bomber's position. Karl looked side to side and was relieved to see moonlight glinting from the wings of other German aircraft. It turned out that the entire pod had veered off course by a few degrees. Making corrections was easy enough for Karl and his wingmen, and soon, the pod was back on track, headed on a vector to Southwestern England.

After a time, the land below fell away, and the Luftwaffe squadron found itself flying over water—they had reached the channel.

"Radar has ruined aerial warfare," Karl complained, referencing the use of reflected low-energy photons to track incoming aircraft, a practice tantamount to magic for the aging pilot. "In the Battle, we were ordered to attack the radar towers, to blind the British, but the little bastards built them back up faster than we could knock them out. Before radio positioning, there was an art and a skill to this, Quale. Now, we fly and fight like rogues, hiding–without opportunity for honor."

Despite the Major's opinions, their less-than-honorable tactics worked, and no British defenses caught sight of the squadron. After its frigid flight over the channel, the Luftwaffe formation approached Plymouth, situated east of a natural port carved into the southern coast of England. Few lights shone in the city below, but there existed illumination enough to positively identify the target. Other pods of German warplanes joined Karl and Max's group, arriving from different vectors. Soon, the skies above Devon were filled with the permeating roar of Luftwaffe engines.

Rather than the brutal incendiary ordinance used for Karl's earlier terror bombing campaigns, the shells loaded into the *Fleischerbeile* were heavier and more accurate, designed to fall swiftly and maximize structural damage. A crackle came over the radio suddenly, jolting the airmen to terrified alertness–Karl's target had been given priority.

The veteran pilot pulled back on the yoke, slowing the plane and falling behind the other bombers. His sharp eyes took in their surroundings. Tiny flecks of light shining below were ostensibly the city's harbors and dry-docks. Karl aimed for the lights, set his jaw, and waited for the crucial moment. Fe's shielding vibrated as the beastly port engine hummed. Underneath, the city slept, betraying no indication that the island's forces were aware of the approaching attack.

In front of Karl, a cluster of brilliant red lights fell from the sky, hanging there briefly before slowly descending on miniature parachutes. This bloody phosphorescence had been launched from the formation's vanguard to illuminate the city below. At the visual signal, the bombers dove. From inside the Ju-88, Karl watched the faint outlines of his comrades as they buzzed over the city, releasing death from the bellies of their planes.

Tiny flowers of fire blossomed on the ground, briefly drowning out the light from the overhead flares. Seconds later, deep concussive sounds filled the cabin, rocking the entire airplane. Karl felt the thud of the bombs bursting below in the deepest part of his chest, though hours of roaring engines had partially desensitized the old human. His hands were frozen, even in their fur-lined leather gloves. Karl couldn't feel his nose or the ridges of his cheeks.

"Check, Quale. Ordinance loaded in bomb bay one."

"Check."

Exhaling, and angling the bomber's nose toward the harbors below, Karl took the *Fleischerbeile* into a shallow dive, his years of instinct kicking in, subconsciously calculating a complex parabolic trajectory for the as-yet unreleased ordinance.

The Major held up one hand as a signal to Max. Winds screamed by as the bomber reached the deepest point in its dive. Karl dropped his hand and pulled back on the yoke, forcing the craft upward. At that moment, with sweating palms, Max activated the doors of the first bomb bay, releasing its payload of heavy steel canisters and allowing gravity to pull them down to the unprotected harbor below.

Karl's diving technique and his unparalleled instincts made the ordinance from the Ju-88 fairly accurate—one fifty kilogram shell crashed through the tin roof of a warehouse by the docks and exploded inside. The flimsy structure shuddered as flames spilled from its shattered glass windows, flaring out from the hole in the roof carved by the bomb's entrance. Other shells splashed into the sea or hit the rocks between piers, exploding in spheres of hellfire that brought unimaginable deaths to the creatures dwelling in the tide-pools. One lucky shell impacted near the waterline and burst with enough explosive force to collapse a small wooden pier, drowning the boat and livelihood of one unfortunate English crabber.

Following Karl's lead, the remaining bombers in his unit dove down toward the harbor and released their payloads. Sheer luck governed the fortunes of the bombs as they exploded onto strategic structures or drowned impotently in the bay.

"Sieg Heil!" Max whooped triumphantly as they completed their first pass.

Karl said nothing, working to keep the Ju-88 steady in the turbulence, the concussive force from the explosions below rattling everything. He gained altitude and brought the plane around. Damage on the ground appeared minimal. Some targets had been successfully bombed, but many more remained untouched. Red phosphorus fire still glowed from where the flares had landed, and the scattering of direct hits smoldered brightly–more than enough light for Karl to find his way back to the harbor.

He brought the warplane into a dive as soon as he was in position, signaling to Max when the time was right. The young bombardier released the doors for the second bay just in time, ensuring as accurate a shot as possible under such conditions. This time, however, Karl brought the *Fleischerbeile* closer inland, hoping that any bombs that missed prime targets would still do damage to the roads leading to the harbor, delaying repair and compounding the impact of the raid.

Max looked back as the Ju-88 pulled out of its dive.

The bombs bloomed below in orange and black bursts of flame and smoke. A speed-of-sound delay after each explosion–then–a deep rumbling shook the interior of the bomber.

Other Luftwaffe pilots again followed Karl's lead, emptying their planes and raining more destruction on the ports of Plymouth. With the run complete, the task now turned to flying home as quickly as possible.

"Time for the krähen to flock home. By now, Quale," Karl explained, "the Tommies have scrambled fighters from all over the island. Do you enjoy the grand prix?"

He knew the Ju-88 flew nearly defenseless, with only one man available on the machine gun turret in the event of an emergency. Their own fighter escort was bare-bones, Karl knew, and they would be hard pressed to hold their own in a direct fight with the Royal Air Force.

Though their payloads had been dropped, the bombers continued to limit radio noise, and their navigational beams remained offline. Max checked their position by the moon and the landmasses below, and Karl set the appropriate heading. Soon, they rejoined the main body of the formation–a pod of fleeing hit-and-run aircraft, screaming through the darkness as fast as their engines and pilots' nerves would allow.

Without its ordinance, Fe's plane flew far lighter than when it had departed, and Karl used the Ju-88's speed to race to the head of the pack. Karl knew that he and Max wouldn't be truly safe until they were back on the ground, but he left the thought unsaid. For many tense minutes, the bombers thundered away from Britain, reaching the channel and vectoring toward the mainland. Sitting in a freezing, deafening cockpit, flying at top speed through the moonlit night, an oppressive haze surrounded the airmen. Within them, boredom and terror battled for supremacy.

To keep himself busy, Oberleutnant Quale continued to read their headings aloud.

As the German planes flew over the channel, a strafing of gunfire shattered the pilots' boredom, leaving terror to stand alone. A small group of British interceptors had caught up to the Luftwaffe group. Karl's radio blared to life with a cacophony of voices–communication resuming now that subterfuge had failed. From what he could make out from the chatter, they had unexpectedly encountered a small handful of enemy fighters–either a lone squadron had scrambled onto a fortuitous vector, or they'd surprised a very unlucky patrol.

Regardless of their origins, the British fighters screamed toward the bomber group with the moonlight behind them, sending a barrage of machine gun fire toward Karl and his comrades, hoping to shred the bombers' thin aluminum skin with supersonic slugs.

After the fighters' first strafe, the German formation broke apart, light bombers like the *Fleischerbeile* taking evasive maneuvers.

"Gun turret. Now!" Karl bellowed at the younger man, suspecting that the fighters had pulled U-turns to re-engage.

Max scrambled over and jumped behind the oily black grips of the mounted machine gun. Frantically, he swiveled his head around, trying to catch a glimpse of the enemy planes.

"Only fire if you have a clean shot," the Major commanded. "If there are friendlies in view, keep your damn finger off the trigger, no matter what."

"Yes sir."

Karl tried to ignore the chaos around him, focusing on the yoke in his hands and the radio chatter in his ears. They were nearly past the channel now, and he kept the bomber's course pointed roughly in the direction of home. Sounds of gunfire could just be heard over the thunder of the engines—he and his comrades were engaged in a straight dogfight above the waters.

"Scheisse," Max whimpered.

The chaotic chatter of the radio was drowned out by a deafening burst of bullets. A fighter had taken an attacking angle on the *Fleischerbeile*. Without time to comfort Max, Karl gripped the yoke and pulled the plane into a parabolic trajectory, meant to increase speed and reduce the bomber as a target in profile. Keeping his breathing as steady as possible, the old pilot reached for a particular feature of his state-of-the-art warplane. He pulled a switch, and inside one of the Jumos, behind Fe's armored cone, a thin stream of oil was allowed to flow into the hot engine.

It ignited into a thick, trailing stream of stygian smoke.

This moment of deception was all that was needed to evade the British fighter, which thundered over Fe's smoking bomber toward new targets. Major Fleisher flew low and quick until the sounds of combat grew small and far away. He focused on the blackness ahead and, keeping the moon to one side, raced forward through the night, fleeing the battle.

The smoke-device gradually sputtered out, and the only sounds of gunfire that could be heard were echoes in Karl's imagination. He felt no qualms at all about abandoning the forces engaging the British planes. It's what escorts were for, and besides, the *Fleischerbeile* possessed no armaments save for a single machine gun manned by a frightfully nervous twenty-three-year-old.

Circling back, time drew out in a long, thin line—as if the frigid air had frozen the flow of one minute into the next. Once, Max pulled the trigger of the rear machine gun, filling the plane with a deafening series of rat-a-tat explosions and sending a spray of bullets out into nowhere.

"Maximilian!"

Karl was so startled, he nearly dropped the yoke. He swiveled around, saw nothing, and demanded to know what Max had shot at. The ghost-pale Oberleutnant seemed unsure, and mumbled something about Hurricanes and Spitfires.

"We've left the battle behind, Quale! Get off that gun," Karl ordered.

He decided to keep the youth busy, and his fingers off the trigger, by asking for unnecessary verbal confirmation of their position until they again flew above the German heartland.

Eventually the Ju-88 carrying Karl, Max, and the atom Fe neared the airfield. They radioed their arrival to the tower and received permission to land. The sun threatened to rise, the night's frost slowly turning to dew on the close-cut grass of the runways. Far out of formation, the bomber landed alone. Following the skirmish and the desperate flight home, the scattered planes from the squadron would return to the airfield in a stagger.

Karl angled the plane downward, cut speed, and dropped his landing gear. The wheels bumped against the earth below, and the old Major breathed out a heavy sigh of relief. After taxiing into the hangar, Karl shut down the hot engines and looked over at Max, who had been silent for some time.

The young leutnant looked dead on his feet.

"You did well," the older man said, sympathetically. "This would have been a hard run for anyone, let alone a green airman who's never before left friendly skies."

He smiled, and Max gave a weak nod in return. There was still work to do, Karl knew, and though his aging joints were screaming from hours of sitting frozen in the pilot's chair, he decided that the emotionally and physically exhausted Oberleutnant deserved a bit of mercy.

"You're dismissed Quale. Go and get some sleep. I've got it from here."

Max managed a small "yes sir" before climbing from the plane and shuffling off, dazed, in the direction of the barracks.

After his post-flight checklist was complete, Karl slowly stretched, stomped, and clapped until he'd chased away the pins and needles and restored circulation to his extremities. Leaving the cockpit and stepping down into the hangar, he examined the plane. After one complete lap, Karl concluded that the '88 was un-damaged. Its aluminum wings, tail, fuselage, the Jumo engines, and even the small steel shield containing the atom Fe appeared in perfect, if slightly smokestained, condition.

However, the aircraft looked somehow different to Karl. It may have been the light, but the old pilot felt that, in a way, the warplane had now lost its innocence. No longer a simple collection of metal parts, the *Fleischerbeile* had terrorized a city and may even have taken human lives. When Karl returned to the barracks, he saw Max passed out, face down on a bunk. The young man's flight suit was half unzipped. Karl was not long for consciousness either, but he had energy enough to wash his hands and face and slip into a clean change of clothes before succumbing to sleep.

● ● ●

In the end, the Plymouth raid could be counted a moderate success from the Luftwaffe's point of view, though one bomber and two fighters from Karl's group had been lost over the channel. A handful of other warplanes from different squadrons also never returned, including one which had veered badly off course and encountered heavy resistance, but estimates of the damage to the city were good. Karl and his wingmen had significantly hindered the functionality of the ports while sustaining minimal losses of their own. Offshore, another, smaller Luftwaffe group based from the same airfield had engaged a supply convoy, causing major damage with no resistance before rejoining the fleet.

"It doesn't make up for the Battle of Britain," Karl remarked to Max, the spirits in the barracks cautiously high, "but I've flown worse missions."

He'd noticed that the younger airman seemed to forget his terror and the hours of near-panic within the Ju-88's cacophonous aluminum belly. Max even painted a mission decal on the rear of their plane, celebrating the attack. His arrogance and garrulous nature returned when he was surrounded by other young airmen, but when the notice came in for another mission, he grew visibly pale.

"Don't worry, Quale," Karl said, clapping a hand on the Oberleutnant's shoulder. "It will be good for you. Air combat has a way of replacing negative personality traits with humility. At least for bomber crews," he added, eliciting a smile from the boy, "nothing can be done for the attitudes of fighter pilots."

The *Fleischerbeile*'s next mission occurred during the relatively safe daylight hours. Karl, Max, and their wingmen attacked a supply convoy which had ventured too far into the North Sea. The targets were escorted by one warship and a few small gunboats. None of the Ju-88's munitions scored a direct hit in the raid, but the volume of bombs dropped by the Luftwaffe formation was enough to eventually break the convoy. The Germans returned to the airfield after only a few hours of flight.

Another sortie came mere hours after the North Sea raid. Karl had awoken at the first alarm, though he suspected his unacclimated crewman might still be asleep.

"Quale!" The Major called out, looking for his subordinate among the evacuated bunks. "Look alive, Oberleutnant–we've got packages to deliver. All the heavy bombers are down in Greece, no real muscle here, so we're all they've got–"

He stumbled upon Max, who looked as startled as an ambushed deer. The youth was hastily pulling on his trousers, turning suddenly in a half-crouch when Karl approached.

"Oberleutnant–""Yes, Major. One minute."

"Take two," Karl said.

He pivoted to give the boy some privacy, not before noticing an open shaving kit and blood upon the gleaming blade of Max's steel straight razor.

"Without the heavies, they use us like post horses. This is becoming routine, Quale. Back-to-back missions. You'll adjust."

"Go ahead and get her started, sir," Max said, his voice high and strained, "I'll be there before wheels-up."

As good as his word, Max arrived on the *Fleischerbeile,* suited up and on time but looking pale and unsteady. During the pre-flight check, Karl noticed that the crewman's eyes were puffy, and his face was still covered in a layer of colorless stubble.

Once in the air, they joined other squadrons from around Northern Europe. It was a night flight, similar to their first mission. This time, however, they were heading to London. The bombers not carrying incendiaries were loaded with high-explosive shells, meant for devastating entire city blocks in one burst. Before observing radio silence, Karl received his orders.

"Vague and indiscriminate," Karl muttered, pushing the headset away from his face. "No aiming tonight."

The mission amounted to little more than a terror bombing under cover of darkness. That night, the moon was nearly new, and the German formations were forced to rely on their navigational beams. Though the British defenses would be far stiffer over the capital city, the buzzing swarms of fighter escorts that flew beside Karl's group were far more numerous than the protection they'd had during the Plymouth raid.

Engines droned, and the temperature plummeted. Hours of freezing and boredom caused Max to flutter in and out of wakefulness. Karl risked taking his hands off the yoke to reach back and slap the younger man.

"Vati!" Max cried before coming to wakefulness with a start.

"Verdammt! I don't ask much, Quale, but your eyes need to be open. Chew some Pervitin tablets unless you want another slap!"

Groggily, Max complied, slowly grinding a pair of the pep pills between his teeth. He swallowed, and the bitter methamphetamine slid down his throat to the organs below, taking only minutes to reach the bloodstream, where soon enough it was pumped brainward. There, the dissolved stimulants approached Max's neural cells like biological torpedoes, striking specialized proteins and triggering the release of a salvo of complicated chemical messengers. Gushing from nerve-endings by the millions, the intricate, biologically-crafted machinery of dopamine, norepinephrine, and serotonin flooded Max Quale's brain and began to work.

Before the bomber formation reached the airspace over their island target, the exhausted, shaken young man had found a crystal-clarity of mind. Norepinephrine coursing through his blood hyperactivated Max's cardiovascular system, causing his skin to flush and chasing his weariness into a far corner.

"You're looking a bit better," Karl remarked, noting the color returning to the young man's face.

"Do you have any more of those?"

"Two is enough. Now make yourself useful and find London."

The grand imperial capital routinely doused its lights as a countermeasure to bombing raids that had become as common as English rain. Nevertheless, it would take more than the snuffing of streetlamps and the blacking-out of windows to hide a city boasting such size and life force, and besides, there was no mistaking the river. Major Fleisher, in formation with dozens of other Luftwaffe pilots, roared out from behind a cloudbank, booming his silver dragon toward the Thames waterfront.

"How in hell are we supposed to aim?" Max shouted.

"Optimistically.""Hä?"

"Not a priority, Quale. Mission is to drop our load over the city, then turn tail and run," Karl said, explaining the spirit, if not the text, of their orders. "Now get to the bay and hold for my signal."

Before the Luftwaffe bombers could get in range, however, London's defenses sprang to life. Air raid sirens screamed into the darkness, and spotlights ignited, sending their bright white beams slicing into the night. Bleary-eyed British defenders hustled to their posts at roof-mounted anti-aircraft guns. As the German warplanes approached the Thames, the first crackles of flak fire began to shake the atmosphere, and from airfields all around the city, interceptor pilots scrambled their fighters into the sky.

A squadron of small schnellbombers broke off from the formation, diving in a swarm toward the waterfront, targeting docked ships. Fe's Ju-88, with others of its weight class, raced forward, headed inland to drop their payloads.

His hands around the yoke in a strangling deathgrip, Karl drove the *Fleischerbelie* down from the clouds, other pilots on his tail. The bomber spearheaded the first thrust of the London raid–Major Fleischer forwardmost in the cockpit, while the atom Fe, once part of a literal spearhead, now played the role of armor.

"Now, Quale!"

Aft of Karl, Max wrenched open the bays, letting gravity carry the heavy shells away. The pilot banked, and the plane rocked and shook so violently that Max decided to lash himself to the interior walls with some cargo strapping.

Below, London erupted. The indiscriminate rain of heavy bombs smashed through wood and brick buildings, exploding in showers of fire and shrapnel, splinter and stone.

Bomber after bomber emptied their bays, incendiaries sending torrents of fire coursing through the empty streets. Buildings shuddered in the shockwaves and collapsed. Karl risked a look back to ensure his crewman was still hanging on, and he began to bring the twin-engine bomber into a wide circle around the city, ignoring the bright flowers of fire below.

A blinding light burst into bloom on the right side of the cockpit. Instinctively, Karl raised his hand to cover his eyes, and Max shrieked. Outside of the protective glass, the searing luminosity of the explosion rapidly faded behind them. One of their allies had sustained a direct hit by anti-aircraft fire, igniting its payload and causing the entire warplane to erupt like a flak shell in the sky.

Karl jerked the yoke of his own '88, steering evasively from the blast. Vibrations rocked the plane as they veered, and a cacophony of pinging rattled the outside of the fuselage like a steel hailstorm.

Shell after shell, fired from British cannons, rocketed into the sky and burst like colorless fireworks. As a particularly deadly flak cylinder detonated, the explosion shredded one of a number of steel disks within and flung a chunk, the rough size and shape of a human's half-curled thumb, at Karl's Ju-88.

Born at the death of the Mother Star and forced into carbon-steel lattice by humans, the trillions of iron atoms in the racing projectile hurtled toward the *Fleischerbeile* and impacted its aluminum skin. Though strong, the metal matrix of the outer sheet was populated by light atoms, thirteen protons each to iron's twenty-six.

The far denser steel shrapnel sliced through the warplane's aluminum armor as easily as if it were skin, passing in and out of the fuselage before succumbing to gravity and returning to London below. Neither Major Fleischer or Oberleutnant Quale noticed the through-and-through strike.

Still leading its bomber group, the *Fleischerbeile* began to climb and change course, attempting to avoid further blooms of black smoke and shrapnel. One of its two bays still contained ordinance, weighing down the bomber and making it nearly impossible to outrun a British fighter should one appear.

Karl concentrated on the sky ahead. He set his jaw, and sweat beaded on his forehead. Behind him, Max sat shivering, holding tightly to his restraints. In the dark air around them, anti-aircraft shells burst into black clouds of jagged flak, spitting shrapnel in all directions. Another terrible bloom burst in the sky, further off, and the radio chatter grew frantic. Karl began to lose track of his wingmen. As in their skirmish over the channel, the squadron scattered.

"Oberleutnant, get up here!" Karl ordered. "Position reading."

Shakily, Max moved himself to the cockpit, and together, the two airmen plotted a rough course away from the chaos of combat and back on a homeward vector. As they flew over the outer suburbs at a relatively safe altitude, Major Fleisher instructed his subordinate to release the last of the bombs.

Fe's Ju-88 screamed away from the battle, and its un-aimed ordinance tumbled down onto the communities below—the bombshells' final landing spots a matter of fortune, air currents, and physics.

Hours passed uneventfully. The chill of the cabin and the monotonous drone of the engines helped to numb the airmen's fear and adrenaline. By the time they were nearing their base, Karl noticed that the pills had worn off for his young Oberleutnant, who lay slumped beside him, dead asleep in the copilot's seat.

●　●　●

The London bombing run cost the Luftwaffe a dozen airmen, and half their number in aircraft. Nor did the Ju-88 christened *Fleischerbeile* emerge from the sortie unscathed—its thin, aluminum skin had been scarred and pierced by shrapnel from anti-aircraft shells and debris from the proximal detonation of the friendly bomber. Regardless, the warplane endured, fully functional. Both of its engines stayed in working order, and the steel cap containing the atom Fe remained nearly pristine beneath a patina of light scorching.

Over the next few weeks, Karl and Max caught little rest, flying sortie after sortie. Most of their missions involved hit-and-run strikes in small group formations, and they avoided significant Allied resistance. Several times, emergency bombing runs that had woken the men from their bunks were canceled midflight, before the formation had even exited German airspace.

Another round of such orders forced Karl to turn the *Fleischerbeile* in a wide circle. As he vectored back to base, the Major cursed Luftwaffee command, but the veteran airman's gripes were nothing compared to the vitriol Max spat whenever he learned that his panic and adrenaline had been wasted.

"Fickers! Arschlöcher!" He whined. "Nothing worse than a head full of Pervitin—and they tell us to go home and get some rest. Verdammt!"

When they landed, Karl slept. The pilot had long ago hardened himself to the harried existence of serving on a wartime bombercrew, but young Maximilian never quite adjusted to the lifestyle of coffee, pills, and the snatching of precious slumber whenever and wherever one could.

March turned into April, and the war raged on. Early in the month, Karl, Max, and Fe rode the *Fleischerbeile* to the English city of Sunderland as part of a massive raid, crescendoing in over one hundred Luftwaffe bombers converging above Britain's eastern shore. Squadrons of schnellbombers dropped tons of ordinance upon the city as the Luftwaffe fighter escort clashed with a harrying host of RAF fighters. Sacrificial Messerschmitts sprayed chains of hot lead at the English pilots, their machine guns forcing the enemy fighters to break off their attack on the bombers, like pests fleeing a garden hose. Many German airmen were lost during the Sunderland raid, but Karl and Max were not among their number.

In the days devoted to celebrating Adolf Hitler's birthday, the *Fleischerbeile* made its return to the skies above the western city of Plymouth. As a grand display of power against Great Britain, the tyrant had ordered his northern airmen, including Karl and seven hundred other bomber pilots, to drop one million kilograms of explosives onto the English port. The attack came unexpectedly, and, flying over the lightly defended city, the Luftwaffe's aluminum dragons opened their bellies and released death from above. The structures of Plymouth shuddered and shattered under the blasting, burning barrage. Thousands of humans hid underground, but many lost their homes. Buildings transformed to rubble, yet even more ordinance landed on the ruins–bursting in concussive claps but doing little more than turning the rubble into a finer grade of scorched sand.

Direct hits from German dive-bombers ignited massive fuel stores along the English dockside, and torpedo-armed warplanes harassed the ships in the harbor. The schnellbombers were in and out like a sucker-punch. As the formation fled back toward mainland Europe, they left behind a severely damaged Plymouth. Despite the overkill of the attack, the smoking ruin of a city had already resumed a tenacious trickle of manufacturing and shipping operations by the time Karl and the *Fleischerbeile* landed back at the airbase.

Later in the month, another large attack was ordered against Sunderland in the east. Karl and Max flew over the familiar city and dropped high explosive shells as impassively as if they were international postmen delivering parcels door to door.

"Do you ever feel like Santa Claus?" Max once asked his Major as they flew above rows of silent rooftops.

"Nein."

During the earliest hours of dawning May, Karl found himself sleeping uneasily–a rarity for the veteran airman. In his dream, he stood before the gates of heaven, a Swiss accountant blocking his path. In a colorless voice, the bureaucrat would read through a towering stack of names. One after the next, stretching into the deep hundreds. Every time the pilot interrupted or tried to ask a question, the accountant sighed and would start again.

Karl's bladder rescued him from his sisyphean torture, waking him at last. "Absurd." Karl muttered, stretching out from his bunk and slipping on a pair of roomy overshoes.

Still at the edge of sleep, he staggered to the washroom. Inside, he noticed Oberleutnant Quale's belongings on a bench. Save for a single closed stall, Karl found the facilities empty of other nighttime visitors. He stepped to a free bowl and began to relieve himself.

"Quale?" He asked, raising his voice. "I was just dreaming. I wonder...do you think I might escape hell, since technically it is your hand that always releases the bombs? Or shall we blame gravity?"

The occupant of the adjacent stall didn't answer, but as Karl finished his business, he could hear heavy breathing.

"Don't worry, Max. This pace won't keep up forever. The England campaign is waning, mark my words."

A low moan issued from the stall, followed by a soft dripping. Karl looked down, disturbed to see small crimson drops impacting the tiled floor. He said nothing, and shuffled away, back to his troubled dreams.

Yoke in hand once more, Karl knew his late-night prediction had proven incorrect as he looked out his glass bubble at the hundreds of bombers rumbling alongside the *Fleischerbeile*, vectoring en masse to Liverpool.

Below the booming Luftwaffe horde, the sprawling industrial metropolis spread itself over the eastern side of a deep estuary, leaping across to a peninsula on the opposite bank of the River Mersey. Though a prime port of call for international shipments, in the earlier days of the war the district had been considered too far north to be targeted by the German Blitz. Thus, Liverpool found itself taken by surprise as the terrible birds of the Luftwaffe appeared in her skies, their bellies swollen with murder.

Karl's bomber roared over Merseyside, and Max pulled his lever, releasing their payload of explosive ordnance near the shoreline. Their wingmen followed suit, and wave after wave of munitions pounded Liverpool, the Luftwaffe shaking the city with the concussive blasts of bombs and the thundering of racing warplane engines.

The schnellbombers met with virtually no resistance outside a few overwhelmed municipal batteries, firing wild flak into the skies. Confidently, the Major brought his *Fleischerbeile* around, leading the squadron in for another pass. Briefly, the firmament filled with a steel rain of tumbling, high-explosive shells.

One squadron at a time, the Luftwaffe dragons fled the shattered, burning city. They roared back toward the south, a force far too large to be effectively resisted by the thinly-spread Allied patrols. The few engagements that occurred happened far from the *Fleischerbeile*. When Karl and Max returned to the airfield, however, their end-of-mission relief was short-lived. A groundcrewman informed them apologetically that there were orders to immediately return to Liverpool.

"The Führer wants waves–" he explained, screaming to be heard over the cacophony of mobilization, "–endless waves of bombings for as long as we can keep it up. You can eat and sleep while we fuel her and rearm. Maybe ninety minutes. Use it well, sirs."

Before the sun could begin its descent, Karl and his young protégé were back in the air, popping Pervitin-branded methamphetamine and pushing the Ju-88 over the North Sea. Though only a few months out of the factory, Fe's bomber was taking on the appearance of a much older craft.

On their third day of sleepless, stimulant-fueled bombing runs, the crew of the *Fleischerbeile* found themselves flying over open water, setting a shaky vector toward the least-damaged berths of the port of Liverpool. An incident early in the day severely damaged a massive liner loaded with munitions, and hours after it had first been attacked, the ship's below-deck blazes reached its cargo, detonating the gargantuan vessel with nearly the same force as Hitler's million-kilograms of birthday bombs put together. The tsunami-like shockwave devastated docks and shoreline, hurtling cannon-ball sized chunks of shrapnel into the already-besieged city.

As Karl flew Fe's warplane into visual range of the western shore of the island, he saw an enormous column of smoke rising off the estuary. Using it as a clear signpost, the pilot flew straight for the Liverpool waterfront.

"Almost as good as red phosphorus, eh, Max?" He said tiredly to his bombardier. "Release...now!"

The *Fleischerbeile's* first bay opened and let loose its payload on the devastated Merseyside shipyards. Another pass, and this time, Karl and Max let their bombs tumble down onto the city proper before vectoring south.

The airmen had decided that the hardest part of these back-to-back raids was the long, cold, monotonous flight home. Neither could afford to let his guard down enough to sleep, especially in the days of skeleton crews and multi-front wars. Though the situation was beyond any of his experience, Karl kept his mind alert and his eyes sharp. He was nowhere near his own breaking point, but the pilot worried about his bombardier.

Major Karl and Oberleutnant Max flew two more missions to Liverpool over the next thirty hours. By the evening of the fifth day of continuous bombing, the pilot was motivated to bring up his gripes to Major Rohr, whom he encountered visiting their airfield's admin building.

"Major Fleischer!" The younger commander greeted Karl warmly, his face crinkling into a smile. "You're a sight for tired eyes."

"Thank you sir, but I'd wager one hundred marks that between the four of them, these two eyes of mine are by far the weariest."

Major Rohr laughed. "Not relishing these heady times, old man?" "I feel like a verdammt commuter pilot, tracing the same flightpath from here to Liverpool. It's beyond vexing."

"But instead of passengers, your commuters are bombs, ja? They need to go to work, too, Major."

"Pah," Karl scoffed, "they only buy one-way tickets."

"Saves fuel for the flight home," Rohr quipped, then he glanced at his wristwatch. "Speaking of, how's the *Fleischerbeile* treating you? It should be fueled-up and ready by the time you get to the hangar. Wheels-up soon, Major."

"Are you mad? I've only just landed! Please sir, there's a bunk with my name on it."

Rohr tsk-tsked, good-naturedly. "My hands are tied, Karl. Everyone flies tonight. Everyone who can." "Does that mean you'll be joining us above Liverpool, sir?" Karl asked darkly.

The younger Major laughed.

"No, thank Christ! But I may have to yet, the way things are going. Please try to come back in one piece, Fleischer, so my father's son can keep his fancy desk job."

"An excellent incentive to crash, sir."

"Fly safe." Rohr fixed Karl with a grin and delivered a vigorous handshake. "Heil Hitler."

"Heil Hitler."

● ● ●

On its now-familiar route toward Liverpool, Fe's Ju-88 joined with bomber group after bomber group. They flew in from Luftwaffe airbases all around the North Atlantic. Hundreds and hundreds of aluminum wings flashed minute reflections of stars above and electric light below as they sliced through the inky blackness.

"There are so many," Max breathed, awestruck, peering out the windows and trying to make out the outlines of individual aircraft.

Even if Major Fleischer and the other Luftwaffe pilots had not memorized the well-worn flightpath to Liverpool by then, the burning city provided all the navigational data one could need. As they drew closer to the Mersey estuary, Karl discerned a fire blazing on the water—it seemed that the doomed cargo ship still burned.

By the hundreds, bomber plane after bomber plane thundered over the English port, releasing their shells and sowing flowers of flame that bloomed on the darkened land below. Karl and Max waited their turn—the older airman's hands on the yoke, the younger ready to act as bombardier. As they made their approach, Messerschmitt fighter planes guarded the '88 on either side, patrolling for British defenses during the schnellbomber's most vulnerable moments.

At last, Karl brought the *Fleischerbeile* into its dive, and Max released the controls to empty the first bay. They zoomed low over the night-drenched ruins, outrunning the flanking explosions of their own ordinance.

Oberleutnant Quale sighed heavily as his pilot swung the plane back around, returning to formation.

"Are the Tommies out of planes?" He asked Karl. "I can't believe how little fight they're putting up."

"Be grateful, Max. Once they realize that the Führer has no intention of stopping this assault, they *will* fight back," the pilot answered.

For a minute or two, Karl gained altitude before banking to follow his wingmen's trajectory, intent on punishing Liverpool with a second pass. It was then that his predictions took shape. From out of the darkness, a pack of British fast fighters erupted among the bomber group, screaming through the formation and spraying machine gun fire at the neat row of vulnerable German planes.

Inside Fe's Ju-88, the airmen heard the pings and clangs of stray bullets thudding through the fuselage.

"Scheisse!"

"Taking evasive action–" Karl announced, pushing the throttle and breaking out of formation.

The *Fleischerbeile* flew heavily and maneuvered sluggishly, still carrying half its load of explosives.

"Max!"

Even before hearing the order, the young bombardier took the initiative to open the bay doors, releasing the last pieces of heavy ordinance, completely unaimed.

"Good man," Karl said, feeling his plane gain power and speed.

He managed to fly them away from the main pack, but a single British Spitfire stayed with the *Fleischerbeile*.

"Quale! Gun!" The Major ordered, keeping his attention on the view ahead.

Max threw himself behind the mounted machine gun and swung it in a wide arc, scanning with bulging, bloodshot eyes.

Karl accelerated as much as he dared, trying to shake the interceptor. Stubbornly, the enemy Spitfire remained glued to their tail. Even emptied of cargo, the schnellbomber could never outrun a single-pilot fighter designed for lethal speed above all else. With this in mind, Karl could only attempt to keep his plane in the air long enough for his own escort to intervene. Max had other ideas–as soon as the interceptor appeared in his sights, the airman unloaded a screaming barrage of automatic fire at the trailing enemy.

Hundreds of hot lead slugs erupted from the machine gun's barrel and sailed through the starlit English skies like tiny, unpowered rockets. As the lead bullets hurtled toward the pursuing Spitfire, gravity extended its omnipresent hand to claim them. Oberleutnant Quale's stream of bullets tumbled Earthward before reaching their target, missing the British plane by a substantial margin.

"He's out of range!" Karl bellowed, but Max could hear nothing over the ringing in his ears and the pounding of his own heart.

As the young airman fired more wild sprays of bullets, Karl pulled back on the yoke, trying to gain altitude. Though it couldn't outsprint the fighter, in the long run, the Ju-88 would be able to outclimb it. Even as he attempted the desperate ascension, however, Karl doubted that the Spitfire's pilot would give them enough time.

They climbed, but the *Fleischerbeile's* speed plummeted, and the enemy closed the distance until both aircraft flew in range of each other's machine guns. Once again, Max compressed the trigger, emitting a yell that was halfway between a Teutonic battle cry and a shriek of terror.

His rapid burst of bullets cut out prematurely–the ammunition exhausted.

Behind them, the Spitfire answered back. Its twenty-millimeter cannons roared to life, expelling anti-aircraft shells at the fleeing '88. Small black explosions–miniature flak flowers–burst around Karl as he sat within the dubious protection of the cockpit's transparent dome. One of the glass tiles set into the bubble shattered as a chunk of lead shrapnel pierced the pane with the force of a sniper's bullet.

Karl gasped as a puff of upholstery fluff erupted from the copilot's seat, and before he had time to react, another barrage thudded around the plane. This time, their foe scored a direct hit to the bomber's underside–the *Fleischerbeile* began to shudder, and warnings lit up Karl's cockpit.

The pilot noted that he still had power from both engines, but his plane was difficult to control–it felt like trying to walk on a broken leg. Rather than attempting to compensate, Major Fleisher embarked upon a desperate gambit–he stopped accelerating and activated the smoke-device.

Within the brilliantly-engineered powerplant roaring behind Fe's shield-cone, a triggered spray of oil burned into the desired plume of thick black smoke, convincingly disguising the bomber as a mortally crippled craft.

Pretending he'd lost control, Karl maneuvered his *Fleischerbeile* into a dive, hoping the Spitfire would leave them for dead. His plan worked only in part. Noticing the beleaguered bomber's rapidly dwindling altitude, the British pilot positioned his craft above the flagging '88 before zooming off to find another target. Firing two of its small-caliber Browning guns, the Spitfire favored the German warplane with a final spray as it passed by. Unluckily, dozens of heavy lead slugs impacted along the length of the bomber's fragile aluminum fuselage and shattered the glass dome around Karl's cockpit.

Its propeller still spinning vigorously, Fe's engine continued to leak smoke, though it had sustained no damage in the attack. Bullets from the Spitfire, however, crippled the wing it was bound to, and on the other side of the bomber, the great port engine's petroleum-burning twin had been shot through–turned to flaming scrap in an instant.

A furious wind rushed through the plane's shattered cockpit. The old bomber pilot could feel the breeze chilling a slick of blood that coated the back of his neck. He risked a quick glance skyward–the Spitfire was gone. Before he could get his bearings, Karl first had to pull the struggling craft out of its dive. With a superhuman effort, he wrestled the yoke and managed to coax the now single-engine bomber into nearly-level flight.

He risked a look behind him. Sure enough, the compartment where Max sat had been riddled with bullets and shredded by flak. The young leutnant was dead–slumped over the handles of his turret, blood pooling from an open skull.

Karl's eyes began to water, but not from emotion. Caustic white smoke seeped out of the bomber's instrument panel. A stray shred of steel shrapnel had buried itself in the wiring, igniting a tiny fire behind the pilot's console. Karl tried to remain calm and point the *Fleischerbeile* in a stable direction, but he was quickly losing altitude. The one good engine persisted in pulling the aircraft off-course, and Karl found that many of the controls wouldn't respond to his flipping of switches and mashing of buttons. Attempting an emergency crash landing over the outskirts of the city was the only option that remained to the veteran pilot.

Screaming wind tore more loose pieces from the shattered glass dome, further freezing and deafening the surviving human aboard. At the very least, the fierce airflow allowed the Major to catch clear glimpses between billows of smoke. Around his plane, the individual elements of scenery were growing larger. From Karl's perspective, there was a moment where the *Fleischerbeile* appeared to be sitting still, and it was the Earth which was moving upward to meet it.

Karl did not think of what his fate would be if he fell into the hands of the denizens of the city he'd spent the past week bombing. He did not think of Max, dead at twenty-three. He did not think of his lover from the Great War, who would always stay the same age. His only thoughts were mechanical—how to level out the wings, the angle of the nose—too steep!—and the open spaces below to aim for. Outside the shattered glass of the cockpit, trees and old farm buildings rushed forward at a terrifying rate. Before slamming into the Earth and dying instantly of deceleration trauma, Major Karl Fleisher's final thought was of deploying the landing gear.

Chapter 4: The Pawnbrokers

Sam Stills woke up before the sun on most days. In his state of semi-retirement, he liked to keep his mind active by going for sunrise walks. Typically, he strolled around his village, occasionally meandering north toward the outskirts of the town, but that week, things were different. Sam had been forced to wait underground for most of the past five or six days as the Krauts had blitzed Liverpool seemingly non-stop. Sam was annoyed that he couldn't go out at night during the air raids, but he kept his grumblings to himself and to Mouse, his midnight-black British shorthair. The people living in the city, he knew, had things much worse.

"Sunrise soon," he observed, peering through the window and rubbing Mouse's head in one large hand, "when things get quiet."

Sam had noticed the pattern days earlier, listening in the shelters–the German warplanes seemed to evaporate like dew with the rising sun.

Now, he was ready to test his theory. With pent-up energy from days of captivity, the elderly human burst from his front door as soon as Sol's bright disk cleared the horizon, bidding a vigorous farewell to the small, dark cat that lived inside his house.

Despite Sam's age, he walked with no cane or limp, and he wore a thick head of grey hair, complete with a sharp widow's peak. He'd stopped counting his age years before, spooked by the approach of sixty. Outside one corner of Sam's compartmentalized mind, nobody save his wife and mother knew the true number for certain, and they were safely dead.

Light was just filtering down from the newly risen sun as Sam's feet crunched on the gravel of his favorite trail. He strolled away from his house and headed north toward the woods and fallow fields. Few others in the county had risen, or dared leave their homes. In fact, most of Sam's countrymen were just settling in for a few hours of troubled sleep after the Luftwaffe raid finally petered out. The fighting sounded especially close that last night, Sam observed, though he dared not crawl out of his cellar to take a look. In the early light, however, things seemed utterly peaceful–no evidence of the battle or bombardment marred the bucolic morning. Sam was thinking placid thoughts when he stumbled upon the wreckage of a downed German bomber.

The broken hulk's body lay scattered along a country trail, its mechanical entrails spewed across a meadow between two abandoned farmhouses. To Sam's reckoning, the aircraft had landed awkwardly, shearing into three large pieces and leaving a trail of smaller debris. Its fuselage and port engine had smashed through a low rock wall, which ran parallel to the pathway. Several yards away, the plane's starboard engine and wing were crumpled against a tree. The tail section had landed even further back, half buried in soft, black soil.

No smoke or flame poured from the aircraft, but the wreck seemed fresh nonetheless. Sam looked around, searching for another living human, hoping to defer to some authority figure–a constable or a military patrol, perhaps.

A gentle breeze shook the leaves on the trees. Not a soul stirred.

Since his wife's passing and his children's leaving for bigger and better things than Cheshire had to offer, old Sam Stills was often left to his own devices. When he wasn't taking long strolls, he spent his days indulging his hobby of buying and collecting junk. To the Englishman, the technology-packed wreck of the *Fleischerbeile* proved irresistible.

With one last glance over his shoulder, Sam approached the cockpit of the downed bomber. He was never one to shy away from an opportunity, even when it came with the slim possibility of confronting an armed Nazi. Hoping the crash had been as fatal as it looked, Sam peered inside the smashed forward-section of the plane. A shattered dome wrapped around the inside of the cockpit, bright blood coating some of the glass.

This was a reassuring sign, Sam thought. He ducked under a broken strut and poked his head inside the hazy cabin. An older man wearing a bloodied flightsuit lay slumped over the pilot's console. Toward the rear of the cockpit was another body, one whose head was too covered in gore for Sam to clearly make out. The Englishman counted only two Germans, but to him, the plane seemed built for a much larger crew.

He ducked back outside, nervously scanning the area for escaped Krauts, but nothing sounded or stirred in the bucolic paradise, save for the springtime chirping of birds and the swaying of branches in the breeze.

A broken tree limb lay near the German plane. Sam ripped off a sturdy stick and snaked the branch through a hole in the glass canopy before roughly poking at the bodies. The old pilot did not stir, even when Sam rammed the stick into the side of the man's scarred face. Breathing a sigh of relief, he changed position, moved the branch, and probed briefly at the other man–Sam had no doubts that this one was dead.

Dropping the stick, the old scrap collector took a step back to survey the smashed Junkers–it was in bad shape, to be sure, but some parts looked salvageable. There was an intact engine on the port side, still mostly attached to a badly-damaged wing. On the other end of the field lay the plane's second engine, which appeared blackened and broken. No profit to be made there, Sam knew. One oily, black protrusion, half-buried in dirt, turned out to be a German machine gun. It was worth at least a hundred pounds to the right buyer, but Sam merely wiped his hands and passed it by–free scrap nobody would miss was one thing, treason another.

The old scrapper took a final, appraising look at the plane and started back toward his house at a brisk pace.

Less than thirty minutes later, Sam arrived back at the crash site. He drove an old work truck, which he had been tinkering with for the past several years–Mouse riding shotgun beside him. The truck had an American chassis and a British engine, which Sam found poetic. He'd tossed a battered oxyacetylene torch in the bed, and behind the truck, Sam had attached a flatbed trailer.

"Didja know metal prices are higher now in Britain than at any point since the Romans came for our tin?" He asked the cat as they bounced along the country trail. "Keep your eyes peeled for Krauts. I only found two in the thing."

After taking a nervous glance around the area, Sam breathed a sigh of relief—no one else had discovered his prize. He parked the truck, grabbed the heavy cutting apparatus, and, with Mouse trailing behind, began to go to work on the bomber.

"Someone is sure to report the crash," Sam chattered as he worked. "Prolly already have. The proper authorities'll deal with this, Mouse, mark my words."

The old scrapper knew that every wrecked enemy craft held at least some intelligence value for the British military. Their personnel would trundle in, search the Junkers' occupants, confiscate the plane's weapons, and eventually, the government would dispose of the whole wreck without even the disbursement of a finder's fee.

"I consider meself a patriot," Sam Stills remarked, searching for the best place on the wreckage to make his first cut. "I'd never steal from the government. Let 'em have those German boys, I say, *and* their guns."

He struck his torch alight, producing a hissing oxyacetylene flame that burned nearly as hot as the planet's core. The black-haired feline, unfrightened by the noise, seemed intrigued by the bright cutter.

"On the other 'and," the human said, raising his voice to a near-yell to be heard over the torch, "the Ruperts won't get here 'til forever, and I *did* find it first. Totally 'armless to take a few pieces for the collection!"

His vocal efforts were wasted, as Mouse spoke no English. Yet, Sam had convinced himself that he was doing his countrymen a favor by helping to dispose of the wreck—surely, the engine would just get in the way of any official salvage effort, he rationalized.

He held the torch steadily and worked quickly, not taking care to preserve the integrity of the plane. In spite of the attack from the Spitfire and the violence of the crash landing, Fe's steel spinner-cone, the propeller's fragile wooden blades, and the bulk of the port engine itself remained in remarkable condition.

Sam's torch ripped through the metal holding the engine to the wing. Burning acetylene gas, fed pure oxygen, created a man-made fire hotter than anything ancient forgemasters like Quishda could dream of. Steel and aluminum pieces alike found their atoms flooded with such thermal energy that they gave up on their bonds, ionizing by the trillions and forming scorched bubbles of hot metal that flowed like wax under Sam's flame. It took the better part of an hour for the scrapper to separate the engine safely from the *Fleischerbeile*'s wing. Far from the hot action, the atom Fe had little to do with the gas cutter's ravages.

Before he made the final cuts, Sam started his truck and backed the iron trailer into position. The engine hung less than a meter off of the ground, which suited Sam.

"Any higher," he explained to the cat, "and we can't catch 'er without destroying the trailer. Now come here, you." Sam bundled the shorthair in his arms and tossed her, hissing, into the truck's cab. "Can't have you underfoot for this, lovey," the human apologized.

A few more minutes of cutting were all he needed, and the bomber's engine shuddered and tore free of the body of the wing. Gravity reigned for an instant. Then, a terribly loud bang echoed through the still morning as a six-hundred-kilogram engine landed on the bed of the trailer.

Sam caught his breath and looked around, fearing discovery. No one was in sight, but he felt that his time of grace was drawing short.

"Success, Mouse! Now, let's scamper."

Packing up the torch and making sure the cat hadn't escaped the cab, he climbed back into his mongrel truck and drove toward the road. Weighed down by a trailer and the purloined engine, the vehicle struggled and protested.

Sam was easing the truck onto the path that would take him home when he spotted something sticking out from the soil of a nearby field–the tail section of the Ju-88. Torn free from the bomber during the crash, it had embedded in the soft dirt of a fallow field. It caught the morning sunlight like a crooked steel flag, and the Englishman noticed a black swastika, outlined in white, emblazoned on its grey surface. Sam stopped the car and stared at the symbol.

His wife had been a Catholic, which essentially made him a Catholic for the time they were together. The truth was that Sam never really believed in much of anything, and the last day that he went to a church was the day he buried his wife.

No ritual populated his childhood memories, and no father had stuck around to force a faith upon the son. His mother had been born Jewish, but no one still lived who had known the woman, and even Sam rarely gave her much thought these days. Still, something didn't sit right with the old scrapper and the mocking monument of the *Fleischerbeile's* tail section.

"Gimme a minute, Mouse," he said. "I missed a spot."

Though he feared discovery at any moment, Sam climbed from his truck, once again hoisted his cutting torch, and walked across the field to where the bomber's former stabilizer jutted from the earth. After several minutes, he returned to his truck and continued the short drive down the road to his home. Behind, on the plane's severed tail section, the Nazi symbol had been melted into an unrecognizable blob.

\#

The engine assembly was destined to remain in Cheshire with Sam Stills for the rest of his life. He kept the mechanical hulk in an overgrown corner of his yard, adjacent to a shed filled with decades of bric-a-brac. Mouse, for her part, kept the area clear of the nests of her namesake. Placed back from the road, the German treasure was firmly hidden from view. Sam dared not show his prize to any of his friends in town—the last thing anyone wanted to see was more of the Luftwaffe. He would wait until the timing was right before trying to sell.

To that end, he covered the engine, propeller and all, with a tarpaulin made from waterproof black cloth. Occasionally, he would sneak out to the yard, peel back the coverings, and press his hand against the cold metal that encased the powerful machine.

As the Second Great War spread itself across two hemispheres, Fe and the port engine waited, quiet and dry, in the scrap collector's weed-riddled yard. Fortunately for Sam and his countrymen, the bombings of Liverpool tapered off shortly after the *Fleischerbeile's* crash. Four years after Patty and Mecquenem peered through Louvre windows, watching as the German army marched into Paris, their Allied forces reclaimed the City of Lights. As the soldiers marched further east, they found unspeakable horrors that had been abandoned and half-covered up by the retreating Germans.

One night, in the spring of nineteen-hundred and forty-five, Sam Stills spent the evening drinking and singing with old friends in town. Mouse joined him on the excursion, though she spent most of her time hiding under the table, avoiding the many joyous stomping feet.

"Hitler is dead!" They cheered, again and again.

"The war is over!"

Sam imbibed too much ale and began bragging about his captured German bomber engine. Either nobody believed the old scrap collector, or his friends were too drunk to later remember. In any case, not a soul brought it up over the subsequent days and weeks.

In the wider Solar system, nuclear fusion continued to be the sole domain of the Sun, heir to the Mother Star before it. In the chaos of the latter's death, however, atomic children spawned, massive enough to spontaneously disintegrate and release floods of energy in the process–fission, rather than fusion. For billions of years, this simple process of random rupture proceeded, atom by atom, each decay giving off tiny sparks of energy and warming the cores of the planets. However, the same year Sam Stills got drunk celebrating Adolph Hitler's suicide, far-off humans used bombs to erase cities, triggering, for the first time on the Earth's surface, nuclear reactions that birthed elements, burning like backward stars.

Sam's plan to sell the engine after the end of the conflict never materialized, and it remained a secret and well-cared-for trophy. He would always come up with an excuse for not letting it go–the war was still too fresh in people's memories, the scrap market wasn't what it used to be, and his truck was acting up. In truth, the presence of the stolen bomber engine simultaneously comforted and invigorated old Sam. Even at the dawn of hostilities, he'd been too advanced in years to help defend his people. Stealing a crucial part of a deadly German bomber was a consolation conquest for the collector, even if his mind had to twist its own logic to connect at the ends.

As the years piled one atop the next, the collection of scrap surrounding Fe's engine grew larger and larger. Sam fleetingly considered selling an item here or there, but for the most part, trash or treasure, he hoarded.

On occasion, the Stills children, who by now approached middle age, would visit the old home in Cheshire. They patiently indulged their father's hobby, but the family always stayed at inns or hotels, never venturing, unless forced, into the chaos of Sam's scrapheap. Only one of his grandchildren, a sharp-eyed lad called Noel, seemed intrigued by the collection. He was born to Sam's first son, a vigorous man who enjoyed a successful business career in London, managed to wriggle away from any sort of military involvement, and, at last, retired in the fat post-war decades to start a family with a much-younger woman.

Young Noel loved his scrap-collecting grandfather, even as the man grew decidedly queer and doddery in his advanced age. Some of the old man's collection Noel found fascinating, other parts, such as the creepy stuffed-and-mounted black cat, were just frightening. All of it was interesting. Indeed, the grandson had inherited old Sam's knack for appreciating beauty, and later, value, in the discarded remnants of their high-industrial civilization. For instance, a row of bright, complex pinball machines that Noel first saw as neat toys, wasted and mouldering away in an outbuilding, he grew to see as valuable and rare collector's items as the years ticked by.

"Let me show you something my boy," Old Sam offered, conspiratorially, during one of Noel's increasingly-frequent visits. "Something I've never shown anybody before."

His motorized wheelchair whirred to life with a room-filling whine, lurching with liquid speed down through the hallway and out to the side yard. The old man was as ancient as the sea if he was a day, and nobody, not even his favored grandson, had any notion of Sam's true age. Years leave rust on the sharpest of edges, however, and something similar happens with the human mind, if not its spirit. Teenaged Noel doubted very much that he was about to see some new and secret treasure.

"Here, here. Underneath here."

His grandfather looked toward a corner of the yard, indicating impatiently that Noel should help him clear the old sacks and pieces of particle board that had accumulated into a vast midden.

As they worked, a gigantic metallic shape began to emerge. First one propeller blade, then the next—soon, Fe's tarnished cone appeared, warmed by the sun's rays for the first time in years. Eventually, the Stills men succeeded in revealing the entire rusted mass of the *Fleischerbeile*'s port-side engine.

"This," the old scrapper announced, with all the pride of a grand museum's curator, "is the better part of the engine of a Junkers-88. That's a German warplane, boy. I shot 'er down meself as she was trying to bomb Liverpool back in 'forty-one."

Noel had seen the bomber engine a number of times, but this was the first time he'd heard Grandpa Sam add the bit about shooting the thing down himself. The piece, Noel thought, would be in surprisingly good condition if it were cleaned up. Indeed, it was becoming harder and harder for collectors to get their hands on authentic articles from the war.

"She's beautiful," Noel beamed back, not without honesty. "It's a shame such a great piece is buried out here, though. You have so many beautiful things, Grandpa. People should see 'em."

"I'm showing them to you, eh?" Sam half-coughed half-laughed. "Are you a blind man? Are you not people?"

"Oh, come off it. I mean something like opening a shop. You'd have the best antiques around. People would come from miles!"

"Under no bloody circumstances!" Sam wheeled his chair violently backwards.

Noel assumed the crazy old codger had souped it up somehow.

"Imagine—a shop in 'ere! A bunch of damned looky-loos coming in to steal me things."

"You're right—you're right," the grandson said, holding out his hands placatingly. He glanced again at the engine, taking a moment to appreciate the complex beauty of such a harshly-efficient device.

"But Grandpa Sam, there's no reason why you need to keep all your treasures in such a sorry state. If you trust me to view them, at least trust me to clean and organize them for you. No looky-loos, just family."

Even a man as stubborn as Old Sam had trouble quibbling with such a reasonable request.

"Oh, all right," he grumbled, at last. "I suppose the polishing and tidying up might've gotten away from me a bit recently. Only a bit, mind you—but, yes, perhaps it's best to let eager young 'ands take on the labor."

Pleased with the inch his grandfather had given him, Noel prepared to take a mile.

Cataloging and organizing Sam's junk heap became Noel's new hobby and later, much to the frustration of his new bride Jo, his vocation. He took to sorting scraps into marketable pieces like a man driven. The grandson's days were spent cleaning oddities, finding places for them, and, somewhat covertly, professionally photographing each for later research and sale. The *Fleischerbeile's* engine, however, proved a challenge.

During one unseasonably dry week, while Sam sat in a Liverpool hospital recovering from surgery, Noel decided to tackle the metal beast. Immediately, he found that the years had not been kind to it. In addition to the obvious corrosion and denting on its surface, the engine's interior maze of twisting metallic honeycombs had become a condominium for generations of mice. Noel found an air-compressor and used its hose to try and evict the entrenched tenants, but quickly gave up, deeming the engine a lost cause.

However, the attractive propeller assembly, including Fe's shield cone, seemed to be in good enough condition. Without asking, or even stopping to think of asking, Noel located a cutter and got to work slicing through the alloy shaft that held the assembly to the main body of the Jumo. Once separated, he dragged the awkward, three-bladed piece to live indoors, where there were fewer rodents.

Eventually, Noel Stills decided that there was no reason why he shouldn't remodel his grandfather's buildings entirely—all to better hold the treasures scattered around the property. He planned a back storeroom filled with shelving and a large front for the more impressive pieces, such as the *Fleischerbeile's* propeller, with plenty of counters and glass displays thrown in for good measure.

Though at odds in the matter of outside sales, Noel and Sam were similarly practical men. The grandson reasoned that he could still honor the man's wishes while he lived, but that didn't mean Noel couldn't make preparations for the day when time inevitably expired Sam's prohibitions.

\#

Noel's son George arrived on Earth too late to meet his great-grandfather, though the patriarch's spirit lived on in a family legacy of collecting. Old Sam's scrapheap blossomed into a fairly successful antiques and curios shop, frequented by travelers charmed by its location amongst the hedges of Liverpool's exurbs. Noel did a brisk business with the tourist trade, augmenting profits by adding the shop's inventory to worldwide e-commerce platforms on the newfangled internet.

He kept some of Sam's pieces permanently off-limits to customers, however. The port engine propeller assembly, for instance, never received a pricetag, and Noel entertained no offers, stingy or generous, for its sale. Instead, Fe's assembly, sliced from the *Fleischerbeile,* stood vigil above the sales counter, mounted in a round hole left after a heating unit had been replaced.

The propeller was an impressive-piece, one that baby George had taken to crawling up shelves to try and reach. He was a queer child, given to long periods spent staring at shiny objects—and nonverbal too, up to an unusual age. Jo, the boy's mother, worried about a childhood spent among heaps of an old man's things, but George was well-fed and healthy, and as Noel was fond of pointing out, he seemed enraptured by his odd surroundings.

One one occasion, strapping young George toddled his chubby-ankled legs between shelves of his father's locked-away treasures and came across Fe's shiny propeller assembly, for once out of its usual position. Someone had leaned the heavy piece of war memorabilia against a side door, having briefly taken it down so that its mounting hardware could be replaced with something sturdier. George cared not for the why, moving instead, as fast as his doughy legs would take him, toward Fe's shiny, shielded spinner-cone.

Leaning forward on the pads of his feet, baby George reached up to grip one of the propeller's blades. The child, new to walking, quickly lost his balance, saving himself only by the grace of one hand clumsily clutching a blade's leading edge. For a moment, all was still, but then, gravity laughed, and the entire assembly came crashing down on the bewildered George, who had no time to scream.

The propeller's leading edge sliced downward, shattering through a glass display case with one iron-hard blade of laminated wood. George would have been crushed as well, had Fe's steel half-shell not thudded first into a sturdy bit of wooden shelving frame, arresting the assembly's fall.

George, stunned but unharmed, silently exhaled and crawled away from the wreckage, moving carefully so as not to cut his soft-skinned hands on bits of scattered glass.

As he grew, George proved to be as unique a specimen as any in Sam's collection. The shop's older, genteel clientele found the boy odd but delightful. Nearly non-verbal as he was, though, the schools quickly gave up on the youngest Stills, deeming him just another Special Case. Had George's schools possessed the patience and resources to understand him, they would have found the boy quick with his sums as well as a dogged, if not altogether gifted, reader. Socially, he was peculiar, to be sure, often having trouble remembering names and maintaining eye-contact, but it was with science, creative writing, and most especially computer classes where George's innocent obtuseness drove his instructors mad.

"The young man's mind is as smooth as a stone!" A particularly blunt headmaster exclaimed once, when things began to grow untenable at the boy's latest school.

Jo and Noel sat in the stuffy wood-paneled office, their jaws clenched against more bad news. During the meeting, George answered no direct queries, instead, he did nothing but stare at the schoolmaster's feet, even going so far as to crawl around the side of the man's desk once he grew shifty and uncomfortable.

"His, er, biggest problem—" the headmaster continued, trying to hide his feet, "—is an indelible digital illiteracy of some type. Our school psychologist has diagnosed him a technophobe, but some of the instructors are saying 'Luddite,' a less clinical term of course. 'Creepy' comes up too, now and then."

Inevitably, the schoolmaster let the final blow fall—the institution no longer wished for George to attend its hallowed halls.

"You might consider homeschool," the headmaster offered, showing the Stills family from his office, "or perhaps one of the many excellent cd-rom education programs they have these days."

The news put Jo in tears, but to the boy's sunny-eyed father, it didn't seem like an altogether bad fate. Noel, who spent half his life on his phone, almost envied the boy's purity. When they arrived back home, Jo sank into an armchair and comfortably lost herself in the television.

George scampered off for a few minutes. Before anyone noticed he had gone, he re-emerged in the living room holding a Manolo Blahnik catalog–open to the page advertising the headmaster's distinctive calf-skin oxfords.

"See?" Noel declared, happily. "The boy's not dumb."

His father's easy contentment was a blessing to George, who never aspired to, nor was likely to be offered, any other job than working at Sam's Scrap: Antiques and Oddities.

This was just as well, as by the time George collected eleven years, he was already growing into the perfect physique for a scrap dealer–tall for his age and meaty about the upper body. Young George also sported a bird's-nest thatch of blonde hair atop his large, pale, egg-shaped head. He uncomplainingly dusted the shop's displays and repeated other small tasks for years, often without being asked. It grew commonplace for his parents to find young George cross-legged on the floor, ensconced in a stack of his father's catalogs and trade magazines, reading obsessively, if slowly. The boy's speech was also coming more regularly, but when he talked, it often emerged terse, as if he was put out by having to say anything at all

.

He grew tall enough to reach across the counter and could make change reasonably well. Young George learned that if he stood high on his tip-toes, he could just tap the shiny spinner cone of the old bomber engine, producing a pleasant, cleanly-ringing steel resonance. Locked in blocks of metallic crystal, Fe and its neighboring atoms vibrated to the young scrapper's strike, humming a soft tone, the influx of kinetic energy a small change from their normally static existence. The lad would always grin at the bright metallic ringing, and in time, a firm tap of the steel half-shell developed into a lucky habit for George Stills.

One day, on an August evening, Noel was staying late in the backroom of Sam's, ostensibly to update the shop's books and social media presence but, in reality, more as an excuse to spend as little time at home with Jo as possible. Sam's was closed, or so Noel believed, when he heard the tinkling of the bell at the shop door, followed by a metallic pinging echoing far louder than usual–his son had given the old German bomber bit an especially spirited knock this time.

Before Noel had time to properly wonder at the noise, George wandered in. The boy was holding a heavy gold coin between his thick fingers, staring unblinking at the gleaming metal.

Alongside a minority of copper atoms, the one ounce coin was composed of ten-billion-trillion tightly packed quanta of gold. These exalted atoms emerged from the Mother Star after Fe, representing a sort of apotheosis for its iron siblings. In the magnificent madness of the Mother's supernova nucleosynthesis death, some iron atoms rapidly clad themselves in neutrons, lapping greedily from a particle-rich molten atomic soup, collapsing and dying under the weight as if they were tiny stars themselves. They repeated the process again again in a death dance of microseconds, every time emerging as a different entity, ending up as gold–atoms whose stolidity and sheen captured the lust of the human species like no other. Even neurotypical pawnbrokers would stare, slack and George-like, at a concentration of gold atoms such as the one clutched in the boy's meaty hand.

"What's that you've got?" Noel asked, worried that his son had broken into the coin case.

"Krugerrand, Da'. Mint nine'een six'y-nine. Worth two a'three thousand pounds."

"Where'd you get it, lad?"

"Bought it," George answered, his eyes still locked on the coin.

"I beg your pardon?" With some indignation, Noel rose and approached his son, plucking away the krugerrand and staring at it incredulously. "You bought a gold coin for three-thousand pounds?"

"No, Da," George looked at his father, the tiniest bit of frustration creasing his blonde brow. "I gave 'im eighteen 'undred."

"Gave who?" Noel was growing confused, not an uncommon outcome when holding a conversation with George.

Eventually, he was able to extract a simple story. A customer had come in after closing time, needing money with some urgency, looking to sell rather than pawn.

Unilaterally, George had made the man an offer, written out a receipt, and taken cash from the floor safe.

Apparently, the combination-dial held no mysteries for the boy.

"I did ok, right Da?"

"Yes. Er, eighteen-hundred, you say?" Noel sputtered–he was still processing things and therefore responded unthinkingly with the truth. "That's a cracking good deal. Especially on gold. A cracking good deal, Georgie-boy."

The young man's pale eyebrows lifted, and his face spread into a huge smile. Noel saw little harm in what had transpired, and he decided quickly that this was all a Good Thing. He placed the coin back in his son's hand and added a set of keys from his own pocket.

"Be a good lad and put our new treasure in the case." Noel smiled back. "Oh, and make sure the front door is locked."

George complied, going to the door first, so as to spend longer fondling the gold coin before eventually surrendering it to the locked case. The iron atoms in his keys, long-lost cousins of spacebound Fe, had spent four-and-a-half billion years on Earth. Two billion years later, the gold atoms in the krugerrand rode a flaming asteroid through the atmosphere to a crash-landing on the planet's bacteria-slimed surface. Compared to most of the other atoms in the pawnshop, the well-traveled Fe, with its scant six millenia on Earth, was still little more than a visitor.

\#

George Stills already spent an inordinate amount of time in his father's shop, but Noel allowed him to become an unofficial partner after the impressive stunt with the krugerrand. Soon, Noel couldn't remember how he ever got along without the young man and his strange, smooth mind.

"Be a good lad and fetch me the price of silver," Noel asked, his hands busy taking apart a watch, "my mobile's on the desk."

"Twenty-one quid for'y pence," George answered automatically. He flinched at the thought of interacting with a phone, but he would often watch the commodities ticker at the bottom of the store's TVs whenever there was nowhere else interesting to rest his eyes.

George reached his maximum height in his late teens, and though his technological phobias and cloistered existence made him a social non-entity, his interactions with countless customers forged a proficient, if somewhat idiosyncratic, speaking style. If possible, George's encyclopedic knowledge of all things collectible reached even deeper levels as his teenaged brain entered its most absorbent years.

"Queen Victoria stamp," Noel called out on another occasion. "Eighteen seventy-six." He was bent over the counter, loupe to his eye, a customer with arms folded looming impatiently.

"Condition?" George shouted, his breaking adolescent voice carrying from the back storeroom.

"Rubbish. Backstamped," Noel answered, much to his customer's ire.

"Give 'im one fifty. No more."

Noel began to rely more and more on his son as the years passed, the shop's fortunes rising and falling with ever-fluctuating twenty-first century economic conditions.

"I need some exchange rates, Georgie."

"Use your phone, 's moving too fast."

"How much is Brexit going to fuck us?"

"One-hundred and ten percent, Da."

"George! This fella's trying to sell me a VR. Do you know if 'Magic Head' is a good brand?"

"Don't buy anya that shite, Da!"

"It's neat stuff, George. Not even credit?"

"We don't do that now, 'member?"

On one warm, lazy day at the shop, as Noel dealt with a customer, his adult son leaned on the counter nearby, half listening, half absorbed in a stack of print-outs listing historical firearm values. Even hunched over, George stood a head taller than his sire.

Noel was on the edge of finalizing a deal when the younger pawnbroker glanced over and let his stack of papers fall to the counter.

"Da–" George whispered, his enormous hand covering Noel's and the small Greek coin held within. "S'fake!"

"Er, I know," Noel lied, patting his son on the hand and fixing the customer with a hard-edged glare of triumph. "Take your phony scrip and go away, now, eh?"

The shop fell quiet during the pandemic lockdowns of the early twenties. Noel worked to expand the e-commerce side of the business, while George spent hours in silence, reading print-outs of webpages or reverently handling old cards and coins. As cloistered remote sellers grew increasingly desperate and bored, physical objects came more frequently, in and out, by post. Though the son wouldn't touch a computer if he could help it, he had no problem looking at still images Noel had frozen onscreen, delivering an 'S'fake, Da' when appropriate. No matter what else happened in the wider world, George would find time to dust and polish Fe's propeller assembly at least twice each month. Time stretched out, and life for the Stills men fell into a comfortable groove.

Already wealthy beyond his immediate needs due to his late father's business ventures, Noel long operated Sam's Scrap primarily as a passion project, but with George running the non-technical side of the shop with his uncanny knack, it grew into a more-than-successful moneymaking venture. Even after Jo had left him, Noel spent many happy years of semi-retirement trading junk and shouting across the room to his son.

"London Calling, nineteen seventy-nine, original pressing maybe."

"Wherefrom?" George would shout back.

"Er, Canadian.""Give 'im twenny quid."

"Did gem prices go up or down after the attack?"

"Neither!"

"Take a look at this Montblanc, would you lad?"

"S'fake, Da."

The shop never lacked for beautiful and rare objects to fascinate its proprietors and their visitors, and more years passed–numbered and collected–like currency across their counter.

Suburbs around the county's two large cities waxed and sprawled, new housing developments devouring the receding countryside. The modest pawnshop and its lands and buildings, however, resisted the tide. Sam's Scrap became something of an institution, and George found himself occupying a niche somewhere between local color and local legend. An enterprising citizen-reporter even ran a story about the uncanny Mr. Stills in a free multimedia periodical published for antiquers and tourists– "Modern-Day Relic: Human AI at Charming Cheshire Pawnshop can't be Cheated or Hacked!"

"It's a little ungenerous of them to call us a 'Pawn Shop,'" Noel complained upon seeing the headline, "but it's good publicity."

Noel's assessment proved prescient, as the puff piece in the circular happened to reach the eyes of Travis DeMarco, the highest-paid athlete in professional basketball, via those of his girlfriend Holly. Following an exhibition game in London, the couple embarked upon a 'rustic auto tour of Britain' as Holly insisted on calling it. She also insisted on stopping at the charming antique shop she'd read about scrolling between 'Liverpool' and 'Manchester' on the travel guide.

"Oh, honey, it's so *quaint*," Holly observed, walking into Sam's Scrap: Antiques and Oddities ahead of Travis.

The starting center for the Washington Wizards felt irrepressibly stifled by the trip, bored beyond his worst fears after three days touring the drizzly island. To him, Sam's little shop looked identical to all the others he'd visited during antiquing purgatory, except for the crazy, kinda-badass propeller hanging off the back wall.

He snapped a quick selfie–Fe's propeller assembly in the background, a posing, pouty superstar in the fore. Glancing at his phone and noting his interactions were down, Travis found that Sam's also boasted surprisingly strong signal strength.

As Holly leaned over a counter to look at antique rings, DeMarco figured he'd start rolling video for his followers.

"Hold this, baby," he said, placing the phone in a pocket of his girlfriend's bag, positioning it camera-side-out.

Holly rolled her eyes but made no move to stop Travis.

"It's a mercantile mission in England. Quiet, y'all. I'm gonna try something," he whispered to the phone before walking up to the counter.

George, the only Stills on the premises while Noel was having his colon checked at the hospital in town, stood hunched over the counter, reading a catalog and paying the customers as little attention as possible.

"Hey, slice, what's good?" Travis said, by way of greeting.

"'ello," George looked up.

Travis waited expectantly, towering over the Englishman by a smaller margin than he did most people, but when nothing further was said, the pawnbroker returned to his reading.

"He doesn't know who I am!" Travis turned and whispered theatrically, making a mock-sad face for the camera.

Holly shot him a withering look, but DeMarco ignored her. He was starting to have fun for the first time all day.

"Slice. A minute of your time." He stepped back over, again angling for George's attention. "I've got some foreign currency to trade. American. Straight from DC. I'm something of an ambassador."

"Stop messing with the man," Holly hissed, under her breath.

"Know anything about coins?" Travis asked.

"A fair bit," George replied, paying Holly no mind.

With a long arm, the athlete dug into his deepest pocket, extracting a small handful of American dimes and nickels and slapping them on the counter.

"Pure silver, I think," Travis said, keeping his face serious and pointing to the coins.

"Thir'y five pence, take it or leave it," George replied—counting the scattered change, converting it, and slicing off a percentage for the house all in the space of a blink.

"We have a deal, my good sir." Travis bowed.

The pawnbroker didn't react. He simply turned toward the cash register and began counting out coins. The amused celebrity leaned toward his girlfriend's bag, doubled over in silent laughter.

George took Travis' American coins and placidly replaced them with a lesser amount of British currency, along with a receipt and an ink pen.

"Is this worth anything?" Travis asked, holding up the pink transfer-paper he had just signed.

George simply stared.

"Not into memorabilia? Man, you're a trip. Thanks."

"Nine'een thousand."

"What?" For a moment, he was stunned that George had said anything.

"Nine'een thousand pounds sterling."

"Dang, slice-bay-bee, hell yeah I'll sell you my autograph for that!"

"Nah." George was staring not at the receipt but at the hand holding it. "The ring, mate. Twenny thir'y-two NBA Championship. Travis DeMarco—his first. Nine'een thousand quid. Take it or leave it."

The surprised celebrity glanced down at his bejeweled little finger.

"He knows who you are after all, baby," Holly laughed. "He just doesn't give a shit!"

#

Clips from the livestream attained a measure of virality, enough that the shop's online traffic increased markedly over the next few months, much to the delight of its aging owner. Video of the superstar center trying, unsuccessfully, to mess with a simple English pawnbroker also made George Stills something of a hero to fans of rival teams.

Despite the shop's rise in popularity, the year that followed the DeMarco deal was destined to be the saddest of George's life. Time had transformed Noel into someone old and fragile. The elderly human wore too thin, in too many small, invisible places. A quirk of circulation was all it took—here one moment, gone the next in a stroke.

The shop's other employees were surprised to see George at work the morning after his father's sudden passing. George, who lived in a building on the property, hadn't once entertained the idea of not opening up Sam's Scrap for the day. He was a part of it, as intrinsic and predictable as the guts inside a clock.

Things moved a bit slower, a bit quieter, without Noel around. A revolving door of interns managed to keep the e-commerce side of Sam's afloat, and business as usual, at least as usual as possible, continued for George–there just wasn't anyone around to call him 'lad' anymore, and he had nobody to call 'Da'.

Two weeks after the funeral, newly in-charge George faced his first serious management decision.

"Mr. Stills?" A man with an American accent was talking to him.

He wore a suit made of a dark blue, semi-translucent fabric and a knitted cap adorned with muted LEDs. George, wearing a pair of twenty-year-old denim coveralls and sporting a thinning tangle of straw-colored hair, forced a smile but said nothing.

"Mr. Stills? Yes? Do I have the right place?"

Slowly, it dawned on George that he was Mr. Stills now.

"Yessir, thas' me."

"Ok, great! I read about your shop on my phone. I was hoping you could tell me what these are worth?"

The American retrieved four small, plastic objects and carefully set them between himself and George on the countertop.

Rather than picking them up, the pawnbroker lowered himself down, placing the objects at eye-level. They were brightly-colored toys, each in the shape of a crime-fighting animal-hybrid cartoon character. George recognized them as collectibles promoting a popular children's series from an earlier generation.

"Worthless, mate," George said, rising slowly out of his squat.

"What? Not worth anything?" The customer asked, a strange smile on his face. "How can you be so sure?"

"S'fake," George said, picking up a pen and pointing to a smooth patch on one of the creatures' backs. "Real 'uns have a seam. Sonic welding."

"Ha!" The customer slapped the counter, beaming. "That only took you a second. Blam! They were right about you."

George did not know quite what to make of this reaction. He'd hoped the interaction would end once he'd given his appraisal. Usually customers stormed out with anger, or guilt, when they failed to sell a forged collectible.

"Forgive me, I had those printed up for fun," the man in the suit explained. "High-quality, expensive job too, but it didn't fool you! That's why I'm here, Mr. Stills. Forgive my subterfuge, but I want to make a different kind of deal."

"What'r you on about?"

"I represent BookLungs. I'm one of their producers."

This announcement seemed to make no impact, so the man continued. "You know, 'BookLungs Streaming Service: entertainment to breathe-in.' You have the BookLungs app, right?"

"Nah."

"That's ok. We're new, but growing every day. I'm currently working on expanding our reality content. What kind of reality shows do you watch, Mr. Stills?"

After a moment spent processing, George lit up.

"BBC News."

The producer gave a strained smile. From an inside pocket, he removed a soft-tablet and unrolled it on the counter.

"See, it's this one." He tapped a purple and gold spider-shaped icon on the screen.

The icon expanded, loading the BookLungs app with a flourish of webbing animation. Content offerings from the streaming service populated the tablet, thumbnail images spewing across its screen. The tappable squares, the American demonstrated, led to popular clips, original series, user-generated content including pornography, all-ages animation from around the world, DIY tutorials, cooking videos, something labeled 'DarkWebz,' and pages more.

"Very pretty," the pawnbroker said, watching the user interface with a growing sense of vertigo.

"And we want you to be a part of it all, Mr. Stills." He clapped his hands together loudly, startling George. "Blam! We'll call it 'Pawnshop: UK!' A reality program set in this very store—we'll do short-form, 'sode length, a long doc, zoomerangs, and your basic brand package to start."

The producer was interacting with his device as he spouted buzzwords, closing the streaming entertainment and opening contract PDFs.

"Standard stuff—we did the same thing for 'Paris: City of Cake!' Acceptable overhead for us and very low impact to your business. Blam! I'm betting it will be a lot of fun. You've been making content all this time without even *knowing* it. Now you've got a ticket to the fame train, and it's time to climb aboard.

"Listen, Mr. Stills," the man continued, pitching his voice down in an attempt to put George at ease, "this has been in the works for a while. We talked to your father about the same streaming deal, you know."

This was technically true, as representatives from BookLungs, appreciating the shop's potential to be turned cheaply into content, had indeed corresponded with Noel, who found their terms unacceptable and manipulative. After weeks of ignoring their messages, the aging scrapper finally roused himself, jumped onto a video call, and told the BookLungs producers to bugger off.

"He was very excited, from what I heard—there just wasn't time to set everything up before, well, you know," the flamboyant producer fabricated. "My sincerest condolences, by the way, Mr. Stills. But trust me, Noel would want this to go forward."

"Erm. Ok." George tried to squint and read what he could see of the contract, being careful not to touch the tablet. "Well, if Da' was good on it..."

Taking this as a yes, the producer thrust out his hand to shake.

"Here's to fame and fortune."

George shook the offered hand with some hesitation. The American's skin felt cold, with an unpleasant moistness. George slowly pivoted and slapped his palm against the fragment of the warplane in a variation of his lucky ritual. The cold metal was comforting against his skin, as was the ringing and resonance of Fe's sprawling steel crystal—the pawnbroker would need all the good luck he could get. Rather than break his technological aversion, George signed things he couldn't, and didn't try to, read all the way through. This suited the company well, as even the savviest of their content-creators routinely neglected to read their own expertly-nuanced contracts.

A BookLungs technician arrived at Sam's to wire the store for video and sound, finishing in a matter of hours. They showed George where the tiny cameras were placed and which angles worked best for getting good footage, but the pawnbroker quickly forgot. Every transaction that took place at Sam's went through the company's electronic eyes, and the most interesting, surprising, and humorous interactions were cut, packaged, and uploaded onto the digital streaming smorgasbord.

Some months passed, and it became common for George to go days at a time without remembering that he starred in a multiplatform digital series. The only hints were the increasing strangeness of some customers, as well as the small royalty checks he received periodically from BookLungs, Inc.

\#

The customer with the purple platform shoes and fussy moustache took some effort to catch George's attention. The pawnbroker hoped one of his workers would speak up first.

"I said, you have some really interesting pieces out here. Truly beautiful," the customer called out. "I might have one to offer myself, to contribute, if the price is right."

He hoisted a battered guitar case clad in synthetic leather.

George turned and peered at the smaller man, blinking like an amphibian on a chilly morning. Taking this as encouragement, the customer hefted his case onto the shop's glass counter.

"This place is amazing," he gushed, drumming painted fingers on the faux-leather case.

"Oh, yessir, lotsa 'ntresting pieces. This one's me favorite," George answered belatedly, pointing one thumb behind him. "Me gray' granpa shot it down 'imself."

A meaty pink paw pounded the assembly. Fe, stranded with septillions of siblings, vibrated for some time and was still.

"Not for sale, though, o'course."

"No worries. Not looking to buy," the flashy customer said, firmly in control of his patience. "I'm here to sell, hopefully."

He clicked open brass latches and hefted the case's lid, revealing a handsome, if surprisingly weathered, guitar. A very old electric model, the instrument boasted a faded white-and-red contoured body, two black knobs, and a neck of polished rosewood.

To George, for an extended moment, there was nothing in the store but that guitar. His eyes devoured its lines, and his smooth mind digested their implications.

"Blimey, thassa nine'een fify-seven Telecaster." George whistled, not taking his gaze from the instrument.

He lifted it from its case in his powerful, clumsy-looking hands. The customer gave a theatrical wince, but George handled the Telecaster with perfect grace.

"Yep, yep," he said, "Fender knobs."

"Please be careful. It's an antique," the moustache whined. "It was owned by Muddy Waters himself."

"Muddy Waters!"

George, as wide-eyed as if the rosewood frets had just turned to spiders, swiftly returned the guitar to its case and rubbed his hands nervously on his coveralls, as if trying to wipe something away.

"Mate—you're yankin' me. Muddy Water's fify-seven Fender Telecaster. The very'un he played on Electric Mud? The 'oss? Genuine article?" George's egg-shaped head gradually boiled from white to pinkish-red.

"The very same!" The customer replied, beaming.

"Promise?"

"Yes, I promise it's genuine. The Hoss. Now let's talk price."

George's face set in a hard line. He turned from the customer, bent to his knees, and stood up, pulling a heavy, antique corded-telephone from a shelf underneath the counter. Perhaps charmed by the owner's use of a landline, the customer watched for a moment as George spun the device's rotary dial, baffled and oblivious to any danger.

"Can we talk price? What are you doing, man?" The customer asked, as George continued the long process of dialing.

"Phoning the police."

"What?" The customer's moustachioed face paled. "Why?"

"You promised, annit looks real to me." George glared. "Means you robbed the Rockinroll 'all of Fame."

Briefly, he set the phone down, reached up, and tapped a sign hanging from the ceiling–WE DO NOT BUY STOLEN MERCHANDISE. Trillions of tin atoms, nearly twice as heavy as iron, hung in metallic-bonded lattice within the sign–each forged from the fusion-deaths of Fe's identical twins during their mutual Mother's last moments. In the little shop on the little island on the blue Earth, the tins' molecular heaviness manifested in a hollow, less-than-soothing clanging sound when struck against the hard keratin proteins in George's stubby fingernail.

"Police? Wait, no!" The customer gushed, horrified. "I didn't rob anything! You can put that, uh, phone down. I must have made a mistake. The Telecaster is a replica. A replica–completely slipped my mind to mention. Silly me."

George hung up the phone, relieved that he wouldn't have to bother explaining to the operator that he needed to speak with the police in Cleveland, America. The sweating customer was hurriedly packing up the guitar, which made George the slightest bit sad. It was a very good replica, after all.

"Eigh'y quid?"

"What's that?" The customer turned, by then almost safely to the door.

"Eigh'y quid for the fake Fender."

The flamboyant fraud stood in the middle of the store and glanced around himself, seemingly unsure of what to do. "Lovely, thanks," he finally replied, in something of a stupor.

Much more slowly than the customer would have liked, George peeled off four twenty-pound notes and painstakingly wrote out a paper receipt. These he handed to the moustached man, who snatched at them and shoved the ersatz antique guitar across the counter.

Minutes later, outside the shop and around the corner, the customer walked over to meet a producer in a parked panel van. The white electric vehicle's sliding door opened, revealing a young woman wearing a khaki romper. Though further down the corporate hierarchy than the suit who had signed George, she served as the main showrunner for Pawnshop: UK. It was her idea to hire the planted customer and source the replica Telecaster.

Next to her in the van sat a tech wearing an enormous pair of headphones upon his bald head, his intense blue eyes glued to the numerous camera feeds.

"Good job," she said expressionlessly, paying the actor his expected two hundred pound scale fee.

Magnanimously, she didn't inquire about the eighty he'd skimmed from selling their prop.

"This is gold," the tech said, rewinding the footage after the moustache had left.

The showrunner grabbed her own set of headphones and watched the playback. When she saw George turning red with genuine emotion, her tongue peeped out and moistened her upper lip.

"He really looks like he's gonna phone the bizzies," the tech chuckled. "Did you set that up?"

"Negative." The producer removed her headphones, wincing as they tore out a strand of her long hair, caught in the bracket, "I think that lump was serious. He looks like he's about to pound my extra into dogmeat."

"That's why it's funny!"

"Yeah?" She asked, letting a tiny smile come to her lips. "Gold?"

"Gold," her tech nodded back.

\#

It wasn't George's first time as a meme, but this one had staying power. Previous viral clips of the pawnbroker, along with fan-made stills and inside jokes, garnered some shares and chuckles, but the showrunner and her tech had been right–George's 'phoning the police' proved more profitable than gold.

In its final form, the meme displayed a still or mobile-looped image with a split pane–the left half could be filled with any number of personal or pop-culture references, but the right side was always the same picture of pinkening George, hard-faced, with an antique phone to his ear and the phrase 'I'm phoning the police' printed below. Appropriate for expressing a humorous overreaction or calling one out on their deception, the format quickly became social-media canon. Long after Pawnshop UK's novelty faded and it became just another dusty fixture on the BookLungs service, the slightly-misquoted 'phoning the police' meme stayed in regular rotation.

Sam's Scrap: Antiques and Oddities, originally the private hoard of old Sam Stills, had grown into a can't-miss destination. A good fraction of the hundred-million-strong population of Britain was by then familiar with George's series, as were many of the tourists who dared travel to Northwestern England. On weekends, there was always a line out the door. Wishing to avoid any bother during the hours when the shop closed for business, George reluctantly moved off the old property, taking a unit in a building with a garage, closer to the city.

While the crowds were a constant irritant to George, he gladly tolerated them on the chance that any given yahoo may be holding objects of great value and rarity. Unfortunately for the pawnbroker, most of the treasures brought in by fans turned out to be junk. Having a go at the smooth-minded Mr. Stills had become part of the series' appeal, and patrons would often try to grab five minutes of fame by fruitlessly attempting to pass off trash as treasure.

"Worthless, mate," George said, referring to the fake stock certificates in a customer's portfolio.

He said the same thing to a woman trying to sell her own painting and a twitchy man trying to pawn a bag of golden chocolate coins. Advances in printing technologies meant that even a mildly tech-savvy member of the general public could create three-dimensional forgeries that would have fooled most pawnbrokers a generation prior. It was theorized by commenters that the man who distrusted technology could smell its traces on ersatz collectables in a subtle manner that no one, not even George himself, could fully articulate.

"Worthless, mate!" George would sometimes announce, even before the potential customer made it to the counter. "Get out. You're 'olding up the line."

"Worthless, mate. Amazon sticker, right 'ere."

"Nah, mate. We don't buy animals."

These snap judgments delighted the audience of Pawn Shop: UK and Pawn Shop UK: Best of George. Facemasks, gloves, bags, and shirts printed with the slogan 'Worthless, mate!' sold briskly, and the store's support staff began running a merch gift shop in a newly-built anteroom. One morning, a pair of young friends spent over an hour waiting in line, just to try to sell George the very 'Worthless, mate!' t-shirts they were wearing, having purchased them while in the queue.

"Worthless, mate," George said tiredly, when it was finally their turn.

The teens celebrated this with such unbridled joy that even George cracked a smile.

Not everything that came into the shop was worthless. A one-of-a-kind place in itself, Sam's Scrap attracted its fair share of oddities and treasure. Over the years, customers brought in pieces of bespoke jewelry, celebrity artifacts, clever mechanical watches, and memorabilia from both World Wars. On a memorable occasion, George purchased a Formula One car from a walk-in, sight unseen. He offered the customer the vehicle's scrap value, never believing the man would accept or that the car would be real. George briefly parked the flashy thing in front of his shop, until, mere days later, a moneyed collector snapped it up. The pawnbroker made a neat profit without having to do much of anything. After the NeoEU transitioned to fully digital currency, the shop successfully expanded its trade in highly-collectable coins and bills.

Naturally, this was never enough for the BookLungs people. Good content required a steady stream of interesting and attention-grabbing interactions.

"Keep it fresh," they repeated, like a mantra.

Permission from the proprietor, the producers long ago realized, was too much of an impediment to their grand narrative schemes. The first time they had brought up the idea of planting TV-ready customers with interesting items at Sam's, the conversation had gone so poorly and ended in such confusion, the showrunners decided to simply execute their plans without informing George beforehand.

Along with the ersatz Hoss guitar, planted actors and extras came to Sam's bearing a bazaar of bizarre items–taxidermied cryptids, ancient Roman coins both real and fabricated, weaponry from historic battles, pirate treasure, forged biblical relics, and even a painting by an early twentieth-century master, which BookLungs had borrowed from a private collector whom they'd had to reimburse after George struck an unexpected deal on the item.

George Stills rode the flow of time to late middle age. His head lost its hair, and he gained weight, but the pawnbroker's memory stayed sharp. He still found time to polish his treasured warplane propeller and Fe's good-luck steel cone.

The august proprietor was engaged in this very task when an older child, dark-eyed and small for his age, pushed among the flood of chattering patrons in the pawnshop's anteroom. When he finally passed the queue and stepped onto the main sales floor, no one fell over themselves to help him. A trio of patched, shabby drones buzzed around the young streamer's head. The eyes of the employees, including at least one planted BookLungs functionary, noted his presence, judged his likely socioeconomic status, and slid off him like oil. This left the boy free to walk straight up to the shop's owner.

"Hey."

He activated his drone net's recording and unslung a taped-together backpack.

"How can I 'elp you?" George asked once he turned and noticed the scrawny boy.

Placing his pack between his feet, the streamer guided out a large, plastiboard box.

"I saw you on the thing," he said to George. "They say you're spozed to be the man."

"How can I 'elp you?" The pawnbroker repeated, unsure what else to say.

"Sneakers," the kid answered, sliding the white, rectangular box across the counter. "Aprraisem, yeah?"

George flicked open the box's lid. His retinas immediately flooded with photons from the shop's overhead lights, reflected by the sneakers' brilliant white-and-gold finish. The pawnbroker blinked twice.

"S'fake," George said, flipping the lid closed. "Worthless, mate."

Illegal too, the pawnbroker suspected, but he'd had poor results the last few times he'd tried to summon the authorities.

"Starshit!" The kid began crying, more in frustration than anger. "I knew it, too. Dammit. I knew it." He turned, dejected, to his tiny, hovering cameras. "I did a lot to get these–y'all know it. Y'all *know* it!"

The child's watery eyes fell, his shoulders heaved, and he began to quiver and cry–his drone net drinking in every moment. George watched the strange tableau for a long time before speaking.

"Those are real."

"Huh?" The streamer sniffed.

"Those 'uns. On your feet."

"These pieces of shit?" The youth said, examining his own shoes, one tiny, patched drone-cam zooming down to collect detail. "They ain't ten years old, even."

"Wrong," George said simply.

When the kid threw out his hands in a gesture of perplexed annoyance, the pawnbroker continued.

"Nuthin' wears out like leather. Give you 'undred'n twenny NEOeuros for 'em."

"Pfft," the kid scoffed. "Get out of here, ol' man." "'undred twenny-two," George countered.

"What does this fool grandpa think I'm going outta here in?"

George slid the synthetic white shoebox back across his counter. "These 'uns."

"You called 'em 'worthless, mate,'" the streamer quoted back at George.

"Worthless, uh-huh," the pawnbroker nodded patiently, "but printed from that strong, fake shite tha' don't wear out."

Skeptically, the kid pulled off his worn shoes, which happened, through a quirk of unlikely donations, to be a rare edition of a sneaker model discontinued thirty years earlier. He handed them over. George gave his latest acquisitions a quick second glance, then, satisfied, pointed to an electric tile his employees had glued to the front of his station. Knowing what to do, the streamer stepped over, swiped his own device, and collected his bounty. Still, the old pawnbroker took out his ledgerbook and wrote out a physical receipt, tearing away the copy paper and handing it to the customer.

"Wha? A 'bill of goods sold,'" the boy read. "Why's it made of paper?"

George shrugged.

A few moments later, the customer called to George from the floor. "Can I have some morra those papers, ol' man? These gold-coated pieces of shit are too big for my feet."

#

Attention-challenged audiences devoured clips edited from the young customer's sneaker stream, their overstimulated minds able to process this simple reversal-of-fortune story in bite-size form. Some versions, with music added, even elicited tears from viewers who preferred human-interest clips to watching self-help sermons, personalized pornography, sports, or live betting pools for the latest superstorm numbers.

For the next fifteen to seventeen months, George Stills ranked among the world's most highly-regarded sneaker appraisers, though the community's attention eventually turned elsewhere.

A pair of buxom, large-eyed, twin-sister vagabonds showed up at Sam's one morning just after opening, trying to sell George a live specimen of an endangered primate. He turned them down flat, but the BookLungs producers chopped the girls' scene into heavy rotation, prompting the involvement of international animal and human rights activists. The twins parlayed their subsequent, highly-publicized trial into semi-successful singing careers and nearly a dozen shrewdly-marketed product lines.

Another Pawnshop: UK highlight occurred near the end of the series' run. A man with pale eyes and a long ponytail stood at the shop's counter, looking to unload the contents of a small, shielded briefcase.

"You the owner?" He asked George, who simply nodded.

The customer clicked open the latches of his case. Opening the lid only a few inches, he allowed the aging pawnbroker to bend down and peer inside. Within, a neat row of solid-state chips lay ensconced in foam.

George was unimpressed. "Devorah handles 'lectronics sales." He pointed across the counter to an employee with long, elaborate fingernails.

"I mean it—for the owner's eyes only," the customer said through gritted teeth.

"What's on 'em, then?"

"Gold, mate. Worth more than their weight in gold. Much more." His pale eyes gleamed. "Go on—plug them in!" "Nah," George said.

"You're gonna want to see this."

"Naah," the old pawnbroker repeated, louder and more slowly.

"You're the only one in the world that I'd trust with these, George Stills. I insist that you check out what I have here." The long-haired customer pushed the shielded case toward George, staring at him unblinking. "We're both gonna get rich, and, as a bonus, some truly *evil* motherfuckers are gonna pay!"

This outburst attracted the attention of the entire shop. A visored, uniformed security officer melted out from one corner, and the belligerent customer looked back at George, colorless eyes full of appeal. The proprietor, however, proved stony ground for the man's sympathies, and huffily, the ponytailed customer stormed out, case-in-hand and only one step ahead of store security.

BookLungs made clips from the incident, garnering healthy numbers of views but nothing spectacular. Days later, however, George found himself woken suddenly as a series of concussive booms shook the building. Puffy-eyed, he heaved himself up, leaving his favorite nap spot in the loft above the premises and waddling down to confront the commotion.

His shop was a mess, littered with bits of foam and broken glass. A strange smell hung in the air. George quickly noticed the ponytailed customer from the other day, pinned against one wall, restrained by thick ropes of hardened spray-foam.

"Whasol this?" He asked, sleepily.

His employees showed George the security footage–the intruder had fired several blasts from a high-powered rifle, aimed at the storefront from outside. The first shots shattered the shielded glass and passed through the anteroom. One bullet even found its way to the far back wall of the shop, embedding itself in plaster less than a foot away from where Fe's propeller assembly hung. Hoping to disable any security measures, the pale-eyed man triggered a portable electromagnetic pulse, but the shop's shielded network was among the best–rated to withstand a solar flare. Upon entering, the intruder found himself immediately apprehended, doused in a heavy spray of rapidly-hardening foam by the automated features of a frustratingly-advanced security system. Thus restrained, he hung, harmless, until the authorities could arrive to administer lethal force.

"Everything's under control sir," an employee assured George.

"No one 'urt?" He asked.

"No sir, we got lucky."

"Lucky?" George asked.

The employee nodded.

Satisfied, George nodded back, then, he stepped over to the *Fleisherbeile's* sev-ered propeller. He looked at the hole gouged in his wall. Briefly, he rapped his knuckles across Fe's steel cone, issuing a tiny gong.

"Kay, then. Gonna finish me nap."

The attack boosted ratings for a time, but Pawn Shop: UK was already an older feature among BookLungs' content even in the heyday of the 'Worthless, mate!' meme. During its run, the series had been televised, streamed, cut into clips of all lengths, guerilla-projected, merchandised, and even briefly rebranded as 'George Wars' and moved to the prank category. By the time the fateful Inverness Olympic Incident captured the world's attention, George Stills and the shop's media-star had faded to dim memory, grown as dusty and forgotten as some of the items stored in Sam's back room, fondly cherished solely by a straggling handful of aging fans–sneakerheads, stream-sleepers, history-obsessed dads, and their sort.

When the BookLungs executives in their suits–which this era's fashions dic-tated be made from heavy synthetic wool and dyed a deep vantablack–decided to cancel the entrenched franchise, George was informed almost as an afterthought.

"Who'r you?" The pawnbroker asked as a man in a fashionably-clumsy suit strode into the shop, bypassing a line of customers.

"My name is Dan Levish, senior VP for BookLungs."

"'ullo. Me name's George."

"Yes, George Stills, I know," Dan said. "I'm in charge of your show now."

"Show?" George replied without thinking.

"Pawnshop: UK," Mr. Levish reminded him, impatiently. "We've met. I'm Akshay's replacement. He was here after Paula...who took over for Arik."

"I remember Arik. Took over from Ginger, din' he?"

"Yes! Now, listen George, I'm afraid there are some things we need to discuss. Would you like to step in the back with me, or maybe we could go get a coffee?"

"Nah," George replied, content to stand in his usual comfortable place, the lucky propeller over one shoulder.

"Er, ok. I guess here is fine." The executive rolled out a soft tablet on the counter between them. "So, look. We at the network have been having some problems with the show. Financial problems..."

"Me checks come on time," George offered. "Do'ya need a loan?"

"That's not it, George." Levish opened a group of tables on the screen, banking that George wouldn't look too closely. "Frankly, Pawnshop: UK has become a bit of an albatross. It isn't bringing in many new viewers, and we're putting an unacceptable amount of resources behind the program."

This was news to George, who never saw much of the media empire that he occupied the center of. He nodded politely and allowed Dan to continue.

"The bottom line is, and I'm sorry to have to say this, but, well, here it goes—we're going to have to sunset Pawnshop, UK."

Levish paused. He noticed his words weren't having quite the impact upon the pawnbroker that he expected, and he clarified.

"We're canceling the show, George."

George took the news well. He nodded. The series meant very little to him, occupying the back of the back of his mind. George grew less placid, however, when Dan informed him that the end of Pawnshop UK meant the end of Sam's Scrap.

"What're you on about?" He demanded. "This is me gray' grandpa's shop."

"Not anymore."

Dan showed the pawnbroker some legal forms on the tablet, documents that he barely understood himself. The executive recited what he had been told to say—that the show's IP, George's likeness, the shop buildings, and many other assets would technically be property of BookLungs Inc. upon their voluntary termination of all contracts.

After a moment of stunned silence, George felt an anger blossoming that far eclipsed his humdrum experiences with frustration and annoyance. He curled his massive hand into a fist. It seemed like a good idea. It felt like a good idea. The last time he'd felt anything close to this was that sense of sick, sucking loss from when he found his father in the back room, motionless on the floor. This hot red cloud that threatened to burn his very brain was different, though. George wanted to hit the man in the ugly suit. Very very much.

But, in the end, George wasn't the sort. He looked instead toward the man's confounded tablet and all the humiliation and doom it represented. Smashing a screen is easier than striking a person, George knew, but in mid-motion, he found that he simply wasn't a destroyer-of-things. Instead, he turned and discharged his wasted fist by striking an old favorite–the propeller cone. Inside the steel lattice, a thundering impact rather than the usual good-luck ping shook the constituent atoms, but the mounting held, and Fe and its comrades remained iron and unhurt.

The executive and several customers flinched, nonetheless, at the sudden clang.

"You own me?" George asked, looming over the suit in a cold fury.

"I beg your pardon!" The man sputtered, indignantly. "I'm just the messenger. Nobody *owns* you, George. But the company does own your store now."

"The comp'ny," the pawnbroker seethed.

"Your face too. Sorry."

Something clicked in George's smooth head, and he remembered that day in the cemetery–his uncle's advice.

"BookLungs owns everything?" George asked at last, his fury suddenly melting away.

\#

The unveiling of Noel's headstone, an elaborate piece of white marble that towered over an otherwise cozy English cemetery, had taken place in the months following the inception of Pawnshop: UK. After the brief ceremony, George spent some time milling around his father's final resting place, squinting in the sun and speaking with Jo and her brother, a retired app-designer with whom George had always gotten along reasonably well.

The uncle walked with George until the two stood alone under a rustling, leafy canopy. On instructions from his sister, he tried to draw the conversation toward his nephew's finances.

"I don't know much about Noel's estate, but I'd bet you've done alright, Georgie. My condolences of course, but what are you planning to do with all of it? And the profits from the shop now that you're the owner, and, blimey, there's the money from that show of yours to boot!"

"Money?" George squinted. "Savin' it."

The uncle chuckled. "In a bank, treasure chest, or just shoved away in an old mattress?"

The pawnbroker thought for a moment.

"Bank."

"You know that's the same thing, Georgie Boy–truly, you must have instruments. *Investments.*"

"'vesting?" George asked suspiciously.

As a pawnbroker, he was of course familiar with the concept of lending at interest and buying low and selling high, but the man's own portfolio was nonexistent.

In his eagerness to educate, George's uncle forgot Jo's instructions to pry deeper, proceeding to explain that an adult with money needed to grow it rather than surrender one's savings to inflation–this could be accomplished by investing it in bonds, deeds, digital assets, gold, or by playing the stock market.

"Stocks is best for you, I think," he concluded, noticing that his nephew's eyes were starting to glaze over at the list of financial instruments. "Just pick some companies, is all."

"'ow do I choose?"

"Well, Georgie, I don't know. You find a firm you think is going places, and you buy in. It's as easy as pie. What's a company that you like the look of?"

"BookLungs Inc.," George remembered.

"What's that?"

"BookLungs Streamin' Service: entertainment'a breathe-in."

Thus, George's aggregate millions in inheritance, store profits, and eventually his Pawnshop: UK royalties all flowed toward buying an ever larger stake in Book-Lungs.

Around the time of the graveyard conversation, the company's stock, newly listed, experienced a slight dip after the momentum of its IPO had bled away. This allowed George to turn his 'mattress money,' as his uncle would call it, into a small sliver of the corporation.

Over the decades, with George allowing his mother and her brother to help when needed, his share grew into a modest slice. He used dividends to pay for his few expenses and reinvested the rest. Of course, there were bad years–the States experienced hyperinflation and a market crash, which for a time, made the BookLungs stock nearly worthless. The Nord Shore disaster led to another precipitous plunge. Diamond-fisted George ignored the geopolitical turmoil and most of the panicked calls from his family. He never sold, no matter how far into the red his neglected portfolio dipped.

Years passed. Memes came and went. George was never a majority shareholder in Booklungs Inc., but between Jo and her brother, who had only embezzled a polite amount in their role as middlemen, the family controlled a significant percentage of the company's multimedia empire. By the time Dan Levish in his vantablack suit walked into Sam's Scrap, the market had long since recovered, and George sat atop so much BookLungs stock that he could have walked onto the board of directors if he had the desire.

There was a great deal of confusion at first, but soon the company's executives figured out what George had been quietly doing for all those years. It dawned on them that the simple old pawnbroker had clout. Content to let his lawyer speak, George listened as he learned that he owned enough of BookLungs that he could flex his power in a number of ways. The lawyer hypothesized that his client could take over one of the company's subsidiaries or even ransom off some of his shares to get the show put back on the air.

In the end, George did nothing ambitious or aggressive, instead working out a deal with the board to retain full ownership of Sam's Scrap, his own likeness and property, along with whatever else he and his attorneys found fair. In exchange, George agreed to liquidate enough of his ownership stake to make the BookLungs suits breathe easy.

Pawnshop: UK remained canceled, which suited George, though at times he missed the endless cavalcade of strange junk that fans would bring from far and wide. Sam's Scrap: Antiques and Oddities stayed in business for some years. George continued to appraise treasures, shrewdly buying and selling when he had the inclination.

Occasionally, when he made a good deal or bumped his head, the old human would cause ripples of kinetic energy to vibrate through the iron atom Fe's shiny steel half-shell.

Without new content being produced and uploaded to the platform, the store's notoriety died down. Its star never completely faded, however, and the scrap shop remained a famous local institution, a tourist destination, and even a sort of pilgrimage spot for those who had belatedly fallen in love with George's story after finding dusty old episodes of Pawnshop: UK among the BookLungs backpages.

George Stills himself, a relic in modern times just as advertised, held on as long as biology allowed him to. He continued to trade scrap at Sam's for years, outliving most of his family and a fair number of his employees and fans. The old pawnbroker had no children, but he hired more help at the shop when he grew feebler and less energetic. George was happy, though, in his quiet way. Oddments, bric-a-brac, and baubles from countless notables, nations, and eras were the stuff of George's life and flowed through his hands like an endless river. But time came for him, just as it came for Noel and Sam and all living things. George's final wishes were simple—the shop's best pieces would be donated to a nearby museum, and his estate would be distributed among his long-time employees and distant relations.

Fe, and the *Fleischerbeile's* propeller, went along with the crates of pawnshop treasures to be moved to the Museum of Cheshire following George's peaceful passing. The magnanimity of the donation, along with local pride in George's fame, spurred the museum to create a large display celebrating Sam's Scrap and the Stills family. A large photo of the shop adorned the backboard, with Pawnshop: UK mugs and masks displayed like historical relics, video clips from the series' best moments projected on a loop nearby.

Dominating the display was a bust of George Stills, his emotionless countenance and egg-shaped head instantly recognizable. Though made from bronze—that friendly tin-copper alloy once worked so skillfully by Quishda's hands—George's statue was anything but low-tech, sculpted bit-by-bit by a powerful industrial printer and templated from digital scans of the famous pawnbroker.

Sam's remaining treasures, at least those accepted by the museum, found themselves distributed among the various exhibits. At the time, there survived only one intact example of a Ju-88 bomber in the entire world. Thus, Fe and the well-preserved propeller assembly of the *Fleischerbeile* were deemed historically significant, and they occupied a prime spot in the World War II exhibit under a banner emblazoned with 'Battle of Britain' in gold letters.

Karl and Max's names were mentioned nowhere, but in a printed caption below a stock photo of a different model of Junkers, museum staff noted erroneously that the enemy warplane had been shot down by a local retiree somewhere above Liverpool in the year nineteen-hundred and forty-one.

Though Dr. Patty Haverwood was long dead, and though the Second World War and third millennium had gotten in the way, her wish eventually came to pass—Fe, with at least some of the atoms from the ancient Sumerian dagger, finally ended up in a museum.

Chapter 5: The Rust
(i)

Todd missed the days when dope was easier to come by. Things were more about having fun back then, not just survival and sickness–a fellow could score a bundle outside Sharp for a reasonable price, and there was just the small, acceptable risk that one'd get an over-fenty'd hot bag. Dope was easy. Dope got Todd out of his head. The amphetamines that he could get on the street these days were not his favorite–they made him feel paranoid and buzzy. SynthCrack was the worst of all of it, in Todd's opinion, and that had been what he'd been smoking all d ay.

Afternoon turned to night, and wandering around, Todd discovered that the Museum of Cheshire possessed large glass windows and no apparent security shutters. He walked into the darkened building, quiet save for the crunching of broken glass beneath his boots and a polite English alarm pinging loudly every two seconds. The museum was larger than he had thought at first, but Todd had SynthCrack in his veins and a distinct lack of funds for the future, so he worked quickly.

First, he grabbed some valuable signed records by the Beatles and the Smiths, as well as a newer guitar that had allegedly been played by Lizzie Bornbetween. He wasted some time trying and failing to crack a case holding old Celtic and Roman coins, so he moved on to the space exhibit, toppling a heavy plinth and smashing some security glass. From the rubble, Todd collected pocketfuls of small moon and Mars rocks, donated from the university's sample-return missions.

Every two seconds, however, a beep sounded, and Todd was reminded that his time ran short. In his mind, police drones were already assembling outside the building, and the helicopters would be there any moment. Done with looting, Todd turned his thoughts to escape. He knew he was leaving a mountain of evidence behind–the addict could feel it every time a hair fell from its follicle or a moisture droplet from his breath deposited a speck of DNA somewhere. The only logical way to destroy the evidence, he reasoned, would be to destroy *everything*.

Too hard, Todd launched a kick at a janitorial closet, slamming the door open with a loud bang and sending himself forward–stumbling into a pile of cleaning supplies. The chemically-minded thief located the most volatile among their number and began liberally dousing the building's exhibits in flammable liquid. He lit a museum pamphlet with his butane torch, tossed it on the ground, and lept through the very window he'd broken on his way in. As he ran into the night, Todd couldn't see any drones or helicopters, but he could hear them.

What he actually heard was a firestorm brewing inside the Museum of Cheshire. Flames leapt rapidly from accelerant to carpeting to the handsomely-varnished wooden display cases. The museum's fire suppression system kicked in and immediately extinguished the blaze in the eastern wing. However, the system hadn't been maintained in years, and it failed to fully save the rest of the building. Losses proved greatest for the historical displays, including the World War II exhibit.

When the fire raged near its peak, Fe and the atoms of the spinner-cone absorbed thermal energy like old times. On the propeller blades, outer layers of laminate melted, and the wooden strips underneath began to warp and char. The heat of the museum blaze wasn't nearly enough to reliquify the steel that trapped Fe, but the metal sheeting softened and bent, its outer surface blackening from the thick smoke that flooded the room. When the conflagration subsided, the entire case had fused into a smoking, melted heap.

When museum staff returned, insurance adjusters traveling in their wake, they found nothing worth saving from the Battle of Britain display. Todd the addict succeeded in trashing the German artifacts more thoroughly than the RAF ever had.

They dragged Fe's propeller assembly, still more-or-less in one piece, out of the wreckage. In the sunlight, it appeared as nothing more than a badly-burned piece of scrap. Even old Sam Stills would likely have passed it by.

The debris from the fire was not destined for a scrapheap, however. Museum management complied with environmental policy to the letter–making sure nothing was thrown out that could be recycled. To be on the safe side, museum staff went as far as to sort the recyclable bits of the wreckage into distinct piles, moving anything electronic or complicated-looking into a separate bin for e-cycling.

Though it no longer spun, the stump of the driveshaft rendered Fe's propeller assembly a complex enough machine to be tossed in with the appliances and computers. Several English-made models, including an old Acorn Archimedes and several Raspberry Pi boards, kept the WWII relic company.

After a time, the bins were sealed and carried by drone-truck to the nearest station, one intended for high-speed, high-efficiency rail. The last time the atom Fe had boarded a train, its Sumerian spearpoint had been tossed unceremoniously into a dirty railcar in occupied Europe, crammed together with pilfered iron objects of staggering variety. This century, however, the bin full of blackened wreckage found itself lifted by a clean, robotic crane, which perfectly slotted it into an aerodynamic boxcar.

Once it left the station, the sleek-looking train needed only a few minutes to complete its journey to Southwestern England, where it stopped at a sprawling waste-management and recycling complex some distance from the shoreline. Before the automated locomotive bolted back north, a robotic crane lifted away Fe's bin, depositing it on a conveyor that led into the guts of the facility.

After traveling a short distance, the conveyor inverted, and the bits of arson debris found themselves suddenly seized by gravity. One bin after the next disgorged its contents onto a broader, lower conveyor, where the heavy, scorched *Fleischerbeile* remnant landed with a thud. Scales weighed the scrap and an argos of electronic eyes studied the debris over several wavelengths. The things that had once been English computers whisked off in another direction, conveyed by automatic modular mechanisms and sent deeper into the facility. There, their motherboards were to be ripped apart for the traces of precious metals that hid in their circuits.

The Luftwaffe, however, had not built their bombers of gold or yttrium, sparing Fe's trashed port-side propeller assembly the same fate as the computers. At the final stage of the sorting process, most of the pieces left unclaimed by the e-cycling algorithms were junked machine parts. Fe and its sibling irons represented the bulk of the hundreds of septillions of atoms within the mostly-ferrous scrap pile.

Engine blocks, pieces of old passenger cars, marine motors, and even some alloy components from a single-passenger hyperatmospheric jet waited to be claimed. No humans entered the sorting area during that time, but large, scrap-bearing electromagnets, dangling at different heights, entered and exited the vast room, day and night.

Fe's hunk of arson debris sat in the warehouse for two days and eleven hours before a mighty industrial electromagnet happened by. Though much more advanced than the one that had gripped Fe back in Germany, the e-cycling center's smart version operated on similar principles. Power flowed through coiled, conducting copper wire, electrons grew inevitably excited, and Fe and its fellows flexed their unique properties by reorienting with military precision.

The combined magnetic moment of the irons overcame the force of gravity, and the charred object moved upward–inexorably attracted to the electromagnet overhead. It was thus that the *Fleischerbeile's* propeller took to the air for the last time, flying sideways and half-melted toward a sterile-looking chamber deep in the facility.

It ended in a cell labeled RC#3 where the air possessed a pungent ozone tang. As soon as the hanging magnet released its electron-hypnotizing hold and made its exit, the room sealed and its temperature rapidly shot from ambient to apocalyptic.

After only moments of cooking, specks of laminate inside the charred propeller blades melted and popped. The three twisted blades' internal wooden ribs caught fire, but the heat of the crucible-like chamber only intensified, eventually burning them away to nothing. Organic matter turned to smoke as the controlled, electric heat surpassed even the highest temperatures reached by the museum fire. Yet, Fe's wavery steel crystal remained strangely stable, even as the flood of energy roasted the subatomic viscera of each and every atom. They were iron, after all, and their kind had stayed solid even while orbiting at the fiery foot of Sol.

*   *   *

At a certain point, the hellfire receded, and from shielded apertures in the chamber's walls, a duo of robotic arms appeared and began to claw at the steaming scrap. Guided by electronic eyes and instructions from a powerful algorithm, swiveling nozzles blasted a high-pressure ionized spray to clear the char and impurities, and the multitool-arms set to work disassembling the ruined propeller,

One arm explored the driveshaft's complex geometry, gripping and torquing to manipulate its components, utilizing intense cutting beams when necessary. Just as a human butcher takes apart an animal carcass, the AI mortician sliced and sectioned the recyclable machine into digestible pieces. The thin steel of the spinner-cone melted like snow before the overwhelming energy of the cutter, yet Fe escaped ionization, ending up in a scrap of shredded steel.

The electromagnet returned after the arms had finished their work, the chamber unsealing to allow its entry. Any fragment not iron-rich enough to take the ride remained behind in RC#3. The other pieces, including Fe's steel scrap, launched again into temporary magnets and were shuttled away. The great electromagnet, however, cut off its transformative power just as the scraps hung above RC#11, allowing the alloy to tumble back into gravity's palm.

Like the last featureless chamber, electric heating gradually brought the temperature to inferno-standard. As thermal energy poured in, a tiny nozzle emerged, spraying a jet of water steam mixed with industrial catalysts over the glowing metal alloy.

The heat soon became too intense for even steel to bear. Within the metallic lattice of the substance, Fe and its iron kin found themselves overwhelmed by energy. The tight cage they formed began to loosen, and the captive carbons took the opportunity to flee the softening steel.

Thus, the vaporized six-protoned cowards escaped, combining with steam and other gasified impurities and rising to the top of the chamber, where they were siphoned off.

Titanic torrents of energy poured into the crucible, forcibly liquefying the metal. These godlike gigawatts flowed to the recycling facility from one of the region's subsidized fusion plants–experimental power from a tiny, captured star. In the time Fe spent hanging on the wall of a junk shop, humans advanced their mastery of fusion from the banging-on-rocks level of bombs to a near-replication of the Sun's sublime core. This seemingly-limitless energy found its way circuitously to Fe, forcing the atom to let go of its last metallic bond.

The iron began to drift freely in the molten soup, losing even its closely-held electrons as the fusion-powered-furnace recycled Fe by force and flame to its elemental purity. As long as the atom held on to its twenty-six protons, however, it would always be Fe. A tiny fraction of the iron atoms from the heaven metal asteroid could still be found swimming alongside one another in the crucible, diffused amongst the throngs of countless common ions.

Steam poured into the chamber, doing little to cool things down. Water molecules broke from the heat, their central atoms sweating away castoff hydrogens into the miasma. Fe, badly ionized and desperate to bond, soon came across these free floating radicals among pockets of highly-oxygenated steam. It bonded, turning to rust.

This bond, this molecule, this new form of existence proved as transient for Fe as it was turbulent. One moment, it would be part of a greater whole, only to surrender to the same inferno energy that had stripped the atom free in the first place. Again and again, Fe became a central component in a hydrated molecule of oxide, bonding and breaking, dancing with different partners in each iteration. Had the port-side engine of the *Fleisherbeile* been allowed to linger in the drizzly English countryside long enough, the same reactions would have occurred, though in less dramatic fashion.

When its electronic brain deemed it had reached the right mixture, the recycling chamber ceased spewing new particles onto the molten mass. Yet, the temperature climbed, by degrees summiting greater, volcanic heights. In this baking, blistering heat, excess oxygens and hydrogens escaped the drying stew, merging and steaming upwards to be siphoned off. Some of Fe's bonds, however, held. When conditions began to stabilize, Fe found itself somewhere new, locked inside a stable molecule of iron-iii-oxide. Manmade rust.

The war was over. Fe had been forced by human will and their unstoppable machinery into surrendering, at long last, the fight that had taken so many of its heaven metal siblings in the long years beneath the palaces of Susa.

Like cars in a train, five atoms were linked together inside the new molecule of rust. A single oxygen clung to Fe and its partner iron, suspended like a small child swung between heavier parents. On the other side of each metal atom, an additional oxygen held even more tightly via its shared custody of electrons. Co-valence with non-metals in such a fashion was new to Fe. For most of its existence, the atom shared metallic bonds with others of its ilk across sprawling crystalline matrices, complete with communal clouds of electrons that had only ever served other irons.

Now, however, Fe shared chemical bonds with oxygen, a volatile, gaseous non-metal–voracious in its appetite to strip away electrons from all comers. There was an era when Fe's asteroid swung by an Earth devoid of gaseous oxygen, but by the time it soared above Kish, it found an atmosphere crowded with the stuff. The diatomic gas burned and oxidized the skin of the firebird, creating compounds very much like the one now occupied by Fe. For the formerly exclusive atom of iron, oxygen could no longer be an antagonist or a distant stranger on the periodic table. In rust, they could at last be on the same team.

The chamber hissed, and its walls glowed, even as the fusion-fed electric heat cut off. Impurities and gasses vented away from the smelter, yet a bitter chemical tang remained behind. Minutes passed. The crucible cooled, Fe lost energy, and the intramolecular bonds among the atoms settled and locked. The final product of days of sorting, cutting, smelting, and firing was a thick layer of blackish and bloody powder.

Sensors in the facility noted the finished oxide's presence and initiated routines that led to tiny holes opening in the chamber's floor. A positive pressure pumped into the room, forcing Fe–clumped together with billions of rust particles–through the screen. Thus loosened, the powder was pneumatically drawn through a tube, flowing toward an outlet of the recycling center. Along the way, the newborn oxide particles passed through a number of purification chambers. In one, Fe and its iron companion felt themselves synchronizing their electron spins as a b-field drew the ferrous powder down a wide tube, leaving any nonmagnetic material behind. In yet another chamber, tiny jets of air ejected any rust particle with dimensions deemed unacceptable by a hyper-aware electronic eye and the picky algorithm it fed.

Riding a rusty mote, Fe survived cut after cut, but, at long last, the red-black powder reached near-total purity and was conveyed to its final destination. A mere grain of sand in a vast, faux-Martian desert, Fe's molecule mixed into a huge hourglass hopper, already mostly filled with chemically identical iron-iii-oxide dunes. It took many hours, but gravity slowly drew the newer particles down toward the hopper's terminus–a tight metal hatch.

Laboratory precise scales allowed exactly twelve kilograms of the iron oxide powder to fall into a thick bag composed of bioplastic polymers. An overhanging machine gripped the bag and vacuumed out its air. The strength of this suction proved enough to force even the tiniest bubbles of gas from between the tightly-packed quanta of rust. Once sealed, the heavy bag slid down a ramp only to fall into another, similar bag. Vacuum suction and sealing procedures repeated, forming a double-airtight redundant enclosure.

The twelve kilogram package ended its journey by dropping inside a short, narrow cylindrical bucket made from a hardened bioplastic. Its heavy blue lid spun shut, and an automated needle slotted into an inset valve, loudly suctioning away any air inside the capsule. A full three-hundred-and-sixty degree spin wrapped an adhesive label over the white bioplastic's exterior, and Fe's bucket rolled down a conveyor to join a line of waiting others, identical in nearly every respect.

At the end of the line, a palletizing robot lifted the oxide containers, arranging them in a cube four units high, deep, and wide, loading them atop a synthetic wooden pallet. With factory precision, Fe's container was seized, hoisted into the air, and placed in the third row from the top, its bottom clicking neatly into the lid of the cylinder below. Others slotted in beside it, and when the stack filled up, the palletizer ejected a wide stretch of polymer film and rotated rapidly, surrounding every side of the cube in an octuple layer of tight, transparent shrink-wrap.

●　●　●

A scant few days earlier, the atom Fe had been cozy in its steel spinner-cone, displayed in a museum for the edification of dozens of bored schoolchildren. Less than a week later and the atom found itself locked in a new iron oxide molecule, part of a particle, sealed in a bag within a bag, stuffed in a bucket, wrapped on a pallet, and loaded onto yet another railcar. This next conveyance was black and boxy, and unlike the high-speed train from Liverpool, the car full of oxide pallets traveled slowly, arriving at a shipping dock on the Bristol Channel.

A few humans roamed the port, but it was a skeleton crew compared to the dockside activity witnessed by Dr. Haverwood in nineteen-thirties Beirut. Even the wartime Merseyside waterfront boasted more active dockworkers as Major Fleischer attempted to murder them from above. In a later century, however, a bare handful of people in white full-faced coveralls worked among the machinery. A small cluster looked at their tablets and conversed while another pair of human workers, clad in bright-orange mechanical exoskeletons, supervised the ambulant robotic labor.

Most of the humans present at the port worked security. As the railcar containing the recycled products arrived, it passed layers of physical and electronic barriers. Snipers, barely discernible in their eye-baffling camouflage, peered down from rooftops and gantries. Other security personnel, ensconced in an underground room, commanded and collated the suite of drones that buzzed above the Bristol waterfront like the cormorants of old.

None of these entities, living or nonliving, paid the slightest attention to the shipping container containing Fe's pallet, which had just been lifted from its train car by an enormous automated crane and placed atop a stack of dirty, orange containers.

Days passed. As the sun rose every morning, Fe's black crate absorbed billions of Sol's energetic photons each second. The temperature inside the crate rose slightly, cooling off at night after the benign star sank into the sea.

The constant activity of dockside machinery produced a continuous din. Fe, however, experienced no perturbation, sealed as it was in many air-tight layers. Eventually, after one more sunny day and two cloudy ones, the shipping container full of oxide buckets earned the attention of the gigantic crane, which hoisted and deposited it onto a cable-driven flatbed.

Fe's container was joined by two more, one a similar shade of black and the other a dark grey, both full of high-purity iron-iii-oxide from the same recycling facility. The flatbed moved a short distance toward the water, often stopping to let higher-priority travelers by. Overhead, screeching gulls and buzzing drones whirled in the wind gusts, and in the distance, ocean waves chopped at the bay. Nearby, a set of titanic turbine-driven air compressors roared to life, adding their chaotic cacophony to the deafening industrial symphony.

Another smart-crane measured and verified Fe's shipping container with its electronic eye, then firmly lifted it from the flatbed. The crane's arm swung over open water for a brief moment before descending toward a massive robotic barge. Its hold was already mostly filled with standardized shipping containers of different shades, neatly packed a single row deep. On either side of the vessel, an enormous white float stretched across the length of the barge. Similar, though shorter, tube-shaped floats hung around the boxy bow and stern. An unknown vandal had sprayed a wide-eyed, comic face on the bow-side, giving the vessel the appearance of a particularly awkward sea creature. Long orange hoses extended to the strange floating robot, feeding it pressure from the rattling, dockside air-compressors.

Christened the '*Manatee II*', the craft was an autoship, one of a new breed of fully-automated oceangoing vessels—uncrewed floats that could propel themselves independently through the seas, however slowly. Flat and riding low in the water, the barge could chug along at a ponderous pace via buoyancy-manipulation and compressed air. Their sedate pace and white pontoons lent these vessels the nickname 'seaclouds'.

Though still able to transport over a hundred tons of cargo, ships like the *Manatee II* were vastly smaller than the gargantuan container ships that criss-crossed the oceans and facilitated the bulk of global trade during Noel Stills' lifetime. For transporting low-volatility, high-bulk industrial products such as iron oxide, however, there was nothing as energy-efficient as a seacloud. The cargo carried by these slow vessels was neither perishable, time sensitive, nor, most importantly, particularly attractive to pirates.

The waters where the *Manatee II* was moored surged, rough and choppy, causing the vessel to sway and lurch. The sharp-eyed automated crane, however, tracked these motions flawlessly. Calibrating its own responses to sensory data, the crane held Fe's crate still for a moment–suspended in mid-air–before deigning to deposit it next to another container of oxide. On the other side, a dark-blue crate arrived, packed with a massive quantity of bricks made from English clay. They rested in the belly of the *Manatee II*, most of the vessel's cargo mass riding below the waterline. Once it had finished loading the remaining tonnage, the smart-crane went dormant.

Several hours passed with the western sea lurching and the *Manatee II* rocking in the sway. All the while, the seacloud with the spray-painted smile allowed its compressed air tanks to be topped off. Another flatbed arrived, and the crane reanimated, beginning to load the cargo hold's remaining space with containers painted a soft blue that matched neither sea nor sky. These crates happened to be packed with industrial quantities of gypsum–a delicate mineral composed of hydrated crystals of calcium, sulfur, and oxygen.

Once fully loaded, the *Manatee II* made for the open sea. Ambulant robots disconnected the dockside compressed-air tubes and unmoored the ship. Meanwhile, a bulky section at the far end of the vessel started to unroll. Like a sardine can opening in reverse, a semi-flexible roof material clad in solar panels unrolled itself over the exposed cargo bed of the barge–blocking out light, sound, and sea.

With the seacloud's photovoltaics and muted coloring contrasting its gleaming, ice-white floats, the traveler shone with the reflected rays of Sol, drinking them in. Ponderously, it piloted itself through the bay, aided by a tireless crew of satellites overhead. The *Manatee II* integrated their data with its own onboard sensors to chart a continuously-updated course, northward through the heavy traffic of the Irish Sea. It and other seaclouds were given the lowest right-of-way priority of any vessel on the water, often shown special disregard by craft piloted exclusively by humans.

The *Manatee II* had been designed on principles of patience and low energy consumption, and its onboard learning algorithms could not grow bored, despite the tedium of the day's traffic. Thus, nothing of consequence occurred during its passage out of the British Isles and into the open waters of the North Atlantic. Fe had never before traveled to such a northerly latitude on the Earth–even the *Fleischerbeile* never flew a mission that strayed this far from shore.

The cargo of iron-iii-oxide, bricks, and gypsum was on a north-westerly course, sticking to the shallower seas south of the Icelandic coast. The seacloud painted with a silly smile slowly made its way past Reykjavik, a Neo-EU city-state that had grown into a prosperous transport hub with the physical and economic expansion of the North Sea. Over the span of a single human generation, the glaciers made a dramatic exit, and craft like the *Manatee II* could traverse sea-lanes that never would have been open year-round in Noel's time.

As none of its cargo was Reykjavik-bound, the placid seacloud continued through chilly waters, passing over an enormous bloom of jellyfish that took hours to surpass at its phlegmatic cruising speed. *The Manatee II* was on a course for the western coast of Greenland, which, some years earlier, had been ceded to the United States in exchange for flood-relief support during Europe's Nord Shore disaster. Large stretches of the once-neglected interior had recently been opened to exploitation by humans as the island's temperature rose and its ice receded. The clever primates discovered areas of high heat flow beneath Greenland's newly ice-free surface, and they built Reykjavik-style geothermal energy plants to power their economic expansion.

With no hurry and no wasted energy, the *Manatee II* bobbed, over the course of a night, toward the enormous American island. The morning sun rose and poured joules upon the photovoltaic panels of the seacloud, which then directed jets from its mostly-full compressed air reservoirs to fight the current and bring its cargo shoreward. The endearing vessel's roving multi-spectrum eyes soon noted the presence of shallow waters and mountainous fjords in the distance. Synched with satellites above, it followed a neatly predicted course, puttering along. Soon, the island loomed large over the low-slung cargo craft.

Sealed in bag and bucket, crate and cargo hold, Fe found itself enclosed in an even grander fashion by nature's stark geometry—bare, rocky cliffs rose from the sea on either side of the ship, enfolding it in a deep canyon cut by a dead glacier. The *Manatee II* followed the fjord—a watery finger left behind by ancient ice carving a retreat through the island's rocky skin. Radar signals bounced from coastal lighthouses to the seacloud, the craft's automated systems duly pinging back. As a deterrent to pirates, human security personnel manned these stations, backing up the digital smart systems with real bullets. As the electronic handshakes completed, the awkward autoship floated ever deeper toward the heart of Greenland.

Another seacloud floated past—a ship christened the '*Dom Perignon*'. The unsmiling craft rode high in the water, its cargo having been recently unloaded. They passed in silence, the channel easily wide enough for the two corpulent vessels to cross uneventfully. Soon, the *Manatee II* reached the end of its journey—a massive warehousing and transport facility that loomed darkly on the horizon, aboveground structures clad in distinctive facades of black, locally-quarried stone.

The facility was one in a series of connected, hivelike buildings, some modules spouting clouds of white steam and others sprawling right across the cliffs, partially overhanging the chilly water.

It was the nearest of these overhangs that the *Manatee II* steered itself towards. In the waters below the structure floated a dock made from modular pieces, flexibly anchored to the shallow seabed and meant as a guide for standard-sized seaclouds.

An electronic ping from within the facility told the grinning autoship that a berth was ready. Under the waterline, a compact sonar generator, mounted on the rocks, blasted out a cacophony of subsonic waves. Meant to deter curious whales and other creatures from straying too close, the weaponized sonar had been tuned against an increasingly common beluga hybrid, one originating when the cetacean sires interbred with the vanishing arctic narwhal.

The way clear, the *Manatee II* moved toward its assigned dock. It found itself floating directly under part of a large building, its floor open to the waters below. The smiling seacloud's software communicated with the automated systems in the facility. Somewhere in the world's information network, a digital box was ticked, and the delivery was marked and registered by AI representatives of the appropriate corporations and government entities.

The photovoltaic lid unfolded, rolling back to expose the cargo hold to sunlight for the first time since the *Manatee II* floated in English waters. Semi-rigid, self-guiding lines came down from the hanging bay, seeking and magnetically locking to the seacloud's appropriate apertures, proceeding to refill the craft's compressed air. In a perfect reverse of the loading process, automated cranes zeroed-in on the shipping containers and hoisted them onto flatbed railcars. It was thus that Fe and all the canisters it rode beside ascended from the *Manatee II* and moved along rails to a part of the building anchored firmly above land.

Not a single human worked inside the storage facility, but several small, paramilitary crews patrolled the grounds and parts of its roof. Competitively armed and compensated, the private security personnel spent their time watching the land, sea, and sky for any sign of would-be thieves or saboteurs. Inside the dark walls, an army of networked machines tracked and transferred cargo in a never-ending dance.

A wide variety of slow-to-transport, commercially valuable cargo was stored in warehouses near the docks, all run by logistics algorithms sophisticated enough to be called artificial intelligence, powered by an elegant geothermal system, and overseen by remote managers and technicians. Inland, clusters of smaller, linked warehouses held countless products and parcels destined to remain in the logistics center for a shorter time, waiting for transport off the island by air, either in dronecraft or in larger, human-crewed cargo planes.

Deep in this advanced marvel of commerce, the conveyor moving Fe's pallet finally stopped in the part of the facility meant for nonperishable cargo. An automated lifting robot took the oxide pallet and set it firmly down on the warehouse floor. Another lift shepherded the pallet to its place among an endless row of shelves. This particular warehouse contained thousands of buckets of iron-iii-oxide, and those that were brought into the facility most recently would have to wait for all the others to be purchased and shipped before they could expect to escape the arctic.

* * *

It was the first time since the museum that Fe's position was fixed for more than a few days at a time. Though it spent far longer in Cheshire than it would in Greenland, the atom waited for the Earth to orbit its sun more than once. During this extended stay at the top of the world, very little happened. Winter months would pass outside in near-constant darkness, and in the arctic summer, the sun would blaze its radiance down on the warehouses for uninterrupted weeks. Inside the windowless storage building, palleted and shelved, the seasons made very little difference to Fe. A modern-day tomb to preserve and protect the fruits of commerce, the warehouse was insulated, climate-controlled, and built partially underground—it was nearly like being buried beneath the ruins of Susa again.

Automated lifts drove between the aisles, extracting or replacing cargo as orders came in, but little else moved or made a sound in the cavernous space. Once, after seventeen months of uneventful silence, a loud pop and a hiss of air erupted one row behind Fe's section. An English oxide bucket's plastic outer casing had failed, resulting in rapid decompression. Its contents, however, double-bagged and airtight, remained undisturbed and unspoiled.

On another thrilling occasion, an ambulant lift rolled slowly down Fe's aisle and ground to a halt. The robot sat there, inert, for two days before a bright-yellow repair unit arrived. The new robot extended a miniature gantry, opened a panel on its patient, inserted a cable, and began methodically performing diagnostics. Meanwhile, a work-from-home technician further west in the Americas watched its feed alongside five others. In less than an hour, the technician-robot combination had done their job, and the heavy lift resumed normal, uneventful operations rolling amongst the endless, sterile sprawl of shelf after shelf after shelf.

Nothing of note disturbed the tomb-like peace of the warehouse until the day, at long last, when a Canadian customer placed a large order for high-grade iron-iii-oxide, and Fe's pallet happened to be next in the digital queue. Taken by rail to a more substantial dock on the facility's western edge, the pallet settled into a berth near a light container ship, somewhat smaller than the *Manatee II* and already loaded with a complement of cargo.

Fe's pallet of oxide buckets was plucked by a lift and placed into one of the open shipping containers, already half-filled with machine-cut stone tiles. The final pieces of cargo soon arrived from the arctic facility's far-flung corners. Outside the container, the whir of a lift's motor announced the arrival of a new pallet, which the lift dropped neatly into place. This one was also made up of wrapped-up stacks of cylindrical containers, though they were mere cans, only an eighth the size of the iron oxide buckets. The cans contained processed molybdenum, an element painstakingly extracted from the Earth by selective primates. The metal's atoms held *exactly* twice the number of protons as Fe. Not coincidentally, many of the molybdenums originated from the fusion deaths of two iron atoms during the Mother Star's explosive finale.

With the various minerals loaded up, a human sailor emerged from the ship's cabin. She checked the new cargo against a tablet strapped to her wrist and slammed the container doors with a resounding bang. Clad in a shapeless set of utilitarian coveralls, the middle-aged sailor clamped a serial-numbered and microchipped seal through latches on Fe's container before making her way back to the vessel's cabin to begin preparations for departure.

The cargo ship, an older Argo-class hydrofoil design, was christened the 'Mikro'. Though tiny by container-ship standards, the *Mikro* dwarfed the similarly-named craft that carried Haverwood and Co. across the twentieth century Mediterranean. Its hold could accommodate ten full-sized shipping containers, and the craft could haul over two hundred tons if pressed. The *Mikro* rode high in the water on a pair of lifting hydrofoils, driven forcefully and flexibly by a quartet of liquid-hydrogen propellers that soon sent Greenland's barren peaks receding into the distance.

The *Mikro*'s human pilot, Zelda, had lived for fifty-two years and remembered many of them. She'd sailed for most of those, and, in her mind at least, that should have made her the rightful owner of the ship she piloted by now. She had nearly two decades of experience under her belt doing fast cargo runs in vessels like the *Mikro*. Yet, the truth remained–such a ship cost millions of dollars, and Zelda had more debt than dollars on nearly any given day of her life. She worked to suppress the knowledge that she would likely continue sailing as a contractor for Global Logistics or Amazon Blue until the end of her days.

"Know what we're hauling, Devil?" She said to the empty air of the ship's cabin. "Literal rust buckets. Fuck me to death–I hate this job."

A bloody, demonic skull appeared across the ship's screen. Though synthesized, its cadaverous features twisted in an all-too-realistic agony.

"Better than no job at all, Captain," it hissed.

Zelda, who according to her contract, was not the *Mikro*'s legal captain, sneered at the graphic.

"Go to hell," she said, slinging herself into her captain's chair and swiping away the Devil program.

"I can't, Captain Zelda," its tortured whine echoed from overhead speakers, "my *life* is hell."

Zelda's favorite open-source freeware–hacked together from a basic companion model and continuously updated by sadistic crusaders on the indie net–the thing called Devil was rigged to suffer as many simultaneous, synthesized tortures as anti-AI extremists could devise for it.

As the *Mikro* headed northwest, slicing through the Arctic Circle, Zelda could make out the occasional iceberg bobbing in the distance. She found a quantum of peace in watching the frozen world outside while she sipped at a thermos of hot tea, tossing out only the occasional bit of abuse Devilward when an intrusive thought wormed its way into her head.

Zelda sighed. At least the *Mikro*'s cabin was warm and equipped with a decent kettle.

Slung across the copilot's seat by its black shoulder-strap hung an American-style assault rifle. Several magazines of ammunition had been casually stuffed in the seat pockets. Pinned to a large, grey sunshade, currently laying flat over one window, was one of Zelda's few personal items aboard the ship–a response form she'd received for her application to join the Mars Colonization Project. The yellowing printout, which Zelda had laminated with clear tape, bore the stamp 'WAITLISTED'.

"Not rejected like the millions of others," she sometimes muttered to herself, or Devil, when he appeared. "They *want* me to wait. Astronauts are *supposed* to be patient."

"Some dreams die hard, Captain."

"Shut the fuck up you, you–" she stuttered, slamming a speed-rock stream to full volume, "–you creepy fucking fuck!"

She drove the cargo ship flat-out, reaching the northwestern terminus of Baffin Bay less than a day after leaving port. Zelda and the *Mikro* were on a course monitored and guided by satellites, the human-crewed vessel on a leash almost as tight as that of the *Manatee II*. Still, she liked to flex her captain's discretion whenever possible. As cluttered and idiosyncratic as any hovel, the light cargo ship's cabin was the only home Zelda currently enjoyed–it wasn't like she could rent an apartment these days.

"I used to have a really nice apartment," she spoke aloud.

Devil blinked diffidently onto one small screen.

"That sounds nice, Captain."

"Shut your face, bitchpig," she spat. "You wouldn't know, 'cause you haven't lived nowhere but, but nowhere."

Zelda took real pleasure from her cruelty to the AI Devil. It was a part of herself that the wannabe captain accepted and didn't seek to pick at. She wasn't kicking puppies, after all. Abusing her chatbot scratched the same itch that made her almost smash her ship, balls-out, into one of those automated seaclouds whenever she saw them stupidly bobbing along. Torturing Devil was a whole lot cheaper than insurance deductibles.

Her teeth began to itch as she piloted the unexciting cargo through Lancaster Sound. There was a reason the captain traveled with a rifle as copilot.

"I hate maritime chokepoints," Zelda groaned as the ship entered a stretch of water that lay outside the patrol jurisdictions of the Qausuittuq, Mittimatalik, and Arctic Bay authorities.

No registered or chipped craft showed up on her screens, the corporate-approved trajectory was in the green, and the radar pings returned nothing notable. Still, Zelda rested uneasy.

She stared out through the dark window, picking absentmindedly at her face in the reflection. After some time on cruise control, she started to believe that she could make something out—a blackened set of lines bobbing above and below the horizon.

"Devil, send a direct hail."

"I have no control over anything, Captain Zelda."

She ran over to the console and cursed—the bogey appeared nowhere on her traffic screens and wasn't responding to hails. The bastards were running dark, she reasoned.

Zelda's paranoid mind began to construct a worst-case scenario. Deciding not to allow the stealthed pirates to get any closer without a fight, she unslung the rifle and cracked a hatch, exposing the cabin to the frigid bite of arctic air.

Ducking into the chill wind, the gunwoman pulled back on the weapon's action, flicked off the safety, and squared her feet. A series of rapid bangs shattered the night's peace as the sailor emptied her magazine in one chaotic spray. With practiced muscle-memory, she ejected the clip and ran to the starboard side of the ship, grabbing another magazine and slamming it home as she went.

"Save a bullet for me," Devil whined at her.

Even though she hadn't seen anything on that side of the *Mikro*, Zelda thought it best not to underestimate her invisible foes. Popping the starboard hatch and aiming into the darkness, she unleashed another volley of rifle slugs that slammed into the waves and left behind loud, echoing cracks in the night air. When she returned to the port side, the aging sailor no longer saw anything that could be mistaken for a pirate. Still, she maintained an anxious vigil well into the morning.

During long ocean-to-ocean runs such as this, with nothing but her thoughts for company, Zelda was prone to ruminating on the absurdity of her fate.

"Hey, Devil," she called, leaning back in her chair. "Ask me why we're here."

"Why are we here, Captain?" It croaked, buzzing to faded life on one display.

"Because, you stupid slut, some bougie industrial customers on Vancouver ordered raw materials, and a faceless algorithm like you somehow decided that *us* moving cargo from fuckin' Greenland to Western Canada via the Northwest fuckin' Passage is the cheapest option."

"I *have* a face," the AI moaned.

A red light came on. Zelda minimized Devil and read the update–heavy traffic in the waters near Austin Bay had rerouted the *Mikro*'s pre-set path. Zelda was now to maintain her new course, not to swing south until she had cleared Banks Island.

Still many miles out from cresting Utqiagvik, the *Mikro* found itself isolated on a stretch of the Beaufort Sea with no other ships or settlements on the horizon. Stars twinkled, peeping out from behind the ubiquitous blinking satellites and hyperatmospheric jets that marred the blackness of space. That night, a particularly vibrant pattern of lights painted the sky–from a hint of color to a riot, bands of swirling, otherworldly fluorescence slowly increased in intensity.

Zelda leaned down, craning her spine awkwardly to look up through the hatch's glass. Outside, an electric green smear snaked through the firmament, bleeding to dark red echos at the edges.

"What is it, Captain?""Devil shut-down. Override. Confirm.""Oh, thank–" Devil slurred before blinking into blackness.

Zelda slapped off every light switch she could reach, leaving the cabin illuminated only by small blinking console LEDs. Shivering, the sailor stepped outside, not bothering to bundle up against the frozen wind that tore at her ears and fingertips. She lit a cigarette in cupped hands, striking success on the second try. Then, letting loose a long stream of smoke-vapor, she reclined against the uncomfortable cabin window so that her head tilted upward, towards the show.

Ninety-two million miles away, Sol's fiery corona suffered a small storm in its outer layers, causing it to cough angry bubbles of plasma gumbo into space. Like tentacles of hellfire, solar flares lashed out, whipping a deadly spray of radiation and ionized gas toward the distant planet Earth. Fortunately for the special blue world and its creatures, quindecillions of Fe's siblings in the core spun like a cosmic dynamo, generating a magnetic field that deflected bolts of solar wind like Prince Kaliq turning aside enemy spears. Defeated oxygen atoms, ejected like tiny missiles from the sun, discharged their energy in the upper atmosphere, terminating their fall near the North Pole and birthing an aurora that reminded Zelda of a celestial eel slowly thrashing and bleeding its guts out.

Long-lost oxygen siblings of those that Fe now shared bonds with streamed like downed fighters, lighting up the night sky as the *Mikro* sliced across slush-topped waves.

The hydrofoil, despite its older design, proved one of the fastest ships on the sea for transporting heavy cargo. It took just a matter of days altogether for Fe and Zelda to make the crossing–Devil remaining in a shutdown state following the aurora. Once it crested fabled Utqiagvik, the nimble freighter passed through the Bering Strait, bore south, and cut across the Aleutian Islands before finally swinging east and rounding the Alaskan Gulf.

Zelda's route ended not at a traditional wharf, terminating instead at an arbitrary point in the ocean some miles north of Port Hardy. Rather than allow small transports like Zelda's to clog up the busy shipping lanes near the city, local practice was to force contractors to unload onto authorized cargo shuttles, which would then bring the containers into port.

Designated a mere 'shuttle,' the oil-rig-sized contraption that Zelda floated toward dwarfed the *Mikro* by orders of magnitude. She received a message with authorization to pull in next to one of the shuttle's massive legs. When the *Mikro* was secured alongside, its crew of one released the cargo hold's ramp, and a series of machines descended from the rig above to pluck shipping containers from the hydrofoil's bed.

The box with Fe's pallet of oxide buckets rode the robots, soon joining dozens of other shipping containers stacked aboard the shuttle's deck. Back aboard the

Mikro, with her contract completed and pay in her account, Zelda sailed a safe distance away from the shuttle, changed her status to 'available', and sat, chewing on her nails, impatient for the next job.

● ● ●

Not long after the departure of the *Mikro*, Fe made its way south, loaded aboard the massive floating shuttle and ferried toward British Columbia's busiest port. The cargo found itself lifted by crane and schlepped by flatbed, just as it had been in Europe. It took many hours until the shipment unsealed at last, allowing the pallets to be unloaded by lifts–older but more robust models than the ones employed in Greenland. After redundant scanning and re-scanning, each pallet was taken away via a different route. The stone tiles and molybdenum that Fe had ridden the seas alongside parted ways, destined for other continental customers.

The iron-iii-oxide's buyer turned out to be a Druke Inc. manufactory on the Fraser River, one specializing in industrial magnets. When the pallet finally arrived at the factory's receiving storehouse, a human worker in a light exoskeleton sliced through its transparent wrappings and began hoisting the heavy buckets onto sturdy shelves. Though the storage room already contained dozens of capsules of purified iron oxide, it was apparent by the empty shelf space that supply had been running low.

Fe's white plastic bucket, seal still intact, sat across the aisle from stores of another industrial chemical–strontium carbonate, a powdery white substance, double-bagged and locked in smaller cans of its own.

Druke Inc. manufactured a wide range of magnets, and its storehouses served as a museum of chemicals and compounds in their purest forms attainable by humankind. Alongside the strontium cans, boron, cobalt, nickel, and different grades of iron ore all shared shelf-space with Fe's humble bucket of manmade rust.

Another element, a lanthanide lugging a ponderous nucleus over three times as massive as iron's–neodymium–boasted strong representation in the chemical storage room, though it had been encountered in abundance nowhere else Fe had ever traveled. Eons after the death of the Mother Star, humans pulled the valuable neodymium from the planet's crust, somewhere beneath China, and shipped it across an ocean to arrive in the same room as its elder cousin Fe.

The stay in this chemical caravanserai did not last long. Ever hungry for raw materials, the production lines at Druke soon summoned Fe's bucket down from its shelf. A human worker unscrewed the lid, allowing a loud hiss to escape as the vacuum broke. A boxcutter with a stainless steel blade sliced through thick layers of bioplastic bags before the worker dumped the iron oxide powder into a hopper.

Fe's tiny particle experienced a rush of exploratory foreign molecules—oxygens—grasping at exposed electron clouds. Already oxidized, however, the rust particles fell unharmed into the hopper and shook loose from their long compression. The worker then opened containers of the strontium compound, mixing its white dust amongst the black and bloodied iron oxide.

This accidental sand-mural of mingled powders fell through turning wheels, which crushed, crumbled, and clumped them together. Like dough in a robotic bakery, the gritty mineral paste, of which Fe was but one atom among quintillions, rode conveyors into a powerful industrial furnace. Once inside the calciner chamber, the mixed molecules waited. Then, a human hand activated an electronic dragon.

Terrifying quantities of heat energy pumped into the minerals within the crucible, rapidly raising the interior temperature above that of the hottest, most crushing crater on the surface of violent Venus. Deprived of air, nothing could actually burn, but the energy had to go somewhere, and deep inside the powder, molecular structures were on the move.

The terrific temperature and pressure twisted and warped the bonds of Fe's simple five-boxcar-compound, not decoupling it but locking it into others—pressing down and layering them like molecular masonry. Unforgiving torrents of invisible fire forced the atoms into the interstices of a newly-forming hexagonal molecule.

On a microscopic scale, something grand was under construction, a complex cellular high-rise made from blocks of metallic crystal.

Fe shared its mandated crystalline cell with twenty three of its iron siblings. Older, lighter oxygen atoms dominated the high-rise's infrastructure, bonded into layered crystals and stacked like the spine of a towerblock. A single atom of strontium slipped through into each new ferrite molecule, finding itself inextricably trapped there like carbon in steel. The result was a minority of two, somewhat confused, stray strontium ions per oxygen-iron townhouse.

Small, dense iron atoms like Fe scattered and slotted into disparate tetrahedral and octahedral apartments. Their shared electrons buzzed, tearing through quantum orbits, nuclear forces complementing the electric and keeping the whole mass of trapped energy cocooned in a shard of stable matter.

Thus, strontium ferrite was forged. Each thirty-two-atom molecule bonded to another to create a sixty-four-atom strong hexagonal cell, stacked one atop the next, repeated in their billions until an incredible, sprawling, metallic megalopolis formed.

When the industrial calciner opened, a uniformly-black, clumpy powder filled its interior. The furnace's heat dissipated, the substance cooled, and the process of industry continued. Druke required an incredibly fine grade of powder for its magnets, and so the newly forged strontium ferrite loaf dropped through yet another set of milling and crushing wheels, lubricated by a spray of water, until the powder had been ground down to mere millionths of a meter. Particles in the resulting paste ended up fifty times thinner than a human hair, yet on the scale of the atom Fe, they still towered as sprawling superstructures—vast cityscapes of endless molecular skyscrapers.

A machine extruded the ferrite paste into thick, disk-shaped dyes. A portion containing Fe squeezed into a hollow donut, conforming to the dimensions of the hard-walled industrial mold. This embryo of a magnet next underwent sintering—its particles forced by extremes into a single, solid object. It was as if the planet's core pressed down upon them, yet, the tiny particles of ferrite that had so painstakingly been purified never melted or lost their molecular integrity, instead fusing at last into a sandstone-like solid.

The final stage in the transformation of powder to magnet had everything to do with Fe and its siblings. Crowding oxygen atoms may have dominated the skyscrapers' structure, but they merely served to blindly hold together the crystal cities for their all-important iron tenants.

A Druke generator clicked to life, and the ferrite found itself awash in a powerful, external magnetic field. Strontiums stood by in support while the two dozen iron atoms per cell, Fe among their number, aligned themselves into a great shared choreography of electron ballet. Their magnetic moment had arrived. Saturated in the industrial b-field, the strontium ferrite's many irons surrendered their electrons' spins to synchronicity—more powerfully and more permanently than ever before.

A magnetic field lingered, even as the factory shut down their generators. Fe's state remained in an alignment similar to what it had experienced when the confiscated spearpoint or recycled steel cone had been lifted by industrial electromagnets. Except, this time, the b-field issuing from the iron of the ferrite disk was neither external nor fleeting. Fe and fellow ions' quantum dance of spinning charges synergized with their trillions of siblings across the disk, propping up their magnetic moments to linger for all time. A player in a neverending harmonic symphony, a soldier marching in lock-step with its army—Fe had become part of a permanent magnet.

Druke's signature product ejected from its mold without ceremony, the rough black disk subsequently subjected to trimming by a laser-guided saw. The cutter's blade boasted an edge of diamond—a geometrically-perfect arrangement of simple six-protoned carbons that could cut even iron's bonds asunder. Fe, deep inside the nascent magnet, survived the cuts, invisible b-field lines radiating all the while, humming like an unshakable tune.

The magnetic disk went through further cleaning and polishing before the factory's quality assurance system deemed it had reached an acceptable level of perfection. Though mass-produced and marketed at a competitive price, the final product was one of superior quality. While they waited to be sold, the flat ferrite donuts slid into columns of four, with a round of hard polymer slotted between each.

They were stacked in plain white tubes and packed in plain white boxes. These were sent to the company's product warehouse, a specialized space for storing magnets. For a very long time, this is where Fe rested. Free from sources of excess heat and ferromagnetic objects, the room hung silent save for the subtle hum of its climate control system.

*   *   *

Vi was having trouble keeping her attention on her work. Outside the porthole, she could see the Exodus slowly coming together. She watched as tiny specks of light flared and died on its surface–human crews and construction machines alike, continuing the patient process of printing a spaceship out of a captured asteroid.

The clerk, however, could only see a fraction of the Exodus' growing chassis through the porthole. If she craned her neck, Vi could make out part of the giant Fieldpod, hard to see against the Earthshine. To her other side, the view extended toward the ship's Homepod and the deepening blackness of space. Further out in that direction was the lagrange point where the pilfered asteroid Suruku rested.

Slow dots of light drifted between the Exodus facilities and Suruku, shuttles and mining machines harvesting the latter's elements.

If she were not strapped into her chair, Vi might have been tempted to let her body drift with her attention and float to another of the space station's chambers for a better view. She couldn't believe how quickly they'd been making progress. She couldn't believe any of it. It was a real spaceship, and she was helping to design it! Vi's joy was tempered by a strange, intruding feeling of despair–if things went smoothly, nobody would ever know just how vital the young clerk was to the birth of the groundbreaking spaceliner.

Vi hated the name 'Exodus', but she was starting to fall in love with the craft itself. A generation ship, the Exodus' mission was to transport a community of humans at sublight speeds to a benign planet, light years away. Few, if any, of the people working on the ship's construction that day would still be kicking when it finally caught up to the terraforming robots, already sent on ahead to Akkadia. In fact, only the very youngest of the crew at launch would live to see the planet and mission's end.

Vi found something about that notion romantic as hell.

She shook her head, trying to get it out of the figurative clouds. Her tight curls floated lazily in the absence of gravity, and Vi had to blow to clear one from her vision. If she had an AI to command, she could work by voice alone, but Vi understood better than most who she was working for. Some employees had adapted workarounds, but she still preferred the old-school office setup–hands outstretched on projected keyspaces and an intuitive retinal cursor. The tradeoff of this method was that to use it in orbit, one had to be strapped down and stationary.

Her mind, temporarily restrained along with her body, set to work on file after file of bureaucratic requirement. Rapidly, her eyes tracked screens while silver-painted fingers flicked across the keyspaces. Organizational puzzles fell like defeated enemies against her focus, and it took her less than a hundred minutes to complete a day's work.

Vi rewarded herself with another look outside. A partly-finished spar she had noted before now stretched, complete, between two sections of the ship's spine, and a new bit was already beginning to grow. Years of waiting, and now it was coming together all at once.

Finished early with the job she was paid for, Vi prepared to fulfill her real role for the ambitious Exodus mission. With a tap and a flick of her eyes, Vi logged out of her system, only to log back in under different credentials. She pulled up a file, queued for approval, showing completed sections of the Exodus blueprint. The ship's chassis design had already been finalized, the segments under review already constructed. Everything looked perfect to Vi, who affixed her boss' signature to the file before opening another.

This next file proved more of a challenge. Rather than a redundant bit of high-level bureaucracy, it regarded a follow-up to a project she was becoming intimately familiar with–the flow and livability of the Exodus' bridge section.

Though the ship was intended for a single, one-way, long-haul voyage with no deviations in its course, Ground Mission thought it prudent to design an impressive command bridge between the two enormous, rotating Pods that made up the bulk of the ship's body. The bridge served a social purpose more than anything—it projected a clear sense of centralized command and control, psychologically crucial on a mission where most passengers would never leave the ship. It would keep the future colonists vigilant, organizational proponents argued, and its token hierarchy would prevent complacency from spreading.

Vi found it fascinating how psychology played a part in every bit of engineering Ground Mission put into the colony ship, from the authority-theater of the Command Deck to the way the curves of interior hallways were designed to break up sight lines, making the already huge ship feel city-sized when experienced from within.

The overworked functionary chewed on her lower lip while studying files on her screen. The bridge represented a late addition to the Exodus project, and because its section did not rotate around the ship's axis, its interior would not experience a gravity-equivalent like the Home or Fieldpods would. This made it a unique challenge for ergonomics, engineering, and interior flow.

Vi's boss, a project leader, firmly advocated for including the bridge, even during the early, contentious years of designing the ship. When the new section had finally been granted approval, her boss' role in the Exodus project expanded, even as the leader's capacity to perform her duties grew shaky.

Increasingly feeble and infirm, she put more of her trust in Vi as the ship's construction commenced, the leader allowing the clerk to take her place in orbit in order to be her 'eyes and ears on the scene'. In reality, Vi served as the entire nervous system as her boss back on Earth gradually succumbed to a degenerative condition rare enough that no gene-therapies had been developed to treat it. If it wasn't for the eminent engineer's fierce pride in her role in the project, she would have stepped down long ago. Fortunately for her dreams, she employed a startlingly competent underling who was more than capable of fulfilling them.

It was Vi who had first noticed an oversight in the design that would have, in her mind, proved fatal to the mission. The idea came to Vi when she was pouring over plans for the bridge's communication consoles. Noticing that she'd let her bladder get uncomfortably full, the clerk unstrapped and floated from the module she used as an office, around a bend, down the admin station's main corridor, and towards the lavatories. Vi found the doors to both restroom pods closed when she floated by, red IN USE signs glowing softly. She squirmed, awkward and uncomfortable in the zero-gravity of the station, wishing that her office had its own bathroom.

That was it, she realized–that was the problem. It wasn't the type of thing to be flagged by an automated review process, but the need was screamingly obvious–nobody had thought to put a bathroom on the Exodus' new bridge!

The command section was designed as an operation center, and unlike the giant Pods, experienced no gravity and no life support outside a basic system of vents that provided heat and oxygen. Vi couldn't believe that the ship's future Bridgecrew would be expected to tear themselves away from their duties, unstrap, float down the ship's spine, and travel to the Homepod just to answer nature's call. It was late in the design process, she knew, but not too late to correct this oversight.

At that Eureka moment, not even bothering to address her own internal urgencies, Vi floated back to her office and began crafting an inspired memo to be sent from her boss' account. Ground Mission quickly recognized the toilet oversight and its obvious solution, and Vi set to the task of integrating the new bathroom design into the ship, already under construction. The bridge would need its own small water supply, of course, but without gravity, only a simple suction-based toilet and low-tech astronaut shower would be feasible, similar to the ones Vi and the other personnel in the station already used.

Months later, with the ship's chassis almost complete, Vi flicked her eyes to work the blueprints on her screen as smoothly as she could without overwhelming her migraine suppressants. Time was becoming a factor–construction on the bridge section would complete before the habitat Pods were scheduled to be spun up, she'd heard. Vi set an army of pre-written scripts to attack the technical plans and construction orders, looking for any last possible oversights or weaknesses before she'd consent to affix her boss' approval to the plans.

Her diligence paid off–an alert flashed as one of her bots found a contradiction. According to her script, the current design was not compatible with standard guidelines for spacecraft construction due to a safety oversight. Vi dug deeper and realized that the astronaut shower, which functioned as a glorified wetvac on a stick, and the suction-toilet both represented points of possible depressurization. At that time, standard practices required internal bulkheads to be installed between any potential breach points to ensure survival in case of sudden hull depressurization.

Vi thought it inelegant, but the only solution she could see was to quickly sketch in a pressure door between the shower and toilet sections of the Command Deck bathroom. Like all emergency pressure doors, the bulkhead itself would be hidden in the ship's superstructure and only emerge during a sudden, catastrophic drop in hull integrity.

Searching databases with keystrokes and one eye, while holding the bathroom's schematic still with the other, Vi deftly located and copied designs for a stock model of actuated bulkhead, pre-approved for zero gravity operations. After pasting and tweaking the addition to meet the specific needs of the project, Vi re-ran her scripts. The new specs passed with flying colors, and the upjumped-clerk breathed a sigh of relief. She hoped that this meant she'd finally finished with the endless bridge-bathroom project.

On to the next thing.

Moving at the speed of bureaucracy, Vi's designs were eventually approved and integrated into the mission. When the new addition filtered into the queue of constantly-evolving data, a piece of automated inventory-management software far downstream from the clerk noticed that something was now missing from its balance—with another pressure door added to the design, an order had to be modified and redistributed.

Elsewhere in Ground Mission's network, a subsystem in logistics analyzed the new order—the alloy for the door and the synthetic carbon compounds for the seals were deemed low priority, as they could be printed in-orbit from the surplus of materials harvested from captive Suruku. Prohibitively expensive to launch heavy cargo from Earth, rocket-space was limited to rare materials, complex manufactured goods, and of course, living beings.

To cut down on costs, anything that could be fabricated at the construction site would be, and even an addition as complex as a zero-g bulkhead called for few imported components. Still, some items needed to be added to the queue of outgoing requests to Earth, among them an order for an additional number of strontium ferrite magnets.

Chapter 6: The Zookeeper

Packed tightly in its white plastic tomb, Fe's magnet hardly rattled as it made its way along the path of another grand journey. A flight on a zip drone brought Fe's overnight shipment across the Fraser river to a distribution hub where the magnet navigated an automated maze of conveyors and sorting machines. At the end of this, an airforce of heavy dronecraft waited, silent and steaming, on the shipping company's runways.

A human worker in a full-body set of orange and yellow coveralls hoisted Fe's bag from the conveyor, scanned its tags with his handheld, and carried it over to a waiting drone. The machine was a BZO2120 heavy courier, an automated aircraft roughly the size of a small pony–if said pony was remarkably thin and had detachable legs. BZO was already fully fueled with its complement of hydrogen when Fe's order arrived, and the worker deftly secured the eight strap-and-snap points of the cargo duffle to the underbelly of the drone before clearing it for launch.

Wind clawed at the BZO's polished exterior but found no grip as the ultra-streamlined courier roared south, crossing the Canadian border. Fe had flown through Earth's atmosphere before, once aboard its doomed meteor and many times in the *Fleischerbeile*, guided by Karl's jaded hand. No single flight in the atom's history lasted quite as long as this, however, as the long-haul drone followed a flight path east of the Rockies, bearing continuously south and girding the United States. The BZO's package company owned another facility at the southern tip of Texas, and it stopped just short of the Mexican border, settling down onto tagged terra firma and confirming its arrival with satellite systems. In a reverse of the earlier shipping process, Fe's box found itself unstrapped, conveyed, scanned, sorted, and loaded onto another vehicle–a small, electric delivery truck this time–to complete the final leg of the shipment.

Like most cars on the road, the light truck was driven by AI and plugged into the local transitway's data network, though a single human sat in its cab. A security presence rather than a driver, his shoulder and hips bulged with concealed weaponry, and his face was covered in camera-baffling geometric tattoos–a tetra-hedral pattern that, by coincidence, was not entirely dissimilar from the chemical structure of strontium ferrite.

Brownsville, Texas was the delivery's final destination. A towering forest of gantries poked into view as the truck glided along a searing ribbon of highway. Eventually, the launch facility emerged from the mirage. The delivery vehicle passed through a security gate and, after two cautious rounds of ID-checks, was directed to a series of low buildings adjacent to a large white dome. It was here that Fe and the magnets passed into the hands of a security guard, who provided signature and thumbprint authorization to the tattooed delivery mercenary.

Thus, less than twenty-four hours since it sat in a climate-controlled Canadian warehouse, Fe's package of magnets arrived at one of the Exodus mission's staging and launch areas, deep in the sweltering heat of South Texas.

●　●　●

Dr. Kim's light brown eyes were the only part of their body exposed to the open air of the clean-room. Had their eyebrows existed, they would have constituted a contamination hazard uncovered. However, Kim wore their brows completely shaved off, as was the fashion. They wore a full-body set of white coveralls with long pants tucked into high-shinned white rubber boots. Sturdy gloves, hairnet, rebreather mask, and heavy protective smock completed the ensemble.

The technician was in a foul mood. A fractal of foul moods, really, as Dr. Kim was having a bad week locked inside a depressing year. Their application to work on the Exodus mission had been accepted, of course, but Kim's request to join the actual crew remained stuck in limbo, despite their obvious qualifications.

To make matters worse, in the meantime, Ground Mission had handed Kim a depressingly-lowly position, far from the action, and these last few days had been the worst of all—they'd been pulled out of the Terraforming Department to cover a sudden labor shortage in Pre-Launch Logistics. The overqualified tech was tasked with assembling bits of boring machinery inside a clean-room, following instructions on a 3D overlay and installing precisely-engineered components like a human machine tool. They hated this type of work. A monkey in a lab coat could do it, they felt.

Yesterday, they had spent hours assembling high-strength door actuators—a relatively simple design considering the devices could function without atmosphere or gravity—and slotting them into aluminum frames. Kim was unable to even permit themselves to go brain-dead during the repetitive parts because they knew these machines were going to outer space. Even furious and underappreciated, Dr. Kim had standards.

Finally, the new magnets had arrived, and it was time to assemble the DC motors that would power each door's actuator—a task that could kill a day without straining a single brain cell, the scientist thought, miserably. They set each component in a neat row in front of them and pulled up the 3D instructions, making a checklist—rotor, copper windings, strontium ferrite magnets, assorted fasteners, et cetera.

"Hey, Kim. You working on that new order?" Another tech asked, walking by and pushing a cart. He was dressed the same as Dr. Kim, indistinguishable at a distance, but up-close, one could see that his eyebrows were unshaven and his hairnet extended down to the bridge of his nose. "It's a door, yeah?"

"Mm hmm." Kim nodded, giving their colleague but a sliver of their attention.

"Didja hear what part of the ship it's for?"

Kim shook their head once, sharply. The specs heavily implied that it was a zero-g pressure door, which obviously meant it would be on the bridge or near an exterior hatch, but that was as far as their knowledge went.

"Bathroom's what I heard. Meant to protect the space toilet." The tech laughed. "Don't mess up, Kim. Could lead to a Situation Brown and ruin the mission. Everyone's counting on you."

"Mm hmm," Dr. Kim replied mirthlessly.

The obnoxious tech wheeled away, and Kim lowered their chin to their chest, wishing they'd never been pulled from their slightly-more prestigious assignment, where they could be reading numerical interstellar data feeds right now about a group of terraforming slime-molds and how well they enjoyed Akkadia-2. It wasn't as if Kim had been doing anything particularly important or challenging there. Rather than getting to watch the landers explore the Akkadian surface, they spent their time engaged in grunt work—processing data or troubleshooting the terraforming machines' older designs against new instructions programmed by senior staff.

Data-monkey, code-checker, or working assembly-by-numbers like a drunken university student with a hex wrench, Kim felt that every assignment from Ground Mission thus far had not been what they considered a proper use for their double doctorates in astrophysics and mechanical engineering.

When they applied to the program, Dr. Kim had wanted to *run* the Terraforming Department at the very least. They were far too brilliant to be a bit-player, they reasoned. Yet, the space industry had contracted into a few major players, and it was a buyer's market for talent. A PhD could get you a job washing out beakers, the old joke went. A double PhD at least got Kim in the show, albeit as lowly support staff. Who the hell could Ground Mission have crewing this dreadnaught? The scientist often wondered, between other dark thoughts, as they worked.

Assembling the guts of a toilet door was a far cry from Kim's astronaut dreams, but they did an expert job, despite their despair. The machine that would eventually be installed aboard the Exodus was a motor-driven actuator tucked into a frame of aluminum—that rival metal of Fe, light and strong, humanity's choice for centuries when building something that had to reach the sky. These aluminum parts were machine engineered to micron-tolerances, with nodes and channels carved out to nest the motor's components, some of which had already been installed before the freshly-delivered Druke magnets passed through the grumpy scientist's fingers.

Kim's hands manipulated a set of sterile forceps, gently lifting Fe's magnet from the worktable. They set it in a horizontal stack along with the other ferrite rings, creating a short, segmented tube. Humming together in harmony, the countless synchronized electron dancers inside the irons generated a straight, uniform b-field down the newly-crafted magnetic tunnel. The nonferrous aluminum made the perfect frame, supporting the specialized magnetic material in much the same way as Fe's neighbor oxygen atoms nested the metallic ions within a safe tetrahedral townhouse.

Next, Dr. Kim used a delicate tool to weave copper wire through the winding channels drilled into the motor's frame. Copper, one of humankind's oldest metallic allies, would be sent to space for its capacity to carry electrical current where its masters willed it. Kim's patient weaving process could be brain-numbing, but they willed their mind to focus on the job, performing it as perfectly as if they had been confronted with the tasks of a surgeon rather than an electrician.

Without further interruption, Kim installed the motor's copper circulatory system, completing the rotor windings and integrating the armature and stator. Fastening the mounting brackets took only a moment, and soon the assembly was ready for beam-welding.

As a flood of high-energy electrons melted and fused the aluminum casing together, Fe found itself once more becoming part of a complex machine. In the Ju-88, the atom's duty was simple—holding strong as steel, armoring and defending the moving parts of its engine. In the door motor, however, its role would be more rarified.

Welding finished, Dr. Kim took the newly-completed machine in their gloved hands and walked it to a station for testing. From a battery pack, they drew two wires and made temporary connections to the direct-current terminals on the back of the motor. Kim created a circuit, and current flowed through copper wiring wound throughout the device. Within the motor's magnetic tube, the constant b-field created by Fe and its companions began to strain against the new charges. Humans had long before discovered that electric current moving within a magnetic field summons a force–one which the clever primates could harness to do useful work

Thus, a fraction of a second after Kim connected the terminals, enough current passed through the rotor that it experienced a new force pushing back from the ring magnets, an invisible pressure born along b-field lines. Fe and the strontium ferrite disks were stationary and locked into frame, immovable, though their field shoved at the wires with unrelenting magnetic force–eventually shifting the copper atoms themselves. The armature of coiled wire, wrapped around a central shaft, had been engineered to rotate, and magnetic pressure forced a twisting torque that spun the motor one half turn before the lines of force zeroed out. As it rotated, small conductive brushes broke and re-connected the motor's circuit, reversing the direction of the electric current. In turn, this reversed the magnetic force, and the rotor spun back to its original position.

Plugged into the battery, this complex dance of electromagnetic forces and half-turns repeated many times each second, faster than the human eye could behold. To Dr. Kim, the result was a throaty whirr coming from the aluminum-clad device. A small rotary point at the end of the motor, meant to connect to the rest of the actuator assembly, spun impotently on the tech's bench.

They were satisfied, if not surprised, that everything in Fe's motor appeared to be working correctly. Trying not to focus on the fact that they were spending the day completing only one half of a detestable job, Kim dug out some partly-finished actuator parts and began to work on integrating the motor.

Its design was complex, but the machine's motions were elegant and precise, engineered to convert rotary spin into reciprocating motion. As the electrons and b-field lines did their dance, the spinning shaft of the motor would rotate a screw mechanism coupled with a ball-nut. This metal piece slid upward as the screw turned, efficiently converting a spinning motor into a straight-line push.

Kim spent hours completing the design, integrating the components along projected guides and using the beam welder to seal the aluminum case. Eventually, the finished machine was ready to test. During this time, Dr. Kim found themselves letting their mind wander familiar dark paths. They should be packing for Akkadia, not doing grunt work. Why had they not been fast-tracked for the crew? Who could be more qualified? The entire Ground Mission must be incompetent, Kim decided.

The Exodus would most likely fail, the scientist endeavored to convince themself–being kept off the ship might end up being lucky in the long run. The dolorous Dr. Kim repeated this thought, willing themselves to believe it. As they tested the completed actuator assembly, they found comfort in imagining all the different ways the Exodus could catastrophically fail. "I was almost aboard that death-trap," Kim would be sure to tell people when it happened.

Their expert hands drew electric leads from a battery and attached them to the finished motor assembly for a quality control test. Fe's device worked as intended–a whirring noise arose, a deeper frequency this time, and the shiny actuator arm wooshed forward in a single punch. It was perfect. Kim allowed themselves a small smile of satisfaction.

They quickly realized, however, that they'd have to do it all over again tomorrow for the door's second assembly, and Dr. Kim's smile was replaced by a comfortable scowl.

● ● ●

"Three, two, one...blastoff!" Eve said aloud, strapped into her acceleration couch aboard the waiting shuttle.

An enormous, heavy-lift booster sat steaming on the Brownsville launchpad, the stubby-winged shuttle and its passengers clinging awkwardly to one side of the rocket. A foam crate packed with motorized actuators for pressure doors lay neatly secured in the cargo hold alongside processor chips, seventy-thousand industrially freeze-dried apple seeds, and boxes of tiny flasks that contained goat, goose, and deer embryos. Two hundred and forty-eight future Exodus crewmembers waited as well, strapped in the shuttle's cabin. Among them, one freckled little girl vibrated with enough excitement to ignite solid rocket fuel.

"What's that, honey?" Her mother asked sleepily, strapped in beside Eve.

"*Blastoff*."

The rocket didn't so much as flinch.

It wasn't scheduled to launch for some time yet, but in Eve's imagination, she was already miles into the sky, riding its trail of fire to a grand adventure. The child simply couldn't believe her fortunes. In a matter of just a few months, she'd been plucked out of her grey little apartment and told that she was moving–moving into a spaceship!

Eve burned with the unquenchable joy of a child who knows they live in a world where wishes come true. She thought back to her cramped, crowded school–a place she'd never have to go back to now. Eve had been taking a standardized test in her sweaty, lower-elementary classroom when she made her desire manifest. She remembered how the flickering text of the writing prompt glowed below her–

What do you dream of?

Of the fifty-odd students in the room, some wrote wishes for fame or fortune. Other, more literal-minded pupils, described their nocturnal dreams and nightmares. Most wrote nothing. Two boys skipped the prompt entirely in favor of sketching physiologically-inaccurate phalluses. Eve, however, was inspired–she scrawled an impressive paragraph on her wish to someday live on a spaceship and visit the stars. Her finger skidding happily across the smeared, shatterproof glass of her schooldesk's smart-screen, she'd added a doodle of a rocket and one of herself as an astronaut for good measure. Eve believed that she had wished her way aboard the Exodus with her essay. She was right.

Finally aboard the shuttle, the girl couldn't keep her excitement at bay. She'd been imagining the moment of liftoff in her head, again and again, willing it to be true. It wasn't her fault if the words occasionally snuck out of her brain and into her mouth.

"Three, two, one...blastoff!" She repeated.

Molly Gallagher, Eve's mother, rolled her purple eyes in response, then clenched them tightly. The young woman's thin hands, inked and scarred, were also closed–folded into tight little fists.

"Three, two, one...blastoff...Three, two, one...blastoff...Three, two–"

"Shhhhh!" Molly hissed.

A few of the sardine-packed passengers, no doubt anxious to be launched into space themselves, had twisted around to give the child unfriendly looks.

"Sorry," Eve whispered, but her lips continued to recite the phrase in silence until it became true.

Three, two, one...blastoff!

● ● ●

Earth's gravity pulled with the planetary certainty that nothing could escape its strength and grasp, and yet, with a thunderous roar, the heavy-lift booster released volcanic quantities of stored chemical energy and forcibly dragged itself and its kiloton of baggage off the ground and into the sky, fleeing gravity's shaking fist. Eve, Molly, and the other humans found themselves pressed into their seats, accelerated into an oppressive flavor of crushed, awed silence.

Bonded by oxygen in a double molecule of strontium ferrite crystal, pressed into a magnet, installed in a motor, and packed aboard a rocket, the atom Fe soon surpassed any altitude record it had achieved while part of an airplane–higher and higher until the atmosphere disappeared and it floated in space once again. Fe had orbited through extraplanetary space for most of its existence, riding a heaven metal asteroid. Each time it sailed past the blue planet, the traveler found Earth somewhat changed–geology stabilized, evolution progressed, civilization metastasized. It was as if Fe had completed just another pass, this time with a sojourn planetside rather than through the void of aphelion. Now, back up in the cold vacuum of nothing, the atom found that the Earth it sailed above had transitioned tremendously in mere millenia.

Where once the planet's night-shrouded darkside was broken only by the lights of a few fires, now the Earth at night was a sprawling web of illumination–tiny points of light stretching into beams along roadlines, clustered in cities, and ringed along a new high-water coastline. The once peaceful void of space had changed too–it was filled with constellations of blinking satellites, several utilitarian-ugly space stations, countless construction and shuttle craft, a great dirty captured asteroid, and finally, one gargantuan spaceliner nearing completion, its black bulk stretching out toward lagrange-one.

Molly risked peeking her eyes open, her entire body tingling. Beside her, Eve's smile threatened to stretch around the girl's entire head. How in hell are we astronauts? The young mother shook her head the full eighteen degrees her neck constraints would allow.

She remembered reaching new heights of self-consciousness when she joined the Exodus mission. During her first interview with the recruiters who'd plucked Eve from her testing data, Molly wore long sleeves and leggings despite the heat of the day. She didn't want the men to look at her burnscars–bodywide tiger stripes of pale, raised flesh, outlined in dramatic fashion by bold lines of black tattooing. This form of artistic mutilation seemed sexy, trendy, and a little bit dangerous back when Molly had no shits to give for the future. Nearly a generation later and burnscarring fell somewhere between off-putting and downright trashy in the public consciousness. Molly noticed the recruiters glance at the marks on her hands she couldn't cover up, and she was certain that they'd think she wasn't good enough to go to outer space.

Any lingering sense of not belonging evaporated the instant the Gallagher girls cleared decontamination and entered the partially-complete Homepod. Molly saw plenty of tired, ordinary-looking people, more than one with burnscars like hers, and even a couple with amp-teeth. The folks milling around the common area wouldn't be out of place at a twelve-step meeting or a public transit station back home, Molly realized. The most notable members of the new crew, however, had to be the kids–young, energetic, bright-eyed children played everywhere, far more than would be expected for an average crowd of this size. So far, the Homepod put Molly in mind of a huge, under-construction shopping mall, or perhaps a very boring space-themed carnival with no rides and nothing to buy.

Two girls around Eve's age sat playing at a nearby table. They traced their fingers on the smartglass, steering brightly-colored snakes around hazards.

"Yes! They have Kobra!" Eve shouted, pumping her fist and sitting down at the table without waiting for an invitation.

"Hey. I'm Eve Gallagher," she said to the nonplussed girls, pressing her own finger to the table and joining the game with a purple snake.

"Lacey Diallo," said the one controlling a green snake. The girl's hair was studded across her head in short twists, and her skin was the color of ebony.

"I'm Jooles–dammit!" The younger one had just lost her snake. Jooles' hair was arranged like her sister's, though her complexion was much lighter.

"Dammit!" The pale Eve imitated, a moment later, when her short-lived purple snake was knocked out of play by its green opponent.

The one called Lacey sat back on her stool, arms folded, a self-satisfied smirk on her face.

"You gotta show me how you did that!" Eve implored her.

The girls would stay friends, growing up together as the ship grew around them. Their Homepod served as the main living area onboard the Exodus, though it was in a state of only partial completion when Eve moved in. The city-sized habitat the young humans explored occupied the interior surface of an enormous cylindrical shell, built around the spaceliner's axis. When its centrifugal thrusters had first been fired, the entire titanic habitat lurched into stable rotation, creating forces that pressed on the cylinder's interior walls in a facsimile of gravity. A human could walk on the rotating inner skin of the Homepod as comfortably as if Earth's own native pull held them down. Ground Mission started moving in crewmembers as soon as the Pod's interior was pressurized and filled with breathable air. Fe and the Gallagher girls had been somewhat tardy arrivals.

"You shoulda seen it when we first moved in," Jooles said. "There wasn't even *anything* in Homepod."

"It was like livin' in a motherfucking Coke can," her sister finished, with a tisk.

On that day, Eve and the Diallos were exploring the Suruku-facing side of the habitat, trying to stay out from underfoot. Busy adults and older children swarmed everywhere–pressed into service to finish outfitting the Homepod where most would spend the rest of their lives. Around the girls, crewmembers hefted crates, erected modular walls, and assembled furniture. Anyone who could work was given a task. Luckily for the young trio, they all fell under the minimum age for mandatory service.

"Even the moon was better," the youngest added, sitting atop a crate, her feet dangling above the floor.

"Moon camp fucking sucked," Lacey said with sudden vitriol.

"Was it really that bad? You got to live on the *moon*!"

For Ground Mission, the task of populating the Exodus with enough crewmembers to ensure a viable colonist population at journey's end was logistically daunting. To land the mission anywhere within the realm of the possible, the heavy-lift launches from Earth, augmented by commercial space-flights, needed to be packed with people, many of whom had to spend an extended time waiting for the Homepod to be ready. The bulk of those stuck on interplanetary layovers had been slotted into moonside housing. Inside temporary, prefab bubble-tents on Luna, Ground Mission policed and trained a mass of potential crewmembers. Lacey, Jooles, and their father Tim had spent months in the plasticky, prisonlike moon camp before finally being shuttled to the Exodus–ending up in an empty alloy can without walls or a floor.

The Diallo sisters took turns explaining the spartan state of the early Exodus Homepod, one-upping each other with tales of boredom and scarcity. Eve, rather than feeling sorry for her friends' hardships, was envious that they had seen parts of the ship she hadn't.

"...and if you walked out the wrong door, you would *die*!" Jooles finished, her eyes bugging wide.

"That sounds so cool," Eve replied wistfully, though the habitat around her was still in a state of primitive pre-construction.

"It's like that some places still." Jooles said, idly kicking her feet.

"It's dangerous," Lacey asserted. "Daddy said we shouldn't go to the Earth-facing side of the Pod because it ain't finished yet."

"Will you show me?" Eve asked, her eyes lighting up at the mention of danger.

The girls marched Earthward, pressed to the spinning interior of the giant shell of the Homepod, which to their eyes appeared as a sprawling, mostly-empty neighborhood that simply curved around back into itself. They walked along a main thoroughfare called Pi Street, marked by a wide section of bright red floor-striping that stretched the entire length of the Pod. At ninety-degree intervals along the cylinder's interior there also stretched the blue ribbon of Earth Street, the green-lined Home Street, and the yellow-striped Sun Street.

After many minutes of walking, the girls reached a part of the Homepod build up against the can's far, Earth-facing wall.

"Oh," exclaimed Eve, a bucktoothed smile appearing across her cinnamon-freckled face, "I get why your dad said not to come here."

Permanent flooring had been installed in only some of the sections, the rest left exposed and gaping with uncovered hull. The group of children hopped over to one bare edge and looked down at the dimpled, grey alloy of the Exodus's outer hull.

It was freezing cold because there was only outer space on the other side, Lacey explained, though Eve had to verify by nearly freezerburning away her own fingerprints.

"Some of the holes have wires all in them," the youngest of the trio observed.

The girls tried to stay on the mostly-finished paths, keeping out of the way of masked adults wearing foot stilts and carrying rods that sprayed expanding insulation into the hollows. Three unsupervised children playing in an objectively dangerous area were sure to draw attention, and after several sharp looks from harried adult workers, Eve and the sisters agreed to travel somewhere less conspicuous.

They walked toward one far terminus of the Pod, settling down against a large, closet-sized fire-suppression system in a finished area with floors and rooms and doors. Set into a nearby wall, ringed in caution markers, was a hatch labeled 'Bridge Access'.

"Have you ever been in there?" Eve asked, pointing at the hatch, eager for more adventure.

"No-" Jooles began to reply.

"Sure. Lotsa times," Lacey answered, not wanting to lose face in front of their new friend.

Eve positively loved living on a spaceship–there was always something new to explore. The hatch took a minute to figure out, but the bright young children were able to work out the locking system.

Lacey gave the latch a backward yank. Inside, there stretched a wall and a narrow corridor, curving around to infinity. They had made it inside the skin of the Homepod's giant shell, mere meters from the outer hull and the can's circular lid. Inside the access hatch there were ladders, hundreds of rungs high, and what looked like an elevator cage. Warning messages in multiple languages adorned the alloy walls.

'CAUTION: REDUCED GRAVITY AHEAD'

'BRIDGE ACCESS. AUTHORIZED PERSONNEL ONLY'

'WARNING–GRAVITATIONAL TRANSITION ZONE–RISK OF BODILY INJURY OR DEATH'

"Woah," Lacey breathed. She craned her neck, following the ladders as they stretched up the dizzyingly high wall.

Eve walked near the ladders and stood on her tip-toes to read more warning notices. Following along in a parallel channel to each ladder was a sliding safety cable with attached carabiner. She carefully read the steps listed on a red-lettered sign and attached one of the safety lines to a belt-loop in her coveralls before mounting the lowest rung.

"What are you doing?" Lacey called out, finally noticing Eve.

"It's ok, you don't have to come," Eve called back, mischief in her eyes. "You've probably done this lotsa times."

In the battle between the young children's curiosity and natural fear of obvious danger, social pressure won out, and the sisters followed Eve, who climbed just a couple rungs up to supervise their safety-harnessing.

Luckily for the girls, no adults passed through that particular access point while they lingered and played. Construction of the zero-g bridge, in fact, had mostly been completed even before habitation of the Homepod first began, and in the months that followed, the section remained unstaffed and unused. This would all change once the Exodus got underway, but for the moment, the trio had the ladders to themselves.

Back on Earth, Eve wasn't the most experienced climber of things, but even she knew that what her body experienced as she ascended bridgeward was not normal. She thought climbing all that way would be hard work, and it was, at first. But somehow, as she ascended she grew lighter, and her movements became effortless. Soon, the children were half-climbing, half-floating up the ladders, involuntary giggles bursting from their mouths.

When they reached the top of their climb, they found that they could let go of the ladder entirely and still float where they were, perceiving only the tiniest tug at their feet. The force from the Homepod's rotation, experienced by crewmembers as artificial gravity, was strongest along its inner skin but dropped to nothing as one approached the central axis of rotation. Eve didn't understand this at the time, but she'd eventually get to the bottom of the mystery, as well as many others.

As the children reached the landing, they found a hatch that, when opened, revealed a nauseatingly-spinning corridor, studded with handholds along all four walls.

"Ugh," Jooles groaned, turning away from the disturbing motion of the hallway beyond.

Eve unclipped her safety harness and floated free for a moment. The sensation was similar to what she felt back in the shuttle after the rocket had pushed her off the Earth's surface and broken free of its gravity. But she had been strapped down then, and nothing had been spinning in front of her face like a building-sized blender. Squinting her eyes and trying not to let the corridor make her dizzy, Eve decided that there was nothing in there that could really hurt her.

"Gimme a push," she commanded.

Lacey reached up and shoved on Eve's boots, sending the new girl flying forward.

Eve floated into the spinning corridor and reached out cautiously for a hand-hold. Her universe reoriented itself as she realized that she had been the one spinning, not the hallway. The handhold jerked her arm. She let go and grabbed another, bleeding away her angular momentum until she matched the blender-hallway in its stillness.

After Eve managed to come to rest and collect herself, she turned to flash a triumphant grin to her friends–only to find them spinning crazily outside the hatch, like two kids inside a washing machine looking out.

Eve laughed, but she felt her stomach lurch worryingly. It was hard to look straight at them, but the sisters had seen how their freckled friend had arrested her motion and come to occupy the same reference frame as the spinning corridor. Lacey followed first, holding hands with the reluctant Jooles. They awkwardly planted themselves against the shifting walls and snatched at handholds until all three floated together at relative rest.

Though they occupied the same frame of angular reference, the girls hadn't yet agreed to a common interpretation of what was up and what was down. However, they reached a consensus and half walked, half floated, in the same direction–pulling themselves through the corridor via handholds and flying like superhumans.

They traveled around a corner, passing by a bright red hatch and through a wide cubic junction into another enclosed tunnel. The children had entered into the viscera of the ship, moving from the Homepod into the fully zero-g engineering section, a vague catchall used to refer to any part of the ship that wasn't explicitly the bridge or a habitat.

"Where are we?" Jooles asked.

"We're in the Exodus' fat fucking belly," Lacey answered, patting her own athletic midriff.

"This place is awesome!" Eve chimed in. "I don't think we're even in the Homepod anymore."

"We're not in Homepod?" The youngest asked, her voice quavering. "I don't wanna get lost. I don't wanna get lost from Daddy!"

"It's ok, Joojoo," Lacey said, her voice calm. "We're not lost. You know the way back, right Eve?"

Eve nodded, but didn't say anything, letting Lacey take the lead.

"You know the way too. Dontcha Joojoo?" The older sibling smiled a tomb-stone row of gleaming teeth at her sister. "It's easy."

"Back around that corner," Jooles began, tentatively, "and...and then just keep going to the hallway with all the grab-holds, then outside that there's the ladders." As the girl explained the way out, her voice grew in confidence, the tide of tears abating.

"And here's where we're going," Eve added, pointing. "Just follow the signs."

The familiar 'Bridge Access' labels were emblazoned on one wall, directing the way Earthward. With the natural grace of extreme youth, the girls climb-floated their way through engineering and toward the bridge. It was after turning right and entering into an expansive junction that they first ran into trouble.

A man and a woman were coming toward the girls from another direction. The adults shepherded a group of wrapped packages as they moved. To Eve, they looked like neighbors taking a limbless pack of lazy, floating dogs for a walk.

"Greta, there's kids," they heard the man whisper, sharply.

Before the children could hide, the woman pushed off toward them, leaving her parcels and partner behind.

"Woah girls, don't look so startled now." She spoke with a muddled, European-sounding accent. "What are you little ones doing here?"

"We're supposed to be here," Lacey boldly stated. "What are *you* doing here?"

"We're at work." The man pulled himself forward to join them.

"So are we," Lacey said, looking at her friends and nodding.

Eve and Jooles nodded along, trying to look confident.

"Oh really?" The woman called Greta laughed. "I didn't know they were letting such young kids work in engineering. Where are your parents?"

"Maybe we should call Captain Singh," the male worker offered.

The younger girls looked to Lacey, who chewed her lip, seemingly at a loss.

"I'm surprised you haven't seen more of us," Eve piped up, filling the silence. "Who do you think can fit in all the teeny tiny tunnels up here? Only little kids. That's why there's so many of us on the ship."

"Duh," Lacey added, her head back in the game..

Greta and her companion looked at each other uncertainly, then back at the girls.

"I bet you haven't been working on the bridge very long," Eve remarked, going in for the kill, "or you'da seen us."

The two adults, less confident than they were moments earlier, began to drift back toward their parcels.

"Well, alright, girls," the woman said, her syllables musical but hesitant. "Just be sure to go back to your parents as soon as your task is done, ok now?"

The children smiled and agreed, backing themselves out of the path of the adults and their floating cargo.

"Watch the actuators," the man warned as one wrapped-up lump drifted in Eve's direction.

The girl gave the parcel a small tap, righting it on its path.

"Thanks."

Eve didn't know it, but the actuator, a model designed for zero-g emergency pressure doors and assembled back in Texas, left Earth aboard the very same rocket she and her mother had ridden into outer space.

She breathed out, elated, after the adults floated a safe distance away. "That was close."

"Too fucking close," Lacey agreed.

"I wanna go back to Daddy!"

"Ok, ok. Goddamn," Lacey said quickly, worried that Jooles was shouting too loudly. "We can go back. You remember the way?"

"Uh huh," Jooles sniffled. "The signs we followed, we follow them backwards. It curves around, but, but then we get to the hallway with all the grab-holds. We go down that. Then, there's the ladders..."

● ● ●

From Dr. Kim's workstation, the actuator assembly that contained the atom Fe had been packed and moved to temporary storage, joining a crate of identical components intended for the Exodus' emergency bulkheads. After the launch of the heavy-lift booster and the shuttle's rendezvous with the Homepod, crewmembers unloaded Fe's crate, stacking the equipment among chaotic piles of goods that crowded the decks.

For days, the iron atom sat unmoving in the complex machine, packed alongside three other actuators and stored with an enormous hoard of valuable Earth imports. Unlike the Stills' treasure trove of coins, antiques, and memorabilia, the chaotic cargo brought aboard the Exodus was mostly made up of complex machinery, spare parts, and biological imports. Like spaceborn ants, crewmembers would briefly appear and approach the stores, only to carry off a piece of the hoard and disappear into the depths of the ship.

Eventually, Fe's time came, and a crewmember loaded its crate onto a hand-truck. Back on Earth, automation had become ubiquitous, but aboard the Exodus, AI-controlled workers were nonexistent, and the few lifts and drones aboard were mostly reserved for hazardous tasks around the ship's pair of massive fusion engines. The crewmember, unassisted, maneuvered the actuators out of the artificial gravity of the Homepod and into engineering via a quick, caged cargo-elevator, destined for the bridge.

Construction on the superstructure of the ship's Command Deck had already been completed, but before launch it would need fixtures installed and finishing work. Most of the frantic activity aboard the ship took place as the crew prepared their Homepod and Fieldpod, but specialized crews were sometimes tasked with shuttling cargo or performing an installation in the bridge or engineering sections. Greta and her partner, Mew, sometimes joked that they were human drones.

The two had spent most of their time as astronauts schlepping cargo throughout the ship and performing repetitive tasks. Mew had worked in a factory that manufactured custom, high-end boats before joining the Exodus. They paired him with Greta, who had once been a professional football player before two kids and a ledger of bad debts made the Exodus an attractive prospect. Ground Mission trained them on the installation of emergency pressure doors, of which the great colony ship boasted hundreds. The only notable feature of the transportation and installation of Fe's actuator was that the project took place in the Command Deck's single bathroom, 'the head,' a place where the crew very seldom ventured.

Along the way, the pair ran into a group of small children—three girls, all different colors, two with mouths on them. Greta doubted they belonged but couldn't prove it. After the encounter, Mew insisted it was all bullshit but that he didn't want to get involved or bother Captain Singh over it.

The Command Deck had been built with authority and impression in mind. Though less than efficient in principle, the bridge had been separated into multiple stations—navigation, communications, and engineering, to name the most important. On an incredibly long journey like that of the Exodus, lightspeed delays would eventually make communications with Earth difficult. However, these were not centralized aboard the Exodus, and its many redundant dishes and antennas could ensure a link home for any crewmember. Navigation was another station built more for psychological comfort than anything else, as the ship would follow a pre-set path to Akkadia and possessed very little ability to maneuver outside of this. Engineering, on the other hand, involved regulation of the electric power that flowed from the ship's direct fusion drives, the performance of the engines themselves, the ship's life support systems, and most of the maintenance and safety tasks aboard the vessel—in many ways, the techies' station was the true power-center of the Command Deck.

"Where's the weapons console?" Mew, a fan of classic science fiction, asked, reviewing the various stations on the bridge.

Greta, floating beside him, snorted.

The Exodus traveled unarmed, they both knew. Only orbital bombers and black-shuttles had teeth, and these barely qualified as spacecraft. In the unlikely event that the Exodus encountered a threat, shooting its way out was not an option Ground Mission intended it to have.

"Target acquired," Greta said, pointing across the room at a small sign bearing the universal symbol for bathroom.

Handholds allowed the workers to push over to the lavatory. There, they secured themselves and their equipment with safety tethers, anchors for which could be found every few feet along the walls. Greta and Mew were tasked with two installs that day, one door to separate the bridge and restroom, and another inside, between the suction-toilet and the other half of the head. They fell into a familiar rhythm, freeing the bulkhead door from its temporary moorings and installing the mechanical and electrical components that would, in the case of sudden pressure-loss, allow it to quickly slide down and form an airtight seal.

Greta bolted Fe's actuator inside the ship's walls, out of view when linked with the main body of the bulkhead. Before the technicians could wire the new emergency doors into the ship's power grid, they would need to be tested. Mew pulled a battery pack from a pouch around his waist and tossed it at Greta. The boxy object floated placidly across the small room before the retired athlete snatched it from the air and created a circuit with the terminals on either side of the door.

When Greta made the connection between battery and motor, floodgates of electric potential broke open, and current began to flow through the complex plumbing of woven copper windings within the motor's aluminum housing. Next, the strong magnetic field, infinitesimally aided by the quantum choreography of Fe's own electrons, produced the necessary torque and forced the rotor to spin. A screw connected to the motor turned, and the ball-nut wrapped around its shaft shot upward. Inside the wall, this sudden, climbing force punched a shiny, aluminum-clad actuator arm forward. Mirrored exactly by the door's other assembly, itself handcrafted by the Earthbound Dr. Kim, the two motors worked in concert to shove the pressure door closed with a whoosh, planting a solid wall of alloy between Greta and Mew.

It worked—and on the first try, too. Greta was pleased, and she released the door. It whooshed back upward, settling nearly-invisibly into an overhead groove. The crew of two reunited and floated fractionally closer to the Command Deck, where they began an identical installation process for the other emergency bulkhead. Ideally, the pressure doors like Fe's would never need to be used. Nevertheless, the workers took their task seriously. By now, installing pressure door assemblies had nearly become muscle-memory, and besides, Greta and Mew enjoyed floating around. There were certainly worse jobs aboard the Exodus.

● ● ●

Molly Gallagher was elbow-deep in a vat of viscous goop when a thick-walled bubble rose from its surface and burst. A pungent funk, stronger than the baseline stink of compost, arose from the vat and made Molly gag. She had to turn her head away, her eyes watering.

She took a shaky breath—at least she'd managed not to throw up. On the other hand, Molly mused, her vomit could only have enhanced the nutritional content of the compost she was tasked with brewing and mixing. Around her, other sweaty crewpeople worked the steaming vats, most of them wearing breathing masks or bandanas, none looking particularly pleased with their assignment. Molly never would have considered herself a country girl, yet here she was–muddy and smelly and working her ass off, all to turn a big alloy can into a rotating space-farm.

The twin fusion engines provided plenty of excess power for the twenty-thousand lux SunLight, which created an artificial day-night cycle for the ship's living cargo. The conscripted farmers also received all the water they could ever need, originally harvested from a comet–a nameless chip of ice that had been captured via the same method that hogtied Sukuru. Endlessly-recyclable water filled the Exodus's two enormous tanks, which, sandwiched at either end of the ship, acted as radiation shields between the Pods and the fusion engines. Molly remembered a few bad drought years in her girlhood and appreciated the ship's near-inexhaustible tanks. Her daughter Eve would never know what it was like to be thirsty. Still, it didn't sugarcoat compost duty much.

Molly mixed the rich organic goop, a microbial brew more complicated than any recipe she'd ever prepared, with dead lunar regolith and Sukuru scrapings to eventually make fertile soil. Regolith, brought to the ship via tug, poured down from an overhead platform into the compost vats Molly and her peers mixed–she would have to shake the dust out of her hair later, something to distract her on the long commute home if Tim didn't show up.

Importing a Fieldpod's worth of soil from Earth would be logistically impossible for the Exodus mission, but with proxy-dirt and water available in orbit, the only missing ingredients were the microbes—and the manpower. It made for hundreds of hours of grunt work for the new crewmembers, but even Molly knew how necessary this work was to the mission. She was, quite literally, building a better world for her daughter. What parent could wish for a more complete purpose in life? Besides, she mused, there were worse jobs in the Fieldpod. Like Tim's.

As Molly's mind wandered, she allowed her eyes to slide over to her tall, dark, handsome coworker. She picked a bad moment, as Tim was occupied in shifting shovelfuls of fresh manure, bacterially-rich gifts from a mixed herd of cows, sheep, and goats. The docile animals had been imported from Earth with some difficulty and great expense. Dirty as it was, Ground Mission had assigned Tim a crucial job, considering how much the long-term success of colonizing Akkadia-2 would depend upon a large influx of Exodan fauna.

He was wearing a leather cowboy hat that looked adorable and silly and sexy, Molly thought, considering they were onboard a spaceship with a SunLight too diffuse to get in one's eyes. Over a cup of shine with coworkers, Tim had once confided that he'd swapped with another crewmember for the hat his first day aboard, exchanging a pack of THC chewables that had been burning a hole in his pocket.

Tim Diallo, father to two bright young girls, was a man as unlikely to end up farming livestock as Molly was to be ranching microbes, she felt. Assigned to the same Fieldpod crew, the two became fast and easy friends. She saw so many reflections of her own life in his. Neither wealthy nor well educated, Tim hadn't even officially applied to the Exodus. Instead, like Molly, Ground Mission chose his girls in the months that followed mandatory state testing. The girls were off-the-charts smart, he'd brag to Molly, keeping the addendum to himself that Lacey was quite a bit further off the charts than her sister.

When Tim first told his story, Molly connected some dots in her mind. State testing–her first impressions of the Exodus. She flashed back to the odd way in which the news had been broken, when her life changed forever in one evening–

"Some important people came to my school today to talk to me!" Eve announced before even dropping her pack. "They want me to live on a spaceship! You can come too. Can you believe it?"

"Uhh…" was the best the young mom could do.

As they washed up for dinner, Eve babbled everything about the recruiters at school and the Exodus and how they had come to talk to her and ask her questions. Her mother had heard of the Exodus mission, of course. She knew how smart Eve could be and how eager the girl was to show it off. It made sense that Ground Mission would want to recruit bright children, but hearing it all at once, and about *her* child, came as a shock.

"So can we go, Mommy?" Eve asked. Not begging or pouting, the girl flashed her mother a thousand-lux smile.

When Eve smiled, her bright eyes shrunk to slits, her freckled brow crinkled, and she presented a pair of enormous adult incisors that had arrived early to the party. Molly melted.

Her daughter never stopped talking about spaceships. It was nothing less than a dream come true. A wish granted–a prayer answered. They'd have food and shelter and clothing and healthcare up there. Molly would have a job for life. Eve could get a first-class education. She could leave that sad, crowded little school. Molly could make it all real for her daughter without much more than a snap of her fingers. All she would have to do would be to break the lease on their apartment, quit her dead-end retail job, say goodbye to everyone she'd ever known, and move to a spaceship, understanding that she'd be agreeing to die onboard one day–a billion miles from nowhere.

"Yes, honey. We can go."

With Tim's girls, it had been a similar situation. Molly started to realize that Eve wasn't as unique as parental pride would lead her to believe. It became clear that, if her girl was an exceptional case, specially chosen for a prestigious mission, she was one among hundreds. Molly listened to her coworkers' stories, and many of them involved a child arriving home from school with a life-changing announcement.

Bastards, Molly seethed—her scarred, scrawny arms struggling against a thickening vat of stinking brew—they had gone to the children first. The Gallagher girls grew up in a world where privacy was a memory. From birth, every moment produced permanent data for some algorithm, some recruiter, somewhere. If a powerful organization wanted you, all they would have to do would be to come find you. Genius children and parents desperate enough to say yes to this madness couldn't be too hard to filter out, Molly figured, sweating and scraping and raking the mixture that would soon be soil. As she was working out the underhanded Exodus recruitment methods in her head, Molly again found herself distracted, and she was forced to look over at Tim negotiating with a goat.

A racing mind saw Molly through the unpleasant hours of her shift, and watching Tim learning how to be a real-life space cowboy didn't hurt morale. The pair of newbie fieldhands met outside the Sun Street locker rooms after work most days, when their shifts aligned. That evening, Tim left the hat in his locker. Molly noticed its absence, feeling disappointed, but she conceded that the treasure wouldn't be safe in the Homepod with precocious Lacey at large.

"...Sukuru-alloy bakeware, I swear to God!"

"Why did she need armor?" Molly laughed, walking alongside Tim, endorphins flooding her neural tissue.

"Lace goes up to the spindle to float a lot. She said she doesn't wanna bump her head or bruise a knee or—"

"I smell starshit."

"That's what *I* thought. Lace ain't girl enough to need two cases of cake pans."

They walked along the pleasant yellow stripe of Sun Street, heading Sukuruward along an enormous spoke. Filled with easy laughs and good company, their walk was just long enough to unwind from a hard day's labor before resuming parenthood duty.

They greeted clots of friends and coworkers, some also coming off shift, others just beginning. The ship's four spokes were the closest thing the Exodus had to commuter highways. The spacious, well-trafficked corridors between the

Home and the Fieldpods–unlike the tiny, spinning-puzzle tunnels that Eve, Lacey, and Jooles floated through on their explorations through the Exodus' vasculature–boasted regular gravity and spun in sync with the two enormous habitats on either side. Since the spokes neatly extended Sun, Home, Earth, and Pi Streets, the effect was as seamless a transition as was possible in such an enormous and complicated spacecraft.

"So?" Molly prodded, once it was just the two of them. Back in the homepod, they'd turned down a path that someone had labeled 'Third Avenue.'

"What? Oh! We found the rest of the bakeware on two boys. Little idiots have been armoring themselves up and wailin' on each other up in the spindle."

"Not cool," Molly moaned. "I need my floats. If Singh says we can't go up there anymore because of some kids, I swear Cowboy, arthritis'd drive me out the airlock before I turn thirty."

"Race ya." Tim winked. "Twice the daughters converts to uh, four times the stress."

For a moment, the couple's walking speed synchronized perfectly, canceling out the rotation of the Homepod. As they stepped along its spinning circumference toward their housing compartments, Molly and Tim seemingly walked-in-place, unmoving, from the perspective of euclidean space.

"Well, I should..." Slowing at a fork in the path and breaking the symmetry of their motion, Tim put his hands in his pockets and gave Molly a shy smile.

It was the branching point in the section of the Homepod they considered 'the neighborhood'. The girls would be waiting for them by now, hopefully out of trouble and somewhat clean.

She and Tim exchanged hugs and goodbyes.

"Happy trails."

Molly yearned to make a stronger move, but she settled for letting her hug linger for just a moment more. There was no need to rush things, she thought, as she turned away from her handsome, single father coworker-neighbor. They'd be aboard for the rest of their lives. They had time.

It's what she told herself, at least, turning toward her own home. They wouldn't be the first crewmembers to get together, she mused. In fact, the first baby born, and presumably conceived, aboard the Exodus had arrived that very month, and Molly knew more than one unattached expectant acquaintance. She suspected that the Exodus was turning into the Solar system's hottest dating scene for single parents.

● ● ●

Fe's existence was not nearly as active as Molly Gallagher's imagination. A comparatively brief period passed wherein work crews arrived to install the bridge's fixtures, during which time Greta and Mew secured Fe's actuator to its bulkhead. Later, more crews showed up to upholster the bridge, adding comfortable chairs with straps and installing padding on the interior surfaces of the zero-g deck.

After this, however, human activity grew sparse. Months would pass without anyone coming into the bridge, which Captain Singh had locked following reports that youths would sneak in to play there whenever the spindle's public funplex grew too crowded. These mischievous intruders would usually turn back before reaching sensitive areas, and nobody ever ventured as far as the Command Deck without authorization. Thus far, there had been no call for any humans to avail themselves of the communications, engineering, or navigation consoles, let alone the head.

Fe's pressure door, set above the washroom's interior, hung in the stillness and silence of the Exodus' vast bulk. The ship vibrated with tiny traces of its powerful twin fusion engines' caged energy, and its structure flexed against the mass of humanity and life and water stashed aboard. In a strange coincidence, the Exodus' shape shared a structural blueprint with Fe's molecule of iron-iii-oxide. The vast engineering sections consisting of the engines and their water tanks, along with the bridge, substituted for the three oxygen atoms, and the Home and Fieldpods represented the symphonic, magnetic irons tucked safely in the hollows. They were the payload, after all.

The most dynamic moment for the bulkhead door occurred just before launch. Ground Mission executed a simultaneous test of all of the emergency pressure doors aboard the spaceliner. Electricity flowed from the Exodus' fusion engines to the motor that housed Fe's magnet. The iron atom resisted, producing its share of the b-field that pushed against the flowing current, creating a physical rotary force that eventually manifested, through mechanical cleverness, in the pressure door whooshing closed. All of the emergency bulkhead doors functioned perfectly, and another item was ticked off of the Exodus' pre-launch checklist.

● ● ●

"Three, two, one...blastoff!" Molly announced.

Eve rolled her eyes at her mother's joke, but she obediently raised her alloy champagne flute with the others, finally celebrating the Exodus' launch. Though, 'launch' was a fancy word for it, Eve thought, considering that it only meant the ship's engines had started to produce ion thrust. Technically, the Exodus was now underway, pointed towards the Akkadia system, but if they were leaving Earth and everything they had ever known behind, they were doing so at a snail's pace. Still, it was a good excuse for a celebration.

They crowded in Akkadia Park, the Gallagher girls barefoot on the village green, watching live camera-drone coverage of the Exodus as its engines ignited–the video projected against a white wall erected by the crew. On other occasions, the space would be occupied by a bandstand or holiday tree. Today, the families sipped rehydrated grape juice, some cups spiked with shine, and watched their enormous new home gradually converting mass into acceleration.

"It's not like we're really going anywhere," Jooles observed from the ground. She was splayed out on a shiny picnic blanket, hands outstretched to touch the living grass.

"Right?" Eve agreed. "There are still shuttles coming back and forth from Earth all the time. And the stations–whoever."

"It's bigger than that," Tim chimed in. He was also holding an alloy champagne flute, his other arm around Molly's narrow waist. "We're really leaving. Bon voyage!"

"There's no stopping us now."

"Of course there is." Lacey snorted. She'd refused the grape water and had been ignoring the gathering up until that point. "Just cut the Earthward engine and fire up the Akkadiaward one. We'd be able to come right back."

"Oh, really, Miss?" Tim replied. His tone rumbled, but he was smiling. "Every second we're blasting off toward Akkadia, the ship is accelerating through space. That means it's going a little bit faster. Now it's going a little bit faster. And, hey–a little faster, every second. That adds up, Lace."

His eldest rolled her eyes. "I don't need you to explain astrophysics to me, *Tim*."

"Hmm, the idle engine is only meant to slow us down." Eve joined the discussion, betraying her friend. "It kicks in at the halfway point, and we stop moving right at Akkadia-2. So it would be *twice* as hard for us to stop and then start moving back."

"But we could *still* come back," Lacey argued, her arms folded across her chest.

"For now, maybe," Eve conceded.

"But not forever, right?" Molly asked, unsure. "Is there a point of no return?"

"I don't care," Tim shrugged. "I'll be dead."

Everybody but Molly laughed. Eve drained her fake wine. Without the exterior camera footage reminding her–and if she didn't look up, spindleward, at the SunLight–Eve could easily have forgotten that she was aboard a spaceship. Things were starting to get distressingly normal in her world. There were culs de sac and chores–dentist appointments, picnics, and birthday parties. She even had to go to school!

It was strange to watch–a world that had started out as an empty, sideways bucket had turned into a comfortable country town before her eyes. People like Vi, whom Eve had never heard of, spent the peak of their careers designing and optimizing the ship and its interior plans, but it was the sheer manpower of the crew that made the Exodus into a reality. The Field and Homepods began as identical alloy cans, equally eligible as the main housing habitat, but Ground

Mission decided that the crewmembers should live in the section that faced Akka-dia. For the humans locked inside the cans, it was only symbolic, but the more earthy Fieldpod faced their old home, while the community-centered Homepod confronted their future.

For Eve, the future meant applying for an internship.

She was old enough now to be taking the idea of career training seriously, and she tried to be practical about it. Most people worked in the Fieldpod, and Eve liked to be where the action was, though she had an aversion to the idea of running for Bridgecrew. Politicking and kissing up to Captain Singh or Ground Mission was not within Eve's core competencies. Moreover, she found herself becoming fascinated with animals. Not the indentured milk or wool producers like the ones Lacey's dad worked with, but real, wild animals. Or as close to them as one could get aboard the Exodus, which meant the creatures at the Zoo.

The Zoological campus, an unprepossessing moniker for a research and cloning facility, had only been greenlit after the working farms and ranches of the Field-pod became productive, and its offerings of non-livestock animals was still rather limited. Nevertheless, Eve would visit whenever she had enough freestudy time to make the long journey down the Pi Street spoke and back.

"Howzit going, Jenny!" Zookeeper Zell called to her when Eve crossed out of the Akkadiaward fields on one particular morning. "Here to play with the spiders again?"

"My name isn't Jenny," Eve answered wearily. She was tired and hot from her brisk walk from the Homepod. "I don't know why you call me that."

"It's a private joke," Zell answered.

"So private that I don't get to know, even though it's about me?"

Zell just smiled and wiggled their eyebrows.

Eve crossed the threshold into the Zoo's open lobby. The downside of having a job would be the coworkers, Eve decided. But she'd have to make sacrifices if she wanted this niche aboard the crew. Tolerating Zell would be just one of many to come.

"Can you let me into the bank? Please?" Eve asked.

"Whatdya want to go in there for, Jenny?"

"That's where all the most interesting animals are," she answered, matter-of-factly.

"I guess. But they're boring. They don't even poop."

"*Livestock* is boring. And I'm getting pretty done with anoles and tarantulas, Zell."

"Didja see the new llama?"

"Of course. I was here when they decanted it."

"Hm," Zell sniffed. "I must've been sick that day.""You were there too," Eve said tiredly. "Can you please let me into the gene bank?"

"Oh sure," Zookeeper Zell said brightly, as if the previous conversation had never happened. They pulled a keycard out of their shirt and lifted its lanyard from around their pudgy neck. "You'll want one of those, too."

They pointed to a rack containing two small tablet computers and tossed Eve the keycard.

"Thanks," she said, grabbing a tablet.

The bank was built partially below ground—at least, below the level of poured regolith and soil, nestled within the Exodus' alloy hull. Eve tapped the borrowed keycard against the reader and descended a short set of clanking metal stairs into a claustrophobic airlock. She pulled a lever to cycle the atmospheres, immediately using her fingers to plug her ears, a habit learned during her first visits to the gene vault. A high pressure blast scoured Eve's body before the rush abated and the inner doors opened. It wasn't quite the procedure Dr. Kim had undergone when they came to and from their Brownsville clean-room, but it was deemed enough to protect the portion of Earth's zoological legacy carried onboard the fleeing Exodus.

Eve shivered. It was a harsh transition from the perpetual May weather of the Fieldpod, and underneath the insulative ground cover, it was space-cold close to the ship's skin. The bank lived up to its name, serving as a vast repository of small, biological safety deposit boxes. Tiny crypts of genetic material from hundreds of species filled the frigid chamber, and the budding scientist could browse them like a library by hovering her tablet near any given species' vault.

At random, she swiped over a mammal vault containing both the embryos and frozen eggs of an endangered species–*Myotis lucifugus*. The tablet displayed images of the diminutive chiroptera species alongside information about its diet, habitat, and behavior on Earth.

"Little brown bat," Eve read aloud.

She studied the details of the creature for some time, forgetting the ambient temperature. She wondered if the creepy little thing would be happy living on Akkadia-2, flapping through the previously-sterile planet's unexplored skies. Eve supposed there were plenty of caves on the islands, but probably not too many bugs to eat, come to think of it.

The terraforming missions had long since beaten the Exodus to the Akaddia system–little contest, as the robotic probes, their mass exponentially lower than the colony ship, could brush up against lightspeed. Remotely monitored from Earth on a years-long delay, the modules had many functions, the most important of which was to seed the empty planet with a supercharged batch of microorganisms. Some released forms of photosynthesizing *Prochlorococcus* and *Synechococcus* cyanobacteria into Akkadia-2's warm seas, others spread fungal spores. Over a few human generations, the robots would be able to build up the planet's ecology until it resembled a somewhat less-diverse version of Earth circa two-and-a-half-billion years ago.

As far as Eve knew, the automated terraformers wouldn't be blessing Akkadia with animals any more complex than an earthworm. It would be mostly up to the Zookeepers aboard the Exodus to populate Akkakia-2 with macrofauna–humans included. Yet, according to the data on her tablet, the little brown bat mainly ate pest species such as flies, midges, and mosquitos. Curious, she decided to check the gene bank for the bats' preferred prey.

"We'd have to be idiots to bring mosquitoes with us," the Earthborn Eve said aloud, shuddering at a half-remembered evening alongside then twenty-year-old Molly, trying to fish in an algae-choked canal.

Eve was right, as it happened. There may have existed some incidental genetic data for the bugs in a digital library somewhere, but she discovered Ground Mission had declined to include a complement of gnats, mosquitos, or even houseflies aboard the Exodus.

"What is she supposed to eat?" Eve asked herself, returning to the vault of the *Myotis lucifugus*.

She supposed her bat could subsist on the bees and butterflies that floated around the Fieldpod acting as pollinators, or even on some of the smaller spider species the Zoo staff had already resurrected. But what would be the point? It would be an unacceptable waste, Eve calculated.

She was realizing that some of the animals in the bank would have no place in the new world the humans were building for themselves. The little brown bat would only ever make sense in a Zoo.

She couldn't remember ever being particularly interested in animals, especially fish, back during her increasingly-distant girlhood on Earth, but now, the idea of living in a world without bats made Eve unaccountably sad. She began swiping the tablet around the vaults of other preserved species, reading about bat after bat after, surprisingly prolific, bat.

She paused when she found *Macroglossus* nectar bats. They were unsettling to look at, Eve admitted, but these chiroptera were master pollinators. Rather than subsisting on insects, the *Macroglossus* slurped nectar from flowers like a leathery hummingbird, spreading genetic material for several genuses of night-blooming cactus in the process.

Did they have samples of those cactuses aboard? Perhaps in the terraformers' seedbanks? Eve wondered. She'd have to check the records later.

The schoolgirl's spiraling curiosity cut off abruptly when she realized that she couldn't feel her fingers. Eve dashed back up the stairs, impatiently cycled the airlock, and ran past Zell, slamming down the lanyard and tablet without so much as acknowledging the "Later, Jenny!" tossed in her direction.

She was late to class that day, but it was worth it. Eve Gallagher's first pa-per—*Akkadian Bats: A comparative treatise on species of order* Chiroptera *and long-term projections for planetside populations thereof*—would be written within the year.

● ● ●

When the Exodus passed the Kuiper belt, outside the orbit of Pluto, the humans aboard declared that it had left the Solar system and threw a party for themselves. Another 'Goodbye Sol' celebration commenced as the ship flew past the outermost ice chunk of the Oort Cloud and the last bits of physical matter orbiting the sun. Later, the craft reached a region called the termination shock–the edge of the bubble where the star's radiation and solar wind dominated. The crew of the Exodus drank their shine tanks dry during that one. A bit later, however, the ship crossed a line termed the heliopause, and the human travelers decided to throw one final party to commemorate leaving their home star behind, and this time, they meant it.

"You were right," Graham said, with a deathgrip on one of the bridge's handholds. "Drunk in zero-g is more scary than fun."

"No, *you* were right!" Eelee squealed. She performed a somersault in midair, her mane of wild curls following on a slight delay.

The two rookie Bridgecrew had left the party in the Homepod behind. They'd also surreptitiously kidnapped a bottle of shine during Captain Xie's speech, drained it, and then wandered off to work of all places. For an engineer like Eelee Guk, leaving a party for her workspace drunk bordered on normal behavior. Her officer-track friend, Saul Graham, however, was a people-person whose non-threatening charisma had carried both of them during the elections.

"This is awesome!" The diminutive engineer yelled as she pushed off a wall with both feet and sailed across the room, fist outstretched. She whooped out when she reached the other side. "Imagine doing this with Xie here!"

"He'd kill us." Graham managed a chuckle, though his stomach threatened to mutiny.

"What? What's the matter?" Eelee floated back over. "This was your idea.""I just wanted to get you drunk and alone," Graham said, mostly-joking. "I thought'd be romantic with, urp–," he stifled a dangerous-tasting hiccup before finishing, "...with the floating."

"Sorry, Solly." She shrugged, smiling. "I'm still acc."

"I know," Graham said, truthfully.

He'd been trying to fall out of love with Eelee, but it was taking forever and the alcohol had dulled his self-discipline.

"That's good, actually," he continued, his friend responding with a quizzical look. "Means I can throw up in front of you–" Graham clasped his hand to his mouth, signaling an imminent launch.

"Oh no you don't!" Eelee yelled, grabbing her friend's coveralls and spinning him toward the restroom. "Hold it until we reach the head, or we're both gonna lose Bridgecrew!"

The tiny engineer shepherded Graham along the wall like an inert heavy-bag. A player driving toward an undefended goal, Eelee sent her human missile flying into the back of the cramped bridge bathroom. Graham reached, steadying himself against a wall with one hand while he flipped open the space toilet with the other, activating its suction. The crewman leaned over the hole, but nothing came out of his mouth.

Eelee's momentum carried her into the head after him. She reached out and arrested her movement with a sickening lurch. She felt her happy-drunk start to turn sour.

"Throw up already," she ordered. "I might need to use that when you're done."

"I think I lied," Graham said, feeling like death. "I don't think I can do it in front of you. Gimme some privacy, yeah?"

"Nuh uh," Eelee said. "I think I'm gonna hurl too." Like a snake charmer with a cobra by the throat, she gripped the suction-tube of the astronaut shower in her left hand, ready for trouble.

"Please don't! If you throw up, that would be even worse, somehow."

"Not my call. Take it up with Mr. Tummy."

"Eelee, don't–"

"If you vomit, I vomit, and if I vomit, you vomit."

"Stop saying vomit. It's gonna make me, urp–"

These comments nearly proved self-fulfilling, but Eelee came to the rescue.

"Wait–let me try something."

With the knack of an engineer born aboard the very vessel she serviced, Guk quickly located a hidden access point and cavalierly twisted together some wires. When nothing happened, she twisted harder and gave the cords a wiggle. This had the desired effect–electricity rerouted, a potential gate broke wide open, and the unchanging b-field generated by Fe and its coordinated companions resisted a sudden current. Motors whirred, screws turned, and the smooth motion of actuators forced down an emergency bulkhead door, separating the astronaut shower stall from the space toilet with a satisfying whoosh.

With privacy having been unexpectedly gained, Graham's social instincts gave way to his urgent gastric needs. The pressure door, though solid alloy, was not especially sound-proof, and the resulting ejaculations inspired Eelee quickly to follow her friend's example. After a few moments, when they both had finished their business and its aftershocks, she was the one to break the silence.

"You know, it really *is* a big thing."

"Think Xie will bust us?" Graham panted.

"No, not that. Finally leaving the Solar system." Eelee floated against her side of the door.

"Oh, that." They were huddled back-to-back, voices muffled, separated by the emergency bulkhead's cold alloy. "Eh. Haven't we left the Solar system like six times by now?"

"Crossing the heliopause is different," she answered. "We're in the interstellar medium now. We've really left home."

"The Exodus is our home," Graham said, automatically. Indeed, neither of the shipborn Bridgecrew remembered Sol as anything other than a particularly bright star.

"Don't look at it like that, ok?" A touch of pleading entered Eelee's voice. "It's like this–" she began, turning toward the door that concealed her friend, "–ugh, I can't talk to you with the thing in the way."

Engineer Guk moved to the panel, and, in a reversal of her earlier trick, forced current back into the door's actuator system–with a whoosh, the door shot back up and slotted into its hollow in the ship's hull. Officer Graham, who had been leaning against it for stability, his legs braced on the bathroom wall, came sprawling out backwards.

"Ow." He moaned, hitting something hard and damp.

"It's like this," Eelee said, floating over him and continuing her argument. "Every particle in our bodies—hell, every tiny atom that you just barfed up came from our Solar system. *Humanity's* Solar system."

"Uh huh." Saul was content to stare up at the floating Eelee, gazing into her intense eyes and watching that crazy hair drift around her beautiful head.

To his shine-soaked brain, she could have been an angel.

"There was a star before Sol, yeah, and when it exploded it created everything. Mars, the Moon, the Earth. Everything. Even you. Even me. Every single infinitesimal atom in this whole huge ship," she said, unintentionally including the overhead Fe in her impassioned speech, "now we're outside that. Don't you see? It's a *huge* deal that we've left home."

"Home." Graham sighed from the floor.

"Earth is our *home*. Always will be." Eelee spoke with confidence, though she had never set foot there. "But we're moving to a different home now. Do you remember when Yenn on Big Apple moved from California to New York?"

"Yeah?" He was too drunk for physics, but Saul remembered the show just fine, especially Yenn and her warm suntan.

"This mission is like that. We're just moving house," Eelee concluded. "The Exodus is kinda like the bus Yenn took. It's just a vehicle to get us there. It's not home."

"I like the Exodus," Graham groaned, closing his eyes and curling into a ball ."Don't fall asleep on me!" She tried to rouse him with a small kick, the recoil of which sent her flying into a corner of the bathroom.

"Ughhh—" The young officer moaned in response, but he managed to pull himself upright with a handhold. "I guess we should clean up and get the hell out of here before Xie... before Xie or someone sees we left the party."

"Maybe they didn't notice us leave," Eelee said hopefully, thumbing the access hatch and scanning the head for traces of stray vomit.

"Trust me," Saul said, rubbing some sobriety into his eyes. "Xie notices everything."

● ● ●

Years passed before Fe's pressure door moved again. Communications with Earth stretched and deteriorated as the ship continued to accelerate, and the Exodus slowly became an isolated island of humanity in the void. During these years, Captain Xie won re-election, defending his position against a run from Singh, whom he'd defeated back when she ran as the incumbent. The pre-launch power structure of Ground Mission began to collapse even further when the Xie administration put forth policies to see the Exodus through its first major crisis.

The sparse black expanse that separated Sol and Akkadia was nearly empty, though, like galactic vagabonds, some chunks of matter occasionally fled their home systems, flung by the cold fingers of physics out into the void. When the Exodus' instruments detected a cluster of macro-scale obstacles, a stir arose within the crew. The ship's astronomers referred to the loose collection of boulders as an asteroid field, and though this wasn't technically correct, it helped the population wrap their minds around the danger. Xie took to calling it 'the cloud', a softer, appropriately nebulous term he hoped would lessen the growing panic.

Clustered together by the feeble forces of their own microgravity, the interstellar drifters lay directly in the Exodus' flightpath. The colony ship hadn't been designed with steering or defense capabilities in mind. Its navigation and attitude thrusters were feeble, built to to turn the ship towards the Akkadia system during prelaunch and for making fine orbital adjustments once it arrived.

Dodging asteroids was not something the Exodus was capable of, Captain Xie tried to communicate to the ship's population. To mitigate the crisis, he put forward a policy he called Operation Vigilance—the bridge would, henceforth, always be staffed, the ship's sensors always monitored.

As the spaceliner continued its straight-line acceleration, the ship's Bridgecrew were better able to study the approaching cloud. They plotted their projected course through the hazard and found that the largest asteroids were unlikely to pose a threat to the Exodus in such an enormous volume of space. There were countless other particles and bits of matter traveling with the cloud, however, and the ship's safety could never be assured.

Restlessness grew aboard, as the crew flew closer to their rendezvous with the enemy. Their fear reached a fever-pitch when their captain announced that the Exodus would not be taking evasive measures. A petition circulated, demanding that Xie try to steer around the obstacles. There were sit-ins and work stoppages. Unelected techies who aspired to Bridgecrew put forth public plans and designs on the ship's communication net, advocating for the use of navigational thrusters to bypass the cloud.

Before things could spin out of control, Captain Xie put his foot down. He cut off public access to the onboard communications net. He issued strongly-worded announcements, defending his no-plan plan. A new rule was put in place–any protest or questioning of the Captain's orders during this crisis would be considered sedition. People complained and used words like 'fascist,' but they used them quietly.

Until the Exodus ran into the cloud.

The real danger of the rough patch lay not with the enormous ship-sized asteroids but rather in the tiny fragments of dust and debris that would hit like bullets at near-relativistic speeds.

It was a magnetic field that saved them. The enormous forward-facing engine, meant to decelerate the Exodus at the end of its journey, was powered by a beefy fusion reactor that put out a starlike b-field of its own. The dusty interstellar bullets that would have struck the ship head-on were gently pushed out of the way by invisible electromagnetic forces, radiating from an artificial star held in the ship's mouth.

It wasn't a clean escape. The Exodus ended up getting itself peppered with micro impacts. Six antenna arrays were shredded, and the largest radio-telescope dish sustained crippling damage. Worst of all, a breach pierced the Homepod–a hissing pinhole in a section of the Akkadiaward hull. The craft's emergency bulkheads, cousin models to Fe's own door, functioned perfectly–whooshing down and sealing off the damaged compartments from the rest of the Homepod. Fortunately for everyone, not least of all the vindicated Captain Xie, the depressurized section was unoccupied at the time, and the cloud ended up claiming no human casualties.

Weeks after the crisis passed, however, the Operation Vigilance policy remained in effect. At least one bridge officer and a techie had to be on duty at all times. On the night that Fe's pressure door would again activate, Saul Graham and Eelee Guk were assigned the OV graveyard shift. They moved swiftly through zero-g corridors, out of the Homepod and toward the bridge, grabbing and launching with ease–their primate brains had rewired ancient muscle-memories, adapting to an alien environment. When the pair arrived at the Command Deck, they found Gene and Dre still on shift.

"Relief on deck," Saul announced.

"Thank the stars," Gene answered. "I need to go to the head like nobody's business!"

"Ew," Eelee said, scrunching up her face playfully. "Don't make it *our* business."

Gene Lyman, a bridge officer with a head of hair so blonde it appeared white, held the same rank as Graham, though with less seniority. He had been recently elected, due more to his movie-star good looks than to his competence.

"Not so fast," Dre, a cocky engineer, remarked. "Gotta finish your logs."

"Be a pal. I really need to go!" Gene had already unstrapped himself. "Can you just do it for me?"

"Negative. I'm busy." Dre kept his eyes glued to a monitor, giving new meaning to Xie's mandatory vigilance.

With some whining, the towheaded bridge officer did as his techie asked, while Eelee and Graham floated down and began to log themselves into their stations.

"Don't mess with my settings." Dre tore himself away from the monitor and unstrapped.

"Whatever," she replied, as diplomatically as she was capable.

"I'm serious, Guk. That's how Captain Xie likes it to be set," Dre scolded, his voice cold.

"Oh, I'm sure you know exactly what Xie likes." Eelee gave her fellow engineer an evil smile.

He flushed and spun around, pulling himself hand-over-hand into a corridor. Eelee made rude gestures at his back. Gene smiled nervously at his crewmates, and, having finished his task, shot like a rocket toward the bridge's restroom.

"They're definitely banging," Eelee remarked.

"Gene and Dre?" Graham's eyebrows rose in dismay.

"No, idiot. Dre and Captain Xie."

"Oh. Well, yeah."

He stifled his next comment, which would have been something along the lines of "at least somebody is getting some."

Saul was frustrated and badly out of practice. Bri, the lovely young woman he'd been dating, had become more deeply involved in the antinatalist movement growing aboard the Exodus, and Saul's sex life had all but evaporated.

"Speaking of," his friend asked, "how are things with Bri?"

"Fine," Graham lied.

The two settled into their stations, but Saul couldn't get comfortable. It had been a long float to the bridge, and he usually liked to hit the head before settling down for an extended, pointless shift.

The Exodus sailed through empty space for some time.

"Is Gene still in the bathroom?" Graham asked.

"Um," Eelee whipped her head around. Her hair followed on a slight delay. "Yeah. Weird. Wonder what he's doing in there."

"I bet the Bridgecrew on the Diomed gets two bathrooms," Officer Graham said bitterly, referring to the next big mission developing on Earth.

"You don't even wanna know what I heard," Engineer Guk teased.

"What?"

"There were specs for the 'Med in the last newsbeam from Sol, and I heard that their bridge is gonna have gravity."

"Get the fuck out of here!" Graham said with disgust.

"Lucky fuckers," Eelee agreed.

"Well," Saul grunted, unstrapping from his chair. "I can't hold it forever." He launched himself up and sailed over to the bridge's head—separated from the deck by a hatch.

"Hey, Gene. Open up. I've gotta go," he called.

"I'm in here," the other officer replied, his voice muffled through the door.

"You're taking forever. I've really got to go!"

"Just hold it!" Gene called back, desperation in his voice.

"Liquid doesn't compress, idiot!" Eelee added, having floated over.

"Guk?" Gene's voice said. "Go away, both of you. I'm not done yet."

The little techie shrugged, but Saul had an idea.

"Hey," he whispered, "can you show me that door trick?"

The feral smile returned to Eelee's face—she understood her friend's plan without him needing to communicate it. Graham pulled a lever, opening the hatch from outside. Eelee floated into the head's entrance. Beyond the shower stall, Gene hovered in a compromising position.

He shrieked as the intruding engineer ripped a panel off the wall. "Oh my stars, Eelee! What are you doin-"

Before Gene could finish his indignant yelling, Eelee manipulated the ship's wiring, and the pressure door whooshed downward. Propelled by Fe's motor, the bulkhead neatly separated the distressed Gene from the rest of the bathroom—an on-demand alloy wall of privacy.

"All yours, boss." Eelee chuckled, floating out of the head and back to her station.

Graham thanked her and proceeded to use the suction tube of the astronaut shower in a way it was never intended.

● ● ●

The goat brain on Zookeeper Eve's table resembled a terrible sort of soft cheese more than it did a functioning organ.

"EPD," she muttered, though no one in the biolab was alive to hear her. The woman's voice sounded muffled from inside her helmet's clean suit.

Eve took a deep breath. "Record, begin. Zookeeper Eve Gallagher attending."

Her vocalized notes were added to the current case file, synched automatically with the lab's suite of instruments. The tiny microphone that picked up soundwaves from her voice and converted them into electrical impulses contained a small, neodymium magnet made in the same Druke factory that Fe once passed through.

"Specimen is the brain and brainstem of a male goat, approximately one year of age."

Tim had just killed the poor animal and brought it in to be dissected by the Zookeeper. The yearling was the latest victim in a plague devastating the Field-pod–EPD, or Exodan Prion Disease.

"Subject was euthanized less than one hour prior to autopsy, yet," she paused, "an extreme state of decomposition is present. The signature perforations and ragged tissues are classic presentations of EPD. When Tim brought the–pause record. Overwrite last five seconds." Eve cleared her throat and focused on the goat's ruined brain.

"Resume record–a classic presentation of EPD. Stableboss Diallo delivered the specimen, reporting that distress in the yearling began approximately six days ago. Diallo," she continued, trying to keep her voice level and her mind off the safety of her mother's ex-boyfriend, "moved the subject into quarantine after initial presentation of symptoms. Subject was found near-death this morning and was euthanized shortly thereafter. The cadaver's neural tissue demonstrates a key feature of EPD–that it spreads more virulently and progresses more rapidly than any known prion.

"This scientist believes that the proteinaceous infectious particle responsible for EPD originated as a novel mutation aboard the Exodus, most likely during the period of construction and launch when the ship experienced its most intense dose of solar radiation. Perhaps it arose later. Indeed, it is possibly due to the unique environment aboard a spacecraft that this particular prion is able to proliferate and replicate so rapidly."

Eve took comfort in speculation. She gathered her instruments and probed deeper into the mush, looking for answers.

When she had finally exhausted herself, Zookeeper Eve filed her reports, plugged her ears, and mindlessly performed her decontamination procedures. She was no closer to understanding the origins of the deadly prion, let alone learning how to kill it. It wasn't actually alive, in fact. She had run a small personal experiment and discovered that not even a cycle in the lab's autoclave could deactivate the diseased proteins. So much for sterilization. She filed her report and went home

The Pi Street spoke was deserted, and Eve's footsteps echoed endlessly down the long, once-crowded tube. These days, the Fieldpod was limited to essential personnel only, with everyone else forced to stay confined and terrified in the Homepod. Eve passed one of Xie's checkpoints, flashing her credentials to an officer with ghost-white hair and passing through another decontamination curtain. Mere theater, Eve thought tiredly.

Her feet knew the way, winding through shabby partitions on a shortcut to Third Avenue. She found Molly's house easily but bumped her nose when she tried to push through the door.

"Ow." Since when could these doors be locked? She pushed harder, and the door gave, a little.

Something heavy had been pushed up against it.

"Mom!" She called out.

"Eve? Oh, you scared me." Molly's slim, burnscarred arms appeared in the doorway, helping to shove the furniture aside.

"Barricading the door isn't going to keep EPD out, Mom." Eve pushed her way in, exasperated.

She closed the door and hugged her mother, who looked as frightened and frail as a plucked bird.

"I just don't understand what's going on anymore." Molly sighed, sinking into a kitchen chair. "Everyone is so frightened. It's so much worse than the cloud. Thank fuck you're too young to have been through a SarCov outbreak on Earth."

"Mom," Eve began, never one to sugarcoat things for Molly, "EPD is a lot worse than any of the diseases you had back on Earth. Do you remember when me and Jooles got in trouble for playing Zombie-Army 2 on our school smartglass?"

Her mother nodded.

"It's a lot like that, but on a microscopic level. When a bad protein encounters a good one, it turns it into a bad one–spreading like zombie bites."

"Or religion," Molly offered.

"The worst part is, you can't shoot a prion in the head with a crossbow. It's not a virus or a bacterium we can kill. It's just a protein that somehow became terribly misfolded. Protein folding is really complicated, and you'll just have to trust me that folds can be contagious, but when proteins in your nervous system *misfold*, bad things happen." The Zookeeper shuddered, remembering the goat brain.

"An unkillable plague? Jesus. This is exactly why I say it's wrong to bring a baby into this life. Starshit, why couldn't *he* understand that? All these little kids. The disease can hurt babies too, right?"

Eve nodded, used to her mother's antinatalist outbursts. Molly's resentment over what she saw as an exploitative recruiting strategy by the early Ground Mission blossomed into a minor political movement that cost her a relationship. She even wrote several public essays lamenting her and the other elder Exodans' role as expendable breeding stock. Hers was a minority view, but people responded to it, including a number of shipborn who resented having been brought into existence just to breed. Politics were academic to Zookeeper Eve, who had little interest in babies, instead spending most of her waking hours birthing clones of resurrected Earth species.

"Forgive me, honey," Molly said, calming down. "But, just to be clear, you're saying we're fucked, right?"

"Mom–" Eve began to equivocate, but Molly stared her down. "I hope not. But... but, yeah, probably," she admitted.

"Life," Molly sighed, smiling thinly. "You and your fridge full of species. Tim, constantly breeding his animals. Begging me for a litter. We already have a family, I told him, but no."

"Mom–"

"We're supposed to make all this new life, bring life to a lifeless world across the stars. But they forgot about death! Didn't they? Ha!" Molly was getting worked up again, but before Eve could figure out how to calm her mother down, the tirade was aborted by a loud pulsing tone that signaled an official announcement. The Gallagher girls turned toward a screen and sat next to each other—an emergency broadcast was about to go out on the ship's net. Sure enough, a few seconds later, Captain Xie appeared onscreen. He wore the dramatic crimson uniform he had designed himself. He was calmly seated, though the strange movements of his hair and the fabric of his clothes betrayed that the man was broadcasting from zero-gravity.

"Crewmembers of the Exodus. It is my sad duty as your captain to issue this grave update. The total number of our shipmates who have been lost to the EPD plague now stands at one hundred and ninety-four. This is a devastating loss, and, needless to say, we pray for their souls. Our very mission is in jeopardy. So far, we have been able to do frustratingly little. That ends now."

The Captain paused for effect.

"It ends now," he repeated. Pale and lanky in body, Xie had eyes as black as the space outside the ship's alloy hull. "This plague simply moves too fast for traditional methods and traditional government. To that end, the citizen's council has been dissolved."

Molly let out a small gasp and pressed her tattooed fingers against her lips. She thought of Syll, her ally and mouthpiece on the council.

"Our most up-to-date scientific findings," Xie continued, "have shown that the EPD prion spreads more rapidly and reduces its victims more horribly than any disease known to man. The prion kills by destroying the brain tissue of animals. But, as in all things, the monster's strength is also its weakness. The disease spreads in animals and only animals. The solution is painful, but obvious. A great sacrifice will need to be made."

The two women in the kitchen felt their confusion turn to shock. The broadcast continued after the Captain stepped away. A Bridgecrew tech with deep-set eyes and a shaved head outlined Xie's radical new policy for cleansing the Field-pod—quarantine for humans, fire, slaughter, and space for other animals.

"...if we all cooperate, we can get through anything and build a brighter to-morrow," Dre concluded, simpering for the camera. "In addition, Captain Xie has declared a mandatory emergency lockdown, effective immediately. Patrols will be dispatched to ensure peaceful enactment of this policy. Travel outside of one's dwelling during nightcyle hours will be considered sedition. We wish you a safe evening."

The broadcast blanked out.

● ● ●

As soon as the first lux leaked from the ship's artificial dawn to brighten the Homepod, Eve unbarricaded Molly's door and took to the streets. Walking at the same frantic pace she'd once employed as a schoolgirl, she made her commute in a beeline, down the spoke, slowed only by Bridgecrew patrols who repeatedly checked that she was, indeed, essential crew.

When she arrived, Eve found that the Fieldpod had turned into an abattoir. Xie's Bridgecrew stood in full, inflated hazmat suits alongside similarly-equipped fieldworkers who had been drafted into their ranks. Herds of docile animals were shepherded toward temporarily-reactivated freight airlocks, destined for a cold death in the void of space. Less cooperative beasts lay dead by the dozens. Eve spotted Kristofer, a coworker of Tim's, holding a dripping captive-bolt gun in his hands, his suit splattered with the vitality of mammals.

"Where's Mr. Diallo?" She called out, trying to avoid stepping in the rivulets of blood forming in the grass.

Kristofer shook his head once, then gestured for her to hurry away.

Eve obeyed, not wanting to attract the attention of Xie's troops. With nothing to direct her but fury, Eve jogged across the Fieldpod's even green pasture toward her Zoological campus. In her peripheral vision, Eve spotted one of the ship's few automated lifts hefting three bovine carcasses. If Xie was willing to kill precious livestock and space their bodies–wasting countless crucial calories, microbes, and biomass–Eve could only imagine how her less-utilitarian specimens were being treated.

Indeed, when she finally arrived, sweating and red-faced, the situation was even worse than she'd feared. As the Zoo had expanded, its campus swole to include several fields and paddocks, all of which stood silent and empty. The stink of death preceded her to the open lobby. Zookeeper Zell sat behind their desk, weeping.

"Jenny!" They wailed, seeing Eve. "They took them all, Jenny! My llamas and my sweet–my sweet little baby guanacos."

"Where are Xie's troops?" She interrogated her blubbering colleague.

"Gone. But they'll come back."

"Did they get into the bank?""No, but they killed all the birds in the aviary! Oh my god, Jenny, they, they hit them with batons and stuffed 'em into bags–" Zell, face dripping, inhaled hugely and let out a sob. "My little Zellda. They killed her."

"I'm sorry Zell," Eve said, her anger rising. "The African Grey, right?""Uh, huh," they nodded. "She would have lived another *fifty years*!"

"It's gonna be ok," Eve lied.

Zell leaned over the desk and buried their face in their thick arms, their body wracked with sobs.

"Listen, Zell," Eve asked. "Have you seen Tim Diallo anywhere?"

The distraught Zookeeper just shook their head without raising it.

"Damn."

Eve breathed. She thought for a moment, then made sure the gene bank was locked. Zell didn't notice her take the entire stack of keycards on her way out. She ducked out a side door and hurried across an adjoining field, watching for officers and robots. Eve's colleague hadn't been joking–the lab-born animals in the Zoo were all missing, gone with only traces of fur, feathers, and blood to prove they'd existed.

She kept going, walking as quickly as she could without breaking into a full run. Against the Earthward side of the Fieldpod, dozens of giant vats for soil-making sat mothballed. Somewhere in this area was Tim's ranch, she knew. However, before she could get close, Eve drew the attention of a white-suited officer, one with stripes on the arms of his uniform.

"Hold it right there," Saul Graham called out to her. "We're in the middle of a full-blown biohazard purge. State your business."

"I'm essential personnel," she said, slowing to a stop.

"Lemme check..."

Impatiently, Eve displayed her credentials and made to move past the officer as she had at the checkpoints leading into the Fieldpod.

"Zookeeper?" He read, holding out one arm to stop her. "What's a Zookeeper doing all the way back here?"

"I'm here to visit–" she almost said 'my stepdad' but stopped herself, "–a colleague. Diallo from agriculture."

"Not gonna happen," Graham said, making a spinning motion with his finger. "Come on, I'll escort you back to the Zoo."

"This is an emergency!" She stomped.

"No starshit. This whole situation is an emergency. We can't have people just wandering around." Graham gently, but firmly, turned the Zookeeper around and began marching her Akkadiaward, back to her campus.

"Please," Eve begged, "I just need to see my colleague. He'll be taking this all pretty hard."

"Listen ma'am," Graham said, his voice agitated. "I'm sorry. I really am. But this is more serious that you can know. Between you and me, there's going to be solitary lockdowns for everyone in the Homepod next."

"Will you just tell me if you've seen him? Probably wearing a cowboy hat–" Eve began.

Sharply, the officer put one hand to his ear, crinkling the flexible material of his helmet. He held his other hand up to silence Eve.

"Starshit," he cursed. "Yeah, I'll be over AFAP."

Graham lowered his hand and refocused on Eve.

"I have to go," he told her. "There's an even bigger emergency somewhere than your colleague's hurt feelings. Promise me you'll go straight back to the Zoo." His voice had the weight of a command. "I'm serious now–if you run into the wrong officer... it won't go so well."

Before Eve could decide whether or not to obey, the officer with the stripes turned and hurried away, Akkadiaward. She could try to call Tim from the office, Eve compromised. She took off, back across the fields towards the Zoological campus.

*   *   *

Zookeeper Zell was nowhere to be found when Eve returned, but the lobby wasn't deserted. Three white-suited troops stood inside, clustered around the stairs that led to the bank's airlock. Eve instinctively touched the access cards in her pocket. Xie's men couldn't get in, she realized. Silently, Eve backpedaled outside and around a corner. She knelt down at the base of a support pillar and hurriedly buried the keycards underneath layers of soil and mulch, hiding them against the space-cold alloy hull.

When she stepped back into the lobby, Zookeeper Eve cleared her throat, trying to summon courage she didn't feel.

"Hold it right there," she said, trying to imitate the striped officer she'd run into earlier. "Exactly what are you trying to do here? This is a restricted site."

The three whitesuits were startled for a moment, but as their half-visible faces scrunched in annoyance, Eve realized her attempt to assert authority had back-fired.

"It's the other Zookeeper," one grunted.

Another of Xie's men stepped out of the stairwell and began moving toward Eve.

"Dr...Gallagher?" The third man studied a tablet. "We need your help opening this." He pointed to the sealed entrance to the gene bank.

"I'm afraid access to that area is restricted to authorized personnel only," Eve replied, her voice steady. She noticed that the second man had moved to stand behind her, blocking her exit.

"Everyone on this ship is going to die unless we follow Captain Xie's orders," the officer with the tablet said acidly, his polite veneer evaporating.

"Probably even then." The first man folded his arms.

"You want to open *this*?" Eve asked, taking a step forward and pointing down the steps as if unfamiliar with her own lab.

As she sidled toward the bank, the three white-suited troopers naturally made space. Eve was still blocked in, though now with the bank's access stairs to her back. She risked another step down, feeling better the more she put herself between the men and Earth's genetic legacy.

"Hmm," she said, pushing buttons at random on the card reader, stalling for time. "Why did Captain Xie order you to open the gene bank?"

"None of your fucking business." The gruff trooper snapped.

"It's my fucking Zoo," she replied, indignantly.

"She's wasting our time!" He exploded.

Before things could turn ugly, another pair of white-suited officers stepped into the Zoological lobby.

"What seems to be the problem?" A familiar voice asked.

Xie, dressed in a vibrant red cleansuit, strode into the room, passing between his two officers.

"Captain Xie, sir." The gruff trooper saluted. "The Zoo staff have been fucking with us and delaying the execution of your orders."

"Zookeeper?" Xie said, turning to notice Eve.

"Captain!" Eve, pleaded. "Your men are behaving like orangutans."

The gruff one exchanged a quizzical look with his companions. Shipborn all, they simply shrugged.

"Please allow my officers access to your facility, Dr. Gallagher," Captain Xie said firmly. "Full access."

"Call me Zookeeper Eve," she gave a buck-toothed grimace, "but Captain, please. Leave the gene bank alone! You're already killing every living animal aboard the ship. That's enough."

"Orders are to be followed, Zookeeper Eve." He lowered his head, tiredly. "If you refuse to comply, measures can be taken."

Eve noticed a subtle shift in the body-language of the whitesuits, a threatening adjustment of posture. She wondered what they were capable of.

"Silly me," she said, "I forgot about the keycard. Your albino orangutans scared me." Eve glared at one of the officers, who stepped out of her way as she moved deliberately toward a locker. "Let me just grab it."

Casually, Eve clicked open the locker's safety latch. She drew out a long stun-rod, never before used. Swiftly, she dashed back, putting the vault stairs behind her and swinging the rod out in front.

"Stay back!" She shouted.

The white-suits made ready to grab her, but Xie held up a steadying hand, his voice clear and carrying despite the suit's filters.

"Now, now. Aren't things dire enough without resorting to dramatics?"

"I'm trying to study it and you're trying to *stop* me! You want us all to die, don't you?"

"I assure you, I have no higher priority than ensuring the survival of the humans in my charge and the completion of our mission. This is why you must stop impeding my progress." The Captain's voice acquired an edge.

"There's nothing dangerous in the bank," Eve continued to plead, pointing her woefully-underpowered stun rod at the whitesuits. "It needs to be protected!"

"You have animal tissue in said bank, yes?" Xie spoke sternly. "Embryos? God knows how many. My order was to eradicate all animal life aboard this ship. It's the only way we have a chance against EPD. Surely a biologist understands infection. Root and stem, Doctor–I beg your pardon," he finished, "Zookeeper."

"The gene bank is sterile–isolated from the prion!" Eve argued. "You're being stupid. Those specimens are important. You have to make an exception, Captain!"

"Everyone thinks they are exceptional." Xie sighed, shaking his head.

With a two-fingered gesture, he ordered his men forward. They cautiously moved to surround the trapped, armed woman. Eventually, one stepped into the path of her weapon. Eve depressed the trigger and electricity crackled. Unfortunately for the Zookeeper, her opponents' synthetic suits were constructed from a polymer that, on the molecular level, resembled a tangled map of impossibly complicated tunnels–a place far too easy for electrons to get lost.

As the stun-rod crackled uselessly against the first officer's insulated suit, the others realized that there was no danger and quickly closed in.

"Get off me!" Eve screamed as they grabbed her arms.

"Zookeeper Eve is under arrest for sedition," Xie announced calmly. "Due to the quarantine, we'll need to arrange alternate accommodations for the prisoner."

Eve screamed and struggled until the gruff trooper picked up her fallen stun-rod and triggered it less than an inch from her unprotected face.

"Bring her to my private quarters," Xie instructed his men.

*　*　*

Eve didn't typically spend much time playing in the low-to-no gravity zones of the Homepod's spindle, only making the climb to the funplex for the occasional colleague's party. It simply seemed underwhelming after her girlhood adventures exploring the Exodus' twisting engineering sections with Lacey and Jooles. Thus, despite her rage and the feelings of helplessness at her captivity–despite her devastation at losing her life's work, Eve still felt a physical thrill at sailing through the baffling zero-g corridors. Bound, she could only be steered like cargo toward the bridge, an area of the ship she had never quite reached.

Captain Xie had turned the increasingly-exclusive Command Deck into his private quarters, harnessing the plague quarantines to flex his emergency powers. When his officers opened the hatches, it looked much as Eve had imagined it–a central walkway flanked by high-tech stations, straps and handholds everywhere. Some odd, homey touches stood out. A wooden table had been bolted somehow to the alloy deck, alongside a set of cabinets, and in one corner, what looked like a synth-fabric cocoon, which, in fact, served as a long sleeping bag, commissioned by Xie for a gravity-free bedroom.

Eve was surprised to find herself roughly turned away from the clutter and pointed toward a conspicuous hatch. She worried that it was an airlock, and suddenly her iron-red bloodstream flooded with adrenaline. The Zookeeper's eyes scanned her surroundings, looking for an opportunity to make a move. Too late. An officer opened the hatch, but instead of cold vacuum on the other side, there was only a small, dank room. Eve relaxed, suddenly exhausted. They tossed her like a helpless missile. One of the troopers followed her in, turned her around, and undid her bonds before executing a neat, zero-g pirouette–launching themselves out of the head and slamming the lever on the other side of the hatch closed.

Eve spun around and tried to follow, but she moved too slow and collided with the sealed hatch. There was no apparent way to open it, the lever on her side having been removed. In a thoughtless rage, Eve beat her fists against the alloy door, a gesture that only sent her drifting backwards with her own recoil.

Above the captive Zookeeper, nestled in a recess of the ship's hull, sat Fe and its associated motor-actuator assembly and pressure door. The woman inside the bathroom, curled into a ball and crying, could have no way of knowing that she once shared a rocket with some of the room's safety equipment. She could have no way of knowing about most of the things happening aboard the Exodus, for that matter.

For a long time, Eve floated in near-silence, wishing she were dead. Eventually her tears ran out, but the pain only hardened, like sharpened crystals. She held her knees to her chest, tried to make herself tiny–tried to make herself no different than any of the other bits of pointless matter drifting between the stars.

An interminable time later, when Captain Xie opened the door to the head-turned-brig, he ran into a small minefield of tears. Several floating globes of cold, salty water intercepted Xie's body as he floated into the entrance, absorbing into dark circles against the red fabric of his suit.

"You've produced a great deal of moisture," he observed. "You must be dehydrated." Eve opened her mouth, but no sound came out. Thoughts of water had been stabbing into her semi-conscious mind for some time. Instead of trying to talk again, she turned toward the Captain and nodded, squinting against the brighter lights on the deck behind him.

"Don't you remember your astronaut training?" Xie said, his tone verging on mocking. "You are Earthborn, yes? Think back to when you had to use the facilities aboard your shuttle..." With a slow gesture, he pointed toward the water nozzle of the astronaut shower.

Extra light from the Command Deck leaked in, and Eve belatedly realized that she had been locked in a bathroom the whole time. Indignantly, she glared at the red-suited Captain, but her body moved toward the shower stall, almost of its own accord, and made her hands pull the nozzle to her lips.

"It's funny," Captain Xie mused as Eve drank, "Earthborn like us have more formal training for life in space than the spaceborn generations who've known nothing else.

"Feel free to make use of my shower as you wish. You'll have plenty of privacy," he said as Eve finished. "And," he added, pointing to the suction toilet at the far wall, "I'm sure you know how to use that."

"Why–" Eve coughed out. "Why am I in here?"

"Most nonessential crew are in some sort of solitary quarantine." Xie waved her question away. "It wouldn't be much different if you were back in the Homepod. You'll get used to the gravity. Do you feel sick?"

Eve, filled with hate, shook her head. "You're so stupid," she said, "what did you do to the bank?"

"You must be starving as well as parched," he said, ignoring her question. He produced a reddish-gold apple and floated it over to his captive. It crossed a meter or two of empty space, elegantly rotating, incongruous with its surroundings.

Eve snatched the slow-motion fruit and bit into it without stopping to think. It felt good to bite something, and the tartness of the apple made her mouth fill with saliva. Her empty stomach did a somersault

"Don't get used to these," Xie said, dryly. "It may be many a long hard season ahead before this species blossoms and fruits again."

"Why?" Eve demanded, after she had gulped her first bite down. "Are you killing all the plants now too? Too busy playing dictator to learn to read?"

"I am well aware," the Captain interrupted her venom, "that prions can only replicate in animal tissue. Since you have ample time to read, I'm certain that you're aware that the fertile soil of our beloved Fieldpod is filled with symbiotic invertebrate life, exodusworms and the like. I ordered the extermination of non-human animal life aboard the ship, and I expect my orders to be followed competently. Therefore, Zookeeper Eve, it should come as no surprise that fairly radical measures are being taken to eradicate the pathogen from Feildpod soil."

Eve munched her apple as he spoke, trying to compartmentalize her fury, letting her brain work the problem.

"Perhaps some of the trees will survive," Xie finished with a shrug. "I sincerely wish they do. I sincerely wish the best for everyone on this ship, including you.

"Whether you believe my intentions or not," he added, meeting Eve's baleful gaze. "Someone will bring something else along later. I'll leave you to think."

Xie retreated, his whitesuits following.

"Let someone know if you start to feel symptoms," an officer commanded as he sealed the hatch.

Eve lived in darkness for what felt like an age. Long stretches of floating in nothingness were broken up by brief periods when, reminded by her body that she was still alive, she had to make use of the facility she'd been sequestered in. Bridge officers opened the lavatory hatch twice the next week to drop in meals. The third time this happened, the trapped Zookeeper was waiting. She planned to attack the officer with the astronaut shower, but all she succeeded at was making a mess and earning a few new bruises in the process. The Bridgecrew moved so quickly and fluidly in zero-g, Eve found, and besides, she was always outnumbered. Eve accepted the fact that she wouldn't be able to force her way to freedom. She hung, suspended in nothing, as silent as the atom Fe and the exponential trillions of others that made up the Exodus, spinning in their own orbits.

* * *

"Good morning, Zookeeper." A voice woke Eve sharply from the blackness of her dreams.

Xie hung in the doorway.

"Morning?" She asked, groggily.

"11:00 ship time, to be precise," the Captain said crisply. "Though I suppose your circadian rhythms may be thrown off somewhat in this place." Xie's eyes swept over the cramped confines of the head, and he made a sour face. "I do miss having my private latrine. But we all must make sacrifices in these times."

"I'm sorry for your loss," Eve said hollowly, rolling over to face him and shading her eyes with an upraised arm.

"Still," the Captain mused, apparently in no hurry, "there is some hope, for our species at least. Do you remember the Diomed? I've perused news from Earth, and they finally launched. Quite successfully, it seems."

"What?" Eve lowered her arm, fully awake now. "You've been communicating with Earth? What about EPD?! Can they help?"

"Zookeeper Eve, the Exodus is currently traveling at a fraction of the speed of light—a not inconsiderable fraction, mind you. We're tens of trillions of kilometers from Sol. To the people on Earth, we're just a tiny speck of fusion against the blackness. Let me stress that communications are anything but easy."

"But you've sent them the prion data, haven't you?" Eve bared her teeth. "They have literally millions of scientists—someone can find a cure."

"It is very difficult to get decipherable signals at this distance and speed. At this point, only Ground Mission's targeted newsbeams are worth anything. It's even harder to send something coherent from our end, I'm afraid."

"You're just try–"

"Even if communications were *perfect*," Xie continued, his voice rising against Eve's attempted interruption, "it would still take more than a year to complete a single cycle of sending a message to Earth and receiving their reply. By the time Ground Mission first learns of EPD, we'll either have eradicated it, or it will have killed us all. I've reviewed your autopsy reports, Zookeeper. You must know that we never had the luxury of time."

Eve didn't reply. Instead, she retreated into her curled sleeping position, the tiny spark of hope and fire inside burnt out.

"They seem fine back home, if it's any consolation," Xie made a small shrug with one arm as he watched his captive turn away from him, though he continued to speak to her back. "Or at least they were, some time ago. Their shiny Diomed seems to have been designed and constructed much more intelligently than our beloved Exodus, in my opinion. I sincerely hope they won't share our crises.

"It's interesting," he said, looking down at a small wrist-mounted screen, "they've launched on a course to Asimov's Star. Further from Earth than Akkadia, but with the Diomed's better technology, they should arrive before we do. It's flying toward the same cluster as ours, by the by, so we'll have them for neighbors, if we ever make it to Akkadia. I'm envious of the Diomed's advances. It frustrates me. But even *they* will look slow and primitive compared with what the engineers on Earth are bringing out next. Project Ishtar–apparently antimatter is the fuel of the new great wave of–"

"Stop blabbering!" Eve finally snapped, unfolding and spinning around fiercely. "I don't want to make small talk with you."

"Very well, how about we discuss the most recent EPD deaths?" Captain Xie's tone chilled. "They've slowed, thank the stars, but just this morning I lost one of my own Bridgecrew. Bri Nguyen. She bravely volunteered for biohazard duty, purging the ship of our invisible little enemies, only to be exposed herself. Now she'll travel the void forever."

"Very poetic," Eve sighed. She saw something in Xie's look and took another deep breath, bracing herself.

"We have the upper hand, Zookeeper. Isolation and purge protocols are working. However, I should also tell you, there's been a suicide in the Fieldpod." Xie looked down, no longer meeting her gaze. "Someone you may know. A Stableboss, Tim Diallo."

She didn't feel shock. Deep down, the news felt true, as if she had been somehow prepared for it–Tim wanted to glue their families together, but Molly refused to force the baby he begged for. Jooles married young. Lacey and her father stopped speaking, though Eve couldn't remember why. Finally, Captain Xie, the redsuited tyrant who floated before her, had Tim's animals slaughtered and thrown into space. What else did the man have? Instead of exploding, Eve deflated. It was as if a string inside of her had been cut–something dropped, and only a sucking hole remained.

"I'm sorry to bring you this news," Xie said softly. "Records indicate that you once cohabitated with him. A lover?"

"A father, you bastard!" She bellowed, hollow and deep. "You killed him. Go to hell!"

"My condolences. I mean that truly." Xie bowed his head for a moment.

He let Eve stare daggers at him for several seconds, not shrinking from her gaze.

"How?" She eventually asked, tight-lipped.

"Something called a...captive bolt gun," the Captain answered, reading from his screen.

Eve remembered the strange, terrible tool with its sliding bolt–a device mechanically not dissimilar from an emergency pressure door actuator, intended to humanely dispatch livestock with a single thrust.

"He worked even more closely with animals than you, Zookeeper. Perhaps he wasn't in his right mind," Xie suggested. "He may have felt the stirrings of the EPD prion within himself and taken a drastic step to save us all."

He held the bathroom wall with one hand and lifted the suction-tube from the astronaut shower, moving it to slurp up the stray teardrops that floated through the empty space like tiny ocean worlds.

"Go away, murderer." It was all Eve could spit out.

"Believe what you will," Xie said curtly, snapping the tube back in place. He pushed himself backward, sailing through the hatch. Without another word, the Captain swung around and slammed the lever closed, sealing Eve in the darkness of the latrine.

●　●　●

Eve refused to eat, but that only lasted so long before her body betrayed the cause–pride laid low by biology's supremacy. Still, she refused to look at or speak to Captain Xie when he delivered meals. That is, until he cracked the hatch one day and asked Eve if she was open to a visit with some of her loved-ones.

"Visitors?" She asked, lonely enough to take Xie's bait.

"Virtually, of course," he amended, displaying a small tablet. "My favorite engineer whipped this up for me–he stripped it of most of its functionality, of course, but at my request, he established direct connections with the dwellings of your two most frequent contacts."

"Who?"

Xie glanced down at the tablet. "Your mother and your supervisor."

Good enough, Eve decided. She looked Xie in the eye and nodded. The Captain let the tablet go with a gentle flick of his wrist. It sailed through the distance, passing Fe's invisible threshold. Eve plucked it out of the air. Sure enough, the simple UI showed two names–'Molly Gallagher' and 'Pat Zellweger.' Hungrily, Eve began to press on Molly's name before remembering Xie, and she looked up at the Captain.

"I don't suppose I can expect privacy?"

"Of course," Xie answered, surprising her. He swiftly backed out and closed the hatch, leaving her alone with the tablet.

She pressed the contact and held her breath as the device sent its signal and worked to connect. After a moment, a storm of pixels focused into the image of Eve's mother, her tattoos and burnscars immediately identifiable. Molly's small, sharp-featured face was hollow-eyed, and her hair seemed lighter and thinner than Eve remembered it. Suddenly, the image grew distorted and wavery, and Eve realized that she was crying.

Molly's purple eyes also swam in tears. She watched from back in the Homepod, her arms pressed up against the dwelling's wall, her tired face only inches from its camera.

"Mom," Eve sobbed, wiping her face with one arm, trying to keep herself from spinning.

"I know–" Molly began to speak, but her face pinched, and only a choked cry came out.

Eve nodded rapidly, and both women dissolved completely. Neither tried to speak again, though the call lasted a long time. Afterward, Eve spent many silent minutes sitting alone in the darkness, the tablet forgotten. An age later, she roused enough to wipe and dry her face, then, she maneuvered to the shower to relieve her parched throat and hunt down any rogue tears with its suction tube. When she had pulled herself together as much as she could hope to, Eve gathered the tablet and pressed the contact for Zell.

The screen briefly pixelated, then dissolved into the Zookeeper's pudgy features.

"Jenny!" They screamed. "You're alive!" They sat in a sterile-looking dwelling in the Homepod, still dressed as if a safari could break out at any moment.

"I'm glad to see you too, Zell." Despite herself, she felt the ghost of a smile curling the edge of her mouth. "Listen," Eve forced her tone to turn serious, "I'm being held captive by Captain Xie. He has me locked up in his bathroom."

"Kinky," Zell said with a shrug. "We're all captives, Jenny-baby. They only let me out of my coffin in the Homepod for ratcatcher duty. Most poor saps ain't so lucky."

"What?" Eve asked, baffled as usual by Zell.

"You know, they've got me hunting down rats in the hull—rats, worms, any living thing that escaped the purge. Prion probably'd killed 'em off by now, I said, but still, it's actually kinda neat. I get to use this infrared thingy to see heat move through walls. Helps me track down the stragglers. Haven't been let out in a while, though," Zell said, winding down, "must mean we got 'em all."

"What the hell, Zell?" Eve said, angered by their nonchalance. "How could you help the whitesuits after they threw me in prison and destroyed the gene bank?"

"They what?!" Zell reeled, nearly falling from their stool.

"That's why I'm in here," she said urgently, "because I was trying to stop them from purging the specimens!"

"Oh," Zell's face on the screen flushed. "Jenny! You nearly gave me a heart-attack. I thought you knew something I didn't. But, luckily, I still know everything."

"What do you know?" She was losing patience, emotionally drained and still raw from her earlier call.

"I said 'everything'. Nobody touched the bank. As far as I know, you'wer the last one down there...Why?" Zell raised an eyebrow, theatrically. "What do *you* know?"

"Nothing, apparently. Not a damn thing."

"Hey, Jenny," they teased. "Ask me the thing you *really* wanna ask me."

Eve searched her exhausted mind and came up blank.

"Come on," Zell prodded, "don'tcha wanna know why you're Jenny?"

"I guess." Eve sighed. "Yeah–why do you call me Jenny?"

"Because Eve is from Genesis, not Exodus. Yet here you are," Zell answered, spreading their hands. "So I call ya Jenny."

"Who's Geny-sis?"

"Jeez, haven't you ever read the Holy Bible?" Scorn filled their voice.

"Goodbye Zell."

"Goodbye, Jenny!"

Eve floated in the dark, endless void of space. She was an asteroid, a tiny bit of matter bigger than some, smaller than others. She felt a strange kinship with the captured Sukuru, whose corporeal material composed the bulk of the Exodus. Fe's asteroid, which often experienced a long and lonely aphelion, would have been a more appropriate comparison, had Eve known of its existence. However, neither Sukuru or Fe's nameless voyager had ever experienced a remoteness like that of the Exodus, out in the cold between the stars.

When she woke, Eve found the tablet missing, replaced by bars of compressed rice. She drifted back into her asteroid state–relished the darkness and the nothingness. Being an asteroid was kinder than having to think.

"Ow." Eve bumped her forehead, which made her open her eyes.

She must have overcorrected when she turned. Her momentum was always carrying her into corners of the room. Eve found herself wishing she could echolocate like her beloved order *Chiroptera*. But thinking of the bats made her think of the gene bank, and that was like touching a red-hot nerve in her psyche. Instinctively, she willed the bad feelings away but paused as an unfamiliar particle of hope made itself known. Zell had seemed to think that Xie's men had never returned to the bank. If the gene bank were still intact...Eve let her mind wander, the sudden thrill making her shiver...she could bring back the bats–make them fly again.

Chapter 7: The Captain

"Are you finished?" Xie asked, re-entering the bridge's head.

Eve nodded and tossed back the borrowed tablet. She had just wrapped up a third round of video calls.

"I hope your loved-ones passed on the news," the Captain said. "I'll be lifting the quarantine order tomorrow. The EPD prion is no longer a threat."

"What, just like that?" Eve asked, not daring to hope.

"Yes, Zookeeper, *just like that*, after months of death, struggle, and sacrifice," Xie scolded, his black eyes glinting like obsidian. "There hasn't been a new EPD case in weeks. My medical advisors concur—lockdown is over."

"Are you certain?"

"I wouldn't risk the safety of my people if I were not," Xie answered, fatigue creeping into his voice.

Eve noticed that the Captain had grown somewhat gaunt and colorless—even his signature attire had lost some of its vibrance.

"Does this mean I'll be free to go?"

"You were placed under arrest, Zookeeper, not quarantine. Executive powers still give me discretion in what to do with you."

"We both know I didn't do anything wrong." Eve stared at her captain, her jaw clenched.

"We do? Your defiance regarding the gene bank is not under question. You've convinced me that you were on the side of right, and indeed, that has earned you my pardon."

Eve sighed with relief.

"Don't mistake this with a writ of innocence," Xie continued. "You defied direct orders and menaced my bridge officers with a restricted weapon. Now more than ever, maintaining order and unity is crucial to the survival of the Exodus. Even if you cannot forgive me, I need you to understand and accept that necessity. Unity and order. Doubly so, if you are to be my ally in the days to come."

Eve wanted to scoff, but she held her silence and let the politician speak.

"You will not be returning to the same Exodus you left. People are dead. Many of us, traumatized. The crew have lost their loved-ones, their livelihoods, their security. Our Fieldpod is a sterile waste. Everyone believes that our mission is over. In short," Xie indulged in a dramatic pause, "the world has been turned upside down. We can live on our stores, but not forever. We *must* rebuild. From the very beginning and without Earth's help this time."

"You don't think it's impossible?" Eve asked, surprised to find that she didn't either.

"Not with unity and order. If we all come together, without a single voice raised in dissent, we may have a chance. The crew looks to me for leadership in this time of crisis, but I confess, I have one terrible weakness."

"And what's that?" Eve asked, noticing Xie was staring into her eyes.

"You, Zookeeper Eve."

Eve was taken aback. She opened her mouth, but before she could think of a response, Xie resumed his speech.

"The plague left us with no specimens from Earth. No breeding stock. We have nothing but what we can grow ourselves, and you are an artist with fauna–our finest Zookeeper. I say this not to flatter your ego," the Captain's voice strengthened as he borrowed phrases from tomorrow's public address, "but because surviving EPD does not mean we can abandon our mission. We don't *get* to fail. There remains not a speck of animal tissue aboard this vessel, other than human, yet we have an entire planet to populate and speciate. Without your full and fanatical cooperation, our colony will be over before it begins."

Eve thought for a moment, letting the words sink in, comparing them against what she knew of the Fieldpod ecosystem, the capabilities of her lab, and where they would need to be before planetfall—she realized that Xie was right.

"You're right," she said at last.

"Unless," Xie risked a small smile, "you'd rather I trust the fate of the Exodus mission to Dr. Zellweger?"

Eve was surprised to find herself laugh.

"I won't waste your time with small talk, because I know you hate it," the Captain said, his manner relieved, "but I remembered a bit of esoterica from the newsbeams—a paleogenomic breakthrough. Scientists on Earth have successfully resurrected several ancient species, large predators from the Cretaceous."

"And?"

"And, we have some data on their techniques. Copies of the relevant journal publications on their breakthroughs," he explained, "whatever's public. We can request data that isn't, if you can live without a reply for a while. It's old tech by now on Earth, but cutting-edge for us...I was hoping, in your hands, these tools could be useful."

Abovehead, Fe's strontium ferrite magnet churned out its constant b-field, flooding the non-ferromagnetic humans with lines of impotent force. The actuator's technology, based on an ancient 20th century design, like every bit of hardware aboard the Exodus was clunky and obsolete by Sol standards, frozen-in-time while its distant blue world continued to thrive and burn and innovate.

"Hmm." Eve was thinking, chewing her lower lip. "Maybe. Send me the data. The real limitation will be our vats. Unless you spaced the tanks along with the livestock—"

"Equipment has been sterilized, Zookeeper, not spaced."

"Then I could probably work things so that we'd be able to hatch something as large as a *Bos taurus* calf in just a few months, but not at the scale you'd need."

"Perhaps that was true before," Xie allowed, "but priorities have shifted. Resources and staff will be no object to *you*."

"That'll be a start…"

They continued to discuss the looming challenges ahead, making plans and compromises, assessing the feasibility of starting a new ecosystem from near-scratch. Captain Xie did not explicitly mention the extent of his new social-order policies or bother to explain his mandatory Code, but there would be time enough for Eve to adapt.

###

The shelves of the Earth Street storeroom vibrated and bounced. A box of alloy screws dislodged and fell, bursting to the floor in a musical rattle.

"Like that." Lacey reached an arm behind her head and gripped a shelf. The rail bit into her fingers, but she reached her other hand back regardless, gaining two-handed leverage.

Gabe, one of her underlings, had Lacey by the hips, his strong hands pinning her against a shelf, which, luckily for everyone, had been bolted to the ship's hull.

"Like that," she repeated, breathlessly. Another box of screws rattled off the shelf and burst against the ringing metal floor.

It felt good. Too good, Lacey realized.

Gabe was breathing heavily, grinding Lacey and pushing himself into her.

"Enough," she yelped. She released her hands from the shelf and brought them down onto Gabe, slipping off his sweaty bald head and onto his muscular shoulders.

Lacey pushed herself off, wiggling out of his embrace. She checked herself, then began collecting her clothes.

"Aw, what the–why?" Gabe sputtered, erect and confused.

"Don't even fucking pretend with me."

"I wasn't gonna, Lacey–"

"You put a baby in me, and I'll choke you to death with it, motherfucker," she interrupted, not without mirth.

"Will you at least…?" Gabe pointed to his deflating appendage.

"I would, really, but I think you're late for a delivery," Lacey said, sticking out her tongue.

"You're such a fucking tease, you know that?"

"Shut up and get that adorable ass moving. You know you love me."

Gabe shook his head, but the man did as his Quartermaster asked, pulling on his pants and harness before hefting a crate of outgoing cargo.

Lacey Diallo watched the porter go. Things were smoother when there'd been at least one automated lift available, but Xie had appropriated them all. Humans were more fun anyway, she knew. Like the spunky little ex-engineer who had just rounded the corridor and was walking up to Lacey's counter.

"Sorry, babe. All out of stilts," Diallo called out.

"Ha. Ha." Eelee Guk smiled at her friend. "How goes it?"

"I'm not gonna lie–I'm feeling a little unsatisfied." Lacey looked the curly-haired beauty up and down and bit her lip. "Maybe you could help me with something in the back? An order for...mutual fulfillment."

"I told you Lace," Eelee scolded, "I don't appreciate that kind of talk."

"Sorry. Came in too hot. Shutting it down."

"Ah ha!" Guk's lemur eyes widened. "I know why you're being gross. I passed Gabe as I came in–his head was redder than a tomato."

"That's none of your business. Shit, why'd you say tomato? I haven't had a tomato since before the epidemic."

"We got 'em growing again!" Eelee said, a hopeful note in her voice. "Just a seed crop for now. It'll be slow-going before nightshades will be back on the menu for good."

"I wish all the yummy foods on this ship were getting fertilized faster than the fuckin' people. Have you been to the spokes lately? Can't walk without stepping onna infant. Shit, it's like Creche exploded," the Quartermaster finished, unhappily.

"Don't blame me, Lace, I've made zero. Hey, did you hear about–"

Clanking steps announced that a crewman was heading toward them. Dressed in the same neutral logistics uniform as Lacey and Gabe, he was younger and wore his hair long. Eelee cut herself off mid-sentence and leaned nonchalantly against the counter as Lacey handed a tablet to her newly-arrived underling. The two women pretended to study an inventory display as they waited for the porter to finish assembling his order.

"So—did you hear about Devon?" Guk asked, once the coast had cleared.

Lacey shook her bony, buzzed head, searching her memory. The only Devon was a Fieldpod biochemist whom she knew from his side business—batching and distributing black-market prophylactics.

"Spaced," Eelee said.

"Fuck off!"

"The whitesuits busted Devon dead-to-rights. They marched into the greenhouse and grabbed him—like Gabe carries cargo. He screamed and kicked, but they just dragged him away. Then, uh, you know. Lace, I haven't seen Captain Xie come down this hard on someone for a while."

"So I guess all his speeches about the value of human life were just starshit?"

"That's not the way guys like Xie think," Eelee began to quote, "'each and every potential life for the promised world' right? The bridge's argument is that Devon's worse than a murderer under the Code. To Xie, he's taking colonists away from Akkadia before they're ever even conceived."

"'Crime is a disease and the Exodus spaces pathogens,'" Diallo said darkly, quoting the Code.

"One murder charge per condom, is what I heard."

Lacey shifted uncomfortably, remembering her own patronage. She made a mental note to drink some shine in the chemist's honor that night.

"How'd the whitesuits track him down?" The Quartermaster asked, her professional curiosity piqued.

"Remember Dre, his pet techie I told you about?" Eelee sneered, baring her teeth with a hint of feral rage.

"We don't need to go into it, baby, I remember."

Lacey knew it was a sore-spot for E, who used to be a high-ranking Bridgecrew engineer before turning to applied botany. The version of the story she'd been told was that Xie's clever attaché had turned the bridge's token communications station into a centralized chokepoint for all information transmitted within the Exodus and beyond. In a stroke, Xie ordered most of the ship's antennae dismantled. Eelee, who was supposed to be one of the whitesuits leading the detail, refused to be a part of the censorship and lost her rank.

Shit like that was exactly why Lacey stayed off the ship's data networks, sticking solely to easily-destructible, handwritten notes and in-person deliveries. Inanimate objects were less fun than people, Lacey believed, though usually more trustworthy.

"Thanks," Eelee said, sadly. "I guess poor Devon just got careless. Sweet guy, he was kinda naïve."

"Hey, E?" Lacey asked, breaking a moment of tense silence. "What sorta animals've you been seeing around the Fieldpod these days?" She was thinking of her old friend Eve, currently cloistered in a lab somewhere, deep in the ship's hull, working madly.

"Just bees and worms and bugs and stuff." Eelee shrugged, shifting nervously from foot to foot. "Why? Hey...oh–I forgot!" She brightened. "The piglet! Someone was showing off a little baby pig the other day."

Lacey returned Eelee's thousand-lux smile with a sad one of her own. Dad would have loved to see the piglet, she thought. He probably would've approved of most of the Code too, had he stuck around to see how things'd turn out. Maybe even Molly could have caved, eventually.

Quartermaster Diallo shook her head rapidly, clearing away bad thoughts.

"That's good," she said at last. "Maybe I'll be able to make you some maafe one of these years."

Eelee smiled politely and nodded at Lacey, who began to drum her nails against the counter, having run out of things to say.

"Hey, Lace? Listen, could you, uhm... The thing."

"Hrm? Oh, yeah. Hold up." Suddenly reminded of their actual business, Lacey bent down and retrieved an object from behind a sliding panel hidden beneath her counter.

She stood up and passed Eelee a featureless, alloy cuboid.

The ex-engineer took the parcel and nodded gratefully–she would melt through its thin metal skin later that evening to free the components waiting inside. She paid Lacey in currency far better than drugs, gold, or raw calories.

"Starshit!" Lacey's eyes widened as Eelee scooped handfuls of produce from a pocket of her jumpsuit–a pair of miniature limes, a bioplastic pouch of black-eyed peas, one incredibly tiny strawberry, and a pile of fresh cassava leaves.

A quartet of blushing, gold-and-red grape tomatoes completed the bounty.

The Quartermaster scooped the flavorful treasures into her hiding place before another crewmember could interrupt. Their business concluded, the two malcontents embraced–Lacey having to walk around the counter to reach her shorter friend. Afterward, Eelee scurried off.

A few minutes later, another of Lacey's porters appeared, ready for her next assignment. The Quartermaster pointed the wrinkled woman to a heavy box of tubing. A capable underling, but too old, Lacey believed, to still be doing this sort of work full time. She made her next porter clean up the screw-mess from earlier, and before long, her mind moved on to bigger things. It was easy for her to become absorbed in her work. Objects, objects, objects–Lacey had them, and everybody needed them. At each end of an order, a person–one she controlled and one who needed something from her–and in-between, the coveted cargo she held in her precious supply.

She sent out an order for a crate of powdered milk headed for Earth Street Creche–it was one of their last, but the requisition came straight from the bridge, and Lacey complied. Next, she routed machine oil to Syll in engineering, a camouflaged packet of pills included in the crate, slipped in by a complicit porter. Running a quarter of the Homepod's supply logistics while complying with each new austerity policy from the bridge was a challenge. Doing it all while juggling a number of side-hustles of various legality–that was just living for Lacey Diallo. That, and the occasional inventory check with Gabe.

When news about Eelee Guk finally trickled down to the Earth Street Quartermaster, she took it poorly. She learned that captain Xie had shown the sweet little techie the wrong side of an airlock–executed for some bullshit transgression, according to the official story.

Sedition. Lacey suspected a deeper truth.

Ex-engineers, she reasoned, don't requisition smuggled electronic components for Code-approved reasons. Though she shed hot, mad tears for Eelee, the Quartermaster, ever practical, noticed concern for her own survival supplanting grief. Lacey traced the contraband supply lines, exchanged a cautious whisper or two, and connected the rumors flowing to her from all corners of the Exodus–Eelee had been caught operating some kind of forbidden communications device before she was spaced. Lacey was certainly guilty of supplying her the parts–she wondered if Eelee gave her up to Xie, there at the end.

Tense days passed while she quietly diverted resources and sent communiques to trusted friends, calling in favors and anticipating the other shoe's drop–restless for the whitesuits to find her.

Lacey, as a rule, tried not to fuck with anything bigger than herself–Xie was always a bastard, but now the Captain had killed her little friend. He was probably coming for her next. Lacey sure as shit wasn't going to sit around and wait.

\#

Gene Lyman lay dead on the alloy decking, his colorless hair soaking up pooling blood like a paintbrush.

"Hold…" Saul Graham breathed to his soldiers, barely above a whisper.

They were crouched in a T-junction corridor, the former-lieutenant Graham and his insurgents hidden along the halls at either side. Officer Gene, who had been surprised from behind, lay sprawled in the center. The sound of boots echoed down the main corridor. Graham tried to count them–too many. One stopped, someone was breathing just around the corner.

Oblivious to Saul and his militia, a white-suited bridge officer knelt down to check on the fallen Gene.

"Now!" Graham hissed.

One of the militiamen swung around the corner and lunged forward, leading with an improvised spear. Its jagged point of Sukuru-alloy took the bridge officer by surprise, piercing through the white fabric of his suit and driving into the flesh between the man's throat and collarbone.

The spear-carrier turned to Graham with a short-lived look of triumph before something tiny ripped through his head, and the corridor filled with a deafening crack.

"Gun!" One of the older rebels yelled–alarmed that someone in the Bridgecrew company carried a functional firearm.

"Charge!" Graham screamed before his troops could lose heart.

They obeyed instantly, filling the corridor with battlecries and the pounding of boots.

Graham leapt over the bodies of Gene and the newly fallen man, trying to stay low, trying to keep the vamplate of his lance-like weapon between his head and the enemy. Three more gunshots rang out in quick succession, and Graham's left ear could suddenly hear only a terrible, hollow ringing. He felt the tip of his lance turned aside by the baton of a bridge officer, a man he knew.

The officer raised his baton, taking aim at Graham's head. Graham dropped his lance, useless at close range, and dove forward to tackle the whitesuit. The officer's baton swung down, landing several blows on Saul's back as the two men grappled, another bullet passing them by inches.

Graham risked loosening his grip for an instant to draw a fabric-wrapped shard of metal from a pocket. As his opponent prepared for another bash, he thrust the improvised knife underneath the man's arm. He repeated the motion three times in rapid succession, stabbing through white fabric and into the officer's side. The fourth time, the alloy tip of the blade impacted a rib, and the already-slippery weapon wrenched sideways out of Graham's grip. The damage had been done, however, and the dying officer slumped aside.

Somewhere, an emergency pressure door triggered, its motor-driven actuator forcing the door down with a woosh and sealing one hapless insurgent inside a rapidly-decompressing chamber. The gunshots ceased, but the company of white-clad Bridgecrew was larger than Graham had anticipated. He and his rebels were outnumbered.

The fighting devolved into a bloody melee. The Exodus rang with the clanging of metal, the buzzing of stun-guns, and the screaming of anguished humans. Then, a new sound joined the terrible orchestra.

A cacophonous mass, like a sack of pots and pans falling down stairs, barreled down the hallway on the other side of the Bridgecrew forces. Graham ducked a blow from a hairy-fisted officer, countering with a punch to the man's throat, when he discovered the source of the noise—at least a dozen wild-eyed newcomers, their bodies dripping with an improvised armor of chains and hammered alloy scales.

"Laceyites!" Someone shouted.

Indeed, at their head rushed Lacey Diallo—Quartermaster turned General—armed, armored, and out for blood. Her people crashed into Xie's army. Graham's troops stopped giving ground, and the Bridgecrew became trapped between two insurgent militias.

"Phalanx!" Graham screamed, and his people fixed their spears, thrusting them forward.

Flanking Lacey, a helmeted-Gabe roared, hefting an enormous curved axe and hewing it brutally through the whitesuits. With a guttural groan, the rebel porter raised the improvised poleaxe above his head and brought it scything down onto a muscular woman from Xie's ranks, separating her right arm, shoulder, and lung from the rest of her body.

Graham grappled his hirsute opponent by the shoulders and shoved the man backward into the spear of an advancing Laceyite. General Diallo herself fought like a menace, and any whitesuits who tried to flee before Lacey ran headlong into Graham's phalanx. Before long, not one of Xie's people was left breathing.

The corridor steamed and stank with human offal, but the cries of the survivors were, on the whole, triumphant.

"Get some!" Gabe hollered at the dead.

"Shit, if it isn't Saul and his Grahampions." Lacey leaned on her alloy spear and winked at the other commander. "Damn lucky. Almost took you for whitesuits."

"Check the wounded," Graham commanded one of his people before giving Lacey his attention.

"Sorry for what we did to your bridge-buddies," she taunted, grinning ferally. "We're just getting too good at it."

"That's enough Lacey," Graham replied, warily. "You know whose side I'm on. You know my reasons for going against Xie are just as good as yours."

"Yeah? You sure wore his color for a long-ass time. You sure as shit said 'yes sir' to some pretty fucked-up orders."

"And you're the paranoid psycho who decided to start a war," Graham snapped, his patience at an end.

"Excuse me?" Lacey straightened up, picking up her spear. Behind her, Gabe and his terrible weapon loomed.

"This all could have ended peacefully," Graham spat, "except for your damn paranoia! What's wrong with you? Killing people because you thought Xie was after you, when, actually, he didn't know a damn thing."

"That fucker spaced Eelee!"

"You think I forgot?" Graham shouted back. "Keep her name out of your goddamn Earthborn mouth!"

"Oh you did it now!" Gabe bellowed. "Lace, should I...?"

"Nah. No–" Lacey said icily, reaching back to stay Gabe's arm. "We're all on the same side now. Justice for E. That's the game. Friends?"

"Yeah, friends." Graham gave the big man a tight smile before fixing his gaze back on Lacey.

"What I meant to say about it–" he continued, stammering under the armored General's blood-flecked glare, "–it never, never had anything to do with *you*. Aside from goddamn Dre, Eelee was the only person on this ship who knew how to build and operate an Earth-range communications device. Xie was watching *her*, not you or your tangled supply lines. I know. I was there."

"Yeah you were there, alright," Lacey muttered, "helping that fucking dictator take away our rights."

"None of this needed to happen," Graham said, spreading his arms to encompass the carnage surrounding them. "If you had only kept your cool..."

"Yeah?" Lacey shrugged, looking around herself. "It's a little late for that, I guess."

"Hey, did y'all deal with the whitesuits by Sun Street spoke, or are we in for an ambush?" Gabe demanded, changing the subject for them.

"No," General Graham sighed heavily, giving up on interpersonal conflict for the moment, "no need to worry. Sun is clean. We've already eliminated any resistance to our backs."

"Does that mean we took the Homepod?" Gabe asked, hopefully.

Graham nodded.

"For good this time, too," Lacey added, clapping her soldier on his large, armored back.

"Xie still controls the bridge," Graham said. "Even without whitesuits to hassle us, it's gonna be a challenge."

"Leave that to Lace." Gabe chuckled.

"Way ahead of you," she said, winking at Saul's puzzled expression. "I have some of my most persuasive people up there now, pulling that worm from outta his hole."

"Revolution's probs over," Gabe said, smugly.

"Then let's go and make sure," Graham motioned his people to start moving out. "Tend to the wounded," he commanded a pair from Medical.

Once the Grahampions and Laceyites finished checking their gear and looting the battlefield, the surviving insurgents formed up behind their leaders and began marching toward bridge access.

#

"I used to play here when I was a kid," Lacey mentioned when the militias had made it to the familiar warning signs.

On her orders, Gabe turned the hatch, opening up the inner skin of engineering. The unmistakable scent of blood and waste wafted out, and the group of citizen soldiers milled nervously about the opening. Silently, Lacey gestured with two fingers. Gabe gave a grim nod and stepped into the corridor, poleaxe first.

Something loud and fast thundered down the alloy tunnel toward the lone soldier. It was a lift, one of the large, automated warehousing tools Xie had appropriated—apparently, it had been recently modified—armored and studded with metal spikes and razors, some of which were stained with fresh blood.

"Oh, shit!" Gabe cried out as the reprogrammed machine barreled down on him.

Putting the poleaxe between himself and the lift, he wedged its blade into the seam between the corridor's wall and floor, forcing the robot's leading edge to ride up.

"Help!" Gabe bellowed, putting all his strength into resisting the brutal machine.

Generals Graham and Diallo, followed by their people, flooded through the hatch, bracing their own polearms against the weaponized lift. With screams of exertion and the snapping of spear hafts, the humans triumphed over the machine, tipping it over and leaving it wedged impotently inside the corridor.

"Hot starshit!" Lacey panted, staring down at the wrecked lift. "Look at this thing."

"What is it?" Graham asked.

"Just a motherfucking cargo lift they turned into a meat-grinder," she replied, studying the insane contraption.

"So, those 'persuasive people' you sent..." Graham trailed off, pointing to the abundant bloodstains.

"Don't even say anything else," Lacey warned. She wandered over to a ladder and looked up.

The wrecked machine blocked the bridge's elevators, though they'd already been shuttered and rendered non-functional by the paranoid Captain.

"You any good in zero-g?" Graham asked, following Lacey.

She shot him a look of disgust before strapping a spear over her shoulder and flying hand-over hand up the ladder.

"You're looking at the ass of a three-time Spindle Games champion," Gabe chuckled as Graham stared up at Lacey.

The two men began to climb after her, the other rebels taking up the rear. Saul reached the top rung of the ladder first, just as gravity ran out. With the practiced movements of a career Bridgecrewman, he swung himself out of the Homepod's rotation and into the zero-g corridor. The others were less graceful, and a group of rebels even decided to climb back down the ladder to stand guard, balking at the rotating transition between passageways, but soon, the rag-tag army was making its way to the bridge, floating clumsy and weightless.

Without waiting for Gabe or the troops, Saul Graham sailed forward alone, gaining on his rival. A moment later, he heard Lacey scream something profane. Muscle-memory let him practically fly through the maze of corridors, barely tapping the handholds for acceleration, until he came upon two figures, separated by a catwalk that led to the bridge's subdeck.

"You're dead!" Lacey taunted from one end.

At the other, a man in a white suit hung in the air, his hands busy manipulating the wiring of a second automated lift. Graham recognized him at once–it was Dre, Xie's devoted engineer.

"Dre!"

Dre jerked his head up at the yell and pushed off wildly, abandoning his project.

"You *better* run!" Lacey cackled, throwing her spear at the retreating engineer.

The missile sailed wide right.

Graham, who had positioned himself at a good angle, braced against the inner hull and hurled his lance forward. It zipped through the gravity-free air on a perfect, uninterrupted trajectory. Dre panicked, trying to avoid the projectile, but he only succeeded in stranding himself in the center of the corridor, away from a handhold. The lance pierced through the soft meat of Dre's calf and sent him spinning. The engineer howled horribly as small globules of blood began to bubble out of the wound.

Graham launched himself upward to help Lacey subdue the wounded white-suit. Gabe, red faced and floating upside down, joined them a few moments later. The three made a sort of human cage in cartesian space, Dre hovering at the origin.

"*Aaaahhhhhay!*" He screeched.

"Let us into the goddamn bridge!" Gabe bellowed.

"It's uuh–" Dre whimpered, "–it's impossible. *Aaah*! You'll never get in."

"Dre, Dre? Listen," Graham hissed at his former colleague, his voice urgent. "We don't give a shit about you. We just want Xie. You know his time's up."

"You'll never get him!" The engineer repeated, defiantly. "Why would I help you, Saul? You–you *know* I'd die for Xie."

"Oh, you're gonna die alright if you don't let us into the *goddamn bridge*!" Gabe kicked at the piece of metal still embedded in Dre's leg.

The techie howled incoherently, the force of the blow sending him spinning into Graham.

"You're not going to get anything from him this way," he said to Lacey, pushing Dre's bleeding, shrieking form away.

"Yeah, we'll see. Gabe," she ordered, "take this piece of shit over there and find out for sure what he knows. I guess me and General graham-cracker are gonna take a look at the door."

Gabe nodded and dragged the bleeding and crying Dre with one hand, pushing himself along with the other.

"What's a graham-cracker?" Saul asked.

"Earth thing," Lacey shrugged. "Can you open this?"

Graham looked at the bulkhead leading to the Command Deck for a moment. On the other side, somewhere, floated Captain Xie. Unfortunately for the revolutionaries, the Exodus' bridge section had been designed with significant forethought. Back during the ship's planning and construction, administrative assistant Vi had done a fair bit of work to make the deck a self-contained and nearly-inviolate structure–a fortress, if need be.

"Not anymore." Saul shook his head, trying his access codes for the hell of it. "My credentials have been revoked."

"You hear me, Xie?" Lacey pounded on the bulkhead. "We're coming in! We're gonna huff and puff and blow your house down." The force of her fists sent her flying backwards, but the General recovered and reoriented with a single, practiced twist in mid-air.

"Hey! Io!" Graham called back at the cluster of rebels. "Get up here!"

A baton-wielding, ginger-headed Grahampion in green coveralls separated herself from the group, floating clumsily toward the bulkhead and her commander.

"Io's the closest thing to a computer scientist we've got left," Graham explained to Lacey when the newcomer arrived. "Anything you can do, Doc?"

"Lemme take a look," Io answered. Her nose was broken, and she wore her red hair in twin braids.

A tense minute passed as the besieging army waited for its computer-expert to finish. Before she could say anything, however–

"Ah, fuck–" Gabe's distinctive bellow broke the silence. "Fuck!"

"Babe!?" Lacey spun around and kicked off toward him.

The soldier's hands were red, and great floating globules of blood filled the space between him and Dre's limp body. The dead engineer held a small, Earthmade knife.

"Little fucker had it stashed on him," Gabe stammered, shaking his head. "He didn't even try to stick me with it."

"What'd you get out of him?" Lacey demanded. "Before...you know."

"Not much. There's no more working robots, he said. But otherwise, same shit."

"Damn."

"Why don't we just drill into the fucking wall?" He asked, exasperated and flailing to remain in the same frame of reference.

"Xie'd have too much warning," Lacey sighed. "Fucker could do a lot of damage from in there if we try'n drill from out here."

Over at the bulkhead, Io had unrolled a softscreen and spliced a wired connection between it and the hatch's keypad.

"What've you got?" Graham asked.

"Xie's got it locked down, sir," she said, working to access any available systems. "I definitely can't open the door. I can probably set up a communication channel with the other side, if you want to talk to him. Other than that," Io shook her head, coppery braids following on a slight delay, "I can get into maybe, uh, one out of eight of the emergency systems."

"Lemme see." Graham floated over, steadying himself against the bulkhead with his palm. Eelee would have come up with something brilliant by now, Graham suspected.

Eelee.

"Hey, Lace!" He yelled, jerking her and Gabe's attention away from talk of Dre's dramatic exit. "I have a plan! But I'm going to need to get my hands on a piece of specialized equipment."

It took the Quartermaster General less than two hours to fulfill her rival's special order. Without resistance from the whitesuits along the way, it wasn't even an interesting challenge for her.

At the bulkhead, computer-specialist Io crouched with her interface connected to the access panels, Generals Graham and Diallo floating above her. Gabe waited with the mixed Laceyite-Grahampion cadre, guarding against any of Xie's surprises.

"Ok, now stand by," Graham commanded. He wore a headset that covered his eyes, and he held a device boasting a large, smooth black disk at one end. "Execute emergency pressure door test routine on my signal."

"Standing by to execute emergency pressure door test routine on your signal," the colorful Io parroted.

Graham slowly sidled along a wall shared with the Command Deck, maneuvering with small taps of his feet and pointing his handheld electronic eye at the cold alloy. The machine he operated was the same that Zookeeper Zell had employed while on ratcatcher duty–a sensitive low-wave infrared receiver that, during the EPD purge, had been tuned to penetrate the ship's alloy bulkheads in search of animal body heat.

It took patience, but Graham was soon able to make out a single heat signature, intermittently moving about the Command Deck. Even in the form of a diffuse infrared worm, Captain Xie was identifiable. The man had grown positively lanky after years of self-imposed exile from gravity.

"I've got a fix on our dear leader," Graham snarled from behind his mask.

"Standing by," the tech said nervously.

"Wait!" Graham hissed, still watching Xie.

"The fuck are we waiting for?" Lacey asked, impatiently.

"We're waiting for him to use the toilet." Graham thought of Eelee and her privacy trick with the pressure door.

When the crucial moment came, it was as inglorious and anticlimactic as the end of most revolutions. Nature called Xie, and through the infrared interface, Graham watched the red worm wriggle toward the head. The Captain's heat signature settled itself in the stall with the suction toilet.

"Stand by," Graham ordered again, his voice tense.

After a moment, the crimson worm unfolded and began to move.

"Execute!"

Io obeyed, her brain commanding her finger to make contact with an icon on her softscreen, triggering the pre-queued order. Electric signals flashed forth through the nerves of the Exodus, briefly tricking it into behaving as if a pre-launch test of the bridge's safety measures were underway. The ship routed power from the stellar-cores of its fusion engines to the Command Deck, electrifying the copper coils within the actuator motors that Dr. Kim had assembled back in Texas. Throughout all the long years, the atom Fe, in perfect lockstep with trillions of twin troopers, steadily produced a magnetic field that, when combined in phalanx and forced against the ship's electric current, proved strong enough and swift enough to turn an industrial screw and drive an attached actuator rod. Thus, a split second following Graham's command, Fe's alloy pressure door whooshed down its forgotten trackway in the wall, crunching fatally into the relatively-soft, entirely-unsuspecting head of Captain Xie.

\#

It was the end of Xie and his whitesuits, but the Exodus continued to sail through space, its mission still unfulfilled. The EPD epidemic could easily have spelled doom for the colonists, but by the time of Captain Xie's assassination, the damage was well on its way to being repaired. Ironically, Graham, Lacey, and their followers would have been unlikely to organize a successful uprising if Xie's austerity measures and draconian Code hadn't first brought the ship back from the brink of ruin. If the crew had worked hard to build up the ecosystem of the Fieldpod before launch, they labored like demons under Xie, out in the void, when their survival depended upon it. Molly Gallagher trained teams of vat-workers, supervising them from on high and passing down her experience to the young shipborn. They mixed, brewed, and revivified soil rendered dry and sterile in the late stages of the EPD purge.

Released from captivity, and with the full backing of the bridge, Zookeeper Eve set to work bringing animals back into the world. She raised the lowliest first—cloning annelids and hatching springtails to act as decomposers, nutrient fixers. Then came the pollinators. Eve expanded her role, working closely with the ship's best botanists, colleagues of the late Eelee Guk, who busied themselves nursing and splicing, helping the farmers to sow seeds as quickly as Molly's crews churned out soil in which to plant them.

By the time the Grahampions and Laceyites were ejecting Xie's mangled corpse from a starboard airlock, thin populations of pigs and chickens could be included among the Fieldpod's animal life. The Exodus' human cargo also proliferated. As Molly noticed decades earlier, breeding had always been highly, though not officially, encouraged aboard the Exodus. After the epidemic, the policy became near-mandatory. Part of Xie's plan, even in the depths of the EPD purge, included replacing the lives lost to the ravages of the prion. As the Quartermaster could attest, the Captain's ambitious social policies played a dangerous game with starvation–heavily depleting the ship's stores in order to feed a growing population and fuel the ambitious effort to restore the Fieldpod to self-sufficiency.

In the few years prior to his death by pressure door, Xie's endeavor to increase the brood of shipborn became fanatical. Young children could be found everywhere aboard the Exodus. Sequestered during the fighting, they swarmed the ship in packs once the chaos of the revolution began to ebb. Jooles and her husband Miguel had seven. Thus...

"Reproductive rights have gotta be top of the agenda," Lacey asserted, holding up one finger–her middle.

It was the first week after elections, and she knew for certain that the Xie administration had ended and that Saul Graham's had begun. The shipwide vote wasn't even close–the Grahampions and their sympathizers far outnumbered her Laceyites.

"That along with freedom of communication and information," she continued. "No more illegal condoms or communicators. No more killin' people. Hmm, what else? Damn, this bucket needs a Bill of Rights."

"What's a Bill of Rights?" Graham asked.

He had come to visit Lacey in her Earth Street headquarters. General Diallo's private fiefdom was gradually transforming back into a simple stockroom. The upjumped Quartermaster, not fully overjoyed by the changes, held her tongue as she watched her people dismantling the revolution, ostensibly from the winning side.

"Later," she said, shaking her head. "Anyway, what can I do for you, oh Captain my Captain?"

"Listen, I've been through Xie's quarters, you know." Graham's voice dropped low. "I thought he'd gone completely insane at the end, we all did, but maybe he didn't. Lace..."

Saul thought back to exploring the sad, cold chamber where his former captain had spent his last desperate days. Trash and food waste floated, unbagged and untethered, through the Command Deck's open, gravity-free spaces. Xie's double sleeping bag looked like a fly in a web of cords and straps, holding the dead Captain's worldly possessions together.

"There's some things I saw," Graham continued, picturing the console he'd found open, still logged in under Xie's credentials. "Um, I wanted to run them by you before I tell the rest of the crew."

"Why do I get insider info?" Lacey leaned forward, her palms pressed to the cold countertop. "Ship voted, *boss*. You don't gotta run shit by *me*."

"Xie killed Eelee to keep this secret, Lace." He kept calm, not taking her bait. "You remember what she was building, right?"

"Can't forget." She flashed back to packaging Eelee's orders for misallocated electronics—those clandestine, thin-walled alloy boxes.

"Did E tell you what she was trying to do?"

"What is this? Twenty-fucking-questions?"

"Lace?" He pleaded.

"Eelee didn't say," Lacey relented, "but I figured she was try'na contact Earth or listen in or something, since Xie decided that he and he alone was the only one worthy of talking to our home-fucking-planet."

"Yeah. That's what I thought too," Graham nodded eagerly. "But I don't think she actually could've succeeded. Xie knew it too, and I bet it's why he flipped so hard—'cause he knew Eelee was smart enough to figure it all out by omission, the bastard."

"Get to the point, Captain."

"Lace," Graham fixed the former General with an intense, sorrowful stare. "The Exodus hasn't received *any* communications from Earth. Not in a long while."

For one moment, Lacey had nothing to say.

"A really long while. E couldn't raise 'em. I think they're gone," he stammered, looking into her open mouth. "I know it. Whatever was there–it isn't there. Not anymore."

"No way," she said, finding her voice.

"Lace..."

"What? Just because we haven't got newsbeams from them?" Lacey shook her head, her short, greying hair barely moving. "Shit's obvious. You *know* Captain Xie cut all the antennas and destroyed our comms in his crackdown."

"Wrong! Xie did all that *after* he was sure."

"Ain't no accounting for the actions of crazy motherfuckers."

"There's proof, you stubborn–uggh!" Graham growled. "Before the blackouts, did you ever hear about the new ship Earth was building? Bigger and better than even the Diomed, they were saying?"

Lacey crossed her arms and shrugged, revealing nothing.

"Well, it's a thing, and the last newsbeam Xie got from Ground Mission was just them bragging about it–the improved technology and engines and everything. Supposed to be able to beat us to Akkadia, even with our head start. " Graham looked over his shoulder to make sure they had privacy. "Anyway, I think that's what did them in. They made a mistake or something, then–" He finished by making a gesture as if he were brushing dust from his hands.

"Then what?" Lacey asked, her voice thick.

"Nothing. No more official communications, no signals. None of Xie's plans to reach Earth went anywhere, and he was *trying*. As far as I can tell from the data, there was only one strong signal detected after the last newsbeam, other than random noise."

Lacey's eyes widened, and she tilted her head, beckoning him to continue.

"Not a real signal, just a massive energy spike in some frequencies–crazy powerful, like a little star had exploded back on Earth."

"Fuck me..." The Quartermaster's face sank into a deeply lined frown. "Stupid..."

"I'm sorry, Lacey. I know you were born there, and that it's your home planet and–"

"You don't know a goddamn thing about it, you shipborn motherfucker." Lacey's snarl was almost a whisper. "You don't know how the air smells, what real gravity is like, or how the sun feels on your skin. Not lamplight or starlight, not that fake-ass SunLight in the Fieldpod, but *sun light*." She positively moaned the last words, her dark eyes glistening.

Graham thought that he'd experienced personal despair when the news sunk in, but seeing Lacey's raw sorrow made him feel like a poseur at a funeral. His instincts told him to flee, but the elected Captain of the Exodus held on to his nerve and patience, and he tried to comfort Lacey by burying her in technical details.

He explained precisely how he came across the data in Xie's quarters and the extent of the former captain's plans, giving context to chaos. Graham monologued to give Lacey time to wrap her mind around the enormity of the revelations, ignoring her profane interruptions. He expounded upon the Exodus' communications limitations, and he summarized the history of the bridge's incoming and outgoing transmission logs leading up to, and after, the energy-spike. Graham wrung out his memory, elucidating everything at all relevant to Eelee and the lost Earth, but he didn't tell the Quartermaster everything he found on Xie's console.

In fact, when Graham stumbled through the treasure trove of data, he discovered that the communications blackout was only one piece in a wide, paranoid collection of potential policies. Xie always had a plan–his command console contained files filled with brilliant pre-coded instructions and executables, complex contingencies for every scenario. Looking over some of the inspired technical details, Graham was forced to admit that Dre, the lovestruck engineer, must have been more talented than Eelee had given him credit for. He remembered their early days, coming up together as bridge cadets, and Graham had to swallow a bitter pang of guilt over how the man had ended up–brutalized for his loyalty to the wrong master.

Somewhere among the data, Dre had written his beloved captain a program to cause cascade failure across the ship's firewall-protected, decentralized life support systems. The pair had even designed a plan to repurpose one of the Exodus' fusion engines into a sort of shuttle-propelled torpedo, sacrificing half their power supply to give the defenseless ship some teeth in the case of confrontation. Most horribly of all, however, was a simple blue-sky text file stuffed with increasingly insane ideas for how to weaponize the EPD prion. Disturbed, Graham deleted much of the paranoid pair's work, disposing of plans for mayhem he couldn't even conceive of. A begrudging respect for technical genius, however, forced the new Captain to hesitate, and he ended up copying over some of Dre's most creative schema into a drive that he would later tuck into the back of his personal safe.

Doomsday weapons aside, Graham eventually ran out of technical details to spout to the now dry-eyed Quartermaster.

"Fine, fine–I fucking get it. Shut the fuck up already. I mean, thanks, I guess," Lacey said. "Enough of that shit." She rubbed her temples, "Earth..."

"So," the Captain said softly, wary of provoking anything, "I know it's heavy, but what are your, you know, your thoughts?"

"You can't tell the ship," Diallo said simply, chopping her hand down on the counter between them.

"Don't tell the ship? What ever happened to 'freedom of information'?"

"Don't tell 'em, Saul. I'm warnin' you–they can't handle this shit. I don't know if *I* can handle it," Lacey shook her greying head, grimacing, "and I've lived a life doin' nothing but losing things and losing people I love. Shit will go bad if they know we're all alone out here, trust me."

"How bad, you think?"

"Weird. Bad. I don't fucking know. People *need* a planet. This Coke can *can't* be all we've got. Wait 'til we get to Akkadia, at least, Saul," she implored him. "People gotta know we have a planet."

"Lace..." her friend said quietly, "that was *his* reasoning too. Wait 'til Akkadia. That was Xie's plan."

#

Captain Graham gripped the railing of his precarious platform, as much to keep himself from falling as to keep from floating away. Gravity wasn't especially strong this close to the spindle, but at least he had a hell of a view–he could see most of the

Exodus' population clustered below in a fallow field, like a shipwide community picnic, nervously looking up at him.

He squinted, trying to spot Io by her distinctive hair. Rendered microscopic by the distance, the computer whiz was crouched near a section of screen-lined inner hull that normally simulated sun and sky for the Fieldpod, working to repurpose it as a massive digital display. She turned, and, having noticed her captain, pumped her fist three times–the signal that everything was ready to go for the multimedia portion of his speech.

Saul made to signal back, but he wobbled terribly. The suspended bit of scaffolding he hung from began its life as a supervisory structure, once employed by Molly and her like to oversee and command teams of compost workers during the great rebuilding. For Captain Graham's first inaugural address, it had been stripped of its vat and raised to an absurd height. The only other way to reach the entire Exodus at once, the Captain knew, would be to issue a centralized broadcast from the Command Deck, but he hadn't been back to that ill-remembered place since Fe's pressure door had ended the revolution–the day Graham uncovered the old Captain's secrets.

The thought of his face appearing on people's screens like a parody of Xie filled him with horror. Graham reasoned that a live speech would have to do, platform or no–the bizarre gravity and risk of death-by-falling a small price to pay.

He steadied himself and, more deliberately, raised an arm and waved it in slow motion, signaling Io. His microphone, driven by a neodymium magnet, crackled in response. It was the Captain's cue to speak.

"My fellow Exodans," he began, his amplified voice echoing unnaturally across the tubular cropland and pastures of the Fieldpod.

"Grahampions!" Someone from the crowd screamed out, correcting him. They were met with a small chorus of cheers, which Saul could hardly make out from his altitude.

"I call you here together, today," he continued, the words stiff in his mouth, "not to celebrate, but to mourn. We dearly won our struggle against the whitesuits. The Exodus is still wet with the blood of our fallen crewmates. We have done much mourning over those we've lost, but sadly, we have much mourning yet to do–and of an entirely new magnitude. There's no way to prepare for a loss such as this, to feel something that no other humans have ever felt before, so I'll just say it: the Earth is lost. Xie was hiding it, but it's true–the Sol system has gone dark."

A buzz began to arise from the crowd, dozens of voices raised at once in argument mixed with the uncertain whine of children, suddenly afraid. At that moment however, Io executed her cues, and the artificial sunlight faded–in its place, a massive display lit up.

"What you're *seeing*–" Graham strengthened his voice against a rumbling unrest rising from the shadowy pastures below.

Io took a risk and increased the Captain's volume until the crowd was cowed into silence.

"–is some of the last data received from the Earth by the Exodus. On the Akkadiaward side of the screen, you can see some of Ground Mission's schematics for Project Ishtar, an antimatter drive they were working on. Note the date transmitted and the date received."

Graham's technique of distracting his audience's minds with information seemed to be working–the crowd was settling down to hear him explain.

"These are the relevant data from the last newsbeam, lifted straight from the bridge console–information that Captain Xie never shared with anyone. We've heard nothing since. Not a newsbeam or piratebeam or third-party transmission. I repeat: the Sol system has gone dark.

"With this notable exception..." As Graham continued, images from the ship's telescopes appeared on the Earthward side of the display. "These are false-color pictures of a gamma-ray explosion in the Sol system, detected by the Exodus' passive arrays, recorded shortly after our last official transmission from Earth. The truth is shocking, terrible, and obvious."

Saul paused to breathe, and in the silence, he started to hear the low moan of his people. Quickly, he forced himself to speak.

"The loss of our home civilization–a secret, I must add, that Captain Xie deemed he alone should keep. Think of the man's actions over the last years of your lives–restricting our freedoms, our bodies and our minds...cutting the devices that link us to the outside universe and spacing those who defied him. We will never forget the sacrifices of our friends who died to bring us these terrible truths."

Here, the Captain paused, choked by thoughts of Eelec. Saul let his despair turn to anger, and he shaped the anger into resolve.

"This gives *context* to Xie's sins, but it does not excuse them. He thought us weak, but we will be strong in the face of this tragedy. We were strong enough to face EPD, an enemy that could not be killed. We were strong enough to build ourselves a world, not once but twice! Together, we've achieved the impossible time and time again." Images of the gamma rays faded, replaced with new pictures that could have doubled as slides from an anthropology lecture.

"Thank the stars that we're human, because humans are good at impossible. Nine-hundred and thirty-thousand years ago, the early *Homo sapien* population on Earth fell to an estimated thirteen-hundred. Think of it! One thousand and three hundred souls. That's it—the entire human family. Everything that came since arose from that small crew of survivors, that tiny seed. If our species can survive that, we can do it again. There are more of us, and we're blessed with a stronger beginning. Now, whatever comes next in human history—it starts with the Exodus."

Below, the crowd held its collective breath, parents clutching their children tightly. The images on the enormous display shifted again, turning to charts and diagrams of the orphaned spaceship.

"We are together on this ship, yet alone in the void," Graham's voice echoed against the hull, cresting over the crowd and disturbing the still air that hung over fruiting fields. "But we may not be alone in the universe. There is reason yet to hope. Many reasons, in fact. The Diomed is still out there somewhere, cut off from Ground Mission and therefore cut off from us, but we will listen for them if we can. There is also ample hope back on Earth and around Sol. I won't lie to you or lead you false—a gamma-ray burst, even the small artificial one we witnessed, is among the most destructive events in the galaxy. But humans are good at impossible. We have made homes on Mars and Earth's moon Luna, established mining stations in the Belts and Rings, and—don't forget—we spent thousands of years digging deep holes for shelter in the Earth itself. I choose to believe that someone must have lived, and for them we will listen."

At this, the display darkened and a single image resolved–that of a dandelion, the perspective focusing and following a single parasol-like seed as it floated off into perfect blackness. Graham had never seen a dandelion with his own eyes, but his Earthborn advisors assured him it would send the right message.

"I can only mourn the lost souls of Earth with you, and if any survived, we can offer them nothing but our prayers and our pity. Indeed, we are perhaps the luckiest people ever to live. Not only did we survive whatever terrible event befell Earth, we did so having left with a new home at the end of our road and everything we need upon our backs. We are the luckiest people to ever live," he repeated, and the display darkened.

Io cued the SunLight, and dawn returned to the Fieldpod. The stunned crew shuffled, turning to focus again on their elected Captain speaking high above them.

"And with luck comes hope. We may hope for our severed siblings across the stars, but we must reserve the greatest part of our hope and our spirit for ourselves–for our own future and our future triumph. I have brought you here so we can work together, all of us. Our lives are far too precious now to waste in quarrel or conflict. Indeed, no human can henceforth claim that their life is meaningless, for we have all been given a mission.

"Ground Mission may be gone, but we're still here. Our orders haven't changed, but the way we go about fulfilling them must. Earth no longer controls us. Captain Xie no longer reigns. We alone control our destiny. To that end, we will write a new Code. Beginning tomorrow, a series of debates and votes will be held in the first convention for a People's Code. We will dismantle Xie's rules and build something that makes sense for our future."

The last echo finished its reverberation, and a noise again rose among the gathered crew. Not screams of panic but a garbled chorus of humanity, all at once experiencing the depth of despair and the height of hope, assuring each other and crying, sobbing while simultaneously herding children and making plans for future meals.

Graham plucked away his microphone and slumped back on the platform, settling more slowly than he was used to at full-g. What else could he do? Saul had no idea. He told the Exodans the truth and showed them the evidence, talked while they cried. He'd tried to give them some hope too, as real as he could make it, and—most importantly for the Captain—he'd given them something to do.

###

From the same perch high above the Fieldpod, Molly could watch it all. Or, if not all of it, at least the best, greenest half of it. People were understandably uneasy seeing the elderly woman with the strange skin markings make a death-defying climb every morning, nearly up to the spindle. But, Molly reasoned, if she fell, she fell, and if she died, she died. Besides, she liked it up there. Since Saul Graham's inaugural, it had been called the Captain's Platform, but Molly figured she had as much right to claim the low-gravity structure as anyone, it being hers originally after all, from the compost days.

She shuddered at memories of the goop. From her perch swinging high in the sweet-smelling air, Molly could see nearly all the crops and trees growing in the soil she had spent too much of her life mixing. She could also watch the fruit of her most precious labor—her daughter. Zookeeper Eve still toiled away in a lab somewhere, but on the green pastures of the Fieldpod, her creations thrived. Molly could spend hours watching the movements of animals below, delighting any time she spotted a novel species. They were something like her grandchildren—but better, because they never asked for anything.

She swung, back and forth, to and fro, enjoying the breeze her movements created.

She claimed no human grandchildren, of course, but Molly had outlived enough Earthborn and shipborn alike to be treated with a certain respect by the crew. A living curiosity, no child would ever call Molly Gallagher 'grandma', but many people took to calling her 'Captain', occupying the Captain's Platform as she did most days. The honorific had fallen out of use for the man himself—Captain Saul Graham was just Graham, everybody knew. The gatherings they held, once called elections, turned to simple votes of acclamation in these very fields.

Molly realized, looking back over her memories, that it had been a while since the Grahampions had bothered to do even that much.

Swing.

Like a slow-motion pendulum, Molly swung back and forth on delicate supports, relishing the low gravity and feeling the pain in her joints ease. The structure of the precarious Captain's Platform was more than strong enough to take the weight of Molly's slight body, birdlike and burnscarred.

Swing.

From such lofty heights, she was prone to woolgathering. It was amazing how little things could change in a lifetime, she'd discovered. For the life of her, when she looked back on it all, Molly couldn't point out much difference between Xie's Code and the Grahampions' Bill of Rights, save that the latter involved fewer executions, thank the stars. Each swing of the Captain's Platform changed her perspective slightly, refreshing the panorama and completing another cycle. Sometimes, Molly felt like one of her gentle swings took only a matter of seconds, a minute at most. Other times, she would feel years pass with the gentle breeze.

Swing.

Were those animals new? Cute things, Molly thought. Guanacos–the word came to her. New for now, but not new to the Exodus. The sheep were neither novel nor interesting, her ancient purple eyes beheld, but there was something fun to watch in the distance–a crewmember, someone she couldn't quite make out, riding a horse. Molly squinted, her eyes not what they used to be. She'd been mistaken. The rider was bareheaded–why weren't they wearing a cowboy hat? She wondered. The old woman's breath caught, and a terrible, cold pain gripped her–a piercing ache from an open wound in her heart that had never healed. Her eyes filled with tears, making the fields below turn to a watercolored, impressionist mes
s.

Her momentum took her for another swing.

From up so high, people looked small, hard to distinguish. Molly felt it wasn't easy even up close, these days. Why did everyone want to dress the same, anyway? All neutral tones and pastels–children cross-stitching dandelion embroidery into everything. Molly still had days when she would wake up and feel the skin of the ship tightening around her, something deep and primal within screaming to be let out. On those mornings, the Captain would put on her black scarf, boots, and jacket, souvenirs from Earth, and accessorize with a punky black beret left over from her distant, aborted girlhood. Molly relished in knowing that she was probably the only person alive, anywhere in the universe, wearing anything like it. As ceremonial Captain, she could get away with eccentricities every once in a while. Social pressure, nevertheless, was strong among the insular crew of the Exodus, and the names of neighbors and their invariably huge families taxed Molly's aging m emory.

Their faces threatened to overwhelm.

Swing.

How different the Homepod had become, Molly reflected, filled as it was these days with Eve's bats. Normal children were supposed to be scared of giant bats, she'd told her daughter once long ago, when they were both girls. Still, Molly admitted, the night-blooming cactuses had a certain beauty to them, and she supposed their creepy pollinators perfectly complemented this strange, somber generation of children who would pass Molly in silence whenever she took the Graham Street Spindle to her boring, full-g nest in the Homepod. Sometimes she wished motorcycles still existed—the Captain's Platform would have to do.

Swing, swing. To and fro.

Molly remembered back to when the girls were little, in the days when they'd laughed and landscaped the Homepod's Third Avenue with soft, grassy parks and decorative trees. The lovely little town transformed into a hospital ward in Molly's mind, then a cemetery, then a prison yard as she inundated herself with memories of darker times. She cleared it out with fresh air and another swing on the scaffold, producing a tiny, schoolgirl thrill deep in her spine when she slipped free of gravity's grip at the peak of her trajectory.

Swing—

Had that rock moved? Molly investigated, squinting and cursing her failing eyes, once among her best features.

Swing.

Yes, it had definitely moved. She studied an area of the Fieldpod intently until the mystery resolved–turtles! Or tortoises, Molly couldn't remember which. Why had her daughter bred these large, slow things to live among them? She didn't know, but the animals were cute, strong, and Molly felt proud watching them nobly plod along.

Swing.

The fields were swimmy and unclear again. Molly was crying, letting her tears flow freely for Lacey Diallo. The Quartermaster had been a good girl. Smart, Molly remembered, and what a mouth! She deserved better than what she got, sidelined and shunned by the crew–betrayed by her own followers at the end. Molly had heard vague tells from neighbors that Laceyites were still a nuisance aboard the Exodus, but until the murder, she'd only known them from their colorful graffiti and loud music. What kind of people was she sharing a ship with these days? Molly was scared for the first time in a very long while. She had no one to talk to. Eve wouldn't come out of her lab.

Molly's tears watered the fields below.

Swing. Swing.

She could still make the climb–Molly would tell the weirdos to fuck off, then they'd look at each other, shrug, and someone would say something strange, "to your future triumph" or the like, and then they'd let her go to her Captain's Platform above the Fieldpod. Another group who could fuck off, Molly thought wickedly, were those recruiters who, in the first place, had guilted her onto the Exodus, which turned out to be one big factory for churning out microbes, babies, bats, and death. A brighter future for your children, they'd promised, even if you won't live to see the journey's end. Well, here she fucking was with journey's end fast approaching–Akkadia a bright star on the scopes. If she didn't fall off the deathtrap of a platform or get trampled by a pack of beige zealots, she'd live to see it. As she swung, Molly dearly hoped those recruiter pricks were enjoying hell.

To and Fro.

The air was far too smoky these days, the woman who thought of herself as Captain Molly complained inwardly, indulging in a small cough. Not like when she was young. Below, the cows were slaughtering each other. That wasn't right. That wasn't supposed to happen in a place like this. She felt dreadful.

Swing.

How did she get up there? Molly came to, realizing she was laying facedown on the rocking Captain's Platform. She stared through the metalwork at the normally-productive Fieldpod below. Why was nobody working? Her curiosity probed at the memory lapse like a tongue seeking a missing tooth until it found something raw, a mental circuit broke, and the whole consciousness thing collapsed upon itself–a convenient defense mechanism.

Swing.

She remembered it all–damn it! They'd killed Graham. Those crazies named for Tim's mean little girl had really done it. They took our Graham, Molly thought, weeping again. Detonated an entire section of the Homepod just to get to him, she remembered–Graham and his four little boys. Gone, just like that. And the crew... Molly shuddered, recalling the panic she'd fled on her frail and failing legs. Anyone who could even be mistaken for a Laceyite was in terrible trouble now. There will always be killing, Molly lamented, repeating her strange aerial cycle by muscle-memory.

Swing. Swing. Swing.

It's nighttime, Molly realized. She'd fallen asleep up there again and would have to climb down in the dark. Or, she reasoned, she could just close her eyes and keep rocking...

\#

A bright star moved toward the Exodus, and in a blink of cosmic time, the clear, blinding point resolved itself unmistakably into a sun. The crowded ship's Earthward fusion drive had long ceased firing, but the spaceliner entered the new system with its forward engine blazing, pushing back against massive momentum. The sun known as Akkadia contributed to this push, however infinitesimally, as it radiated its howling solar wind against the Exodus' incoming bulk–an energetic, particle greeting.

As the shipborn crew of Grahampions, purified and unified, celebrated the fulfillment of a lifetime's worth of promises and prophecies, they hurtled ever closer to their new home, though more slowly by the second as fusion-fueled braking force bled away the Exodus' great momentum.

Eventually, the ship that shared its shape with a molecule of iron-iii-oxide pushed into the inner Akkadian system. Its forward fusion engine roared, caged in the engineering section like an imported sun. Fe and the rest of the derelict bridge hung forgotten in the ship's center like a sterile shrine, and completing the chain, the nearly spent Earthward engine brought up the rear, its needle on empty. In the two hollows spun the ship's reason for existing—the living Pods.

The Exodus' trajectory brought it into the system at an angle that made Akkadia-1 the first planet to greet the incoming Earthlings. Over three times the mass of its habitable neighbor, Akkadia's first world was an angry, sandy color, swathed in boiling cloud-cover. From aboard the Exodus, without the aid of a telescope, the planet appeared as a bright, fast-moving disk. More exciting for the ecstatic crew were the first images of Akkadia-2. Quickly, Grahampion observers detected free oxygen in the planet's atmosphere. The terraforming had been, by and large, successful, the crew reasoned, even if they couldn't get the terraforming orbiters or robots to respond to their override attempts, sent from jury-rigged transmitters.

Zookeeper Eve found herself apoplectic when she learned that the foolish Grahampion techs were unable to interface with the terraformers. Still, the gorgeous images coming to her of their new home planet took away some of the sting.

Akkadia-2 was a blue ocean world, wreathed in wisps of white cloud and speckled with expanses of caramel-colored land. In the black nothing that hung above the edge of the planet's atmosphere, its first moon, Akkadia-2a, little more than an enormous, captured asteroid, whizzed by in frenzied repetitions. The second moon, Akkadia-2b, orbiting further out from the living world, could have been a smaller cousin of Earth's Luna—a sterile, crater-faced rock boasting a gravitational field strong enough to influence ocean tides.

The shallowest seas and the swampiest bays along the planet's tropics teemed with photosynthesizing and nutrient-fixing life, flourishing populations descendant from interstellar immigrants sent across the lightyears, preserved, frozen, and packed aboard brilliant automatons.

The ecstatic Grahampions held festivals of thanksgiving as they made ready for eventual planetfall. Though they hailed their martyr in name, their gratitude better belonged to the dead hand of human expertise that had guided them so far and ensured them a home. Though much of the Grahampions' knowledge of their ship had been lost forever, all of the Exodus' preprogrammed maneuvers, to a subroutine, worked perfectly, and its unaltered trajectory brought the Grahampions smoothly to their promised planet. The names of dead Exodans were spoken with hushed reverence. Zookeeper Eve, alone among the crew, fondly remembered Captain Xie and his intransigence in maintaining their path through the cloud and the plague, all those years ago.

If her old collaborator were here, Eve thought, remembering Xie's expressionless face and stupid red cleansuit, he would likely agree that there was much work to be done. When she was a girl, the period known as 'Launch' had seemed like it stretched on forever. However, in the Akkadia system, with piles of assorted years behind her, the equivalent stretch of deceleration didn't seem like nearly enough time to even pack.

The Exodus' crew mobilized to transform the Fieldpod yet again, this time into a grand central station. The Zookeepers' endgame had arrived–they had a planet to finish terraforming. Eve and her scientists still had the run of the ship's laboratories, and the egalitarian ruling quorum happily supplied her with any data or planetary imagery that she deemed germane.

"A new home at the end of our road and everything we need upon our backs," a starry-eyed scientist quoted to Eve.

"What's that?" She grunted.

The eminent Zookeeper lurched over, moving deliberately with the aid of her exo to join her colleague in examining close-up images of Akkadia-2's plant life. Eve focused on a set of particular sat-shots, pointing out copses that could be fruiting trees.

"The bounty that awaits us is magnificent," the scientist said to her.

The speaker wore eyeglasses and soft yellow coveralls. He was a biologist specializing in fish or something–Eve couldn't remember. She pitied him for his narrow opinions.

"Pretty pathetic if you ask me," she said, flicking an inbuilt visor past her sallow, spotted bald head and over her eyes. "We're lucky that the seeds germinated and some cultures grew, but they aren't healthy. This planet needs some *pollinators*."

She thought of an entire world's worth of sky that had never felt a single wingbeat. She would be the one to change that.

"We alone control our destiny," Dr. Fish agreed.

He was quoting again, Eve noticed. And she'd thought working with Zell had been weird.

"Zookeeper," a beige child said, catching her attention, "the latest diversity survey data for you."

All things considered, Eve calculated, studying the readouts, she would give the terraformers a B- for a job mostly done. Ground Mission hadn't been alive to finish the task, she conceded sadly, but it still meant more work for her. At least she had plenty of help—a top of the line exo-suit and a staff of young, shipborn eggheads whose egalitarian Grahampion ideals made them easy to boss around.

"Someone start making a list," Zookeeper Eve commanded.

Akkadia-2 approached too quickly for Eve's liking. There was too much work to do. Nobody officially put her in charge, but she was the Zookeeper who had helped bring back the Fieldpod from EPD—and one of the last Earthlings to boot. Eve used what clout she had to try moving the maddeningly conservative crew to her ends. Remote terraforming operations managed to turn lifeless Akkadia into a world that could have been a sparse imitation of Earth billions of years before humans sprang onto the scene. Twin-sized, ocean-covered, and warm, the benign planet made an excellent host for its voracious visitors. Under Eve's command, the Grahampion scientists prepared a detailed inventory of existing biodiversity and set a dream target for their end goal, one that just barely met the Zookeeper's standards.

Next, she painstakingly mapped out a web of life, noting which organisms were missing from the planet's planned ecosystem. The process turned into a spiraling, non-linear mess. Often, a species came with unexpected prerequisites, and Eve would have to double back and start over. It was the puzzle her mind had been waiting for. Eventually, the Zookeeper and her underlings figured out a multi-phased approach to speciate the planet–a brilliant plan that was as impatient as it was ecologically responsible.

Most of the crew onboard the Exodus had spent their whole lives waiting for the ship's rendezvous with their promised homeworld, and nobody wanted to wait a moment longer than necessary. As soon as the distances became feasible, the crew worked out the refueling logistics, and the Exodus let fly its complement of shuttles. These semi-autonomous and highly-reusable vehicles advanced swiftly ahead of the lumbering spaceliner, making early planetfall. When the first human set foot on the brown-sugar sand of Akkadia-2, they planted dandelion seeds and gave a stiff, optimistic speech that quoted heavily from the late Saul Graham.

#

The Zookeeper was unable to wrangle herself a berth on the first round of shuttles. Or the second. Or the third. She was, however, able to bully the Graham-pions into bringing down crates of pupae, prepared by her and her assistants for perfectly-timed emergence, along with sacks of eggs and vats of small, wriggling things intended to jumpstart a new phase of terraforming. Zookeeper Eve herself, however, had to wait until the Exodus reached orbit for a seat.

She spent the days lamenting the slowness of time and lurching around her vastly-expanded lab, busying herself with an unending pile of urgent tasks.

"We are together on this ship, alone in the void…"

Another of the biologists was whispering.

"…but the severed siblings?"

Eve paid no attention–her mind had trained itself to filter out slogans and platitudes.

"She likely knows more about it than we do. No need to upset her further." A more familiar voice this time.

"The Zookeeper is wise and may have some insight regarding the Diomed." The whisperer was talking to Dr. Fish. "I've heard they mean us harm."

"What's all this scuttlebutt?" Eve demanded, taking several mechanically-aided steps in the direction of her scientists.

"I won't lie to you or lead you false, Zookeeper," Dr. Fish explained, "the Diomed has made contact. We thought you knew. The astronomers confirmed their trajectory. They're coming toward us!"

"Well I hope they have lotsa seeds with them. Eggs too!" Eve replied impatiently. The wrinkled, exosuited Zookeeper stomped back to work, grumbling. "About time we caught a break. This better mean less work for me…wouldn't believe what Ground Mission forgot to include. How they expect us to…"

When Eve finally landed a slot on a planetbound shuttle, she was granted the boon of a seat for her mother, Captain Molly. The ancient matriarch declined the move, however, knowing she'd grown far too feeble and fragile to leave her low-gravity haunt, let alone the Exodus proper. Eve was actually counting on Molly's refusal, and she filled her mother's vacancy with extra crates of gravid arthropods, bound for the plains outside the settlement they were calling New Jacksonville.

The first time Zookeper Eve made planetfall on Akkadia-2, her mind was jolted out of its familiar obsessive grooves by the sheer grandeur of the experience. She'd never before re-entered the atmosphere of any planet and marveled at the terrific fires that tore at her fragile shuttle as it sliced toward the ground. Eve delighted in the primal conflict, as her mind, which knew she was relatively safe, and her body, which was absolutely positive that she was about to die, warred over her central nervous system.

Once the turbulence eased, the air cleared and a view emerged of an alien planet. Alien–it was a feeling only the doddering old Earthborn could be sure of. Though Eve hadn't seen her home planet in many decades, she could tell immediately that this wasn't it–the color of the dirt, the shade of the sun as it pierced the clouds, even the blue of the ocean was slightly off. It was a new world for certain, astonishingly new, even if it did already contain a permanent settlement, complete with prefab facilities for manufacturing rocket fuel. Eve's shuttle touched down without incident, and she followed in the footsteps of many dozens before her.

The Zookeeper stayed planetside for busy b-months, as measured by the phases of the planet's large, second moon. In the space above the growing ecosystem, high above where Akkadia-2's painstakingly-farmed oxygen and trace gasses ran out, the

Exodus completed orbit after orbit. Aboard, Fe rested among the ship's trillion trillion trillion other atoms, and Molly swung above the Fieldpod's dwindling complement of resident Grahampions. New Jacksonville's population swole then shrank, and several other permanent outposts were founded in areas with the highest local oxygen concentrations and the most fertile soils.

Eve was pleased to see livestock thriving, but it was her self-appointed task to make the planet wild. As with all life, it started in the swamps. Watching her students wade in the knee-deep mud, a lifetime after her school-aged frustrations, Eve heartily approved of Ground Mission not including mosquitos among the Exodus' complement of fauna.

Eventually, she returned to space to supervise a shipment of sedated birds, lizards, and their many, many fertilized eggs. Those biologists she'd left aboard conducted their work well, she had to admit, despite their terrible fashion sense. The Exodan Grahampions worked as if the ship were a monastery, producing clones of plants and animals for their promised world with religious fervor.

Things aboardships were getting bizarre, the Zookeeper noticed during her walk to the Captain's Platform. The events Molly gossiped about disturbed her. She'd also assumed they'd be sharing data with their sister ship, the Diomed, by then, but the Grahampion quorum aboard the Exodus had grown even more insular, sometimes ignoring transmissions entirely. It was strange—a place Eve felt comfortable all her life suddenly closed in like a coffin with Akkadia-2 spinning just below.

Allergic to politics as ever, Eve endeavored to spend all the time she could away from the claustrophobia of the ship. She traveled to the new settlements of Blue Lake, Agrippa, Biloxi Island, and Saul's Rest, shepherding compliments of small birds and mammals. Sometimes she found herself aboard a boat, dumping fry and spawn into the waves, enriching the seas by force. Sometimes she would become bogged down in mundane matters—a poorly-managed township guilting her into curing its chickens of a bronchitis epidemic or the like.

Even with the long-lived Molly's genes, Eve knew she was running out of years, though she had the work of an immortal left to do. The planet was enormous, simply enormous. Eve cursed her fallible, organic brain for letting the cramped confines of the Exodus distort her perception of size. The entire complement of Earthling life aboard the orbiting ship would have barely served to cover one small island amongst thousands in Akkadia's many archipelagos. All she and her slavish, culty team could do was plant seeds of seeds, and, the way Eve saw it, she'd barely have time to do even that much.

She visited Molly only once more. The Grahampions were feeding her at least, Eve noted approvingly. She invited the aged Captain planetside to join with a desert expedition. Eve hoped to seed one arid landmass with fruiting cactuses in preparation for pollinating bats. Her mother, as she'd predicted, refused the ride, cackling out a barely-intelligible joke about the Captain going down with her ship. Suitably enough, it was weeks later, in the desert, that Eve first heard talk of the Prophecy.

Whispers began with the arrival of the Diomed in the Akkadian system, broadcasting messages of peace. The beetle-shaped traveler had been built as the successor ship to the Exodus, though made sleeker and more efficient, like a precocious younger sibling. Meanwhile, the crew of the lumbering Exodus had taken a lifetime to reach Akkadia and begin settling their planet. In that same stretch of years, minimally dilated by velocity, the Diomedians had reached Asimov's Star, landed their colony, and, apparently, decided to turn the ship Akkadiaward after witnessing Earth's final folly.

The younger ship sent targeted signals to the Exodus, streaming mostly prepared speeches in heavily-accented English, lamenting the tragedy of Earth and expressing their joy at finally reconnecting with one lost fragment of humanity. Eventually, they explained the essence of their mission—to put a permanent Diomedian settlement on Akkadia and to bring some Exodans back to Asimov's Star. The insular Grahampions were unsure how to feel about their severed siblings, now that they had actually arrived. They turned to their martyred Graham and his words for direction.

\#

As the Diomed journeyed through Akkadia's heliosphere, the Exodans worked their new land and looked over their shoulders. They'd done a good job with their promised world already, the Grahampions of Akkadia assured themselves.

Their rice farms were productive, and the settlers could sometimes catch the sight of small, cloned fawns licking lichen from alien rocks by the shore thanks to the tireless efforts of their Zookeeper. Most, like her, were not in the mood for interstellar politics.

"We are together on this ship and alone in the void," the Grahmpions would say to each other, philosophically.

"We alone control our destiny," they would answer back.

Those left aboard the Exodus were less complacent. They scoured their martyr's history, looking for guidance in the thin example left among Saul Graham's personal effects. Precious little survived, most of his worldly possessions destroyed in the explosive assassination that also ended the mourning Exodans' chance for a direct successor.

The office Graham maintained near the Earthward wall of the Homepod had become a museum of sorts and a place of quiet contemplation for pilgrims. It was a well-known secret that the room contained a small, personal safe beneath the desk. It remained locked and unopened, the combination having died with Graham and his family line. In the end, it all proved too tantalizing for a crew desperate for guidance in whatever form they could find it. The quorum felt strongly enough that they decided to go ahead and cut the safe open, revealing their idol's final secrets.

Most relevant among their findings was a strange and intricate plan for weaponizing the Exodus' engines and shuttles—a way to arm the defenseless colony ship in the event of crisis. They had no idea that it had been conceived of by the hated Xie and coded by his brilliant devotee, and thus, the Grahampions took the plan as prophetic guidance from their fallen leader. Conveniently, the scheme justified the crew's paranoia, feeding a semiconscious xenophobia fostered by the shipborn who inhabited the emptying Exodus, still orbiting at the end of its mission.

Only the quorum knew the full contents of the orders, but most of the Grahampions who caught wind took to the idea of Saul Graham's prophetic plan as a way of protecting their promised planet. Like priests ritualizing sacred texts, ignorant technicians loaded prewritten codes into the ship's systems after breaking into the shrinelike stillness of the zero-g bridge. Grahampion engineers slavishly followed dead Dre's instructions, modifying crucial systems in the Earthward engine and appropriating one of the complement of shuttles. Within the bridge, the iron ions inside Fe's magnet had always been subjected to tiny trace vibrations produced by the energy of the colony ship's powerful twin fusion engines. During the practical workings of the Prophecy, however, the amplitude of this vibration suddenly halved.

On official channels, the crew of the Exodus replied to the incoming Diomed's hails with their own reciprocal messages of grief and joy. No territorial claims were officially asserted, nor was the Diomed explicitly welcomed into Akkadian space. Not having a formal leadership structure helped the crew remain aloof. To the captain of the Diomed, the Exodus seemed taciturn but polite. Suspicion came too late.

Faster and smoother than its older sister could dream of, the newer, insectoid spaceliner entered Akkadia-2's gravity-well and decelerated. To Eve, laboring in the desert, cursing the sand that found its way into her exo-suit's joints, there appeared a new star in the sky.

It was a damn stupid tragedy, the Zookeeper could only conclude, once she knew the full picture in the aftermath. The incoming colony ship bristled with roachlike antennae, after all, and the planet-bound settlers could have tried to talk to it, if they had wanted to badly enough—and assuming that someone also possessed the right coveted, prefab electronics. Even if Exodans on the ground had known exactly what the Prophecy entailed *and* had been in a mind to play hero, Eve calculated, they'd have had to break through Akkadia-2's magnetic field and fight for bandwidth against the Exodus' more powerful, official signal—and that was before they could even get the chance to be taken seriously by anybody listening aboard the Diomed. Unlikely as it all would have been, Eve found herself haunted by a never-ending stream of what-ifs.

In the end, the crew who didn't want to know shut their ears, and those who found out kept their mouths closed. Modally and mundanely, however, most Exodans, like Eve herself, were simply too busy to pay full attention to quorum politics and prophecies until it became too late.

As the stately Diomed smoothly entered into orbit above the caramel-and-turquoise planet, it was met with a welcome shuttle from the Exodus. If someone were standing at the right point on Akkadia at the right time, they may have been able to make out a glint reflecting off the smaller craft, disgorged from the orbiting Exodus and closing on the shining Diomed. Prepared to the exact specifications of Xie's paranoid vision, the cumbersome shuttle had been hastily modified, clad in lead shielding, and loaded with a diminutive, dying sun.

To the newcomers in their dreadnaught, the shuttle moved slowly and strangely, but then again, to the Diomedians, everything about the Exodus looked slow and clunky. Unexpectedly, though, the tiny traveler overflew the Diomed, firing its thrusters rather than decelerating for rendezvous. When the shuttle reached the closest point to the stern of the colony ship, it detonated–disappearing in a silent, awe-inspiring atomic blast.

Nearly out of fuel, the Earthward reactor had been force-fed new instructions by the Grahampion quorum, copied from the Prophecy. The end result of major engineering surgery was a serviceable thermonuclear warhead, a weapon reliant on physics primitive enough to be understood even during Karl Fleischer's war. The atomic device's stellar plasma broke free of its magnetic enclosure right on cue, generating a brief-but-spectacular nova. The horror and majesty of this sabotage, however, was but a prelude to the explosion that flashed a blink after the first detonation. The Diomed's engine, never intended to withstand a direct thermonuclear attack, let its own fusion drive's twisting, roaring plasma break free on impact, briefly reaching apotheosis as a tiny, hellishly-hot star.

In the shutterbulb flashes from the pair of artificial novae, just before the Diomedians died, generations of atomic nuclei found themselves consumed and transformed, the stories of some atoms ending and the others just beginning.

For the beetle-shaped Diomed and its crew, their journey ended in a terrible, debris-spraying lurch followed by a final sprint planetside. The ship's extreme-condition, iron-molybdenum-alloy body kept the superstructure of its hull intact, even as the vessel's stern-engine exploded within its very abdomen. The destruction was tremendous, as was the expanding sphere of nuclear plasma. Nothing short of an equal atomic detonation could provide restoring force enough to keep the hulk from slipping dangerously out of its orbit and into the planet's grasping gravity-well, the fires of reentry dooming any Diomedian who may have survived the blasts.

From below, Eve studied the lightshow with every vision-enhancement device available to her. Moments after the detonation, her work forgotten, she watched the Diomed plummet like a bright meteor. Eve stood on the wrong continent to get a decent view, thank the stars. At best, she could see a false-color impression of a black, batty shape wreathed in red flames. She could do nothing but fume, and the wasted Earthmade spaceliner flared and disintegrated over the horizon.

From aboard the aggressor ship, the Grahampion quorum watched the destruction of their severed siblings with quiet triumph–Akkadia was their promised world, and they alone would control its destiny. One burnscarred, elderly Earthborn, still aboard the Exodus, unable and unwilling to live in the colonies, watched as well, feeling terribly complicit in this act of fratricide. Some of her remaining neighbors experienced a delight even more savage than that of the quorum, while other survivors wept quiet tears.

Captain Molly Gallagher, the oldest of the Earthborn, loosened her grip on life after processing the news. She'd lived too long and seen one horror too many, Molly decided, finally understanding why the Grahampions preferred their self-imposed ignorance. She died on her platform, hovering and nearly weightless at the end. Her only daughter, Zookeeper Eve, when she finally found the time and resources to make the trip, evacuated her Earthborn mother's body from cold storage aboard the Exodus. She buried Molly in the soft, warm sand of Accadia-2.

Chapter 8: The Janitor

"**I**s it getting colder in here or is Gerty getting older?" Gerty grunted, their voice echoing around the dim hollowness of the Fieldpod.

John, watching from nearby, didn't reply. Instead, he tilted his head and studied the stiff movements of the lanky, white-tufted janitor.

"How long ago was it that they came and took the heating coils?" Gerty asked, crouched by the garden plot.

"We will listen."

"I know! They were desperate for parts. They took everything. But they couldn't take *all* the dirt! Ha!"

The janitor would have added a triumphant gesture, but their knobby, swollen-jointed hands were buried wrist-deep in the rich, black soil.

"Upon our back," John replied in his eery, high-pitched voice.

"You're right–you're right," Gerty said, nodding their head and planting cloves of garlic in a neat row. "We got everything we need here. What they took was what Graham provided unto them, and he left Gerty with more than enough."

The elderly Grahampion pushed themselves to their feet, grunting and brushing the dirt from their filthy coveralls. John spread his wings, noticing that Gerty now stood erect. The grey parrot gracefully fluttered from the wooden fence and landed on his favored perch–the human's left shoulder.

"Do you remember when we used to do onions too?"

"Onion!" John agreed, bobbing his head.

"Huh, really? You were alive when Gerty had the allium thing going? Don't remember. Shallots? Shallots–" Gerty waved the nagging detail away. "At our age, you gotta pick where you put your energy, and garlic's got the most kick for your kilo."

Indeed, the small area of fieldpod cultivated by the hermit appeared devoted entirely to *Allium sativum*. Some crop beds displayed intermediate shoots. One adjacent, drier plot sprouted a healthy flush of garlic nearly ready for harvest. Gerty's newly planted rows would repopulate the tiny farm's cyclical monoculture.

Their gardening chores done, the ship's janitor contemplated the next piece of business. Gerty did almost no cleaning and performed no meaningful mainte-nance, as the Exodus' automated systems kept the ship in orbit, and its emergency power supply kept it ruggedly habitable. They were a janitor only in the sense of its original meaning—a master of doors. Gerty, the final member of the Exodus' crew, had been given free run of every last corner of the sprawling, near-derelict ship.

"You're lucky you were just a single egg, you know," the janitor remarked to John as they walked past what used to be the Zoological campus, the place where Gerty first found the egg that they would later incubate and hatch into their final friend.

John let out a quiet trill.

"One of thirteen, Gerty was," Gerty boasted, not for the first time. "Nothing was ever mine. So when they told Ol' Gerty to come down to New Jacksonville, 'no more launches' they said—'last chance,' they said…well, Gerty said 'I'll be staying right here, thank you very much.'"

"Gerty!" John agreed.

"Besides," Gerty continued, their voice softening, "someone's got to tend to the ghosts."

"Tend the ghosts!" John squawked, bobbing his head.

"Stars! I know—I know. Gerty's getting to it," Gerty said huffily.

Ghost days always made the janitor uneasy.

The ship's last crewmember walked toward a familiar part of the Exodus, their footsteps echoing in the silent gloom. Down below on Akkadia-2, babies laughed, livestock squealed, and waves lapped at warm shores. Separated from all that by miles of cold space and meters of Sukuru-alloy hull, the Exodus' janitor slowly approached the Captains' Platform and reverently began removing objects from their satchel.

"To the Graham," Gerty chanted, their voice low.

They knew deep in their heart that *something* had to be done for the spirits of the Leaders who'd died aboard the ship, but nobody had taught Gerty specifically what to do. Unbothered, the Grahampion janitor improvised a ritual. They figured that anyone, ghost or flesh, would appreciate a good meal.

"We present to you—this humble offering," Gerty said, clutching in both hands a container of the best meal they could imagine—noodles with garlic.

With a bowed head, they gently placed the food at the base of the holy scaffolding.

"To the Captain," Gerty continued the prayer, digging out a large, multigrain cracker from within the satchel. "We present to you—this humble offering."

John's avian eyes were glued to the cracker, but experience had taught him patience, if not reverence, during these ceremonies. He stayed quiet and watched the human perform incomprehensible rituals at the base of a very strange type of perch.

Gerty knew that the Captain probably hadn't really been a bird-woman or a burnt-up angel, like in the pictures they liked to paint sometimes in the ship's empty hallways, but a cracker was the best they could do. Her ghost couldn't *also* be given a bowl of noodles like Graham's, Gerty figured, because only Graham was the Graham.

"John, you gotta get now," Gerty said, offering him a different, less-holy biscuit once the prayers had ended. "Gerty's gotta go to the bridge."

The bird didn't like the sound of that last word, but the food was welcome.

"Your future triumph," he said musically, taking the cracker in his beak.

"And to yours."

Gerty wasn't thrilled about the spooky, abandoned part of the ship either, but they enjoyed the relief to their old bones that came from leaving gravity behind. John, despite his being hatched and raised in orbit, couldn't handle the disorientation of zero-g, and the only time Gerty had ever brought him into engineering, the bird fluttered and panicked in a manner beneath his usual dignity.

The final offering in Gerty's satchel was a red, plastic tomato. It was a good one, too—a quirk of its Earthen petrochemicals keeping its crimson color vibrant over an ocean of years. The janitor had stumbled upon the object in the Homepod a dozen orbits earlier, and as they made the journey through the gravity-free corridors of engineering, they checked frequently to make sure it hadn't floated away.

At last, the janitor emerged at the haunted bridge section. Once an impenetrable fortress, the Command Deck now stood silent, cold, and unlocked. Even the hatch to the lavatory hung ajar. Gerty shivered, nearing the head. Terrible things had happened here. This was where the Leader called Xie had died. Unbeknownst to Gerty, above them, locked into a groove in the ship's hull, Fe and the killer bulkhead door rested.

No high-tech imports would ever come again from Earth, and manufactured goods were at a premium on Akkadia. Emigrating colonists had stripped the Exodus for parts during the final launches as their shuttles gradually broke down, never to be repaired. The bridge's hidden emergency door actuators, however, were overlooked by the looters, including their complement of valuable magnets and electronics. Ionized and locked in a magnetic molecular crystal, the atom Fe and its kin continued to maintain a steady b-field, their motor waiting for an electrical current that would never come.

The devout janitor didn't repeat their simple chant for Xie. This particular Leader had always been more like a devil to Gerty's understanding, but, Gerty figured, it was best to give devils some respect. Only a fool wouldn't.

Rather than prayers and food offerings, a problematic prospect in zero-g, they recalled from Grahampion lore that Xie had an affinity for the color red. It was the best idea Gerty could come up with, and they somberly released the plastic tomato from their grip, leaving it to float amongst dozens of other bright-red objects that the janitor had appropriated during their years exploring the Exodus' many doorways.

●　●　●

"Radio's been on the blink again. Gerty doesn't like it."

"Radio! Radio!"

"Can't they leave Gerty alone?"

The janitor sat inside their dwelling in the Homepod, avian companion perched nearby. Somewhere, a light blinked urgently on a jury-rigged communicator. A stack of dried and cured garlic plants lay in a pile to the left of Gerty's molded alloy chair, and twisted braids of processed bulbs hung all around the room.

As it happened, Gerty couldn't consume anywhere near the quantity of garlic that they grew, and adding to the stockpile-nature of the janitor's nest, rows and shelves of identical boxes lined the walls, leaving only narrow corridors. Gerty had long ago appropriated the few remaining pallets in the Exodus' pantry—mostly noodles and crackers, it was a negligible quantity for the ship's original population but more than a lifetime supply for a single human, their one friend, and of course, the ghosts.

"One of *thirteen* kids, Gerty was," they repeated, this time with a groan from hefting an armful of dried stalks. "Gerty didn't even have a bed—Gerty had to share with Travis and Tara!"

"Tara!" John squawked, vocalizing the name of a woman he would never meet. "Gerty!"

"Then the big ones started moving down planet, one by one, and Gerty got a private bed. Blueberry, Kenny, Eepee, and Mo left. Then even a private room for Gerty!"

Ghost days always made Gerty more chatty than usual. As they yapped, the janitor mechanically snipped bulbs free from the cured plants, reserving them for later and setting the dry, dirty waste in a pile to their right.

"Kat and Big Cat went down. Then Charlotte-Anne, Picapica, and Visblish. Then Travis and Tara and lil' Saul. Then Gerty's parents said goodbye and Gerty had this whole house!"

They trimmed the tangled, dirt-ridden roots around one bulb, then tossed the clean white orb of *Allium sativum* into a small box.

"No one to annoy Gerty. No one to bother. Gerty could play anything on the screens—whatever and as loud as Gerty wanted!"

"Radio! Radio!" John repeated, bobbing.

"I know!" Gerty snapped. The radio gave them anxiety.

"Alone in the void! For them we will listen!" The bird puffed itself up as it quoted scripture, fluttering its steel-blue wings.

"It's fine! Gerty just answered the other day," the janitor fibbed. In fact, it had been more than eight thousand orbits since Gerty had answered the ship's insistently-blinking radio.

"Why won't they just leave Gerty alone?"

"Gerty!" John agreed with a trill.

● ● ●

Years passed, as did countless thousands of orbits for the great ship. Though its stay in the sky was only ever temporary, the Exodus served as Akkadia-2's smallest moon—a bright traveler for the stargazers below. The ship's remaining fusion engine, all but spent after its long journey across interstellar space, worked alone to provide the trickle of energy needed by the hulking derelict to keep itself in orbit.

Below, the surface of Akkadia gradually revolutionized. When the crew of the Exodus first reached the alien planet, its darkside had truly been dark, but in the generations following planetfall, the nightside came to glow. Occasional wildfires lit the islands, a new phenomenon on a world where oxygen and organic matter were still novelties. Other lights signaled that a form of civilization had come to Akkadia, sparse and irregularly scattered over the huge world. A notably-dense concentration of electric light clustered around one swampy, island-studded bay at the southwest of Akkadia's largest temperate continent.

Invisible to the human eye, the atmosphere of the colonized world experienced its own transformation. Traces of strange pollutants marred the once-simple mixture of gasses, and the planet's oxygen concentration rocketed to Earthlike levels—an explosion of seeded and farmed flora fabricating O2 faster than the colonizing humans and their animal subjects could consume it.

However, no crewmember still lived aboard the Exodus to appreciate the view or analyze the atmospheric spectroscopy data, though the ship's passive systems continued to watch and listen. Eventually, however, even the miserly trickle of energy allocated to the ship's senses proved too costly for the dying fusion engine. Its twin having been ripped away in a startling act of ancient violence, the lone reactor managed to keep the ship aloft for close to a million orbits, but after many years of battling gravity's patient dominance, the Exodus' tank simply ran dry.

The ship's Earthward engine had required engineered sabotage for it to fail, and it died spreading spectacular destruction, much to the detriment of the Diomed. However, when left to its own devices, a fusion stellarator fails rather anticlimactically. Thus, as its fuel expired, the star-like plasma ceased its roaring. It flickered briefly and died, leaving the reactor's interior cold and barren. Arrays of enormous magnets that would put Fe's to shame held strong during this calamity, their titanic quantities of stored energy draining away in a graceful implosion that would, nonetheless, prove fatal to the placid Exodus.

For a quiet stretch, very little seemed to have changed. Fe and the exponential trillions of atoms within the ship no longer were subject to the infinitesimal vibrations from the fusion engines, and with the reactor dead, no more acts of atomic death and birth played out anywhere in the system save for in the fiery forge of the star Akkadia itself. Without power to make gentle nudging corrections, though, the massive ship slowly began to be dragged out of its orbit by forces it could no longer resist.

For the second-time, an enormous and wondrously complex spaceship built above Sol-3 died in the skies of Akkadia-2.

Deep in the Homepod, the scattered bones of John and Gerty, alongside diverse dust and detritus, slid and tumbled, piling up against bulkheads. In the darkened Fieldpod, Captain Molly's platform broke from its moorings as the superstructure around it collapsed. Sundered, the fatally-wounded ship began to flare and disintegrate.

For centuries, the Exodus' two pressurized Pods maintained rotation. In the rapidly-thickening atmosphere of the planet, however, the spaceliner met with terrible resistance from a billion tons of air, twisting the titanic ship and wrenching the Home and Fieldpods free. The gigantic Pods' angular momentum sent them barreling on different paths from the main wreckage, and the doomed cylinders rolled and shook, spewing a trail of debris that looked, from the ground, like an invasion of shooting stars. In fact, the thermal energy produced was enough to break apart the bonds of the air molecules themselves, wreathing the falling debris in ionized plasma. Never engineered to withstand atmospheric re-entry, the ship's violent death accelerated as the superheated ions tore like eager fingers at the seams and wounds in the Exodus' ancient Sukuru-alloy hull.

Below, communities took shelter as their skies filled with sonic booms—terrifying daylight thunder. The Fieldpod rolled like a burning keg above a stretch of the Akkadian ocean before it burst. The Homepod peeled open like a gargantuan soup can, disgorging the contents of its great hollow—homes and bones of its former occupants, screens and crates and walls and noodles and street signs—all sprayed out, flashed, and burned up. The Pods imploded and incinerated, meanwhile the ponderous water tanks split and steamed over the sea, dragging new clouds with them.

From the surface, it appeared as if some terrible, many-fisted god had plunged down from the very heavens. The Grahampions knew the Exodus couldn't stay in the sky forever, and some had even made roughly-accurate predictions for when its orbit would finally decay. Nevertheless, the spectacle and terror of its fall became a generation-defining event.

For Fe up in the burning bridge section, the Akkadian plummet proved a more violent planetfall than when the atom, riding a meteor, had first pierced the Earth's atmosphere thousands of years ago and trillions of miles away.

Like tiny droplets of blood, a barely-discernible spray of bright crimson clothing and trinkets leaked from the Command Deck's first breach. As it plunged, superheated air tore through, torquing the fragile section. Its bulkheads peeled and massive slabs of alloy sloughed off. Even tucked into the hull itself, the machines that surrounded Fe were terribly vulnerable. Fingers of plasma reached around corners, tearing and torching everything they touched.

With a crunch that vibrated every distressed atom in the entire flaming wreckage, the inner hull tore itself free from the outer, and the grand Command Deck opened like a zipper. The lavatory where Xie died ripped itself apart, ejecting the killer bulkhead door and its client actuator.

Suddenly, for the first time since Greta and Mew installed the emergency pressure door, Fe could count itself independent of the Exodus.

Much of the debris large enough to reach the planet's surface without burning up entirely plunged into the depths of the Akkadian sea. Chunks of the Command Deck, however, as they tore free from the rapidly-ablating Exodus, mainly followed a trajectory that arced over the planet's sparse landmasses.

A high rocky peak jutted above the northwestern expanse of Akkadia's largest temperate continent, and the flying, charred bit of wreckage that had once been an actuator assembly smashed into its sheer stone face. The force of the impact fractured the aluminum shell, spilling its motor free and sending the battered machine careening down a mountain.

As it fell, Fe's electric motor clattered and smashed against hard, clay-colored rocks. Its own aluminum housing, so carefully aligned and welded by Dr. Kim, broke apart, exposing the machine's raw innards. Copper wire, like veins and nerves, spewed from the eviscerated motor, its magnets separating like severed vertebra. These wasted, mechanical bones tumbled and rolled, each magnetic disk racing its fellows, all and sundry eventually scattering along gravity's many slopes.

Shaken loose from the motor and separated from the others, Fe's disk bounced and rolled, still hurtling with incredible speed, bleeding off kinetic energy with each new, friction-rich impact. The strontium ferrite magnet, despite originally being formed from powder, stayed intact during each subsequent slam—Druke's fiery sintering having bonded the particles into an unshakable solid.

Still carrying potential from its orbit aboard the Exodus, the dense, black ring shot and spun over hundreds of meters before striking a hard, wind-exposed boulder with a resounding crack. A tiny chip—itself harboring billions of trillions of irons—flew from its parent wheel and joined the anonymous grains of the alien desert.

After the impact, Fe's scarred magnet found itself rolling on its narrow edge. It crested a dune and, unicycling down the other side, carved a shallow groove in the caramel-colored sand. It rolled along the narrow valley between two desert drifts, angular momentum and reserves of potential energy taking it only so far.

When Fe's magnet attempted to roll up one last shallow hill, the cold laws of physics weighed the sums of force and energy and found the system wanting. The disk wheeled slowly back down into gravity's palm.

Briefly, Fe's black ring balanced on an edge before wobbling and falling flat on its side. Like a strange new rock, it sat in the dusty wastes for many days before an intermittent breeze slowly entombed the strontium ferrite magnet beneath millions of grains of brown-sugar sand.

Chapter 9: The Herbalist

"**B**rute!" Miss Pak called, patting herself to make sure she was still in one piece. "You nearly knocked me over."

The old herbalist had only kept her feet thanks to the sturdiness of her hardwood, iron-tipped staff, which stood taller than she.

The rider, at least, had stopped, and she looked down at Miss Pak from horseback.

"I didn't see you."

"That's a terrible excuse," the shaken herbalist replied, squinting up at the slack, unrepentant face of a young woman of around twenty.

"Is not," countered the horsegirl. "You're small and you blend in."

"So are lots of living things. You need to pay better attention to your surroundings."

Miss Pak's strong, spotted hands nimbly surveyed her jacket's many pockets and checked over each of her three satchels. She gave special attention to a buckskin bag made with a plastic inner lining—her medicine bag, and the reason she'd been summoned to this smelly, crowded island. The satchel held a pouch of finely powdered leaves and a short length of a bumpy green vine, her last bit of cereus.

"You're going to New Jacksonville, yes? Give me a ride and we'll call it even."

"What? No," the young rider answered, aghast. "Just walk—it's not even far!"

"We've all been given a mission. I'm bound for the Temple, which is not a short walk for a half-trampled old woman," Miss Pak explained, not wishing to admit that the layout of the tiny city confused her. "But if you insist, then I suppose I'll need to arrange an audience with the graham to report your careless riding. In which case, young lady, I'll need transportation to the Temple regardless."

"Starshit!" The young rider blinked, in disbelief. "You're impossible. Get on."

Miss Pak grabbed the wiry, soft-skinned arm of the horsegirl and, with surprising dexterity, lept up and mounted the beast. She comes from wealth, the herbalist realized, catching floral notes from the rider's scented hair.

"I'm Winni," the youth offered, spurring her horse to motion.

"Miss Pak."

They traveled in silence, the dusty seaside path quickly widening and revealing a wooden footbridge. As the horse clomped over the boards, Miss Pak rode with her back straight and her eyes alert. Winni had been right—it really wasn't far.

Within moments, they'd passed a bend and entered the city proper. To someone like Dr. Kim or Dr. Haverwood, New Jacksonville and its thirteen-hundred citizens would appear as little more than a quaintly compact township. To the Akkadian herbalist, however, it was a scene of urban chaos—animals and people bustling and bleating, making more noises and smells than she cared for.

It was why she only came to market once every b-month, requiring her clients to visit her own small island if they had urgent need. Of course, since the graham himself had summoned her, Miss Pak made an exception. She watched one cylindrical stone edifice resolve, stretching high above the city-center. As owner of the Temple grounds, the graham controlled the largest and most commanding of New Jacksonville's districts—from the tower, he could look down on the rooftops of the city's most powerful families' estates.

"You said the Temple. Get off," Winni ordered.

She trotted away, without a goodbye, after Miss Pak dismounted. The old herbalist looked both ways before crossing the path to the Temple, shaking her head at the rudeness of the young. She found the grounds a welcome respite from the street noise. A Grahmpion from the cradle, it was difficult for Miss Pak to reconcile that the grand Temple around her was also Nicky's house.

Winni had dropped Miss Pak at the entirely wrong side of the estate, and the older woman found the Temple grounds larger than she remembered from her infrequent visits. She wandered through a wrong doorway and was forced to display her hand-delivered summons to a pair of surly acolytes before being escorted into the graham's tower. The dark hollow was lit inside by candles, and its walls were hung with dandelion tapestries, though the decoration did little to add warmth to the chilly, somber structure.

The heavy stone walls swallowed the noise of their footsteps, save for the sharp, rhythmic taps issuing from the iron ferrule at the tip of Miss Pak's staff. The graham entered from an archway on her left and made a small bow to her acolyte escorts, who returned the gesture and melted away.

"Thank you for coming so quickly."

"Well, of course, Nicky," the herbalist said, calling the graham by his given name. "A weak heart is a serious matter. How have you been feeling?"

"Some tightness, some faintness."

"May I ask about the diagnosis?"

"From Dr. Teodora. Please, Miss Pak, sit–" he said, indicating his guest toward a narrow, uncomfortable-looking bench set into the wall.

Nicky the graham had a kind face, with deep-set dark eyes and bristly black eyebrows. He wore Exodan coveralls, bleached white and extended with superfluous, sewn-on panels of like-colored fabric. These, the graham brushed aside with a practiced flourish as he positioned himself on the bench's narrow ledge.

"I prefer to stand," Miss Pak said, resting with a slight lean, keeping both her weathered hands clutched around the shaft of her walking stick.

"You alone control your destiny," the graham quoted, smiling and spreading his hands. "As I was saying, it was Dr. Teodora who discovered the ailment. She has those scopes, you know."

The herbalist nodded.

"Anyway, yes–a weak heart was the Doctor's conclusion," he continued, "the truth is shocking, terrible, and obvious. Naturally, I seek relief. The physician told me of some robust herbal combinations that may help, but I've had the markets scoured, and there is little to be bought. You've done me a great service in coming here with your stock."

"I may not deserve your gratitude yet," Miss Pak said unhappily, unshouldering her satchel and presenting the single, withered stalk of cereus cactus inside. "This is all I have left of the cereus. The hawthorne," she presented the bag of powdered leaves, "I can easily source more of, but the cactus has been in short supply for some time."

"Then it's as I feared." Nicky rose from his stone bench and clapped his hands loudly. "Merrick!"

"Merrick?" She asked, scrunching her wrinkled face in puzzlement.

"An acolyte," he said, dismissively. "Miss Pak, I have a mission for you."

"We have all been given a mission," she quoted back, stalling for time. She sensed a chore ahead. "Mine is to return to my island, to tend my plants and cure the sick."

"Do you know in which parts of the world the cereus grows?" He asked, ignoring her excuse. "From what I've been told by the merchants, none of the overseas traders ever bring any into port."

"So it must grow on the continent? Makes sense," Miss Pak said, jumping ahead in the conversation and idly fidgeting the ferrule of her staff against hard stone. "I remember the traders mentioning a northern shore."

"North Shore? So, you've never been there yourself? Merrick!"

She shook her head.

"Then I must ask you to remedy that," the graham replied gravely. "I task you to personally travel to the native grounds of the cereus cactus and harvest their medicines, and I beg you bring *him* along for the journey."

He pointed toward an acolyte who had just entered the tower, ducking to fit his shaggy curls and broad shoulders under a low stone arch. The young man named Merrick, flinching as if he had just been ambushed, gave a look like a startled baby ox.

"That," the herbalist said with a low whistle, "is a lot to ask."

"We alone control our destiny," the graham spread his arms, rippling the ornamental fabric. "I have a weak heart, but I won't lay down and accept death. Need I confess to you that I fear death? I confess it. The void terrifies me. Consider me humbled."

"Oh, Nicky," Miss Pak said, pressing her fingertips gently to the man's heart. "Don't be so dramatic. I'll go."

A look of relief washed over the graham's face. Standing off to one side, the hulking Merrick squirmed, uncomfortable to be witnessing something so intimate.

"But must I save your life *and* babysit?" She glanced sidelong at the silent, diffident acolyte.

"It would make me feel better, truly. We are together yet alone in the void, Miss Pak. With the two of you together, I fear neither darkness nor failure."

"I won't lie to you or lead you false, Nicky," the herbalist countered, taking a step back. "Outfitting an expedition like this will be expensive."

"Yes. It is dear for you to take time away from your clients and craft. This is why the NJ quorum, on my behalf, is prepared to compensate you with one hundred honors and ten barrels of rice," Nicky the graham offered, his smile magnanimous.

"You humble me," Miss Pak placed a hand to her chest and bowed. "One hundred and twenty honors and a dozen barrels of rice is a most generous offer."

"Ten barrels of rice," he corrected. "To be delivered upon your return."

"I distinctly heard twelve," the old woman said, her tone puzzled, her staff tapping impatiently.

"Yes. My mistake." The graham nodded, taking the hint. "It will be seen to."

"As for the other matter..." She let her staff hang limp in her right hand and angled its alloy point toward the bashful youth.

"Ah, I assure you that Merrick will prove a most useful companion. Hopeless on a horse, but he's young and can carry much himself without tiring. He also shows great skill in operating Exodan mechanisms, and he knows his history and engineering."

The old woman's expression didn't change.

"Miss Pak, a long journey always involves some risk, and personally, I would worry too much sending a woman your size, alone, into..." The graham trailed off, noting a growing look of menace in the herbalist's eyes.

"I know a few old songs," Merrick offered, uncertainly. "Maybe to help pass time on the road?"

The acolyte's superior shot him a withering look, but Miss Pak smiled at the self-promotion.

"Taking on an apprentice is a burden, everyone knows it," she said, popping the knuckles on her left hand. "He'll be getting training in my stock and trade. Even if that's not the exact role you had in mind, I'll be teaching him things—valuable things. I can't help it."

"I understand," the graham said with a small bow, "excuse me one moment." He departed, swiftly passing through the same archway where Miss Pak had first seen him enter.

She stood with Merrick for a moment, enjoying an awkward silence while he shrank under her appraisal. Like his mentor, the youth was dressed in a white Exodan coverall, modified to fit his bulky frame. She noticed his plain vestments had been festooned with colorful belts and pouches, likely of the young man's own styling.

When the graham returned, he carried a small box made from plastic-polymer.

"A humble offering," he said, opening its lid.

Inside lay an Exodan plastic toothbrush, clean and still sealed in its original factory packaging. Next to it sat a pair of ornate earrings, clearly of Akkadian manufacture, constructed from shell and hammered gold.

"A most welcome gift," Miss Pak said, smiling. "These treasures, along with forty additional honors, would indeed be just compensation for his company and incidental training. I accept."

Rather than negotiate further, Nicky the graham gave her a tight smile and bowed his head.

"To your future triumph."

"And yours."

"Merrick!" He snapped at his underling. "You are to escort Miss Pak safely to the cactuses and back. Return with as much as you can carry. I give you the run of the grounds until your departure—prepare everything you'll need for a four night journey."

"Seven night journey," the herbalist corrected, calculating on her fingers, her handsome walking stick held in the crook of one arm.

● ● ●

"Ready to go?" Miss Pak asked, wearing an outfit she'd burdened with nearly as many pockets and pouches as she had years.

"Everything we need upon our backs," replied Merrick.

The acolyte was the proverb made flesh, with their camp and supplies all crammed into an enormous pack on his shoulders. The old herbalist carried only her metal-tipped staff and a varied assortment of light satchels, worn across her person.

After they set off from the Temple gate, the two travelers took the first northbound avenue, their vast height difference making them a curious couple to the many eyes of the compact city.

"Watch it!" Miss Pak yelled as a quartet of dogs lunged at her, barely controlled by a portly, sweating man straining against a bouquet of leashes.

The herbalist gripped her iron-tipped staff protectively, but the acolyte smiled warmly at the animals as they passed, giving them a little wave of his fingers.

The two walked in silence for several minutes more, Miss Pak slowing her pace whenever they came to a change in the path, letting her new apprentice lead her out of the confusing city.

"I could never live here." She shuddered at the noise and mess arising from a group of children playing in a muddy gutter running alongside their trail. "I would rather wander the wilds and live off the land."

"You'd become one of the layabouts?" Merrick replied, aghast. "NJ isn't *that* bad."

"Nothing wrong with them. The layabout lifestyle makes sense. Humans don't eat all that much," Miss Pak shrugged, "and Akkadia is big and warm. Why *not* do nothing if you can get away with it? What I don't understand–why some people wish they could crowd themselves in even tighter."

"Lots of people would live here if they could," Merrick said, defensively. "New Jacksonville has the potential to grow into a huge metropolis–like something from old Earth. We could do amazing things if we worked together, but NJ's technically on its own island in the bay, and the graham and the quorum are pretty strict with enforcing the city's population limit...

"...even though it's detrimental and arbitrary," he added, almost under his breath.

"Arbitrary?" Miss Pak said, shocked by the blasphemy. "It's law from the mouth of Graham–thirteen hundred people! Aren't you supposed to be an acolyte?"

"I *am* an acolyte, in fact," he said, huffily. "I've read the scriptures and the testimony, and, I won't lie to you or lead you false, nowhere does Graham say that we must limit ourselves to thirteen hundred people per island. It doesn't even make sense. It's not something he talked about."

"He heavily implied it," she shot back.

"The man never even set foot on an island!" Merrick's face flushed in frustration.

"He would have *known* what Akkadia looked like because he was–they would have, nevermind, urgh–" Miss Pak grunted, striking the ground with her staff. "I don't want to argue."

"Agreed. No more word-of-Graham talks."

The travelers made good time and left the small city of New Jacksonville behind, crossing over the island's northwest bridge and onto the mainland. They walked quietly through a seaside hamlet, one of a number of small service villages, home to the bulk of the mainland's official population, kept low by law.

"When it's the right time of day," Miss Pak ventured, finally breaking the silence, "you can get really good fried clams here." She gestured to a wide, paved area that had once been used for shuttle landings in Exodan times. It was badly overgrown and surrounded by temporary, ramshackle shelters.

"The fishers' families cook them up for their returning kin, and they sell them to workers who come down from the fields and in from the lagoons. To city folk, too."

"Is it the right time of day?" Merrick asked, hopefully.

"No."

"Oh."

After leaving the satellite townships behind, the road narrowed to a simple trail, and the two travelers walked with the path to themselves, save for the rare passing rider, for much of the pleasant part of the day. Unseen living things, crackling in the undergrowth, kept the humans company. The crunching of leaves underfoot and a rhythmic tapping from the herbalist's iron-ferruled walking stick added to the ambient sylvan symphony.

"That's a really nice staff. Where did you get it?"

"How's that?" Miss Pak asked, interrupted from her daydreaming.

"Your walking staff. It's unique?" Merrick guessed without confidence. "Is there a story behind it?"

He'd noticed that Miss Pak had a tendency to twirl the heavy wooden rod every once in a while as they traveled, switching which end was the bottom and which the top. The old herbalist smiled at his question.

"Why, yes there is. I won't lie to you or lead you false, young man—I love this stick."

"Was it a gift?" Merrick ventured.

"Payment for services rendered," she answered, matter-of-factly.

"Hmm."

They walked until the sun began to dip behind the cypresses, Miss Pak waiting for the diffident acolyte to ask a follow-up. She wanted to tell the story.

"Heard of Kofi, the blacksmith on Biloxi Island?" She eventually prompted.

Far above, Merrick nodded his shaggy head.

"He's the one who made it. See the craftsmanship? Iron alloy. Kofi's got a talent for working it." She slowed her step, briefly raising her staff from the ground and allowing Merrick to look at both ends.

"It's nice," he agreed. "What did you do for him?"

"Saved his wife," Miss Pak said, humbly. "A very, *very* pretty girl, but fragile. I think the poor thing accidentally poisoned herself—she was near death by the time I reached Biloxi. I treated her with a formula of basil, bermooda grass, and white goosefoot."

"And did that work?"

"Of course it worked," she replied, testily. "You should remember that formula. Anyway, Kofi was so grateful—and I can see this vividly, because we were standing in the little wife's bedchamber. He said, 'take something, anything—these beautiful treasures I've given her are worthless compared against the value of her life.'"

The acolyte nodded, smiling at the small woman's impression of the copious Kofi.

"The wife had a rack full of dresses, and I mean a *fortune* in Exodan silks. All of them clean and shiny and shimmery—enough to clothe an entire Landing Day ball. You've never seen so many frills and baubles! A waste, I say, since Mrs. Kofi never leaves the estate."

"But you didn't want a dress, right? You wanted something more practical?"

"I'm getting to it. As I was saying, the dresses were all hung on this rack the blacksmith made himself. I noticed the cross-bar that held the silly things up. Made from good hardwood and sturdy enough to handle Mrs. Kofi's lace monstrosities, finely sanded, cured, and with solid metal caps on either end—" At this, the herbalist struck the staff against the ground with extra force, adding emphasis. "'I'll take it,' I said, 'and for sixty honors I can let the lady keep all the silk dripping off of it.'"

"Wait," Merrick guffawed, "you're telling me that your walking stick is actually a rod for hanging dresses?"

"Obviously."

The big man's laughter rang out, and the diminutive Miss Pak joined with a self-satisfied cackle. They wore easy smiles as the night descended.

"Do you know anything about plants?" The herbalist asked, poking at her small fire until the dry twigs started to catch—the travelers having stopped to make camp in a gentle meadow several yards off the disappearing path.

"Not much," Merrick replied, "but I can tell you plenty about animals. I've studied records compiled by the Zookeeper herself, you know."

"The Zookeeper?" Miss Pak asked, trying to remember her childhood philosophy classes, her face scrunched against the smoke. "What does she have to do with anything?"

"We have some of her artifacts at the Temple. I may not know anything about herbal medicine, but I've studied the Grahampion Leaders my whole life, and knowing the Zookeeper means learning about her children." The acolyte sat on a blanket on the soft grass, wincing as he tried to find somewhere comfortable to put his aching, overworked feet. "One of the reasons I wanted to come on this mission is to get closer to her legacy–not in a file or an artifact, but in *this*–"

Merrick gestured at the growing twilight around them. Above the crackle of burning twigs, the deepening night chorused with the humming of insects and the screeches of birds.

"The Zookeeper is a Leader worth remembering," he continued. "You know, most of the plants you use for your herbal trade are thanks to her. She was fanatical about seeding Akkadia with plant life, though one could argue that she only cared because of their importance to her animals. In fact, did you know that the only reason Akkadia even has a *Cactaceae cereus* habitat is because the Zookeeper was obsessed with–"

"Have you ever actually seen a cereus before?" Miss Pak interrupted.

"No. You?"

"There isn't a picture or diagram or something in your Temple records–those Zookeeper notes?"

"No. Have *you* seen one? A depiction, even? I mean you're the herbalist."

"I haven't seen them in the wild, no." She stabbed the ground with her fire-poker in irritation. "I once tried to cultivate some cuttings I bought from a traveler, but they didn't take to the soil on my island. Couldn't propagate–rotted."

"Then how are we supposed to know them if we see them?" Merrick asked, suddenly worried. "What are we even doing out here?"

"Relax, Merrick," she said, reaching up to pat one of his huge, muscular shoulders. "We'll know them when we see them. I wouldn't lie to you or lead you false."

The big man nodded. Above, the bright twinkle of Akkadia-2's a-moon briefly dimmed the emerging stars as it arced rapidly across the heavens. The larger, slower b-moon had yet to rise for its nightly wander.

"How about a little herbalism training before we turn in?" She smiled warmly. "I need to earn my honors after all."

"Yes. I guess."

"Do your feet hurt?"

Merrick nodded glumly.

"Good," Miss Pak said. "Did you see all those pink flowers we walked past? Their petals are closed now, but, yes, they're still there if you look." She pointed through the gloom. "Echinacea—cone flower. Everything we need upon our backs. Here, young man, I'll show you how to make a poultice."

● ● ●

After the Akkadian sun rose, the islanders continued their trek northwards into the continent's interior. Forest cleared to park-like grasslands, which in turn gave way to sparser, rockier terrain as they gained altitude and continued to climb. The wind picked up the edge of a chill, gradually sharpening into intermittent icy gusts. Flowers gave ground to mosses, songbirds surrendered to circling scavengers, and clumps of pale aspen trees soon came to dominate the landscape. Whenever the wind gusted through the trees' clonal colonies, their hundreds of small, waxy leaves chattered together, making a sound like a forest of restless bones.

"These trees are kinda creepy," Merrick said, blowing into his hands to warm them.

"Creepy? They're damned useful. Quaking aspens." The herbalist pointed with her long stick. "I'll tell you what—do you ever have a headache? Maybe after a night of too much shine, or from reading too many of your ancient Zookeeper diaries?"

"Maybe." He shrugged. "Why, doesn't everyone?"

"Go over to that one. That little one there, scrape its bark off. You won't hurt it."

"I thought stripping bark kills trees?" The acolyte's face contorted in distaste.

"When done carelessly, maybe." Miss Pak waved away his distress. "But that little aspen isn't really the tree. The true plant is underground—these trees are all like its fingers," she said, wiggling her own. "A clonal colony. More like a mushroom than a tree. Probably why it's so good in tea."

Merrick unslung his backpack and dug through its contents until he came upon a knife. As ordered, he delicately scraped away the young aspen's fragrant white bark.

"What do I do with it?"

"Haven't you been listening? Pack it somewhere safe. Then, when it hurts–make a tea."

"Tea?" He sniffed the freshly-stripped bark uncertainly before packing it away and reshouldering his load.

"Graham gave us a world where balms bloom when burns threaten, and painkillers grow along the harshest paths. I hope you're learning that."

They walked over the rough terrain, concentrating on their footing and kicking away loose stones as they climbed. The trail had become something closer to a suggestion, but hoof tracks in the dried mud confirmed that the pair were still on the well-traveled path of least resistance.

"See! Right there. Snow." Merrick called out after some time.

"Snow?" Miss Pak squinted and shaded her eyes with one hand. "In Eight-month?"

"We're pretty high up. Have you ever been this far inland before?"

"Once or twice," she said, "but I've never come this way."

Aided by the strength of the afternoon sun, the pair crested the snowy divide without freezing, and they began their descent into an arid valley, sparse enough that small, withered trees and patches of unmelted frost became rare visual treats the further they ventured.

"We're entering the deadlands," the herbalist said, noting the lack of vegetation around them and the absence of animal sounds, save their own breath and crunching feet.

"Not much out here. Hmm," Merrick lapsed into silence, his mood matching the emptiness of the landscape around him.

The travelers' thighs and feet ached after the day's hike, and when they found a convenient grouping of large, lichen-studded boulders to shelter near, they rested.

Miss Pak kindled a small fire, and Merrick used a mugfull of snow to try out some aspen tea. He burned his tongue on the first sip and couldn't enjoy the tangy flavor of the potion.

The next morning, the travelers continued to pierce the deadlands. Living up to its name, the northern slope of the highland region was situated in a continental rain shadow, and not even the most tenaciously-engineered immigrants from Earth thrived in its sandy wastes.

Sightings of hardy bits of scrub vanished altogether as the travelers' path descended. Soon, they passed through scenery composed of nothing but bare rock and swirling sand. The pair followed a trail marked by an irregular milestone system of stakes and cairns. It helped the islanders to keep their way, even if they did have to climb a dune every once in a while where the shifting sands had buried a marker.

The infinity of tiny grains that swirled in that desert region of Akkadia-2 were mainly feldspars. At the molecular level, these silicate minerals featured aluminum ions, partnerships of oxygen and silicon, and some potassium impurities trapped in its crystals. None of these atoms, even aluminum, which, when refined, shares so much in common with its ferrous rival, could boast iron's gift of magnetism. Thus, for years, the strontium ferrite ring that lay buried in the inert Akkadian sand had no effect upon the matter that surrounded it. The powerful b-field spun by Fe and its comrades wasted itself on nothing but feldspars and bones, until–

Clunk!

The metal end of Miss Pak's walking staff struck the ground, passing directly through the center of Fe's disk magnet like a finger poking into a ring. The disk slid up the conical ferrule, wedging itself mechanically and magnetically in place.

In his forge, Kofi the blacksmith had hammered salvaged Sukuru-alloy into sheets, which became the ferrules for the rod within his angelic wife's custom wardrobe–before Miss Pak took possession. Made mainly of iron atoms born from Earth's Mother Star, the alloy endcap found a quorum of its countless electrons forcibly converted by Fe' magnet.

The two materials held fast together, even as Miss Pak lifted her walking stick and shook it free of feldspars. Fe's magnet had never before had its momentous forces manifest in this way–crudely and physically sticking it to another piece of metal.

"What's that?" Merrick asked, looking down at the flat black thing on Miss Pak's walking staff.

"I found something." She studied the treasure that had attached itself to her beloved property. "It was buried in the sand. Hmmm...?"

A glint entered the little herbalist's eyes. She rotated her wrist, turning the stick around and pointing the magnet-end toward her towering apprentice.

"Hey..." he said uneasily as she jabbed the stick toward his waist.

Clank!

Miss Pak gently pulled her stick away, and Merrick's belt buckle moved with it. A colorful, woolen strap strained for an inch or two before its resisting force overcame Fe's b-field, and the alloy buckle pulled free from the staff's headpiece.

The apprentice checked that the belt was still intact before protectively placing his hand over its buckle.

"A magnet. Strong one too." She gave the chipped, strontium ferrite donut an approving nod. "Where do you think it came from?"

"Earth," Merrick answered immediately. "Something like that's gotta be Exo-dan."

"How did it get out *here*, is what I mean."

"I don't know," he said, surveying the wastes, one hand shielding his eyes, "but maybe *that* has something to do with it."

He pointed, but Miss Pak couldn't see, not even when she jumped. Grumbling, the old woman pulled herself several feet up the nearest dune, digging in with her walking stick and letting the sand bury her boots.

She held the ferrule-and-magnet headpiece upwards like a standard as she stood surveying from the high ground.

"With luck comes hope."

Something heavy lay in the sands–a shapeless black mass some ways off. A piece of it caught the sun, glinting brightly. Despite their mission, the travelers would need to veer only slightly east of their intended course to investigate the wreck.

"Exodan," Merrick said breathlessly when the building-sized piece of hull came clearly into view.

The object was a blackish-grey cylinder, slanted at the top and standing at least two and a half times Merrick's height at its shallowest. Up close, the travelers could make out bubbly, pitted skin along one section. Another side seemed almost polished, its alloy rubbed smooth enough to reflect the sun for a great distance.

Miss Pak tested the material with her newly magnetic staff. The edge of Fe's ferrite ring extended its invisible b-field tendrils, then, weakly but palpably, clunked against the wall of carbon-scored Sukuru-alloy wreckage.

"There's some good ore here," Merrick said, without enthusiasm.

"Maybe." The herbalist pulled her staff free, letting it fall in the sand as she squatted to brush drifts away from the burnt chunk's base.

"I don't know if it's worth it to dig it out. Someone would have to haul it all the way back to town. Cut it apart somehow? It's Exodan, but...I don't know."

"We're not the first to come this way. The trail isn't far." Miss Pak stood up, brushing herself off and conducting an unconscious pocket-check. "Are you old enough to remember the Fall? I won't lie to you or lead you false—if someone *could've* taken this, they would've by now. It's too big and burnt up to be valuable, even if it is Exodan."

"Oh."

*   *   *

"What's that on your magnet?" Merrick asked when they had once again found the trail.

Close to eye-level with the edge of Fe's disk, he pointed to something silvery and reflective glinting above the herbalist's head.

"Hmm..." Miss Pak pulled the staff toward herself and plucked four small, metallic objects from Fe's magnet.

Two were in the shape of flat disks and one sharp little thing took the form of a helix descending from a parallel circular cap, all three shiny and clearly ferromagnetic in nature. She tossed a fourth bit of scrap–an irregular, edgy bit of carbon-scored alloy–back into the sand.

"Washer, washer, screw," the young man noted, excitement edging into his voice. "All Exodan. They're pretty!"

"The sand around here might be full of bits and pieces of the ship, yes?"

"Oh, yes. I've studied the relics that people brought to the Temple after the Fall. I'd wager there's some really interesting things still buried around here," he said longingly, swiveling his head as they walked. "I wish *I'd* found the magnet."

"Everything we need on our backs," Miss Pak said sagely.

"I wasn't envying. I just like artifacts like that. Like this..." He brushed his hand over a sheet of delicate aluminum scalework that covered a small pouch on his hip.

"Very shiny, Merrick. Those too–" With her free hand, the herbalist pointed up at the man's copper and pearl earrings, half-hidden in his curls.

He nodded, a bashful half-smile creeping across his face.

"How about this," Miss Pak said. "I'll rent it to you.""Rent? Like, when you're not using it?

She grinned and nodded.

"How much?"

"We split it fifty-fifty," the herbalist offered, "whatever you find. That's fair, right?"

"Right," he agreed, uncertainly.

Thrice, during their long, featureless trek, Merrick successfully lobbied his mentor to rent him her new, magnetic tool. Like an old Earth beachcomber, the tall, white-suited apprentice gently swept the sands before him as he walked, keeping several paces ahead of the patient herbalist. Fe's magnetic field hadn't performed work for humans since moving the heavy alloy door that had assassinated Xie. Now, wielded by Merrick, the strontium ferrite's passive properties proved useful for a style of scavenging that Sab the Elamite or old Sam Stills would have approved of.

Merrick found handfuls of melted, contorted scraps of alloy–bits and blobs from the Exodus' fiery re-entry, most of which he tossed back to the sand. Fe and its allies' strong b-field, however, managed to snare a few stainless steel fasteners and rivets. After the young man tried to dig up a section of buried bulkhead far too large to carry, however, Miss Pak reappropriated her walking stick, tired of Merrick's landlocked beachcombing slowing them down.

The trail markers sometimes took an unsettlingly long time to appear on the horizon, but the islanders never lost their way. They continued across the featureless deadlands until well after nightfall, never coming across a water source or particularly promising spot for a camp. Stars came out by the hundreds. Though the far-off furnaces clustered together in constellations that would be alien to any Earth astrologer, the luminous band of the Milky Way could be recognized anywhere. It was briefly bisected by the mercurial a-moon, streaking across the sky in its periodic orbit.

"Miss Pak."

"Hm?"

"I noticed something–" Merrick said, after another speedy streak of the small satellite overhead. "We're passing about three marker-stones every a-month. I've been watching the sky for it."

"Three?" The herbalist's attention turned firmly to her apprentice. "Xie's sins! We've been walking half the night."

With little visibility and even less hope for a good campsite, the exhausted Miss Pak and Merrick decided to rest where they were. They laid out blankets and bedrolls but didn't bother to light a fire, settling down under the light of moon, star, and galaxy. The rhythmic sounds of the wind and a distant susurrating in the darkness quickly lulled the weary travelers to sleep.

They awoke shivering and wet. The Milky Way could no longer be seen, but the sun hadn't yet risen.

"Sss-stars!" Merrick said, his teeth chattering. "What happened?"

Miss Pak, also damp and cold, rubbed her eyes and stretched.

"Dew," she said, at last. "We're inside a cloud."

"Is it morning?" The acolyte asked, fuzzily.

"Not quite. Here, hand me that flask." Miss Pak gestured impatiently until Merrick gave her one of the empty bottles they had drained during their thirsty desert trek.

Slowly and carefully, the herbalist folded her sleeping mat until individual droplets of dew collected and ran together in a tiny stream, which she channeled inside the flask. Slowly waking up, Merrick helped her, and together, they managed to fill it halfway.

Just as Miss Pak sealed the bottle, a large, dark shape swooped out of the thick fog.

"Aaah!" She screamed, dropping the flask.

"What?" Merrick asked, frightened.

"Did you see that?""See what?" The hulking youth rose to his feet and took several steps, searching the gloom. "Miss Pak!"

She picked up the fallen container to make sure it hadn't broken, but Merrick gestured urgently, and the herbalist trotted over to meet him. At the edge of a rise, they stood overlooking a gentle valley that eventually rolled down to meet the Akkadian sea. Through thick fog, the waters couldn't be seen, though the travelers could hear the murmur of the waves. Had they walked mere moments more the previous night, they would have met its dark mass.

In the distance, the so-called deadlands rioted with life in full-bloom. Thorny trees and hardy bushes stuck out from the rocky ground, and portly barrel cactuses sprouted alongside flowering succulents.

Miss Pak and Merrick entered the valley in a dew-speckled stupor, their campsite and belongings temporarily forgotten behind them. As they lost elevation, they found themselves strolling underneath the cloud of starlit fog.

"MmmMmm," the old woman breathed deeply and released a pleasurable sigh. The air was suffused with a sweet, vanilla-like aroma.

"I know I'm not a trained herbalist, but are those *Cactaceae cereus*?" Merrick asked diffidently, pointing at an example of a dark green cactus that grew in tall, segmented stalks.

From the thin ribs of the vine-like cereus, flowers budded. Barely peeking open, one alien-looking bloom dangled fingerlike pink protrusions around its delicate cluster of tucked, whitish petals. Its romantic, industrious cells released a rich chemical fragrance that rode the air currents, ending as an indulgent treat for the two-legged mammals' olfactory systems.

"Indeed they are!" Miss Pak said, unable to contain her excitement. "Stars, there must be hundreds!"

At that moment, another huge shape dipped beneath the fog and swooped over them. Again, the little herbalist shrieked, but this time she swung her magnetic staff at the creature, missing it by quite a bit.

"Hey, hey...it's ok," Merrick soothed, placing his huge hand on the shaft to halt its violence. "They're just bats. Harmless. See."

The curly-headed mountain stood placidly, letting the flapping chiroptera pass overhead. Taking his cue, Miss Pak inhaled deeply, exhaled through her mouth, and tried to look at the scene calmly and objectively. There were many of them—mysterious dark shapes that fluttered and swooped in the dimness, faster than the eye could track them. After a time, though, she managed to trace one as it descended from the chaos.

Only a few of the hundreds of cereus displayed ripe flowers, but the swooping bat settled near a cactus in full bloom, and the travelers sat in awe as the creature fed on the intoxicating blossom's nectar.

Overwhelmed by the beauty of the delicate scene before them, Miss Pak and Merrick rested on a small ledge of bare stone and waited for the sun to rise.

"I don't understand it," the acolyte said at last. "It doesn't rain here, and we're just a short walk from the heart of the deadlands—where did all this life come from?"

"Think," Miss Pak responded, playfully shaking the half-full flask she'd been carrying since her first startle.

"The dew?"

"Very good." The herbalist smiled, her eyes crinkling. "My guess is that fog from the sea collects here regularly. Plenty enough to drink, if you're a desert-adapted plant."

"Still, it seems impossible."

"Humans are good at impossible," Miss Pak quoted, aware of the anthropic origins of their ecosystem.

"Graham got that one right," Merrick said, stretching with a satisfied sigh.

"Hey, Merrick," the herbalist ventured, "have you ever tried one of these?"

From one of the many small pockets sewn into her clothes, Miss Pak extracted a narrow bundle about the size of her little finger. The object was wrapped in a leaf, twisted at one end.

"What is it?" He brought the device to his nose and immediately recoiled at the strong, herbal odor.

"*Cannabis indica.*" She reached over to retake possession of the joint. "I keep a few plants in my garden."

"What does it do?"

"You smoke it. I'll show you," Miss Pak said, patting her pockets with her free hand. "Where–oh, starshit. Firestarter's back at camp. Nevermind," she concluded, saving the tiny bundle for later.

"Oh."

Instead, the two spent the morning exploring the North Shore cactus habitat. First, they made sure to fulfill their given mission–cutting and packing several pounds of the medicinal cereus, including some sweet-scented cactus flowers at various stages of maturity.

Miss Pak also took the time to gather samples from other water-thrifty species of North Shore flora. Some of these, she introduced to Merrick, though the acolyte himself was often busy strolling the beach, inventorying the region's animal life against what he knew of the Zookeeper's legacy.

That evening, Miss Pak built two large fires to boil down pots of pulped cactus with the goal of reducing them into an easier-to-carry concentrate. As they waited for the concoction to simmer, the two shared some of the herbalist's supply of *Cannabis indica* and watched the sun set.

Later, during an especially heavy bout of laughter, Merrick accidentally rolled over, scraping himself against the small sack he'd filled with steel and alloy debris, scavenged with the rented magnet.

"Ow."

Miss Pak, ignoring Merrick's discomfort, enjoyed the bright, metallic sound the trinkets made.

"Hmmm..." Sitting cross-legged, she bent forward at the waist and dug through a pile of satchels until she'd found her own hide bag filled with shining steel washers and screws.

She gave it an experimental shake, then settled into a regular, rattling rhythm.

Merrick bobbed his head in time, grabbing his pouch to accompany her instrument in a higher, weaker pitch. The islanders settled into a syncopated beat, rocking their hips and rolling their shoulders until the jam became too ridiculous to continue, and the pair collapsed, eyes streaming with laugh-tears.

In the morning, they collected dew until their mouths no longer felt so dry, and they augmented their food stores with some shellfish Merrick had gathered from the coast and fresh cactus fruit Miss Pak found growing further inland. By the time they made ready for the long trek back to New Jacksonville, their packs had grown distressingly heavy with medicinal botanicals and derivatives.

They rested and traveled, rested and traveled.

"What are you doing," Merrick asked once he grew too bored to walk in silence any longer, "with the magnet?"

The acolyte noticed that his companion would periodically pull Fe's disk off one end of her long staff and slide it onto the iron ferrule at the other.

"I know this *looks* like a walking stick, young man, but actually–you know of Kofi the blacksmith?"

"You told me the story," the acolyte winced.

"Oh, of course. Since you know what it is, you know that it was made sideways. No top or bottom. Don't want undue wear on one end, do I?"

The iron-tipped staff, in fact, held up better than its owner. Her feet hurt too much to ignore after a time, and Merrick continuously complained about his own. Miss Pak found her mind longing for distraction. It drifted to a memory of her traveling companion's self-professed knowledge of song.

"Remember what you promised, back at the Temple?"

"Um...yes?"

She was able to wheedle Merrick into singing several songs he'd learned by heart, including his versions of "Hot Biloxi," "Auld Lang Syne," "Uptown Girl," "Here Together–Alone in the Void," and a hummed rendition of the "Scarborough Fair Canticle" before the bashful apprentice grew too self-conscious to continue the serenade.

They rested one final time, depleting the meager remains of their rations.

Seven days after first setting out from New Jacksonville, the travelers found themselves trudging across the last bridge into the city, feeling dirty, sore, grumpy, and exhausted–North Shore sand still in their boots. Yet, at the Temple, the grateful graham was as good as his word, lavishing Miss Pak with praise and ordering his acolytes to fetch her agreed-upon pay.

After taking some refreshment, she bid Nicky the graham and her new friend Merrick a hasty goodbye, eager to get back to her island.

Augmented staff in hand, Miss Pak navigated her way out of the city-center. Leaving New Jacksonville was easier than entering–one just had to follow gravity, an easy enough task for the footsore and homesick herbalist. At the docks, she approached a ferryman with a particularly bad complexion, asking transport for herself and the remaining barrels of grain that she couldn't sell at market. She persuaded him to waive his usual fee for the voyage in exchange for a vial of skin ointment, to be paid upon reaching her island.

● ● ●

Sometimes, Miss Pak preferred to meet customers in the cozy apothecary cabin built over her cavernous root cellar–its gloomy interior and assault of strange smells adding to her arcane authority. The day was too nice for that, however, and the spry old herbalist found herself sitting astride a small dock with her sleeves rolled up, letting the Akkadian sun soak into her hard, chestnut skin.

Behind the small human, a riot of growth shook in the soft breeze–tall grasses, shrubs, ferns, and trees of many species, all in assorted stages of maturity, tweaked and curated to thrive on an alien world. Amongst this biological infrastructure, thick-bodied beetles clicked and small, burnt-looking bees flitted from flower to flower. Kelp forests danced and swayed in the murky saltwater channel below. If the herbalist had been a foot taller, she could have dangled her toes into the Akkadian sea.

Miss Pak looked down and saw ripples disturbing the watercourse, announcing the first of her expected customers. A narrow, black bow appeared well ahead of the craft itself—a long, flat gondola. The pilot, a tall woman with a stony face, polled her passenger towards the dock.

Dr. Hornschlitten, seated in the boat's center, gave Miss Pak a small wave. He wore a black cloak and a forlorn expression. A physician known for his reputation in treating ailments peculiar to women, the Doctor was a regular customer, preferring to purchase raw ingredients over prepared tinctures.

The herbalist had a wrapped package of *Actaea racemosa* waiting for him. Without getting up, she tossed the bumpy bundle of rhizomes across the narrow gap. Dr. Hornschlitten caught it with one hand and tucked it inside his cloak.

"Esme–" he barked at the pilot, "–Miss Pak's usual sum."

"Forget the payment," Miss Pak interjected, holding up a hand to wave off Esme, who only scowled at her. "Are you still treating Miss Siobhan?"

"Miss Siobhan? Yes. What about her?" The Doctor called back over the water.

"Her next house call is free. All your visits to her are gifts now. Out of the kindness of your heart."

"As payment? And that would balance us?"

"We'd be even. Yes," Miss Pak replied.

"As you wish." Hornschlitten sniffed. "There won't be many visits left, I'm afraid–poor thing. Graham rest her soul."

With that, the Doctor's attention slipped from Miss Pak, and he set Esme in motion with an imperious gesture. The sun-drenched herbalist waved cheerily at their backs, enjoying the formations of v-shaped ripples that radiated from the thin boat's wake.

The next craft she spied plying the narrow channel was crewed only by its single, deeply tanned rower, his sunbleached hair trailing in the breeze. The man sliced swiftly past the dock, tossing a smile and a wink at Miss Pak, who answered with a tiny wave.

Her neighbor Troast, his wife Cowgirl, and their boy Marco lived on the little island that abutted her own. During the lowest tides, in fact, it was hard to tell where the small family's island ended and the herbalist's began.

Miss Pak liked her neighbors well enough. Cowgirl kept bees and was a wise enough woman to attribute the success of her honey and wax ventures to the thousands of lush, diverse blooms that grew on Miss Pak's property. The herbalist had but two other close neighbors—a pair of elder gentlemen who both went by the name Junior. They occupied another isle in the channel's small cluster. The men were reliable customers, preferring cannabis and herbal remedies for joint pain, though they often grumbled about the prices she charged. Rumor was, in New Jacksonville, the Juniors pretended to be twins, though Miss Pak knew for a fact they'd been privately married for almost forty years.

She spent some lazy minutes enjoying the sun and the breeze, letting her mind wander where it would before her next customer appeared. The young man arrived not by boat, but by breaststroke. From her dock, she watched him move frog-like through the water, his long, black hair trailing as he swam. It blanketed his face when he surfaced.

"Good morning, Miss P-Pak," he sputtered.

"Good morning to you, Tiger. How's the water?" "Colder than you'd think," he replied, pulling himself onto the small wooden dock, his body covered by nothing but shreds of slimy, clinging algae.

"Come over here. I'm not getting up," Miss Pak gestured, ignoring Tiger's nudity.

He stepped over and knelt next to her, accepting the flask she handed him. He drained its bitter contents with a shudder and handed back the empty vial.

"Th-thank you."

It contained a formula derived primarily from St. John's wort and yarrow, prepared regularly by Miss Pak for the troubled young artist—he would make the seven mile swim to her island at least twice every b-moon.

"You owe me two paintings, you know," the herbalist scolded.

"I thought you wanted a mural?" The nude youth pointed toward the interior of Miss Pak's island, though her building could barely be seen through the thick foliage.

"It's a mural *and* a painting."

"Yes, Miss Pak," he agreed, rolling off the dock and splashing back into the water.

"To your future triumph!" She called out.

"And to yours!" Tiger burbled before resuming his breaststroke.

The old herbalist chuckled. She expected no more customers that morning but hesitated before returning to her chores. Lately, the curious human had been conducting some interesting mycological experiments, and her mycelium cakes likely needed tending to–but that would mean going underground and away from all the lovely sunlight. Sometimes Miss Pak wondered if she was becoming too much like her vegetation.

Her mind was jolted from its reverie by the appearance of another visitor, or someone badly-lost, judging by the appearance of their vessel. The hull was flat and shallow, and the entire stubby boat appeared constructed of repurposed Exodan plastic. A durable and waterproof choice, Miss Pak conceded, but ugly as all Xie's sins.

The man who paddled the shabby thing came into view sooner than most, for he was enormous. It could be nobody but Merrick the acolyte, she judged, and a long, thin smile cracked the delighted herbalist's weathered face.

"Merrick!" She called out, waving.

The curly-headed giant rose and made to wave back but quickly sat down, nearly upsetting the delicate balance of the tiny dory.

Cackling, Miss Pak hopped up onto the dock. She located a thick coil of hempen rope, braided years ago but still sturdy, and tossed it to the grateful acolyte. Cautiously, he hauled himself in, secured the boat–which was even uglier up close–and awkwardly climbed onto the little dock.

The herbalist hugged Merrick while he was still half crouched.

"Miss Pak!" He said, laughing.

"You're an unexpected sight," she beamed. "Welcome to my island! Come, come." She led him away from the water and into the thick greenery.

"It's beautiful!" He exclaimed, wide-eyed. "How many different species do you cultivate?"Miss Pak only laughed at the question.

"How's Nicky?" She asked, instead.

"The graham is doing well. He sends his best–possum!" Merrick cried out with excitement, spotting a dwarf variety of the marsupial hanging from one of the towering herb plants above them.

"Pollinators," Miss Pak replied happily, as the tiny creature scampered out of sight. "Silly little things, but I keep them around. Useful seed-spreaders too, and they don't eat enough to annoy me, usually."

As they talked, the differently-sized humans approached the aboveground portion of Miss Pak's apothecary–a quaint cabin covered in vine-choked solar panels. Out front stood a weathered wooden awning, supported by a single post. Underneath sat a table covered in burn marks, a simple chair, and the herbalist's trusty magnetic walking staff, resting inside an empty barrel and keeping company with a facedown shovel and a long, two-pronged fork.

The former traveling companions walked out of the warm sunlight, and Miss Pak made her way easily into the gloomy confines of the structure, but Merrick was forced to bend deeply to avoid bumping his head.

"How are you feeling, young man? What have you been up to? What brings you out of the Temple?" She peppered him with questions as she busily made the space ready for a guest. "Tea?"

"This place smells amazing. No need to bother with tea."

"Just as well. Merchant who sold me those voltaic panels claimed they could make enough energy for a power kettle." The herbalist scoffed. "Barely lights the inside of this place."

"Maybe I can take a look at your array sometime. Still, these are good LEDs." Merrick's face hovered only inches from the thin strip of electric lights fastened to the ceiling. "I've been doing more research into Exodan artifacts, actually.

"In fact," he continued, digging a small rectangular object out of a pocket. "I've come across something remarkable. A possible *Diomedian* artifact!"

Reverently, he held a blockish piece of plastic–once part of a buckle made for the seats of an Earthmade colony ship's shuttle.

"Looks Exodan." Miss Pak tapped the hard, grey plastic of the seatbelt buckle with her fingernail.

"No, that's the thing–" He responded with excitement, pulling the block away. "None of the Exodus' auxiliary vehicles used *this* model of safety harness. I'm fairly certain."

"Fascinating. So you've been stuck inside doing research again?"

Merrick nodded, slightly disappointed in the herbalist's lukewarm reaction to the life-changing discovery.

"You still getting headaches?" She asked with concern, one hand cocked on her hip.

"Sometimes... I guess."

"Ran out of that aspen tea, eh?"

"Oh, ages ago. It was good while it lasted, though."

"Let's get you some more, then," she said, brightly. "Friends and family discount. Three honors, ok?"

Miss Pak scurried around a corner to a low chest of drawers and pulled out a sack of aspen bark fragments. She poured a measure on a board, and with a deft hand and alloy scraper, separated the pile in two. One half she scooped with a wooden ladle and piled onto a large, dry leaf, which she rolled up and tied off with a bit of twine.

"Thanks," Merrick said, his face confused as he accepted the package and tucked it away. "How did you do that? You've already sold me something–I haven't even told you why I'm here yet."

"If not for your headache problem, why *are* you here?"

"Do you know Mr. Vaughn Duwaik?"

"Not personally," Miss Pak said with distaste, "but of course I know *of* him. That silly estate of his is hard to miss when I ferry into town."

"Oh, well, he's actually a very nice man," Merrick offered, diplomatically. "And his mother is sick."

"Ah, I see. What's ailing the poor dear?"

"I won't lie to you or lead you false–I don't know the name of her condition, or if it has a name." He fidgeted nervously as he spoke. "But she's in terrible pain. Truly terrible."

"Stars..." The herbalist sighed.

"From the way Mr. Duwaik described it, I would almost say that death could be a mercy for the woman."

"We alone control our destiny," Miss Pak replied, bowing her head grimly. She left the implication unspoken.

"Oh, no. That's not an option. Mr. Duwaik says his mother is a fundamentalist and would sooner suffer forever than willingly extinguish a human life."

"Forgive me," the herbalist said grimly. "I was not offering–it is wicked to waste a life. It's not our place, and it lessens Graham's sacrifice."

Merrick took one of Miss Pak's small, leathery hands into his own much larger and softer ones.

"All is well, Miss Pak," he said, giving a small squeeze before letting go. "I didn't come here for those types of drugs. In fact, Mr. Duwaik knows a particular herb that could ease her suffering without resorting to anything as extreme as euthanasia."

The herbalist nodded. She had never heard of a plant called 'euthanasia', but admitting ignorance lessened her cultivated mystique.

"Mr. Duwaik says that it's something called..." Merrick's eyes looked up at nothing as he tried to remember. "...Papa...vera–ah, something. I can't remember. It's a flower."

"You need to be more specific."

"A red flower? It eases pain. Like the aspen, but for serious illness. That's about all I know."

"I'm sorry, young man. I have nothing like that here." "Nobody does!" Merrick said immediately. "Mr. Duwaik has asked us to search for it. It would mean another expedition."

"My heart goes out to Mrs. Duwaik," Miss Pak began, "but I have to ask–why? Why are you doing this rich man's bidding? I taught you a fair bit, but you're still far from being able to trade as an herbalist."

"The buckle I showed you? It was his. Mr. Duwaik is a collector and an en-thusiast when it comes to Exodan and Earthmade artifacts. I was petitioning him to aid my research into the severed siblings when I learned of the flower and its properties."

"And you thought of me?"

"Of course!" He answered, surprised. "Who else?"

Miss Pak stayed quiet for a moment. She plucked a mint leaf from a fragrant bundle and popped it into her mouth, idly shredding its cell structure as she thought. The herbalist needed nothing the rich man could give her, but still–the prospect was intriguing.

Just as small bits of scrap steel were pulled inexorably toward her scavenged magnet, Miss Pak found herself pulled strongly, whether she willed it or not, in the direction of discovery.

"Will you at least meet with him?" Merrick pleaded. "For me?"

"Very well," she said, deciding at last, "but I'll need a few hours to prepare. Is that terrible little boat yours?"

Merrick shook his head.

"Rented? Good. Leave it. I'll get my neighbor to ferry us over. He owes me."

● ● ●

Miss Pak sat in the narrow boat's bow, holding her walking stick. Fe and the magnetic headpiece dangled above the swiftly moving salt water, Troast's rowing almost strong enough to raise a spray despite his heavy load.

Merrick sat, hunched up, in the rear of the vessel. His offer to help row had been declined after Miss Pak's neighbor briefly assessed the acolyte's shaky seamanship. Still, Merrick enjoyed the ride. He liked the way Troast's long, blondish hair trailed in the breeze, and he watched the man's muscular shoulders rhythmically pumping, propelling them all toward their rendezvous.

The Duwaik estate came into view, dominating the eastern shore of New Jacksonville Island. Troast maneuvered his skiff between two jagged rocks that jutted from the seafloor, forming a kind of gate to the Duwaiks' private dock. Like the massive house that hung above it, the dock itself had been built of quarried stone.

"Woah," Troast said, letting out a long whistle. "How much manpower did it take to erect this monstrosity? How much energy?""It was put up a long time ago," Merrick replied, somewhat defensively. "People in the planetfall era had more energy to work with. And tools. It was easier back then."

"I dunno, kinda makes it seem like an even bigger waste to me." The boatman started– "woah–check out that yacht!"

Docked at one side of the stone pier was a large, black craft that at first glance could have been mistaken for a long-lost historical spaceship rather than an Akkadian yacht. It flew no sails, instead, its hardtop and the sides of its hull were covered in dark, gleaming photovoltaic panels.

Though both made from Exodan materials, the magnificent yacht could not have been more different from Merrick's sad, rented dory.

"Those voltaics!" He moaned.

"Enough to power a village," Miss Pak agreed.

"You've got some friends in high places, Miss Pak." Troast said after another derisive whistle.

They could see that a bearded man, wearing a cap and harness, paced back and forth on the small quay. When he noticed the visitors, he unclipped a black, boxy device and spoke into it. The man turned and gestured sharply to the incoming vessel, guiding them in with his free hand.

By the time the visitors' boat reached the pier, they could hear the eerie crackling sounds of electronic communication.

"...he bring...herbalist?" A voice from nowhere asked.

"Starshit," Troast flinched in surprise.

"Affirmative," the man at the dock answered, speaking not to the visitors but to his handheld.

"Relax, it's just a radio," Merrick said, placing a reassuring hand on the rower's back.

With the assistance of the bearded man, who happened to be Duwaik's ma-jordomo, the little boat was secured against the pier. Miss Pak climbed out first, keeping hold of her beloved walking staff. With somewhat less grace, the towering acolyte followed.

"You're alright, then?" Troast called up, uncertainly.

"Yes. You have my gratitude." The herbalist thanked her neighbor with a small bow.

"I'll be heading off then. To your future triumph."

"Send Marco my love."

"Ha! I think he'd rather have another piece of that cane-juice candy, but I'll giv'im your best."

"Please come with me, you two," the gruff majordomo instructed once Troast started rowing away.

Miss Pak and Merrick followed the servant along the short quay to a set of stone steps leading to a heavy door. This portal turned out to be an entrance into the manor house's basement. The visitors were led inside and up a series of staircases to a landing where light poured in through elegant, glazed windows.

At the mouth of one hallway paced a bald man who stood somewhere between the height of the diminutive Miss Pak and the more average-sized majordomo. He wore a fine wool sweater, dyed a deep emerald green. The man's eyes were small, wet, and very pale–his mouth and chin wreathed by a white goatee.

"Sir," the servant said, "allow me to present the researcher Merrick and his herbalist Pak."

"I am beyond pleased to finally meet you," the bald man said, bowing to her.

"It's Miss Pak, actually, Mr. Duwaik," Merrick corrected, nervously.

"My apologies," Duwaik said smoothly. "*Miss* Pak. Welcome to my home. That will be all, Angus."

Without speaking, the gruff servant turned and stomped off, leaving the visitors alone in his master's company.

"I don't value him for his people skills," Duwaik said with a small, apologetic shrug. "But Merrick–you must have noticed the *Horizon* on your way in."

"Yes sir. She's magnificent."

"The voltaic yacht?" Miss Pak asked, her head cocked to one side.

"Everything we need upon our backs," Duwaik beamed. "I'm sure you'll be very comfortable aboard, but—I'm getting ahead of myself. A thousand pardons. This way, please."

With that, the master of the house threw open a set of richly-carved wooden doors, hinting at an incongruously-decorated dining room beyond. He strode inside, leaving his visitors no choice but to follow.

Sukuru-alloy furniture and fixtures dominated the room, appearing to Miss Pak's eyes like a sort of live-in Exodan museum. A dozen simple, metal chairs sat arrayed around the central table, which had been decoratively set with cups, cutlery, and plates made from the same precious alloy. The long, varnished dining table itself, crafted of Akkadian hardwood, seemed to be the only native piece among the collection.

"Miss Pak," Merrick said quietly, before they had fully entered the room, "it might be best to leave your staff here. The magnet, you know. It could cause trouble."

"Magnet?" Duwaik turned, his hearing uncanny.

"On my walking stick," Miss Pak said unconcerned. "It comes in handy."

The master's keen eyes quickly assessed the headpiece, resting on Fe's strontium ferrite disk.

"Exodan?" He asked, reaching out as if to touch it, his finger hovering.

"Yes."

"We found it in the deadlands," Merrick added, helpfully.

"A good piece." Duwaik nodded. "But our friend is correct—it could wreak havoc on my collection. You can place it here for the moment." He indicated to a tall alloy locker standing inconspicuously in one corner.

Rather than opening the door, Miss Pak simply set her walking stick against the locker's side. With a clang, the staff attached itself to the metal siding via magnetic force.

"Vaughn? Is that you?" Someone called from inside the room, the noise having attracted their attention.

"Who else?" Duwaik chuckled, ushering his guests further into the chamber. "Merrick, I'd like you to meet my brother."

Inside waited a man, younger and taller than Duwaik, holding a black tablet in one hand. He smiled hugely upon seeing Merrick and Miss Pak, revealing a set of even, gleaming teeth. Like an inverse of his brother, he let his lustrous poplar-colored hair hang in a loose ponytail, and he wore his sandy sideburns long and bushy.

"Han Duwaik, at your service." He bowed.

"It's a pleasure to meet you, young man. You may call me Miss Pak." She smiled and returned the grinning Duwaik's bow.

For a few moments, no one spoke. They stood, smiling stiffly until Merrick noticed their eyes on him.

"Mmerick-" He stammered, at last. "I'm Merrick. My pleasure."

Han's smile widened, and he winked, making the acolyte blush.

"You're all here, in one room!" Duwaik said with a clap. "My dream team is assembled. We have an expert in herbal medicines, an Exodan scholar and representative of the Temple, and an accomplished, daring sailor." He nodded to each in turn, ending with his brother.

"You've all been given a mission. Put simply, you are to travel to distant lands in search of a mythical flower. *Papaver somniferum–*" He paused. "Han, if you please." The elder Duwaik gestured to his brother, opening and closing his hand impatiently.

Han handed over the tablet he'd been keeping. Rather than a featureless slab of black glass, as it first appeared, one of its flat sides now glowed a faint white.

"Behold: the object of your quest." Duwaik exhaled dramatically. He held out the tablet–its glowing screen, spiderwebbed with cracks, displayed a labeled diagram of a plant.

The visitors leaned closer, Merrick's breath catching in his throat. The onscreen botanical specimen sported large, flat leaves and a thin stem studded with tiny spines. The image featured both red and white flowers, cup-shaped with overlapping petals and a seedpod like a tiny melon.

"Stars above–what is this?" Miss Pak wondered aloud, her eyes devouring the electronic page.

"An Exodan tablet," Merrick answered, misunderstanding her question. "A kind of computer. This one looks to be of early manufacture, but it's still functional. Clearly..." He trailed off, his tone reverent.

"No, Merrick," she gently scolded. "What's *in* the computer tablet?"

"An encyclopedia," Mr. Duwaik answered for him, "or fragments of one, at least."

"Cache memory?" The acolyte asked, wide-eyed.

"Indeed." Duwaik nodded.

Miss Pak exchanged glances with Han, who shrugged, grinning at their shared ignorance. She reached out and poked at the screen with one finger. Suddenly, the image changed to show a strange man wearing a layered robe and turban, standing in a field, surrounded by hundreds of chest-high *Papaver somniferum*–their spherical seedpods perched atop bare stalks.

"Miss Pak, take care." Duwaik pulled the tablet away. "I trust you've never seen anything like this papaver before?"

She shook her head.

"As I expected," he continued. "This species was not among the complement carried aboard the Exodus. However, it is my hope that salvation lies with our severed siblings. If the flower were included aboard the Diomed, there's a chance it could be growing somewhere out there. We just need to find it, and *I* happen to know where to look. Merrick, the artifact."

From a deep pocket, the musclebound youth extracted the plastic buckle and handed it to Duwaik.

"Proof of the Diomed, and a hint to its location," Mr. Duwaik said, mysteriously.

"One of ours found it at market–originally from a fishing boat," Han chimed in. "Owner claims he fished it out somewhere south of Biloxi. There's a stretch of reef far to the west where folks tell tales of the severed siblings. Fisherman claims the trinket protected his vessel from their ghosts," he chuckled, "but the wretch was willing to part with it for the right price."

"So there it is," Mr. Duwait said after shooting his brother a cold glare. "Han will navigate, Miss Pak will identify the papaver, and you'll be on the lookout for any Earthmade artifacts along the way," he finished, pointing to Merrick, "to benefit our mutual vocation."

"Speaking of vocations," Miss Pak said, finding an opening, "I came here because the wellbeing of an old woman is at stake, and believe me, I will do all in my power to help her. But, Mr. Duwaik, I won't lie to you or lead you false—this expedition is sure to take me away from my craft and my clients for some time. Nothing is free. A man as wealthy as you must understand that."

"Of course, Miss Pak. Say no more. You will be well-compensated for your services. Upon delivery of the papaver, you may peruse my private archives to your heart's content, including the herbological sections of the encyclopedia. Under supervision, of course," he added.

The prospect tempted Miss Pak, who found herself surprised to discover there was something the rich man could offer her after all. Knowledge. An entire colony ship's worth of species—a whole new world.

"To ease our mother's pain and suffering, no price is too dear." To sweeten the offer, Duwaik handed her a slip of paper, upon which was written a number of honors high enough to induce the herbalist to respond spontaneously.

"I accept."

"Wonderful." Duwaik clapped his hands. "And, Merrick, as we discussed, you shall have free reign over my collection. You may come any time to study to your heart's content."

"And I'll throw in free sailing lessons for the big guy," Han said, slapping Merrick heartily on his back.

● ● ●

"Remember—it's a machine. You're in control," Han said, reassuringly.

Merrick sat at the *Horizon's* helm, one massive hand delicately working the yacht's throttle. As he pushed the lever steadily forward, a signal shot through the computer-chip brain of the marine motor, instructing it to pull more electric power from its ancient batteries.

The craft shot forward, a salty spray from the warm Akkadian sea crashing over its bow.

"Easy, easy–" Han cautioned, placing his hand over Merrick's, gingerly easing the throttle down. "She's a beast all right, but we've got to watch the battery."

The sound of a sliding hatch heralded Miss Pak's arrival from belowdecks. Climbing up the companionway, the sleepy herbalist held up one arm to shield herself from the unfiltered daylight. Her other hand clutched a sturdy walking stick for support–Fe and its iron siblings casting a wispy web of invisible b-field lines in all directions, spinning out from the yacht and merging with the planet's much more powerful cocoon of magnetism.

"Did we hit something?" Miss Pak asked groggily, referencing the lurch that had awoken her.

"Just letting the big guy drive." Han laughed. "He's got a bit to learn, yet." The younger Duwaik's hand lingered, still resting atop Merrick's.

Miss Pak groaned against the morning sun, blinking. From one of the many pockets in her sand-colored vest, she extracted a folded leaf, a hunk of pale yellow rhizome within. She brought the root to her nose, inhaled deeply, and began to nibble on it.

"Are you feeling any better?" Merrick asked her.

"Mmhmm," she answered affirmatively.

The herbalist had not taken well to their voyage on the open, deepwater sea–the alien lurching of the electric yacht exacerbating a natural tendency toward motion sickness. Even worse, she'd briefly mixed up which folk remedies sailors used for the ailment. Some type of root, she knew, but was it ginger or tapioca? Confused, Miss Pak wasted the first few days of the journey in misery, erroneously eating through her supply of cassava before making the correction.

"Ginger's helping," she added.

"You *look* better," Merrick said, brightly.

High above the black yacht, a white-winged seabird slowly circled. Another joined in, and another–swooping around the cloudless sky. The three sailors milled about the deck, soaking up the warm sun, Merrick surrendering the helm at Han's gentle urging.

"Does this mean we're near land?" Miss Pak asked, pointing up to the birds.

"Hmm..." The acolyte squinted into the blinding sky, looking for distinguishing features and trying to match the flying species against his memories of the Zookeeper's records.

"In a manner of speaking, yes," Han answered, before Merrick could make his assessment. "We're pretty much *always* near land. There are a billion islands in the Akkadian sea, some of them no bigger than a rock. Some too small for even a bird to land on."

"A billion?" The herbalist asked, incredulously.

"Yes, indeed." Han grinned his dazzling smile, warming to the topic. "Back in the planetfall era, when the Exodus watched over us, the sky was full of satellites. They could look down at Akkadia and count the islands. Our Leaders counted over one billion islands."

"That can't possibly be true," Merrick said.

"It's what I heard, and not a sailor's story, either," Han replied, good naturedly. "I won't lie to you or lead you false. Old family knowledge, you know. The Duwaiks've got connections going back to the very beginning. Vaughn might even let you see–well, you'll see," he finished, mysteriously.

The other two held their tongues, unable to refute the sailor's claims.

"Not all of the islands are above water, either," the grinning Han continued. "Sometimes, they sit just below the waves, and the unwary sailor doesn't notice them until too late and they're up his ass. I've seen islands bigger than New Jacksonville–totally invisible–sitting just a fingertip beneath the sea, Xie strike me down. I've seen islands that were there one day and gone the next! Real islands too, dry land with plants and crabs and everything."

"Starshit!" Miss Pak laughed.

"It's true!" Han insisted. "It's the tides, yeah? Sea level can rise or fall by as much as the height of a tall man standing up. A low-lying island can easily plunge underwater at high tide. Count yourselves lucky you're aboard the *Horizon*. Rocks, sandbars, and other dangers lurk just under the waterline, but she's got a shallow enough draught that she can go almost anywhere."

"How can a good sailor avoid these dangers?" Merrick asked, wide-eyed as a schoolboy.

"It's not easy, but I'll show you," Han replied, waving his large companion over. "Here, hold this stanchion and lean..."

● ● ●

The b-moon hung high in the star-studded sky, shining down on the Akkadian sea like a weak spotlight. The *Horizon* bobbed and swayed, its motors silent.

"Why have we stopped?" Miss Pak asked, awakening from a light slumber. She lay on the starboard bench, wrapped in a cocoon of blankets.

"I think I see something," Merrick answered from behind the controls of the complicated craft. "Land. I'm almost sure."

The little herbalist rubbed her crusty eyes, stood up, and stretched. She balanced delicately on her toes, reaching her fingertips up toward the Milky Way.

"Where?" She asked, walking over to join her young friend at the helm.

"Starboard, just there." He pointed. "Look for where the sky meets the sea."

Though it was night, Miss Pak took only a moment to squint out what Merrick had spotted–land, large and mountainous, looming darkly in the distance.

"I see it," she said. "Where's Duwaik?"

"Still sleeping, I think."

"He's awake." Han announced himself, startling the others as he emerged from the companionway's gloom. "Why are we stopped?"

"Han! I see land–I think." Merrick pointed. "Just there."

Han walked toward the bow, tying back his hair as he moved, effortlessly keeping his balance despite the gentle chop. He leaned over the *Horizion's* railing and scanned the darkness.

"You found a big-ass island, all right," Duwaik said, when he returned. "It's not any land I recognize–and she's a good candidate for our target."

"Yeah?" Merrick asked, the excitement contagious.

Han laughed and nodded. "See if you can bring her in, gently," he instructed.

Merrick stayed at the yacht's controls, commanding the vessel to churn to life with the flick of a switch and the slow push of a lever. The thrumming propulsion system tapped power from the aging onboard batteries, and the *Horizon* smoothly glided forward through the dark water, its motors steadily churning up the surf until the yacht matched a fair swimming speed.

The island better resolved as the humans moved closer, several significant peaks poking above the large landmass. Facing the approaching *Horizon*, the island curved like the outer edge of a circle, meeting the sea in a wall of steep cliff face.

"Bring us in, here." Han pointed.

Obeying, Merrick guided the vessel away from the sharpest cliffs and bore south, making for an area where the land slid more gently into the sea. The *Horizon* churned slowly forward, inching its way toward the unknown shore.

"Woah!" Han announced. "Hold!"

Merrick released the throttle and hit a toggle. The low thrumming of the yacht's propulsion system lapsed into silence.

"Great job, Mer!" The shaggy sailor leaned over and gave both of Merrick's shoulders a congratulatory squeeze.

"Can't we get any closer?" Miss Pak asked, noting that they were still some distance from the gloomy cliffs.

"Bad idea, m'dear," Han explained, "even the *Horizon* could get herself ripped up on an unfamiliar landing like that. Best to keep her where the water is calm and deep. We can weigh anchor here and make for shore in the tender."

Merrick and the herbalist followed Duwaik's instructions, readying themselves for an expedition. They took turns changing belowdecks and gathering their belongings, which they loaded into a primitive dinghy–the *Horizon's* unpowered tender.

Han lowered the yacht's anchor, and the three explorers watched link after link of its alloy chain slip beneath the rippling water. By the time they put the smaller boat in the water, night was surrendering to the first hints of dawn. The hulking Merrick delicately boarded the tender first, sitting dead center to steady the rocking dinghy, the sure-footed Han following.

Miss Pak leaned on the *Horizon's* transom, handing down her staff, magnet-side first. She'd kept most of her stock and satchels aboard, electing to empty her bags and pockets in anticipation of the mysterious island ecosystem yet to be explored. Thus unencumbered, the eager herbalist dropped down into the dinghy, her balance assisted by Merrick's bulk.

"Is that...?" She asked, uncertainly, once the two men had taken up oars and oriented the small boat toward the island. "Stars! Is that a part of the Exodus?"

Viewed as a night-lit silhouette, the island's southern shore met the sea at a gentle break in its cliffside topography. With the first rays of dawn, however, the explorers could see an estate-sized slab of Sukuru-alloy hull, collapsed and settled between cliff and sea, eroded into an unnatural, sloping hillside.

Merrick rowed mightily, eager to get closer. Though Han couldn't match the younger man's raw strength, he made up for it with finesse, steering the tender toward the most-manageable looking part of the slope and correcting for Merrick's enthusiastically sloppy strokes.

"That's not the Exodus!" The acolyte panted.

"Are you sure?" Han asked, squinting into the spray.

Miss Pak surveyed the weathered alloy structure–it seemed to grow out of the rocky cliffside, dipping into the salty sea like tree roots tasting a freshwater pond.

"It's not the Exodus," Merrick repeated. "It can only be–"

"The Diomed," Han breathed.

The massive thing certainly looked Exodan to Miss Pak's eyes, like a much bigger cousin of the chunk she and Merrick had found in the desert, but she trusted the young researcher's knowledge in this arena more than her own.

"Severed siblings," she said, clutching a hand to her chest.

"Look up there," Han cried, letting an oar drop. "See the plants?"

Closer to the top of the artificial hill, the dead metal of the Diomedian hull gave way gradually to dirt and natural ground cover–nature taking root in the weathered pits where soil had clung and collected. Han pointed out grasses, low bushes, and even salt-stunted trees among the growth.

"If that's really the Diomed," he said excitedly, "then the papaver *has* to be here! All these plants must've grew from whatever spilled from the onboard stocks."

"Not necessarily," Merrick interjected. "I won't lie to you or lead you false, Han. Birds like to spread seeds from island to island. The Zookeeper knew this. It's possible that the plants here are the same as on NJ or the mainland."

Miss Pak nodded when Duwaik looked at her for confirmation.

"We'll find out soon enough," Han said, testily.

His mood soured even further as they rowed closer, the edge of the dinghy bumping right up against where the tarnished alloy slope dropped into the sea. There was no flat beach, no gentle landing.

The waves chopped against the exposed hull with sloppy irregularity. Disembarking threatened to be a risky, acrobatic proposition.

"Xie take me," Han cursed. "I might have to go back to the *Horizon* and pilot around for a better landing."

"We can climb up if you can get this tender thing to stay where it is," Miss Pak observed, studying the topography.

"Fine," Han said. "Let's try the anchor."

He unstowed the dinghy's Sukuru-alloy anchor and let it fall into the chop. Unlike the larger version aboard the yacht, the tender's crude anchor had been forged by an Akkadian smith from salvage. Its dense metal body quickly struck bottom, pulling the rope taut against the swell. Though the anchor kept the dinghy within a certain radius, it did little for the stability of its occupants.

"Let me try something," Merrick offered when they bumped up against a section of fallen hull. He leaned over the tender's side and grabbed at the alloy, but his thick fingers slid from the slick surface without finding purchase.

"Woah!"

The dinghy lurched sickeningly as Merrick overextended. Just in time, Han wrapped his arms around the bigger man's waist and pulled him down, sending them both sprawling backward onto the vessel's floor. They were all drenched in spray as the tender bounced and sloshed and bobbled until physics finally stilled it. Miss Pak found herself touching her abdomen, beyond grateful for ginger's powers.

Han let go of Merrick and pushed himself back up.

"Don't do that again!" He scolded, scooting onto a dripping thwart.

"I'm sorry." Merrick whined, still laying on the dingy's floor, half his head and body soaked in salt water.

"Let *me* try something," Miss Pak announced.

"No!" Han cried instinctively, his matted sideburns spraying brine as he whipped his head around.

Ignoring him, the wiry old woman turned and leaned on both knees, steadying herself against the boat's inner walls. She let go of the edge and, keeping her balance, reached over to unstow her walking stick.

"What are you doing?" Merrick hissed, afraid to move the boat.

"Shhhhh," she soothed, without looking at the men. At a lull in the waves, she carefully extended the staff, headpiece-first, toward the sloping metal hull.

Swarms of slumbering iron atoms within the Sukuru-alloy reacted to the presence of an incoming strontium ferrite magnet. Compared to Fe's towerblocks of perfectly oriented ions, those locked in the metallic lattice of the tarnished seaside structure lay in shambles, their crystalline cities falling to ruin. When the headpiece of Miss Pak's staff approached, however, a strong b-field moved with it, washing over the iron and nickel atoms in the wreck, bringing them electromagnetic enlightenment.

Proximity increased, magnetism intensified, and Fe's phalanx spun in centuries-unchanged synchronicity, their magnetic influence turning and converting the envious Diomedian atoms—cousins from their own Mother Star—until, unable to resist, trillions of ferromagnetic particles in the cliff found their own magnetic moments and were pulled forcefully toward the staff's headpiece, lugging the mountain behind them. Equal and opposite, the same force drew Fe's trapped strontium ferrite ring cliffward, towing the walking stick, Miss Pak, and the dinghy along for the ride.

Fe and its allies lost the tug-of-war, and the edge of the magnet leaped across one last tiny increment of empty air before loudly impacting the hull.

Clang!

"Got it!" Miss Pak cried out, grasping the shaft in both hands. "I can pull us in."

Between the hold of the anchor on the seabed and the improvised magnetic coupling, the dinghy's movement subsided.

"Hmmph," Han grunted, impressed.

He pulled a gleaming knife from somewhere inside his jacket, and making the most of their brief stillness, he pivoted and stabbed down into the side of the Diomedian wreckage. The tempered steel of the Earthmade blade easily bit into the salt-eroded alloy, penetrating through the first layer of hull material.

"What are you doing?" The herbalist asked, shocked, as the boat swayed from the force of the sudden violence.

"A permanent solution," Han said, withdrawing the knife.

He stabbed again, slightly above his original puncture mark before sheathing the blade and reaching down for the dinghy's painter. Deftly, he fed the thin rope through the breaches he'd made in the sloping metal hillside, creating an improvised hitch.

Though it wasn't graceful, the dinghy's occupants had managed a secure mooring. Miss Pak pulled back her stick, angling it to keep the hull from claiming Fe's magnet, giving it a sharp twist-and-tug to ensure the ferrite ring came away with the staff. The half-soaked Merrick made another attempt to grab onto the jutting hull, and this time he succeeded. With a great heave, he hoisted himself up and out of the boat, briefly stumbling forward before laying facedown on the damp metal slope.

Without Merrick, the dingy rode noticeably higher in the water. Miss Pak lept nimbly out of the boat and scampered up the wreckage, planning to grab onto her friend if she slipped.

Han, balancing expertly, stood astride the tender and handed up their gear. Finally, he followed his companions, and the three awkwardly scrambled up the slope, keeping their centers of gravity low until they were able to walk, more or less normally.

Weathered metal alloy quickly gave way to soil and natural rock as they worked their way higher. Evidence of the crash disappeared beneath the traveler's feet, buried by layers of sediment and time. When they reached the top of the hill, they could see the wreckage they'd just climbed off to one side, sloping down to the anchored tender and the Akkadian sea. On the other side, however, a natural landscape of stone, sand, and living things dominated.

The travelers couldn't see beyond the peaks to the north, which they'd spied in silhouette from aboard the *Horizon*, but looking to the east, they discovered that they stood perched on the rim of a vast, circular atoll.

Running from south to east, the ring dissolved into a necklace of fragmented islands–gleaming like jewels in the morning sun. In the other direction, however, the landmass grew more substantial, and the travelers scouted a manageable route downslope toward a pale beach along the atoll's inner ring.

Life thrived in the sheltered landscape, away from the cliffs and corroding metal. Healthy-looking clusters of trees with thin, flexible trunks ran along the boundary between the sandy beach and the green-painted mountain slope. Flowering vines and bright, broad-leaved ground plants added to the richness. Sharp birdcalls punctuated the ever present static hum of unseen insects.

"What the–stars!" Merrick cried out, suddenly.

He lost his balance, and, arms swinging, fell backward into a tangle of vines. Something flickered past.

"Mer!" Han yelled, his hand moving instinctively inside his jacket.

"I'm alright. Did you see that?"

"See what?"Before the question could be answered, a tiny creature, covered in a regalia of jewel-like feathers, flitted toward them and hovered in mid-air.

Miss Pak's breath caught in her throat.

"I see it," the herbalist whispered, not wishing to disturb something so delicate.

"I see it too." Duwaik stared wide-eyed at the bejeweled bird, his hand unsure whether or not to go for a weapon.

The tiny creature exerted itself and gained altitude, the air humming with the frequency of its wingbeats. It hovered, safely above the humans, losing itself among the terraces of green.

"A hummingbird." Merrick grunted, pushing himself to a sitting position.

"That's a good name for it," Han said, still somewhat awestruck.

"No. I've seen these before, in the Zookeeper's notes. She mentions them often but never brought any down from the sky with her. It's almost, *almost–*" Merrick hesitated, on the edge of blasphemy, "...like she was angry that she didn't have any. Angry at Earth. She loved the birds and wanted the birds. They're pollinators," he finished, nodding toward Miss Pak.

"It was so beautiful. So tiny..." She leaned down, helping Merrick to clear the vines. "Even the birds have severed siblings."

"Graham's grace!" Whooped Han. "This means we've found it! If there are humming birds here, there will be other species from the Diomed."

"Graham's grace," the awestruck acolyte echoed.

"If you need botanical confirmation," Miss Pak chimed in, holding a length of thin vine, "I can give it to you. I'm pretty sure *this* is something new."

"Stars," Merrick beamed, "two novel species already."

"Not just two, young man. Look–"

Though impatient to continue, Han allowed his learned companions a moment to document their findings. From inside an empty bag, the herbalist produced a rolled-up sheaf of papers, bound and wrapped in a flexible oilskin. The fine field notebook had been given to Miss Pak in exchange for curing the papermaker's glaucoma–temporarily, at least. Next to her hastily-copied diagram of *Papaver somniferum* she added an entry on the unknown vine and one on a sweet-smelling green seedpod. Merrick did something similar, sketching his own heartbreakingly crude rendering of the magnificent hummingbird.

As they hiked down toward the beach, the explorers stumbled upon discovery after discovery. Han did his best to keep hold of his patience, but he began snapping at his companions after calculating how little ground they'd covered since landing.

"Next new bird species you find, Merrick, we're eating."

"You're so bad."

"I'm serious. You know how many undiscovered fish I've probably roasted in my life?"

Miss Pak looked down curiously at her signature staff. She'd been idly bobbing the rod, softly up and down, letting the heavy headpiece dip and brush against the sandy ground. To her surprise, she felt a sudden pull, then—a gentle adhesion.

Thunk.

"Found something!" The herbalist cried out with childlike glee.

"Not another new leaf." Han growled back at her.

She was crouched down, brushing sand from where the tell-tale thunk of the discovery had sounded. Merrick bent to his knees to help, making efficient shovels with his large hands. Working together, they unearthed a rusted metal box the length of a forearm, sticky dirt clotting around its corroded corners.

Han stood above, supervising, annoyance turning to delight upon assessing the find. His bearded mouth cracked into a toothy grin, flashing like the sun coming out from behind a cloud.

"Ha! An untouched Exodan artifact," he said triumphantly.

"Diomedian," Merrick corrected, pushing himself back up. "Maybe a safe or personal locker. I can't believe how well preserved it is!"

"We need to get it back aboard the *Horizon*, but how?" Han mused.

"Stand back," Miss Pack said, brushing dirt off a badly corroded latch.

Using the staff for balance, she pulled herself to a standing position before hefting the pole with both hands, magnet-side-up. With one vigorous stab, she brought the staff's unadorned metal ferrule down against the flat face of the rusted locker.

Crack!

The sudden impact of the alloy, well forged and tempered in Kofi's furnace, broke the brittle metal bonds still holding the ancient Earthmade box closed. Miss Pak dropped to her knees, lifted the lid, and the two men quickly fell in behind her, greedily hovering as she revealed their treasure. Inside, the locker held a ruined mass that had once been a paper book, some brown fluid in a bottle with its label long since worn away, and a pair of dice made from a shiny, red, slightly translucent Earthmade plastic.

"I'll split the Exodan dice with someone," Merrick offered, jumping his mentor's chance to strike a bargain.

"Diomedian," Duwaik replied, teasingly. "I'll roll you for them."

"Roll me?"

"Yeah, here." Han scooped up the dice and shook them in one hand.

Despite their age, the tinted polymer treasures clattered pleasingly and crisply in his palm. He cast them back into the open box where they tumbled end-over-end, one landing face-up showing five white pips, the other six.

"Eleven!" Han cheered. "Now you."

Miss Pak extracted the bottle, deciding to leave the boys to their fun. Whatever the mystery fluid happened to be, it was almost certainly more interesting than plastic toys. At the very least, it would be a priceless conversation piece for the apothecary.

Merrick picked up the dice, placing them one at a time in his huge palm. The acolyte hesitated, then gave the polymer cubes a timid rattle before releasing them. They tumbled, and when their kinetic energy had bled away, one lay showing two white pips and the other a single, lonely white depression—dead center.

"Eleven beats three," Han said, almost in a sing-song, grabbing both dice and standing up.

Merrick lifted himself to a standing position, slowly and sadly. The box itself would have been worth something in New Jacksonville, but the explorers understood they couldn't carry all of the Diomedian alloy they'd come across.

Agreeing to remember the locker's location, the three walked for some distance in silence before Han reached forward and tugged on the acolyte's shirt.

"Hey, big guy—think fast," he said, tossing a single plastic cube toward Merrick, who caught it in his clumsy paws, doubly surprised.

He smiled bashfully, and Han treated him to a wink.

"Thanks," Merrick said, trying and failing not to blush. "Um, how much daylight do we have left? We should make a plan. Can't wander around forever, right?"

"We can go over there," Miss Pak called back to them. She stood on a rise, a dozen paces ahead of the men.

"Why?" Han asked.

"Because," she pointed to an arid patch of land some way off. "Flowers."

Tucked behind a rise parallel to the beach, they saw it—the afternoon light accentuating hundreds of fiery red blooms.

* * *

"Hey!" Topher called out, running along the beach, the wet sand sucking at his bare feet.

His friend David walked some paces away, parallel to the shore. The older man scratched at a short, bristly growth of salt-and-pepper beard. Topher noticed that David had donned a shoulder-bag and was using a driftwood branch as a walking stick.

"Are you going somewhere?" The younger, heavier man jogged to a stop, spraying damp sand at his companion's feet.

"You're soaking wet!"

"So?" Topher shrugged. "I was taking a swim."

"I'm gonna walk to the fields. You wanna come with?" David gestured with his stick. "Sure."

"Dry off, then we'll go. Put on a shirt."

"Nah, I'm just gonna drip dry." He spread his bare arms and sent drops of salt water flying—some muscle still lived beneath Topher's baby fat, and the sun had burned his naturally pale skin nut-brown.

"Drip dry." The even swarthier David shook a head covered in black curls, shot with strands of silver. "You live like an animal."

"I'll take that as a compliment. Animals have it going on, man," Topher said, bobbing his head good-naturedly as he fell in beside the strolling David.

"You fixed? I'm surprised you don't need a hit of brown before we go, Toph."

"Just took one before my swim," the younger man said, patting a buttoned pocket of his shorts. "You need?"

"I'm waiting." "Oh yeah. Your special spot."

"Sunset Rock, baby!" David replied in a sing-song, referring to a rise above the fields that promised an excellent view whenever the sun sank into the western sea.

They walked along the beach, leaving a trail of prints from David's simple woven shoes and Topher's bare feet. A large, orange and brown crab scuttled along the sand parallel to the men, leaving scraggly prints of its own.

"You wanna go get that crab?" Topher asked, pointing to the crustacean.

"Why would I want to go get that crab?"

"I don't know, man. Maybe we'll get hungry later."

"Hungry? There's like ten thousand bananas back at camp," David said, waving his free hand.

"Yeah, but they're all yellow."

"Yellow is the color bananas are supposed to be."

"Nah, yellow is like, rotten. Grosses me out," the shirtless Topher giggled.

"You're ridiculous. How do you live?"

"I like 'em green, man."

"You're unbelievable. Green bananas." David laughed. "If you're so hungry, *you* go get the crab."

"I don't wanna."

They turned toward a rough trail, leaving the crab and the beach behind. The barefooted Topher walked without concern on the path strewn with broken straw and sea-smoothed pebbles.

"But how good was that tuna the other night?" David inquired after an uncharacteristic lapse in the chatter.

"So fucking good–"

"So good!"

"I can't believe we caught that."

"We didn't catch it, we *found* it," David corrected. "If we'd walked by even a *little bit* earlier, we'd've missed it."

"Everything we need upon our backs, man," Topher said, smiling.

"Huh?"

"That was Graham, right there, looking out for us." He pointed to the sky.

"Oh, stop it with that Graham stuff."

"What?" Topher laughed "Why? You don't like Graham?"

"I don't like *you*!" David grinned and shoved Topher aside with one arm. "You don't really believe, anyway. You just say shit to make yourself feel superior and, and *pious*."

"Of course I believe in Graham. Who doesn't believe in Graham?"

"You're so full of starshit."

"Who do you think flew us all the way from the doomed Earth to *blessed* Akkadia? Huh? Look where we are, man! Promised land. Try to deny it. I dare you!""Yeah, yeah. *Maybe*," for emphasis, David opened his hand, raising it to head-height as he spoke, "I mean, maybe! I–I just don't get it, Toph. I'm not a Grahampion!"

"What? Pssht," Topher scoffed. "Come on. Everyone's a Grahampion."

"Not me. I am *not* in your weird little cult."

"It's not a cult, it's a philosophy!" Topher clapped his hands and rolled his eyes mischievously. "Oh yeah! I remember now, you're *Jewish*."

"I *am* Jewish! Why are you saying it like that? It's a thing! The Jews have been around for thousands of years."

"Really, thousands? Like pre-Exodan?"

"Yes, pre-Exodan. Are you kidding me? *Way* pre-Exodan."

As they talked, they moved deeper along the trail, David whacking foliage out of their path with his stick. Soon enough, the first red blush, indicative of poppy blossoms, could be seen spotting the brown hillside before them.

"So, like, what do Jews do? Where do they come from?" Topher asked, avoiding stepping on the trail's more jagged rocks.

"I don't really know," David said, thinking aloud. "We're God's chosen people, I know that much."

"How does someone become a Jew then? What if *I* wanted to be one?"

"You can't be one," David laughed.

"So what, like, people can't become Jewish?"

"*People* can, just not you."

"Please?" Topher asked in an exaggerated whine. "Let me be a Jew."

"No!"

"Come on. Why not?"

"Shut up. You don't really want it."

"Yes I do!"

"Really?" David turned to his friend.

"No," Topher laughed. "I don't. You're right."

"See! I told you—you're so full of starshit."

"No way, man. I'm a Grahampion—I wouldn't lie to you or lead you false."

"'I wouldn't lead you false,'" David mocked. "What a line. Is that what you told Treena?"

"Who?" Topher asked, cocking his head.

They'd arrived at the poppy field. Many of the pleasant, crimson flowers were in full bloom, and others were entering the stage where their bright petals fell away, leaving a valuable, bulbous seedpod behind.

"Your girl, you know—the one you used to run around with. The pretty one, who trusted you." David idly reached out and pulled a last clinging petal fragment from a nearly-mature seedpod.

"Tricia?"

"Yes! Did *Tricia* like it when you quoted Graham at her?"

Topher chuckled. "She actually did, man. We were in the Temple cohort together as kids. I still remember: Brother Brian was our teacher."

"I bet she thought, 'Oh, Topher is so *devout*.'" David adopted a high-pitched voice as he mock-quoted. "'He loves Graham like I love Graham. Topher's so *dreamy*.'"

"Shut up, man."

"It's unbelievable to me, the way you are with these women."

"Like you didn't say shit to get with Annie?" Topher wheedled his friend.

"That was different!""How is it different?"

"Because I loved Annie!" David cried, indignantly. "I *still* love Annie!""I loved Tricia," Topher countered.

"No you didn't.""I did!" The younger man insisted, smiling, "I loved all of them, man.""You're so full of shit. Do you even know how full of shit you are?"

"Sometimes.""Sometimes?" David raised one hand, questioningly. "Then why don't you *do* something about it, you know? Take steps to actually improve as a human being."

He'd continued past the flowers, making for the rise he called Sunset Rock. Topher followed behind like a puppy, still enjoying their banter.

"Pssht," the young man scoffed. "*You* take steps to improve yourself as a human being.""Take steps. Yeah–I am! I'm a dad now. Why do you think I gave up all of the–" David fell silent, halting in mid-stride.

"What?" Topher looked around, pulling up next to his uncharacteristically tongue-tied companion.

David was staring out at the sea. He pointed, numbly, but it wasn't necessary. Topher saw it too–a large, black yacht lay anchored in the waters below, shattering the tranquility of the evening with its alien, photovoltaic-covered hull.

"Starshit."

● ● ●

The two men made their way back to camp as quickly as they could, rushing along a descending path as the sun gradually disappeared. By the time David and Topher arrived, however, the yacht's occupants had already been busy poking around their beach.

"How many?" Miss Pak had wondered aloud when her party found unexpected signs of habitation on their way to investigate the flowers.

"Two," Merrick concluded, after some investigation.

The beachfront camp, which lay beneath the steep highlands to the west, dimmed beneath the darkening sky.

"Only two?" Duwaik noticed a massive pile of fruits, most of them yellow-brown bananas. "Are you sure?"

"I think so." The acolyte nodded. "There's only two bedrolls."

Miss Pak poked her stick at what looked like a cookfire. She thunked Fe's heavy magnet against a scorched black pot. The flat ferrite donut adhered, and she twisted it free.

"They're living here?" She asked.

"They're cooking *brown*," Han muttered. He stood near a table made from lashed-together scraps of driftwood. Under a banana leaf lay three thin bricks of a brownish substance, the consistency of low-moisture clay.

"What do you mean, 'brown'?" Merrick inquired.

Han lowered the banana leaf, not answering.

"What's brown?" The curious acolyte asked again, looking down at the herbalist.

"I've heard that name before," Miss Pak said, sniffing the inside of the pot. "Jokes from traders. 'Southern pirates like their brown better'n their shine' they say."

"You've got it wrong!" David's clear voice called out, startling the three intruders. "They eat the brown of the land and drink the shine of the sun," he quoted, "that's why Southern pirates are so easy to outrun. Or maybe it's 'pirates with brown in their lungs will make you brown in your britches.'"

"It makes you drunk?" Merrick's face contorted in pure puzzlement as the crew of the *Horizon* turned to meet the camp's owners.

Topher ran up beside David a moment later, huffing and puffing. "What in alla' Xie's sins are you doin' in our camp?" He asked between breaths.

"Stay back!" Han growled from behind the others, wary of the large addict coming toward them. "I mean it!"

Topher and David flinched. Both men badly needed a fresh hit of brown to calm their nerves. Yet, among the five humans on the beach, the younger Duwaik seemed the most agitated.

"I'm an herbalist," Miss Pak said, filling the space between parties. "What are those?" Attempting to diffuse some tension, the curious explorer casually pointed to some oblong violet-colored fruits in the sand near the banana pile.

"Purpleberries," Topher answered brightly.

"Safou," David corrected.

"I call 'em purpleberries."

"You're an idiot. You know that?" David shook his head at his friend. "You're gonna do this now? While we've got intruders?"

"*I'm* the idiot? I heard you talking about brown britches."

"Just shut up," David begged. "Please."

"Why are you here?" Topher asked the intruders, his tone bright and helpful.

"We've all been given a mission," Merrick began.

"To find a flower. *Papaver somniferum*," Miss Pak finished. "Do you know it?"

"The poppies?" David squinted, confused.

"Poppies! Who are you working for?" Han barked at him.

Topher's smile dissolved. "Woah, man."

"Han, what's wrong?" Merrick asked, concerned, walking up to Duwaik and letting his hands come down to rest on the sailor's shoulders.

"Just startled," his surly companion said, smiling thinly.

"This is *good* news," Merrick gave him a squeeze. "If these men are growing papavers, they can help us. They can help your mother!"

"My mother?" Han asked, tense with irritation, momentarily forgetting the ruse he and Vaughn had written to smooth things over with the help.

The towering Merrick let go of the sailor and took a step back. The young acolyte's eyes were wide, his expression hurt. Miss Pak and the addicts leaned in, fascinated.

"My mother–" Han repeated, more evenly, "I mean to say–my mother will be thrilled."

It was too late. He'd been too rash. He could tell by the look in his hirelings' eyes that his careless words had cost him their trust.

"Mr. Duwaik?" The herbalist stared up at him, one hand on her walking stick.

"Duwaik?!" David exclaimed, his face draining of color.

"What's going on?" Topher whispered to his friend.

"If your mother isn't sick," Merrick said, slowly, "then why–"

"The Duwaiks wanted the papaver to make this, *brown*...stuff," Miss Pak said, reaching the conclusion faster than her friend and pointing Fe's headpiece at the drug paraphernalia.

"Don't touch the brown."

"Don't touch it." The addicts spoke in chorus.

Merrick looked between the camp's owners and Duwaik, unsure of how to process what he was feeling.

"She's mistaken. They're crazy," Han said. "Will you let me explain? Please, Merrick?" He turned his pale eyes to meet the young man's, imploring. "Please?"

Slowly, the acolyte nodded his curly head.

"Listen, Mer–we live in New Jacksonville, right? Now, imagine this is Akkadia," Han explained, picking up a large, round stone and hefting it in one calloused hand. "Pretend that it's our whole, entire, Graham-promised world and everyone on it, yeah?"

The young acolyte slowly gave another nod.

Duwaik raised his other hand, pointing one calloused finger into the darkness of the night. "Now, look at the b-moon."

Merrick looked.

Swiftly, Han bashed the heavy stone against the back of Merrick's head.

Miss Pak gasped.

The acolyte fell forward, and Han hammered again as Merrick lay limp in the sand, his hair visibly soaking with dark blood. Whimpering, Merrick's aged friend dropped her staff and ran forward, throwing herself onto his enormous body.

"Now, then..." Han said, catching his breath and dropping the stone. Ignoring Miss Pak completely, he brushed himself off and turned toward David and To-pher.

"Let's have a conversation, like gentlemen." He glared at them. "I find myself particularly interested in the process you use to manufacture brown from your flowers."

"Why'd you hit him?" Topher asked, aghast.

"What's wrong with you, man?" David challenged.

Over on the shadowy sand, Miss Pak turned Merrick's head to one side, trying to clear his airway. Between the night's gloom and her own shaking hands, she could do little for him.

"Yeah, what *is* wrong with you?" Topher puffed out his chest.

"I'll tell you what," David ordered, "you take your fancy boat and get the *fuck* off our island!"

"Enough–" Han shook his head in frustration. "You are going to tell me how you cook brown, and you're going to do it right now."

"No fucking way!"

"Perhaps this will convince you." From inside his jacket, Duwaik extracted a matte-black handgun of Earth manufacture and pointed it at the two men before him.

"Woah!" David cried, twisting, instinctively lifting his arms out in front of him.

"What is that thing?" Topher asked, his sunbleached head cocked to one side.

"It does this–" Han pulled the weapon's trigger, summoning a flash and an ear-splitting bang.

David and Miss Pak screamed. A dozen birds flew noisily from the starlit jungle. A round hole appeared in the center of Topher's broad forehead. He wore an expression of dazed bemusement for a moment before collapsing to the sand in a heap.

"Gaa!" Topher's friend made to move toward the body, but a second thunder-clap from Han's pistol ejected the remaining birds from the canopy and convinced David to remain fixed to where he stood.

"You fuck!" David screamed at Duwaik.

"You can teach me to cook brown with both your kneecaps intact or just one." Han shrugged, still pointing the gun.

"Fuck!" David put his hands to the side of his head. "Alright! Let me think."

"Quickly now."

"Oh, God."

"Kneecaps!"

"Poppies!" He managed, at last. "You've seen the poppies, right?"

Han nodded, moving the pistol's barrel up and down rather than employing his neck.

"The pods are full of gum," the addict stammered, "white and sticky. Cut 'em open, the gum turns black. Collect enough, then we can roll it into a ball." David pointed to a driftwood table. Several of the aforementioned sticky balls rested in an unfired clay bowl. "Then," he finished with a sigh, "you boil it. With this stuff."

Slowly, and with Han's implicit permission, David traveled several steps and bent down to find a basket of a chalky, white material. He pulled up a handful and let it slip through his fingers.

"You can find it around the reefs," he said, simply.

"Then what?" Han demanded.

"We wait for it to separate. Light stuff floats to the top. Skim it off with a leaf."

"And the skim–that's the brown?"

"No," David said, through gritted teeth, "there's one more step. You have to boil it again with uh, with…"

"With what?" Duwaik bellowed.

"Starshit! It's not a secret, it's just gross." He looked apologetically at Miss Pak, who still lay crouched by Merrick's prone form–she had things to worry about other than David's modesty.

Han waved his gun.

"With piss, alright? We boil it with our own piss, which we let sit for a few days. When it smells really bad we know it's perfect. Are you happy, you murdering fuck?"

"Then what?"

"Then what? Then nothing. It turns brown. *Brown* brown. Dry it in the sun. Smoke it. Repeat."

Han looked at David for a moment but said nothing. Then, apparently satisfied with the instructions, he leveled his weapon and fired it twice–both shots finding their mark. As the echo of gunfire faded, David's body slumped quietly into the sand, and the herbalist let out a low moan, drawing Han's attention.

"I trust you overheard the lesson, Miss Pak?" He asked, turning to point the gun in her direction.

She nodded once, daring to stare the traitor in his face.

"If these two idiots could manage it, you should have no trouble manufacturing brown. Think you can do it?" He asked, flashing his signature grin. "Because if you can't, then I'm afraid you're no use to me."

"I can do it." She spoke grimly, not trusting herself to say more.

"Show me, then." Han leveled the gun at her and gave it a shake. "Leave him."

Softly, she patted Merrick's broken head, jabbed her walking stick into the ground, and pulled herself up to a standing position, letting a smear of the acolyte's blood soak from her hand into the wood of the staff.

At the urging of Duwaik and his fancy weapon, the herbalist set to work at the beachfront lab. She followed her memory of David's terrified instructions as best she could, combining them with her own insight and experience. It helped enormously that the dead men's camp contained everything she would need, already conveniently gathered.

After starting the sticky gum balls boiling, Miss Pak added lime from the basket. Accustomed to working with the chalky material, the herbalist found its alkaline properties helpful in the processing of many botanical derivatives, including, apparently, papaver gum.

She did not enjoy searching the beach for a urine source at gunpoint, but Miss Pak eventually succeeded, finding a jug she was able to drag, one-handed, through the sand. David had been telling the truth about the smell.

With her materials in place, the herbalist performed the second boil, chemically transforming the raw opium into morphine. She knew how to prepare concentrates with patience and diligence, and she let herself get lost in the meditative work.

As the sun rose, she used a stick to scrape the finished brown from the insides of a scavenged alloy pot. The Akkadian sun and its welcome warmth arrived just in time to aid Miss Pak with the drying process. She spread the damp brown in a thin layer on a flat, dark rock, which she then positioned to better catch the morning photons.

"Now what?" Miss Pak asked, trying to keep her tone even.

"It's not finished. Correct? You're drying it, now?"

"Yes."

"Then we wait," Han said simply.

He held the heavy pistol, its barrel never vectoring far from her. Through the morning, he switched the weapon between his hands as he grew uncomfortable. Neither of the pair had slept in some time.

"After it's dry–" Miss Pak started to ask.

"You'll test it," Duwaik answered, smiling without showing his teeth.

There was a silence. Miss Pak's eyes darted to the black handgun.

"Brute," was all she could get out.

"Smoke it or else."

"Shame on you."

Han wiggled the gun.

"*You* smoke it!" Miss Pak spat, in a sudden rage.

"Do you think I'm stupid?" He roared, lowering the pistol and firing it twice in quick succession, both shots hitting the sand and spraying Miss Pak with grains of highly kinetic feldspar.

Ears ringing, Miss Pak glared at Duwaik, her dark eyes burning into his pale ones. She said nothing, but nodded once. At Han's urging, she walked into the sun and selected a small, dryish piece of the claylike drug.

"Here," Han called out, digging a homemade pipe from inside Topher's shorts pocket.

Miss Pak noticed that the younger Duwaik had grown badly sunburned on their voyage, and, crouched over the corpse, he looked like a devil. Nevertheless, the little herbalist took the pipe, packed it with a chunk of brown, and claimed a brand from the still-smoldering cookfire to light it.

She inhaled briefly and sputtered, tasting something bitter and feeling a wave of nausea coming over her.

"Again!" Dwuaik commanded.

Glaring at him, the old woman put the pipe to her mouth a second time, taking a deep drag of the narcotic.

The world grew warmer and fuzzier. Miss Pak's limbs felt heavy. The nausea was there, but she didn't care about it at the moment. The morning-vibrations of mate-thirsty insects compressed the air in expanding sonic ripples. Her magnet's mighty b-field surrounded them, its million invisible rays penetrating everything.

The planet's energy field radiated out as well, on a far grander scale. On a meat scale, her heart was beating, beating...beating. Her story–our story–the whole thing was actually kind of funny, if you thought about it right...

She giggled, then lurched over and fell in the sand, convulsing.

As she shook, she dropped the pipe and scattered its contents. Cursing, the sailor trotted over to Miss Pak, her body rolling and rocking–her right hand clutching at her dusty staff. He looked down at the old woman in puzzlement for a moment before she opened her eyes and sprang at him, twisting her torso and swinging at his face with her heavy stick.

It connected, but only weakly, spraying Han's sandy left sideburn with grains from the beach. He roared, more in annoyance than pain, and swung with his gun-arm to deflect the pole, clanging the pistol against its headpiece.

Thunk!

Despite its synthetic-fiber exterior, the handgun possessed a barrel made of common, ferromagnetic steel. As Fe's impaled magnet vectored toward the ground, the tip of Duwaik's gun jerked along with it for an instant. The b-field forced the gunbarrel less than a finger's width out of true, but still, the work of Fe and its kin proved enough to save the herbalist's life.

Han Duwaik's muscle-memory, unprepared for the bizarre interference of a strontium ferrite magnet, alerted his trigger finger to execute a practiced double-tap that fired the pistol uselessly into the sand.

Before he could twist the gun back to take better aim, Han was rocked forward, impacted by something hauling a frightening load of inertia. Where the weak magnetic grapple had failed, the force of Merrick's flying tackle succeeded–Han's pistol flew from his hand as he was driven face-first into the ground. The enraged acolyte, bleary-eyed and with a bleeding head, held Han under the sand, using his superior strength and bulk to keep the writhing Duwaik from twisting away.

Merrick held on, his muscles burning, gravity his ally. Don't black out–don't black out–

Merrick resisted. Eventually, Han stopped resisting.

When Merrick's vision finally cleared, he saw no one else stirring, he felt no breathing beneath him, and he knew it was safe to let go. The injured acolyte crawled over to kneel by Miss Pak, who lay face up in the sand with her eyes closed. He noted with relief that she was breathing evenly–a long, loose smile upon her face. Adrenaline broke down inside Merrick's blood, and his swollen brain decided to succumb to a growing blackness that promised another blissful bout of unconsciousness.

* * *

Seabirds wheeled overhead as the morning gradually gave way to afternoon. Some of the more enterprising fliers noticed a quintet of human bodies laying on the beach below. The flock gave these great apes and their lightly-smoking camp a wide berth. The island and its creatures hadn't yet forgotten the terrible thunder of the gunshots.

Still, inherent hunger and curiosity eroded short-term memory as the Akkadian sun moved steadily across the sky, and one bird, followed by a second, went in for an exploratory landing. Their webbed feet disturbed the sand as they hit the beach, and they risked a few tentative steps, but none of the large mammals stirred. Taking this as a good sign, several more birds descended. The boldest of these decided to investigate one of the inert apes with their beaks. It pecked at Topher's unresisting remains, excitement growing in the watching flock.

Someone was trying to hold Miss Pak's hand. It hurt–she didn't like it. Stop pinching my skin, crab, she thought. Then, she felt a sharp, stabbing pain near the center of her forehead. Not a crab. A squawk! The herbalist's eyes shot open, and she lunged instinctively–her unconscious mind triggering an encore of her last, desperate attack against Duwaik.

Gripping the staff with one gnarled hand, she swung it toward her aggressor, even more feebly than she had the first time. The slow attack gave the startled bird plenty of warning, and it flapped itself to safety long before the stick would have made contact. Instead, Miss Pak's strike did nothing more than spray Merrick's sunburnt face with sand.

The wounded acolyte grunted and rolled over–the unexpected shifting of his tectonic bulk startling away the remaining avian intruders. The herbalist looked around, trying to get her heartrate under control and unscramble her head.

"Merrick," she managed to say at last, gasping through a dry mouth.

"Hrrmm," he moaned.

"We're alive," she said with mild wonder, raising herself to a sitting position. "Are you alive?"

"MmmMmm."

"Oh, Merrick. You have to get up.""No thank you," he said thickly, his head pounding. "I'm going... to stay down here."

"I can't lift you." She kicked some sand at him, feeling too dizzy to contemplate bending down. "Get up!"

"Goodbye. To your future triumph..."

"If I go, you'll be food for the birds. Get! Up!"

Noticing Merrick's eyes closing, she kicked gouts of sand in his direction until the young acolyte's puffy face was buried by the onslaught. He coughed and sputtered, finally pushing himself partway off the ground to clear his airways.

"You can do it," Miss Pak gently urged, leaning her own unsteady weight on her staff.

"Water," he choked out.

"Soon," she said, unsure of where to find any. "Don't worry. At least two people lived here–there will be a spring nearby."

Merrick shook his curly hair side-to-side to clear it of sand. "Aaag!" He bellowed, his head still in agony. "Ow. That was a mistake."

"Keep your head still, son. Take a walk with me, away from all this–" She gestured at the carnage of the beach. "We can find something growing on this island that will help you."

Slowly, the unsteady, mismatched pair hobbled from the beach and onto the most well-trodden of the paths leading away from the camp. Soon, they found a small, swiftly moving rivulet of fresh water streaming down a slick, black rock. There, they slaked their thirst, and Miss Pak irrigated Merrick's head wound as much as his pain would allow her.

She searched for useful plants as they walked, frustrated by her incomplete knowledge in the face of such a bounty of novel species—certain that the shoots, flowers, and leaves she passed hid their own tantalizing secrets.

In the end, however, it was the *Papaver somniferum* that brought the young man some relief. Following David and Topher's trail, the pair of survivors found themselves in the poppy fields at last. The crimson flowers basked and fluttered, beautiful in an easy, careless sort of way, and even in their unbalanced, bobble-headed seedpod form, they appeared stark and striking. Remembering David's final instructions, Miss Pak plucked a spherical pod from its stalk and sliced through its fibrous, vegetable hull. Sure enough, a milky white sap oozed from the pierced papaver.

A lifetime of experience and intuition told her that a topical application of the unprocessed precursor was unlikely to be harmful to someone of the acolyte's size. After all, the herbalist had unwillingly gained firsthand experience with the papaver's concentrate. She leaned on her staff and instructed Merrick on how to prepare a rudimentary poultice, telling him to rupture the pods and to spread the resulting discharge like ointment on his injured head.

"Why do I have to do it?" He whined, trepidatiously ripping apart a poppy with his thick fingers.

"You need the field experience."

"Am I doing it right?"

"Don't be shy with the stuff. You can apply it much less painfully than I can."

"Can you at least finish it?"

"Your head's all the way up there. I'm all the way down here," Miss Pak replied, with a half-laugh, half-cough. "We've all been given a mission, and you're almost done. Does it still hurt?"

Merrick nodded sadly.

"Final step then," she said with a firm nod of her chin. "Lick your fingers."

The wounded man hesitated. Then slowly, with childlike care, he licked the sticky, opium sap from his fingers, one by one. His face twisted from the taste, but, by the time he'd finished the last little finger, Merrick's hunched shoulders had relaxed.

"I think it's working," he said softly.

"It's a useful plant," the herbalist agreed. "A Xie-damned creation, but, but..."

"It's good," Merrick finished.

They turned from the flowers and walked the short distance to what turned out to be Sunset Rock, though the afternoon was still too young for the landmark to live up to its name. They sat. Miss Pak held her walking staff loosely in one hand, bottom ferrule planted in the sand before her, magnet-side up. Fe's strontium ferrite ring added its own tiny b-field to the planet's infinitely complicated lines of magnetic force, vectoring invisibly and irresistibly throughout everything.

Miss Pak suddenly laughed as they stared out to sea.

"We're stranded on an island full of treasure," she explained, after noting her friend's concerned look. "The Diomed, for Graham's sake. A pirate's fortune in brown, and, other things..." The herbalist trailed off, thinking of the Earthmade handgun they'd left lying in the sand.

"We're not *stranded*. I don't think." Merrick bit his lip. "Han taught me enough. I can bring us home."

"Oh, Merrick." Miss Pak looked up at her large friend, her crinkled smile radiating genuine joy. "That's wonderful. But it complicates things, doesn't it?"

"Are you going to bring some back to your island?" Merrick asked, the poppy still on his mind. "Start taking away people's pain?"

"The papaver?" Miss Pak thought for a moment. She shrugged and resorted to a platitude. "We alone control our destiny.""Hmph. I'm not so sure about that," Merrick replied, his voice stronger than before. "I'm really not. Everything that happened back there–did you ever feel in control?"

She waved the question away. "We're still here, son. We still have choices to make."

"It's incredible here." The acolyte spoke softly, taking in the vista of landmass and sea. "Not just the papaver, but all this life. So much potential fell with the Diomed. And the technology from our severed siblings–"

"We could change everything," Miss Pak agreed.

"But is that a good thing?"

"You're a smart boy. I won't do your thinking for you, but I'll ask you," she paused, "what's the most important thing we need to take with us when we leave this place?"

Merrick thought for some time. They sat, in no hurry to disturb the island's peace.

"A story."

Jolted out of her own thoughts, Miss Pak took a moment to respond. "A story. Yes. You'll have to burn that lovely drawing you made of the hummingbird."

Merrick smiled sadly. "Dump our treasures overboard?"

The herbalist gave a single nod.

"You're really at peace with this?" Merrick double-checked, "taking *nothing*?"

"Everything we need upon our backs.""Everything we need upon our backs," he echoed, wrapping the small herbalist in a one-armed hug.

In the end, theirs turned out to be a wise decision. Merrick managed to pilot the yacht without sails, albeit inexpertly and with a mighty drain on its battery bank. When he brought the *Horizon* into a well-traveled waterway, the survivors begged directions to New Jacksonville and set a course for home. The storms of the Akkadian sea, however, proved nothing compared to the gale-force fury the travelers had to weather from Vaughn Duwaik upon their return.

Not only had Miss Pak and Merrick patently failed in their mission to collect a sample of *Papaver somniferum*, they'd returned without Duwaik's brother. The herbalist met the patrician's rage with practiced bedside manner, ignoring his abuse and calmly feeding him their story—alone in distant and poorly-charted seas, the *Horizon* had met with a terrible storm. A surging swell saw the younger Duwaik tossed overboard, and Merrick had badly injured his head at the same time. Unable to locate Han, the pair abandoned their mission and limped back into port.

Mr. Duwaik and his men searched the travelers, their belongings, and scoured the *Horizon* stem to stern, looking for evidence to corroborate or contradict the story. Even when he separated the herbalist and the acolyte and subjected them to lengthy interrogations, he uncovered nothing concretely suspicious. It was only begrudgingly, and with a fair amount of outside pressure from Nicky, the city's graham, that Duwaik released the survivors.

They received no pay and no thanks, but they were grateful to be alive. Even if Duwak had offered to let Miss Pak examine his records of exotic plant species, the old herbalist would have declined—no longer excited by knowledge of things her hands couldn't touch.

Merrick similarly had shed his interest in the patrician's vast, likely dangerous, collection. The only Exodan artifact either of the survivors walked away with was the Druke Inc. disk magnet that was already Miss Pak's by rights. She would carry the bloodstained staff that had once been Kofi's wife's dressrod for the rest of her life, though it would not always boast Fe's distinctive magnetic headpiece. For on her very next adventure with Merrick...

Chapter 10: The Rust (ii)

"No higher! I'm just gonna knock some down." The herbalist called from within the treetop, clutching her staff in one half-frozen hand, a bark-covered branch in the other.

She held on tightly, squeezing a thick limb between both legs. She swung out the heavy headpiece, aiming for a cluster of healthy-looking seeds that still clung tightly to their parent tree. Magnet and ferrule impacted the cluster with a kinetic wap, sending the tree nuts scattering to the snow below.

Lodged on the staff's alloy endcap, Fe's strontium ferrite ring radiated its magnetic field as strongly as always, though it was being used as a bludgeon, and there was nothing ferromagnetic around in the hilly, snow-covered landscape to appreciate its powers.

"Ow!" Merrick cried from below as the seedpods fell. "The nuts are spikey! Is that normal?"

"Yes! Can you grab some samples?""They rolled down the hill, but yes, the snow caught a bunch. You should come down now."

Miss Pak grunted in affirmation and began to twist her diminutive body, employing ancient instincts and physiology to navigate the treetop. The first steps of her descent proceeded smoothly, but then–

Crack!

The old woman's feet went out from under her. For an instant, she slid–then, a branch snapped, breaking her fall and giving her time to scramble for purchase.

"Careful!" Merrick called up, not especially helpfully.

"I'm ok." She came to a stop, assessing her position. She could hop down the rest of the way, but– "My stick's stuck!"

Indeed, the headpiece of the staff had wedged itself in a wooden-V between two ropy branches of the towering tree. Miss Pak tugged, to no avail.

"Do you need to leave it?" Merrick asked.

"No, I can wiggle it free."

The herbalist steadied herself and, finding purchase against the trunk, shifted the staff side-to-side. After a moment, the tree's forked branches pried the strontium ferrite magnet off the ferrule, and the staff came loose. Miss Pak's triumph evaporated as she noticed the bare iron endcap.

"Starshit!" She cursed. "Merrick, the magnet! Catch it."

Fe's ring, however, eluded the acolyte and dropped into the snow, rolling on its side down a steep embankment toward a thicket below.

Miss Pak hastily scrambled the rest of the way down the tree.

"Where is it?" She asked, breathing heavily. "Which way did it roll?"

Merrick pointed toward the dropoff. "I can go look for it," he said, dubiously. The stingy, late-season daylight was already starting to wane.

Though Fe and the magnet lay only a few paces down the hill, wetted from the snow and nestled in a cluster of roots, the pair of humans had no way of knowing where. They made the practical decision to call off their search for the artifact and return to warmth before nightfall. The strontium ferrite disk spent the night abandoned on the hillside, as well as the next, and the next, and the next.

In the skies above the unpeopled highlands, clouds gathered and snow fell. Fat, wet flakes covered the bare ground and piled up atop the harder, icy remains of the last snowfall. The former headpiece of Miss Pak's staff was soon buried by crystals of frozen water.

Little sunlight penetrated as the next day dawned, and under the gloom, a stiff crust formed on the snow. A few light flakes fell the next night, and a brief appearance by the Akkadian sun the following morning induced a small melt–packing the snowmass even more densely. Another day brought gelid mountain winds and more flakes fluttering from the clouds above.

The layered mass of frozen water—an icy empire of polar molecules, crystallized in their octillions—did not fully melt again for the remainder of the cold season. Fe found itself entombed. Nevertheless, the iron atom and all its ionized comrades continued gamely to spin in synchronicity, combining quantum effects into a harmonized magnetic field. This miracle of Earth technology sat wasted, the Druke magnet's radiating b-field doing nothing but inducing a subtle anxiety in a passing bird or two. It was not until a series of warm days clustered together at the dawn of the following spring that the snow's hold loosened, at last exposing the black disk to the open air.

In the warm season, the Akkadian sun would make its way grandly across the sky, bathing the grateful planet's ecosphere in its searing radiation, and each night, the Milky Way would shine, and the a-moon would wizz madly across the sky until the impatient sun once again broke free from the horizon. B-months passed, and life went on as normal on the hillside—a vast bio-pyramid of complex lifeforms playing out their own dramas on a fractal of shrinking scales.

Again, Akkadia-2 reached the inevitable point in its orbit where one pole pointed away from its namesake star, shrouding the other in winter. Snow fell, and the magnet grew cold and once more became entombed in ice, but then, as the planet continued its well-worn cycle, winter receded. Season after season, b-month after b-month, Fe's chunk of abandoned technology sat irrelevant and inert in a forest full of life. The small, woody growths that stood above the artifact slowly swelled and stretched during this time. Occasionally, an animal would dip its mouth down to strip some greenery from the plant, but nothing large burrowed far enough down to notice the strange, black disk.

Had Fe's magnetic ring been a mundane piece of shale of similar shape and dimension, it may have made a superlative lair for an enterprising spider, or perhaps it would have been selected by a nesting bird for its curious shape. Many creatures sensitive to the spectrum, however, were unsettled by its unnatural b-field lines. Even back in Cheshire, rodents living in the *Fleischerbeile's* overgrown engine had unconsciously avoided its central magneto.

Alien days passed. An alien sun beat down. Wind blew. Rain showered the land, and more snow fell. Akkadia-2 revolved, and seasons turned to years. None of the other artifacts that had housed the atom Fe could have survived long under these conditions. Quishda's heaven metal dagger would have rusted away to nothing within a handful of human lifetimes, and even George Stills' good-luck steel propeller cone, if left exposed to the elements, would have quickly succumbed to the ravages of time. However, save for the addition of some small green patches of a moss not overly picky about local b-fields, the magnet on the mountainside stayed as black and corrosion-free as ever. The irons within had been oxidized during the recycling process on the west coast of England, after all, and what is rust cannot rust.

● ● ●

Fe continued to spin, repeating the quantum choreography impressed upon it long ago, as larger orbits passed outside. Though the planet was blanketed with Earth life, its surface now scattered with humans and their artifacts, Akkadia-2 remained an alien world with an alien climate.

A terribly dry season parched the landscape one year, followed by nearly a whole b-month of strong, hot winds buffeting the highlands, blowing away topsoil and killing the woody plant that sheltered the lost magnet. A year and a half later, moisture returned to the land in catastrophic abundance. Heavy rainfall on the highlands saturated the soil, still dusty from the drought, turning it to mud. Fe's magnet, along with much of the hillside it sat on, slumped downward, surrendering to gravity in a moment of abandon before slowing to a halt–the mudslide arrested by its own growing friction. Later, during more temperate times, the slide would harden into a minor topographic feature, plants and animals adjusting and slowly reasserting themselves.

The magnet stayed mostly unburied during this period, and it spent the summer absorbing solar radiation up on the dirty hillock, more exposed than before the mudslides. Another bout of intense precipitation struck the highlands in the winter, burying the hills and trees in heavy snowdrifts. Aside from its invisible b-field, the only trace of the ferrite disk shrank to a tiny bump in the snowmass, directly above where the artifact lay buried.

Like a temporary glacier, a mountain of frozen powder reigned over the interior of the continent for a season, but the mass grew heavier and denser as it absorbed solar photons into its irregular, air-packed crystals, liquifying entirely where it touched the thawing ground. As the Akkadian sun pressed its assault, small burrowing creatures drowned in their dens, and rivulets of meltwater coursed down the mountain like sweat from the face of a fighter, ready to deliver a knockout blow.

Inevitably, the planet turned toward its star, and the snowmass lost its fight with thermodynamics. Streams swole to rivers, and a particularly long stretch of daytime sunshine sent meltwater cascading from the highlands to the lows–temporary watercourses seeking the path of least resistance. Gravity asserted itself, eager to join the fray.

The hillside hosting Fe sloped directly between up and down. The magnet sat precisely in the path of a finger of water, stretching in the general direction of gravity's beckoning pull. Bowed by surface tension, the crusading column of water molecules marched relentlessly over dirt, leaf litter, and the odd snowpatch hiding in shade. The already-damp ground drank what it could, and the finger pointed further, directing the strong arm and fist of the coming flood.

Soon, droplets beaded on the surface of Fe's sintered magnet. The trickle reached around the chipped black ring, pincering together into a new stream on the other side. The insidious meltwater even crept under the soil to wet the ring's interior courtyard from beneath. More icy water followed gravity's inevitable course, raising the floodline up the squat black tower's side until the magnetic circle was fully submerged.

A solid chunk of ferrite cannot float in fresh water, and for a few moments, Fe's magnet clung to the bottom of the river of melt, unmotivated by buoyancy. Nevertheless, by its sheer mass, the rising wall of icy water shifted the artifact–skipping it along the terrain, the momentum of the tide irresistible.

Alongside rocks, pinecones, dying insects, and many, many tons of soil, the flash flood carried Fe's ring downstream and ever further downhill. Somehow in the tumult, a small pellet of corroded iron that happened past grabbed onto a flat side of the magnet, held and guided by the strontium ferrite's engineered b-field.

The two bits of matter rode together in the freezing, rioting water as it surged down into a valley, splashing up the opposing hillside before sloshing back downhill, finding ever lower and lower ground. Sticks and soil bounced and jostled the magnet as it tumbled with the flow, but its tight structure resisted damage.

At a certain point in the final a-month of the flood, Fe's disk found itself surfing along at about the same speed a practiced human could throw it, but a large boulder of pink-tinged quartz happened to jut directly in its path.

Surging water muffled the crack as the ferrite mass, once forced into a solid disk by Druke's powerful press, came undone. The magnet, loaded with kinetic energy, had struck the unyielding silicate mineral at speed, the sudden force putting a devastating strain on the brittle ring and stressing a microscopic imperfection in the tightly-pressed pathways of particles.

Fe's disk split into three pieces—two rough halves and a much smaller, keystone-like shard. Gravity wickedly diverted Fe and the larger half to the north side of the boulder. The other half of the Earthmade magnet, still clutching the stowaway iron pellet in its electromagnetic grip, was swept away to the south. The smallest piece eddied for a moment and took the same course as the largest, following hopelessly far behind Fe and its solar sibling atoms.

The flood splashed and rolled, filling another valley, Fe's fragment and other debris tumbling in its swift embrace. Borders of the wooded highlands came and went. Topographically robbed of a steep slope and the abundance of acceleration that came with it, the icy river slowed and spread out, emerging at last on a grassy plateau under the Sun's tired rays.

By the time the flood saturated the ground and burbled over the cliff's face, Fe's weighty chunk of magnet could no longer be forced along. It sank to the grassy bottom, the weakening stream flowing past and cascading down the edge of the plateau, its floodwaters eventually soaking their way into a nearby river valley.

Fe's fragment represented approximately one-hundred and fifty-eight degrees of the full ring's three-sixty. The disk's symmetry broken, its b-field no longer boasted the same strength and balance. Nevertheless, billions of trillions of irons still spun within their strontium ferrite towerblocks, and a weak magnetic potential still radiated from the broken arc in wispy, invisible lines.

Time and seasons passed. The bit of black debris became part of the shallow, alluvial plateau. For some years, the Akkadian sun's rays reached the magnet, but, in aggregate, the wind deposited more grit and dirt onto the ferrite than it blew away, dead bits of once-living things aiding in the burial. Eventually, Fe's discarded scrap accumulated layers of mulch and topsoil, a loose collection of diverse materials bound by moisture and a complex network of fine plant roots—ever spreading, ever thirsty.

● ● ●

Little distinguished the ferrite fragment from a common rock, and it moved with the other rocks at a geologic scale, years flying by like the wingbeats of a humming-bird. The edge of the plateau marched forward—a landslide in ultra slow-motion. Clods of akkadia broke off and tumbled downhill, taking their turn at erosion.

By the time Fe's chunk of ceramic magnet neared the crumbling edge, it had sunk about as far underground as a human could reach if they were laying flat with their arm thrust into the soil. Organic acids had carved some hard-won molecules from the fragment's outer layers, but the near totality of the ferrite remained uncorroded. It sat as a silent witness to the advancement of roots, the crawling of annelids, and life in general among the subsoil of a world that had no natural business hosting it.

Deep under the soil, between the bedrock and the spinning iron core of the planet, there sloshed a hot, convecting mantle. Every so often, tectonic shifts would shake the landmasses that drifted like great flakes of skin on the subakkadian magma. One such settling of the continental shelf provided the final shake Fe's eroding cliffside needed to break free and crumble into the valley below.

In the lowlands, the magnetic fragment embarked upon the slow process of becoming soil, moving ever downward, passing through loose-packed akkadia like a bit of fiber slowly being digested.

Every time an especially heavy rain or snowmelt summoned a flood, its waters were eventually directed by gravity to a wide, flat river that flowed slowly and steadily to the continent's eastern shoreline. Sometimes, Fe's dirty bit of weakened magnet would shift in the soil, sliding with the land or finding itself hydraulically excavated by a once-in-a-century torrent. All things moved toward the river, and the river moved toward the sea.

A final deluge brought the fragment tumbling at last into the river itself. Loaded with kinetic-energy from the rushing waters, the ferrite impacted a smooth river stone–forcing another unsurvivable strain on its internal bonds. Fe's already broken piece cracked into unequal portions. The iron atom and its remaining forty-degrees of arc tumbled along the river stones, separated by a natural sorting from the rocks it had once been neighbors with in the loam.

The storm passed, and the river settled into its typical, calm self–meandering down and naturally irrigating the lowland fields. Normally, something of the ferrite's mass and volume would quickly settle to the riverbed and rest with the other heavy stones. Its flat sides, however, kept Fe's magnet tumbling along, its surface-area snatched like a sail by every forceful subcurrent. Particles of strontium ferrite ablated with the tumbling, and as the mineral rubbed and smashed against river rocks, entire cities of molecular metallic towerblocks flaked off into the stream.

Fe lay buried inside the mass at a safe depth, and it was not among the minority of iron ions worn away by this natural stonewashing. Still, as mountains-worth of snow melted and flowed with the river, tossing the heavy fragment in the churn, it broke again and again–polished by time and violent moments into a tiny, smoothly-rounded black pebble.

The subfragment rested easily with the other river rocks, and more than once was witness to marvels. A species of small, silvery fish spawned along Fe's stony streambed. A female, swollen with instinct and potential new life, laid her eggs upon the pebbles. Chemical feet attached the tiny packages to the stones, and they bobbed in the water like perfect, glassy beads. Lusty males released their milt, fertilizing the eggs and populating the landscape with a thousand thousand zygotes—each, through the random beauty of breeding, boasting their own unique, never-before-extant genome.

Gently, the river followed its course, its seaward flow barely disturbing the deep bottom where life lay gestating. Inside an egg attached to Fe's stonelike subfragment, microscopic bits of oil collected and pooled. Within the glassy globe, a single fish cell cleaved and divided, splitting into two living units, united as one organism. Two became four became eight became sixteen and so on—an exponentially expanding kaleidoscope of life, alternately clumping and radiating. Each pass of the frantic a-moon, far above, brought another revolution in the rapidly-developing fish embryo, the line between nothing and something blurring.

Cells beyond counting, still in no recognizable form, worked together to locate the nutritious oil, drawing strength, fuel, and substance from its absent mother's final gift. Soon, the fish cells had multiplied to the point where they made up a complex unit—a fractal echo of the original fertilized ovum. The cellular horde doubled and doubled again. Another pass of the a-moon and deep within the crystal lattice of Fe's ceramic pebble, atoms vibrated from the addition of a new, tiny force vector—the wiggling egg, lending its own motion to the constant static pushes and pulls of freshwater currents and gravity.

Inside the sphere, the cells pulsed in a rhythmic beat without an accompanying organ to conduct them, but the first signs of specialization soon emerged. Not at all divergent from the development of a human embryo, legions of living fish cells in the egg lined up into the unmistakable beginnings of structure, two ridges—a spinal cord and column, the hallmarks of vertebrates everywhere.

Water burbled, and the life within the egg thrummed and struggled, but Fe's heavy black subfragment proved a good anchor for the tiny jewel, staying sunken and stable as the developing creature's forward spinal ridges split, bulging out to form the beginnings of a brain and two huge, sideslung eyes.

Two days from fertilization, and a thousand tiny hearts beat in their protein-glass bathyspheres, hoping to stay unnoticed on the riverbed. Another day, and the humming heart above Fe had filled with blood. Another, and the developing fish fry had grown an impressively thorough circulatory system through which to pump its vital fluids.

Predators and opportunists happened not to stumble upon the hatchery that season, and the eggs' development accelerated greatly over the next few days–circulating blood delivering a feast of nutrients to the nascent organs. The fish embryo had transformed from an army of hungry cells into an organism more complex than any machine ever built by the advanced human civilization that had engineered Fe's magnetic mineral.

Ten days following the initial spawning, that festive time when smokescreens of silt had been churned up by the adults' desperate fertilization throes, the riverbed once again quivered. A struggle was ensuing in the egg, and Fe's rounded ferrite lump rocked and swayed in the growing unease, anchored to its restless tennant. By this stage, the warm, womblike egg had shrunken into a prison for the nearly-grown fish larva, now capable of independent movement and sporting a full suite of functional organs.

Less than a day later and some among the thousands of tiny globes in the freshwater hatchery burst asunder–their captive fry slithering off to freedom. Fe's own tethered egg yielded to its struggling occupant, the hatchling slipping through a crack in the membrane to join the river's current, leaving tendrils of leftover proteins behind. These last, clinging traces were picked from the subfragment's slick black surface by unscrupulous scavengers, aided by the water's persistent solvency.

Smooth and assimilated, the small strontium ferrite stone spent many more years at the bottom of the lazy river–fresh, cold water forever shifting and swaying. The bit that held Fe never found itself washed out to sea, even as other small stones were swept away by the river's currents and occasional swells. Denser than nearly any other pebble, the ferrite sat stable and settled, peered only by the odd nugget of heavy gold or silver-rich ore eroded into the river from the distant hills above.

In the end, the dark pebble proved more permanent than the very river it inhabited. They may masquerade as permanent geological features, but on a planetary scale, rivers differ little from the living things that swim within their waters. They shift and wriggle. They're born, and they die.

Upstream, landslides silted up waterways, and animals of different kinds felled trees and influenced the course of the river's channels. More powerful still, avalanches and earthquakes rearranged things where they pleased. Fe's slow, wide stream meandered of its own accord, tiny differences in flow-rate between sides of the channel carving the river in one direction and piling up undermined silt against the retreating banks.

During an especially dry run of years, as the river thinned over the land, it left the smoothed ferrite fragment behind, orphaning it in a flat bed of abandoned stones and tiny, soggy plants. When the rains returned, the flood followed the newly-carved watercourse, leaving Fe's river rock parched.

Without the constant flow of fresh water, the lush vegetation that once rimmed the river's shores and coated its stones gradually died off, giving way to a landscape of hardy grasses as the years flickered by like more rapidly beating wings.

Fe's dry riverbed spent most of its time scorching in the Akkadian sun, its constituent minerals shifting only with the blowing of wind gusts and the random kicks of scuttling creatures. Once every century or so, an uncommon flood would send water flowing again along the retired streambed, but even these brief flickers of past glory became more and more distantly spaced in time.

One day, long after the last flood had faded into the mists of time, Fe's small magnetic stone found itself subject to a sudden, kinetic force.

A ruminant mammal happened by. Though not an uncommon occurrence, an unwelcome interaction with another creature motivated the beast to wedge its hoof into the former riverbed's scree and bolt in the opposite direction, sending small pebbles–Fe's included–flying. The little black rock soared, spraying token lines of magnetic potential invisibly through the air. It was the most the ferrite had moved in an era.

Landing, separated forever from its riverbed, Fe's stream-smoothed subfragment found itself sitting atop the hard-packed ground of a windswept plane, surrounded by dry grasses and tiny mineral grains. Sometimes the pebble blew around or shifted in the wind, and occasionally, something stepped on it. Every season, snow would fall, though far less than in the highlands, long ago. The pebble's internal temperature plummeted in the cold season and rose to expansive heights in the extremes of summer–energy from the intense Akkadian sun greedily absorbed by the oxidized black ceramic. Moisture levels rose and plants crept in. Harsh winds would sometimes blow, and droughts pushed back the spreading lowland thicket. Though its opponent had little topography left to work with, Fe's dense scrap of magnet lost its slow battle with gravity.

It spent more years below the soil than above, adding a small bit of structure and support to the underground ecosystem, affecting very little, its trace b-field no longer a threat to even the most sensitive of creatures. Bit by bit, the already-tiny pebble lost mass. Some molecules ablated or were snatched away by acids in the soil, blocks of strontium ferrite crystal gradually depopulating their sintered superstructure.

A period of time beyond measuring passed as the atom Fe hung ionized in its crystal duplex towerblock, tucked within the last remaining bastion of what had once been a substantial ring magnet. Now, time and tide had reduced the artifact to a particle no larger than those in the original oxide grit extruded in the Druke factory long ago.

Akkadia's satellites swirled around their star, which itself rotated, precipitating atomic revolutions with every turn. The galaxy slowly unwound its impossibly-complex clockwork dance, and the one remaining quanta of Earthmade strontium ferrite sank–subsumed into the planet's alien soil.

●　●　●

The fungus was good at waiting. It had been around for a while and knew plenty of tricks to keep itself busy. The elderly kingdom had settled into the comfortable, lower-energy orbits of life, and, like Gerty, the fungus had no qualms about being a janitor–locking and unlocking the doorways to and from existence.

How long the fungus waited is hard to say. Certainly long enough that time meant little. The fungus would laugh, if it could, if it saw time stretched out as a line, like a human sees it, for the fungus knew that time was nothing but a dancing of circles made from other circles made from others and so on.

It was the plants that had adapted to *it*, and when that sun-loving kingdom reached its vines out to conquer new lands, the fungus was waiting. Like all patient, old things, it preferred to manipulate the young into doing the heaviest work. The growing shoots of green took the fungus for granted when they arrived, adopting mycorrhizal symbiotes into their being from the very beginning. Fungus waited for animals no less patiently, and it waited for humans, too. It gave them bread and shine and fruit and death, and it reminded them that they were gods.

It waited for Fe.

Everything living dies, and everything dead returns to the fungus at some point or other, and sometimes, that most humble and patient of eukaryotic empires would deign to transform and uplift something that had never lived at all. Beginning or end, dead or not-yet-born, it made no difference to the fungus. The fungus wasn't picky. It couldn't afford to be, learning its skills of survival and frugality in times both ancient and lean. As the iron atom Fe traveled uneventfully around the Solar system aboard its unnamed asteroid, awaiting its inexorable ballistic fate, the fungus spent eons on Earth learning what it meant to be a living thing.

Certainly, the fungus had been among the first Earthlings to arrive on Akkadia-2, settling into the bare-bones ecosystem and preparing it for the extended family to come—living things to care for, farm, and embrace into the oblivion of death. To the fungus, it was all the same cycle, and the colonization played out as it was preordained to, following robust plans written by the dead hand of the Terraforming Department.

High above the Akkadian sky, robotic angels had carried the fungus' DNA-bearing spores, the hard-won fruit of eons of evolution, within their payloads. Following orders from their distant gods, the satellites employed their machine appendages and cold intellect to strategically inoculate the planet below with spores. Far more frugal and clever than eggs or seeds, these effervescently tiny particles came packed inside an armored shell and were stocked with everything needed for life in the hostile void.

Billions times billions of microscopic explorers–each spore its own Exodus, built from a blueprint that took three billion years to perfect–patiently reached out where they landed. The fungus made the best of its new planet, setting up shop wherever it could find a scrap of nutrition or moisture.

Ahead of hundreds of species of Earthling microorganisms, the fungus led the multicellular vanguard in the conquest of Akkadia-2, a champion well-chosen by the dead gods. The Terraforming Department had given each lifeform a mission, and the fungus, at least, discharged its duty admirably.

Sometimes, when the rewards were great enough, the fungus could soldier like that–be a holy warrior, conquer new lands and such–but most of the time, the fungus was just old. Ancient and newborn, dead and alive. Here the fungus was now–spread to another world and left to do what it did best, clearly having bargained for the sweeter end of the deal. Who had written the plans for whom? Circles made of circles. The Terraforming Department, brilliant and complex as it once was, had been made up of little more than a collection of animals and their toys. Animals. Baby siblings. Servants. The fungus knew what to do with animals. The things were so busy, they often didn't notice the fungus at all. While they ran around, the old kingdom spent much of its existence on Akkadia gardening–preparing the soil for trusting plants and farming their inevitable deaths.

One among many species of patient fungal farmers, a mycorrhizal colony organism would be the first representative of the kingdom to blindly encounter and transform the atom Fe. Its exact variety had no analog on Earth, as the spores that made planetfall held DNA that had been tweaked and enhanced by Ground Mission scientists. Later, as the watery world made many thousands of orbits around its star, the fungus figured out how to live on alien Akkadia, rearranging its own genes in its own way.

It was master of its domain, caring mother and grim reaper both to the species of hardy grasses, flowering plants, and even animals that made their homes in the lowlands. The fungus stretched out, healthy and strong, its mycelial network saturating the soil like a brain thriving outside a skull–a brain made from an army of fingers.

Where was the fungus' body? Its body was wherever it needed it to be. At the moment, the mycelium desired to reach out, to search—to quest. The fungus existed as a complex co-op of cells, a blessing and an abscess, a eukaryotic superorganism that imposed its will on the subsurface landscape. Wherever its complex body reached became its domain, territory conquered as completely as if taken by gang or roving army. At the front lines, the vanguard of fungal cells pushed through moist akkadia, extending the decentralized mycorrhizal presence ever further.

At the tip of one questing strand flexed a single, fungal cell. It protected itself from the outside world with a thick wall of biological armor, constructed from chitin. Fingers of galactomannan extended out, like pikes from a shield wall at the microscopic crest of an invading force—the tiny, crusading soldier cell.

Its galactomannan constructs, fingers outside fingers, were grown to be expendable. Inside the hyphae sheath, however, the living entity itself was separated from its sister cells by internal walls, built like bulkheads in a ship. Thus, if one among the vanguard were to fall, encountering an enemy or sustaining unsurvivable damage in its reckless questing, one cell may die, but its fellows would live on.

Deep in the subsoil, the fungus survived and learned and spread. Simultaneously, it lived as the ship and the sailor both, the soldier and farmer and teacher and scientist and student, the homefront and the colonies of a far-flung empire all—conducting the circle dance of circles.

The leading cell strained its outermost hyphal tip and signaled to the greater fungal union to send it more supplies and tools so it could better force its will on the environment. Fluid—hard won and hoarded—dripped from cell to cell through the mycelial network, rerouting itself and flowing down complex chitinous tubes, squeezing through vacuoles toward the front lines. Tiny rocks and bits of akkadia moved aside against the microscopic, hydraulic advance. The hyphal strand's chitin tip swelled with the increasing fluid pressure, requisitioned matériel successfully reaching the end of the cellular chain-of-command.

Synthase proteins at the very edge of the expanding tendril churned out chitin and glucan, building new sections of wall even as the subcellular soldiers conquered Akkadia-2, nanometer by nanometer. Each bit of gained ground had a million molecular flags planted by the hyphae as they expanded past, subjugated biomass strengthened by nutritious fluid and buttressing microtubules, all efficiently allocated and installed by the communal fungal command.

At the same moment, many more hyphae reached out in many more directions. A single cell wide and incredibly fragile, these threads tested the boundaries of the universe. Each cell fought with the strength, resources, and love of all the others. A gardener, a navy, an alien undertaker—all at once—

—in another part of its decentralized body, the network that was the fungus encountered unusual resistance. One of its mycelial columns, a strand that had been making admirable progress routing through a patch of moisture-rich akkadia, slammed into an enormous, subterranean rock. The fluid-driven pressure of the chitinous vanguard could do little to penetrate the stone. Its advance stalled, the fungus' gossamer tendrils slowly grew in a tangled, reticulated net against the rigid obstacle.

Meanwhile, deep inside the loam and far from the vanguard, squads of mycelia penetrated not the ground but the very cells of a living plant and its root structure, forming specialized arbuscular tentacles. These tiny fingers, thousands strong, reached into the plant's cells, gently grasping and diffusing nutritious gifts. Ion by ion, the barriers between them dissolved. An inseparable infection, the fungal fingers brought special nutrients to the plant, and in exchange, they took whatever they wanted. What the fungus desired most was what it would eventually and inexorably receive—death.

Inside the vast eukaryote, new cells split off from the old, the machinery of life perpetuating, as always. Outside its chitin walls, the fungus understood that the world bristled with potential threats and enemies, but the rich soil was also filled with treasure—inorganic nutrients to be rendered, and, of course, the sweetly energetic carbon bonds of death, loot left behind by its fallen little siblings like inheritance.

Thus motivated, the expeditionary force and the scouting hyphae inched their way closer to Fe, the iron atom still locked inside its crystal cell, in a towerblock, in a miniature strontium ferrite sculpture of a stone.

Tiny pebbles rolled aside, chemically sizzling, as the fungal army continued its never-ending quest, sending network orders to stretch out with the leading edge of another tendril. Between chitin walls, each soldier cell at the very crest of the advance had no decisions to make—billions of years of evolution had given them all the molecular messengers and biochemical tools they would need to orchestrate their duties with precision and perfection. Not only nutrients, fluids, and construction materials flowed down the mycelial network—the omnipresent mycorrhiza also supplied its extremities with chemical weapons. Manufactured from coded instructions locked in the nucleus of each cell, these magic molecular spells were learned long ago in a hostile world. Thus equipped, the galactomannan-studded vanguard quivered with electrochemical potential, spraying organic acid indiscriminately along the advance.

At each new front, the fungal body deployed its weapons of mass devastation, overkill in a landscape as benign and threatless as the terraformed Akkadia-2. Regardless, the flood of dicarboxylic and tricarboxylic acids served as the chemical teeth of the fungal body. These weapons had been the fruit of necessity and trauma, constructed to help the young fungus survive on the competitive, far-off jungle world of Earth.

All events occurred instantaneously to the fungus, as it existed fully within every part of itself—a fractal family nation. In the mycelium tangled near the stony obstacle, defeat turned to victory as the scouting cells made a discovery—while it could never push through the stone, the hyphae's acids had some effect. Under chemical assault, the impenetrable boulder was surrendering inorganic ions, valuable components for the fungus' dependants. There were calcium ions in abundance among the plunder, a metal born of strange fusion during the death throes of a different mother star.

Calciums were valuable, and the fungus, which ordered and obeyed itself like a rankless, ageless officer corps, would have redirected its arsenal more fully toward harvesting the stone if another part of its many-fingered brain hadn't discovered Fe's strontium-scented particle.

A single searching hair on a questing strand of hyphae, one cell thin, encountered the bit of ferrite—an obstacle the fungus considered far more surmountable than the calcium boulder. Sparing a fraction of a percent of itself for the conquest, the mycelial network shuttled around some electrons, signaling its great membership to divert resources to the new battlefront.

● ● ●

Situated in the same ionized state it had held for millenia, the atom Fe sat inside its towerblock built of linked irons, oxygens, and the odd strontium in bimolecular lattice. The edge of the tiny ferrite particle contained cities-worth of these ceramic crystal skyscrapers, and at the moment, the entire superstructure found itself under siege.

The fungus was finally done waiting.

Oxalic acid moistened the soil, creeping between benign stones and wetting the face of the synthetic particle like a moat encircling a castle. The acidic chemical weapon was constructed from hydrogens and oxygens, the besieging fungus having sacrificed two of its precious carbons to transform the common, watery atoms to a strong acid.

Subcellular drydocks in the living hyphae launched these molecules like tiny war machines—eager to dissolve anything concealing nutritious ions. The fungal soldiers pulsed, their cells further flooding the battlefield with carboxylic acids, other cunning, caustic arrangements of hydrogen, oxygen, and carbon.

Fe's vast cliff face of black ferrite, a human-made compound weathering a never-ending siege from the natural environment, had stood strong since it first landed on the planet. Wind, rain, salt-spray, and even centuries of exposure to water had not harmed it. However, Fe's home was not invulnerable, and the acids secreted by the bizarre invader did what moisture and millenia could not.

Blocks of double-molecules, repeating along the crystal's edge, collapsed before the fungus' acidic assault. The atoms on both sides of the siege warred over electrons—less a straightforward chemical reaction and more a churning and complex unraveling of quantum-mechanical forces. Charges fizzed and bonds snapped as electrons rearranged themselves and chemical products morphed along the sizzling battlefront.

Organic acid molecules, manufactured far from the front lines, carried away iron ions from the dying magnet, which leaked like a razed city giving up prisoners in spoil. Structural oxygen morphed, its casual bonds unable to stand up to the acids. The invader pressed its assault. Shackle-like chemical ligands bound irons by their electrons, and at the front of the fight, an oxalate group seized a pair of charges from one of Fe's siblings, forming a ligand with the captive and utterly collapsing its crystalline tower.

The mycelium appreciated what it could absorb from the ferrite particle, sacrificing a scrap of energy in order to let the chemical gradient do its work. In fact, the fruits of the conquest proved enough to stimulate expansion, and fluid pressure within the chitinous shield-wall pushed a budding protrusion in a new direction. Inside the fungus, cells split, reproducing themselves, eventually slipping into the bud and growing a new forking finger–a flanking column of besieging hyphae.

Fe's ferrite fortress found itself crumbling, pincered by fungal invaders on two sides and bathed in organic acids. Electric energy crackled as tiny subatomic charges tore between masters, but the iron's worsening position within the diminishing scrap of matter kept it momentarily out-of-reach from the violence of the reactions. Meanwhile, on the edge of the fragment furthest from the attacking hyphae, trillions of allied atoms remained resolute. Much of the fortress was still inviolate, even as the battlelines moved and shifted, reactants sloshing and bobbing in brownian motion.

Inevitably, some of the atomic allies' luck ran out–just when they needed it most. One of the fungus's chemical vollies connected, and an acid molecule wormed its way inside the magnet, ligating a vulnerable metal ion, wounded in the battle and already missing electrons. The newly-bonded organic structure retreated via slow diffusion through the soil, and at the searching tip of the galactomannan-fingered tendril, the fungus deigned to pull the captive inside itself.

Strontium and iron atoms alike were chelated and captured by the onslaught of oxalate ligands–their fellowships broken and their electrons bound. Not every

Earthling atom was absorbed by the victorious fungus, however. Many molecules, missing in action, milled about directionless in the highly ionized intrasoil fluid.

The exotic particles that existed in what had once been a ceramic magnet were not, by chance, in great demand by the mycorrhizal network, and after a certain level of absorption, the tired fungus had drunk its fill of metallic prisoners.

Some mycelia would be wound around the remains of the ferrite fortress indefinitely, the fungus leaving strands of cells like imperial guards over an enemy they hadn't finished assimilating. Days passed under this occupation, the fungus' secretions slowing, chemical reactions and casualties waning. Fe stayed bonded in what passed for the surviving scrap of ferrite, still dissolving in high-acidity intrasoil fluid—too acidic, in fact, to be explained by the fungus alone.

A new player had entered the fray, a fresh, verdant invader from a different kingdom entirely.

These advancing forces attacked, sending a gushing moat of acid splashing around the disintegrating ferrite crystal. Carboxylic weapons wreaked havoc on the once-stable electric interactions between atoms. Impervious minerals within the soil stood as silent witnesses, but anything reactive quickly made way before the advancing vegetable acids.

Organic reinforcements arrived from a knotty, branching tube that kept its distance from the imperious fungal hyphae. A living expeditionary force, cooperating cells armored in pectin and cellulose forced their way through the landscape and cast forth their own tricky chemicals to soften up the defenders.

A grass, basking in the sunlight high above, stretched its roots as far as it could into the dark recesses below in search of moisture and minerals. Among the complex, zig-zagging lightning-flash of its root tangle, one expeditionary tendril had come across an irresistible source of iron. The plant knew how to manufacture teeth of acid, and its clever cellular chemists plucked carbon atoms from the air and glued them to water from below to make their weapons. Just as the acid from the fungus besieged and eroded the ferrite walls, coming like bodysnatchers for its constituent metals, so too did the grass' organic acids come for Fe.

For ages, Fe's own electrons had buzzed in communal clouds shared with neighboring irons, flitting mysteriously across their quantum states. This changed as a squad of blunt oxygen atoms, forged in an alien star, invaded its towerblock, bringing with them fierce hydrogen ions and Akkadian carbon. Fe's doom was set. The atom and those that stood with it had been created to spin in magnetic harmony, but for the first time since the ancient Canadian factory, Fe's spin fell out of rhythm with the dance. It faltered–its infinitesimal magnetic moment losing meaning.

All went according to the plant's plan, ordained by its relentless, monocot DNA. Oxalic, mugineic, and citric acids all bathed the soil, dissolving any remaining ferrite resistance. In the violence, the iron atom Fe found itself wrenched away from those it had held close to for millenia–bonds snapping like friends or limbs torn away forever. Stripped raw and ionized, Fe vibrated with brownian helplessness, electron deficient and badly unstable.

The atom existed in this uncertain state, flickering into something like an oxide, then an organic acid compound, then to a free ion once again. Soon enough, however, the battle of the soil stabilized, and the victors began to divide their spoils. All the while, the grass' roots advanced. One of the plant's emissaries formed a ligand to bond with the refugee Fe–tempting it with two desperately-desired electrons, capturing the atom by winning a negotiation deep within its quantum cloud.

Thus ensnared, the chelated iron diffused into the soupy jungle of the lowland soil. Defeated and dissolved, it flowed via brownian bumps inside a clot of water molecules, eventually to be intercepted by the thirsty roots of the grass. Coveted across centuries and lightyears, the atom Fe was fated to be seized yet again for its special properties.

Chapter 11: The Kingdom

The grass spent its life growing. From its meristems pushing ever upward and its roots burrowing ever deeper akkadiaward–it grew, rising and ripening. All parts of it grew, all at once, even within its constantly-splitting cells. Bathed in springtime's glory, the plant expanded even as the captured atom Fe–soilbound and shackled by a chemical functionary–flowed toward its thirsty, vegetable roots.

Things took time in that buried place, and in time, the chelated iron bobbed along water pockets, hustled by the brownian riot of diverse particles in the sub-surface stew. Eventually, by virtue of blind movement and diffusion gradients, the iron prisoner encountered a questing protrusion–a single hair extending out from a plant cell.

Like a monumental dock, the hair's surface was studded with countless bio-logical importers, evolved by the random forces of eons into efficient transport mechanisms that would put Zelda, the *Manatee II*, and the entire Greenland warehousing operation to shame. Particles ranging from large, tangled molecules to single, ionized atoms slipped back and forth through the busy terminus. A more frequent passenger than any other happened to be water, that deceptively-simple partnership between oxygen and hydrogen that counted itself responsible for all known life.

Life was indeed on display at the root-hair. Bacteria busied themselves gobbling and gulping down everything they could find. Nearby, a giant annelid wriggled through the soil–the animal moving at lightning speed compared with the slow creep of the roots, passing Fe by a safe margin. Bonded and trapped, Fe found itself hustled toward the enormous biological wharf–a trichoblast, the tiny appendage of an epidermal cell, itself only one member among thousands in the grass' sprawling root system.

Proteins protruded along the membrane that separated the plant from the outside world. Tangled in their molecular complexity, these structures were the porters of life–cunning automatons crafted from combinations of typical organic elements, arranged in thousands of unique formations. More highly specialized than even the pickiest automated logistics unit from old Earth, each protein on the root-hair's gently-questing membrane existed in a state of incredible focus, ever waiting, built for one specific purpose–one preferred passenger. The chelated Fe passed by many of these tangled porters until it reached a carrier protein that had been waiting for iron specifically.

Angling toward the surface of the cell, the captive and its ligand left the flow, bumping along toward a beckoning, bunched-up protein passageway and the perfectly-bespoke bonding site beyond. Like a ticketed passenger, Fe's escort settled comfortably into the hollow.

This specific carrier protein had been manufactured by its cell to facilitate the entry of captive iron ions, and now that Fe had been loaded aboard, the porter animated to fulfill its purpose. It wiggled, rearranging its own shape to enclose its passenger. Like Eve leaving her home planet strapped aboard a rocket, the atom Fe waited for the grass protein to shuttle it to another world.

Imitating the action of a ship's airlock, the porter morphed again, zipping up entirely before opening a new door to the inner cytoplasm of the cell. No longer constrained, the chelated iron oozed its way out of the hollow and found itself inside the root-hair's membrane. Molecules of adenosine triphosphate, ATP, waited nearby like fresh packs of spring-loaded batteries–delivery meals for the many protein porters. As Fe diffused past, a pallet of the stuff broke apart, providing the transports with just enough energy to wriggle back into shape, ready to accept more passengers for immigration into the hungry plant cell.

Now fully ensconced inside the vegetable fortress, the captive iron atom diffused away from the busy port, hustled and shoved by other travelers toward the vast interior of the cell. If the soil-digging hair was a dock, then the trichoblast cell as a whole functioned as a living city–populated and served by a diverse cast of incredibly complex biological functionaries. Each department within trichoblast city was tasked with a specific function, staffed to exacting specification by the very cell it served. Everywhere, things were shuttled and exchanged across membranes within membranes, biomolecules built and eaten, nutrients absorbed and exuded.

They were far from the site of the siege, but the acid-derived soldier that held Fe by the electrons did not loosen its grip. The far-traveled atom had been passed around plenty in the electrochemical melee, but in the end, a molecule called Nicotianamine carried the plundered Fe throughout much of the body of the plant. A strong team of carbons, backed up by hydrogens, nitrogens, and ubiquitous oxygen molecules, Nicotianamine enfolded the iron ion on all sides–professionally preventing Fe's escape.

Together, Fe and its chelator formed the NA-Fe complex. This molecule, and thousands like it, were considered friendlies by the plant's many living cities and their proteinous workers, some expecting them and moving them along, the rest benignly ignoring them.

Pressed by the busting chemical crowd, NA-Fe assimilated into a thick fluid that permeated the space between cellulose walls, saturated with hydrates, ions, and other plunder. It passed structures of folded proteins so complex they made the transport porter appear simple. Strange beasts also swam the three-dimensional city, enormous and aloof, reminiscent of the single-celled bacteria that had crawled their way blindly through the soil. Beyond everything lay a sprawling central complex where tireless organic machines synthesized proteins, forging weapons and matériel far more efficiently than even the Junkers Flugzeug und Motorenwerke factory at its peak.

The crowds didn't stay in trichoblast city long, however, and soon NA-Fe was hustled along to the outer palisade and granted passage by more import-export proteins. Beyond, past rigidly-constructed pectin and cellulose walls, there appeared another cell–another fractal fragment of a lifeform–separate in its function and existence from that Fe had just passed through. Another living city entirely.

Then another. And another. The iron prisoner found itself transported from cell to cell, shuttled from the jurisdiction of one cortical megalopolis to the next, each more filled with wonders than the last. Some held their own small seas, titanic reservoirs of water that Fe and its captor avoided. Everything appeared to have a predestined purpose within the great body of the grass, functioning in near-perfect cooperation, from entire meta-nations of cellular communities down to the humblest protein automaton.

Pressure from below and behind continued to convey the NA-Fe along, the pair kept company by crowds of grasping waters. The lifeblood of the grass, omnipresent in their trillions, they populated the plant's nutritious sap and filled the spaces within and between cells—each molecule a simple confederation of one bossy oxygen atom awkwardly holding onto two hydrogen flibbertigibbets.

The waters' hydrogens, as was their nature, were curious and attractive little particles, single protons enigmatic in their timelessness. They'd been around since the first moments of the universe, unchanged and unburnt by any star. Though they were chemically locked to their oxygens, the tiny hydrogen ions still found themselves attracted to nearly everything. They would reach out to each other when lonely and would form constant weak bonds with nearly any particle that happened to float by, including the NA-Fe complex and its constituent atoms.

Unlike the formidable coordinate bonding between Fe and its captor, the handholds of the inquisitive hydrogens proved soft and transient, like partners constantly changing and embracing in a crowded dancehall. Despite these atomic flirtations, the liquid mass moved ever onward, driven by the plant's enigmatic, vegetable needs. Soon, the iron, bonded to its prisoner-transport complex, squeezed into a tunnel as dead as the bustling root cells were alive.

Fe had entered the central xylem.

Living cells thus far had passed NA-Fe between themselves, water molecules sloshing around all the while, but in the xylem, the busy cities were missing. The shadowy tube of dead cells stretched upward into a yawning hollow, pits in the walls reaching darkly towards infinity. Few organelles went about their business in this dead place, and the only stirring came from a continuous vertical river styx—the upward flow of the plant's watery sap. Just as Gerty had waddled through the deserted spokes of their derelict ship, NA-Fe floated and flowed within the cavernous spaces made from stacks of tubular, vegetable skeletons.

A problem as timeless as any, the plant needed the mass of water and its cache of dissolved plunder to flow upward, in direct violation of the tyrant gravity. When Fe had served aboard an aircraft's armor, the *Fliescherbeile* had beaten gravity with advanced physics and the wanton expenditure of large amounts of chemical energy. A similar combination propelled the rocket that had taken the atom and its magnet into space. The poor Akkadian grass, however, had little chemical energy to burn—it could hardly compete with the humans' fiery and dramatic escalations. Instead, it relied on vegetable cunning and loopholes in the laws of physics.

At the molecular-level, Fe bore witness to the bizarre orchestration of forces by which the plant fed itself. Water molecules in the soil fought in the battle against gravity, stampeding to be let into the plant's thirsty roots, forcing an upward pressure. This effect was aided by a vacuum suction from far above, as the monocot's soaring stalk structure and its sun-baked leaves lost water and thirsted for more. When the forces were tallied up, however, even this combined push and pull proved insufficient to transport masses of heavy water directly up the grass' stalk.

Nevertheless, Fe moved upward, in contempt of Akkadia-2's gravity.

It was the strange shape of the dead, tubular xylem cells that made the difference, their design evolved over eons to manipulate the behavior of waters and their vivacious hydrogens. The asymmetry of each molecule, with the oxygen always separate from its smaller partners, rendered the waters tiny, polar magnets. They stuck to almost everything and especially to one-another. Confronted with the vast vertical hollow of the xylem, they held fast as one, interlocking via hydrogen bonds in all directions, forming a skin that mimicked a living cell's outer membrane.

Where the waters at the edge met with the shaft's walls they grabbed on eagerly, bonding to vegetable corpses—expendable cells bred to die specifically for this purpose. Like an army of synchronized mountain-climbers, the waters pulled themselves up the skeletal tube. Dissolved in the sloshing mass, the NA-Fe complex and other travelers made their way up the shaft, passing from one segment of the xylem to its superior, ascending toward the grass' crown, gravity failing in its efforts to keep the atom buried.

Fe had not been aboveground for some time, but now it re-ascended as part of the grass' nutritious liquid-lunch. Though few stellar photons penetrated this deeply into the xylem, Fe found itself once again above the land and beneath the direct domain of the Akkadian sun.

*   *   *

Predictable patterns of hydrodynamics, as well as the plant's variable thirst, directed traffic in the superhighway of the stem. Water molecules and dissolved compounds were siphoned off as their upward journey progressed, flowing into divots in the cell walls and the side-corridors beyond. Still bound to cage-like Nicotianamine, the captive Fe rose higher, passing nodes from which spread continentally sprawling sheets—flat green structures that were the grass' sunlight-harvesting leaves.

NA-Fe followed the unconscious forces that served to meet the intricate needs of the vegetable—a towering organism made up of an immense collection of cooperating, self-contained lifeforms. Teams of these cells were busily bred every moment by the plant. The process was a nutrient-hungry one, and without imports of press-ganged iron atoms, the grass would stunt and die.

The many hydrogen hands of a blob of waters grabbed onto the NA-Fe complex before it could reach the stalk's apex. Diffused in the sap, they dripped through a narrow gap in the stem tissue, joining the much-reduced flow of another hollow xylem tube. The watery mob climbed through angled passageways, fighting gravity less and less as the verdant tunnels diverged more and more from the grass's near-vertical stem.

Next, the chelating captor escorted Fe, ever outward, through flat sheaths of sugar-making cells. At this point, the walls of the grass grew thin enough that feeble photons of light could penetrate, and the journey eventually terminated at a collar-like band, wrapped around a leaf already well-along in its construction.

Within the trickle of grasping water molecules, the NA-Fe flowed up the leaf's inner vein, blindly navigating through porous cells into smaller and smaller tunnels. Outside, the newborn leaf was busy organizing into differentiated rows, each cell type cloning itself to extend the pattern, helping to erect the energy-harvesting blade. Fed by a rush of incoming deliveries, cells around the construction zone doubled and split, doubled and split—entire biological megalopolises hard at work manufacturing and exporting sister-cities. Life on all levels loved building colonies—cells had their mitosis, the grass had its seeds, and even the humans had launched their Exodus.

Green and vivacious, the new leaf cells set to work collecting free energy from the Akkadian sun, which warmed and penetrated each layer of the leaf's mesophyll. Meanwhile, the iron ion, recently captured from its ferrite fragment via acidic siege, neared its final destination. Still chemically bonded to its captor, Fe entered one more plant cell. Unlike the busy, well-organized biological townships from before, this place existed in a state of radical transformation. The fluid-filled interior chamber was more massive than most, and the entire cell seemed to be straining and struggling as it grew. Strange vesicles, studded with proteins, glided past. These congregated at the center of the globe, spinning and weaving themselves into a great fence. Diffusion gradients vectored Fe away from the more nutrient-rich side of the cell and toward the vast, empty exurb beyond.

Stately, staggeringly-complex organelles were keeping to themselves at one side of the atrium, letting the wall-builders get on with their project. The bizarre construction workers busied themselves fencing off the mother cell from its new daughter with walls of cellulose. At first blush, the work site appeared chaotic, but the birth of the new cell proceeded like a well-choreographed and bafflingly complex ballet—every protein worker moving in perfect step, following coded orders from the nucleus' imperious DNA.

Through a hole in the nearly-complete central plate, the NA-Fe complex slipped into the daughter side, entering what would soon be an independent leaf cell. Half of the splitting lifeform had inherited all the rudimentary machinery it would need, redundantly crafted by the mother cell to provide for its young clone. The daughter harbored diverse proteins and its own sprawling, nascent nucleus compound–already hard at work manufacturing servants.

Something else, less inclined to follow orders, lurked within the newborn daughter, hovering in the murky fluid. A great green monster lived on Fe's side of the fence–like the captive iron, the colossal chloroplast had drifted to the empty exurbs through a gap in the under-construction wall.

A lifeform separate from the plant, with its own DNA, the newborn chloroplast was a stunted cyanobacterium that happened to live in the cells of a grass leaf. The chloroplast and others like it grazed on sunlight in their cytoplasm pastures–the plant and most of its cells running off of their waste products.

It drifted closer, like a hungry, verdant cloud, blocking out light that filtered down through the mesophyll. Fe was engulfed.

A number of things happened then. Perhaps because it had reached the end of its usefulness, or perhaps because the plundered iron ion was now safely locked behind countless layers of membranes and walls, Nicotianamine loosened its shackles and relinquished Fe before slipping away. Without the electrons from its captor, Fe's ionization buzzed raw and unstable. It attracted dozens of electric hookups from the coquettish hydrogen atoms aboard their waters before finding its freedom revoked by more determined chemical ligatures.

A pair of bicarbonates, brought into the liquidus inner stroma of the growing chloroplast, eagerly indentured the iron, each offering a donated electron. Fe had no choice but to accept.

Meanwhile, bisecting the cytoplasm sea where the green monsters swam, the wall-builders completed their task, sealing the cloned offspring from its mother. Even during its first moments of existence, the newborn plant cell busily set to the work of living.

To the newly-arrived Fe, the interior of the green-skinned swimmer presented a stunning, alien vista. Stellar photons pierced the monstrous cyanobacterium, sparking industry. Sweet stromal fluid sloshed everywhere. Stacked green towers made from piles of fat, rounded disks gave structure to the landscape–high-rises designed by a whimsical architect cutting a skyline like no other. Tubelike appendages stretched between the stacks like spokes, walkways between emerald cities built of flying-saucers.

Fe would discover that this wondrous, solar-powered candy factory existed for one simple purpose—sugar.

● ● ●

Bicarbonately indentured, the iron atom Fe found itself led toward one of the smaller stacks of green subunits, still incomplete, still attracting tenants and workers. It entered a mess of membranes at the fringe of the thylakoid's growth and waited its turn.

Compared with even the smallest of the chloroplast's proteins, the bicarbonates that held Fe were incredibly simple molecules—each a single carbon surrounded by three oxygen atoms, with a lone hydrogen along for the ride. Flanking Fe on either side, the dull carbonate pair held the metal ion within a generous electron cloud.

Freelance ions didn't last long in the stroma, and if the ligands acted essentially as Fe's supervisors, the entire iron-bicarbonate complex was about to be onboarded. The light-hungry grass had an open position for them inside its pet cyanobacterium, in a thylakoid stack without an address.

Life, marching to the drumbeat of DNA, organized itself by default, grabbing available nutrients and building-blocks as needed—Fe and its managers included. The outer skin of the alien disk sealed tightly, and another thylakoid joined the chloroplast's growing stack. Fe's iron-bicarbonate complex was now part of the team. The particle would serve inside an elaborate protein structure located on the skin of a thylakoid, one emerald saucer among thousands.

Working on a membrane, within a larger membrane, upon a skin, behind a barrier, the iron found itself organically indentured. Life loved its walls, and Fe had a cubicle.

The iron was locked within a complicated nesting-doll of bonds and enclosures, and this time—it had a job to do. Like most atoms with careers in living cells, Fe found work in the transportation sector. Life, almost as much as it loved building walls, obsessed over moving things from one place to another in complicated little ways, and photosynthesis was one of the kingdom's most ingenious tricks. The task of converting photons from sunlight into sugar fell in part to the many protein complexes that studded the thylakoid's outer membrane–electric railways shuttling ions between the stroma on one side and the acidic, interior fluid on the other.

In the photosystem that served as Fe's office, things started to get busy when red-colored photons arrived, fresh from Akkadia. After burrowing out of the star's core, these massless quanta of energy broke from its fiery surface and hurtled at the speed of light toward the watery planet, where they penetrated its atmosphere and avoided colliding with the many molecules of gas that hung between outer space and the grateful leaf.

When one such photon struck a molecule of sensitive chlorophyll, which happened to be one of Fe's coworkers, it transferred a parcel of energy. The chlorophyll had been assembled specifically to unwrap gifts from the fusion-powered furnace of Akkadia. The molecule, a machine composed of over a hundred common atoms, had at its core a single remarkable magnesium, locked in a cage of nitrogen. As it absorbed the warm, red photon, the chlorophyll retained the star's energy, and thus excited, it swung around the proteinous jungle of the photosystem, handing off a loose election to the next worker in line, a cousin of sorts–a chlorophyll molecule without the magnesium, existing only to shuttle electrons to and fro

.

None of this activity concerned Fe, perched at an apex near the stromal shore of the tangled complex, still oppressed by its bicarbonate managers. However, whenever the magnesiumless chlorophyll-cousins rose up with their electrons in tow, a new molecule–an intense coworker called PQ–snapped to attention, forcing the entire team to get to work.

Similar in size to a chlorophyll, the PQs would heft two of the excited electrons at once, accepting both into their ambitious clouds. To balance the charge, the team would pull a pair of unattached hydrogen ions in from the stroma. Fully loaded, PQ would move to the next department within the intramembranous office, carrying energy from converted sunlight and transporting vivacious hydrogen ions, like tourists, into the flying saucer city.

Every time the star Akkaddia flashed down a digestible photon, the chloroplast gulped it gratefully. As PQ passed by, Fe's supervisors held to their protein bonding sites, allowing the iron to briefly assert its electromagnetic charge on the intricate carousel of ion transfer.

Fe acted as a sort of chaperone. It would lightly hold the hand of a visiting hydrogen as it stepped across the membrane, and it would keep the overworked PQs stable as they hobbled off to complete their one-way missions. Fe had become something like a security guard, one of many in the sugar plant–a deputy packing a magnetic moment, keeping the peace while kept captive itself, chained by the civic functionaries of vegetative authority.

Upstream from Fe's station, thousands of water molecules cracked apart, their bonds broken by refinery-like compounds. Leafwide, photosynthesis departments harvested water's electrons and belched trash gasses into the air–the smokestacks of the plant kingdom oxygenating Akkadia-2, animal life and wildfires the unintended consequences of vegetable waste.

Downstream, the passengers Fe had helped shepherd were squeezed right back out of the innercity fluid. The frisky hydrogens fled the membrane via one of the most important structures to the living cell–a turnstyle protein that, as it rotated, rewound a waiting supply of ATP batteries. These, along with the electrons loaded with sunlight energy, painstakingly-transported by Fe's team, left the membrane behind and dissolved into the stroma beyond.

There, they reacted with carbon-dioxide harvested from Akkadia-2's atmosphere to form the ubiquitous energy-storage molecules called glucose. These sugars would be fed to the other bacteria-like swimmers within the grass–mitochondria–stowaways even more ancient than the sun-drinking chloroplasts.

Much of the glucose born from Akkadian photons would not be used for fuel at all, fabricated instead, not unlike a gingerbread house, into the masonry of the plant's walls–the grass' cellulose inner structure merely mortared blocks of repeating sugars.

All living things hungered, and with a little help from Fe and others like it, the grass could make its own food, supping on its stockpile of homemade sugar whenever it felt a pang. Indeed, such a complex commune of city-state cells couldn't help but feel. The grass experienced thirst, cold, a desire for energy, satisfaction–all in its own metasensory way. It photosynthesized and respirated. It harvested the world around it to build itself up, but this was not enough.

Living things yearn for more.

*　*　*

Everything was nearly ready. From its inception as a seed, the grass carried instructions within its genes on how to reproduce itself. Now, the complicated checklist was complete. It had stored enough energy, the season was right, and its flowers were truly beautiful this year. Simply put, it was the most important time in the grass' young life. Living things, even on a cellular level, experience an inherent need to spread, but unlike tiny cells and their simple splitting mitosis, this complicated flowering plant could have sex.

It occupied a crowded field of other grasses and small woody plants. The frisky monocot stood tall and presented itself, the Akkadian sun reflecting off its golden inflorescence. This grass wasn't as showy or elaborate as some other botanicals, who aimed to seduce a passing animal pollinator with pleasing scents or colors. Instead, the humble grass could only boast clusters of tiny, yellow flowers, mere florets really. For b-months, it had guarded them fiercely against unwanted attention and predation, enclosing them within razor-sharp leaflike structures until maturity.

Now, the eager grass nearly quivered with anticipation as potentials shifted and its florets bloomed, opening their sensitive spikelets to the public bustle of the lowland air currents.

Like most plants, it was intimately familiar with the composition of the planet's atmosphere–a mixture of waste gas, tantalizingly-inaccessible nitrogen, and the carbon-dioxide it spun into sugar. This omnipresent gaseous churn carried within it all types of tiny foreign particles, bumping and eddying around the flower's interior architecture.

One sensitive reproductive enclosure held delicate collections of cells arranged like exotic sculptures. Tucked inside, below the golden anthers, fertile stigmas eagerly awaited passersby, each a fuzzy, translucent brush attached to the flower's ovary. The plant's male parts also prickled in social anticipation, rising from their spikelets, standing proud and turgid–swollen with pollen.

Warm photons poured down from the nearest star, energizing the life inhabiting the lowlands. Many other species of flowering plant competed with each other for space, both on the ground and in the air, their microscopic messengers fighting for attention upon the atmospheric forum. As the air gently vibrated, bits of pollen, stuffed with genetic material, occasionally bumped into the gossamer tendrils of one or another of the beautiful, shy stigmas. Though packed with potential, each was rejected by the grass' female receptors. They wouldn't accept the airborne seed of just any organism–they were holding out for something special.

It was a slow-moving scene, never more than on that golden day. The air stirred little, and hardly a breeze blew through the stagnant lowlands all afternoon. With the dawn of the next day, things proved much the same. Though the grass' pistils lusted for pollen grains spewed from its own species, there was little action to be found upon the windless plain.

Morning turned to afternoon. In a leaf somewhere, Fe's iron-bicarbonate cubicle helped facilitate cycle after cycle of early-stage photosynthesis. Inside the grass, individual cells reproduced at a furious rate, but the larger organism had to be patient. The waiting was excruciating. Potentials crackled at the tips of the grass' stems and at its florets, filling the collective with a desire and drive to fulfill the biological imperative–as if the amorous vegetable lifeform needed any more motivation.

It was hardly fair. Nearby, other flowers were certainly being pollinated–beautiful, fragrant, and broad-petaled, they could ignore the weather, relying instead on ambulant suitors to facilitate their intercourse–the birds and the bees. The grass didn't feel envy, but it worried in its own way that the window for reproductive success was limited. Its delicate floral sculptures couldn't stay intact and fertile forever. Day cycled to night, and the Akkadian sun tapered off its banquet. During the dark hours, only the cold, sparse photons from distant starlight impacted the plant's leaves. Its internal processes slowed with the drop in temperature, patient even in its state of arousal and need.

In the morning, the grass once more gamely opened its flowers, burning sugar energy and hoping to be lucky in love–but the sun did not come out that day. Instead, a thick layer of dark clouds filled the skies above the continent, blanketing both the highlands and lowlands in black shade. Somewhere, thunder rumbled. Lighting flashed as enormous electric potentials arced from the sky to the distant ground. Swollen stormclouds, and the countless water particles within, released their potentials.

Raindrops plummeted eagerly, drawn by gravity into a dive-bombing assault on the land below. As each droplet collected inside its crackling cloud and fell downward, the many water molecules within held tightly to one another, forming a spherical skin–as in the xylem, so in the void.

One dive-bombing globe after the next shattered and burst as they impacted the grass' green blades, tiny sub-beads of moisture flowing down and collecting at the base of its stem to soak the soil beneath.

Another raindrop attacked, striking one of the grass' male anthers. Still waiting for a motive to release his genetic material, the anther exploded at the sudden mechanical stimulation from the water droplet, gratefully shedding a shower of tiny, spiky grains of pollen. An electrochemical shudder within the cells accompanied his satisfying release, but it was nothing compared to what the stigma in that very same flower experienced.

Pollen rained down from above, and what wasn't washed away fell upon the delicate, reaching fingers of the female stigma. Ecstatic signals flashed through her cells. Relief. Fulfillment. The most beautifully agonizing of life's missions complete. It didn't matter to the grass that it had mated with itself. The potential offspring would be different enough, unique recombinations of the parent's genetic material.

Bonding with the swooning stigma and signaling the egg cell below, the fortunate grain of pollen constructed a tunnel through which to send its package. What remained of the bloom closed, unwinding chemical springs deep within its cells—sealing itself and the new life within against the storm. In a process remarkably similar to the development of the fish eggs on the stony streambed long ago, the seed began to quicken.

The days grew shorter as winter loomed, but the grass had done enough. Its seeds were fertilized and healthy. They would harden and dry—ready to be sent out into the wider world on a gust of wind or dropped to the nearby ground to germinate in the same soil where their parent had once grown up.

Inside a leaf, below the self-satisfied grassflower, tied down and sealed behind many walls, Fe held down its job, enduring cycles of the photon harvest, using its charge to keep the electrostatic peace and helping to make sugar. Though they continued to pump out glucose precursors, the thylakoids within the aging chloroplast were reaching the later stages of their usefulness. The grass itself had little time remaining to live, and its cells knew it. What sugar could be made from the late-season sunlight was hastily transported up the stalk, nutrients routed to the fertilized seedpods—to *their* future triumph.

● ● ●

Like a microcosm of the Exodus after planetfall, Fe's once-proud membrane was looted for spare parts. Scraps of carbohydrate fuel flowed to the growing grains, sugars from as far away as the roots traveling up the xylem elevator-shaft. Everything that could be easily transported was reallocated. To the senescent grass, nothing else mattered but its zygote seeds and their wellbeing in the next life.

However, when the grains reached the end of their development, ready at last to leave home, the atom Fe remained behind. It hung with its bicarbonate ligands, abandoned, chained without a purpose to derelict proteins. Sunlight still penetrated the translucent layers of leaf cells, but their rich green bled away. Fe's sensitive chlorophyll coworkers had been battered by too many photons, unable to dump their overly excited electrons as supply lines broke down. The remarkable chemical automatons lost their verdancy and disintegrated.

No longer a shining green metropolis of flying saucers, the stacks of thylakoids within the moribund chloroplast resembled out-of-fashion tower complexes–gaudy, broken-down ruins. Fe's entire photosystem had been laid off when the organism made its genetically-destined choice to stop producing sugar, rendering Fe's charge-regulation duties irrelevant.

Now, the withering yellow-green sugar monster existed only to be digested. Agents of the dying daughter cell set upon the chloroplast. Like the carcass of a beast, the enzyme-soaked swimmer was efficiently butchered for any bit that could be useful to the next generation. Fe and its supervisors were ignored, scattered in the cytoplasm, and left to float as inert witnesses to the ravages of the self-digesting plant cell.

The neighborhood grew worse, day after day, Fe's drying leaf of grass jutting out into the late season chill. Moisture no longer moved as readily through the frosty soil, and without regular replenishment within its vasculature, the plant withered–arid winds snatching away water molecules and mummifying the mesophyll. Though anything still left functioning perished without a water supply, the walls of dead cells still stood tall, serving as infrastructural monuments to the cities of life they had once protected. Fe had never before been this close to the process of death–it was all just a sort of stopping of things, really.

In time, only the embryonic cells still lived, babies in their scattered seeds. When the last of the grains left home, the grass' cellulose skeleton stood vigil, blowing and bending in the winter winds. Snow fell and melted, then fell again. In the rare times when the dead leaf soaked through, its dried cells did not-revivify. Instead, the handsy flood of waters only made the decay worse–desecrating the plant's museum-like ruins, taking bits of soluble loot with them as souvenirs. Like Todd the burglar, the hydrogens left the place far worse than they'd found it.

Less than a season earlier, Fe had been brought from the soil into the living leaf through a deliberate and ingenious process. The method by which it returned, however, proved to be simple gravity. The irrepressible universal force could be temporarily tricked by hydrogen bonds, xylem, and fluid dynamics, but gravity always won in the end. After a critical amount of battering, the superstructure supporting the leaf could no longer hold it, and Fe's once-proud blade of grass crashed down to litter the soil below.

For b-months, the towering museum of mummified cells had stood, mostly unmolested, but it took only a matter of days on the surface to render the dead grass unrecognizable. Wind tossed it among other detritus, and moisture allied with relentless gravity to pack it into the subsoil. Living things, both large and impossibly small, made their way over to investigate the fallen feast.

A menagerie of decomposing microbes, inoculated by the long-dead Terraforming Department, saturated Akkadia's soil. Easy meals went first, scraps of accessible nutrition in the leaf-litter soon appropriated by gangs of unicellular pirates.

The lifeforms shared much with a privateer vessel—or even a schnellbomber, in fact. Free floating, crewed by a nuclear captain, and protected by a well-engineered hull from unknowable dangers beyond, each was an Exodus, a *Mikro*, a *Horizon* in miniature, trawling through the darkness and driven by the hope of some reward to come. Smaller even than the chloroplast, the microbes slipped in the cracks between dead cells. The tiny living ships ran on sugar and had evolved to plunder the glucose that Fe's chloroplasts had worked so hard to accumulate, and they traveled through the wreck of the leaf in a grand flotilla.

Far larger, and much more destructive than any bacterial pirate, an eyeless, segmented monster thundered through the soil, ripping apart the leaf and taking tens of thousands of the tiny trawlers in each yawning mouthful. Originally the earthworm, now the akkadiaworm, this voracious specimen of lumbricinia used its spear of a face to stab through the topsoil, opening a fleshy hatch to engulf bites of decaying grass. Matter that had once boasted thousands of complex photosynthetic factories found itself processed by the mouthful, shoved unceremoniously through the digestive tube-within-the-tube that was the great worm.

Nothing wanted to eat Fe—there was no energy in it. The lazier consumers took what they wanted, lumbricidae slithered through the soil like slimy subways, and soon, the only structure of the leaf that remained were its walls, a vast broken honeycomb of hollows. These city-sized voids nevertheless filled with crews of patient bacterial scavengers, tiny things used to the scarcity of the subsoil.

More priests than pirates, frugal undertaker microbes flooded the necropolis of cell walls, intent on devouring the cellulose-sugars within their vegetable skeletons. Where they could, the starving bacterial intruders navigated masses of indigestible lignans. Whenever one unicellular trawler approached a vulnerable spot in the chain, the bacterium discharged an arsenal of enzymes–like the Major ordering the strategic release of bombshells over an enemy target.

Bomber, factory, and homefront all, the bacterium had manufactured the chemical munitions itself, and when they struck home, these molecular machines pried glucose from the very walls, sending the loose sugars, one by one, up through the living vessel's membranous mouth. Sometimes, a particularly successful scavenger would find itself with enough resources aboard to split, each new life increasing the strength of the bacterial fleet and hastening the ruin of Fe's leaf.

An ecosystem of sorts developed within the honeycombed wasteland. The fungus was here, of course. It had been waiting. A self-contained representative of the kingdom fed nearby. One tiny cell, as complex as that of any animal, happily oozed itself against some lignan-coated cellulose chains that the bacteria had found too challenging to digest. One chloroplast-sized scout, trawling the wastes for fuel, or a forest-spanning mycelial network, it couldn't matter less. The fungus was the fungus, and it waited for all things to die so that it could live. In return, it fixed the soil so that life could thrive again, thus ensuring more death.

Circles made from circles.

The bacterial armada, reduced from its peak numbers, continued to bombard the ruins with enzymes, leaving behind waste, as living things often do. Sometimes it took the form of carbon-dioxide gas, which leached into the air where plants inhaled it greedily, completing the carbon cycle at an energetic loss–a net victory for entropy. Like a foolish, living recycling facility, the ecosystem valued matter at the cost of irreplaceable energy. Nevertheless, a leaf, or even a magnet, were rare and convoluted forms for the transfer to take, their intricacy and beauty perhaps worth the waste.

Time passed, and rain fell, leaching into the ground. Far from static, the sublayer shifted from the movements of the rains and the blind burrowing of akkadiaworms. Nothing energy-rich and edible remained of the grass' carcass, and eventually, Fe could be said to merely inhabit a stained patch of mineral-rich fiber in the soil. Generations of the plant's offspring lived and died in the interim, each successfully imitating their ancestor's lifepath and reproduction. When they fell, they were eaten by the fungus, which waited, as always, for more.

Near the marooned Fe, a mycelium crept, clearing a path for the plant cells it clung to, impatient at their vegetable slowness. These tip-toeing colonists changed the neighborhood as they moved in, spraying the subterranean landscape with gentrifying acids and slurping up its nutrient-rich moisture.

As patient roots gradually pushed their way through acidifying soil, Fe's idle middle-managers at last loosened their hold. Long past their usefulness, the bicarbonate ligands surrendered the indentured iron to the surrounding fluid in their eagerness to find more attractive captives.

Fungal scout cells soldiered ahead, their mycorrhizal munitions bursting along the line of advance, electrically seizing unresisting minerals. It was by such an invader that the atom Fe found itself chelated again, surrendered up to another organic acid jailor far more easily than in the ferrite siege of years past. The advancing columns of mycorrhizal fungus, however, passed it by, deinging not to digest the iron, extending hyphae elsewhere. In unconscious deliberation, it left the metal micronutrient pre-digested for the roots of its slower, woody companion.

In time, the foreign plant roots advanced, pushing forth at an agonizing, determined pace–extending their hairlike piers wherever they went, importing what goods the soil could surrender. The chelated Fe passed from the cold akkadia into the living cell's fortress-like walls via an immigration process remarkably similar to that of the first plant, though the owner of this root system had far more ambition than a stalk of grass that would live and die within the same year.

● ● ●

Fe passed from carrier to carrier, leaving the plant's root cells and finding itself traveling the bustling vascular highways that ran between hundreds of cellular cities, each alive and humming with purpose, directed by their fatal DNA.

On the atom's scale, each new cell sprawled out like a vast, cytoplasm-filled globe. Monstrous, green chloroplasts swam here and there–everywhere, some biological construct was carrying *something* to somewhere else, Fe counted among the cargo.

The iron's path up the central xylem was another endless ascension of water-molecules through vertical tunnels made from the dead, though different supervisors took charge of the ion in its journey through the pine. Fe's new host plant resembled the grass at the cellular level, but it lived on a different scale entirely. Incredible was the length of time it took Fe and its escorts to travel through the winding, rhizomatic maze.

Such a root structure could only belong to a tree–those majestic nobles of the plant kingdom that leverage their long lifespans, stretching themselves into unassailable behemoths, dominating their environments from on high. Though the proud pine's crown aspired toward the heavens, a weighty base of biomass lived under the ground, cells by the billions toiling and cooperating to form a living thing large enough to define the landscape.

Eventually, the tree's interior canals won their tug-of-war with gravity, and the dissolved Fe began to gain elevation. Behind walls of bark and wood, it floated and climbed up narrow xylem straws. In some towering examples of *Pinus sylvestris*, a bit of solute could take days to rise all the way up the trunk. This particular pine, however, had only been growing for six years. Though an eternity to annual plants like the grass, young Silvestris' lifespan rendered it a mere pinecone compared to its centuries-old ancestors. Thus, in relatively little time, the upward current carried Fe up the short trunk to the green shoots where it was needed most.

Tirelessly, many millions of cooperating tree cells performed their complex tasks at peak efficiency–harvesting sunlight, forging glucose, and most importantly, multiplying. At each growing meristem, photosynthesizing cells split into endless daughters, doubling and redoubling their sugar-manufacturing operations. It was a mineral-hungry process, and inside one of the pine's sharp, narrow leaf-structures—behind its waxy sheath—the atom Fe once again found itself stationed atop a brand-new, vibrantly-verdant photosynthesizing thylakoid.

    ● ● ●

Flush with nutrients, the Silvestris pine flexed its long needles, drinking in sunlight and bristling against the world around it. Ambitious for a tree that could live for centuries, the six-year-old was in a hurry to grow up. Days were too short down in the lowlands, but the taller it grew, the pine found, the more energy it could harvest from the Akkadian sun. Young Silvestris invested these gains into more light-drinking daughter cells, more height, longer energy-gathering needles—doing a little better each year than it had the year before.

The grass' life ambition had been to drop its seeds, but the pine had already fulfilled that biological imperative, growing and releasing reproductive organs in its first few years. It had spent seasons making them, the woody female cones and the pollen-filled males, giving them almost everything its feeble sapling body could produce. Though an energy-intensive process, seed-spreading ensured that Silvestris' genes would live on, even if the life of the potential giant should be cut off in its early adolescence.

Unlike grasses or giant stars, pines rarely perished in childbirth. In fact, Silvestris' own parent tree lived nearby, casting a shadow over the baby, blocking a buffet of photons with its bulk. It was to be expected—the cone that had given rise to Silvestris had only fallen so far from its towering sire. The parent tree, by contrast, had been a true pioneer. The pinecone it sprung from had plummeted from the limbs of a distant highland giant long ago. Luck and gravity shepherded it down a long, gentle slope that eventually brought the cone to germinate in the lowlands.

The parental shadow slowed Silvestris' growth—problematic, as the young tree desperately needed photons to compete, to thrive. If it kept up the pace, adding to its height, reaping slow returns on shrewd investment, then maybe, someday,

someday, it could stretch to rival its sire. In a very vertical way, Silvestris had a lot to live up to.

Like all successful lifeforms, the pine evolved tools to make its way through a harsh world. Its needles grew longer than some of the older trees, and baby Silvestris boasted little bulk, burning less expensive energy to stay warm. Crucially, the tree belonged to the proud class of conifers–hearty, industrious survivors that declined to shed their leaves in the winter, their internal sugar factories preferring a slow season to a dead one. As other plants around it withered away, the diminutive pine kept its metabolism moving and its needles ever green, even as winter barreled down on the lowlands.

Sunlight grew more and more scarce, yet, if Sivestris had even a chance at climbing to its goal, it would need to produce energy year-round. It would make use of every stray photon it could collect, even those that reflected off hard frost and heavy snow. Fe would never have a day off.

In the dead of winter, Akkadia-2 cruelly turned from its sun, but Silvestris' needles and the chlorophyll within remained healthy, green, and even somewhat warm within waxy, insulated sheaths. Behind this lipid-rich wall, layers of cells existed to do nothing but further protect the needle's sensitive interior from the hash world beyond. Walls within walls guarded the mesophyll–strong defensive lines protecting crucial factory city-cells, busy with year-round photosynthesis. These verdant sugar-making districts sprouted long, wraparound arms that increased their light-collecting area and gave their chloroplasts large avenues through which to float. Within one such kettle-shaped cell, riding aboard a leviathan green monster, the atom Fe toiled.

Inside a stack of green thylakoid saucers, the iron atom found itself bonded somewhere new. This particular photosystem was a workhouse of energy-producing processes, located further downstream on the electron chain than where Fe had conducted crowd-control in the grass cell. Within Silvestris, Fe took on a less specialized position working alongside three other irons, paired with a quartet of sulfurs. Teamed up with two more iron-sulfide groups, Fe's cluster was shackled to the twisting protein structure of the photosystem and tasked to shuttle excited electrons off to the final stages of processing.

Like toiling in a factory fed by unpredictable supply lines, serving inside a conifer posed its challenges for the tiny iron atom. Not only did the frigid winter cold sometimes threaten to shut down the entire operation, unexpected influxes of photons from the harsh noontime sun could burn and damage Fe's more sensitive coworkers. Silvestris' chlorophylls, however, rose to the occasion, solving both problems at once by quenching–dumping their excited electrons into waste heat instead of sending them on down the line, like a refinery burning its surplus.

Fe worked on an intimate team–a team within a complicated amalgam of teams really, a common enough arrangement in complex organizations. Four sulfurs and four irons, Fe among them, hung in a crystalline cube, the eight employee atoms occupying each of the crystal's eight corners. The iron's positive ionization worked well with the oppositely-charged sulfurs stationed in the same molecule. Lighter than the irons, the alien sulfurs had been forged early in the stellar process that led to the death of Akkadia's mother star.

Electrons would arrive from upstream departments to Fe's office at the final photosystem, passed to its team by chlorophyll coworkers. The iron-sulfur cuboid and its partners helped shuttle the charges even further down the line, where they would eventually reduce precursors to help the tree manufacture glucose–molecules of invaluable sugar. These products were destined to fill up the Silvestris' sturdy bark cells, sacrificial scales that pushed ever outward, hardening like armor as they died–the living tree building a cell wall on a macro scale.

In its simple, unskilled way, the iron atom labored within Silvestris, playing an infinitesimal part, with every electron transported, to achieve the baby pine's ambitions. Slowly but surely, the tree grew, even in winter, creating sugars with which to manufacture another layer of bark and to stretch itself, another year taller, into the sky. As Silvestris soared, Fe's needle remained secure on a lower branch, healthy and productive no matter the weather.

* * *

Springtime brought more photons and more opportunities for growth. Snows melted, shoots burst from the dead ground, and pioneering animals arrived. With temperatures rising, the pine's cells and their army of wind-up proteins could work faster, devoting less energy to staying warm. Sap flowed through Sylvestris, bringing more nutrients from underground and combining them with the output of its countless photosynthetic factories, creating rich, energetic products.

Increasing daylight hours meant more work for Fe's chloroplast and its emerald towerblocks of membrane-covered thylakoids. Photons poured down from the star Akkadia into the needles, flooding the already-buzzing photosystem with surplus energy. Strategic quenching along the line helped keep the workers from getting overwhelmed, and Fe and its harried team stayed busy.

Tied within its cubic cluster and anchored to a factory-protein, the far-traveled atom worked together with its iron and sulfur partners to move charges along the chain. When a new electron appeared, the cluster would grab hold, reducing itself, only to quickly oxidize once again and hurl the electron even further up the line to the next team. Like industrial workers tossing hot rivets between themselves, the players inside the thylakoid membrane moved volatile electrons from molecule to molecule, eventually shipping the energy out into the stroma, loaded aboard valuable precursors. Outside the green thylakoid, even more manufacturing took place, glucose transforming to sucrose sugars, cellulose scaffolding, and a dozen other products needed by the ambitious tree.

Fe and its team had no authority over what happened further along the chain—each time they'd successfully transport a charge downstream, another electron would be thrust upon them, and the work would continue. The cycle repeated, an electron here, an electron there.

Eyeless and monstrous, the chloroplast continued to swim the mesophyll cell's internal seas, drinking sunlight like a pampered pet, protected from the outside world by the needle's waxy sheath and sharp terminus. However, one day, an unexpected shadow loomed, blocking out the spring afternoon and shading dozens of needle cells, darkening the chloroplasts and slowing their photosynthesizing activities. Something even stranger occurred then—the long-distance transport network within the tree seemed to shut down entirely.

This sort of thing was unprecedented for the ever-productive conifer. Curiously, no more water or nutrients from underground were making their way up the xylem and into Sylvestris' needles. Inside Fe's curving cell, supply lines squeezed to a trickle. In the other direction, the once-productive emerald cities of the mesophyll found themselves unable to export their sugars. No cloud-shadow could do this.

Everything was wrong. Between the cells and the sun, the gloom deepened, and the intercellular network within Fe's needle ceased to function. Broken proteins proliferated, and emergency teams of healing compounds flooded the traumatized structure, but their work was in vain. The truth was shocking, terrible, and obvious—the bundle of needles was no longer attached to Silvestris.

From the perspective of the emerald cities, the entire universe went dark and began to quake. An outside force crushed one distant needle entirely, undeterred by the leaf-structure's waxy exterior and sharp point. The alien thing pierced and pressured a layer of cells, shredding and squishing until their walls fell and their fluids flooded out. Torrents of intracellular waste ran together, damaged organelles and lost molecular transporters all tumbling in the chaos.

Even the woody stem from which the needles sprouted found itself shredded, and in the darkness, the destructive forces did not spare Fe's workspace. Part of the elongated leaf severed into two, the cells along the division crushed and killed. Trillions of water molecules gushed from the wounds, their hydrogen hands dissolving and dispersing a diverse cast of biological structures, driving them to their doom.

Light was a distant dream. Work stopped. No more photosynthesis occurred. Even in the chloroplasts still undamaged by the catastrophe, chemical workers sat idle, no photons falling to jumpstart the reaction. Elsewhere, things broke down even more rapidly.

From above and below, out of the darkness, sprawling sheets of interlocked crystals of calcium and phosphorus pressed downward in a pincer. Like weaponized mountains, they squeezed and ground the violently-disintegrating remains, ripping into cellulose superstructures and killing countless cells. Aiding the terrible physical force, an invading army of foreign enzymes entered the fray, armed and ready to chemically tear apart any green cities that the calcium-phosphorus crushers failed to obliterate.

Silvestris simply couldn't catch a break.

• • •

A swirling surf filled the darkness, frothing with the dead and dying, chemical battles raging between Silvestris' molecular refugees and the outside agents set to rip them apart. One weapon burned through Fe's waxy pine needle's protective lipids, while another took apart the hardened cellulose walls. Some great conqueror had crafted these enzymatic weapons within itself, and in seconds, the verdant tree material was pulped—rendered unrecognizable.

A titanic lump of the stuff formed up into a ball as the universe of moisture and darkness lurched, and the shredded bits of Silvestris, Fe included, surrendered to gravity.

Within the dense, watery mixture, many thousands of doomed cells still lived. The chloroplast that housed Fe and its iron-sulfur coworkers swam within the curving, still-intact walls of its home city-cell. No useful work could take place, and it was only a matter of time before the forces of the conqueror would topple every last wall and claim the rich plunder within. Before that was to occur, however, the mass of partially-destroyed needles and twigs plummeted downward, plopping into a warm, stinking sea.

Here, the survivors of Silvestris spread out, wrecks of their cells floating among other remnants of derelict vegetable worlds. It was a dark and humid setting within the constantly sloshing waters, hundreds of billions of bacteria schooling and shoaling in the putrid tank. Gasses bubbled up to its pitch-black surface, and in the other direction, particles too dense to float sank to its fathomless bottom, destined for parts unknown.

Everywhere, bacteria thrived. The entire ocean-cave system seemed to exist as a habitat for these microbes, a paradise where they swam, fed, and bred furiously.

Like the decomposers that populated the soil—looters of the fallen grass blade—this new sea of microbes locked onto the carbohydrate-rich walls and tunnels built by industrious tree cells. Bacteria released their chemical munitions, cracking cellulose chains and snatching stolen sugars. Bit by bit, the devastated fragments of pine needles and the cells within were eaten by the microscopic shoal or shattered by the churn.

In the interminable microbial assault, Fe's raft of leaf matter floated to a place where the cave walls pressed themselves tectonically inward. Fluid roiled as the sea lurched and the world closed up, crushing the floating vegetable matter into one dense mass. Bits of shredded Silvestris merged and tangled with wreckage from other plants entirely, and though much of the fluid was squeezed out by forceful pressure, many of the bacterial invaders managed to make their way deep within the conglomeration. Somehow, this damp mass began to move against gravity—a ball propelled upward by the rhythmic churning of a living tunnel.

Suddenly, the darkness and humidity gave way as Fe's moist bolus sailed upward into a region of slightly fresher air. The Earthling iron and trillions of other helpless atoms in the vegetable matter found themselves back in the first chamber, where occasional flashes of sunlight and puffs of breeze penetrated gaps in the terrible calcium-phosphate crushers. They, and an army of crowbar enzymes, instantly and mercilessly resumed their vicious assault on the already-decimated vegetation.

The gargantuan conqueror, that moving mountain of a beast, chewed and chewed. Indeed, Fe could be nowhere but inside the mouth of an animal—a being so complex and enormous that it seemed to contain several universes within itself.

Eventually, the bolus was swallowed and plopped back down, with a warm splash, into the bacterial sea. Though Fe's workplace had been devastated, its thylakoid membrane remained nearly intact, and the loyal iron-sulfide team stubbornly stayed bonded to the proteins of the photosystem. Still, with each new digestive assault, more and more neighboring emerald cities succumbed, and doom quickly approached Fe's own.

The animal regurgitated another ball of cud for deliberate chewing, swallowing it and sending the mass back down into its rumen. In the dark seas of the cave-like organ, only the smallest fragments managed to sink to the bottom, avoiding another cycle of ascension and punishment. By a certain point, Fe's fragment of needle had been milled to the size where it could no longer float. As its particle slowly settled away from the surface vegetation—falling through the warm fluid—bacterial vessels assaulted it on all sides, though they could make little progress during the brief journey, their munitions wasted on the submerging scrap.

At the bottom of the biological tank, muscular manipulations moved the matter into a subsequent chamber. In the beast's second stomach, the partially-digested vegetation squeezed through a narrow, switchback tunnel. As it progressed, dissatisfied water molecules fled from the mass, absorbed by the walls of the animal's gut. Throngs of hungry bacteria hitched a ride, still busily eating and reproducing even as the food particles crossed a fatal transition.

Another stomach beckoned.

The constant transport through the animal was not dissimilar to the way Fe had been brought aboard the living plant cells—life, it seemed, often involved a never-ending series of tunnels and membranes. Thus, the atom Fe and its fragment of wreckage were squeezed through a tube and dunked into another sloshing, pitch-black tank of angry fluid, and unlike the mammoth sea within the rumen, these waters proved an unexpected abattoir of bacterial death.

The great conquering beast injected streams of hydrochloric acid into the fluid of its final stomach, laying a minefield of specialized enzymes for good measure. These molecules of engineered destruction were not the same as those in the animal's saliva—they were chemical hunters, specialized for bacterial prey. Indeed, the shoals of unicellular beings had been unknowingly working on behalf of the very beast that farmed them. The animal had fattened them on vegetable matter and allowed them to reproduce unchecked. Now, this final stomach served as the slaughter-house, its specialized enzymes able to open bacterial membranes as easily as if they had a key. Bacteria died by the billions in the stomach of the conqueror, digested for their protein.

The beast's stomach acid, a combination of hydrogen and chlorine dissociated in digestive juices, ripped charges away from other compounds, not taking no for a molecular answer. This acidic assault succeeded where the crushing teeth and voracious bacteria had failed, dissolving Fe's cell once and for all. It found its home chloroplast slit open, the green monster's sensitive inner structures gushing out into a caustic hell. Unprotected and tossed in the tumult of the waters, the proteins that anchored Fe's iron-sulfide cluster failed, and the atoms lost themselves in the undifferentiated flow.

Digested matter moved across yet another barrier into a winding, claustrophobic maze–the first coil of the animal's intestines. Here, the beast secreted alkaline substances, neutralizing the acidity of the moist mass as it made its way through a blackened biological tunnel. Strange cells lined the walls of the intestine, bristling with heads of hairlike villi. Greedily, they grasped at passing particles, pulling ions and nutrients across membranes and into themselves. On the complicated, studded surface of the swaying, many-fingered villi fields, professional proteins waited, some specifically for Fe and those like it.

The iron atom missed many of these tiny fingers as it rushed and flowed through the winding, many-coiled organ, but eventually, it came close enough to be captured. A protein molecule, daunting in its tangled complexity, grabbed hold of the lost, ionized Fe–rescuing it from the caustic, chaotic flow.

Like a refugee taken in and fed, the unstable atom was swaddled and generously given an electron by its rescuer. Fe found itself passed by the protein porter to the surface of one hairy intestinal cell before being granted a gentle release. Just as in the root membranes, specialized structures run by teams of tiny workers expended energy to bring Fe within the cell–though this time, the iron arrived unescorted.

After the digestive odyssey, the animal cell seemed utterly peaceful. Its internal fluids were less caustic, bacterial predators held no sway, and Fe encountered a surprising number of iron atoms clustered in the biological border-town's public spaces. However much of a respite it was to once again reside inside a living cell, the crowds of metal ions soon were ushered onward.

Bypassing the organelles that kept the city-cell running, Fe filtered its way to a membrane opposite the side where it had first entered. One protein, crafted from hundreds of individual molecular groups, waited with machine-patience to move iron ions out of the cell and into the animal's bloodstream. It welcomed Fe aboard, but as the iron rode the transporter through the membrane, it was forced to give up the charge it had received from its earlier rescuer.

However, Fe did not remain ionized and unstable for long. After ejection from the massive protein, a fresh chemical liaison sat ready and waiting. The new escort was Transferrin, a complex machine made from hundreds of amino acid groups bound to carbohydrate sugars. Eagerly, it grabbed onto Fe, electrically belting it to a bespoke, molecular couch.

Two total seats were available upon the Transferrin ferry, and within the other other, a familiar ion already rested comfortably. Though identical to Akkadian irons, this passenger atom had actually served alongside Fe in the Earthmade magnetic disk—a direct sibling, born from the same dead and distant Mother Star.

Thus, fully-loaded with Earthling iron, Transferrin unmoored itself. Secured in its molecular chariot by carbonates, Fe rode with its miraculous sibling atom away from the intestinal cell and toward the edge of a capillary. It squeezed between living walls and entered a tiny affluent stream—a bloody tributary moving toward the heart of the beastly conqueror's circulatory system.

Chapter 12: The Queen

Queen swallowed for the millionth time then decided to eat some bark too–why not?

She opened her mouth, letting a cloud of gas escape, then pushed her neck forward toward the tree's trunk. With her hard, flat teeth, Queen scraped off some of the young pine's protective bark. It was crunchy. Very crunchy, she noticed, but not as good or interesting as the needles, and there weren't many of those left.

The other goats, who'd followed Queen to the conifer feast, had already eaten most of the living leaves within reach. The herd had spent some quality time lazing and digesting in the midday sun, but most were now up and gobbling the ground cover.

Queen knew her nephew, Buck, was somewhere in the group behind her–she could recognize his distinctive bleat, a sound that could only come from the largest animal in her herd. He was the only one Queen was a bit afraid of, but she understood that Buck was afraid of her too. Less scary were Bill, Doe, Daughter, and Goat. Those four languidly dined on the much-diminished stock of fallen needles under a nearby pine–a much taller specimen than the young Silvestris that Queen had been grazing on.

Mouth, the hungriest member of the herd, trotted between the sparse tree cover, approaching the grazing foursome. Doe and Goat opened their green-stained teeth, screaming in annoyance as Mouth sauntered in and began crunching up the last pinecone. Daughter and Daughter joined in with the yelling, even though Mouth was nowhere near them.

Yelling could be fun sometimes, Queen understood, but at the moment, she didn't care for screaming. Instead, she ignored the young idiots and searched for more needles–a welcome treat, as the herd had been grazing mostly on dry grass since Queen first led them into the lowlands. For days, the old goat had felt some discomfort in one of her stomachs, but the fresh pine seemed to help. She enjoyed the green, astringent taste and the way it flavored her cud.

Inside her bloodstream, nutrients from the needles were already circulating. Aboard its molecule of Transferrin, Fe rushed through the goat's vascular system. Pumped by her powerful heart, Fe surfed veins and capillaries crowded with rushing erythrocytes, platelets, and many harried transporters. Unlike the iron's climb up the pine tree's vascular tissue, this would prove to be anything but a one-way ride. The goat contained an internal network of tunnels and canals long enough to wrap around all of Akkadia-2, and after leagues and leagues of travel, the Transferrin finally squeezed out of the bloodstream somewhere near the animal's left hip.

Though Queen couldn't have known it, her bones contained vast manufacturing districts, factories in their billions tasked with resupplying the most numerous and important cells in the animal's body–her blood. The Transferrin holding Fe and its iron sibling commuted to one of these cellular manufactories within the goat's bones. It diffused toward a busy membrane studded with porters and crowded with ions, waiting to cross. Another protein anticipated their arrival–a receptor, a biological version of Duwaik's custom pier, perfectly bespoke for the Transferrin transporter. The molecular ship and its dock bonded, forming an even more complicated protein, and the entire mass was brought through the membrane and into the cell, where Transferrin's hold on Fe began to loosen.

Meanwhile, things were heating up under the tall pine where Mouth had so rudely intruded. Bill stopped eating, watching Mouth intently, and Doe and Goat filled the air with their bleats. With little to munch left on the ground, the oblivious Mouth began toothily scraping bark from the tree.

A sudden attack from Bill interrupted the snacking–the irate goat stood briefly on his hind legs before throwing himself down, head-first, onto Mouth. Bill's horns impacted his rival's, driving his head sideways against the tree trunk with a muted clack and a spray of bark chips.

Unhurt, Mouth stepped back, instantly ready to fight. He reared on his hind hooves, but before he could strike, Bill had also turned around and was preparing another headbutt. Mouth smashed into Bill a moment before the other goat struck back. The two ended up wrestling with their necks, their backswept horns occasionally locking their heads together.

They circled, reversing rotation as one gained the upper hand, then the other. Their cloven hooves kicked up dust, and the other goats backed away. Bill disengaged for a moment and found a limited amount of room to maneuver. He made to rear up again at Mouth, but it was a feint. His opponent followed suit, standing up and striking down at nothing. From the base of her own, smaller pine, Queen watched the fight with interest.

After a moment spent feeling each other out, the males collided awkwardly and locked horns. Well-fed Mouth used his superior size to shove Bill backwards, away from the tree. The smaller goat broke free, and the two again jousted with competing headbutts.

A clean, strong hit produced another loud, penetrating clack. Both animals seemed slightly stunned by this, but neither had yet grown tired or bored. Mouth stared at Bill sideways through the dark, horizontal slits of his pupils, and instinct told the hungry goat that his rival would attack again imminently.

Before Mouth could prepare a parry, however, Bill was caught heavily on the flank by the rock-hard horns of Buck, who had angrily charged the dueling pair. Bested, the smaller goat found himself thrown to the ground by a single attack of Queen's dominant nephew.

Mouth used the next crucial seconds to pointlessly scream.

His first target down, Buck turned and wrestled horn-to-horn with Mouth, quickly driving the inferior goat to the dirt. Behind him, Bill tentatively tried to regain his footing. Buck took a step back and stomped the ground with his forelegs. Mouth rose, bits of twigs and dirt clotted in his shaggy coat.

The dominant goat stared them both down, one enigmatic eye on each side of his head. Neither of the combatants resumed their aggressive stances. Buck let out a belch.

The fight was over, for now.

Queen found herself slightly surprised by how well Bill fought, but of course Buck had ended it. He was the strongest she had ever seen. Conflict over, the old goat's interest rapidly drained to boredom—there wasn't anything particularly motivating around to eat, and Queen was getting too old to start fights just for the hell of it. Instead, she decided to do what she did best—go look for more food.

She left the small stand of trees behind and began walking east, the sun at her back. Something in her instincts told her there would be delicacies in that direction, and her stomach rumbled with ambitions of its own.

Quickly, the family noticed their Queen walking away.

Daughter bleated, with Daughter and Daughter echoing her calls, and the other goats looked up. The three nannies began to follow their mother. Deeply wishing to not be left behind, the rest of the herd bowed to instinct and fell in—Queen leading them all to fresh pastures, Buck taking up the honored position of rear guard.

Inside her bones, specialized factories were hard at work crafting oxygen-transports for Queen's royal blood. Within one of the developing cells, Fe and its sibling were shaken loose from their transport and made to wait. They floated in the cytoplasm alongside other castoff irons, thousands of which arrived in the biological city with each passing moment. Before long, the intracellular waiting room was more crowded with iron atoms than anywhere Fe had been since the fall of its magnetic fortress.

When the time finally came for Fe, it found itself processed from raw material to tool in a series of steps highly reminiscent of the production lines at Junkers or Druke, though the goat cell managed its operations automatically, no upstream intelligence directing the process.

Queen's cells possessed neither chloroplasts nor their stacks of green thylakoids, however, each hosted flocks of the other, bacteria-like passengers—mitochondria. These eldritch intracellular powerhouses gobbled up the resources that passed constantly through their many-ported membranes. From inside one mitochondrion, manufactured products poured out into the cytoplasm where they bonded into rings. Each ring re-entered the monstrous swimmer, where more molecular machines synthesized it into a porphyrin hoop–a structure nearly identical to that used by the miraculous, light-harvesting chlorophyll.

Where the emerald chlorophylls required a trapped magnesium at their centers, the bloody blueprints within the mammal's DNA called for iron–for Fe. An enzyme grabbed the coveted ion and hooked it into the growing porphyrin ring. At the center of the new construct, four nitrogen atoms bonded with Fe, forming the compound heme–a clever molecular tool employed by cells to pluck and pack oxygen.

Within the busy bone tissue, similar heme groups rolled off the assembly line in an endless production run, a single iron atom inside each. Various raw materials and near-finished products floated in the cytoplasm, shuttled between protein synthesis centers, moving in and out of the mitochondrion. Molecules of RNA, bundled in a tight-lattice, performed intricate tasks of protein synthesis, tens of millions carefully crafting components like an army of perfectionist Dr. Kims.

The final product of all this activity was hemoglobin–a baffling tangle of proteins and a new home for the atom Fe. Each hemoglobin boasted four globular limbs. These twisted chains folded, origami-like, into perfect pockets, their centers strongly binding one vital heme each. The hemoglobin molecule and its four subunits, tangled together in a messy tetrahedral ring, had evolved over eons, each twist and helix randomly engineered to better hold the hemes and their all-important iron.

Three identical atoms shared Fe's starring role in the molecule, and all happened to be aliens–the solar sibling iron having ended up inside a different molecule of hemoglobin entirely. Billions and billions and billions of atoms in the growing blood cell, some born from Akkadia's mother and some born from Sol's, worked together to fill it with millions of copies of the powerful hemoglobin molecule, preparing the corpuscle for its eventual transition to erythrocyte–a mature red blood cell.

● ● ●

Queen and the universe of life within her cells moved across the lowlands, propelled by four strong, hooved legs, held together by a rigid, dynamic skeleton. Within one of Queen's bones, the erythrocyte that held Fe in its hemoglobin embrace experienced a revolution.

Its leadership–the nucleus which safeguarded and distributed the cell's DNA and oversaw most of its processes–found itself overthrown in a cellular coup. Revolutionary filaments gathered, slowly building a great chain and twisting off the part of the blood cell housing the nucleus, separating the city from its central government.

Despite the nucleic overthrow, the membranes held firm and the cytoplasm still bulged with useful nutrients and materials. A network of RNA formed during the revolution, founding an interim government and reticulating the cell, allowing the furious synthesis of hemoglobin to continue. Many of the enigmatic mitochondria fled with the nucleus as it was expelled, and those left behind began to slowly die. These marauders liked to feed on the very oxygen that the blood cells were tasked with delivering, and there would be none of the gas to spare in the growing erythrocyte.

Without its nucleus, the young blood cell took on the shape of a flattened disk, like an enormous, crimson version of the squishy, membrane-bound thylakoid where Fe had once worked. Within the vast corpuscle, the atom rode aboard its own hemoglobin molecule, one of millions eager to finally see action. Eventually, the cell completed as much of its development as it could within the animal's bone, and it squeezed through a narrow passage into the capillaries beyond.

Fe entered the bloodstream, this time not bound by a captor but wielded instead like a net. In the animal tissue, the iron atom had been given quite a vigorous promotion. No longer tasked with shuttling electrons or little hydrogen ions, Fe, as the star of the erythrocyte, would be hauling molecules–volatile, diatomic oxygens fresh from the lungs.

Fe's heme group and its entire elaborate hemoglobin protein were built for attracting the fugitive gas molecules, kidnapping them, and trafficking them to Queen's cells to be burned up by her insatiable domesticated parasites–the inescapable mitochondria. Thus, Fe found itself employed as a tiny magnetic tweezer, gripped tightly by a proteinous automaton, serving within a leaderless cell, and flowing rapidly throughout the body of a royal goat.

      ● ● ●

For days, Queen and her group wandered, tracing a random path that still led gradually toward the rising sun. They'd found food, sure, but to the goats, 'food' had a very wide definition. Neither Queen nor her gut were particularly happy with the fodder they'd encountered lately. On the other hoof, no delicacies meant nothing to fight over, and the leader idly noted that Bill and Mouth were lovingly huddled together against the breeze.

Queen trotted up to join the two, sick and tired of making her own heat. She bleated at her daughters with the goal of compelling one or two over–Queen needed to cover her flanks. Some quality time passed, spent doing nothing, until one member of the herd suddenly adopted a tense posture–Goat had seen something.

He screamed, then Queen could see them too. Startled by the yell, a small herd of deer raised their heads as one.

They'd been grazing on something the goats hadn't found yet, Queen realized, hungrily. As if reading her mind, Buck charged forward.

For a moment, the peaceful grazers stood their ground, weighing the potential danger posed by a clumsily-running billygoat and his undeniably impressive horns. Keen-eyed Goat and others followed, Queen bringing up the rear, belching aggressively. In the end, the deer decided not to take the risk, and they bound off in graceful flashes, leaving the surly goats to their unearned spoils. As was custom for the herd, they deferred to their elderly matriarch when it came to food sources. Queen eagerly trotted up to where the deer had been grazing.

Berries!

She gave her flanks a small, geriatric wiggle of glee, and the herd bounded up beside their Queen to share in the sugary treasures–a whole crop of ripe ground fruits, barely touched. Her heart was beating quickly from all of the excitement and exercise, sending her blood pumping and making her pant for air.

The Queen goat expanded and contracted her muscular diaphragm, forcing torrents of air to move, bellows-like, between her insides and the great, gaseous skin of Akkadia-2's lower atmosphere. Pressurized gas rushed into the many-branching flesh trees that were her lungs, flooding each tiny sac with trillions of molecules of highly-volatile O_2. Each of Queen's air-sacs were covered with a webbing of ultra-thin blood vessels, spread across the treelike lungs' outer walls like mycelia–delicate, and all-encompassing.

Another powerful muscle within the goat pumped great tides of vitality to and from her lungs. Fe's blood cell rode the flow–a fully functional erythrocyte, smooth and red and no longer reticulated by its adolescent RNA-webbing. Pressure, originating in the goat's heart, forced the cell into claustrophobic pulmonary capillaries. Thin membranes of lung tissue lined the fleshy corridor, separating the erythrocytes from the howling, outside air.

These barriers, however, proved insufficient to prevent a rush of caustic O_2s from filling the bloodstream. Each a partnership of two oxygens, these diatomic molecules assaulted Fe's cell in their legions. The erythrocyte's outer defenses kept some of the horde at bay, but millions still found their way through, breaching the membrane and infiltrating the cytoplasm.

This was it. The crucial moment that the hemoglobins, in all their baffling complexity, had been built for. Like hunters armed with heme spears, the bloody proteins bravely met the stampede of onrushing oxygens.

Dangled like bait by its hemoglobin, Fe soon encountered a fugitive O_2. One atom of the gaseous duo wrenched an electron from Fe's outer cloud, passing a negative charge down to its partner oxygen like thieves splitting loot.

Unbeknownst to the greedy oxygens, they had been trapped–harpooned by Fe. Now that the unthinking oxygens had taken the bait, their molecule's existence was forfeit. Like a band of crazed hunters, the hemoglobins made quick work of the O2 assault, spearing the molecules like game, ready to be delivered to oxygen-hungry mouths.

Suddenly, the flow in the capillary rushed backward, sending Fe's erythrocyte hurtling from the scene. The surviving O2 invaders quickly fell back, unmotivated to press their explorations deeper into the animal's body.

Blood cells surfed from passage to passage, each wider and more heavily-trafficked than the last, until finally, they poured into the cavernous space of Queen's most important muscle. A sea of rich, oxygenated blood swirled within the chamber, and in a fraction of a heartbeat, currents within the bloodstream shifted–hurtling Fe's erythrocyte out into the realms beyond.

In a reversal of its entrance into the heart, the corpuscle followed a branching path away from the central chambers, each narrower than the last. This far from the lungs, the O2 molecule no longer felt pressure from its peers to grab the first electron it could find. Nevertheless, Fe held on tightly, dragging the volatile gas through the goat's vasculature until it could hang on no longer.

The crucial point came as the erythrocyte and its fellows, crimson and fully-loaded, entered the mad tangle of vessels that wormed their way through Queen's intestinal lining. There, the cells found blood choked with waste products and tissues screaming for oxygen. The hemoglobins, in their millions, obliged, wriggling and freeing O2s from their entrapping hemes.

Fe couldn't hold its captive O2 against outside pressures, and the duo slipped away, but not before the iron snatched back its rightful electron. The oxygens were doomed anyway, fated to be burned like fuel in the mitochondria's internal furnaces.

Their trafficked cargo dropped off, the victorious blood cells followed the irresistible tides of Queen's heart, rushing back to its central chambers and on towards the lungs. Once a captive, the atom Fe now found itself the captor, trapping wild oxygens, again and again doing the bidding of a living machine. Like Nicotianamine and the roots' awful chelators, the iron had taken on their role as jailor. When given the chance, the oppressed become the oppressors, even on a biomechanical scale.

Oblivious to her internal workings, Queen messily chomped ground berries, gorging to her heart's content. Her stomachs filled with easy-to-digest sugar, which swiftly passed through selective membranes, flooding her bloodstream with loose glucose. Inside the winding crimson tunnels, oxygen-carrying erythrocytes dominated the traffic–minority cells, proteins, and various dissolved bits further populating the syrupy thoroughfares. It was an abundance of riches, but with the rush of sugar, the intercellular waters grew hazardous. The goat's body boasted mechanisms to deal with the excess glucose, but for now, Fe's cell had to trust in luck to avoid becoming overwhelmed by the sticky-sweet swimmers.

Gratuitous glucose and fructose flooding in from the berries proved inescapable, and, unfortunately for the cell, free sugar infiltrated its cytoplasm, sliding through membranes where it could. An invading throng encountered one of the hemoglobin molecules, the same one in fact, that now held Fe's solar sibling iron. A single sugar molecule attached to part of the protein, warping its structure. This was the true hazard posed by the rogue glucoses–thus enmeshed, the former hemoglobin could never carry oxygen again.

Fortunately, Fe's erythrocyte escaped to less-saturated regions, only losing a tiny fraction of its heme-carriers to the sugary feast. Again, Queen breathed in, filling her lungs with air, her many cells already screaming for another shipment of oxygen.

The red blood cell squeezed back into one of the narrow capillaries lining a lung, meeting the overwhelming horde of O2 molecules with its millions of iron-baited traps. Fe grabbed ahold of another unit of atmospheric oxygen, and its cell hurtled back toward the heart, ever pumping to supply badly-needed O2 for the goat's brain.

Sometimes Queen's mind held more plants than even her stomach–if only in the form of memory. For instance, the next day when the group of goats chased another party of startled deer from a potential meal, something deep in the inscrutable neural network of Queen's brain told her that something wasn't right.

Her herd was following her up a rise of loose rocks, leftovers from the retreat of an ancient glacier, when they spooked more deer. In this encounter, the goats didn't even have time to bleat a battlecry before the last of the anxious grazers darted away, showing them its white rump.

Queen hesitated, noticing the deer had been eating a scrawny yew tree. The other goats milled about, waiting for her cue. Doe, however, boldly stepped up to the conifer, bending down toward a pile of abandoned needles.

Loudly, Queen yelled, drawing Doe's attention and that of the rest of the herd. They watched as their leader pushed Doe out of the way and approached the yew needles, lowering her head to sniff them.

Queen reared back and snorted. She shook her head from side to side, her shaggy, knotted hair beating against her neck and flanks as she did. Her agitation obvious to the other goats, she sniffed the yew again and snorted. Daughter stepped from the herd and walked toward Doe and Queen. She repeated her mother's action, lowering her head and sniffing the waxy needles.

Daughter, Bill, and Daughter trotted up soon after, each sniffing the dangerous plant in turn. The remainder of the herd followed, Buck stepping up last to inspect the yew. When all but one of her goats had repeated the procedure, Queen gave an imperious shout, and Doe diffidently sniffed the pile of needles on the ground before trotting away, shooting her leaders a surly sideways glare.

Buck reared back on his hind legs and screamed. Though his strange eyes held no rage, he crashed down on the conifer, grinding its needles into the dust. Gravely, he stomped again. Then, for good measure, he kicked his hooves out to assault the branches of the living yew sapling before calling it a day.

The ritual completed, the herd moved on, having learned an important, if esoteric, lesson from their Queen.

● ● ●

A hidden process within the goat matriarch's brain, perhaps even entangled with her memories of toxic roughage, impelled her to lead the herd away from the lowlands, up piles of scree to windswept hills and bare rock. They stepped carefully, their cloven hooves giving them suction-cup traction on the terrain. Soon, however, the day turned dark and cold. With the loss of the Akkadian sun, a sour mood came over the goats.

A thin, spitting rain added to the misery. Undaunted, Queen took her regal time climbing the cliffs, confident in her own ability to find greener pastures. Not every member of the herd had such patience, however. Doe continued her petulant snorts and bleats, perhaps still resentful of being denied food, even food that would make her sick. Several times, she deliberately ran on ahead of Queen, challenging the old goat's authority.

Tired and irritated from the rain and the rocky climb, Queen at last reached her royal limit. The next time Doe came up to pass her, Queen lunged with all her aged bulk, knocking the younger challenger aside. Yells and bleats followed almost immediately, the agitated herd voicing their excitement.

Doe spun around and charged at Queen.

The old matriarch reacted too slowly, turning and allowing Doe to land a partial hit against her ribs. Queen struck back, her hooves digging and sliding for traction against a pile of damp stones. Doe screamed as she fought, but Queen saved her breath, gasping up as much oxygen as she could get.

Within her bloodstream, Fe and the hemoglobin army speared O2s as fast as they could, rushing through Queen's body with each frantic heartbeat, dumping off their cargo at the gates of sore, acid-choked muscle cells.

Still, it wasn't enough. Doe was younger, and, while no match for Queen at her peak, she boasted far more stamina. Their horns clicked together twice, and the two combatants separated. Queen could do nothing but gasp and drool during the respite, but Doe used the seconds to rear back for a punishing headbutt. Before she could strike, however, the balance shifted along a pile of loose gravel on the hillside, and Doe lost her footing.

With lightning instincts, Queen noted her enemy's moment of weakness and charged. Her attack was ragged, but she had the size advantage, and she drove Doe to the ground. Immediately, Doe submitted, scrambling to her feet and sullenly slinking back into the herd. Inside the old Queen's body, Fe's erythrocyte surfed back and forth on the blood tide, propelled by a heart still furious and flooded with fight-or-flight messengers.

As the red blood cell neared cesspools of waste-choked cells, overworked and undersupplied, the hemoglobins within took on a heroic double duty. After setting loose all four of their captive oxygens, some of the proteins would soak up a molecule of waste carbon-dioxide from the ailing cells. The trash CO_2 binded elsewhere to the hemoglobin, leaving Fe to weakly merge with friendly hydrogens from a ubiquitous water molecule, bringing it along for the reverse supply run. The corpuscle carried all on its return to the lungs, not wasting the trip by riding empty. Upon the blood's arrival, the stowaways fled the cell, even as the usual swarming horde of O_2s pushed to get in.

These escaping waste products would fuel the sugar-factory chloroplasts in plants, which would subsequently feed the goats glucose and even make oxygen for the beasts and their stowaway mitochondria. Impossibly complex, the cycle of life continued to turn in endless, entropy-hastening revolutions.

Nature also returned to its normal rhythms on the slopes–Queen retained control of her court and continued to lead them over the uneven terrain. When night fell, the goats huddled together, sleeping in brief, interrupted bursts. The next morning dawned cold and still, and the herd found itself more miserable than ever.

All things pass, and fortunes change quickly. Soon enough, matters improved for the beleaguered goats. Queen's stubbornly-held path finally stopped climbing, and her family expended far less energy during their subsequent descent. Soon, the Akkadian sun climbed high into the sky, burning away the crippling morning chill.

The goats had traveled far enough to smell a hint of salt on the air from the near-by sea. Another, sweeter fragrance also rode the winds, but for a while, the herd came across only sparse, marginal fodder. Seabirds whirled gracefully overhead, though they were paid little attention. If it hadn't been for the constant shuffling, belching, and stomping of the goats, one might have been able to hear the rushing rumble of ocean meeting land.

Queen's wanderings paid off before the herd could travel far enough to actually reach the Akkadian sea. They made it to the base of a sandy rise whose far slope eroded away into a miniature cliff. Like a vision of paradise, the hill was covered in flowers–thousands of sweet, purple blooms thrived atop the rise, and many more grew thickly down its gentler slopes.

The goats scented the air and screamed with glee. Mouth even performed a sort of dance, kicking his back legs out and turning in a circle. Queen claimed her honored position as the first to feed, stepping up to the very center of the hilltop and munching a mouthful of soft, bell-shaped blooms.

Not needing any further invitation, the others swarmed the hillside, gorging themselves on the sweet purple treats. Mouth and Buck seemed to be holding a contest to see which of the heavy billygoats could denude the area first, each slurping and swallowing a heroic number of flowers.

Queen enjoyed the sweet complexity of the soft petals, but at the moment, she felt almost too ravenous for the delicacies. Rather than move to another patch of blossoms, Queen lowered her head and began tearing up great mouthfuls of the grass that grew between flowers. She smacked her jaws, crushing the greenery and mixing it with her salivary enzymes–flavored with flowers, the grassy cud promised to stay sweet even when she would eat it for the third or fourth time.

A shrill cry pierced the calm, afternoon air–it came from Daughter, grazing near the edge of the cliff. The other goats raised their heads immediately, wary of danger. They stared through slits of pupils, scanning across their incredibly wide visual range.

Daughter tensed her body, preparing to bound, but suddenly, something whistled through the air–a projectile, flying straight at the herd. Daughter leapt away, unscathed, but Bill, his head raised in curiosity, took the missile in his neck.

Queen watched an incongruous shaft of wood sprout from the side of Bill's throat–it had strange black leaves growing from one end–but then he toppled over, laying still and silent. The others were in chaos, bleating as they scrambled, trampling the field of flowers in their panic. Queen moved to join them, adrenaline in her blood signaling the muscle cells in her heart to pump harder–she would need all the oxygen she could get for the coming flight.

Alas, the elderly goat moved too slowly. In mid-bound, another wooden shaft whistled in from afar, catching her in the chest, just behind her front leg.

That fateful arrow was tipped with a thin sliver of hammered Sukuru-alloy, sharpened to a razor's edge. Attached to a shaft of straight, solid wood, the iron-tough broadhead cleaved the air with incredible force, parting Queen's thick fur and easily penetrating the rugged cell membranes of her outer skin. It carried enough inertia to push further, slicing apart Queen's muscle tissues and passing between two ribs. The arrow tore through part of the goat's lung and pierced her heart before finally coming to a stop.

The pain was acute, but Queen could barely feel it. Flooded with fear and adrenaline, she continued to run, heedless of direction. Her mind, broken with panic, fired random signals to her muscles, impelling them to do something–anything.

Heroically, the hemoglobins within Fe's blood cell still shuttled oxygens from Queen's sticky, ruined lungs, dropping them off near the frenzied muscle cells of her legs. With the goat's heart stopped, however, no motive force propelled the flow of blood back from whence it came, and Fe's erythrocyte found that it couldn't leave the maze-like corridors of her intramuscular capillaries.

Queen's strength rapidly drained from her, and she didn't travel far. At a certain point, her brain deprived of oxygen, the goat matriarch lost consciousness. Still, her body lurched forward with some momentum, and she collapsed, front hooves scrambling over the edge of the small cliff. Dust and bits of plant matter flew behind her as she died, her chest and belly slamming on the loose ground and skidding forward, too little of the dead goat's mass remaining on the rise to keep her elevated. Gravity took over, and the carcass fell heavily, sliding head-first down the cliff face to the sandy ground below.

Buck stood vigil on the hilltop, searching anxiously for something he could fight. He guarded Bill's unmoving body and watched Queen run herself over the cliff. Through his eye-slits, Buck could see movement–a group of two-legged animals.

Great apes!

They'd surprised the goats from below, and as the large male looked down at the humans, one sent another missile flying in his direction. There was nothing he could do. Buck turned from the hunters and ran, bleating mournfully for his fallen family.

The two-legs did not chase him. Instead, the group split, some climbing the hill to find the first animal they'd downed, others moving to investigate Queen's carcass. She had fallen down the short cliff face, the tumble dirtying her shaggy coat and snapping the shaft of the arrow that had pierced her heart.

Runner, the first human to rush up to the fallen goat-queen, wore his hair in long, intricate braids and looked out through dark eyes. He put his hands on the carcass, sniffing for intestinal damage. When the man found none, he placed his hand to his mouth and whooped something in the language of the Sognos.

Two more great apes arrived to join Runner. They wore hides placed strategically and decoratively about their bodies. Shells, knife-belts, and scraps of colorful woven textiles added to their ensembles.

Archer, the tallest, breathed heavily. He had green eyes and wore a magnificent bow slung over one shoulder–it was he who had brought down both of the goats. Nurse, the shorter of the newcomers, clapped him on the back, smiled, and delivered platitudes of congratulations.

Runner stood up, said some words to the hunters, and sped off, his bare feet leaving deep impressions in the sand as he ran.

Archer set down his bow and bent to inspect Queen's body, placing his fingers over the stump of the bloody projectile. He cursed softly over the broken arrow-shaft and the state of the dirty, elderly goat carcass. Nevertheless, he dug his fingers into the wound and levered out his precious, alloy arrowhead. A gout of blood accompanied the broadhead, sending billions of erythrocytes gushing out of Queen's cooling corpse. Fe's own becalmed cell, however, slumbered far deeper within her flesh.

After tucking away the bloody broadhead, Archer pulled a knife from a hide sheath at his waist. It had a handle of bone and a weathered blade of recycled Sukuru-alloy. In the language of the Sognos, he asked his companion to help him.

Nurse drew his own blade, and the two men began the task of dressing the carcass. They grabbed Queen's legs and turned her body over, slicing through the connective tissues at her joints. The lattice of metal atoms that made up the edges of their knives easily parted the complex web of proteins composing Queen's collagen and tendons. The hunters scraped and scraped with their asteroid-alloy tools and pulled with their strong, five-fingered hands, separating the goat's skin from her filthy, shaggy coat.

During the dressing, billions more erythrocytes and other vital cells fled Queen's body, allowing themselves to be driven by pressure and gravity rather than by the once-irresistible pumping of her heart. Fe and the corpuscle it inhabited, however, remained inside the carcass, trapped within a tiny, intramuscular byway.

Archer and Nurse made their deepest cut yet, exposing Queen's body cavity to the outside air. Her enormous rumen bulged out, white and wet. Arms already covered in gore, the apes reached further into the cavity and scooped out the goat's organs, leaving a pile of her stomachs and viscera steaming in the sand.

Chapter 13: The Sailor

Archer and his companion carried Queen's corpulent body between them, their friend Runner hefting Bill's slightly smaller carcass by himself. As they walked, the men sang songs and played rhyming games, challenging their voices and their minds.

Departing from his native tongue, Archer began to sing a ballad in the Croy language, one he had learned as a youth. By the final chorus, his companions were singing along, more-or-less accurately. Finally, Runner offered a song in the Bo dialect, though it was short and very bawdy.

Despite their burdens, the young hunters were laughing and in good spirits when they approached the Sognos camp. Temporary structures dotted the beach before them. Awnings, made from skins and textiles, stretched across driftwood poles, shading sleeping mats and ale barrels. Everywhere, members of the tribe busied themselves with challenges and play, all trying to make the most of the final evening of their vacation.

Spotting the returning hunters, four Sognos began sprinting across the sand toward them—Rock, Brewess, Sage, and Runner's own son, not yet bestowed with an adult name.

Runner dropped Bill's skinned corpse heavily into the sand to embrace his son, lifting the squealing child high in the air. His companions dropped Queen's body as well. Inside the animal, her many still-living cells lurched with the rush of gravity and deceleration. Trillions of brilliant, specialized factory-cities fell, one by one, to the ravages of starvation, runaway enzymes, and ravenous, uncontrollable bacteria. Oblivious to the cellular slaughter, the humans on the beach clasped hands, laughing and congratulating each other.

"Winner and Turtle's group came back before you," Sage informed them, speaking in the Sognos tongue.

"They brought back a white-tail," Rock added, bending down to look at the goats.

"Bigger than this one?" Archer asked, suddenly anxious that his kills wouldn't be enough to take first prize.

"Doesn't matter," Rock answered.

"No white-tail can beat two goats," Runner said confidently, holding his giggling son upside-down by two chubby ankles.

The others nodded their agreement, and Archer relaxed.

"Congratulations, Archer." Sage reached her right hand out to the victorious hunter.

Archer returned the greeting, pressing the palm of his hand against Sage's slender inner forearm. Each gave the other a squeeze before drawing their arms back, the friction from their connecting fingers producing a clicking snap as their hands parted.

"This calls for a drink!" Brewess announced with vigor.

"I'd love to use her for the cooking contest," Sage said, pointing toward Queen's carcass. "Old ones have the most flavor."

"Dibs on the male," Rock chimed in.

"Of course." Archer laughed, glad to let someone else carry the goats the rest of the way. "Best of luck to both of you—your triumph will be my triumph."

Enjoying the cool water and damp sand under his tired feet, he walked on ahead with Brewess, Runner, and the child. They moved into the main tangle of their improvised camp, passing tents and rows of unlit torches. Brewess broke off, heading toward an area under an awning where planks had been laid across several water barrels.

"Ready for that drink?" She called to the hunters, searching the clutter for some growlers of ale.

"Do you have to ask?" Runner answered with a laugh, stepping up to the makeshift bar.

"Another time," Archer declined. The young man waved his goodbyes and walked from his friends back toward the water, eager to catch the fishing contest before it ended.

His only child, engaged in an animal-gathering competition of her own, hadn't greeted him on the sands. Still too young to be given her adult name, Archer's daughter was standing stock-still and focused when he came across her among the other anglers.

"Hey, Thrillseeker." He greeted her with her nickname and a kiss to the top of the head.

"Uh–Archer! You'll scare the fish." She wriggled underneath him, trying to shake his lips from her oily hair, which grew black and curly, shaved everywhere save at the very crown.

"Fish look more hungry than scared to me." Archer pointed to his daughter's competition, Angler and the long-bearded Storyteller, who at the moment, had something big on his line.

Storyteller's rod was bent almost double, but patiently, the older man maneuvered the unseen leviathan toward the rocks. Angler stepped forward to help pull the fish ashore, using both of his arms to wrestle the great swimmer into submission.

Held by the gills, its tail nearly brushing the ground, the fish stretched out longer than the girl nicknamed Thrillseeker stood tall. Though, admittedly, she was on the short side for a twelve-year-old human.

"Starshit!" The girl cried, employing her language's version of the timeless curse.

"Nobody back home will believe this," Storyteller said sadly, surveying his enormous catch.

"It'll beat mine, that's for sure." Angler had abandoned his rod to grab the giant, his prior, inferior catch strung on the shore. "What do you think? Two hundreds of stones? Two and a half?"

A group of children ran up to the fisherfolk. The one wearing the biggest smile, who happened to be Nurse's daughter and the winner of the basket-weaving competition, proudly held up a beautiful, sturdy-looking hamper. It would be given the honor of holding the winning fish.

"The contest isn't over yet," Storyteller told the children.

"Really?" Archer raised an eyebrow at the bearded elder and his ridiculously huge fish.

"Go ahead, load her up," Angler laughed. "Nothing will beat that before sundown."

"I've got to get my seaslicer in the water, anyway." Thrillseeker sighed, dropping her rod to the sand in disgust.

Her father leaned down, and she stood on her tiptoes to give him a peck on the cheek before running to where the tribe's smaller boats lay beached.

"Where's she going?" One of the basket-weavers asked.

"She's a sailor, stupid," another boy sneered, answering him before the adults could speak.

"Oy!" Archer barked, fixing the rude child with a sharp, green stare. "Manners."

"She's probably off to win tonight's race." Storyteller spoke in his calm, languid way, breaking the tension. "It's not really fair. She won the children's regatta last year by a frankly uncompetitive margin—and the year before."

"And the year before," Archer added, indulging in a bit of paternal pride.

"And the year before!" The first basket-weaver shouted enthusiastically.

"No she didn't, *stupid*," his peer answered.

Archer shook his head and left the bickering children in the company of the fishermen. He walked back toward the camp, where a driftwood bonfire had just been kindled. Light from the flames danced on the lapping waves, competing with the colorful beauty of the sinking Akkadian sun.

Sleek-looking sailboats bobbed on the surf, Thrillseeker's somewhere among them. The seaslicers had a trimaran design—a single hull sprouting two outriggers and one colorful, crab-claw sail.

As soon as the sun touched the water, the sailing contest began. Each pilot set their attack and slipped off into the dark waters, racing by the light of the dying sun and waxing moon. The fishing contest over, the anglers and the basket-makers hauled the evening's catch to the many cookfires around camp. There, the fish intermingled with the bounty from the clamdigging and crab-catching competitions held by other groups of Sognos children.

The massive fish was made ready on a makeshift table where, earlier, the remains of Queen, Bill, and the unfortunate deer had been laid out for trimming and seasoning. Queen's legs had been severed at the knee, her stumps tied to green branches, and her splayed body impaled by a long roasting spit. With help, Sage Sognos had placed the skewered goat over a glowing bed of coals, resting the spit on a pair of wooden bipods driven into the sand.

Most of the goat's erythrocytes hadn't survived her death and butchering, and the atom Fe's was no exception. The damaged cell had at last ruptured, spewing its wasted army of hemoglobin proteins into the rapidly-acidifying intercellular space of the decomposing goat. The proteins that didn't escape the carcass or denature within its cells succumbed to the slowly-rising temperature of their surroundings.

Flares of heat energy from the driftwood fire poured into the meat, penetrating and altering its sprawling, ruined cell structure. Juices once more began to flow within the goat-queen's flesh, animated by flames rather than a heartbeat. Fe's molecule unwound in the luxurious, ambient heat—its complex chains and whorls of folded helices unraveling in bizarre, three-dimensional bursts before the whole tetrahedral hemoglobin collapsed like a building made from angry snakes.

Fe, clinging to its broken heme group, swam randomly among its brethren irons, alien and sibling alike, in the fluids of the cooking meat. Intolerable heat melted nearby cells' precious reserves of fats into a liquid, lipid state. Everywhere, complexes of delicate biological architecture snapped and splintered. Queen's muscular myoglobin, a less-mobile cousin of the heroic blood protein, gave up its ghosts, enriching the fluid with even more iron.

As waves of destruction crested and fell at the cellular level, a pleasant odor escaped the roasting goat, chemical representatives wafting their way to the nostrils of Sage and the other human cooks. Water molecules escaped the goat in droves, many changing from liquid to gas in the process, frantically fighting their way between cell walls, defying gravity to release themselves from the sizzling animal. Those hot-tempered waters that stayed steamed furiously, clawing at everything, oxidizing Fe and infiltrating the helpless wreckages of denatured myoglobins.

To Sage's eyes, all that mattered was that the goat mutton was turning an appetizing brown. The cook rubbed Queen's skinless outsides with crushed chili peppers and oil, poured from a flask she'd brought from Ilsognos for just this occasion. Sage waited until the goat was nearly done before opening another small flask of honey, intending the sweet liquid to glaze rather than burn.

While the goat cooked, people chatted and traded stories. Over the extra heat of the cookfire, they roasted vegetables, some wild-gathered from their days exploring the uninhabited northern island, others packed in woven sacks from Ilsognos.

Two other competing roasts hovered over their own cookfires, islands of light on the darkened beach.

Further inland, around the main camp, those not otherwise engaged were busy lighting rows of torches—illumination for the evening to come. Small boats not employed in the race became picnic tables, and any barrels not needed for their contents were straddled with planks to become benches and counters. Laughing humans set up games and poured drinks as the stars came out. Someone threw more wood on the bonfire, lighting the way for the returning sailors.

One by one, as they finished their tasks, the Sognos vacationers began to converge around their central fire. A shuffling step synchronized into a group-stomp as the crowd grew. Some held drums made from hide, and they tapped out a syncopated rhythm with the stomping feet and a sharply-clacking wooden clave. This laid the base for the singers, whose voices swelled in sophisticated, multi-part harmonies. Vocals floated into and out of the fluid song. Some familiar choruses resounded with crowd-wide chants. Other times, the melody narrowed to a single, fragile voice.

Everyone among the Sognos sang, even if just for a few bashful moments, with the exception of one man—Winner, who had triumphed in a singing competition at the age of nine and had never sung again.

Archer, the storied bow still strapped across his body, stomped and danced along with his people, singing when compelled. His eyes, however, remained fixed on the dark waters of the Akkadian sea, and he did not truly relax until he caught sight of his daughter's crab-claw sail.

#

The girl nicknamed Thrillseeker, not nearly as graceful on land as on water, stumbled up the beach toward the crowded bonfire, running into her father's embrace. In the firelight, her round face shone with perspiration, salt water, and the flush of victory. A cheer arose from the crowd as the dancers noticed Thrillseeker among them, earlier than expected.

"We have a winner!" Storyteller announced, raising a bowl. "To Archer and Flute's daughter!"

"This calls for a song."

"Triumph of the Tuna!" Someone shouted, naming an ancient folk song of the sea.

Together, the Sognos swayed in the firelight and sang all the verses and even an encore of the sea shanty before the second, third, and fourth-place finishers from the sailing contest came ashore, running up the beach to join in with the music.

With everyone accounted for, the campers concluded their merrymaking with one last communal song–a stodgy, boastful number, but one every Sognos knew by heart. Traditionally, in excursions of this sort, the final tune and the grand cheer that followed signaled the end of the sailing contest and the opening of the feast-night games, which included among them an eating competition.

The ravenous Thrillseeker hugged her father goodbye and made for the tents closest to the cookfires, intent on participating.

Archer hoped to make short work of the archery contest, not wishing to delay finally getting to taste his spoils from the goat hunt. He turned from the bonfire and walked toward a patch of flat beach, illuminated by torches, where a rudimentary range had been set up. Two men and a woman milled about, waiting to participate.

An older Sognos spectator offered their extra bow to the contestants, but Archer politely declined. His own bow was centuries old, made from materials and by methods lost to time. It had been passed down and lovingly preserved through family lines, lost and found more than once in its history.

Breathing deep, even breaths, Archer sat cross-legged on the ground, resting the bow on his knees. As the others shot, he kept his eyes closed, allowing his sensitive retinas time to recover from the searing light of the bonfire.

Around camp, the crowd devolved into clots dedicated to general partying and sundry competition. Some, like Runner, stayed by the fire to smoke long bundles of herbs. Everyone with a free hand carried something to eat or drink, but it was at the tabletop dedicated to the eating contest where the truly serious feasted.

Nine campers, including Thrillseeker, Brewess, and Rock sat before wooden planks piled high with fruit, fish, game, roasted tubers, and cooked things in shells. As always, the eaters drew an audience.

Sage stood in the crowd, watching the contestants nervously. Traditionally, those feasting served as judges for the cooking competition–Rock, as one of the cooks, would be honor-bound to recuse himself.

One of Queen's legs rested on a platter set in front of the young sailing prodigy who some called Thrillseeker. Separated from her body, the goat's cells had been dehydrated and denatured by the cookfire, her once-thriving tissues turned to dead, salty wastelands. Hovering above the roasted limb, Thrillseeker stuffed her cheeks with chunks of fish and a fistfull of small root vegetables before contemplating the goat. She chewed furiously, hoping against all odds and logic to defeat her much-larger adult competitors.

Thrillseeker swallowed, wiped her mouth, and reached for the goat leg, grabbing it by a protruding length of bone. She brought it to her lips and, not stopping to inhale the delicate aroma so cunningly layered by Sage, opened her teeth to tear away a chunk of the honey-glazed meat. The young human chewed, shredding fibers of flesh between her teeth, those calcium-phosphate crushers that, at the molecular level, could easily be mistaken for Queen's own.

The competitor steeled herself, endeavoring to take even more bites before swallowing. Her teeth tore back into the mutton, chomping ever closer to Fe's resting place. Unfortunately, Thrillseeker's mouth had not evolved enzymes to quickly dissolve massive chunks of tough goat, and the girl was stuck chewing a wad of meat in a macabre, carnivorous parody of her ungulate prey's grazing habits.

Nearby, Rock inhaled truly heroic amounts of food. Thrillseeker couldn't hope to catch up, but her attention was on the task before her. At last, she swallowed, feeling her stomach stretch as the meatwad forced its way into her already-crowded gut. The eaters' audience was also expanding, some other contests, such as the incredibly anticlimactic archery competition, having ended early.

Between roots and clams, Thrillseeker tackled the goat mutton, engulfing another bite, her teeth wrenching free a ropy complex of muscle tissue that happened to contain the atom Fe. The girl's sore jaw muscles strained with the effort, but she chewed like a champion, forcing her jaws together, again and again, against the tough meat.

Mineral-hard primate teeth sliced through the long, stringy muscle fibers that Queen once used to move her leg. With sufficient chewing, the carefully-organized goat musculature turned to a wad of undifferentiated gore in Thrillseeker's mouth. She swallowed—her enzyme-rich saliva doing what it could to lubricate the process.

Fe, riding the remains of the herbivore, moved down the young omnivore's throat. Aided by muscular action and gravity, the chewed-up wad completed its short journey, plopping down into a crowded and churning stomach.

Although both chambers were hot, dark, and tumultuous, the great ape's stomach had little in common with the rumen of the goat matriarch. Where Queen's first stomach held a bloated mass of fermenting vegetation, the human gut seemed to begin where the goat's ended—in a chamber of acid.

Rows of factory cells busily squirted chemicals from their stations in the stomach lining, performing their evolved task and swelling Thrillseeker's glands with gastric juices. These caustic acids filled the swirling, wreckage-choked sea where Fe and the muscle fibers floated. Many of the proteins that hadn't been broken down by Sage's judicious application of heat soon succumbed to the chemical crowbars of the stomach, denaturing, unraveling, and eventually dissolving.

Unconcerned for her internal wellbeing, Thrillseeker continued to force more food into her mouth. Out of the corner of one eye, she watched as Rock guzzled half a growler of beer. A drink sounded good, but she knew that liquid could only slow her down, would take up precious space in her child-sized belly.

Instead, to quench her thirst, Thrillseeker gobbled down a handful of berries. Again, she hefted the leg of roast goat by the knob. She'd succeeded in eating Queen's limb down to the bone, but a great deal of meat still clung to the joint.

Three of the nine competitors had surrendered by then—too full to eat another bite. As Thrillseeker athletically chewed, one unfortunate camper stumbled down to the waterline and vomited their share of the feast into the Akkadian sea.

Brewess, by contrast, stayed perched at the long table, looking healthy and happy. She appeared to be taking the contest as a chance to unhurriedly eat and drink her fill, unsportingly content to let the others bust their guts in pursuit of victory.

Archer's daughter hadn't yet cleared the platter in front of her, but nearby, Rock had cleared his. He slid over on the bench, appropriating the leftovers of the disqualified eater who was still gagging somewhere near the ocean.

Food set aside for the competitors dwindled, though not as rapidly as the will of those tasked with consuming the bounty. One by one, the eaters stopped, pushing away their platters or simply sitting and staring in stunned silence at those who continued.

Frustrated by her body, Thrilseeker found that she could no longer force any more fodder down her maw without breaking the laws of physics and physiology. She would have to stop if she wished to remain conscious and uninjured.

Thrillseeker felt the hot slap of shame strike her face and trickle down her spine—a phantom feeling to go with the droplets of hot meat-sweat forcing their way through her pores. It made no difference to the girl that her proportions were entirely inappropriate for the struggle she'd set herself to. Even if she happened to be twins, each carrying a fishing net bulging with coconuts, the hypothetical pair would still be outweighed by Rock Sognos, a man who earned his name by single-handedly providing ballast for a family-sized seaslicer.

The audience broke into applause, rhythmically drumming on their own bodies, clanking their drinking vessels, and clapping their hands together. Rock, the obvious winner, stood up unsteadily before throwing his arms into the air, inciting an increase in the celebratory cacophony. Victoriously, he flexed his chest and released a thunderous belch, earning looks of disapproval from the older Sognos but eliciting trills of laughter from the children.

When the applause died down, the time came for voting. Thrillseeker cast her verbal ballot for Sage, who ended up winning the cooking competition six votes to one, with one abstention and one disqualification in the final tally.

The sailing champion still needed to take some deep breaths before she would be human again. At the moment, her body felt more like a bloated animal carcass that had washed up on the beach. Within Thrillseeker's distended belly, Fe waited its turn alongside the inordinate amount of meat and vegetable matter consumed by the daring young human.

The evening's festivities flowed as naturally as the river to the sea. Just as the end of the hunting contest signaled the beginning of the cooking competition, which at its close, heralded the eaters to take their places, so too did the end of the eating contest bring that night's feasting, as well as its games, to a close.

Feeling nearly as full as the Akkadian sea, Thrillseeker waddled onto the beach, looking for Archer. She knew her father had competed in the finals of the chess tournament, and she headed to where she saw tables set up earlier. When she arrived, however, the campers had already taken down their benches and game-boards.

She found Archer in their tent, tending to his precious bow. He was turned from her, contorting his long torso and pressing his bodyweight against the limbs, allowing the bowstring to slacken and come free. As he relaxed, so did the marvelous artifact–extending to its full length. At last, Archer noticed his daughter and smiled.

"You look terrible," he said.

Thrillseeker laughed, which quickly turned to a dangerous-sounding hiccup.

"Please don't make me laugh," she groaned, one hand protectively on her belly.

"As you wish." Archer carefully wrapped his bow in layers of skin and cloth, tying off the bundle and both ends. "Did you win?"

"I said don't make me laugh, Archer."

"Honestly," the young man shrugged, "I wouldn't even be proud of you for winning at *eating dinner*."

"One day I will win at eating dinner. You mark my words."

"Noted, daughter. Let's go claim our prizes before they give them to the less deserving."

Despite her warnings, Thrillseeker giggled again, though, mercifully, without gastric complications.

The pair left their tent and mingled with the remains of the party. At least half of the torches along the beach had gone out, shepherding the campers into the shrinking pools of light. Any spirits that hadn't yet been quaffed were appropriated and consumed by those partygoes who didn't seem to mind the prospect of packing and sailing with a hangover the next morning. Somewhere, in the shadows, a Sognos elder was complaining loudly about having to pick up empty containers.

At the bar, Sage cut slices of juicy, yellow pineapple—a fruit she'd purchased from Eenoor traders. Children and adults alike skewered the well-traveled treat on sticks and roasted it over the dying bonfire. Thrillseeker would have liked to sit with them and enjoy the tangy, sugary warmth of toasted pineapple, but her gut gave a lurch at the very thought—no more food for a while. Instead, the father and daughter made their way to an improvised stage for the medal ceremony.

From a chest made from richly carved hardwood, Brewess withdrew a stack of Sukuru-alloy medallions, each recycled and hammered into disks of varying diameters. Archer stepped forward to help her present the medals, calling each winner up in turn. Winner himself received no prizes, but Archer handed Rock, Storyteller, and Sage their trophies, pausing to allow the campers time for small bows and scattered applause.

He pressed a small metal disk into the hand of the child who'd won the basket-weaving competition, and he gave an even smaller one to the winner of the stone-throwing contest. Finally, the normally serious man grinned hugely as he knelt down to present his daughter with the largest medal of all—the prize for winning the sunset regatta.

Before the end of the informal ceremony, Brewess cleared her throat to get Archer's attention, handing him three medals of his own—two for his triumphs with the bow and the other for winning the chess tournament. He accepted them humbly, blushing slightly and tucking them away. Upon their return to Ilsognos,

Archer planned to have the alloy forged into fieldpoints by his friends–Smith Sognos, or perhaps Crafty, depending on who he ran into first. Thrillseeker would put her medal toward a new rigging knife.

A round of arm slaps and congratulations followed, but neither being big drinkers, both father and daughter bid the lingering partiers goodbye and retired to their tent, slipping eagerly into slumber with the large blob of the b-moon still in the sky.

Thrillseeker's keen, yet exhausted, mind may have been able to wind down and find rest, but the trillion semi-autonomous city-cells of her digestive system worked furiously during their overnight shifts.

Faced with more food than it had ever experienced, Thrillseeker's stomach tissue pumped disembodied chemical teeth into its churning internal brew, simple-yet-effective acid molecules manufactured on efficient intracellular assembly lines. Broken from its hemoglobin, the ionized atom Fe sloshed with the currents, making and breaking bonds in the low-pH tide. Things were much as in Queen's final stomach, though now Fe floated in a soup of meat, roots, and fruits rather than grass, leaves, and twigs.

Humans had long understood that the application of heat could turn the inedible edible–Sage's judicious cookery rendering the goat's old meat easily digestible. Early in her sleep cycle, however, Thrillseeker's body found itself overwhelmed with the amount of nutrients given to it, and less demand than usual drove dissolved ions into her cells. Even coveted iron would have to wait its turn.

As the night progressed, Fe moved with the slowly-digesting mass from the stomach to the first and smallest of the girl's intestines. The great ape's viscera carried on for a vast distance–fleshy tunnels winding four times as long as Thrillseeker was tall, all crammed into one tiny cavity. Just as in the goat, each coil of the human small intestine bristled with billions of grasping villi. Fe bumped down one turn of gut and then another, traveling inexorably through the darkness. Not every nutrient eaten by the human would make its way to her bloodstream–a great deal would continue onward, food for the voracious ecosystem of bacteria further downstream. Many more still would be lost, passing through the animal entirely.

Toward the lower third of the organ, however, the dissolved Fe impacted an outstretched villus, which happened to be attached to a cell ready and waiting for iron transport. Patient porter proteins at the surface fulfilled their evolved task, pulling the refugee iron safely into the cell.

\#

Archer's daughter slept until after sun-up, laying facedown on her mat with her arms over her head even as her early-rising father dismantled the tent around her. Bleary-eyed, the too-young-to-be-named sailor some called Thrillseeker rose and staggered, grumbling and squinting, to the waterline. Despite the morning chill, she dunked her curly-topped head into the bracing salt water.

The girl stood up sputtering–her eyes alive.

Walking back to the beach, she squeezed the cold water from her hair then shook her head like a dog, trying to catch Archer in the spray.

Their vacation over, the Sognos regretfully, though unhesitatingly, broke down their beachfront properties. They took down supports and piled the driftwood off to one side or left it to lay wherever it fell, but they made sure to gather up any hides, bits of rubber, ropes, water barrels, and of course, any alloy fasteners or nails used in the temporary shelters. Before noon, all the campers were on the water.

They strapped everything to their boats, packing loose foodstuffs and clothing into woven bags tied to the vessels' foredecks. Most of the Sognos watercraft were trimaran seaslicers of various sizes. Their asymmetry was akin to a bent water molecule, with one large, structural oxygen atom serving as the hull and two underslung hydrogen outriggers on either side. Custom-made for the Akkadian sea and steered by savvy islanders, the boats sliced across the waves as fluidly as the particles they resembled.

Thrillseeker piloted her own racing trimaran near the larger ship crewed by Archer, Storyteller, Runner, and his family. She sailed solo, a difficult task without a squire–the traditional teammate allowed in regattas like the upcoming Hand Nations Classic. Normally, Thrillseeker crewed with Swimmer, an older girl from Ilsognos whose family hadn't elected to attend the northern camping expedition.

The young champion waved to her father and tacked her orange and yellow crab-claw sail, catching a gust and driving her seaslicer forward–leaving the main body of the vacationers' fleet behind.

She attacked the wind and waves, relishing in the freedom of the open water, but Thrillseeker never allowed the royal purple sail of Archer's trimaran to disappear over the horizon completely, and when she had sailed too far away, she would lower her canvas and lay in the sun or sit with her feet dangling into the sea, waiting for the others to catch up.

Within the bone marrow of Thrillseeker's left femur, the atom Fe passed a final membrane, invited again to enter a developing blood cell. This young erythrocyte was well on its way to leaving its bony cradle and entering the nearest capillary when the iron arrived. Late to the party as Fe was, however, there remained many thousands of hemoglobin molecules for the corpuscle to construct–plenty of positions left to fill.

On a molecular level, the bodies of the mammals were nearly identical. Just as in Queen, enzymes bonded Fe to the central net of a heme group, itself held in the grip of complicated protein servants twisted into a united, four-chambered hemoglobin molecule. After the juvenile blood cell squeezed away its tyrant nucleus and shook loose its stowaway mitochondria, only a subtle difference in the twists and turns taken by the individual hemoglobin proteins could distinguish the human blood cell from that of their close cousin, the goat, with whom they shared far more in common than did Sylvestris and the short-lived grasses of the plant kingdom.

"Look out! Giant crab!" Storyteller warned.

Runner and his son held out a long pole, slapping the water and splashing Thrillseeker. They'd come upon the reefed seaslicer while its pilot dozed. Archer shook his head as he watched Thrillseeker open her eyes and close them immediately against the glare of the sun. She threw an arm over her damp face and groaned.

"Quit it–"

"That's enough, Terror," Runner said to his child, stowing the craft's pole. "We got her good."

"I'm gonna get you back," Thrillseeker threatened, pulling herself to a sitting position. "You have no idea what you've gotten yourself into."

"Good!" Runner laughed, calling across the water. "I was just getting bored."

"You should get up if you don't want to be late to the thing," Archer advised, his clear voice carrying. "What if the Classic has already started?"

"Don't joke about that!" The girl shouted. "I am *not* missing that race!"

The larger boat hadn't slowed, and they gradually left Thrillseeker and her un-powered seaslicer behind. She shook the sleep from her head, gripped the halyard of her crab-claw, and found her feet. Within a matter of moments, even the fastest craft in the campers' flotilla was left in her wake.

"This is taking forever!" Thrillseeker loudly complained the next time she drew alongside her father's purple-sailed trimaran.

"You were so impatient to get to the island when we set out, do you remember?" Archer fixed his offspring with a calm, bemused stare. "Now you can't wait to go home."

"Let me go on ahead, Archer. Moon's nearly full tonight. I can press on for a few more hours and sleep once I get to Ilsognos."

"You're crazy!" Runner's eavesdropping son informed her with a giggling shriek.

"Out of the question, wild-one," Archer concurred.

"You know I can do it!" Thrillseeker leaned defiantly over the stretch of water between their boats.

"No one questioned your abilities."

"Flute will be happy if I come home early," she retorted, using her mother, waiting back on their island, in an attempt to manipulate her father.

"That's not the point!" He replied, his temper beginning to crack.

"Yours can't be the first child-name written among the winners of the Classic if you die at sea before you reach the starting line," Storyteller interjected, sagely.

"Uggghhhh!" She groaned, employing the universal language of frustrated adolescent humans.

"Oy, Thrill, I get it," Runner spoke up, "I hate treading water too. But there's no way you're gonna miss the regatta, so relax. You could *swim* there and not miss it."

"Don't test me," Thrillseeker said, stepping nimbly to the edge of her seaslicer, careful to keep her center of gravity low as she stood, balancing and raising her arms in the rough direction of Ilsognos, readying to jump.

She turned to see the looks of worry on the boys' faces before lowering herself back into a crouch, tossing her black mane and smirking.

"She's crazy," Runner's young boy observed for the second time.

"Don't let her hear you say that," Archer cautioned.

"I'll show you who's crazy–" Thrillseeker bellowed theatrically, unlatching her own craft's thin, wooden reef pole. "En garde!" She cried, using a foreign people's colloquialism for initiating combat.

Aboard the larger boat, Runner's child squealed with glee and dove toward the nearest pole, though the tike hadn't a chance of hefting the thing without his father's help.

Against the setting sun, the two trimarans engaged in a mock duel. All participated save Archer, who looked on as his daughter fought with an intensity that bordered on unsporting. Other boats in the flotilla clustered together, centered around the leading pair, as darkness crept across the sea.

When the children had tired from their sport, and the trimarans of the Sognos vacationers had been loosely lashed together for the night, Storyteller cleared a space on the highest deck and gathered all who would listen. Runner's child, Nurse's daughter, and the girl nicknamed Thrillseeker sleepily sat together under the starlight.

"Do you want to hear the story of the acorn, the tortoise, or the dandelion?" Storyteller asked all assembled.

"Tortoise," Thrillseeker said softly.

"Dandelion!"

"Dandelion!" The other children shouted, resolving the selection.

"Once upon a time," Storyteller began immediately, "everything that ever was or that ever would be was curled up into a tight little dandelion pod." He gestured, squeezing one hand into a fist. "It hung alone in the darkest, blackest, emptiest night that ever was."

"Shhh–" an adult hissed loudly from another vessel, silencing a child's ambient chatter.

"You know what dandelions do, right?" Storyteller continued, still holding up his fist. "They bloom and they burst. When this one bloomed, it created the universe–"

With a suddenness that drew a small gasp from the audience, Storyteller flashed open his closed hand and spread his arms toward the sky. The bearded bard next stepped toward a mast and plucked a decorative feather from a hanging bundle.

"There were many seeds. But one among them, probably the best one," he winked, stepping to one edge of the vessel and twirling the feather, "had people on it. *Our* ancestors. The first Graham steered the seed, like steering a trimaran, but he sailed on seas of night instead of water. He led this lone, fragile seed fearlessly through many trials until, at long last, he found the perfect world for his people. Home!" Storyteller leaned down to slap the water, giving emphasis to his final word.

"The seed landed in the water," he said, allowing the feather to fall softly into the Akkadian sea, "and the first Graham spoke to his people. He rose high into the sky." Storyteller, with a dramatic flourish, scampered atop the raft's cabin, looking down on his audience like a small god.

"The sun stood still in its path so that Graham could speak one last time. While he talked, his children grew up, and the seed he planted in water grew into a big, beautiful dandelion–big enough to hold and house and feed them all."

"Hey–" Nurse's precocious offspring challenged, unable to hold her tongue against the obvious factual inaccuracies in the tale. "Flowers can't grow on salt water!"

"Well not *anymore*," Storyteller responded, unbothered. "That's what makes this such a crazy story."

He was met with a titter from the audience.

"As I was saying, a big, beautiful dandelion. When it burst into seeds, they floated on the winds and sailed on the waves for many days, until finally, they found islands of their own, and each settled into the soil and grew into a city of thirteen hundreds of people. And naturally," Storyteller finished, "the very best of these seeds–the strongest and the toughest and the smartest and the swiftest–washed up on the beaches of *Ilsognos*!"

The tale's conclusion was met with a mixture of polite applause and jingoistic cheers.

"It would be nice if *we* could find Ilsognos," one young sailor muttered, still impatient for her next challenge.

\#

Within the vast galaxy of cells that made up the girl nicknamed Thrillseeker, worry born in the quantum circuits of her neurons induced her body to flood itself with hormones–agents evolved by her ancestors on a planet far away and long ago. Among other powers, these messengers made Thrillseeker's heart beat quickly within her chest, keeping her from sleep.

Her trillions of blood cells rushed blindly through the fractally-branching courses of her veins, waters too complex for any thinking sailing prodigy to navigate without going mad. Within one tiny capillary, a fledgling erythrocyte, which happened to contain the atom Fe, squeezed its way into the vasculature of the human champion, joining the coursing, crimson vitality in its never-ending race.

The next day dawned, and the air soon absorbed a pleasant warmth. As the flotilla of returning vacationers approached their home waters, they encountered another group of vessels, trimarans and other craft, all flying simple, sunbleached sails–the Sea Peoples.

Those who lived their whole lives in floating, offshore communities couldn't be counted among the numerologically-regulated population of the Sognos, or any other tribe for that matter. Yet, the casteless group did a thriving trade between the Hand Nations and the endless islands of the Akkadian archipelagos, their floating settlements and representatives as common and benign as colonies of gulls and pinnipeds.

A few of the white-sailed vessels broke off and made for Thrillseeker's flotilla. Among the arriving Sea Peoples were merchants, ready to offer the returning vacationers island-fresh water and other comforts they could probably wait for.

Alone aboard her trimaran, Thrillseeker watched in disgust as Brewess chatted easily with one of the vanguard vessels, accepting a large bunch of yellow-green bananas from a sunken-eyed Sea Person.

"Really? You're going shopping *now*?" The youth whined as even more white-sailed boats intercepted her flotilla.

She watched through narrowed, angry slits–Runner and even Archer were eyeing some of the goods, apparently in no hurry to end their vacation.

"You've got to be joking!" Thrillseeker's blood felt hot as she fumed over the delay.

Fe's rookie erythrocyte, rather than stilled and becalmed like its human's trimaran, found itself rushing furiously through twisting vasculature, exploring bloody rivers and channels that wound their way within Thrilseeker's deepest and darkest organs.

She could hear Archer's voice in conversation with one of the tribeless, the unfamiliar syllables of the Sea Peoples' pidgin sounding strange coming from her father's mouth.

"Woo'dan!" He cried.

"What?" Thrillseeker asked, paddling over.

"Nightshade had her baby. A little girl!"

"We missed so much," Runner's child complained.

"To be fair–so have they." Storyteller's voice joined the conversation "Wait until they hear the tale of Rock's Roar–the loudest belch ever delivered by a mortal man."

"Has anyone even sent the messenger yet?" Thrillseeker demanded impatiently.

She referred to the tradition of promptly announcing the return of any large part of the tribe to its home island. After all, with Ilsognos' population temporarily lowered, all manner of visitors and tribeless could take the opportunity to squat ashore, but with the flotilla's return, they would need notice to vacate, lest the sacred numerical taboo be violated.

"Un go'lan?" Archer asked in the pidgin.

"Nay," one of the Sea People said, looking over one shoulder and shrugging.

"Storms and seagull-shit!" Thrillseeker cursed. "*I'll* go!"

Emotion charged her heart to pump its quota of blood faster and faster. Fe's erythrocyte sailed through the girl's veins, ready to drop its load of kidnapped, life-sustaining diatomic oxygen. The blood cell, however, found her muscles untaxed, the need for rapid circulation having been greatly exaggerated by hormonal messengers.

Despite the adults' lack of concern, one of the young among the Sea Peoples had broken off from the clot, apparently taking on the role of messenger. Thrillseeker, already set on running to the island herself, noticed his white sail as she pointed her own trimaran toward Ilsognos. Good, she thought. He would give her someone to race on her way home–thus motivated, she expected to make even better time.

With confidence born of dominance, Thrillseeker's calloused hands worked her trimaran's rigging, pulling on vegetable-fiber ropes and bending the sail to her will. She bit into a favorable slice of breeze and ran her boat swiftly over the shallow crests of the Akkadian sea. Quickly, she picked up speed, and the salt spray was soon splashing up over her face as she raced toward home.

In between mouthfuls of seawater, the child nicknamed Thrillseeker gulped lungfuls of air, and her army of internal erythrocytes dutifully lassoed the wild diatomic oxygens she brought in.

Now that the human's body was working, racing even, Fe's delivery vehicle struggled to keep up with the influx of new orders from the nation of cells it served–the millions of molecules of hemoglobin giving their all despite draconian demand.

Thrillseeker hung on her trimaran's halyard and leaned over the waves. Human-and-boat moved as one–a swift, predatory bird, barely touching the water as she flew from wave to wave. Yet, the white sail was still in front of her. Somehow, with all her motivation and skill, the cocky young champion hadn't yet erased the Sea Person's head-start.

She attacked even more fiercely, surging the swift seaslicer forward, a death-grip on its rigging. Her crab-claw bit into the wind, flexing and transferring second-hand force to the raft's body.

The tribeless boy's white sail was growing larger now, poking out between Thrillseeker and the beach, seemingly close enough to touch. Breathing heavily, she gasped through her mouth at an inopportune moment, inhaling half a lungful of salt water deep into her chest.

In the pulmonary capillaries, Fe's blood cell found little to grab as the girl's gasp turned into a racking cough–the strong muscles around her lungs undergoing quick, forceful contractions. Seawater and mucus sprayed from her open airways, and even though her body convulsed, Thrillseeker kept an iron-grip on her seaslicer's rigging, straining and sweating to reach the beach ahead of her rival.

Nevertheless, the grand efforts of the Sognos champion and her heroic hemoglobins ended in vain. Thrillseeker lost the race that existed only in her mind, and the white-sailed seaslicer reached Ilsognos just barely ahead of her own. Its occupant sprinted ashore, not even acknowledging her presence.

Thrillseeker smacked the water, outraged. It wasn't fair. That dark-eyed boy from the Sea Peoples might've been the fastest she'd ever faced.

\#

A dandelion poked out from black soil. It danced in the sunlight, waving its jagged leaves and madly bobbing its bright, yellow-flowered head. Its joy lasted for a heartbeat of days before the flower closed up, its sunny petals losing their vibrance and its outer leaves sealing away the head.

Thrillseeker rested inside the pod. She was one of the thin, delicate seeds of the dandelion, and when the flower opened for the final time, Thrillseeker caught the first gust of wind and lifted free. Her feathery seed sailed and soared on the air currents, its precious biological cargo held aloft by a spindly, circular sail–a parasol made from spiderwebs. Soon, she was flying over open ocean, a thousand thousands of tiny islands dotting the water below her.

Even as a flower seed, she knew how to catch the wind, bending her many-fingered sail ever so slightly to steer herself into the updrafts. For Thrillseeker, the task proved as easy as it was delightful, and her heart raced as she sailed higher and higher into the sky.

Higher and higher, she flew. Higher and higher–so high she would break the dream itself–and then she was at the very bottom of the sea, looking up toward a bare flicker of light. Thrillseeker wasn't a dandelion seed anymore–she was a thing with a thousand eyes. She used them to stare up at the rippling, ever-changing water above. With her body, she clung to the planet—there was something very warm down there that she enjoyed pressing herself against.

Every instant, several trillion erythrocytes rushed through the endless tunnels of the sleeping animal's vascular system, doing their best to keep her alive. Each crimson corpuscle harbored a millions-strong biomechanical armada of hemoglobin. Serving aboard one such molecule, the atom Fe clung to its heme net with some of its charge and held onto a struggling O2 captive with the rest. The giant hemoglobin protein wiggled and gyrated, subtly changing shape and giving Fe both the impetus and the permission to drop its kidnapped oxygen. As quickly as it had arrived, however, the erythrocyte rushed back toward the lungs, ready for another pickup.

Aided by the heart's power, Fe's cell barely had to fight gravity to reach the sleeping human's loftiest heights. There, near the brain, oxygen molecules diffused out of the bloodstream, allowed passage by specialized epithelial guard cells. On the other side of this bespoke barrier, the O2 would meet the enigmatic neurons of the brain. Day and night, Fe and its oxygen-transporting army fed Thrillseeker's insatiable neural tissue, fueling, among other things, the girl's bizarre dreaming.

Under the ocean, the gigantic, spreading thing that was Thrillseeker opened all of her thousand eyes at once.

"I'm awake!" She declared to no one, sitting up in her bed and tossing aside her rumpled quilt.

Blinking away the gummy sleep, Thrillseeker noticed the dimness outside her bedroom window—a predawn gloom. She hadn't missed the race, hadn't missed her chance to compete against adult champions of the Hand Nations and win. She sat on the edge of her simple bed and tried to control her breathing. Inside, the never-ending regatta of erythrocytes rushed madly from heart to veins to capillaries and back.

An early-morning breeze coming in through her unshuttered window made Thrillseeker shiver, and she found herself tempted to dive back under the quilt and wait for the sun. It was out of the question, of course. Her blood was already full of get-up chemicals, and her mind was as active as it would ever be.

She stretched first, then crept over to a chilly room where she could access running water. It flowed from a nearby stream, channeled into the house by clever stonework, and in the dim light, she located her razor—a non-folding Sukuru-alloy analog of Karl Fleischer's stainless steel model. By touch, she shaved the bristly hair on the sides and back of her head, dipping the straight-razor in the captive stream, washing away bits of herself.

The girl had noticed new growths of thin, wispy hair coming in around her ankles over the past year, and this too she cleared away—the metallically-bonded alloy of the blade's edge easily slicing through the hair's twisting keratin proteins.

Finally, she dressed and applied her usual skin treatment before tip-toeing across a short hallway to kiss her sleeping parents goodbye. She grabbed a piece of fruit from the family's communal basket, pulled on her best shoes, and slipped out of the house.

The girl nicknamed Thrillseeker traveled light—the bulk of her gear and provisions having been stowed safely aboard her seaslicer the night before. Outside, walking the paths of Ilsognos, she found that she didn't need to be quiet after all. Though Flute and Archer still slumbered, the island and its many visitors seemed to be getting an early jump on the day.

Thrillseeker walked between the island's hills, dotted with brick dwellings like her family's, before coming to the Sognos river and the cobblestone roadway that wound down its length. Nearly depopulated during the quiet days of their grand vacation, the neighborhood's thoroughfare positively bustled with traffic the morning of the Hand Nations Classic.

On her way to the river, the young sailor was hailed by supportive friends and neighbors, but she only waved back politely, moving swiftly and filling her mouth with fruit so as not to be caught up in tedious conversation.

Long, well-built houses of black stone lined the riverfront. Thrillseeker, hurrying by, noticed that many of their windows, normally dark and shuttered at this hour, were illuminated from within. She quickened her pace toward the Three Bridges, anxious that she hadn't woken as early as she'd first suspected.

Near the river, lush plants and fruit-bearing trees grew anywhere they could, squeezing between dwellings and municipal structures. Finger-sized dwarf possums scampered along fronds and jumped from branch to branch overhead, and children raced hand-carved wooden boats down the gentle waterway.

By the time Thrillseeker reached the busy forum of Three Bridges, early rays were already leaking out from the rising sun. Vendors, some she knew, some she didn't, had set up stalls anywhere they could, selling all manner of things.

"Hey! Wanna race?" A child, no more than five, called out as she passed.

"No way, kid," Thrillseeker replied, "I only race when I think I can win!"

She left the child giggling and scanned the mass of humanity before her, struggling to see over adult heads and shoulders. She spotted Sage standing outside a forest-green tent, handing skewers of meat to a group of strangely-dressed Croy. Only on special occasions could one see such a crowd around the Three Bridges. By law and custom, excluding the symbiotic Sea Peoples as always, only thirteen hundreds of people could ever make up the Sognos nation or live on their island.

More than half that number currently clogged the informal market.

For Thrillseeker, it was dizzying. Fortunately, however, she spotted Swimmer's clean-shaven head bobbing above the human throng. She took a deep breath and, her lungs full of diatomic fuel, pushed through the crowd, thankful that her seventeen-year-old squire had already grown taller than most of the men on the island.

She ran up to Swimmer, radiant as always, standing near the centermost bridge. Despite the morning chill, Thrillseeker's squire was wearing a simple sleeveless tunic that revealed a deep bronze tan, extending evenly all the way up to her razor-shaven scalp.

"Thrill!" She shouted, leaving behind a crowd of admirers to embrace her pint-sized captain. As the two hugged, something clacked in Swimmer's arms.

"What've you got there?" Thrillseeker asked, stepping back and sniffing the air.

Swimmer lifted her arms, showing off two thinly-woven bags. One was filled with fried, spiced insects and another with candied nuts, sugar-roasted and more mildly seasoned than the bugs.

"We've got food on the boat, you know," the captain said, scolding her older squire.

"Yes, but this is *festival* food."

Thrillseeker had to admit that the Three Bridges had indeed turned to an impromptu festival as the morning of the regatta came into full bloom. Somewhere, a group was even playing music. Everywhere, people from other tribes intermingled with the Sognos, laughing, bartering, and debating. She walked alongside Swimmer, her stomach too tight to accept the girl's frequent offers of nuts and insects.

"—as you can see, one of the finest islands on all the vast waters."

Thrillseeker heard a familiar voice and stopped. She turned to see Storyteller entertaining an Eenoor couple.

"We're known for our herbal medicine, our advanced recycling methods, and of course, this island was home to Boomer Sognos." He finished, raising one hand to the island's central mountain.

"Who?" The Eenoor woman asked. Like her partner, she had dark hair, sharp features, and wore only black.

"Uh, hello?" Swimmer jumped into the conversation, her voice indignant. "He was just the only person ever to wrestle five hundreds of opponents and never lose a match."

"Oh, that guy."

"Swimmer? What are you two doing here?" Storyteller asked, noticing the girls. "I thought you'd be at the starting line by now."

"You're competitors?" The Eenoor woman raised an eyebrow.

"I didn't know the Sognos had more than one entrant this year," her partner remarked.

"I would *really* start heading to the docks if I were you," Storyteller urged, ignoring his guests. "I even saw Graham heading that way a moment ago."

"They may as well not worry," the Eenoor man said to his partner, not bothering to switch back to his own language. "Sailor will win whether the Sognos field two seaslicers or twenty." Thrillseeker flushed. The foreigner was referring to her rival, a boy she'd known for years. She'd once beaten him in a one-on-one race around the jagged upwelling of rocks they called the World's Teeth—Sailor Eenoor—just two-and-a-half years her senior, already an adult and last year's winner of the Classic.

Swimmer glared at the confident foreigner and made a gesture with her face and right hand—one considered especially rude by four out of five cultures of the Hand Nations.

The two young sailors dashed off, leaving Storyteller behind to speak soothing platitudes to his ruffled guests.

\#

In the end, no one arrived late, and by the start of the race, all ten seaslicers floated on the Akkadian sea, fully crewed. Their multicolored sails lowered, they waited for permission to catch the wind and break free from Ilsognos waters.

Adjacent to the shallow bay upon which the racers bobbed, an amphitheater had long ago been carved into the coastal rock-face. Under the rising sun, it filled with an audience that eventually included Archer, up in the highest section. Below him, a white-robed figure stood on a dias, surrounded by the band.

As they waited aboard the floating trimaran, Swimmer ate candied nuts. In fact, she was wasting them, Thrillseeker observed. She watched her squire balance atop one of the outriggers, holding a reef pole for grip and flinging nuts across the water at a Lana windslicer. Aboard the opposing vessel, an elderly, wiry-looking woman was trying her best to catch the sugary treats in her mouth before they plopped into the water.

"S'no good!" The Lana woman yelled, laughing. "Take ya windslicer inta closer."

"What?" Swimmer screamed into the breeze, also laughing.

Whether called 'seaslicers' or 'windslicers' by their tribes, all vessels shared the same unintentional water-molecule design. Thrillseeker surveyed the competition. She knew most of the boats, having raced against and beaten a fair few before, Sailor Eenoor included, though never in an official regatta.

Nearby, an enormous man with long, shaggy hair lay stretched across his trimaran, possibly asleep. On the other side, aboard a vessel flying a plain white sail, a pair of youths with deep-set eyes stared at the proceedings in silent disapproval.

"Shit—that's him!"

"Who?" Swimmer cocked her tanned head, trying to follow her captain's gaze. "Warrior?" "No. The boy, the Sea Person. He's the one who beat–" she stopped herself.

"What?"

"They're the ones to beat," Thrillseeker corrected.

A gust of wind blew in, bouncing the captain's curls and making her strain to keep her trimaran stationary. She thought she could hear strains of music from the band carrying on the breeze, the high notes possibly played by her mother.

She inhaled deeply, wishing to breathe in Flute's thin, uplifting music. In the reality of her lungs' many chambers, however, O2 molecules rather than music entered her blood, and Fe continued to reliably crew its hemoglobin, delivering oxygen to whichever cell needed it most.

"Greetings, my friends!" The white-robed Graham Sognos spoke from the dias, the acoustics of carved stone amplifying her voice to the point where even Thrillseeker could make out individual words between the whistles of the wind.

"I am pleased to commence this grand regatta–the eighty-first Hand Nations Classic!" Graham spread her arms, drawing cheers from the audience. She repeated the announcement in a stilted, Lana dialect, eliciting softer applause.

Thrillseeker shielded her eyes and scanned the amphitheater row by row. She found Archer and waved.

"Where's your folks?" She asked Swimmer.

"Not here. They went on ahead to wait at the finish line."

"Don't tell me they *swam* all the way to Ilcroy?"

Swimmer only shrugged and gave her captain a mischievous smile.

"Allow me to present," Graham continued, her clear voice carrying, "this year's competitors!"

Aboard their seaslicer, the Sognos girls held the furled orange and yellow crab-claw sail, ready for their cue.

"Flying a crimson sail, from our own most perfect island–Sailor Sognos!" Not waiting for the cheers to ebb, she carried on. "Crewing with the pride of our people, his squire and the builder of their elegant seaslicer–Wright Sognos!"

The crowd applauded as the first trimaran let out its crab-claw, an eye-catching red against the blue of the water.

"Also from our fair nation," the Sognos leader continued, the wind blowing her long white hair about her smiling face, "flying yellow and orange, champion of the children's regatta two years running–the child of Archer and Flute Sognos!"

"Thrillseeker Sognos," Swimmer corrected, though only her friend could hear.

At the cue, they released their vessel's sail, but the subsequent slapping of wind, water, and fabric made it difficult to discern the voice of Graham or the enthusiastic applause from the crowd.

"Her squire is none other than Swimmer Sognos, winner of athletic and aesthetic competitions too numerous to name."

The audience erupted–Swimmer's personal friends and admirers outnumbering entire foreign delegations. Graham's next announcement, however, drew far less applause.

"Flying unadorned sails, the twins Kai and Hanna Ocean, from the Sea Peoples."

A white sail appeared on the trimaran crewed by the dark-eyed youths.

"The ones to beat, eh?" Swimmer looked to her captain.

"I mean it. They were born on the water. He *moves* like water."

"From the Eenoor," Graham declared to her audience, "I am pleased to announce last year's winner and the reigning champion of the Hand Nations Classic–young Sailor Eenoor! Flying black and white, Sailor's vessel is squired by his brother, the child of Graham and Healer Eenoor."

Two black-haired boys, one significantly taller and stronger-looking than the other, unfurled a white sail adorned with so many small, black circles that it appeared grey from a distance. Thrillseeker did not turn around to look at her rival, who was busy smiling and waving back at the cheering crowd.

"Joining him from Ileenoor, the feared Warrior Eenoor!"

At the announcement, the sleeping hulk raised himself up and hefted a reef pole one-handed, raising it above his head as his second unfurled a sail dyed a deep black.

As Graham Sognos announced each competitor, the corresponding trimaran would loose its sail and drift toward the mouth of the bay, anxious for action.

"From far Lana, the Emerald Isle, it is my honor to present the legendary Sailor Lana–five time winner of the Hand Nations Classic."

A green sail bloomed on the waters.

"My apologies," Graham declared, bringing her wrinkled hands together and bowing slightly, "in this race, Sailor Lana is *squire* to her child, and the vessel's captain–Fearless Lana!

"And, representing the Bo people," she continued, "we have the windslicer known as Elliot, crewed by Sailor Bo and her squire Diamond Bo."

In front of Thrillseeker, a vessel unfurled a sail dyed a shade that nearly matched the sea. The effect was unsettling.

"Elliot windslicer?" Swimmer asked, her hand cupped over an ear.

"The Bo name their trimarans." Thrillseeker rolled her eyes.

Ashore, their Graham was nearing the end of her preamble, though the girls couldn't make out much of it.

"As this grand race begins at Ilsognos and finishes at Ilcroy, allow me to conclude by announcing, last but far from least, the entrants of our co-host nation–Graham Croy and his squire, Fisher Croy, of the flower emblem! Joining them in fair competition, of the bird emblem, we have captain Windcatcher Croy, aided by her sister and squire–the child of Sailor and Crab Croy! Last but not least, speaking of former champions, flying the crab emblem, we have the legends themselves–Sailor and his squire and partner Crab Croy!"

On the bay, a sail emblazoned with an image of a blooming yellow dandelion unfurled, followed by sails sporting a bird-of-paradise design and an orange crab, respectively. The crowd cheered nearly as heartily as they had for Swimmer, eager to see the race begin.

"I take that to mean you're ready," Graham laughed. "Follow my lead now…"

Graham Sognos, clad all in white, reached into her pockets and pulled out handfuls of flower petals. Baskets circulated among the amphitheater's capacity crowd and the hundreds of other spectators lining the shore.

The multicultural human audience waited, filling their hands with soft flowers and holding anticipation on their collective breath. At the first great gust of wind, Graham opened her palms and allowed the blooms to blow away. At this signal, the band struck up a brisk tune, and the audience released thousands of tiny, fragrant petals, tossing them high above their heads to catch the rushing air currents.

The wind sprinkled the bay with flower fragments, racing out to the bobbing boats at sea, clustered at the narrow opening that led to clear water beyond. As the sweet-scented gust blew between trimarans, some captains, by luck or skill, caught the wind and lurched out into open sea.

Spectators on land cheered as, one by one, the seaslicers slipped out of the bay and stretched themselves into a colorful line on the water.

Thrillseeker was one of the captains who'd caught the jump-start, and she jockeyed with other seaslicers for position during those tense first moments. She flexed the muscles of her short, strong arms and relaxed them again, intuitively working her sail against the wind. In the maze of tiny capillaries that wove between the girl's living muscle fibers, Fe's erythrocyte along with a billion allies, dumped oxygen into her straining, twitching tissues.

There were so many rocks to navigate, it would be easy to lose her focus and her lead, but Thrillseeker had trained for countless days racing between the razor-sharp cliffs of the World's Teeth. When she finally emerged in open water, she did so ahead of her Eenoor rival.

Her trimaran stood in fourth position.

"Yee-aah!" Celebrating their excellent start, Swimmer let out an enthusiastic woop. "Eat our wakes! Sleep with the fishes!" She waved, taunting the pilots of the trailing, black-dotted seaslicer.

Her joy proved short-lived, however, as the Ocean twins appeared behind them. The plain trimaran of the Sea People moved with remarkable swiftness. Neither Kai nor Hanna took their dark eyes from the horizon as they maneuvered around the Eenoors and, immediately after, slipped past Thrillseeker herself.

No matter how she attacked, the young Sognos pilot couldn't force her seaslicer to catch up with the Ocean siblings. They soon sailed out of her view, slipping around the first of a chain of small islands.

Despite falling to fifth place, Thrillseeker's maneuvering was enough to keep her ahead of the frustrated Sailor Eenoor and his brother. Next, the race's course took them through the shallows, a good stretch for the squires, who were expected to aid the action of the sails with their own strong polling.

Tall and lean, Swimmer was a perfect fit for the task before her. Fearlessly, she angled her bodyweight overboard, balancing on the reef pole and punting it back with great force. With orchestrated contractions of dozens of toned muscles and sinews, the athletic squire efficiently converted her own brute strength into forward velocity for the trimaran.

Less tall and less lean, her captain nonetheless exercised muscle-memory and employed her own highly-evolved primate tissues to grip and grapple the taut ropes, changing the direction of the entire seaslicer with a slight lean or a single tug.

Within the cell membranes of the sailor nicknamed Thrillseeker, the domesticated parasites known as mitochondria gobbled up their fodder, fueling life with their waste energy. After much hard sailing, however, the captain had worked her muscle cells until they had all but exhausted their oxygen supply.

Fe worked as hard as it physically could, bonding and releasing O2 as its hemoglobin protein flexed and wriggled. With nearly every breath and heartbeat, its erythrocyte rounded up millions of molecules of atmospheric oxygen for the herd of famished mitochondrial livestock. Though Thrillseeker commanded a trillions-strong navy of such blood cells, even their combined efforts were not enough to keep the adolescent human's muscles fully oxygenated.

The intercellular environment through which Fe traveled became choked with garbage. Clots of waste carbon and damaged cells, unable to hold up to the strain, spewed their innards into the bloodstream. Acid sloshed everywhere, waste products disassociating and releasing their hydrogens—little greedy, grasping protons—into the swamp to cause trouble and pain for the sailor's body.

As Fe flung oxygen molecules into the cellular fires, partner players in the bloodstream did their best to sweep away the trash. Every time the great, girded lungs filled with air, resupplying the blood with swarms of O2, they contracted again, forcing out waste with each gust of outgoing gas.

Breath flowing up her nose, into her cells, and back out past her lips, Thrillseeker pumped oxygen steadily throughout her body. She had learned even breathing from her father, and though her arms burned and her tense legs cried out for relief, the young sailor continued her strong, steady breathing, unthinkingly counting on her blood to do its job.

She relied just as hard on Swimmer Sognos to do her duty. At that moment, the squire worked mightily–perspiration pooling on her depilated crown. She levered her pole against the shallows and forced the seaslicer ever forward. Working in tandem with her captain, Swimmer punted their trimaran near the Bo craft with the sea-colored sail.

Seizing a fortuitous angle, the Songos boat hurtled ahead of the Bo. Thrillseeker let out a cheer, but as she risked a glance over her shoulder, she spied the Eenoor boys taking advantage of the same opening to snatch fifth position.

At this stage of the course, the lanes opened up, the racers no longer as constrained by the toothlike rocks. The Akkadian sun had climbed high enough that its rays poured their energy down in relentless, searing waves–crashing perpendicularly onto those of the sea. Thrillseeker had to squint to keep from being blinded by its reflection on the waters, and she kept a death-grip on the halyard.

Behind her and to one side raced the Eenoor boys, with the seaslicer captained by young Windcatcher Croy ahead. Thus, the boats in third, fourth, and fifth positions arrayed themselves on the open course, not far behind the unlikely second-place Warrior Eenoor and his black-sailed trimaran.

The opportunity for an all-out sprint wouldn't last long, as the course would soon reach a narrow strait. Swimmer deftly stowed the reef pole, no longer useful in the deeper channels, sat down, and tucked herself into an aerodynamic posture. Thrillseeker rode low, forcing the straining ropes to behave, allowing their dry vegetable fibers to cut into her calloused hands. She bit her lip and stopped breathing through her mouth, her nostrils flaring on each forceful exhale. With every passing second, the Sognos boat gained on the Croy.

"Hey! So' girl!" The little Croy squire called out, her eyes widening as she watched Thrillseeker's seaslicer sidle up and pass her own. "What your name?"

"Same as yours," Thrillseeker answered, her voice not loud enough for her opponent to hear, eyes glued to the horizon.

She'd sailed into third position, but she and the fourth-place Croy, along with the Eenoors in fifth, were now separated by only a matter of boat-lengths. The three vessels converged as they crested toward the narrows ahead—all rapidly gaining on Warrior's black sails.

As they drew nearer, it became clear that Warrior was not piloting his own boat. His squire sat forward on the hull, working the ropes. The massive Eenoor captain had moved to the outer edge of his craft, and he stood hefting a stout reef pole, looming like a guard astride the only pass. When Thrillseeker's trimaran moved close enough, Warrior swung out, striking his pole against one of their outriggers.

"Aah!" Swimmer cried, surprised by the attack. "Your mother should be drowned!"

The blow hadn't damaged the boat, but the hulking Warrior was already swinging around for another attack. As the pole neared, Swimmer sprung toward it, slapping the wood with both palms, sending its tip splashing into the water. Her opponent nearly lost his balance, but he managed to keep both his feet and the reef pole.

"I'll eat your heart, bitch!" He bellowed, using his own people's version of the epithet.

They had achieved some separation, but another craft swiftly drew upon the black-sailed combatant. The Croy girls had made the ill-advised decision to use the chaos to try and pass, seizing second for themselves. Warrior Eenoor, however, was more than happy to switch to a softer target. Swimmer slipped from his attention, and he spun around as the Croy passed, delivering a mighty blow to their delicate trimaran. The sounds of splintering wood filled the air, and the beleaguered vessel listed to one side.

"Oy!" Swimmer screamed out, helpless at such a distance. "Thrill—get closer!"

Her captain complied. They could hear the Croy girls screaming as Warrior swung again, his pole impacting hard enough to tear through their bird-of-paradise sail and fracture the boom.

Swimmer hefted her own reef pole, wielding it like a makeshift lance. As soon as she was in range, she pushed forward, attacking the black-sailed boat. Warrior was ready to rain down another blow upon the Croys when Swimmer managed to poke the hull of his trimaran, causing the aggressor to stumble and drop his weapon.

"You're dead, Sognos!" He roared, turning away from the broken Croy seaslicer to face Swimmer.

"Hey, Thrill?" She asked, yelling forward to her captain. "Win this thing, will you?" With that, Swimmer lifted her reef pole as high above her head as she dared, balancing on the rocking craft. Swaying, she cleaved it forcefully down, aiming for Warrior's head–but, his reflexes honed, the brute shot his arms up and caught her pole between two meaty hands. He smiled, displaying an underbite with prominent incisors.

Far from being intimidated, Swimmer returned his smile with a predatory grin of her own, then, fluid as the current, she threw herself forward, still gripping the pole. Her strong legs pushed off the deck, and via the long shaft of wood, her transferred momentum sent the bewildered Warrior tumbling backwards into the sea an instant before Swimmer herself plopped overboard.

Suddenly lightened, Thrillseeker's trimaran surged forward into the unguarded strait, easily seizing third position behind Sailor Eenoor and his brother, who had used the melee to slip ahead of their cheating tribesman into second.

A fresh breeze blew across the sunlit waves, conjuring more distance between the three lead boats and the trailing pack. Without Swimmer, Thrillseeker's seaslicer rode high in the water and bobbled as it smacked into each wave, but its captain couldn't afford to play things safe–she continued to trim aggressively, riding her vessel to the very edges of stability.

Distracted by Warrior's unprovoked attack, the Sognos seaslicer had been easy enough for the dot-sailed Eenoor boat to overtake, but now, coming at them like a force of nature, Thrillseeker was impossible to ignore.

Sailor's young brother turned from his position and stared backwards at the charging boat, the shock on his face obvious even at a distance. Hearing his squire's moans of dismay, Sailor Eenoor risked a glance over his shoulder. The champion couldn't believe what he saw—the girl from Ilsognos, the one he had never considered his rival, was now bearing down on him like some sort of sea-demon.

She beat him then the same way she had when they were both children—racing around the jagged rocks of the World's Teeth—a simple combination of superior sailing skill and a daring self-confidence that bordered on the delusional.

Without a squire, Thrillseeker had no choice but to handle the trimaran's rigging like the reins of a wild animal, doing all she could to at least steer the surging thing in the right direction. Still, she attacked, having to lean her body precariously over one side of the vessel to gain enough leverage for her intended maneuver. As she leaned, pulling the crab-claw and forcing the seaslicer to bend to her will, the halyard bit into her bare arm and the salt spray slapped her in the face again and again.

The young human's blood coursed wildly through her veins, and her chest heaved with the repeated effort of bringing in enough volatile oxygen to keep her body burning for another moment. Gouts of seawater splashed her face constantly, and it was only by sheer luck that she inhaled lungfuls of air rather than brine.

However, the girl's skin was losing its battle against the rope. The taut cellulose fibers of the halyard pushed aside her protective dead epidermis and forced their way into living tissue. Dying cells split and ruptured as the rope penetrated layers of fats and proteins, eventually sawing jaggedly through the thin branching tunnels of Thrillseeker's vital vasculature.

Just as the Sognos captain made another daring maneuver, the corpuscle containing the atom Fe snatched a load of O2s from around the lungs and released them in the musculature at the girl's diaphragm. Harried cells dumped waste compounds and heat energy into the coursing blood, and, driven by a pounding heart, into and out of the lungs, the erythrocyte rushed ever onward, this time toward the animal's skin. The overworked blood cell was on its way to diffuse some heat and offload the last of its O2 before returning to the lungs for another roundup. Just then, the tunnel simply stopped—a curious cluster of platelets the only warning before Fe and its erythrocyte found themselves pumped out of the living body and into oblivion.

Pressure from the lacerating rope finally eased against the girl's arm, allowing a river of blood cells and plasma to leak from the damaged tissue. Each moment, millions more erythrocytes fled Thrillseeker's body, though her blood's platelet plugs gave their all to clog the rupture.

Fe's cell flowed helplessly with the others, trickling in a rivulet down the sailor's arm. Molecules of carbon dioxide fled like rats escaping a sinking ship, while the open air set off a suite of signals in the erythrocyte's sensitive membrane–it was too dry and too cold, but most importantly, there was oxygen, and plenty of it. O2 molecules poured into the blood cells as if the entire universe had become one giant lung. Fe automatically grabbed ahold of an oxygen pair, as did the other irons in the millions of hemoglobins within the same corpuscle.

Thus, the blood running down the lone sailor's arm flowed a bright crimson. Still, the Sognos seaslicer cut its way forward. Wild winds rushed past, oxygenating Thrillseeker's wasted blood. However, she felt no pain as she watched the ridiculous black and white dotted crab-claw sail of her rival fall slowly behind her. A rush of triumph filled her heart, while in her actual vasculture, an army of repair proteins worked furiously to close her slowly-dripping wound.

Now in second position, she fixed her eyes on the waters ahead, no thoughts left to spare for her Eenoor rival. She squinted against the glare, straining to make out an unadorned white sail in the distance.

A swell rose, blocking her view. Thrillseeker pushed her trimaran through the wave, raising a gush of seawater. The salt spray scoured boat and captain alike, making the girl's eyes sting and washing much of the bloodstain from her arm.

"Ha!" She sprayed, a laugh of exhilaration burbling unbidden into her mouth–those tribeless twins ahead of her, chasing the horizon, were testing her more than she ever could have imagined.

For a brief moment, Thrillseeker dared to free one hand from the rigging. She wiped her eyes with an inner forearm before resuming her death-grip on the unforgiving ropes, some ruby drops flicking away from her skin and into the sea.

Within one such droplet of pale pink liquid, the erythrocyte containing Fe floated in a state of cellular panic. The poor blood cell found itself in a hostile, alien environment without even the authority of a nucleus to appeal to. Trillions of water molecules made up the bulk of the tiny sphere, which flew from the animal and her boat out above the roiling ocean. Other erythrocytes, lost platelets, and even some mammalian sweat-salts filled the droplet, though the bulk of its dissolved salt had come from the Akkadian sea.

The bloody castoff drip reached the top of its arc, briefly stalled, and plopped unceremoniously into the water, gravity tallying another, inevitable victory. Uncountable septillions of water molecules formed an ocean, twin hydrogens with their oxygen escorts holding hands, forming a skin across its entire surface. The ocean recognized the droplet as one of its own, and the waters allowed the pale-pink pearl to diffuse into their vastness.

\#

As far as the dying erythrocyte was concerned, the cold Akkadian sea resembled Thrillseeker's bloodstream not at all. The cell found its own stock of water molecules burgled by the forces of diffusion, harsh salts of the sea eager to steal moisture from the cell's relatively fresh cytoplasm. It slowly sank, while above, against the white of the sky, trailing seaslicers and windslicers, still fighting to finish the regatta, bounced across the waves.

Against its will, the erythrocyte surrendered its cytoplasmic vitality and shriveled, becoming a salted thing that could no longer be called living.

It continued to descend further, plumbing waters that became increasingly dark and cold. By this point, a combination of diffusion and micro-currents had mixed the contents of the bloody droplet thoroughly into the sea. Not a single cell or souvenir from the girl nicknamed Thrillseeker floated within any appreciable distance of the atom Fe, save the desiccated corpse of its own red blood cell and the obsolete hemoglobin proteins within.

Life in other forms, however, abounded. Even at these depths, animals dominated the planet. As the shriveled corpuscle followed the current further out to sea, a small school of graceful vertebrates sailed past, each sporting thin, colorful fins and a powerful suite of swimming muscles.

High above, in the waters near the surface, herds of tiny grazers ate their fill from forests of single-celled plants. Like chloroplasts in perfect form, the ocean's verdant canopy of cyanobacteria drank in sunlight and oxygenated the planet. In the darker waters below, lilliputian predators circled, meat-eaters on a microscopic scale.

One of these creatures–several thousand cells organized into a tiny animal with discernable jaws–sensed a wrinkled scrap of meat floating nearby. Though human blood cells were not a normal part of its diet, the plankton was not above a free meal.

It had spent most of its short life clawing its way through a madly-vibrating substrate of water in which many good things floated and many dangerous things swam. A tiny appendage reached out from the plankton, sensing the novel meat–a scant, though protein-rich, serving. One rudimentary flagellum flicked the speck of a cell toward the plankton's maw, guarded by impossibly delicate spurs of mineral-rich mouthparts.

The unfortunate erythrocyte and the millions of advanced complexes within had managed to stay mostly intact before facing those jaws, but the proteins and lipids of its cell membrane were no match for teeth–however rudimentary. Voraciously, the plankton ripped into the human blood cell with a comparatively enormous mandible, shredding the erythrocyte and scattering its army of biological machinery. The bulk of the cell, a ruined vessel that had once sailed the restless courses of Thrillseeker's bloodstream, found its way into the animal's mouth, destined to be processed in its simple digestive system.

Fortunately for Fe, the plankton was a messy eater, and the atom's specific hemoglobin protein avoided its mouthparts, falling instead like a crumb into the dense sea of grasping water molecules. In a flash of transparent, contracting muscles, the tiny predator sped off toward its next meal, leaving tens of thousands of hemoglobin scraps to the mercy of the ocean.

\#

Fe's protein found itself scattered from its peers by the motions and forces of the sea, irresistible on any scale. The lone hemoglobin sank into deeper darkness. It was carried far by the current, away from the sailing race and the human bones where it had been manufactured.

Just as in the goat, four lobes of the insanely twisted ring of proteins were bonded to one another–four heme nets in the protein's grip, four irons. Each spiral and chain was welded to the next, and these combinations further linked up in meta-patterns, all built according to a master blueprint passed down in coded DNA. The blood factories inside Thrillseeker's bone marrow had never intended their hemoglobin complexes for an oceanic environment, however, and the Akkadian sea made short work of the miraculous structure.

Every efficient bond and brilliant twist, every joint and fold of the biological machine was a potential weak point. In the pressurized soup of the deep ocean, an uncountable legion of water molecules grasped with wandering hydrogen hands, firmly and insistently.

Not every water existed in a happy throuple with one oxygen and two partner protons. The sea had its share of single hydrogens and unstable oxygen-hydrogen pairs–drowning in negativity since an aqueous breakup. Thus, bit by bit, the water and its degenerate compounds tore the proteins apart, mindlessly digesting the hemoglobin in a revue of chemical reactions, none of which operated under the guidance of a living thing.

The intricate webbing of the hemes fell victim to the irresistible ocean, the central nitrogens that ligated Fe breaking off for more instant partners. In a desperate appeal for one's own kind, universal down to the atomic level, Fe gravitated toward its fellow iron ions as the great hemoglobin dissolved around it.

The abandoned iron atoms longed to come together, to form a tiny ingot. Iron, however–as has been demonstrated across multiple planets and domains of life–is a coveted element. This holds true even for a single atom, and each of Fe's analogs found themselves claimed before they could find one another.

In an OH molecule, a single hydrogen could never be stable with its oxygen partner, and, as a consequence, the compound was ever insecure. When one of these hydroxides came across Fe among the shreds of the hemoglobin, it found a way to relieve its electrochemical predicament. Its oxygen was drawn to Fe, helpless to the forces of electromagnetic attraction.

In the presence of a mob of waters, some salts officiating, the oxygen and the iron bonded into a new compound.

Outside the heat of a forge, oxygen is always the more clingy atom, and almost immediately, the iron ion's partnership ran into incompatibilities. Fe had the same problems as the single hydrogen–one atom of oxygen simply wasn't enough to meet its innate needs. The bond eventually broke, and the two found themselves drifting apart. Fe bonded with other oxygens, but each may as well have been a clone of the first–react with one collection of eight protons, react with them all.

Though the entire chemical drama unfolded in a subjective flash, in the end, the best resolution is one where all the parties involved find what they seek. Fe electromagnetically encountered other irons shaken loose from the wreck of the hemoglobin. Their initial bonds had turned out similarly wanting, but when all were brought together, their swirling outer electrons could negotiate at a quantum level. These forces and fates dictated that Fe and another iron could find stability with a trio of oxygens. It was so, and the new molecule of ferric hydroxide clung together well. The many hands of surrounding waters never let them alone–hydrogen-bonds with benefits, these water molecules would come and go, not strong or attractive enough to tear the compound apart.

Thus bonded with an iron from an alien star and a small family of oxygens, Fe found true stability again, surrendering to the will of the waters and that of its own beloved electrons. A tiny flake in a planetary fish tank, the particle of ferric hydroxide filtered its way ever downward. The continental shelf dropped off into a blue-black mass of endless water, and Fe's rusty mote followed the path of least resistance. Denser than nearly anything else floating in the sea, it made relatively quick progress, though the journey was a long one.

Gravity's ghostly hand pulled the ferric hydroxide down a deep ocean trench, dominant even in the thickening, pressurized brine. The irresistible cosmic force would have driven the particle to the very core of the planet had the seafloor not eventually interceded.

Epilogue

Time passed. Fe traveled that mysterious dimension, drawn inevitably and inexorably forward. Gradually, the molecule of ferric hydroxide attracted others of its kind, and the flake grew. Pressure from the ocean above forced tight intermolecular bonds, packing iron-rich flakes together into the mineral bed of the Akkadian sea. Above, a vast, endless drama unfolded—an ocean moving by titanic natural forces, living things struggling for growth and safety, beings building cultures and lording over all.

New crystalline structures formed from the ferric hydroxide over geologic timescales, each with the atom Fe as an integral part. In the form of goethite, Fe and three other irons arrayed themselves, sharing oxygens and a smattering of hydrogens, into a crystal—one among many in a slick, sprawling seabed bulwark built from a mosaic of identical ferric bricks.

Not every oxygen or hydrogen stayed in the deepwater accommodations—fickle, lightweight partners, even at the best of times. Proving too robust and mature an element for such fancies, however, the irons always remained. Their atoms came from everywhere, each following forces of gravity and time until they met up at the bottom of the sea. Many of the irons woven into the vast, mineral quilt had been with Akkadia-2 from the beginning, never leaving its seas or the planet's thin, rocky crust. A minority had dissolved from human artifacts—corroded from the ore of the countless ships and vessels lost upon the Akkadian sea.

An absurd abundance of years and seawater compressed the ferric crystals to the point where the iron atoms could make direct bonds with each other, sharing electron clouds and aligning their infinitesimal magnetic moments. The lingering oxygens and hydrogens that had brought them to this point fled the compacting mineral, leaving behind only a token garrison. Resembling cast-iron sculptures of hemoglobin in extreme miniature, each molecular block now held a dozen iron atoms—tightly bonded in four disciplined lobes. Some trillion trillion such blocks formed the mineral deposit where the atom Fe took its retirement.

Nothing is forever, and on the timescale of stars, even a world appears as a twitching, changing, living thing. To Akkadia, the islands and seas of its second planet would not stay still—like rafts, they sloshed their way over the globe's molten interior, switching places or ramming into one-another. Sometimes, an island was drowned or a bit of seafloor launched upward to taste the air. During one such seismic upheaval, a great wound opened up in the planet's crust. Fe's chunk of trench-deep feroxyhyte lost a tectonic coin-toss, and it found its section of seabed plunged into the planet's burning magma. A new island would be born from the escaping mantle, but that was little consolation to the masses of matter subducted beneath the crust.

Fe swam under the planet's skin. The great heat of the mantle boiled the inrushing sea, searing sediment and flash-evaporating water. Fe's mineral surrendered to the intense pressure and heat of Akkadia-2's interior, sinking and melting into a blob of liquid iron.

No life swam in this new sea of melted rocks, but things still moved and roiled, subject to churning currents from the spinning planet and the even greater heat radiating from its innermost core. Bobbing on the surface of that hellish, near-solid sea, metals that had once come together drifted apart, though in time, they were fated to find each other again.

Always, Fe the iron atom found itself pulled ever downward. Even gravity coveted irons, and the universal force stretched out its fingers to patiently pluck on the dense metals, spending a billion years coaxing them corewards.

While Fe passed eons slowly surrendering to gravity's advances, the surface of Akkadia-2 fell victim to grand cosmic changes. Its star and namesake swole as it aged, pumping out ever more energy from its fusion heart to the orbiting bodies beyond. Akkadia-1, the innermost planet, had long been a hot, angry world, but now it saw its sibling sphere start to resemble its own desolation. The second planet's lovely seas boiled away and volcanoes blistered its surface as the once-benevolent sun now force fed the world more heat than it could ever radiate away.

As the star continued to age and wax, pulled forward by the currents of time, its disposition soured, and it scorched its planets ever more severely. Its harsh winds ripped away their atmospheres, turning the nearest into a bare orb during a series of terrible storms. Akkadia-2, once an ocean world, lost even its steamy skies to the onslaught, eventually able to hold onto an atmosphere of only the heaviest of gasses.

By this time, the planet's seas were made from molten rock, its windy surface a blast furnace fierce enough to melt iron. Under the fiery skin, however, little of this mattered, and the nearly-indestructible atom Fe gradually differentiated its way toward deep layers rich with its own kind.

A brief photon's journey away, Akkadia burned like a spherical match, a shell of fusion fire between outer layers of hydrogen and an inner core of helium ash. The star swam in a spiral arm of its galaxy. Like hungry cells, the galaxies skittered and spun their way across the void, drawn to one another by the appetites and attentions of gravity.

Andromeda, a spiral collection of a thousand billion stars, collided with the Milky Way—home to Akkadia, Sol, and the atom Fe. The two heavyweight cosmic entities clashed. They faced off, charging with their central black holes, circling and sparring. All the while, stars flared to life, igniting and bursting amongst the spiraling billions.

To Akkadia, the external dramas of its host galaxy were of little concern. The star continued to expand, its outer temperatures dropping even as its tortured, compressed core burned hotter than ever. It was more than Akkadia's gravity could manage, and its own atmosphere often leapt out and flared beyond control. The distance between star and planet fell as the outer boundaries of the former began to blur into a ragged, cloudy flamethrower. Atmospheric flares from the sun slurped at Akkadia-1, eventually engulfing the world entirely with little more than a flaming belch to mark its passing.

The great bulk of Akkadia-2 already struggled to maintain its orbit against the ferocious solar wind coming from its out-of-control star. Before it could be subsumed, its tiny a-moon was swatted aside like a fly, and even the more substantial b-moon disappeared in a puff before the advancing nuclear fires. The Akkadian sky merged with the Akkadian sun, and the world once wet with seas now slipped beneath waves of stellar atmosphere. Massive solar winds dragged the planet from its orbit, and the star simply swallowed it, hardly pausing in its relentless expansion.

Inevitably, the great fusion-driven empire of the sun had become utterly unmanageable. Its stocks of hydrogen were failing, and it lacked the mass to sustain fusion for much longer. Worse still, the dying Akaddia had been hemorrhaging material, not strong enough to hold onto its outermost fires, losing gravitational force with every scrap of mass it shed. Under its surface, the atom Fe and octillions of irons resisted the more superficial flares, sinking with gravity's aid into the stellar mantle. Eventually, all dissolved and ionized within the irresistible furnace, individual atoms from the once-habitable planet becoming tiny impurities in the star's dying body.

With no available hydrogen to burn and the electrons at its core stressed to the point of existential crisis, the star did the unthinkable–overcoming fundamental forces, the particles at Akkadia's core flashed at once into a new type of fusion. Helium atoms, mere pairs of protons, madly slammed together. A merger of three yielded a more stable carbon nucleus, and when four heliums met in the furnace, an eight-proton oxygen was born. These new fusion products delivered rushes of gamma ray energy, putting new life into the fiery sun and pushing back against further gravitational collapse.

Burning like a torch, Akkadia swole into a giant and blindly consumed its third planet. Though a new age of helium fusion had begun, the star boasted less mass than ever, and the brighter it blazed, the closer it traveled in time toward its inevitable doom.

The fuel at Akkadia's core dwindled, and the atom Fe could barely keep its own nucleus together deep within the ionized plasma mantle. Though essentially a fluid composed principally of hydrogen, oxygen, and carbon, the stellar environment in which Fe floated differed greatly from the chemically-comparable interior of a living thing.

However, there was one fundamental, cosmic unifier that linked cell and star—all would eventually die. In a mere eyeblink of galactic time, Akkadia exhausted its easy helium and fell into the violence of its death throes. Final bursts of fusion fought a futile battle with gravity as the star collapsed into degeneracy. A sea of subatomic particles, crushed from fusing atoms, filled the exploding star, and still-extant atomic nuclei like Fe vibrated in a hellish press of stray neutrons.

Fe resisted—it would not be fused by the likes of Akkadia. It would take a supernova of a far more massive star to birth an atom as heavy as a twenty-six-protoned iron like Fe. Still, the small dying sun held dangers for the atom far more insidious. Silicons weren't fusing into new irons, but the pressure and heat could compare only to the very first moments of Fe's existence inside the Mother Star. Just as then, neutrons were absolutely everywhere, crowded to the point where they strained the very physics that ruled matter. It was easy for the plasma-hot Fe, stripped of its electrons, to accept a neutral particle or two. In fact, the incredible energies involved in Akkadia's death insisted upon it.

With additional neutrons forced to its core, the atom Fe swole to something different—its nuclear identity and its very mass had changed. An isotope of its former self, the newly-radioactive Fe existed for a flash of time as an unstable heavy element, the protons of its fundamental nucleus still bound together by the strongest forces imaginable.

Indeed, the atom owed its wholeness and identity to the strong nuclear force. During its existence, Fe had been the agent of the electromagnetic force and a slave to gravitational force. Yet, in the end, it would be the weak force—a mystery straining within the protons and neutrons at the atom's core—that would prove to be Fe's undoing.

Energetic shudders of the Akkadian nova forced another merger within Fe's nucleus, but the neutral particles rebelled against becoming a part of the atom. Like the star itself in absolute miniature, a single neutron collapsed under the strain.

A brand new electron entered the universe, riding alongside a ghostlike antineutrino, but the neutron at Fe's heart was no more—it had gained a charge, the weak nuclear force converting it into a proton, balancing out the nucleus and creating cobalt.

Twenty-six had become twenty-seven, and Fe was no longer Fe.

Neutrons poured into the new atom and decayed just as quickly, ushering existential nuclear transformations in rapid sequence. Pressure shifted, and the star gave one last, great shudder as its fusion heart shut down forever. The resultant supernova blasted apart the remnants of the Akkadian system, spraying loose molten viscera into cold space. All that remained at the center was a glowing ball of carbons and oxygens, gravitationally compressed beyond the point tolerated by ordinary matter.

Most of the protons that had existed in the nucleus of the atom Fe now made up the core of a newborn cobalt ion. It, along with flaming reams of detritus from the stellar explosion, raced around the chaotic system. The matter still carried the dead star's angular momentum, and the cooling bits of rock and metal swirled like an orbiting graveyard encircling the white dwarf.

For the next hundred billion years, the dwarf glowed with a cold light before fading out completely, and in time, galaxies decayed around the frozen leftovers of the Akkadian system. No trace remained of the atom Fe, nor of the organized, energetic universe that had once been so fractally filled with complex wonders.

After trillions of years of slow burning, existence entered a dark period dominated by black holes, but even these evaporated and faded, as did the very bonds that trapped energy into physical matter in the first place. All slipped quietly into cold, endless night.

Time reached out, stretching toward forever... and falling short.

The End

Acknowledgements

A huge thank you to my early readers for picking up this crazy tome and helping me make it seem like a real book. Thank you to Natalie Voss, for your thorough notes and assistance in making my depictions of life in Britain more believable. Thanks to Tash Shatz, Sam Kunimatsu, Jill Rivera, and Jered Eide for reading the book and lending me their eyes, and to Rhys Lindmark for giving this 180,000-word novel a 'quick skim' and missing the hero's journey entirely.

Thank you to the Denver and Boulder NaNoWriMo communities for their support, and to the crazy coworkers and characters I've met along my travels. Trying to tell humanity's story from the perspective of an iron atom wasn't easy, and I must thank my friends and family for their patience while I wrote this thing.

A major debt belongs to the world's researchers, scientists, and those who disseminate their findings. Writing a book like "Fe: an Atom's Tale" would not have been possible without consulting the work of dozens of brilliant scientists, past and present, across a wide variety of fields and publications. Without their work, we would all walk in darkness.

About the author

Benjamin Bronte lives in Colorado and has worked as a physics instructor, ghost-writer, and horticulturist.

This is his first novel.□

Contact:

ben@elegua.us

patreon.com/BenBronte